THE
LAST
WITCH

I

M.J. LAWRIE

Copyright

For my loving husband. Without him and his support, his encouragement and positivity, my stories would never have made it to paper.
And also for Lowie and my sister. My first fans.

And for you, the reader.

Please Note:
This is a dark, paranormal fantasy romance series and contains explicit content and darker elements, including mature language, violence, torture and non-consensual sex. It is not intended for anyone under 18 years of age.

Chapter 1

It must be raining. The leak's always worse when it rains. I watch the water travel along the ceiling and drip off the glass light bulb above my head. Small droplets land on my bare feet and slide between my toes. The bulb flickers and the sound of electricity buzzes as it mixes with the runoff. Maybe it will make the bulb explode. Perhaps I'll get lucky, and a shard will find its way into my neck. Who knows. Stranger things *have* happened. It flickers again as I sit and watch it. Only that and the constant ticking of the clock hanging on the wall makes any noise.

That bloody clock.

Put in here with me for no other reason than to remind me of all the seconds I'm wasting away down here. It says it's nine o'clock, but I have no idea if that's nine in the morning or evening. This grey concrete box I currently call home has no windows. Being below ground, why would it?

God, I'm thirsty. My mouth's unbearably dry from the dirty cloth I have gagging me. It cuts into the corners of my mouth, peeling and rubbing away my skin with every bit of movement.

Roger peeks his head out from under the heavy wooden door ahead of me. His little ears twitch as he raises his nose and sniffs the air before scurrying over.

He's quite cute for a rodent.

The little brown mouse always comes to say hello. His feet tickle as they clamber over my legs. But seeing there's nothing here for him to eat, he returns under the door, making escape look so easy. But I can't even get to the door, let alone go through it. The deadbolt on the other side is always locked.

I shift, hoping to ease the pain in my extremities. My arms ache like hell behind my back. The chains linked to the cuffs around my wrists are attached to the wall behind me, and they rattle as I shuffle. I can't move more than two feet from this spot.

The tickle in my throat that started two days ago is turning into a full-blown cough. I'm not sick. It's the spores I've started to breathe. The mould's getting worse. I can taste it as it creeps across the walls, getting closer.

Like me, the cellar's neglected and forgotten.

Like me, it's been left to rot.

The bulb gives one final flicker and then...*pop*. I'm plunged into darkness.

Great. And not a single shard in sight.

I continue leaning against the cold, wet wall with my legs stretched out in front of me. And I wait. Wait for food and water. Wait for the daily, silent glance from Mr Simmons to make sure I'm still alive. Wait for the mould to start growing on me. Or for Roger to begin eating my toes.

But I don't wait for freedom. Or kindness. Or forgiveness.

Not any more.

I think now I'm just waiting to die.

As my eyes grow heavier, the monotonous ticking and dripping begin to fade away.

BANG.

What the hell was that noise? It sounded like...

BANG.

There it is again. Gunfire I think, followed by the high-pitched screams of the women, and the fearful bellows of the men who all live above me. A few moments pass, then I hear footsteps. But they're not the heavy, slow, purposeful almost bored footsteps of Mr Simmons, my keeper who brings me food and water once a day. These footsteps are rushing. Running. Tripping over themselves.

The heavy clunk of the deadbolt is followed by the door flying open. The bright light from the hall floods the room blinding me for a moment. But I still manage to see who stands in the doorway.

It *is* Mr Simmons.

The heavily built man wears a simple black suit that barely contains his frame. And he is usually all business. Very stern and severe. But now he's sweating. Panting. Terrified!

'Up!' he orders, storming towards me and going straight to the lock keeping my chains connected to the wall. 'Get up, girl.'

Although my joints are stiff and my body's weak, I get to my feet. The screaming and shouting from upstairs continue. As does the gunfire. Followed by a loud animalistic roar. It's not like any animal I've ever heard. It's almost demonic. Mr Simmons watches the door, his hands halfway through getting the key in the padlock. He doesn't seem to be breathing as he just stands there watching with wide eyes.

He's waiting.

But no one comes through the door. Not yet. He finishes undoing the lock, takes hold of the chain and grabs my arm, pulling me in close.

'The house is under attack,' he tells me. 'I need to get you out of here before they find you.' I want to ask who's coming. I want to know what the hell is happening. But with this gag in my mouth, I can't say a single word.

The light in the hall suddenly goes off leaving us in less than no light. I feel Mr Simmons trembling. His quickened and frightened breath land on my skin.

From the end of the hall, someone begins to whistle. It's a child's tune. One I remember.

Somewhere over the rainbow.

It echoes down the long concrete corridor. It's a playful song. A sweet song. But whistled at us in the darkness by someone who has one of the bravest, strongest and most fearless men I've known trembling, has me filled with utter dread.

Simmons' hand grips me tighter. So tight, I think my bone will break. But the terror of whoever, or *whatever* is at the end of the hall has me backing closer to him.

The whistling stops as quickly as it started. The silence is deafening.

'They can't be allowed to get their hands on you,' Simmons whispers. I turn, but can't see his face. There's just the blackness of my prison.

Is it finally happening? Am I getting out of here?

In a quick move, he wraps my chains tight around my neck and pulls.

'They can never find you alive. I'm sorry.' The more I struggle, the tighter it gets. My hands are bound behind my back. I can't do anything but fall to my knees and try to get the slightest breath.

He's killing me.

Snap.

The chain tumbles from my neck and lands on the cold floor. They're followed by a heavy thud. I slump, landing on my side, panting and gasping for as much air as I can get while my eyes stream and my head throbs.

He just tried to kill me!

Bastard!

The light from the hall suddenly flickers back on and I see Mr Simmons. His body is facing me, but his head is completely the wrong way around. I scream and try to get as far away from him as possible.

Someone clears their throat.

I freeze, too terrified to turn. Too terrified to breathe.

They start to laugh.

Slowly, shakily, petrified...I turn.

A man is kneeling beside me, covered in blood. His clothes, his hands, his face, his lips are smothered. But there's no sign of any injury. His thick dark hair reaches to his shoulders and is a wiry, tangled mess which matches perfectly with his thick untamed beard. But it's his eyes that fill me with terror. They're completely black.

'Bit chilly for shorts,' he laughs, a malicious grin creeping across his lips as he runs his filthy finger up my leg and circles it around my knee. He takes in sight of my body. My bruised bare legs. My grazed knees. My chest. And when they settle on my neck, he licks his lower lip. I'm trapped between a dead man and his killer. His breathing gets heavier, and the lines and scars on his face become deeper and much more pronounced.

He traces his finger along my cheek and sweeps my matted red hair out of my face giving a low moan as he does. The sensation of red-hot needles being dragged across my skin erupts over every inch he feels. I jerk my face away. He doesn't like that. With an annoyed grunt, he grabs my chin and forces me to look right at him.

'What ya doing down here, hmm? Have I found Hooper's little chamber of terror? Or pleasure?'

I struggle to get my brain to communicate with the rest of me. I want to scream. I want to try and get away, but all I can do is lay frozen in terror as this beast of a man towers over me.

He leans in close and runs his nose up my throat sniffing me like some kind of animal, sending a cold shiver up my spine and forcing a whimper up my throat.

Oh, God...there's blood in his teeth!

They're not natural teeth either, but jagged and sharp. I let loose another involuntary scream and try to free myself from his grip. But of course, I can't. No matter how hard I try.

'Shhh,' he says softly as I thrash and kick. 'No need to scream, little lady. I'll be gentle. I promise.'

He bares his teeth, and goes for my neck.

I scrunch my eyes closed. This is it. I'm going to die.

But after a few seconds, I'm still very much alive. I can hear his breathing in my ear he's that close. But he does nothing.

When I open my eyes, he's looking at the gag in my mouth with deep concentration and uncertainty. As he inspects it in more detail, his eyes widen and flick up to mine in surprise.

'Is that what I think it is?' he demands, grabbing my face and leaning in real close for a better look. 'Bloody hell. It is! Well, well, well,' he mumbles. 'It's your lucky day. Seems I won't be killing ya after all. There's someone upstairs that would just *love* to meet ya. Let's go.'

With that, he grabs my arm and drags me out of the room, the chain trailing behind me.

I thought that if I were ever to leave this damp and windowless dungeon, it would be as a pale, stiff corpse. It's been two years after all. But as I'm led away now, by a beast who almost tore the head off the man who just tried to kill me, I know I'm in far greater danger than merely being murdered.

Who the hell is he taking me to?

Upstairs is a massive contrast to what it is below. Clean to the point of obsession. Tidy and filled with expensive antiques all out on display boasting wealth and connection for the family that live here.

Christa and Harry Hooper own this eight-bedroom country home, complete with a hidden dungeon in the cellar. It's nestled safely away in the heart of Dartmoor where only those who would know where to look would find it. But usually, the polished wooden floors, floral rugs and priceless pieces of furniture aren't covered with blood and bodies. I seem to forget how to walk as the Beast pulls me past what's left of four men I recognise as house staff piled up at the base of the stairs. Their limbs all tangled up. Their eyes are wide and glassy. They're covered in so much blood. I can't look away at the horror in front of me as he pulls me closer and closer to their corpses.

I know each of their names.

But I couldn't care less that they're dead.

Inside my mind, I'm hysterically screaming and wailing. But outside, I'm silent. Fear has overridden everything. Fear that I'm soon going to join them. He's watching me and laughs to himself as my legs turn to jelly.

I'm taken to the main hall where the front door comes into view. The light from the lounge sneaks out through a crack in the door, and the shrill screams of Christa and the furious yells of Harry reach my ears from inside. They're alive and by the sounds of it, being tortured. Christa is hysterical. Howling and weeping as God knows what is happening to her. Harry's bellowing threats, warning someone to get away and leave her alone.

There's another voice. One I don't recognise. It's calm, polite and soft. A dramatic contrast to the others. The Beast stops by the door to the lounge, and his grip becomes even tighter making me cry out in protest. He silences me with an angry glance and a snarl before taking hold of the chain trailing behind me. The Beast busies himself securing me in place, wrapping the chain around the leg of a heavy ottoman unit beside me. The soft voice of the stranger inside the lounge drifts through the air.

'Now, now,' says the stranger who remains out of sight. 'Calm down, Mr Hooper. You are upsetting your wife. May I suggest you just tell me what I want to know and I will tell my colleague to stop hurting her.'

His voice is eerily calm and has a hint of amusement within in. It unsettles me more than the Beast does. Every word is said with clarity and grace.

'Don't tell me to calm down!' Harry yells with a ferocity I know well. I can see his face as clear as if he was screaming at me. 'You tell your minion to get his hands off my wife, NOW! I know very well who you are and why you're here, but you're too late. It's gone.'

'Gone?' the stranger asks. 'What do you mean, gone?'

'I mean your chance is gone. There's no way I'll throw in my lot with you. And neither will my son. So, as I said. Your. Chance. Is. Gone!' His words are vicious and stern. He means what he says. 'You'll never succeed. You'll never find my son.'

The stranger continues, 'My men and I would welcome you back into the fold gladly, Mr Hooper. You and your son. Seeing as you and your boy are the last Hooper's left, and it's vital to me that that changes. Come with us. You'll have all the women you want. All the money and luxuries you could dream of. You will want for nothing.'

'And what? You'll breed us like common bitches? I have no interest in joining your cult. The Hooper's will never help you, and you'll never succeed. I've made sure of that.'

'What do you mean?'

'Ever heard the word...vasectomy?' Harry laughs. 'I won't further the Hooper line, and neither will Junior.'

Christa screams again, sending a cold wave of fear over me. What are they doing to her?

'STOP IT, YOU DERANGED PSYCHO!' Harry yells. 'HURTING MY WIFE WON'T CHANGE ANYTHING!'

'Oh, Mr Hooper. Less of the *"deranged psycho"* if you please. Let's try and keep our manners, shall we?' There's frustration creeping into the stranger's voice which only makes him sound more terrifying. 'You are lucky that vasectomies are reversible. If you wish to remain here, fine. But I will not leave until you tell me where your son Junior is. As well as the other man I was asking about. You will tell me-'

'I told you-'

'I know the lies that you have told me. That you haven't seen your son in more than five years and that you have never seen the other man I am looking for. If you were anyone else, I would have killed you for that. I truly do detest liars. You are lucky I need you alive. Your wife on the other hand... I do not. So, you will tell me where they are, and start talking to me with respect. Or she will suffer the consequences. Give me what I want, Mr Hooper, and I will let her live. Tell me where those boys are.'

What the hell are they talking about? Vasectomies? Furthering the bloodline? They're looking for Junior?

The Beast shoves me against the wall returning my full attention back to him and points a finger in my face.

'Stay!' he growls, before heading towards the room.

I pull against the chain, but I'm stuck firm. Tethered once more to this house. I need to get away from here. The stranger is torturing Christa. And if Harry won't give up the information they're after for her, there's no hope in hell he will for me.

The front door's in sight, but restrained like this it might as well be on the other side of the planet. I pull and tug, but it's hopeless. Even if I were at full strength, I wouldn't be able to break free. The stranger continues to talk calmly beyond the door and seemingly pays no attention to the Beast as he gestures for someone to join us out in the hall. I keep trying, desperate to get away.

Soon, a tall man with ruffled blonde hair in his mid-twenties follows the Beast into the hall, closing the door behind him and cutting off the stranger's voice altogether.

Blondie tucks a knife into his jacket pocket with bloody hands as they make their way over. The closer Blondie gets, something odd happens. The air around him seems to vibrate. I can feel a pulse through me like a small wave of energy. It's unlike anything I've ever felt before and makes my hair stand on end. It's enough to distract me from pointlessly struggling. As he gets closer I realise, it's him! His presence alters the air somehow.

Blondie stops close. I feel smothered in this unnatural sensation. What the hell is this? What is he? His teeth are normal. His eyes are a very human hazel colour, not black like the Beast's.

'Where the bloody hell did you find her?'

'Chained up in the cellar behind a hidden door. That Hooper prick's been hiding her. First, I thought that maybe she was just his little plaything. She's cute under all that filth. But then I saw this.' He grabs my chin, manhandling me so Blondie can see my face and the gag in my mouth clearer. I try to get away from his grip, but he just digs his nails in.

'Holy shit!' Blondie whispers.

'Yeah.... and look at her hair. Only *they* have that red hair.' There's excitement in his voice as he lets me go with a little shove.

Blondie's scanning my face. Looking at the gag and my hair before his eyes finally lock onto mine. He gives me a kind little smile. Almost coy. There's kindness there. Odd, considering the situation.

'Maybe. Why is she so...battered? If you did this to her, he'll kill you. You know that, right?'

'I didn't touch her,' the Beast insists, holding his hands in the air. 'I saved her from his manservant who was trying to throttle her. I mean, I was going to bite her. But when I saw that gag, I brought her straight up to you.'

Bite me? Surely, he doesn't actually mean...

'Grayson needs to see her before we jump to any conclusions. He'll know for sure.' He points at the gag. 'Don't take that off, Hendrix. She's wearing it for a reason, and until we know *what* she is, I think it best we play it safe.' Watching me, he rubs his chin in contemplation. 'Grayson's still questioning the Hoopers.'

'Has he got anything from them? Do we know where the little shits are yet?'

'No, not yet but we're just getting started so...' Blondie shrugs, still keeping his eyes on mine.

'Maybe Grayson should let me take over. I'm much better at getting people to talk than you are.'

'You end up killing everyone we interrogate, Hendrix,' Blondie replies tiredly, gesturing to the pile of bodies by the base of the stairs. 'Just watch her. I'll tell Grayson what you've found. That should cheer him up.'

'Yes, *sir*,' Hendrix replies dryly.

Blondie turns and heads back to the lounge with a final quizzical look to me over his shoulder. He closes the door and leaves us out in the hallway.

I panic.

I don't want to be taken in there. I don't want to see the man that I assume is their leader. I start tugging and yanking the chain.

Hendrix slams me back against the wall in a swift swipe without even turning to look, knocking the wind out of my lungs and stunning me as my head bangs the wall.

'Move again, and I'll break your skinny little legs,' he warns, slowly turning to look at me with his eyebrows raised and a condescending smirk. 'Would be a shame to batter that body of yours even more than it already is. So just behave.'

The lounge door opens wide, and we both turn to look.

'She's just out there with Hendrix, Boss,' Blondie says. 'Want me to bring her in?'

'Absolutely, Collins. I'd love to meet her,' the stranger replies.

Chapter 2

Collins takes hold of my chain and snaps it in two, separating me from the ottoman like it's a mere paper chain instead of a thick iron one.

My survival instincts kick in. I thrash and scream as he tries to lead me into the lounge. But he's phenomenally strong and barely struggles against my efforts. With my arms still cuffed behind my back, I don't stand a chance. But I can't *not* try to get away. When we reach the door, I slam my foot against the frame and refuse to budge. He looks down at me as I shake my head and sob, pleading with him not to take me in there.

'Come on, now. Don't make this difficult.' As he takes another step forward, I lift my other foot. 'Miss...lower your feet.' Again, I shake my head and plead with my eyes for him to let me go. 'You're going in that room with me, and that's all there is to it,' he says. 'I know you're scared. That's wise, but fighting us will only make it worse for you.' He returns my feet to the floor and places his hands gently on my shoulders. 'Listen to me closely and do as I say. Keep your head down. Speak when you're spoken to, and mind your manners. Grayson has a real thing about manners.' He throws a nervous smile my way as I whimper. 'You'll be okay.

Just be honest, answer Grayson's questions, and he won't hurt you. Come on. He's waiting.'

The lounge is precisely as I remember it, despite not setting foot in here for over two years. It's big and filled with way too much stuff, all of which is pretentious, garish and unwelcoming.

Just like my captors, Harry and Christa.

The walls are covered in a hideous red and gold paisley wallpaper with a massive painting of Harry's precious racing horse above the marble fireplace ahead of me. In an L-shape are two sofas that match the walls, and above our heads hangs an enormous golden chandelier. The large oak panelled window to my left is nestled between two glass cabinets that usually displays the crystal and silver. But they've been stripped bare. The drawers to the large wooden antique oak desk are now lying broken on the floor. Paper and books are strewn all over the place, and the shelves that line the walls each side of the enormous marble fireplace straight ahead of me have been emptied.

In front of the fireplace, tied to two red velvet armchairs, are Harry and Christa. Harry's a big man with a nasty face, no hair and a grey moustache. Christa is a third his size. Her bleach blonde hair is usually neat and wavy. But now it's plastered to her face by blood and tears. Neither share a look with me for too long. Their focus seems to be on the tall man with dark hair standing in front of them, with his back to me. He's in a white pressed shirt, smart black trousers, and holds himself easily.

When he begins to turn, I lower my head and look at nothing but my feet which stumble over themselves. Collins stops in the centre of the lounge and steadies me as I stagger to a halt, keeping my head down as instructed.

The slow, purposeful footsteps making their way towards me across the wooden floor bring with them the same sensation of energy I felt with Collins. I have to close my eyes to focus on my breathing and hope I don't pass out with dread.

He stops in front of me. 'You found her, Hendrix. Yes?'

'Yes, Boss. Chained to the wall in a hidden room down in the cellar,' Hendrix replies in an incredibly respectful tone. 'His manservant was trying to kill her. He had that chain wrapped around her neck. Good job I found her when I did or-'

'Was she in this condition when you found her?' he interrupts. 'sir?'

'Did you hurt her in any way, Hendrix?'

'I found her exactly as ya see her. But look here...' Hendrix grabs my hair and yanks my head back suddenly. I snatch it away keeping my eyes closed and my head down, terrified to face anyone.

'Alright, Hendrix. Let's try and be a little bit gentler with her.' He places a finger under my chin and slowly lifts my head. As soon as he touches me, I flinch, and he lets me go. 'It's alright. I'm not going to hurt you. Open your eyes. Let's get a look at you.'

My body's shaking as adrenaline and terror courses through me. I couldn't open my eyes even if I wanted to. I give the slightest shake of my head.

Please, just leave me alone.

'I said open your eyes, Miss.'

The heavy breathing of Hendrix gets louder as he positions himself close behind me. Collins squeezes my arm slightly, reminding me of his warnings. I open them but keep them down. I feel that when I see him, I'll be seeing death. My death.

He steps closer. My body feels like it's shrinking, trying to make itself smaller as these men surround me. I'm trembling and almost hyperventilating. Tears start spilling down my cheeks as I begin to openly sob.

'Easy. Calm down, Miss. There's no need to cry.' He bends his knees ever so slightly and lowers his face. Again, he rests his finger under my chin and lifts so I have no choice but to see him.

Our eyes meet.

I don't know what I was expecting, but it certainly wasn't this. I begin to calm, feeling like no one this serene and gentle looking could ever hurt me.

'Hello,' he says with an easy and confident smile. 'My name is Grayson. Nice to meet you.'

Withdrawing his hand, he takes a step back to look at me, and I, in turn, look at him. He must be in his late twenties. His dark brown hair curls ever so slightly in a neatly styled way and falls just above his equally dark brown eyes. He has the slightest bit of stubble over a strong jaw, and everything about him is stunning. I'm astonished to see such beauty in amongst such horror. I almost don't notice the blood on his clothes and hands. The smudges of it on his cheek.

But as I look at him, there's something off. The way he smiles. It seems genuine, but the kindness in his features doesn't reach his eyes. It's unsettling.

The weakness of my body from a severe lack of food, exhaustion and shock hits me. The room spins, my legs buckle, and I fall.

'Whoa,' He catches me before I hit the floor and keeps me on my feet holding me close as I slump against him. He's solid. I feel his muscles through his shirt, and he holds me with ease. I lift my head which lolls ever so slightly and try to push him off, but he won't release me.

'If I let you go, you will fall,' he insists, scooping me up in his arms and carrying me to one of the sofas. The room continues to swirl around me as he sits me down. 'You're not going to be sick, are you?' he asks, kneeling on the floor in front of me. I shake my head as everything shifts in and out of focus, and I take a few deep breaths. 'That's it. Try and keep calm. I don't want you fainting.'

He's looking at the dryness of my lips and the thinness of my body. 'Hendrix, fetch some water and something for her to eat from the kitchen. This poor girl is half-starved and extremely dehydrated.'

Hendrix turns and leaves as instructed, returning with a glass of water and a bar of chocolate a moment later.

Grayson raises his hands making me violently flinch. 'It's alright. I just want to take that thing out of your mouth so you can have some food and water before you faint. You are hungry, dehydrated and no good to me unconscious.' He has his hands an inch from my skin and is waiting. I shrink back, scared to death. 'Let me put it this way,' he says with a twinge of exasperation. 'It is better if you do as I ask, then force my hand to persuade you. I need you awake, so please, let me take it off. I will not ask again and I would hate for things between us to turn unpleasant.' He watches and waits as I look between his bloody hands and his dark eyes. 'I promise. I'm just going to take the gag out of your mouth. That's all.'

I nod. I don't want him close, but getting the gag off will vastly improve my situation. He lowers it from my mouth so it falls around my neck, and then quickly lowers his hands. But he doesn't remove it entirely.

'Here...' he lifts the water and holds it to my lips. I lean over, not taking my eyes off him for a second, ready to try and run if he attempts to hurt or touch me. I take a sip, but my throat is so dry, I cough and splutter, despite how desperately thirsty I am. I shuffle away, lower my head and just hope that he leaves me be.

'Mr Hooper. Why on earth do you have a young woman tied up and gagged in your cellar?' he asks.

But Harry doesn't speak a word in reply.

Grayson gets to his feet and rests his hand on my shoulder making me twitch, but he doesn't take it away. Instead, he squeezes it affectionately and strokes me with his thumb back and forth, making me uncomfortable with his familiarity.

'I am afraid I have to insist that you answer my question, Mr Hooper. Or I *will* hurt her.'

'Do what you want,' Harry says viciously, looking me up and down with disgust. 'She's nothing to me.'

I move away slowly from Grayson and his hand, watching it cautiously.

'My apologies. I was not clear.' He slides his hands instead into his pockets. 'If you continue to refuse to cooperate, it will be your *wife* that suffers, Mr Hooper. Not *her*.' Grayson gives the slightest nod in my direction and continues to smile that unsettling smile. 'I am finding myself getting bored with her fingers. Maybe I should take something else from her? An eye perhaps?'

Looking at Christa, I notice the three fingers lying in a bloody puddle on the floor by her foot. Now I know what had her screeching. They've been torturing her. She's slumped forwards, panting and sobbing, barely conscious. A spark of something stirs inside me. The fear and panic shift, making the slightest bit of room for something that resembles...justice.

'Who is she?' Grayson asks.

'She...' Harry begins, but he hesitates. He doesn't want to say. Should I answer?

I look at Harry and see the hatred he still has for me for just breathing, and I think...no. I won't. Not unless I'm asked directly.

With a formidable authority, Grayson orders Collins to take another finger from Christa. I watch as Collins, without a moment's hesitation, reveals the bloody blade from his pocket. With a lot of screaming and thrashing, he cuts off another of her fingers. I scrunch my eyes closed and fight the bile climbing up my throat as I hear her being mutilated a few feet away from me.

But still, I keep quiet.

Better her than me.

Harry roars as her finger lands with a small little thud on the floor joining the others.

'Who is she?' Grayson asks calmly over Christa's screeching.

'SHE'S NO ONE!' Harry's watching horrified as Christa continues to scream. 'A MAID TURNED THIEF. THAT'S ALL!'

'Your manservant was attempting to kill her rather than allowing us to find her. Seems drastic for nothing more than a thief. Who is she?' Grayson asks again.

'I TOLD YOU!'

Christa falls unconscious.

'I'm sure.' Grayson gives a small laugh before turning his back to Harry and instead, looks at me. His eyes shine with excitement as he sits beside me, looking at the gag still around my neck. 'This word here, Nexasanguinum.' He gestures to my gag and looks me square in the eye. 'Do you know what it means?'

I shake my head.

'It means, *bound by blood*. The word itself, is written in blood. *Your* blood.'

I remain silent and stare straight ahead.

'Why would you be wearing this?'

I give a slight shrug and shake my head.

'Hmmm. Curious. Maybe you don't know. Tell me your name.'

I try to speak, I do, but nothing at all comes out. My voice has abandoned me completely. Through fear perhaps? Or maybe the attack from Mr Simmons. All I manage is little more than a squeak as I continue to shake all over. His eyes stare into mine as he reads me.

'You are absolutely terrified, aren't you? I wonder, is it me that you are afraid of? Or them?' He gestures to Harry and Christa.

I can't help but look at Harry. As soon as those nasty eyes meet mine, I look at the floor.

Grayson sees and asks, 'What the hell have you been doing to her, Hooper?'

'None of your damn business,' Harry spits back.

'You've kept her hidden. Kept her prisoner. Kept her secret. I demand to know why?'

'Go to Hell, abomination.'

'Careful. I warned you where your lack of manners would lead, didn't I? You vulgar human being. Look at what you've done to this girl.' Grayson looks at Collins. 'Kill his wife.'

'NO!' Harry bellows, pulling at his restraints. 'Please, don't!'

'Then tell me the truth. Who she is?'

'I TOLD YOU!'

'Fine. Collins, slit Mrs Hooper's throat.'

Collins readies his knife. The blade rests on the nape of her neck, and he applies enough pressure to pierce the skin.

'LILLY!' Harry yells suddenly. 'HER NAME IS LILLY HOOPER. OKAY? SHE'S MY NIECE!'

Chapter 3

'Your niece?' Grayson has a rather fake disbelieving smirk. 'I thought you were the last Hooper? Well, you and your son. Now you are telling me you have a sister? Not only that, but she had a daughter? That's a fair few more Hoopers than I was led to believe existed. Surely you weren't lying to me before? No…you can't possibly have a niece.' Grayson's playing with him like a cat would play with a mouse, enraging my prideful uncle even further. And what's more, the revelation that I'm family hasn't surprised him one bit. I think maybe he knew as soon as he saw me.

'I *had* a sister. *That's* her daughter.' All I get is a slight nod from Harry. No eye contact. 'Are you happy? Now leave my wife alone. For God's sake, man.'

'Where is your sister now?' Grayson asks.

'Dead. She died seventeen years ago when the girl was five,' Harry says, nervously eyeing the knife still at Christa's neck. But Grayson is watching me with a chilling calm.

'Lilly…. that is a very pretty name,' he says sweetly, crossing his legs and leaning back on the sofa. 'A pretty name for a very pretty girl. My name is Grayson. Grayson Kendryk.' He nods behind me. 'The man who found you is Hendrix Spencer, and the man standing by your aunt, is Cailean Collin. But we call him Collins. I wonder, have you heard of me?' He secures eye contact with me once more and emanates ease, calm and control. Nothing around him seems to faze him. The bodies in the hall, the severed fingers on the floor, or the thin, frightened young woman sitting beside him.

I shake my head. I have no idea who he is.

He seems to be thinking as he looks me over. About what? I have no idea. After a sudden intake of breath, he turns and looks at Collins.

'Remove the handcuffs from Lilly's wrists.'

What? He's setting me free?

Yes!

With my hands free I have a chance of getting out of here.

Collins steps forward to do as he's been asked, and I'm more than happy to be rid of the cuffs. I eagerly hold out my wrists behind me.

Hendrix steps forwards. 'Boss, do you think that's wise? She could be dangerous.'

'Nonsense. Look at her. She's skin and bones. And besides, she knows better than to try and run. Don't you, Lilly?'

Hastily, I nod. Anything to get my arms free.

'Precisely.' He leans in towards me as Collins makes his way over. 'Just so you know, if your hands go anywhere near that gag of yours without my express permission, you will sorely regret it. Do you understand me?' He waits for me to agree. 'I mean it, Miss Hooper. Do as I say and everything will be fine. Disobey me, and it will not be. Am I being clear?'

I nod. I believe him. Completely.

With no effort at all, Collins breaks the handcuffs and removes them from my wrists entirely, dropping them to the floor by my feet with a thud. The freedom feels amazing. But sore. My arms have been behind my back for so long, moving them so they're in front of me is slow work. The bones click, and the muscles stretch as they try to remember how to work. It hurts, but it's a good hurt. Like stretching out a dead leg. Grayson's eyes furrow as he sees my pain.

'How long have you been like this?' he asks as I settle my hands on my lap. 'Christ!' He snatches my arm and pulls up my sleeves revealing dark bruises and bloody welts from where I've been pulling against my restraints for so long. 'You must be in agony!' Glancing over his shoulder, he glares at Harry. 'What kind of man does this to his own family?!'

I snatch my arm away and slide back across the sofa keen to get some distance. Collins returns to my aunt's side with a disgusted glance at the metal cuffs on the floor.

'Lilly, I'm not going to hurt you.'

I jerk away as he reaches out.

'What is that?' Grayson asks Harry. 'Why does she flinch away from me?'

'She doesn't like being touched,' my uncle mumbles. 'Never has. It's called haphephobia.'

'Fear of touch. I'm familiar with the condition,' Grayson muses before sliding away an inch and holding his hands up by his head. 'Then I won't touch you, Lilly. You have my word. Here...'

He hands me the glass of water. I take it, and this time it goes down a little easier. I keep the glass in my hands, using the coolness to rest against my wrist hoping it will help ease the throbbing. But I don't trust him or his apparent kindness one bit and keep a watchful eye on him.

'I know you are afraid, and that the attack you just suffered below the house must have hurt your throat, but can you *try* and answer my questions? Why have they done this to you?'

My smile disappears as I run my fingers along the raw skin in the corners of my mouth caused by the gag.

Grayson pulls off his tie and dips it in the remainder of the water.

'May I?' he asks, holding it just by the corner of my mouth. 'The tie will touch you. I won't.' I nod, and he gently cleans the wounds. I watch him as he concentrates. How can someone so terrifying be so...tender? And why is he being so kind to me when he's actively torturing my aunt and uncle?

'If it hurts too much to talk,' he says, lowering his tie and looking me in the eye. 'Just give me a nod or a shake of your head. I need to know, are these people your aunt and uncle?'

I give a slight nod, which my uncle doesn't like at all.

'*Girl*, you better keep your mouth shut! You have no idea who you're dealing with. He's not your friend!' Harry's voice sends a cold shiver straight down my spine and despite myself, I lower my head.

Grayson slowly turns his attention to Harry. 'That *girl*... has not opened her mouth nor said a single word since we found her. I suggest you do the same. Unless asked a question, Mr Hooper, I recommend you keep your foul mouth shut. Or the next thing we cut off will be your tongue.' The way Grayson speaks is slow and purposeful. Not an ounce of anger, just a ton of menace. But it works, and my uncle remains silent. But I am also very aware that not a few moments ago, a man that I have known my entire life, the closest thing to a father I've ever had, just tried to kill me rather than see me in the hands of these men.

Returning his attention to me, Grayson carries on.

'I just want answers to a few questions I have. Your uncle's manners and refusal to cooperate has got many people killed and landed him and his wife in this position. But you will help me, won't you? I am not here to hurt anyone. Least of all you.'

I give a small nod. I have no intention of being tied up again or losing digits.

'Good girl. I knew you and me would be friends.'

'She isn't what you think,' Harry insists.

'I think denying what she *is*, is rather redundant. Her gag and the fact that you would rather see her dead than anywhere near me, tells me everything I need to know. You filthy traitor. You call yourself Hooper. You are the furthest from a Hooper I could ever have imagined.'

'You have no idea what she's capable of,' Harry tells him darkly. 'There's a reason why she was locked up. She's not...normal.'

Grayson looks between us warily but seems to decide that Harry's talking nonsense.

'I don't like normal so that works out well. You know who I am, Hooper. You know what I am, and now you have seen what I am capable of. So, if you think this malnourished, frail and frankly traumatised little thing frightens me, or your words will scare me off, you are very, very mistaken. I suggest you stop acting like a fool. I understand that may be hard for you, Mr Hooper, but please, do try.' Grayson shows me a smile and even throws me a wink.

But Harry's not done.

'She has to be contained. She's evil, Grayson. A monster. A fucking murderer. You have no idea.' My hands are shaking. I try hard not to let his words get to me. But after everything he's done, he dares call *me* the monster? I'm getting angry as he continues listing all the words I've heard a hundred times before. Liar. Bitch. Psycho.

'ENOUGH, HOOPER!' Grayson shouts, making me jump. 'Now, you and I both know that the reason you hid this girl is because...she is a witch.'

My insides feel heavier than lead.

Harry laughs and shakes his head. 'I don't think so.'

'Harbouring a witch is punishable by death, Mr Hooper. Hiding her from us...is much worse.'

'Good job she isn't a witch then,' he insists.

'You are lying,' Grayson starts speaking through his teeth he's getting so frustrated. But he doesn't ask me directly what I am. Just Harry. 'I really hate being lied to. She is a witch. There is a binding spell currently dangling around her neck. Admit it now, *Please*.'

Harry and I both remain silent as he holds his cynical stare.

'Right,' Grayson sighs, slapping his hands on his knees and moving closer to me. 'Then there will be no problem in me removing her gag. Will there? I mean, if she were a witch, and was given back her magic, I would be more inclined to think that you and your wife would be the ones in danger here. Not me. You are the ones that locked her up. You are the ones that just tried to have her killed.' He reaches out for me, his hands going to the gag still tied loosely around my neck. 'We will soon find out where her loyalties lie. Just to be clear, Miss Hooper. Witch or not, I will not harm you as long as you behave. Saying that however, if you feel the need to exact some revenge on your captors, I heartily encourage you to do so.'

'DON'T!' Harry yells as Grayson gets in touching distance. 'GET YOUR HANDS OFF HER, YOU FUCKING FREAK!'

Grayson's hands stop just by my neck. 'Freak?' Grayson repeats quietly. I see a darkness in his eyes that makes me thrilled I didn't insult him at any point.

Collins stands straighter. Hendrix gives a low growl. All three men react to that word, the insult aimed at their leader, and if I did care about Harry, I'd be afraid for him right now.

The atmosphere in the room intensifies as Grayson lowers his hands from me, and turns instead to my uncle. Well, Harry certainly succeeded in stopping him removing the gag. But I'm pretty sure he'll regret how he accomplished it.

'Did you just call me a *freak*?' Grayson slowly gets to his feet and walks towards him. The predator stalking his prey. Harry's eyes grow wider in fear the closer Grayson gets. Considering the circumstances, Harry seems pretty unharmed.

I get the feeling that's about to change.

'I think the only *freak* here, is you, Mr Hooper. I see the way she cowers as you speak. The terror she has about being touched. She's *yours*, is she? And in what way is she -*yours*? She's a pretty little thing. I bet that's why you kept her alive, isn't it? So you can make sure she's *yours* whenever you want her to be-'

'If you're insinuating-'

Grayson's angry. His voice is brimming with it as he cuts Harry off. 'You mistake my manners for leniency. I have spared you any real harm because you are after all, still a Hooper-'

'You murdered my staff, mutilated my wife, and now you accuse me of interfering with my own niece! Is that your version of manners?!' Harry replies astounded.

'Why else would she be so afraid of touch?'

'I wouldn't touch her even if she weren't related to me. She's a vile, filthy, disgusting Witch-'

'A witch, huh?' Grayson looks at me over his shoulder with a triumphant smile before turning back to Harry. 'Your son is no witch. You are no witch. But she is. The red hair alone is a giveaway. All Hooper witches had that lovely hair. Never mind the gag or the fear she clearly instils in you. She's a Hooper witch. And you will pay for hurting her. You will pay dearly.'

Panicked, Harry turns to me. 'They're here to take you away with them. You know that, right? To do whatever they want with you. You think they want to be your friend? Getting into your knickers, that's what they want. And if you say no to them, they'll force themselves on you. They want to further our bloodline. Make more Hooper's. Make more witches.' Harry doesn't get to say another word before Collins, looking utterly disgusted at his words, slams his fist hard into Harry's face. His nose explodes with blood, and I flinch at the sound of the bone breaking.

'You're vile,' Collins tells my uncle before looking at me and shaking his head. 'No one is going to touch you like that, Lilly. We would never.'

But every cell in my body is on alert at the mere suggestion. I sit even more nervously on the sofa with my hands gripping the edge of the cushions. I reach up for the gag.

'Don't,' Grayson warns. 'Don't even think about listening to his lies. If you remove that binding spell and turn on me, there will be consequences, Miss Hooper. Please, do not force my hand. I do not want to hurt you. Truly.'

'I can't...' I whisper.

'You can't? Can't what?' he asks, his eyes narrowed in sympathy as he hears the fear and strain in my voice.

'I can't face any more. Not again. I can't. Please, please let me go.' I look at them all standing there, with blood on their clothes and death on their hands. 'If you *are* here to hurt me, please kill me instead.'

'You did not actually just ask me to kill you?' he asks sadly. He takes a step in my direction.

I get to my feet and sprint to the door, but I'm much weaker than I thought. I'm clumsy and slow. Grayson catches me easily. He lifts me up as I thrash and scream, desperate to get away. Desperate not to be hurt by anyone anymore.

'NO!' I shriek. 'GET OFF. PLEASE. I BEG YOU!'

'Take it easy, Lilly,' Grayson says loudly over my screaming while tightening his grip. 'You're not going anywhere, so calm down.'

'Please don't hurt me.' I keep trying to get free as terrified sobs escape me.

'Lilly Hooper!' he barks. 'Look around you. You're completely surrounded and you can barely stand. Stop trying to run, and settle down before you hurt yourself,' he warns in my ear.

My head falls forwards as I cry. I give up trying to get free from his arms that are wrapped tightly around me, and I just sob desperately.

'Please don't hurt me, Grayson. I beg you.'

He turns me, keeping me wrapped in his arms as he looks down at my tear soaked face.

'Please...' I cry. 'Please...'

'Listen to me. My men and I do not rape women. I don't like the accusation that we would, so get that out of your mind right now. We're many things but not that. We do bad things. But only to people who deserve bad things. I believe the people in the hall, the people who have locked you up, left you hungry and cold, left you fearing the touch of another, I believe that they deserve bad things. And I know that they...' he points to Harry and Christa. 'They definitely deserve bad things. Don't cry.' He places a hand on his heart. 'I swear, us finding you has been the best thing to ever happen to you. I assure you. Now please, calm yourself.'

His dark eyes fill with sincerity. He reaches up and wipes my tears with his thumb. It's a kind gesture. One I do appreciate. But it creates the familiar agony that I always feel with physical contact. An instant sensation of violation and dread that makes my skin feel like it's being burnt with hundreds of needles over every inch he touches.

'Do you promise?' I ask weakly.

'I promise. I just can't let you remove that binding spell until I know that you won't turn on us. You clearly don't trust us and you are very emotional. I won't risk our safety. Or yours. But I promise that you can take it off soon. When you are calmer. When we both trust each other a little more. Fair?'

His hands settle on my hips as he looks down at me with gentle kindness. I lay my palms flat on his chest as a mark of trust, and nod.

'Good girl.'

'He's lying!' Harry spits blood onto the carpet. 'Look at what they've done to Christa. They've murdered everyone you know. You'll be passed around. Is that what you want? You'll be tied up. Their hands will be all over you, touching you!' Harry continues tormenting me, knowing exactly what to say to make me panic. I fear touch. I can't stand it, and as he says these things, I see them in my head. All the things that could happen to me play out like a film behind my eyes. My hands cover my ears as it gets harder to breathe.

'Please, make him stop.'

Grayson lets me go and stands over Harry who shrinks back at his mere presence, but there's nowhere for him to go. Grayson holds out his hand to Collins who, without needing to be told what to do, places the knife into it.

'You tell her we're going to hurt her. Touch her in nasty ways because you know that is what she is frightened of. I think it is you who are the vile, filthy and disgusting thing here. This is what happens to men who touch women without their permission in my world.'

With incredible force, Grayson drives the knife into my uncle's wrist, almost severing his hand altogether.

'We take away their hands.'

As Harry yells, Grayson twists the knife making his screams of agony even more unbearable. I've never heard a man scream like it! Blood spurts from the wound as Grayson yanks out the knife. He rests the tip above his other wrist.

'You...you can't do this!' he stammers eyeing the knife. 'You need me. I'm a Hooper!'

'So is she. And so is your son. I bet he'll accept my offer if she won't. Not so cocky now, are you? Knowing your life isn't as safe as it was before we found her. You're not the last Hooper, and I have no problem killing a man like you. Unless you have some information that can change my mind?' He keeps the knife pressing into his skin. 'I want to know where your son is.'

'I told you,' Harry's voice is shaking and getting weaker as the steady flow of blood from his wrist gathers by his foot, creating a large puddle. I don't know if it's fear that has me silent, letting this happen. Or the sense of justice that finally he's getting what he deserves.

'Last I heard he was in Paris spending his inheritance. I haven't seen him in over five years.'

'Your son isn't in Paris. Or anywhere in France. I looked. I want to know where he is, Hooper!' The tip of the blade digs in, piercing his skin.

'I told you, last I heard my son was in Paris! I swear!' Spit flies from his mouth as he speaks, desperate for Grayson to believe his words. And he does.

'What about the other boy?'

Other boy? Harry only had one son.

'I told you,' Harry's starting to slur. 'I have no idea who you're talking about.'

'Yes, you do. I know you do. He was here. Two years ago. He is one of my men, and I have it on excellent authority that the last place he was seen was heading inside this house. And he hasn't been seen since. I want to know the following. What was he doing here? Where is he now? And where is the Journal? WHERE IS HE?' Grayson's calm composure is gone. Replaced by this menacing interrogator. His anger's so terrifying, it even makes Harry flinch. 'TELL ME!' He takes the knife and digs it into his throat.

'I DON'T KNOW WHO YOU'RE TALKING ABOUT!' Harry yells, desperately trying to get away from the knife. 'I SWEAR!'

'Mid-twenties. Stark white hair. Violet eyes, you really couldn't miss him. So. One last time or I will drive this knife straight through your fat neck until it comes out the other side. Where is he?'

My stomach hits the floor, and every bit of breath leaves my lungs.

I know who he's looking for.

Oh shit. What the hell do I do? I'm so distracted by my own panic that I only just now realise that the room has fallen silent and that everyone, absolutely everyone, is looking at me. Grayson has a considerable frown as he looks me over and then he points at me accusingly.

'What did you just say?'

'Me?' I ask in a shaky voice. 'Nothing.'

'Yes. You did. You whispered a name.'

'Did I?' I ask in a weak, fretful whisper. I give a shrug and shake my head. 'I don't-'

'Miss Hooper. You are lying to me. I can see it on your face. I can hear it in your voice. I warn you, lie to me again, and I'll tie you up next to your uncle. Do you hear me?'

His threat and the tone in which it's delivered turns my blood cold.

'We made a deal. You would not lie to me, and I will not hurt you. I will ask you again. The boy I'm looking for, with white hair and lilac eyes...have you seen him?'

All I can do is sit here, frozen. Grayson looks back to Harry, digging the tip of the blade in a little deeper.

'Wait!' Harry gasps. 'Wait, wait!' His eyes move frantically between Grayson, the knife and me. 'The man he's looking for, it's him, isn't it?' Harry waits, his eyes firmly on me. 'It is...he's the one that got you into all that trouble. That's who he's looking for?'

'Trouble?' Grayson asks. 'What trouble?'

'Don't. Don't you dare, uncle Harry.'

'You said you never saw the man I'm looking for,' Grayson accuses, glaring at Harry.

'I never saw him, no,' Harry says. 'But she knows.'

'She does?'

'Of course she knows who you're talking about. She just said his name. Toby. Toby Smith. He used to sneak into her room through the window.' They're all watching me, and the panic on my face is as clear as day. 'Two years ago,' Harry says hastily, eyeing the knife. 'She ran off with him and then he dumped her back here six weeks later. Toby. Her boyfriend.'

'Boyfriend?' Grayson says in disbelief, lowering the knife. 'You, you and he-'

'Was,' I say weakly. The mention of Toby makes me want to curl up on the floor and sob. 'Okay. Okay, I know who you're looking for, and yes, we were together, but I don't know where he is.'

'Tears... Grayson, don't fall for her little act,' my uncle scoffs at me as I quickly wipe them away, hating that they fall at the mere mention of Toby's name.

'Shut up,' I snipe. Harry's getting paler and paler as he continues to lose blood but he's always been a stubborn man. He'll die when he wants to and not a moment sooner. He isn't done trying to break me yet.

'One wrong word. One innocent touch. One argument where she loses her temper. That's all it takes. Even if she doesn't mean to. She can't control herself. She doesn't *want* to control herself! That girl is dark and dangerous.' All eyes turn on me. 'Why don't you tell them why you were down in the cellar? About what you did when you tried to run away?' Harry's throwing me under the bus. It's him or me, and he won't give up without a fight.

'What did you do? Why were you in the cellar?' Grayson asks.

I open my mouth to speak, but nothing comes out. I have no idea what to say because I can't tell him the truth.

'Whatever happened, whatever you may have done won't change my promise to you. I won't hurt you as long as you are truthful.' I trust the sincerity on his face. It's a risk telling him anything. But what other choice do I have?

'You heard about the Miller farm massacre?' Harry asks before I can say a word. 'She killed six innocent people in those six weeks she ran off. Murdered them all in cold blood. Even your man couldn't cope with her, so he brought her back. And she will do the same to you in a heartbeat.'

'Stop talking, Harry!' I warn.

'The Miller farm massacre?' Grayson asks. 'I read about that in the paper. It was humans.'

'If Simmons and I hadn't gone in there and moved those bodies, we'd have Witch Hunters swarming all over us. Making it look like a human affair was near impossible, but we did it so we didn't suffer for her actions. She ran away, lost control of her magic and killed those men. I had to lock her up. It was the only way to keep us all safe.'

'That wasn't me.'

'One man was found pinned to the roof of that barn by a pitchfork. Another had every single one of his bones broken. Another literally torn to pieces. His entrails wrapped around his neck like a scarf. That's who she is. That's what she does. I could go on.'

'I would rather you didn't,' Grayson replies, looking at me with uncertainty.

'She can't be trusted, Grayson. She will kill you and your men, and anyone else who so much as looks at her funny. That binding spell must never be removed. Or she will destroy us all. You take that binding spell off, she'll turn on you. I guarantee it. You can't allow yourself to be fooled by the fragile little girl routine. You can't!'

'If you're so scared of her, why not just brand her?' Hendrix asks. 'Much more effective way to keep her in line.'

'Because,' Grayson answers on Harry's behalf while gesturing to the gag. 'Only a Witch with magic can brand another Witch. To sear the binding spell into flesh will only work with magic. But this he can do. Bind her magic. Lock her away.'

'I had to be cruel. I had to be tough. After what she did-'

'You tortured me long before I ran away.' I look at Harry, hating him with every fibre of my being. 'Since I was five, you made my life a living hell.'

He looks at me the same way as he says the words he would say after every time he raised his hand to me.

'You, *girl*...are a monster. And you got what monsters deserve. And Grayson will do far worse than lock you away when he sees the real you.'

I look Harry straight in the eye. Something I was always too scared to do. My fists are clenched, and my hands are trembling, but not through fear. Not this time. Everything he's done to me, not only the last two years but since I was five, and he calls *me* a monster?

I can't help the laugh that comes with my words. 'You think out of the two of us, that *I'm* the monster?'

'You killed those men. I know it-'

'What about what you've done?' I take a step towards him. 'What you let happen to me under this roof?' Grayson steps slightly to one side, giving me a clear path to face my captor. 'In the seventeen years I've lived with you, you have starved me. Beat me. Humiliated me. Encouraged the cruelties that your wife and your staff would put me through for sport. Before putting me in your cellar, you locked me up like an animal upstairs in that attic every day for almost two decades. You took everything from me, Harry. Simmons just tried to kill me!' The anger coursing through me is like acid burning at my insides. 'My mum died and left me in your care. I was five years old. A child. You were supposed to look after me.'

'I did my best!'

'TWO FUCKING YEARS I'VE BEEN DOWN THERE! ALONE! IN CHAINS!'

'Bloody hell...' Collins whispers. 'That's inhumane. How could you do such a thing?'

'What the hell was I supposed to do with her?! Take her on holiday? Let her go to school?'

'How about feed me! Clothe me! Protect me!'

'If anyone got the slightest inkling you were here, we would all have been taken by Hunters. We all would have been executed. Even knowing a witch is a death sentence. You can't control yourself, just look at what you did to your poor, stupid mother. How could I let you out in the world?'

'I was five when my mum died. How can you blame me for something I can't even remember? Am I the mad one for thinking this was all a pointless waste of energy on your part? You could have just left me alone. Hell, you could have just killed me! You didn't have to make me suffer like this.'

'It was my duty to keep you away from the world. To keep you in line. You lose your temper and look what happens. People die!'

'I NEVER USED TO BE LIKE THIS! I DON'T WANT TO HURT ANYONE!'

Harry looks to Grayson. 'You need to listen to me. I've seen her angry. I've seen her upset and believe me when I say you're completely unprepared for it.'

'Maybe he's right,' Hendrix grunts. 'Boss, she could be dangerous. If she's really been in that room for two years, I'm not sure she's gonna be all that stable.'

I don't give anyone the chance to say another word as I take one more step towards the ever-weakening Harry.

'This has nothing to do with anyone else so stop trying to bring them into this. This is between us.'

'I should've known something was going on when you started acting out.'

'You mean fighting back!'

'I never saw it coming. You and a boy. I mean, who in their right mind would want a girl as damaged as you?'

'I can think of someone.' I want to choke on the words. 'You didn't seem to care about him wanting me, though did you?'

'I don't know what you're talking about,' he says, looking away to the floor. His denial is infuriating. 'Lies. You're a liar.'

'Call me a liar one more time, and I'll show you a real monster.'

'Slanderous lies-'

'I mean it. I'll rip out your tongue and make you eat it. You make me sick. Even now there's no remorse. No admittance that what you've put me through is nothing less than sadistic.'

Grayson's footsteps get closer until he stands by my side, looking at me with a sort of pity in his eyes. It's the first flicker of kind emotion I've seen in them.

'Someone here has been inappropriate with you, haven't they?'

I stare at Harry and dare him to say a word. But he won't. Not about that. Not about...him. My blood's pumping so fast I can hear it. I don't think I've ever been this angry.

When Grayson's hand attempts to take mine, I snatch it away.

'Don't fucking touch me. DON'T!'

'I'm sorry. I didn't mean-'

'WILL YOU CONTAIN HER!' Harry yells at Grayson. 'BEFORE SHE KILLS US!'

'Boss,' Collins calls nervously. 'I think we should-'

'What?' I snap angrily. 'Put me down? Lock me up? I DIDN'T KILL ANYONE! I NEVER HURT ANYONE! THE ONLY ONE WHO HAS SUFFERED HERE IS ME! HE'S LYING TO YOU!'

Grayson's hands raise up. 'I believe you. No one here is going to hurt you. I promise.'

'Oh, I know,' I snarl with bitter tears streaming down my face. 'That's never going to happen. Not again.'

Grayson's eyes flick behind me for the briefest of seconds. An action I'm sure was more subconscious than conscious. I turn and see Hendrix making his way slowly towards me. A knife in his hand. His black eyes are firmly on me. Collins is watching me too. His fists clenched.

'SHE IS A FUCKING MONSTER!' Harry shouts, pulling against his ropes. 'WILL YOU BLOODY LISTEN TO ME?! SHE'S A MURDERER. A MANIPULATIVE BITCH. A LIAR. SHE'S EVIL!'

That's it. There's no more I can take. No more I *will* take. My whole body is vibrating with fury. I'm panting with hatred. In a quick move, I reach out and snatch the bloody knife still in Grayson's hand. He tries to take it back, but I've already pressed the blade into the cloth around my throat and sliced.

As soon as the binding spell leaves my body, I feel it. My magic's free and flowing through me a hundred miles a second, making me breathless and dizzy, but strong. After being separated from it for so long, it swirls inside my chest and claws at my skin desperate to get out. Begging me to use it. It's seeping from my pores and feels fucking fantastic.

Without my magic, I'm nothing more than a helpless girl.

But with it...I'm a force to be feared.

Even by a man like Grayson.

And definitely by Harry fucking Hooper.

Chapter 4

This is precisely why Harry didn't want that gag to come off. His shitty binding spell that's kept my magic bound for so long was his only protection from me. But not anymore.

Now, I'm free.

Grayson steps back and watches me carefully. Gently, he tries to talk to me. 'Lilly...I need you to-'

With a gut-wrenching surge of magic from deep inside, the glass in every mirror, every window and every cabinet shatters simultaneously with an almost deafening crash. And I send shards of glass flying in all directions. My anger guides two large jagged pieces as they soar through the air making a clear whoosh as they go, before stopping at the necks of Collins and Hendrix. The knife in my hand is pointed at Grayson who took too many steps towards me, making him close enough to hold the tip of the blade against his throat.

'You try and hurt me, and I'll kill every single one of you,' I warn in no uncertain terms.

Now I have them all standing stock still with their hands up by their heads watching me nervously. I let go of the hilt and lower my hand, leaving the knife covered in Harry's blood floating in the air. Grayson attempts a step back. The blade follows him.

'This is not necessary. We are on your side.' He presses his lips together in a tight line. I'm making him angry. I couldn't give a shit!

'*I'm* on my side. That's enough. Just stay still. I need a moment with my uncle.'

There's a storm raging outside in the darkness, and with no windows keeping it out, the wind and rain join us in the lounge. The heavy curtains billow against the gusts and the loose papers over the floor fly around us. My magic becomes a hurricane of fury that demands to be let loose. It's seeping out into the world, making anything not nailed down, shudder and shake. I should step away, remove myself from the situation so no one gets hurt, but I can't. I turn my full attention back to Harry.

'What do you want? An apology?'

I take some very deep and purposeful breaths as I prepare to say the only thing I have left to say to him. The only question that I need answering now. The most important question in the world.

'Was it you?' I ask.

'I have no idea what you're talking about.'

'Yes, you do. Tell me, Harry. Was it you, or was it him? Who killed her?'

'Who did he kill?' Grayson asks, but this is between us. Not him.

'Did you do it?' I demand. 'Or was it Toby?'

'When you knew the answer to that question, you went mad. I may hate you and everything you are, but I will not willingly unleash your darkness onto the world.'

I make my way closer to him and laugh as I look into his cloudy grey eyes one last time.

Come on, Red...just do it already. You know you want to.

In the corner of my eye, I see him standing there like a ghost. His devilish smile and eyes that shine with evil intent.

'Do it' he mouths.

He's there for a second before he fades as if made of smoke, nothing more than a memory that still lingers desperate to crawl out of my head into the real world. I know that. Toby Smith isn't here. Not physically. But his voice and his face, the way he thought and made me think, is more real to me than the blood my toes are standing in as I stand before the man that ruined my life.

'Who did it?' I repeat. 'You, or Toby?'

'Will knowing bring you peace?' Harry asks.

'Yes.'

Harry leans forwards, as much as he can, given his restraints. A nasty sneer appears on his face.

'In that case, bite me, Lilly Hooper. You disgusting, monstrous, lying murderer.'

Hatred. Utter hatred fills me as he just smirks.

'Everything that happened to you, you deserved. Everything. All of it. If I could do it all again, I would. I hate you. Your mother regretted you. Your father disowned you, and when you die, no one will mourn you.'

With a hateful scream, my hands erupt in fire. Black and white flames cover my skin, but it doesn't hurt. It never does. The heat is me. It's mine, and I control it. The flames reflect in Harry's eyes and in that second, he knows. He's looking at death.

His death.

He screams as a black and white streak of fire leaves my palms and shoots towards him. Every inch of his body is ablaze in a second. His screams fill the room as it burns through his clothes and onto his skin. It's ravenous and unnatural. He thrashes and writhes against the ropes as my magical fire consumes him. My aunt regains her senses just in time to watch her husband burn. She screams a blood-curdling scream before turning hysterical, which makes me laugh. As her screams get louder, so does my laughter.

'Holy shit. Look at her hair!' Hendrix calls out in sudden urgency. 'She's fucking Broken, Grayson. She's a Broken Witch!'

'I can bloody see that, Hendrix!' Grayson bellows back.

'Hooper's right! She's dangerous! Boss, you have to put her down!'

I spin round and turn my full attention to Grayson.

'You can try,' I tell him with a snarl. 'I would stay there if I were you.' I nod to the knife still at his throat. My fire still burns in my palms, and I'm more than prepared to use it against them. I'm done being threatened and controlled. I'm done being afraid. 'It's my turn to ask the questions, Grayson. And we'll stick with your rules, shall we? Refuse to answer, and someone will get hurt.' His dark eyes narrow on me, but he remains still. 'Why are you looking for Toby?' I demand.

'Just calm down. I'm not a threat to you.'

'You will tell me how you know Toby Smith, or I will use that chunk of glass to cut Hendrix's head off.'

Grayson lifts his hand slowly and vibrant blue streaks of lightning start crawling over his palm.

'You are threatening a fellow witch. Two fellow witches,' he adds, nodding to Collins. 'And a very temperamental vampire.' He looks to Hendrix. 'We're on your side. For now. But if you do this...we won't be.' The lightning weaves between his fingers threateningly. I can hear it crackling, and I know that it'll pack one hell of a punch if he sends it my way. 'If you cut anyone's head off, I will kill you.' Grayson gestures to my hands. 'Put it out and calm down. And you...' he looks past me to my shrieking aunt with disgust and hatred. 'SHUT UP!'

Christa quietens but continues to whimper. As Grayson resumes trying to reach me, I look at him with the same smile Toby would wear. I always loved that grin of his.

'I'm a witch, just like you and I only want to help. Lower the glass you have at my men's throats before you kill them. Lower the flame and stand down-'

'Before you kill me?' I laugh, shaking my head. 'I really don't care if your men die. I don't even care if I die.'

'You don't care about anything...right?' He gestures to my hair. 'Look at what's happening to you.' The long, ratted mess of red hanging over my shoulders is changing. I can see it as much as I can feel it. The power inside me is merging with overwhelming anger and hatred, changing me not just inside, but outside too. Turning my lovely red hair, a stark, chilling white. Just like Toby's. The need to make anyone other than myself suffer is consuming me. There's no guilt. The conscience that should prevent this violence is lost.

'Your eyes too. They're changing colour. Look.' He points to a sliver of broken mirror by my foot. I look at the reflection and I don't see me. I see a girl with Toby's white hair and his lilac eyes.

'What the...' I whisper in confusion. 'What's happening to me?'

'Drop the weapons and I will tell you,' he repeats as I lift my head to look at him. With another look at the two men I have pinned he loses his patience. 'DROP THE KNIFE!' he yells.

The confusion of what's happening to me is nothing compared to everything else I'm feeling and for some reason, I do as I'm told. The knife at Grayson's throat lands with a thud on the floor. Hendrix grabs the glass suddenly with his bare hands and throws it to the floor before making a beeline for me. But he's suddenly tossed across the room by an invisible force and hits the wall with a heavy thud. As he gets back on his feet, I prepare to kill. But Grayson stands between us. He raises his hand in Hendrix's direction and pins him to the wall with magic.

'No one touches her!' he says firmly. 'You stay out of this, Hendrix. Do you hear me? You stay away from her.' He lets him go and turns back to me. 'The pain and suffering that these people caused you is taking over. It won't stop till you end it, do you understand?' He gestures to my aunt and uncle. 'Finish it, Lilly. End this now and put it all behind you for good. Or you will lose control.'

I turn my attention back to my aunt and uncle. Harry's stopped moving. He's nothing but a burning mass of flesh. My eyes and Christa's meet. She sobs and pleads for me to let her go. All these years it's been my screams filling these halls. My tears. My desperation. But not today. Her face is the one twisted in fear and horror. She's helpless, not me.

I spread the flame to my aunt with a simple swipe of my hand and she disappears screaming beneath a swirl of black and white. The fire on my own skin dies down as the fire on theirs rages on.

'You were right,' I tell him. 'I feel much better now.' The anger's gone. The misery and hatred have left me completely, and now all I feel is...nothing. I feel nothing.

Grayson takes my face in his hands and stares straight into my eyes.

'No, don't do that. Don't turn off your emotions. Don't give in to it. Toby does, and you know what that turns you into if you let it. He's a cruel, nasty piece of work. That's not you.'

I have no idea what he means, and I don't really care.

'You have to focus,' he insists. 'Listen to my voice and calm down. I can see you changing, and if you let it win, if you don't let your feelings back in right now, you may never come back. They can't hurt you anymore. It's done. Everyone that hurt you is dead.' His eyes flick from my hair to my eyes. He weaves my hair between his fingers and waits. 'This hair needs to be red. Not this. Come back.'

'Why are you looking for Toby?' I ask again. 'If he's one of your men, I can't trust you.'

'He was. But not anymore. He took off two years ago with something of mine which I want back. Which I *need* back. That's all,' he insists. 'You can trust me.'

'He took something from you?' I ask.

'Yes. A book. A very important book.'

'Was it red? With the picture of the star on the front?' It has to be that one. Toby treated it as if it were made of gold.

His eyes grow wider. 'You've seen it! Do you know where it is?'

'No. He took it when he left me.'

'All I want is that book,' Grayson says matter of factly. 'I don't care about Toby.'

'And Harry's son? What do you want with him?'

'You and he are the last Hooper's alive. Letting a magical bloodline such as yours die out is a terrible waste. I wish to make him an offer. That's all.'

'What offer?'

'To come live with us. He'll want for nothing. If he chooses to further his bloodline, we will support him financially. If not, then he is still welcome. Do you know where he is?'

'No.' I lower my hand and with it, my threat. 'Look, I don't know where Toby is, and Harry's son left this house after they had a huge row. Last I heard, he'd taken a chunk of cash from Harry's bank account and run off to France. So the story goes.'

'And Toby?'

'He left me two years ago and took that book with him.' Those words are painful to say.

'You loved him?' he asks.

'I did,' I answer truthfully.

'And now?'

I shake my head. 'No. Not after...not after everything that happened.' The fire in my belly making me ready to fight fizzles out and I'm left with the realisation that I've just murdered the last people in my life I called family. I don't feel bad that they're dead, I just regret that I was the one that killed them. I turn away lost in confusion at my conflicting emotions and stare at the fire that continues to spread throughout the room. My hair returns to its usual dark red, slowly, from the roots to the tips, and tears silently fall down my face as I accept what I've done.

The sound of feet walking over the broken glass and pieces of debris is followed by a firm hand on the base of my back. Grayson's touch, although uncomfortable, is strangely comforting. I drop the final shard of glass at Collins' throat, and the room falls still and silent. The inanimate objects remain inanimate, and except for the two human pyres, there's no magic to be seen.

Grayson opens his mouth to say something, but there's nothing he could say that I want to hear.

'Don't. I'm calm now, you can drop the act. I've told you all I know and let your men go.' I turn and watch him as more tears fall down my cheeks, feeling so worthless and filled with such regret. 'Harry was right. I'm a monster.'

'You are not a monster. Believe me, I've seen monsters.' He tucks my hair behind my ear as I lower my head and stifle a sob. 'What you are is troubled and traumatised from years of abuse. That's not your fault. It's theirs,' he says pointing at Harry and Christa.

I see the gag on the floor.

'I'm sorry I took it off when I promised I wouldn't.' I reach down to pick it up.

'You don't need that,' he tells me, taking it from my hand and putting it in his pocket. 'You don't need to be bound, Lilly. You just need to feel safe, and you are now. You listen to me. They were the monsters here. Not you.' I turn so my back is to him, and close my eyes to stop the tears.

He walks around me and lifts my chin. Opening my eyes lets loose the pools of tears, but he wipes them away with his thumb.

'You're a Witch too.' I reach up and stroke the hand that was covered in lightning not a moment ago. 'I thought me and Toby were the only ones.'

He wraps his fingers around mine. 'You are the last one to be born to date, but yes, I am a witch. Just like you. You are not alone.' His confident and calming smile appears. Maybe it's in my head, but that smile still seems...off. 'It's done. They're dead. You can leave all this behind you.'

'Thank you.'

'For what?'

'For saving me.'

He laughs softly. 'No problem.'

'You should go.' I lower his hand but find myself reluctant to let it go. 'I don't know how to stop the fire when it leaves me. It was nice to meet you, Grayson Kendryk. Good luck finding your book.' I let go of his hand, and it falls to his side. 'And if you ever do find Toby, tell him I'm dead. I really don't ever want to see him again.' I walk to the door past Hendrix and Collins who watch me in stunned silence.

'Lilly, wait.'

I stop and turn on the spot. Grayson's wearing a dazzling smile as he slides his hands into his pocket and stands taller.

'My offer extends to you too. Come with me.'

'What?'

'Come with me. I can take such good care of you. No one will ever hurt you again, and I'll help you learn to control your magic.'

He waits. His eyes never leave me. His smile doesn't falter for a second, and his confidence and authority fills the air. I can almost taste it. But I'm reluctant.

'I don't want kids. I won't further the bloodline for you.'

'I still want you to come with me. I still want to help you.'

'I don't know you. How can I trust that I'll be safe with you?'

'The world is still full of Hunters. We're almost extinct because of them. We can keep you safe. My men and me. At my house. In my Coven. There will be no more bars on your window. No more chains around your wrists. You will never go hungry. No one will strike you. You'll be safe. Free. I swear it. There is nowhere safer or more comfortable than with us at my home. What do you say?'

'Free?'

'Free.'

I've never been free before. And if anyone can offer me freedom, if anyone can protect me from Hunters and myself, it would be another witch. When I nod, his smile grows and excitement etches across his face. I feel the same expression on my own as suddenly I'm filled with positive hope for my future. I've been pulled out of hell and given a second chance.

On the very top floor of my uncle's home, at the far end of the long landing, is a white door with a large deadbolt screwed to the outside. I pull it across and unlock it. The hinges creak against two years of rust as I push it open. Beyond the door is a thin flight of wooden stairs. I flick on the light switch, and a single bulb at the very top of the stairs flickers on. Slowly, I make my way up the stairs with a pit in my stomach, even though I know that there's no one behind me ready to lock me in once I'm inside. When I reach the top, I come to yet another door and another deadbolt. I slide it across and push it open.

The smell of damp and dust is pungent. It's drawn into my lungs as soon as I take the slightest breath. I flick on the light switch and see the room I called home for most of my life.

The attic.

It's enormous with a high ceiling, but the room is actually filled with very little. Harry would store his broken furniture up here. One of which was my old double bed that still sits beneath a grimy porthole window. Next to that is a wardrobe missing its two doors and rail so I could never use it. Not that I had any clothes to put in it really. Just old T-shirts and a couple pairs of jeans left behind after my mum died. Those and her black Dr Marten boots. I pick up her old rucksack by the door and think about what to pack. I don't know why. I have nothing.

I stroke my neck where a beautiful silver pendant used to rest. It was given to me by my mother the night she died. The delicate seven-pointed star surrounded by a knotted triangle was a family heirloom. Her mother gave it to her, and she gave it to me. She slid it over my head before tucking me into bed. That's the last memory I have of my mum. The next day, Harry woke me up screaming in my face that I'd killed her. That she was on the bathroom floor, dead. I was five and suddenly very alone in the world.

No, not alone. Surrounded by people who hated and feared me. Even after all these years I still don't know what happened to her. In my darkest moments, I would cling to the necklace and talk to my mum. I would pretend that she was sitting beside me. But two years ago, I woke up in chains in the cellar, and my necklace was gone. The only thing that made me feel safe. The only reminder that there was once someone who loved me, was nowhere to be seen.

Maybe it's in here?

At the base of the bed, covered in two years worth of dust and cobwebs are my mother's black Dr Marten boots. I slide them on even though they're heavy and ill-fitting, but they're worth the blisters. They're not as precious to me as her necklace was, but they're all I have now. That and the book that she would read to me every night. A black leather hardback copy of *Grimm's Fairy Tales.*

I loved those stories.

Her reading to me and showing me all the illustrations before bed is another treasured memory I keep close to the forefront of my mind. I used to sleep with it like a security blanket and kept it under my pillow when I wasn't reading it. The bed still has the same sheets on, and nothing's moved since I was last here.

The book must be here too. I lift the pillow, but it's not there. I look everywhere, but neither the book nor the necklace are here. I turn to leave the room for the last time and see a glimpse of myself in the cracked mirror resting against the wall. I look half dead, and I'm beyond filthy. I'm thinner than I've ever been. Lifting my jumper, I run my fingers along my visible rib cage. I'm skin and bones. Barely recognisable from the last time I caught sight of myself in a mirror. The only things that have remained the same are my green eyes and red hair.

I ate up here, slept up here, and I cried up here. A lot happened to me in this house. Painful and fucked up things. Some of the worst were Toby's doing. But also, the best. I know that having Toby in my life changed who I was. Before I met him, I wouldn't hurt anyone. But I know, deep down, that by the time he turned his back on me I was someone else entirely. I saw a glimpse of her downstairs just a few moments ago and that girl, that version of me with white hair and lilac eyes, she's Toby's girl.

And she's more than capable of causing the bloodshed that happened at the Miller's farm.

Problem is, there's a gap in my mind. A hole where six weeks of my life has disappeared.

Six weeks.

Faded from my memory like they never happened. It was in those six weeks that six men were murdered in the most unusual ways that the police had ever seen. But thanks to Harry and Mr Simmons, they ruled it as a human affair. It was in those six weeks that Toby vanished from my life. And it was in those six weeks that someone died. Someone close to me and I have no idea who was responsible.

I can't think of that. Not now. Not feeling this vulnerable and volatile. I have to keep myself together. I won't risk anything changing Grayson's mind and leaving me here with nothing but bad memories and ghosts. If he knew that I have a gap in my memory right around the time Toby disappeared with that book, I don't know what he'd do or if he'd believe me that I really don't know what happened.

One thing's for sure. I can't let what almost happened downstairs happen again. I can't let Toby and his influence affect me like that anymore.

I turn and leave the room closing the door behind me, and go in search of my mother's necklace and fairy tale book elsewhere.

The downstairs hall is filled with smoke and dust. Black and white flames block the lounge door, and there's a loud groan followed by a sudden crash as the magical fire in the lounge weakens the ceiling, causing the room above it to crash through it.

'We need to go, Little Witch,' Hendrix urges as he appears from somewhere behind me. 'Before that happens to the rest of the house.'

I take a step back giving him more than enough room to pass without touching me as he disappears outside into the rain carrying two large boxes and whistling his creepy lullaby.

'Ready?' Grayson asks, appearing next to me. Collins follows Hendrix, also carrying boxes. He glances back at us both looking apprehensive but disappears outside into the storm.

'Almost,' I tell him. 'I just need to find something.'

I turn down the hall into my uncle's library. It's a relatively large room with a heavy oak desk below the window and a grand piano in the corner. The walls are all lined with shelves housing books. This is where I would spend a significant portion of my day. Mr Simmons would have me in here studying for hours. There was nothing else to do with me, Simmons would say, so he would spend his time teaching me anything and everything. I start pulling the books out handfuls at a time, frantically searching for my mother's fairy tale book. If I see the cover, I'll know it straight away. I scan them littered over the floor.

Nothing.

I search the desk for the necklace.

Nothing.

After a couple of minutes and with no luck, I start to panic. I can't leave without them. My Uncle's bedroom maybe? I run out of the library and back to the stairs, but there's thick smoke everywhere, and the heat from the flames are suffocating. I make it up the first couple when a hand grabs my wrist.

'You can't go up there!' Grayson insists. 'This house is coming down. We need to go.'

'I can't leave without them!' I argue, pulling my hand free and taking the stairs two at a time up to the top as he calls after me.

The left side of the house is entirely ablaze. The white door to my room is lost in the inferno, Harry's bedroom is to the right. I have time till it spreads. I throw open his door and start searching. The drawers have been emptied, the cupboards searched, and everything of value is gone. Is that what was in those boxes they were carrying? Have they robbed him? Maybe the book and the necklace are in one of those boxes. Maybe not. It's too big a risk not to look now. If I leave them behind, they'll be destroyed for sure. I have to keep looking! I search frantically for what I've lost, but it's getting obvious they're not here.

Devastation and loss erupt inside me as I start to sob. I continue to hopelessly search, tearing through his room like a hurricane. But nothing. My sobs turn into screams, and I start throwing and smashing everything and anything I can get my hands on. I'm not looking for anything. Not anymore. I'm just destroying. Destroying his possessions. Destroying the horrors he put me through. Destroying his life, like he destroyed mine. It's not enough Harry's dead. I want him to suffer more.

The room's filling with smoke and the fire's getting closer, but still, I yell and cry, tearing apart his room. All the hurt, anger and sadness that I've never been able to express is exploding. And I can't stop it. Grayson wraps his hand around my wrist.

'Lilly, we have to go,' he says firmly in my ear. The room starts to groan and the windows crack as the fire beneath us burns through the floor.

'I can't leave without them!' I cry.

'What? What can't you leave without?'

'My mother's necklace and her book. *"The Brothers Grimm"*. I can't leave them behind.' The despair I have in my heart pours out of me. As I fall to the floor, he comes too. 'I've lost everything. I've destroyed everything. There's nothing left.'

'Yes, there is. There's you. You're still here, and you have us now.'

I just cry, unable to speak anymore as it all washes over me. I don't care that I can see the flames out in the hall. I don't care the room's thick with smoke.

'Shhhh,' he soothes. 'You *are* going to get through this. I have you now, and you are safe with me. Let's get you out of here.'

He scoops me up in his arms and carries me downstairs.

The rain's coming down hard and it's freezing outside. The wind's vicious and I'm not wearing nearly enough to make any real attempts to keep warm. As I shiver in his arms, he tightens his hold on me pulling me closer to his chest. He walks away from my uncle's house and stops by a black Mercedes. We turn back to watch the roof collapse. The flames grow higher and fiercer despite the wet weather.

'Are you ready?' he asks.

'Ready for what?' I lift my head, and he rests his nose by mine. His eyes drift to my lips, and he leans in to kiss me, but before he does, he says quietly.

'To be free.'

Chapter 5

Lying on my back, I look up at the rafters.
The sound of rain hammering the tin roof is all I can hear.
I sit and look at my surroundings.
I'm in a barn.
Piles of hay and broken farming machinery line the wooden walls.
As I move, my body cries out in pain. But I have to get to my feet.
It's all I can think to do.
The floor's slick, making me slip as I stand.
I see the door! Ten metres or so away.
With my first step, I lose my balance completely and slam down onto my hip with a heavy thud, screaming an obscenity as I go.
But I won't give in. I'm getting out of here.
Putting all my weight on my hands, I hang my head trying desperately to muster the strength to get back on my feet.
'One last push... come on, Lilly, you can do this!! On your knees...that's it, now push up. There... good girl.'
My pep talk pushes me on. Getting me closer and closer to the door.
Talking to myself. The first sign of madness, so Harry says.
I'm well past that!

I wipe my hands on my shirt to clean them, but it's pointless.
I'm absolutely covered. The floor is too. I'm surrounded by a
thick river of red.
With a deep readying breath, I turn my attention once more to
the door ahead of me.
Why does blood have to be so fucking slippery?

I jerk awake from my recurring nightmare, and as I lie here, I feel something I've never felt before. Fresh, clean, crisp sheets. I'm in bed. A large, comfortable, but unfamiliar bed.

The events of the previous night crash like a horror movie into my brain. The violence, the fire...Grayson and his men. Harry and Christa's death. Grayson and the kiss! Oh no... who's bed am I in? It takes me a moment to get the courage to roll over and look.

Empty. I'm alone. But where?

All I know is I'm in a dark and reasonably large room that's in an immaculate condition. There's everything you would expect to find in a bedroom. A double bed, wardrobe, dressing table and bedside cabinet. All the furniture looks antique and very, very expensive. There's a closed door to my right and another straight ahead of me. I can feel my magic, so I'm not bound. Not defenceless. That's something.

There's a small digital clock on the bedside table telling me it's three in the morning, and a bedside lamp by my head casting a low glow in the room. Next to that is a large glass of water with a couple of white pills and a note.

The pills are painkillers.

The kitchen is downstairs if you get hungry. Second door on your right.
I'll be back to check on you in the morning.
Gx

I swipe up the pills and swallow them down with the entire contents of the glass. It's no good, I need more water. My mouth's beyond parched, and I ache everywhere. I notice my wrists have been wrapped neatly in white bandages, and I'm wearing boxers and a large black T-shirt with short sleeves. I've been strip washed and put in men's clothes. My hair seems to have been rinsed and pulled back in a rough ponytail. I'm suddenly feeling very vulnerable at the idea of Grayson undressing me while I'm unconscious.

Who does he think he is? Why would he think that's okay?

My palm slaps my forehead.

I kissed him!

Stupid girl...stupid, foolish girl!

That's a great impression to give him. What must he think of me? I'm a crazy murdering psycho that will kiss you as a way of saying thanks...that's what.

The last thing I remember after our kiss is him sliding me into the front seat of his car, buckling my seat belt and driving me away from the burning rubble that was once my home. After that...nothing.

Slowly and on shaky legs, I make my way to the door on my right. Cautiously I open it, flick on the light and see it's a bathroom with a toilet, shower and sink. I rush over to the sink and drink till my belly's full. But it growls fiercely as I shake with hunger.

I need food.

But I can't go out there dressed like this! I don't know who's out there or what they want with me. I open the wardrobe door and inwardly cry when I find it empty. My already overwhelming sense of vulnerability is pushed into overdrive by my severe lack of clothing.

I go to the second door and rest my hand on the doorknob for a ridiculous amount of time. I have to tell myself to stop biting my lip before I chew it off. Fuck it! I have my magic and besides, what else could possibly happen to me that hasn't already?

I pull it open and head outside.

Stepping out into a massive hallway, my mouth literally opens in a well-formed O. This place is unreal! The clean white walls are a stark contrast to the dark mahogany beams in the high ceiling, and there are three long spiralling clear crystal chandeliers with black pendants dangling below, all equally spaced from one end of this seemingly endless hallway to the other.

My uncle's house was big, but this...this is mind-blowing! My bare feet are cold on the wood, but I'm too engrossed in taking in all this beauty to care. As I walk, the top of the staircase comes into view, and with a quick glance back I take a mental note of which one of the many doors belongs to the room I just left.

The walls are decorated with stunning pieces of art. As I walk, I admire the various landscapes and portraits hanging above the carved wooden panels which follow the hall all the way to the stairs. I look down nervously to see if anyone is below. But I don't see anyone. The stairs turn three times before reaching the ground floor, and there's another flight of stairs further along the hall leading up to yet another landing. I take a nervous step back and clumsily knock into a small round pillar displaying a blue vase with a dragon and phoenix painted on each side. I hold my breath waiting for it to crash to the floor.

It wobbles but steadies.

Above it is a painting I actually recognise. The red and yellow poppies against the dark background was one of Mr Simmons's favourite pieces. He would spend hours trying to recreate it, but could never get it close. I lean in, seeing the brush strokes he never achieved and with it, the small signature at the bottom.

'Fuck me!' I gasp, realising what I'm actually looking at.

'Maybe you could buy me a drink first?'

Every nerve explodes at the unfamiliar voice. My reaction sparks my magic and as I spin around to see who's behind me, the blue vase soars through the air.

'Whoa!' A man laughs, catching it just before it slams into his face. 'Easy there. Grayson's not too keen on people playing catch with seventy-five grand's worth of ugly vase.'

He lowers the vase that's obstructing his face, returns it back to the pillar, and looks at me with a smile.

His straight, almost black hair falls over his electric blue eyes which shine even in this dull light. He brushes his hand through his tousled hair in a failed attempt to tame it. He has the same hard jawline as Grayson but no stubble, and he's built just like him. He's younger, mid-twenties maybe. And he has a cheeky half-smile that makes my heart flutter. As he stands there in black joggers, barefoot and bare-chested, my cheeks flush. My eyes linger on his six-pack and perfectly formed body before he clears his throat, snapping me back to his amazingly beautiful face. The corner of his mouth twitches further into his half-smile, and he holds a hand out for me to shake.

'Hello. I'm Gabriel.'

'Like the angel?' I whisper like a fool.

'Yeah,' he chuckles. 'Like the angel. No one's likened me to an angel before.'

But he bloody is! He's beautiful!

'So, I told you my name. You're supposed to say your name now. Or you could carry on gawking. If you prefer.'

What the hell's wrong with me? I'm just staring at him like a stunned mute.

'Gawking it is, then,' he laughs, retracting his hand before slowly walking towards me. I instinctively back away. Each step he takes forward, I take one back until my heel doesn't feel the floor anymore and I fall backwards. With a small yelp, I reach out to stop myself from falling down the stairs, but there's nothing to grab except air.

Shit! I'm going down!

'Woah!' He reaches out and wraps his fingers around my wrist. I'm pulled back to safety and land in his arms. My hands are gripping his shoulders so tight my fingertips are white. 'Are you alright?' he asks. When I don't answer, he leans down to my face. 'Are you alright?' he asks again with that smile still firmly in place. His eyes look straight into mine, unblinking and beautiful. I'm stunned into this ongoing silence.

I nod and drag my eyes away, staring instead at my hands.

My hands which are touching his skin. This isn't right!

I let him go and take a small step back creating some distance between us. After a minute of unbelievably awkward silence, he walks around me, intentionally giving me plenty of room. His eyes don't leave me until he reaches the stairs and starts walking down them, his hand stroking the dark mahogany bannister as he goes.

'I'm heading to the kitchen for a drink and some food.' He turns back and looks at me over his shoulder. 'You're welcome to join me if you like. Unlike Hendrix, I don't bite.'

I follow him down, despite the voice of reason inside my head screaming, *"Hide! Run away!"*

The grandness of upstairs is a shadow of what it is down here. The entrance hall is magnificent! Beside the stairs is an enormous white marble fireplace. To my left, there are two sets of double doors an equal distance apart and straight ahead of me with stain glass panels is another set of double doors that lead out to a further entrance hall and the front door. To my right is yet another set of doors, these ones are thick and heavy. In the centre of this vast space is a long wooden table decorated with a vase of red Calla lilies. The hall carries on further behind me bending to the right, and I can hear the clinking of glass coming from that direction. I follow the sound keen to find the mysterious Gabriel. I walk across the lobby and as Grayson said in his note, the second door on the right leads into the kitchen. It's a large and rustic room with white walls and exposed wooden beams. The wood floors end here and change into grey stone slabs. In the centre of the room is a large fitted island with several tall stools surrounding it. The patio doors beyond the island lead out into a garden which is shrouded in darkness and behind me is another fireplace made entirely of bare bricks which take up almost the whole wall. The units are light wood with granite surfaces, and standing by the sink pouring us a drink with his back to me is Gabriel.

He turns, holding two glasses of amber liquid in his hands.

'You like whiskey?' He perches himself on one of the stools before sliding a drink over to me. 'Everyone likes whiskey. Come sit with me.' He takes a slow sip and runs his fingers through his hair once more, gesturing for me to join him. I sit, taking the tumbler in my hands and hitching my t-shirt down as far as it will go. I sip the whiskey, wishing he'd given me something to eat instead.

As if on cue, my stomach gives an enormous growl.

'Hungry, huh? I can fix that.' Gabriel gets to his feet and opens the fridge door. 'We have chicken, apples, chocolate...' He starts grabbing various things before returning to the stool next to unload them all. 'Eat. As much as you like.'

I can't actually remember eating a fresh piece of fruit. It's been years. I eat grapes, an apple, a chicken leg and then turn my attention to the bar of chocolate.

'God, that's really good,' I groan in delight. 'Chocolate. Actual chocolate.' He watches with satisfaction.

'Want anything else?' he asks.

'No. Thank you. It's been a really long time since I've eaten anything without mould growing on it. Thank you, Gabriel.'

He gives a small polite nod. 'My pleasure, Lilly.'

'You know my name?'

'Grayson told me when he brought you home last night,' he says, dunking his finger in a jar of chocolate spread and sucking it clean.

'Last night?' I look at the clock above the door. It's almost five in the morning. 'How long was I asleep?'

'You passed out in Grayson's car on the way home and slept all day. He tried to stay awake so you could see a familiar face when you woke up, but he was tired. Collins too. I said I would wait up for you instead. I hope you don't mind.' His vivid blue eyes flick quickly over the scars on my arms and the bandages around my wrists. I lower them down onto my lap feeling far too exposed. 'So...' he says with a forced cheeriness noticing my discomfort. 'What do you think of The Orchard?'

'The what?'

He opens his arms wide, 'The Orchard. It's the name of the estate.'

'It's beautiful.' I tell him with complete sincerity. 'I feel like I'm making it a mess by being in it.'

'Nonsense. I saw you admiring the painting upstairs. Do you enjoy art?' he asks.

'Not particularly. But it's not every day you see a real Van Gogh hanging in someone's hall.'

'Most people think it's a copy.' He shrugs, breaking off a bit of the chocolate and putting it in his mouth.

'That painting's worth-'

'About four million,' he says casually. 'Yeah. I know.'

'It's also been missing for the last seven years. It's stolen.'

'I won't tell if you won't.' He winks and I feel myself redden again, making him give a small chuckle.

'Who washed me?' I ask looking down once more at my bare legs. 'Because I didn't say anyone could wash me or undress me.'

'Grayson did.'

I huff and shake my head, wrapping my arms around me protectively as I do.

'To be fair, Lilly. You were in a bit of a mess. He burned what you were wearing while cursing your uncle to hell for what he did to you.'

'He told you about that?' I complain, hating that suddenly everyone seems to be helping themselves to my life. And my body. 'What did he say?'

He goes to speak when a light from outside suddenly turns on and the door leading out to the garden opens. I jump to my feet on high alert and back up behind Gabriel as Hendrix skulks in. He closes the door and gives the slightest nod in our direction.

'Gabriel.'

'Hendrix,' Gabriel replies. I can hear their mutual disinterest.

He walks past and his eyes settle on me. 'I see you've met Little Witch. Glad you're awake, finally,' he drawls, looking me up and down making my blood run cold. He doesn't look away until he disappears through the door. I want to wash his stare off me.

'He's disgusting, but he won't hurt you. No one here will hurt you and not because you could turn them into a human torch,' Gabriel adds with a light-hearted laugh, but I don't share the joke. I see my aunt and uncle burning at his words and shake away the image from my mind. 'Sorry. I have a dark sense of humour. But seriously, you're perfectly safe here.'

I give a small unsure nod and lean against the counter with a sigh.

'I killed my aunt and uncle,' I whisper sadly. 'What kind of person does that?'

I look at him as if he can answer me. Now I'm out, I feel awful about what I did.

'Hey, no. Don't do that. Grayson and Collins told me how they found you.' My eyes start to brim with sad little tears. When one spills over and tumbles down my cheek, he gets to his feet and settles his hand on mine with a concerned furrow on his brow. 'Killing those people was not your mistake. Not making them suffer for the rest of their days was your mistake. Don't you feel bad for what you did. They deserved it. And a lot more besides.'

'You're a Witch too, aren't you?' I ask quickly, steering the conversation away from murder.

He wipes my tear as another falls. 'How did you know?'

I hold my hand an inch from his chest watching it intently.

'Because I can feel it.'

'Feel it?'

I move my fingers as if playing with the air. 'There's a hum around you. The air vibrates. It does with Grayson and Collins too. But not with Hendrix.' Whatever it is weaves between my fingers as I move them. 'It feels *really* beautiful around you.' I smile fondly at the feeling.

'That's not the only thing that's beautiful,' he says. I look at him with surprise. 'I-I'm so sorry,' he stammers. 'I am being way too over familiar. And after everything you've been through, the last thing you need is some stranger-'

'D-did you just call me beautiful?'

'Noticed that, huh? And you're sensing my magic,' he tells me, sliding his fingers between mine. 'I wish I could feel it. It's supposed to be an incredible feeling.'

'I can't feel it around Hendrix.'

'You wouldn't. He's not a Witch. He's a vampire,' he explains. 'The only vampire left actually. Grayson said you can make fire and move things. Is there anything else you can do?'

'No. That's the lot. What about you?' I ask.

'You want to see?' Suddenly he's excited.

I give him a smile and a nod. Just before he speaks, his eyes darken. The whites disappear entirely, and those ocean blue eyes are replaced by blackness. It's horrible.

'Lilly...stand on one leg!' My leg shoots up off the floor, and I can't lower it at all. 'Touch your nose,' he says.

Again, my body follows his instructions, and I stand there with one leg up and my finger resting on my nose. He waves his hand casually; his eyes return to startling blue, and I get control back over my body.

He can control people?! That's a power no one should have. The blood drains from my face as I start backing away and his excitement disappears altogether.

'I'm sorry. I didn't mean to scare you.' He raises his hands in a bid to show me he means no harm. 'I'm so sorry. I shouldn't have done that. I've made you uncomfortable.'

'Is it just actions?' I ask, my mouth suddenly dry. 'Or can you make people think whatever you want them to? Are you using it on me now?' I'm backing away, and his face gets more distressed at my reaction.

'No!' he insists. 'I swear I'm not. You knew what was happening and you remember it completely-'

'Don't do that to me again.' I want it to come out as a warning, but it sounds more like a plea. If some of the people I'd known in my past had that ability...God, help us all!

'I won't. I swear.' He rests his hand on his heart before backing away. 'I will never use it on you again. You have my word. Please, forgive me?' I watch him, nervous to move or say anything else.

'Gabriel?' comes a soft, delicate voice. I look up and see a pretty blonde woman about my age wearing nothing but a T-shirt and hopefully some underwear. She sees me and stops. Her placid features harden for a brief moment. 'I wondered where you'd gone. Who's this?'

'This is Lilly. A friend of Grayson's,' he explains.

'Lucky Grayson,' she says, gliding through the kitchen and pouring herself a glass of water before turning to Gabriel and giving him a small lingering kiss on his cheek. Her perfectly tanned legs and unmarked skin annoy me. She tucks her long straight hair behind her ear and flicks her hazel eyes in my direction.

'I'm Ava,' she says. 'A *close* friend of Gabriel's.'

'I told you to stay upstairs tonight,' he says a little coldly to her. 'You want me to call you a cab home or something?'

'Nope,' she giggles, leaning in and whispering something into his ear. Her eyes glance at me for a second as she does and I know she's claiming him as hers.

He leans back from her. 'Just...go back to bed. I'll be up soon. Okay?'

'You better,' she smirks, biting her lower lip and running her manicured fingers along his arm before leaving us alone once more.

'I'm sorry. That wasn't what it looked like,' he tells me quickly. 'She's just a friend. No one special-'

'It's none of my business,' I reply. 'If you need to go-'

'I don't. Honestly, she's a friend.' He stands with me and keeps smiling.

'To be honest, I could really use some alone time.'

'I would have thought you would have had enough of that.' He attempts humour. I don't think it's funny in the slightest and his smile starts to slip. 'Let me take you back to your room at least.'

'No,' I say quickly. 'I would like to stay here. In the open where I can see an exit if needed.'

'An exit?'

'Gabriel, I really don't want to seem rude. But I'm completely overwhelmed and really very frightened right now. And in my case, that can sometimes be a lethal combination. Please, go back to your girlfriend and-'

'She's not my girlf-'

'Gabriel, please. I really would rather you left.'

'It was my magic, wasn't it?' he asks sadly. 'I freaked you out.'

'This is all freaking me out. Please...I'd really like it if you could leave so I can just have a moment to acclimatise.' I'm getting tired of repeating myself.

'Okay then.' He swallows hard and walks around me. 'It's been a pleasure to meet you. And I'm sorry if I made things awkward.' He gives me a small formal bow and makes for the door.

'Wait!' I call when he's almost gone. He stops and turns, looking hopeful that I've changed my mind. 'You said it's just actions you control, so anything I feel is me feeling it...right?'

He nods as his frown deepens. 'What's on your mind?'

With a deep breath, I nervously ask, 'Can I touch you?'

'What?' He stands a little straighter. 'What do you mean, touch me?'

'Like, can I put my hand on your shoulder?'

He returns and takes my hand in his so he can place it flatly over his heart.

'Help yourself,' he whispers in my ear.

I lay my hand on his chest feeling his heart beating frantically and rest my other hand on his shoulder.

'Nothing...' I breathe, looking up at him, confusion etched on my face. 'How can that be?'

'Charming,' he grumbles with an eye roll.

'I didn't mean it like that, it's just... never mind.' That was embarrassing. I resume my seat, intentionally avoiding his stare which I can feel burning a hole in my back. He's still there. I can sense him. The vibrations in the air increase and I feel the warmth of his breath on my neck making every hair on my body stand to attention.

'It's been really nice meeting you, Lilly,' he murmurs in my ear before he leans in and gently plants a small kiss on my cheek. 'Welcome to The Orchard. I think you'll really love it here.'

I turn and see his beautiful eyes taking me in. I could get lost in that shade of blue. Which is precisely why he needs to leave.

'Good night, Gabriel,' I whisper.

'Goodnight, Lilly.'

He leaves me alone with a horrifying realisation.

I touched his skin...and it didn't hurt!

Only one other person has had that effect on me.

Toby.

Chapter 6

I'm trembling as I hold out both my arms straight ahead of me. My fists are clenched. My fingernails digging into my palms so deep I can feel blood.

I look straight ahead, trying my hardest not to show how afraid I am.

But I shake violently. And my breathing is nothing less than panting.

'Ten,' Harry snarls as he points my aunts riding crop at me. 'Ten, and you will count, girl.'

He takes my hands and twists them, so the soft skin of my underarm is exposed.

He raises the cane above his head, his face contorted in hatred, before he brings it down on my arms with as much force as he can muster.

I don't hold back as I scream.

'COUNT!'

'ONE!' I cry.

'Lilly. Lilly...wake up, sweetheart,' Grayson's voice echoes over my counting and the crack of the cane breaking my skin. His words pull me from my nightmare and back to the waking world.

When I feel a hand on my shoulder, I lash out, hitting whoever's touching me in a desperate bid to get them away. My magic erupts in a violent pulse, and I hear a smash.

Grayson yells.

I open my tired eyes to find I'm still in the kitchen, tucked up on the floor with my head on my knees.

Grayson's mug of coffee has exploded all over him. He's busy wiping the scalding liquid off his hands and doesn't see that the curtains by the patio doors are alight with my black and white fire. When he sees me staring at them in horror, he turns.

'I got them.' He kicks open the door, rips the curtains down and tosses them outside before turning back to me with a quick exhale of breath. 'Bad dream?'

Reaching down, he helps me to my feet as I stumble over my words, desperately apologising.

'It's fine,' he insists. 'No harm done, Lilly. I assure you. You may owe the curtains an apology, however,' He looks down at his soaked white shirt. 'And my dry cleaner.' He's wearing a suit again, but there's not a trace of blood to be seen. He lifts his head, his eyes twinkling as he sees me. 'I am very glad to see you.'

Collins comes charging into the kitchen looking ready to fight and scans the room until he settles his eyes on me. I sidestep behind Grayson, unashamedly using him as a human shield.

'It's alright, Collins. We're fine,' Grayson tells him firmly, gesturing to the door where he appeared from. 'You can go.'

He leaves, and Grayson turns back to me. 'You're alright. He won't hurt you. He was making sure we were safe, that's all. That's all any of us want for you. To be safe.' He runs his hand down my arm, and I shrink back as he touches me. He lifts his hands an inch from my skin reading my reaction. 'Sorry. Of course. Your haphephobia. I won't touch you if you don't want me to.'

'Grayson! Your hand!' His skin is badly burnt from grabbing the flaming curtains. 'I'm so sorry. It was an accident. I didn't mean to. I was having a nightmare and my magic...sometimes it just... I'm sorry!'

Shit!

I start panicking, and it gets harder to breathe.

'It's okay. I'm not mad, or hurt.' The cupboards begin to shake. 'Hey, hey,' he comforts. 'You're absolutely fine. Calm down. I know it was an accident.'

I take a breath and close my eyes. When I open them, he's bending down to pick up the bottle of wine I found last night. And drank.

'Did you drink all this?'

'I'm sorry.'

'Stop apologising.' He puts the bottle on the counter and pours another coffee. 'Do you take milk?'

'No,' I say quietly, embarrassed at passing out on his kitchen floor. He hands me a big black coffee. Perfect. It's a taste I haven't had in a long, long time.

'I was worried when you weren't in your room. Hendrix came to tell me you were asleep on my kitchen floor. He was a tad nervous about waking you up. Did you get enough rest?'

'I'm sorry about the wine. I was just-'

'It's fine. I told you.' Grayson pours himself a coffee as I stare at his hand. 'It hurts but it will heal very quickly. Please don't worry.' He stretches out his red fingers. 'I can heal most injuries. We all can. This will be gone in half an hour or so.'

'We?'

'Collins, Hendrix, Gabriel and I. Courtesy of a spell we did a few years back. The smaller the injury, the quicker we heal. I hear you met Gabriel last night?'

'Yeah.'

He seems to be waiting for me to add to the conversation, but I have no clue what to say. They can heal themselves? Because of a spell? I'm struggling to process all the information that's being given to me. Forty-eight hours ago, all I had to think about was when I was going to get some food, or if Roger would start nibbling on my toes. Now I'm in a house with witches, a vampire, and the man who saved me is talking about spells.

'What other spells can you do?' I ask, unintentionally glancing at the bandages on my wrists and the scars from the punishments my uncle would dish out. Maybe he can get rid of them for me.

'Not so many now I'm afraid. We have a lot to talk about, and I know you must have a dozen questions for me, but first things first. You need more painkillers. I saw you had the ones I left you.' He takes a pot of pills from his pocket and empties two into his hand before passing them to me.

'Second. Your bandages need changing. Those marks from the cuffs will more than likely scar I'm afraid.'

I nod. What're a few more scars.

'Then I really need to talk to you about Toby-'

'I need some clothes.' My words come out a lot louder than I intended. His eyebrows arch up in surprise. He clearly isn't used to being interrupted. 'And, I know we kissed but... I'm not comfortable with you undressing me,' I add clearing my throat which is painfully tight.

He gives a small short laugh.

'You were filthy, Lilly. I had to wash you. To make sure your injuries didn't get infected if nothing else. The fact we kissed played no part in that. But I am sorry that it made you uncomfortable. That wasn't my intention. And I have someone getting you some clothes as we speak. No women are living here, so we had to make do with those for now. It was all we could find that would fit you.' He gestures to what I'm wearing.

We're interrupted by Hendrix who clears his throat as he stands in the doorway.

'Boss. You have a phone call. The New York office. Something about a secretary wandering off with sensitive information.'

'Thank you, Hendrix,' Grayson replies with a heavy sigh. 'I'll take it in my office. Work beckons I'm afraid. Make yourself some breakfast, and I'll be back shortly. Help yourself. I won't have you go hungry. What's mine is yours.' He gives me a courteous nod before heading towards the door.

Hendrix lingers in the doorway. Again, his eyes scan up my body and that disgusting sneer makes an appearance.

So that's what a real Vampire looks like? Huh, modern fiction really has it wrong!

Thankfully he doesn't stay, and follows Grayson out of the room. I wonder what classes as work for a man like him. But not for long.

The sun's up, and it's only now I see what lies beyond the patio doors. Along with the burnt remains of Grayson's curtains, I see endless greenery. Acres and acres of perfectly manicured lawn with clipped box hedging and stone statues surrounded by rose bushes and colour coordinated flowers. The garden rolls down to what looks like a boating lake in the distance with a magnificent willow tree hugging the bank. In the distance is open countryside and woodland. It's a scene of undoubted beauty. About a hundred metres in front of me is a patio with a huge outdoor swimming pool slap bang in the middle, surrounded by sun loungers. Beyond that is a large three-tier stone water fountain that sprays water in all directions. It's what I imagine heaven looking like. Open, empty and free.

I long for the open space. More than I long for clothes. So I put down the coffee, open up the doors, and head out.

The cold air bites and gets stuck in my throat. But the sky's perfectly clear and the sun's shining. I pass the patio till I feel the grass beneath my feet.

That's when I stop.

I wriggle my toes, feeling each blade that nestles between them and observe my skin in the natural light. I'm so pale. Almost grey. The scars on my skin are more visible than I've ever seen them. A strong breeze blows a few loose strands of hair across my face, and the smell of rain from last night's storm still lingers in the soil. I raise my arms either side of me and lower them again, so my palms lay flat on my thighs and then I do it again, and again.

'Thinking of flying away?' Grayson asks, standing next to me watching my unusual behaviour.

'It's tempting,' I reply. 'Everything okay with work?'

'All fine. I'm more worried about you, not a misplaced folder containing the email addresses of a few business associates.'

'You have a job? But you're witches.'

'Yes well, being witches doesn't pay the bills,' he jokes. 'Never mind all that. How are you feeling?'

'Overwhelmed,' I sigh. 'This is the first bit of sunlight I've seen in two years.' My lip starts to tremble. I can't cry. If I start, I don't think I'll ever stop. The tears I have inside could wash me away if I let them. I look back out at the vast space before me so he doesn't see me trying not to fall apart. 'I never thought I would feel the grass between my toes ever again.'

'You thought you were going to die down there,' he says sadly.

'Worse,' I tell him. 'I thought I was going to survive down there. I would have taken death happily from the minute I woke up in those chains. After everything...' My voice trails off.

'What happened to you? The marks on your body and those men in the barn? Collins told me what they found. Did you kill them? You and Toby?'

He wants answers. And although he sounds caring and concerned, I know he's desperate for information. All I want right now is to enjoy this moment.

'Would you mind if we talked about all that later? I just need to let my head catch up with everything.'

'Sure,' he sighs.

I return to enjoying this moment, right now. I lower myself down on to my knees. The morning dew settles on my skin and the blades of grass sit between my fingers. I rip up a few and smell them. 'In the summer, Mr Simmons would open the window of Harry's library. When the gardener mowed the lawn, the smell of the freshly cut grass would come in through the window.' I smell the grass once more, delighting in its aroma. 'When you grow up with so little, it really makes you appreciate the small things, you know?'

He squats down next to me, resting his elbows on his knees and takes the torn grass from my hand to smell. He doesn't share my sentimentality and drops it to the floor.

'Whatever happened to you at your uncle's home, I want you to know that it's over. No harm will come to you here.' He reaches out a comforting hand and rests it on mine. The usual hot, sharp pain erupts on every inch he touches. I flinch away from him, and he retracts it immediately.

'Grayson, I have a problem with being touched. It takes time,' I say a little annoyed. He knows this. 'I would really appreciate it if you could just give me a little space. I don't want to lose control and hurt anyone.'

'I understand. And I apologise,' he says softly, getting to his feet. 'Come inside. You must be freezing. We can have a chat.'

'Can I go for a walk first?'

'You will get cold.' He looks at my legs, bare feet and short sleeved top.

I throw him a forced smile. 'I don't mind the cold. Please?'

He nods. 'As you wish. Take some time. Clear your head. But please, stay close to the house.'

'I will. Thank you.'

He leaves as I take off in the opposite direction, eager to explore.

I find a tennis court, pool house, greenhouse and an impressive lake with a small boat. If I knew how to swim, I would be tempted to take it out onto the water.

After another twenty minutes or so of walking, I come to a large brick wall with a single archway in the centre. A black iron gate sits slightly ajar tempting me inside. I walk through it and realise why they call this place The Orchard.

Set out in hundreds of straight lines that disappear into the distance and eventually merging into thick woodland are countless apple trees. I can't even begin to guess how many there are. I take a leisurely pace, walking past line after line of flourishing fruit trees decorated with beautiful red apples that make the air smell sweet.

'Can I try one?' I ask when I feel the air begin to hum.

'That's a creepy talent,' replies Gabriel. 'I usually enjoy sneaking up on people.' He reaches into the branches and plucks an apple. 'I think we can spare one.' Gabriel hands me the fruit before taking off his leather jacket and holds it up for me. 'Put this on. You must be cold.'

'I'm fine,' I lie. I'm freezing, but I don't want to be an inconvenience.

He holds out his jacket further and shakes his head.

'Not gonna take no for an answer. You're in shorts and a T-shirt. And it is winter, Lilly,' he insists. 'We can't have you getting sick.'

'I'm not the ideal person to make jump,' I tell him as I slide on his jacket. 'You're more likely to end up bursting into flames or slamming into walls than getting a funny scare.' I pull the leather jacket tight around me, thankful for the warmth as he laughs softly to himself. 'That's nice,' I gesture to the leather bracelet that looks like a cuff around his wrist. It has beautifully carved knots and intricate patterns in the flesh of the leather. He holds it out for me to see.

'My mother made it for me before she died. It's supposed to bring the wearer luck.'

I take his hand in mine and pull it closer. It really is stunning and so detailed.

I soon stop looking at the accessory and start admiring the hand I'm holding. Everything about this man is stunning, even his fingers. My hands hold his, and I'm lost in wonderment at how it feels to touch him. There's no pain. No discomfort or feelings of dread. Human contact is massively overrated to those who can bear it. I can't. So when it feels nice like this...I savour every second.

Finally, he clears his throat making me drop his hand and look up at his cheeky grin and curious eyes.

'I was told you didn't like to be touched. Am I an exception?'

'I'm sorry about your mum.' I change the subject fast. 'My mum's dead too. It sucks.'

'Yeah,' he sighs. 'It's a real shit.'

I take a bite of the apple.

'That's amazing,' I tell him. I haven't had an apple that wasn't bruised or stale in a long time. It's juicy, crisp and the freshest a piece of fruit can be.

I look up at the clear blue sky through the branches of these beautiful trees, listening to the birds sing their morning song and feel nothing but fresh air and freedom. I'm in heaven.

He picks an apple for himself and takes a bite. 'We've grown them here for decades.' He looks around him enjoying the beauty of our surroundings for himself. 'I love mornings like this. Sunny but cold. It feels fresh, don't you think?'

'Yeah.' We continue walking.

'Why are you out here alone?' he asks. 'Did Grayson not want to join you?'

'I'm sure he would have if I asked him to. I don't want to be a bother. Talking about being a bother, I'm really sorry about last night. I was rude. And I hope I didn't offend you or your girlfriend.'

'She's not my girlfriend,' he says with a casual air. 'I'd had too much to drink at the pub. She drove me home and helped me upstairs. I passed out. Guess she decided to stay over.' He runs his hand through his hair but it falls straight back over his eyes which are watching me, and the corner of his mouth is hitched up in that half-smile of his. Why does hearing that make me happy? 'You know you don't have any shoes on.' He nods to my naked feet.

'I'm aware,' I say not caring in the slightest that I'm freezing and my feet are actually throbbing. 'Some things are worth feeling uncomfortable for. I've not felt grass beneath my feet for a while.'

His eyes flood with sadness, or pity maybe. I don't like it, so I make a mental note to myself to keep the depressing talk to a minimum.

When I've finished the apple, I tuck my hands in the pockets of my borrowed jacket and wrap it tighter around my body with my nose snuggled in the collar, breathing in the scent of sandalwood and vanilla. It smells like him. And I really like it.

'How old are you?' he asks as we continue walking.

'Twenty-two-ish.'

'Ish?'

'I'm not exactly sure when my birthday is. I know I was five when my mum died, and that was seventeen years ago.'

'You should pick a birthday. I'll get you a present.' He nudges my shoulder playfully as we walk.

I chuckle at his suggestion. He's funny. And sweet.

'Being here is more than enough. How old are you?' I throw his question back.

'Twenty-five-ish,' he says, trying not to smirk.

'Ish?'

'Well... I've been twenty-five for a while.'

'What does that mean?' I step on something sharp and lose my footing.

'I've gotcha.' He grabs my arm keeping me on my feet. I hold onto him to steady myself, and again, stare in surprise as my hand rests in his. He strokes my skin ever so slightly with his thumb sending tingles through my whole body. 'Damn, you are so fucking beautiful,' he whispers to himself before looking at me like he forgot I was there. 'I am so sorry. I won't say that again,' he laughs, embarrassed. 'I think it's the hair. Redheads are just...' as I laugh at his reddening cheeks, he looks to the floor, grinning from ear to ear. But his grin turns to a frown. 'Oh shit, you're bleeding.'

I've cut my foot. But it's not too bad. I put some weight on it but wince as I do. Before I can utter a word of protest, he scoops me up in his arms and starts walking back to the iron gate.

'I'm sorry if me holding you is uncomfortable. Grayson mentioned that you don't like being touched, but I don't want you to be in any more pain than necessary. You'll be in agony if you walk back to the house with no shoes. Can you bear it till we get back?'

'I can bear it,' I tell him.

I can more than bear it.

Sitting back in the kitchen on one of the stools with my foot on his knee, Gabriel cleans the cut and puts yet another bandage on my body. He also has a large bowl of warm soapy water ready to wash my wrists. I can't stop watching his skin on mine. It's hypnotic feeling his hands on me and not being filled with dread and pain. He unwraps the bandages around my wrists. The pity in his face doesn't go unnoticed when he sees the marks, and although his hands are gentle, I hiss and wince as the wounds are wiped clean. Every time I do, he tells me he's sorry.

'Those cuffs really dug into your skin,' he says. 'I can nearly see bone.' He finishes wrapping them. 'All done,' he says, resting his hands over mine. We look at each other, and I feel his thumb trace back and forth over my knuckles. 'How does it feel?' he asks quietly.

'Fine,' I reply with a dry mouth and butterflies in my belly.

The loud ding dong of a doorbell makes me violently jump as the lightbulb above us pops and showers us with glass.

'It's alright. That will be your new wardrobe,' he assures me, patting my hand which has grabbed hold of his tightly. He goes to stand. To leave!

'Will you stay with me?' I ask, not letting him go. I hate sounding so pathetic, but I feel safer with him around.

'Of course. For as long as you like.' He returns to the seat and carries on tending to my wrists.

The front door opens, and I hear someone walking into the lobby. The clacking of heels on the wooden floor tell me it's a woman.

'The traffic was a bloody nightmare, and the shopping centre was heaving. But I think I have enough for a while at least,' a soft, delicate female voice says as she walks through the lobby towards us. I think to myself, please don't be Ava. When she walks in all I see is a pair of feet in kitten heels and a horde of shopping bags walking towards us. She can't see where she's going because the bags are completely blocking her face from view as she makes her way closer.

'Gabriel... be a love and take some of these, would you?'

Shaking his head and rolling his eyes in amusement, he heads over and lightens her load.

'Where is she then?' she asks, dumping the bags on the island and looking around the room until her big silver eyes fall on me. It's not Ava, but a dainty young woman in her very early twenties with waist length brunette hair, pale complexion and light freckles.

'Oh, look at you! You're gorgeous!' She has the biggest smile as she nudges Gabriel's arm.

'Yeah,' he agrees, throwing those blues in my direction. 'She is.' I feel myself blush which only makes him smile more.

She doesn't take her eyes off me as she struggles to untie her hands from the many bag handles wrapped around her wrist. Finally free, she rushes forwards holding out her hand.

'I'm Amara Jayne. You must be Lilly. It's a pleasure...an honour, really.'

I didn't know my hands could get so sweaty so quick as I eye her outstretched hand.

Take it. Shake the poor girl's hand!

But nothing happens, and her happy little smile starts fading. Hand still outstretched, she takes another step towards me.

'I've heard a lot about you. Mainly your dress and shoe size.' She gives a nervous laugh and looks at her still outstretched hand that I can't seem to take. My heartbeat quickens and I actually back away from her. No one's offered me their hand before. Every time someone's touched me it's rarely been my choice. I genuinely don't know what to do! I don't want to be touched, but I don't want to offend her either.

'Oh...shit, yeah Amara, Lilly has a slight phobia. She can't shake your hand. Nothing personal,' Gabriel tells her. Amara quickly retracts her hand.

'I'm sorry. I didn't know,' she whispers to him. 'Why did no one tell me that?'

'Why haven't you got her normal clothes?' he whispers right back.

'I had instructions!' she argues, her voice still low. 'Grayson was specific.' With a big sigh, she turns her attention back to me. 'Well, Lilly, if you need anything else, let me know. I hope you like what I chose.'

'What Grayson chose,' Gabriel mutters.

'Is he home?' she asks him, her hands on her hips.

'Upstairs. Tell the lazy sod to get his arse out of bed.'

'Will do.'

He leans down, and they kiss each other on the cheek before she leaves the room.

'I don't know why I did that,' I say embarrassed. 'I just froze! What the hell is wrong with me?'

'Amara's harmless,' he tells me while rummaging through the bags. 'She won't hold that against you. Not sure what you're going to think of this lot.' He pulls out a silver silk strap top and hands it to me. He's pulling out more, and it's all very similar. Thin, dainty and sleek. 'Daft mare. It's winter, and she's not got you a single jumper. Oh, hold the phone...' He pulls out a pair of jeans and I almost pull him over as I rip them from his hands. Without a second to waste I slide them up my legs and ease the discomfort of being so exposed that I've had since I woke up.

'Is there *anything* with sleeves in there?' I ask desperately.

'There are tank tops, dresses, heels,' he looks up at me over the bag. 'Not much in the way of sleeves I'm afraid. I-I have some long-sleeved tops you could borrow. If you want to cover up?'

'Really? That would be great,' I sigh with relief.

He relaxes into a smile, scoops up all the bags and gestures to the door. 'Come on. I'll help you unpack and fetch you some hoodies from my room.'

My fingers play with the edge of the fresh bandages on my wrists as I sit watching Gabriel putting my new clothes in the wardrobe. There's a tap at the door before Grayson walks in. He looks between the two of us and the many bags.

'So, you met Amara then?'

I nod. If you can call staring at her and not saying a word meeting.

'Did the fresh air do you some good?'

'Yes. Thank you.'

'Good. When you are done up here Gabriel, bring Lilly with you to my office.' As he speaks to Gabriel, his tone is nowhere near as gentle.

'Sure thing,' Gabriel replies with his head still in the wardrobe.

'She will need something to eat-'

'I'll get on it.'

'Her bandages-'

'Already done.' He pokes his head out from behind the door. 'I'll bring her to you fed, watered and ready to fill us all in within the hour.'

Fill them in? On what?

'Good.' Grayson turns and heads out the door but turns back and stares at Gabriel.'Remember what I said, Gabriel. *Pas pour toi.* I mean it.'

They both stare at each other for an awkward amount of time, neither one blinking. If I had a knife, I could cut the tension with it.

'I know. I got that loud and clear last night. Thank you for the reminder though, *brother.* I'll bring her down in a few moments. Okay?'

'Good.' And with a small nod to me, Grayson disappears.

'*Brother?*' I say stunned. 'You two are *brothers?*'

'Yeah,' he sighs. 'Didn't you know? I'm the boss's baby brother. Here,' He throws me a red tank top, a black bra and matching pants and socks. 'Get dressed.' He points to the bathroom and sits on the bed. 'And maybe have a shower. You're a little ripe,' he teases playfully, but I take the hint and head to the bathroom. I look back before I close the door.

'He's a bit scary, isn't he?'

'He can be. But if he's in your corner you're pretty much untouchable. And he's definitely in *your* corner. He's extremely protective and loyal to us all.'

'Well, for the record, I speak French,' I tell him.

'You do?'

'Oui. Je parle bien,' I reply, telling him I speak it well. 'And I'm not here for anyone. So his warning, *Pas pour toi?* Not for you? Really? I told Grayson I won't be furthering any bloodline so if either of you think that's what I'll be doing...you can think again.'

'Wow, he was right. You are feisty,' he says with a soft chuckle. 'Well, he's just reminding me that you're a little fragile. He doesn't want you to feel uncomfortable, and I can be a bit...friendly, sometimes.'

'You don't make me uncomfortable,' I tell him. 'And...I like that you're friendly.' In fact, he makes me feel much more at ease than any of the others. Hendrix and his teeth. Grayson and his temper. Collins and his knife. Gabriel is much more relaxing to be around. 'Now excuse me. I stink and need a shower. Apparently.'

I hear him laughing as I close the bathroom door and I find myself giggling too.

The shower cubicle in the corner is very modern with three different knobs and a large rectangle head that sticks out covering almost every inch of the shower.

I have no idea how it works. At Harry's house, I had five minutes with a sink and a flannel. I've never had a shower, but I refuse to ask Gabriel for help on how it works.

I can do this!

I turn the first knob and the shower springs to life. I jump back so I don't get wet but give myself a mental pat on the back for figuring it out. The water's warm, so excitedly I take off my clothes and step in.

'Oh my god!' I bellow.

'You okay?! Lilly?' Gabriel calls through the door. 'What's wrong?'

'Nothing! I'm brilliant!' I start laughing as the water covers me completely. It warms me through my skin to my core. 'This shower's amazing! Holy fuck!' I hear his soft chuckle as I continue to enjoy myself.

'There's shower gel and shampoo by your feet,' he calls. 'I'm going to grab you some clothes from my room.' I look down and help myself. I use way too much shower gel, but it feels incredible covering my body in this sweet-smelling foamy soap. The various cuts sting as the shampoo, conditioner and shower gel comes into contact with the raw skin. But I can deal with that. Easily. I rewash myself three times. Every time I think about getting out I just can't do it. This is the most relaxing experience I think I've ever had. By the time I'm finished, my hair smells of coconut and my skin, of cherries. I've never been so clean. My skin's never felt so soft.

I dry off and get dressed. The clothes I've been given are small, but they still hang loosely on me.

When I open the bathroom door, Gabriel's gone. I feel so out of place. Everything here is so nice and expensive. I'm scared to touch anything in case I break it. I stare at the door waiting for him to come back and I tell myself that I'm okay. That he'll be back in a moment and no one here wants to hurt me. But I don't believe my words. Not really.

Fuck, I really wish he would come back.

After a few minutes of watching the door, I force myself to sit at the dressing table on the small stool in front of the mirror and begin brushing several year's worth of knots out of my hair. I look at myself in the mirror as I work the bristles through the strands. The red marks in the corners of my mouth from the gag aren't as angry as they were but they're still there. As I keep looking at myself, I feel like I'm looking at a stranger. This girl looks different than the one that used to wash her body in a sink every morning. Different than the girl who loved Toby. She's someone new. I'm a little bit nervous about getting to know her. But excited too.

With my hair knot free, it reaches to my waist. It's got long. I kind of like it. I stand and lift my top so I can see my belly in the mirror. Tracing my fingers over the two scars that rest just above each of my hip bones, I wonder how they got there. They weren't there before the missing six weeks.

And I still can't get over how thin I am.

Gabriel walks in and glances at my body before looking at the floor. I pull down my top and turn quickly. Oh bugger, how much did he see?

'I'm sorry. I didn't see... I mean...' he clears his throat, still looking at the floor. 'Here,' He quickly holds out a black hoody for me to take and places a pile of other long-sleeved items on the end of my bed. 'They'll be big for you, but they'll keep you covered and warm.' I slide it on, keen to gain the extra layers. It smells of him again. Vanilla and sandalwood. I feel so much better covered, but the unease is still very present. He glances at me briefly as his feet shuffle and I can't stand this sudden awkwardness.

'I have scars,' I tell him. 'Can we move on now?' I tuck my wet hair behind my ears and wait for him to respond.

He looks up at me and nods. 'I didn't really see anything. I promise. Come on, best not keep my brother waiting.'

Following him downstairs I can't believe I didn't clock they were related sooner. The resemblance is obvious. Their faces are too similar not to be. He hasn't mentioned what he saw anymore and has returned to his former self. Chatting away and smiling as we head down. He stops outside the large doors in the lobby that look like they belong in a medieval castle.

'Go on in. I'll go make you a sandwich. I'm determined to get some meat on those bones of yours.'

'You're not coming in?' I ask a little too desperately. I look at the door and back to him. 'Is it just Grayson in there?' My fingers are knotted together so tight they hurt. I step closer and look up at him. 'Can you come in with me? Please?'

'I will. In a few minutes,' he replies patting my arm encouragingly.

'What does he want?'

'To talk. That's all.'

Images of my aunt and uncle tied to chairs spring into mind. He wanted them to talk. What if he asks me something I don't want to answer or worse…something I *can't* answer. I step back, distancing myself from the door.

'I don't think I can go in there,' I say quietly, more to myself than him.

'I'll be right behind you. He wants a few moments alone with you. That's all. I'll make you some food and be right in. Okay?' Again, he gestures to the door. But I don't move.

'Is he going to hurt me?' My voice is uneasy and shaking a little.

'He won't hurt you. He just wants to talk.'

'That's what he said to my aunt and uncle,' I mutter.

'Just be honest. Answer his questions and whatever you do…be polite. He has a real thing about respect so don't be rude.' He re-tucks a loose strand of hair behind my ear, and our eyes lock. 'Go on. You'll be fine. I'm right behind you.' He attempts an encouraging smile. 'It's going to be fine.' He opens the door slightly before walking away leaving me standing nervously outside the intimidating room.

But that's nothing compared to the intimidating man that awaits me inside.

I knock.

'Come in, Lilly.'

The door's heavy so I slide in through a small gap before closing it behind me. Straight ahead at the far end of the room between two large windows is an imposing dark grey metal fireplace. Like the one in the entrance hall, the breast reaches up to the ceiling. The walls behind me are covered in books and the wall to my right is a map dotted with different coloured pins. Some of them are linked by string and have post-it notes on them. The room screams classic elegance, power and authority.

It's very him.

Grayson doesn't look up from the pile of papers and books on his large antique oak desk.

'Come in. Make yourself comfortable.'

Nerves prevent me from speaking or walking. When I don't reply he raises his head and realises I'm far from comfortable. Purposefully, he sets his pen down and gets to his feet.

'Come in, Lilly. Please. We have a lot to talk about. I keep telling you, you are perfectly safe.'

With a small swipe of his hand, one of the chairs on the other side of his desk pulls out.

'Have you eaten?' he asks as I sit.

'Gabriel's getting me something.'

'Good. I'm glad you two met. What do you think of my brother?'

There's a hint of annoyance in his voice, and his brow raises as he speaks.

'He's nice,' Is my chosen answer.

'Oh yes. Gabriel can be very nice. Especially with the fairer sex.'

'I didn't know you had a brother. He didn't come with you to my Uncle's house. Are there any other witches I'm to meet?'

'No.'

'Why didn't he come with you?'

'He was busy. With Ava.'

He's very short with me. I'm getting the impression he doesn't want me talking about Gabriel, so I change the subject.

'I can't begin to tell you how grateful I am. But, why do I get the feeling that there's something you want from me? I meant what I said back at my uncle's. I won't be used to further my bloodline.'

'I know. And I already told you that I have no intention of forcing you to do so. However, there is something I do need your help with.'

'Really?' I ask. 'What could I possibly help you with?'

'Something very, very important,' he says. 'But before we get into that, I have a few questions. Will you answer them for me?'

'I'll...I'll do my best, Grayson.'

'Good girl.'

Chapter 7

Gabriel's words are swimming around my head. Be honest. Be polite. I need to keep my answers simple. Harry always told me that I was an awful liar. That lies were written on my face like words on a page. Grayson isn't a fool and lying to him isn't a good idea.

'Gabriel tells me that you are a Sensitive? How long have you had that ability?'

'Am I?'

'You tell me.'

'I don't know what that means so how can I answer you?' I say a little sharper than intended. He's acting like he's trying to catch me out. When his eyebrows raise in response to my tone, I lower my head to show that I didn't mean any disrespect. 'I'm sorry. What I meant to say was, I don't know what a Sensitive is. I don't know anything about magic or witches.'

He rises from his chair and walks around the desk. I watch him like a hawk, half expecting him to lunge at me and start tying me to the chair as he did with my aunt and uncle.

'Grayson, I'm really sorry. I shouldn't have spoken to you like that. Please, don't-'

'Lilly, calm yourself.' He takes the seat next to me, crosses his legs and leans back comfortably. 'I know we didn't meet in the best circumstances. But I am not going to hurt you. We're just talking. Okay? Please trust me. As long as you behave, I'll behave. Deal?' He gives me a smile, and I'm quick to nod. 'Now, being a Sensitive means that you can sense magic. The humming you feel in the air around my men and I is our magic. So, I'll ask you again, now that you understand the question. How long have you been a Sensitive?'

I answer clearly and with as much respect in my voice as I can muster. 'I felt it for the first time with Collins,' I say slowly and concisely.

'That's very interesting.' He has a knowing smile as he looks briefly out the window. 'Very interesting.'

'Is it a bad thing?' I ask.

He turns back to me and shakes his head.

'No, Lilly. That is a fantastic thing.' He's watching me with fascination. Like I'm something thoroughly interesting, but all I am is extremely anxious. 'I would love to know what your first manifestation of magic was. That is to say, when and how you got your first ability. Tell me about it. How old were you?'

'I was four, maybe. I moved things. Then my fire came about four years ago.'

'That's remarkable. Absolutely remarkable,' he says quietly before looking at his hands. He asks the next question without making eye contact. 'Did you know that Toby was a Witch?'

'Yes. I did.'

'Did he tell you about me?' He lifts his gaze, hungry for information.

'No. He didn't talk about any others. I actually thought we were the last ones,' I laugh at my own words, embarrassed by how naive I was. The last two witches in all the world finding each other and falling in love. It would have been a sweet story. If Toby wasn't, well...Toby.

There's a knock on the door and Gabriel walks in holding a plate in the air. I could slump in a heap with relief.

'Food,' he says, looking at Grayson for permission to come in.

With a nod from Grayson, he comes in, hands me the plate and I tuck in happily to the ham and cheese salad sandwich.

'You like ham then,' he says happily, leaning on the desk and folding his arms. 'How are we getting on?'

'We were just talking about Toby,' Grayson tells him. I stop chewing. Isn't he done with the Toby talk? I swallow, and suddenly my stomach is closed for business. I can't face another bite. Why on earth does he want to talk about him? 'Her uncle seemed to believe he was Lilly's boyfriend,' Grayson tells Gabriel like I'm not here.

A small scoff erupts from Gabriel. It gets my back up a little.

'How did you even meet?' Gabriel asks. 'I thought your uncle kept you hidden in the house?'

'He did. For the most part.'

'So how did you two meet?' Grayson asks.

'Erm.' I take a second to think how best to answer. 'Well, I was hanging out washing and he sort of...appeared.'

'Your uncle made you do chores?'

'Harry would only really speak to me when he wanted to vent.'

'Vent?' Gabriel asks.

'Yeah. He had...anger issues.' They share an angry look. 'I was put under the supervision of a man called Mr Simmons. He kept me busy.'

'The man who Hendrix stopped from throttling you to death?' Grayson enquires.

I nod. 'He knew what I was and was hired to keep me under control. Mr Simmons used to be in the military. Secret ops or something.'

'So what happened between you and Toby?' Grayson asks.

'Two years ago, we had a fight, and he left. I've not seen him since.' I hope that's enough information for him.

'I assume he knows you're a Witch?' Grayson asks.

I nod.

'How long were you two together?'

Images invade my mind of Toby and our time together. The good and the bad.

'Lilly?' Grayson says a little impatiently pulling me out from my momentary daydream.

'Three years. Can we talk about something else please?'

'Three years!' Gabriel says suddenly in disbelief. 'How did we not know-' Grayson holds up his hand silencing him and leans forwards a little more to me.

'Is that three years including the time you spent in the cellar?'

'No. Three years before the cellar. I was about sixteen when we met.'

'So he knew about the late manifestation of fire?'

'The what?' I ask.

'That you manifested your fire four years ago. He knew that?'

I nod. 'He actually taught me how to do it,' I admit. 'Toby taught me how to use my fire and helped me practice moving stuff.' I stop talking as I see how they are both looking at me. With furrowed eyes and suspicious expressions. 'Have I said something wrong?'

'He helped you manifest fire?'

'Yes,' I answer nervously.

'How?'

I keep my eyes down and shrug, too embarrassed to say.

'Lilly, please tell me how he helped you,' he repeats, but I remain silent. With a sigh he says, 'Can you tell me what you two fought about when he left?' Another stint of silence from me and he groans. 'It is imperative we find him.'

'Knowing why we fought won't help you.'

'Is there *anything* that you can tell me that might?'

'There was something he mentioned once. A brother. But I got the impression he was dead. Other than that...he didn't really talk about his life away from me.' He nods and the two brothers share a look of disappointment. 'He had a friend. A female friend,' I add in the hope that I can be of some use.

'What was her name?' Grayson asks shifting to the edge of his seat and staring at me intently.

'I don't know.'

'What did she look like?'

'I never saw her face. Sorry.'

'So how can you be sure if she was a she?' Gabriel asks, folding his arms and looking at me.

'I just know,' I say hoping that that will be enough. But of course, it's not. They both look at me expectantly, so with a sigh, I accept that there's no getting past letting them see how pathetic a girl I really am.

'Because he would...' I run my hands through my hair before letting them slump onto my lap. 'Well, when I got jealous, he would make me watch them together. She would wear a hoody, and she would face away from me while they were...together, but it was always the same girl. She had long blonde hair that would fall out the front of the hood.' I lean back and refuse to look up at them.

'He made you watch him screw someone else? Why would he do that?' The disgust in Gabriel's voice is apparent.

'Toby said I was weak. And that exposing me to hurt would build up a tolerance. I got jealous? He would sleep with other girls. I got frightened of something? He would expose me to it even more. That's it. I don't know where the book is. I don't know where Toby is, and I don't know anything else about the girl other than the colour of her hair and that she liked being watched while having sex with the man I was in love with.' I bury my face in my hands in shame. 'Can we please just move on from Toby?'

Grayson kneels on the floor in front of me and gently pulls my hands away so he can see me.

'Toby is a callous and nasty individual. I'm very sorry that he treated you so poorly. I won't ask any more questions about him. Okay?' He gets to his feet and returns to his chair leaning back and once more looks at ease. It makes me feel at ease too, and I'm pleased that we're moving on.

'I know you said you have no idea where Junior may be. Your cousin? But if you have any information that might help us locate him, any friends he had? Or places he liked going?'

'I didn't really know him,' I reply. 'He was at boarding school and then went travelling as far as I'm aware. I wasn't really included in family matters.' He looks disappointed. 'Why do you want to find him?'

'Because other than you, he is the last known Hooper. If there is any chance of continuing the bloodline, I have to try. Besides, he's of magical descent. He is entitled to a place with us. Are you certain you can't help in finding him?'

'I would if I could, Grayson. Sorry.'

He quickly moves on.

'Can you demonstrate what you can do for me please?' He raises his hand and the blue lightning snakes between his fingers as a demonstration. He wants me to show him my magic.

'You've seen what I can do,' I tell him. 'The fire and-'

'I have seen you angry and your magic affecting your environment. I want to see what you can do. I want to see if you can control it.' He gestures for me to stand. 'Show me.'

I get to my feet which are unsteady and reluctant to obey his command.

I imagine my magic as a bright red light when I attempt to use it intentionally. It's a glow that's always in my chest, and when I want it, I channel it out, sending it through my body and towards what I want to use it on. I see it in my mind. A swirling mass of red waves on a stormy ocean, and send it to the fireplace to create my fire. It's controlled and calm but still the unnatural black and white. He gives a small approving nod and continues to wait. Gabriel's looking at the flames with his arms folded and a deep furrow on his brow. He doesn't seem impressed. He seems suspicious. Wary.

'Why is it that colour?' Gabriel asks suddenly. 'It's like his. Is she Broken too?' Grayson silences him by raising his hand but keeps his eyes on me.

'Broken? You keep saying that and I have no idea what it means.'

'What else can you do?'

Me being *"Broken"* isn't up for discussion. Yet. But I'll find out. I just need to wait for the right moment to ask. So instead of pushing it, I continue my demonstration.

The sound of something sliding across the desk makes Grayson's eyes flick in that direction, and he smiles proudly. Resting on the blade's tip, at the very edge of the desk, is a rose gold miniature knife letter opener. He reaches over and inspects the knife before putting it back on its side.

'Very well controlled.' He admires. He gestures for me to return to my seat, but I remain standing.

'Can you do any of that?' I ask.

'I have Telekinesis. The ability to manipulate objects around me, and this,' he wriggles his hand and shows me his lightning before once more gesturing for me to sit. 'This is called Energy magic. It's like lightning. Your fire is called Elemental magic.'

'And you can control the actions of others?' I ask Gabriel, who nods with his half-smile back in place.

'It's called Mental magic. Power over the mind,' Gabriel tells me.

'Collins is strong. Like superhuman strength.'

'Physical magic. The ability to heal or manipulate your strength,' Grayson explains.

'And Hendrix is a vampire.' Again, another nod as nervous laughter sneaks out of me. 'Wow,' I whisper letting all this sink in.

'Sit down, Lilly,' Grayson says. 'Let's talk about-'

'My uncle told me I was the last, but then I met Toby-'

'Lilly, sit down,' he repeats when I continue standing. 'I want-'

'Are we the only ones or are there others?' I ask Gabriel. I'm so excited to learn more. Gabriel stands up and has such enthusiasm on his face as I beam at him. 'Do you all gather together and make spells on a full moon?' I tease.

'It's just us,' Gabriel laughs. 'And we're more inclined to gather for a beer than spells I'm afraid.'

'Well, that sounds fun too!'

'Well, I'll gather the Coven as soon as possible,' he says with a chuckle.

'It's a date.'

He looks into my eyes and says quietly, 'I'll hold you to that.'

'I SAID SIT DOWN, LILLY!' Grayson shouts suddenly, making me jump and sink into the chair with my head down. The smile that was stretched across my face and the excitement about learning more about Witches has abandoned me.

'Grayson!' Gabriel scorns quietly. 'Take it easy.'

Grayson's eyes flash angrily to his brother before settling back on me.

'I apologise for my outburst. But I won't repeat myself,' he warns. 'I asked her to sit. I expect her to sit. Not ignore me completely and talk over me.' I sink back further into the chair. His tone alone is terrifying never mind his angry expression.

'I'm sorry,' I say in barely a whisper. 'I meant no offence.'

'I accept your apology,' Grayson says, getting to his feet. 'But to avoid future misunderstandings let me make this perfectly clear to you, Miss Hooper. I do not tolerate rudeness. I detest lies, and I will not repeat myself. Ever. The sooner you learn this about me, the more enjoyable you will find your time here.' I would run screaming and crying if I could rid myself of the paralysing fear he's just forced on me. My magic is bubbling up from my chest. My own built-in defence mechanism ready to attack with or without instruction from me. The more afraid I feel, the stronger it becomes until it starts seeping out. The lights in the room flicker. The pictures hanging on the wall begin to shake.

'You're scaring her, Grayson.' Gabriel looks nervously at the less than inanimate objects.

'My warning goes for you too, little brother. You know I demand more respect than this. So stop flirting with her and start doing as you're told.' They watch each other for a moment until Gabriel looks away to the floor. Grayson's in charge. The conversation is over, and Grayson's point has been made loud and clear.

I close my eyes and try to control the surge of power that's desperate to explode. I'm strong but unpredictable, and I don't want to anger the only people that have so far tried to help me by hurling them or their possessions around the room.

'Okay. Okay, easy,' Grayson soothes, resting his hands over mine. I open my eyes and see him on his knees in front of me. 'I am sorry I shouted. Perhaps I was too hasty in my reaction. I really didn't mean to frighten you. Forgive me?'

He remains on his knees looking up at me. The soft grip he has on my hand is as uncomfortable as ever. I nod because what else can I say or do? I don't want to leave The Orchard. I don't want to be on my own again. If I have to work around Grayson's rules, I will. It's a small price to pay for freedom.

'Take some deep breaths for me,' Grayson says, leading by example and taking in a long deep inhale. I copy, and after a few minutes, the room settles. It's nice to know that I can be calmed. Even if it's him that set me off in the first place.

Grayson gets to his feet with a smile and reaches out his hand. 'Let's take a break. Come with me.'

'Where are we going?'

'I'm going to give you a tour of your new home.'

We walk out to the entrance hall leaving Gabriel behind. Grayson leads me forward to the stained glass doors and out to the front of the house.

At the end of a very long gravel driveway is a set of thick, black, heavy, electronic gates set between a high, solid wall that stretches on and on clearly marking the boundary between us and the outside world. The driveway leads straight back up to the house finishing by a huge stone water feature of an angel with her wings spread wide and water cascading down on a platform beneath her feet. Running alongside the driveway are dozens of apple trees. Parked around the stone feature ahead are several cars. One of which is the black Mercedes Grayson brought me here in. And behind that is a large garage.

Looking back, I see the front of the house. The pillared porch and arching windows make it look like something from a period drama. It's made of dark grey stone and is three storeys high except in the corners where turrets are giving an extra floor. It extends round the back, giving it an east and west wing.

'Holy shit…' I gasp. 'You live in a castle!'

'It's impressive, huh?' He looks up at the house with me.

'You know it is!' Outside in the air and with him smiling easily at me, I find it easier to talk to him.

'Come on,' he says happily, nudging me playfully. 'Let's carry on.'

Back in the lobby, he opens the doors to our right and gestures for me to go in.

'This is the dining room.'

Inside, the walls are covered with light wood panels and above us is a domed ceiling with a crystal chandelier hanging centrally over a large oak table big enough for twelve at least. Again, there's an impressive fireplace made of white marble and a large set of doors with deep red velvet curtains that lead out to the garden. We walk back out to the hall and into the next set of double doors beside it.

'This is the lounge,' he tells me.

In the centre of the enormous room is a large cream sofa with two armchairs either side. The high ceiling curves into a dome again with a matching large crystal chandelier hanging in the middle. Same as in the dining room. The floors are the same wood as the rest of the house, but this room has a rustic rug of red, blue and white stripes almost reaching the walls, the lower half of which are oak panels and the top halves decorated in yet more exquisite paintings of stunning landscapes. Decorative vases and antique furniture are placed beautifully around this massive room, and yet again, there's another grand fireplace. This one's made of gold and marble with carved pillars reaching up to the base of the dome. In the corner by the window is a black grand piano with a stool. And in the other corner, tucked away almost out of sight is a record player with hundreds of vinyls neatly stored in shelves next to it. The dining room and lounge combined are the same size as Grayson's office. This place is enormous! He leads me out past the stairs and his office, towards the kitchen. Opposite which is a set of double doors. He opens them up.

'Game room,' he tells me. Inside is a pool table sitting in the centre of a large, light room with wooden floors and high ceilings. In the far left are a couple of sofas facing a television and bar stocked with bottles of spirits. There are two large glass doors at the far end. Peering out I see they open up into the garden.

'I like this room.' I swipe the balls across the table and fail to pot a single one. 'Do you play?'

He rests his palms on the large table and watches me.

'I do. You?'

'Once. I was terrible.'

'Remind me and I'll teach you,' he insists.

We leave and go back into the hall and turn right. The hall splits and continues to the right and to the left. At the end of each corridor are more doors. He takes me right and leads me inside.

'Wow!'

'The Victorian conservatory,' he tells me as I walk inside a circular room made of glass, giving me a complete view of the grounds. There are cream sofas and loungers placed all around. It's all very elegant. The windows are all open letting in the fresh air and in the middle, is a small fish pond built into the floor with Koi gliding through the water.

'Holy shit, Grayson, your home is...this is all...'

'Why, thank you,' he says with a small courteous bow. 'Would you like to carry on?'

'Lead the way!' I'm eager to see more. The only other house I've been in was my uncle's. The Orchard is so much nicer.

We walk back along the hall to the door at the other end.

'Palm house,' he says. 'Otherwise known as big, greenhouse.'

The room's hot and filled with plants.

'You like gardening?' I ask leaning in and smelling the various flowers. He nods. 'You, Grayson...are full of surprises.'

'You have no idea.' He grins. The tension from inside his office is gone, to which I'm very relieved.

We return to the hall and walk past the kitchen and the game room, back into the extraordinary entrance lobby.

'Come on. Upstairs next.'

We climb up to the first floor.

'There are six bedrooms on this floor. Each has their own bathroom. There are also two extra bathrooms, a few cupboards and a room we shove junk in,' he explains as we walk. He points out which room belongs to Collins, Hendrix and now me. The hall bends to the left allowing more space for the sheer number of rooms this house holds.

We return to the stairs going up instead of down. I like it up here. The hall goes in a big square so I can walk around the twisting staircase and look down to the lobby floor. As I stand at the top of the stairs, there are two large double doors both to my left and my right. He walks to the ones on the right.

'This is my bedroom, and that one there,' he gestures to the other double doors opposite. 'Is Gabriel's bedroom. We are the only ones who sleep up here.' As we walk along the landing, I admire the art covering the walls. There are pieces I recognise and know from Mr Simmons that they are missing. Rembrandt's *The Storm on the Sea of Galilee* and Vermeer's *The Concert*, hang bold as brass right in front of me.

On the other side of this square balcony are three more doors. Two of which are bedrooms, he tells me.

'What about that one?' I ask, looking at the third door in the far corner. Like his and Gabriel's, they're double doors.

'That room used to belong to my brother. Bias.' A solemn look washes over his features as he stares at the set of doors, and his tone drops lower as he talks. 'Bias died a few years back. He was our youngest brother.'

'Oh, Grayson, I'm so sorry. What happened?'

'I would rather not talk about it.' He attempts a smile, but it's so full of grief I can't help but rest my hand on his arm in comfort.

With a small tap on my hand, he continues walking around the landing and back to the stairs.

'Come on. We haven't finished yet.'

He takes me back to the first floor and turns right, past my room and towards a set of doors at the end. I assume it's a bedroom, but when I walk in I gasp in awe! I can't believe what I'm seeing.

'Grayson, this is... I mean...wow!'

'The Library,' he says. 'It's the whole of the west wing. Twenty-two metres long. Ten metres wide. Twenty-two thousand books at the last count and home to the largest selection of occult reference books in the world. As well as all the mainstream greats. Dickens, Shakespeare, Tolstoy...' he opens his arms as he walks into the very centre of the room. 'This...' he looks lovingly at every corner of this grand room. 'This is my baby.'

'Your baby's amazing! I've never seen anything like this.'

The books are housed in oak carved bookcases that not only line the walls, but jut out, creating aisles. There are tables and great big armchairs for reading. Above us is a gallery overlooking the room with yet more books, and at the end of the library is a large, lit ornate marble fireplace warming the room. I can't wait to curl up in front of it with one of these books. The cream ceiling has dark wooden beams going across from one end to the other, and two large full height bay windows are giving outstanding views across the gardens. I charge across the room pressing my nose against the glass in excitement.

'Is that the ocean?' I ask, pointing into the distance. I've never seen the ocean before. As I strain to see it, he walks up behind me and gently slides his hands onto my hips. As he does I tense. He feels my reaction but keeps them there.

'We are a couple of miles from the coast here. If you walk in that direction,' He gestures into the distance, pressing his body against mine. 'You will reach the cliffs. I will take you for a walk one day. It really is stunning. My brother and I own the land right up to the edge.'

'How long have you lived here?' I ask. My attention shifting from the amazing house and views, to the powerful and frightening man holding onto me.

'Forever.'

I look back at him. All this beauty and he's taking me in completely. He turns me by my hips and firms his grip, holding me in place.

'Do you like The Orchard?' he asks.

'I love it, Grayson. I'm so thankful to you for letting me stay here.'

'I don't want you to be thankful. I want you to be happy.' He glances down to my lips. 'Lilly...I would very much like to kiss you.'

My breath hitches as he leans in. I raise my hands to his solid chest and stop his approach. I barely touch him, and he halts.

'I'm sorry, Grayson. I can't...' but he's still looking at my lips. He's dangerous and frankly terrifying, even if he is incredibly attractive and has saved my life. 'I'm just not ready to be kissed. By anyone. I'm sorry.'

'You never have to apologise for not being ready to kiss me,' he says sweetly.

'What's that?' I ask nodding to the fireplace, hoping to distract him without insulting him. Disappointed, he lets go and walks towards the sizeable woven tapestry hanging pride of place on the wall. It's black with an intricate silver seven-pointed star in the centre. Simple, but very bold.

'We call it the Arcane star. It's a representation of the most powerful type of witch ever to exist. An Arcane Witch. Have you ever heard of an Arcane Witch before?'

'No,' I tell him still looking up at the tapestry. 'But my mother used to wear a necklace with a seven-pointed star on it.'

'She did?'

'Yeah.' I run my fingers along my neck, missing the small piece of jewellery immensely. 'Is that what you are? Is that why you're the Coven's leader?'

He laughs and shakes his head.

'I wish I was an Arcane Witch. That would have made my life a lot easier, but sadly no.' He points up to the image. 'Do you see how the star has seven points? Well, each point refers to a different realm of power. There are seven realms in total. Telekinesis, Elemental, Sensativa, Energy, Physical, Mental and Sight. All witches are born able to access at least one of those realms. Gabriel, for example, has Mental magic allowing him to alter and control people's minds. Collins has Physical magic which allows him to heal and have extraordinary strength. I have Energy.' Raising his hand, he creates his lightning. 'And Telekinesis, of course. Most Witches are born able to access one realm, but some like me are lucky enough to possess two. And then there's you. You have three. Telekinesis, Elemental, and Sensativa.'

'So, what makes the Arcane so special?'

'They are special because they can access all of the realms.'

'All seven! That's a lot of power. Is there an Arcane alive now?'

'The last one died five hundred years ago,' Grayson tells me. He's not looking at the star anymore but at me. 'Before she died, she did a spell to protect us all from a terrible threat. Witch Hunters. You see, five hundred years ago Hunters launched an attack on us all without warning. We didn't even know they existed until it was too late. Their mission was simple. To hunt and kill every single witch on the planet without mercy or exception. We were massively outnumbered and extremely unprepared. Soon there were hardly any of us left. With the risk of extinction and heartbroken at watching all the bloodshed, the Arcane did a spell. A spell that prevented witches accessing their magic.'

'Why?'

'So we could pass for human. Hunters could track us via our magic. We had to give it up so we could hide. Cutting us all off from our powers meant we could live in the world without prejudice and the threat of death hanging over us at every turn. For years children were killed. Families torn apart. Innocents were being tortured. We needed to disappear.'

'That's awful.' I feel my heart break a little. 'That's so unfair! What happened to the Witches after the spell?'

'They're still here. Well, their children's, children's children. They are called Descendants. You met one earlier. Amara Jayne. If she were alive five hundred years ago she would have magic. But with the Veil up she doesn't. Your uncle and your cousin are descendants too. Hunters would love to get their hands on the Descendants, even now. To them, they're all still Witches. Even without their magic.'

He turns and looks back up at the star, but now it's me that can't stop looking at him. I'm dying for more information.

'What's the Veil?'

'Magic exists in a place called the Arcane Realm. Think of it as a world that lives right next to ours. An invisible world.'

'Like an alternative reality?'

'Sort of. Yes. But instead of people occupying it, it's just pure magic. Five hundred years ago the two worlds overlapped, but the Arcane did a spell and created a veil between us. We call it the Arcane Veil. It stopped the magic reaching us.'

'Okay...' I say more to myself than to him. I need a minute to take it all in. All the information about the Hunters, the Descendants, the veil. I'm determined to understand. The world is so much bigger than I ever imagined. So much more complicated. How can a girl that spent most her life living in the confines of her uncle's house ever expect to understand it all? As I look up at the star, a connection sparks in my brain.

'The book you're after, it has a seven-pointed star on it.'

'It does.'

'It's connected then? The veil, the book, the Arcane.'

'The book is, in fact, a Journal. One written by the Arcane Witch in a language that only an Arcane Witch can read. Inside is the spell she used to put up the Veil. As well as the spell to bring it down.'

I whip my head around understanding what he means to achieve. Understanding why the book is so important to him.

'You want to bring the veil down, don't you?'

He smiles.

'That's why you're so desperate to find it! You want to bring back magic!'

'Yes. We want to return magic to all the Descendants of the world so they can come out of hiding and take back their freedom. If we don't, we'll all be killed by Hunters for certain. But we need your help.'

'I'm supposed to help you?' I say slowly in disbelief. 'I told you, I don't know where Toby or the book is. Why won't you believe me?'

'I do believe you. But finding Toby is not how you can help me.' He takes a step closer to me as we stand beneath the star. I'm so enthralled by what he's saying I don't care he's close again.

'Magic manifests, and then it's done,' he says. 'I got both my realms when I was six. That's it. No more. You have been manifesting them for years. First your Telekinesis. Then years later your Elemental magic. Then two days ago you manifested Sensativa.'

'What does that mean?' I ask nervously.

'It means that you will keep manifesting till you are finished. Until you become a fully formed Arcane Witch.'

I can't help but laugh. That's funny. I soon stop when he looks a little annoyed at my reaction. Is he serious?!

'Hang on. You're not joking, are you?' I step back and stare at him like he's crazy. 'Are you actually saying you think I'm this...Arcane thing?' I shake my head as he nods. 'No. I'm sorry, but you're very mistaken.' Is that the only reason he wanted me here? When he knows I'm not this Arcane Witch, will he kick me out?

'The last Arcane Witch was called Rebecca Hooper. Only Hooper witches have ever been Arcanes. Why do you think I was so keen to find Harry's son? If you all died out, the Veil might never come down. Why do you think I came to your house? Why do you think that your mother would have a necklace that represents Arcane power?'

My mouth won't close.

'I'm not an Arcane,' I tell him. 'I can't be.'

'I grew up with Rebecca. I know an Arcane Witch when I see one, and you, Miss Hooper, are an Arcane Witch.'

'You're wrong!' I insist 'I'm sorry but you're just wrong, Grayson.' I shake my head and step away from him. The enjoyment from the lovely tour, the beautiful library...it's all gone.

He steps closer.

'I'm not wrong. You are the single most important Witch alive. The most powerful. The most amazing-'

'Stop it! I'm not those things. I'm not,' I insist. 'So if you think I am, you're wrong. If that's why you brought me here, then I may as well turn and leave now. Because I'm not going to live up to your expectations.' I'm suddenly furious. Angry tears start appearing, so I turn away. He reaches out to take my hand, and I yank myself away.

'Why are you acting like this?' he asks. 'What have I said to make you angry?'

'Do you really think if I were as amazing and as powerful as you say, I would have let myself suffer like I have? You think Rebecca Hooper would have let what happened to me, happen to her?' I shake my head again and wipe my tears on the sleeve of Gabriel's hoody.

'Hey,' he says gently. 'What happened to you wasn't your fault. Don't talk like that.'

'I'm no one, Grayson. Not your Arcane. Not your answer to the Veil. I can't control the magic I *do* have, never mind piling on four more realms. I'm nothing. I'm no one and life has been hard enough being no one.'

'Are you afraid?' he asks, still looking concerned as I almost yell at him. 'Or do you think you're just not worthy? Because let me tell you,' he walks straight up to me and takes my face in his hands. 'You are worthier than anyone I have ever met. From what I've seen, you have faced the absolute worst of humanity. You have been beaten. Starved. Tormented. And I suspect much worse. Yet you are the one that still stands. *You* are the one that is free. All those people at your uncle's house are dead. You're not. Toby's on the run. Living in the shadows like a coward. Not you. Some people would have killed themselves long ago if they faced half of what you have faced so don't ever call yourself nothing. Don't ever think you are no one because you are the most important someone to exist.' He looks at my lips and wraps his fingers in my hair. 'You are everything I have been looking for in the last five hundred years.'

I never knew my mouth could dry so fast. His closeness and his words have stunned me completely.

'How old are you, Grayson?' I ask in a whisper.

'Twenty-eight.'

I remember Gabriel in the orchard this morning. He said he was Twenty-five-ish.

'How long have you been twenty-eight?' I ask.

With a sly smile, he says, 'Five hundred and fifty three years.'

'Oh my god,' I whisper, my voice lost to shock. He's centuries old!

'God had nothing to do with it.' He leans in and kisses me. His mouth claiming mine as well as his arm which wraps around my back. He pulls me in, holding me close to his body. I don't close my eyes. I don't push him away, because honestly? I'm scared. I pull back and cover my lips with my fingers.

Our eyes meet, and he's smiling that smile again. And still, it doesn't reach his eyes.

'I want you to help me bring magic back, Lilly Hooper. There are hundreds of Descendants depending on us to save them. I need you to help me bring back witches. Only an Arcane can. Will you help us?' He's searching my eyes for an answer. A sign of what I'm thinking.

Someone behind us clears their throat and I spin round to see Gabriel watching us. I walk a few steps away from Grayson, embarrassed that he more than likely saw us kiss.

'Grayson,' Gabriel says coldly. 'Billy's here. He wants to know when you want the men back.'

'Tell him I'll be down in a moment,' Grayson replies happily. Gabriel looks to the floor before leaving the room.

'Will you help me?' Grayson asks, bringing my attention back to him. 'Will you help me bring back magic?'

Grayson walks me back to my room, and before he leaves, he asks me to think about everything he's said. I can't give him an answer. How can I? I have no idea what any of this really means. Is it a good idea to bring back magic? Is he right about me? I don't know these people. Not really. I have no idea if I can trust them.

After an hour of staring out the window with all the information Grayson has shared with me swirling around my head, I watch the sun sink lower into the horizon. Soon, the first stars I've seen in years blink into view. It distracts me for a while and gives my brain a chance to slow down.

He thinks I'm an Arcane Witch. He needs the Journal Toby has run away with. A journal that only I can read. He plans to return magic to the world. He and Gabriel are five centuries old! Jesus! I bury my face in my hands. Yeah, like that will help. I don't know what frightens me more. If he's right about me and I'm due another four realms of power, or if he's wrong and I have to deal with a disappointed Grayson. I don't imagine he would take it very well. On top of all that, I let him kiss me. I slam my fist into the wall in frustration and groan.

As I sit in the dark, I occasionally sense a witch walk past the room. Every squeaky floorboard, every voice or loud noise has me on high alert. My heart will wear out if it keeps beating like this. Before I get into bed, I slide the dressing table across the door. The duvet keeps getting tangled in my feet and the pillow feels like it's smothering my face. Finally, I give in and accept that I'm just not used to being so comfortable. I slide down on to the floor, rest my back against the bed and bury my face in my arms. I pull myself in, making my body as small as possible and fall asleep feeling afraid, confused and overwhelmed.

I'm barely aware that I'm being lifted off the floor. The room's still dark as I'm laid gently down on the bed. In my half-asleep state, it's much more comfortable. The duvet's pulled up around my neck, and I settle down. Whoever has lifted me into bed, sits beside me and as soon as I feel their hand stroke my head, I know who it is.

'Gabriel?' I whisper.

'Yes, Lilly?'

'My mum had a necklace. It was a star,' I tell him sleepily. 'Did she know?'

'Know what?' he asks.

'That I'm the Arcane Witch?' His hand continues to stroke my head, and I'm struggling to stay awake.

'I think so. Yes.'

'Did Toby?' His hand stops. 'Is that why he wanted me?'

'Go back to sleep.'

'Night, Gabriel.'

'Goodnight, Lilly.'

I wake with a start as the sound of a door closing disturbs my sleep. I sit and look around. It wasn't a dream. The dressing table's been put back to where it was against the wall and Gabriel's put me into my bed.

When I hear Hendrix's booming voice calling to someone from outside, I know I won't be able to sleep if anyone can just walk in here. I get up and put the dressing table chair under the handle of the door. Feeling that little bit safer, I crawl back into bed determined to keep my mind as empty as possible so I can actually get some sleep.

I just hope I don't have a nightmare.

Chapter 8

'Try it!'
'I don't want to.'
'I don't care if you don't want to, Red. I'm telling you to.'
'I can't control it. You know I can't.'
He glares at me. The anger and frustration coming from him is unnerving.
'Do...It...Now!' Toby's jaw tenses as he starts descending on me. His hands are balled up into fists, and every muscle in his toned arms are visible.
I stumble back, but he reaches me and wraps his fingers tightly around my wrist.
He stops with his nose against mine and his angry breathing in my face.
'Do it, Red, or I'll punish you.'
'I don't know how, Toby, please-'
He quickly raises his hand.
I flinch, but he just strokes the hair from my face before sliding his hand along my cheek and resting it on my throat.
I swallow and wait for his punishment.
'Turn around,' he orders.

I spin so my back is against his chest. His hand needlessly holds me in place by my throat.
His other hand plunges into my jeans and into knickers making me gasp at the sudden invasion.
'Do it,' he growls as his fingers move. I look at the tree in front of us.
'I-I don't know how. I've never done it before! What if something bad happens?'
'Do it for me, Red, or I'll never touch you again' he whispers in my ear. His fingers go deeper as I reach up and wrap my fingers in his hair.
I'm so afraid of him and yet I crave him more than anything. I'm biting my lip and panting.
'Do it. Or you'll never see me again. Is that what you want? For me to leave you here alone, with them? With Harry and Christa?'
'No, Toby...please don't leave me.'
I look at the tree as he works me closer to an orgasm.
'Then do it for me, Red. Do it. DO IT NOW!'
The tree erupts in bright orange flames as I cry out in pleasure.
'I knew it!' he laughs, watching the fire climb higher. The fire I created.
Magic I didn't even know I could do.
'I fucking love you, Red. My very own Arcane.'

'LILLY! LILLY, OPEN THE FUCKING DOOR!'

A series of loud bangs wake me from my uneasy sleep.

I can't see anything! My eyes are stinging. I can't breathe. I try to speak, but all that comes from me is violent, agonising coughing.

'She's in there. I can hear her!'

Another series of bangs and more yelling.

'OPEN THE DOOR!' Gabriel bellows desperately. 'YOU'RE GOING TO BURN TO DEATH!! LILLY, PLEASE!'

Burn to death? Shit, the rooms on fire!

'LILLY HOOPER, OPEN THE DOOR!'

My movements are involuntary as I try to fight the overwhelming smoke and heat to do as Gabriel's ordering me. It's no good. My arms buckle, and I can do nothing but lie here ferociously coughing, despite his compulsion.

'COLLINS... KNOCK IT DOWN!' he shouts.

The door explodes, sending splinters of wood in all directions. I'm pulled into a sturdy pair of arms and lifted off the ground.

'Gotcha.' Gabriel carries me out. The air gets clearer. It's getting easier to breathe.

'Get that fire out before it burns the house down,' Gabriel orders the others before looking down at me. 'Can you hear me? Open your eyes.'

I feel my body moving and hands on me but can't do anything. My voice is gone and my consciousness teeters on oblivion.

'Where is she? Is she okay? Is she breathing?' Grayson asks in a panic, skidding to a halt on his knees beside me as Gabriel lays me on the floor. Despite my eyes being a streaming mess and everything spinning wildly around me, I see his bright blue eyes full of worry.

'You still with us?' Gabriel asks.

'Sorry,' I cough.

'Get it out!' Grayson yells at the others and pointing towards the fire. 'Before my house goes the same way as the Hoopers'.'

'It won't go out!' Collins yells back.

'What do you mean it won't go out?' Grayson jumps to his feet and heads to the burning room. 'Use the extinguisher!'

'We tried! It's not working. It just comes back!'

I reach up and stroke Gabriel's face to get his attention. He looks down at me, worry and anger in equal measure. This is precisely what I didn't want to happen. I had a nightmare and my magic externalised. I told them when I came here. I warned them that I can't control it.

'You have to knock me out.' My voice is a hoarse, cracked mess. The flames are mine. I can create them but putting them out is a different issue altogether. Especially when they weren't created intentionally.

'As long as I'm conscious, they won't stop,' I tell him. 'Knock me out.'

'I'm not going to hit you!' Gabriel says firmly, but he has to. If he wants the fire to stop, I have to be unconscious.

'Boss, it's getting worse!' Hendrix calls over, the pointless hissing of the ineffective fire extinguisher echo down the hall. 'Little Witch, put it out!'

I take Gabriel's hand. 'Do it. Or the house will burn. Please, I don't want to be told to leave!'

He shakes his head looking pained, but I nod and do my best to smile, letting him know it's okay. He strokes the hair from my face and kneels over me.

'I can't hurt you. Not after everything you've been through. If you give me permission, I'll tell you to sleep. Will that work?'

I shake my head and look at the others fighting the flames.

'It will if I'm unconscious. It always does. Harry had to, sometimes.'

He looks at the flames that are crawling out of my room into the hall and at the three men trying desperately to put it out, but it won't. It never does.

'We don't have time...hit me,' I cough and struggle to get a good breath. He's starting to cough too as the hall gets thicker with smoke. 'For god's sake, Gabriel!' I say desperately. 'Your house will burn to the ground! I don't want to be sent away. I don't want Grayson to be mad at me. Hit me. FUCKING HIT ME!'

His hands twist in my hair, but he still hesitates.

'Do it. Do it.'

'I'm sorry, Lilly. Forgive me.'

He slams my head into the floor sending me into darkness. *Good boy.*

The muffled, distant voices start getting clearer and closer.

'She's waking up,' Gabriel says urgently. I feel a hand holding my arm. 'Lilly, can you hear me? Are you okay?'

'Ow,' I groan, shifting and reaching up to my throbbing head. 'Very, very ow.'

An anxious Gabriel helps me sit. On the other side of the bed is a rather angry, twitching Grayson.

'Is the fire out?' I ask in a panic. 'I'm so sor-' The brutal bout of coughing that erupts from me is agony. I feel like my lungs have been shredded.

'Easy,' Gabriel soothes, putting a glass of water in my hand. 'You breathed in a lot of smoke. Drink this. You'll be alright. And yes, the fire went out as soon as you were unconscious. Everything's fine.'

The ice-cold water's most welcome. Grayson's annoyed expression is less so.

'Everything's fine?' he mumbles. 'It's not fine. This is far from bloody fine.'

'I had a nightmare,' I croak, trying to explain. 'It was an accident. My magic is...tricky to control.'

'Tricky?' Grayson hisses. 'You almost killed yourself and could have burnt my house down! If Gabriel hadn't gone to check on you when he had, you could have died in there! That fire is not tricky, Lilly. That fire is lethal! You created it in your sleep? What on earth were you dreaming about?'

I've really fucked this up. So far, I've scolded him, burnt his curtains and now set his house on fire. He is really angry.

'This is not okay,' he barks, getting to his feet and pacing up and down. 'This is not acceptable.'

I push myself off the bed and get to my feet, brushing off Gabriel who's trying to steady me as I do. 'I'm so sorry. I'll go,' I really don't want to, but to spare them the aggravation I will. 'I'll leave. You've done enough for me.' As I leave, no one says a word. But when I get to the door, a hand slides into mine. I'm pulled back by Grayson who holds me close to his chest. He wraps his arms around me and buries his face in my hair. I hate being held like this, but the sheer relief that he's not going mental at me is a lot stronger.

'You don't have to go. I'm not mad, you just scared the hell out of me. I thought you were going to die. Don't ever, ever do that again. Ever.' He holds me at arm's length and inspects my face. 'What on earth were you dreaming about?'

'If you're right, and I'm your Arcane...we're all screwed.'

He and Gabriel both start to laugh. I wasn't joking.

'As long as you're okay, that's all that matters,' Gabriel tells me.

'Indeed. The sun's up. Have a shower. Change your clothes and come downstairs for something to eat,' Grayson instructs. He points to the door in the far corner. 'Your bathroom is through there. We've had to move you. You're on the top floor with us now. We can keep an eye on you up here. Come on, brother. Let's leave her to it.'

He leaves the room followed swiftly by Gabriel who glances back at me over his shoulder with a less than natural smile. When the door closes, I stand uncomfortably in this new room. It's twice the size of the other room I was in, with wooden floors, paintings of landscapes hanging on each wall and a large dressing table against the wall to my left. The bed's a large wooden four poster that sits between two large windows and everything's cream. The curtains, the bedding and the walls.

I strip off my smoke drenched clothes and walk into the bathroom. It's bigger than the one downstairs but has the same shower. Plus, a free standing cast iron bath. I get in the shower and sink to the floor with a groan. I'm going to fuck this up. I know I am. I'm a ticking time bomb, and I'm just waiting for me to blow. Even if they aren't.

There's a small tap on the door which sends me straight back to my feet.

'Don't come in!' I shout rudely.

'I wasn't planning on it,' Gabriel calls back. 'I have some more clothes for you. Your new ones went up in smoke, so I'm giving you some of mine for the time being. I'll leave them on your bed.'

I stare at the door praying that it doesn't open. I don't want anyone to see me naked. Not with all these...marks. He's right on the other side, I can hear him leaning against the door.

'Lilly?' he says finally.

'Yeah?'

'I'm sorry I hit you.'

He goes before I can tell him that there's no need to apologise. He did as I asked. He did the only thing he could do. I feel terrible for making Gabriel feel bad, and I feel awful for letting Grayson down. Why can't things just be simple?

I've been pacing my new room for what feels like the whole night. Yesterday was a disaster. I'm so ashamed of myself for losing control the way I did. My hunger is almost crippling me. But I just don't feel brave enough to face them. Humiliated. I'm absolutely humiliated. I could go downstairs, grab something and be back before anyone sees me. I'd much rather lie low for a day or two.

Slowly and as quietly as possible, I open the door and peek out onto the landing. Nothing. There's no one around. I tiptoe out and reach the top of the stairs but stop dead when I hear the loud ding-dong of the doorbell. I stay frozen to the spot, foot still in the air, and wait.

'John,' Gabriel greets. 'Glad to see you made it.'

'Of course we came, sir. The Kendryks call, we answer. It's both our honour and our privilege.' I peer over the bannister, careful to remain hidden, and watch Gabriel greet a tall, smarmy looking man with greasy black hair. They shake hands, and John even gives a small bow as if he were addressing royalty. Two other men are close behind, and each gets a handshake from Gabriel as they bow. Collins lingers to the side watching the welcome.

'Grayson's ready for us in his office,' Gabriel says, stepping back and opening his arm wide towards the enormous room. He's being polite, but is obviously bored and disinterested in the meeting. 'After you.'

They all follow, and Collins closes the door behind them leaving the entrance clear. I take my chance and make a quiet run down the stairs and whizz past the office towards the kitchen.

Safely in the kitchen, I grab a banana from the fruit bowl in the centre of the island before turning to leave. When I do, I slam into someone and fall back on the floor landing flat on my arse.

Quickly pushing myself up on my elbows, I see the greasy haired man Gabriel was talking to grinning down at me. John.

'Here. Let me help you.' He leans over me, holding out his hand. I shuffle back and get to my feet avoiding the outstretched hand like it's about to explode, telling him I'm fine. He shrugs and looks me up and down.

'What's your name, gorgeous?'

His voice is as slimy as his hair and sets me on edge. I go to leave, but he sidesteps in front of me blocking my path.

'Where are you going?' he asks, checking me over. 'Stay. Talk to me.' His smile's stomach-turning and his suit, which is extremely ill-fitting and ancient, smells of damp.

'I have to go.' I could slap myself for sounding so pathetic. When he doesn't move, I once more attempt to sidestep around him, but he blocks my path. 'Move. I have to-'

'Not seen you about before. You from the camp?' he asks, ignoring my words.

'I don't know what you're talking about.' I go to try and get past him again but no such luck. I groan as he blocks my path.

'I like you. You're pretty.' He reduces the space between us with a big step forwards waking my magic, readying it for attack. I should have stayed upstairs. Hunger be damned. 'I would really like to take you out for a drink sometime.'

'I'm not interested,' I say as firmly as I can and taking a deep breath in a bid to control my magic. I take another step forwards and he laughs as he yet again blocks my path. 'Move. Let me past.'

'You should treat me with more respect,' he says, leaning in closer and losing his smarmy grin. 'Not a good idea to piss of Grayson's men, ya know. I'm just trying to be nice.' He keeps coming as I back up until my arse hits the counter and I have nowhere else to go. 'I don't see a ring on your finger, so you must be open for business. How about you and me go for a private little walk? I could show you a good time.'

'Let me past.'

'C'mon. Don't be shy. If you show me yours,' he raises his eyebrows and stares at my chest. 'I'll show you mine.' His hand rests over his crotch.

Who the hell is this guy? He licks his lips and continues to openly stare at my chest.

'I'm going to ask you one more time.' I try to hold my tone. 'Let me past.' He leans in close. I shove him, but he barely moves. 'Get your greasy, vile little face out of mine before I punch it,' I warn.

'HEY!' we turn and see Amara standing in the doorway looking at us. 'Get away from her, John!'

'Piss off. This doesn't concern you.'

'Move!' I warn him again.

'Make me,' he laughs.

'You have no idea who you're messing with,' Amara warns, nodding at me. 'She's not someone you want to annoy.'

'Oh please, what's she gonna do?'

I knee him in the crotch and shove him hard, knocking him over.

'I think she'll whack you in your special place,' Amara laughs as I head towards her. 'You okay, Lilly?'

'Fine,' I reply. 'But I have to go before I do something I regret.' The magic inside me is screaming to get out. I need to get somewhere safe.

'Of course, go.' She steps aside.

I keep going till I reach the open space of the entrance hall and stop dead when the door to Grayson's study begins to open.

Shit!

I can't go back to the kitchen, and there's no way I'll get to the stairs unseen. I inwardly scream as I just stand, frozen like a statue. The magic inside me is clawing at my skin, and I don't think I can hold it much longer.

The two men that came with John leave the office, followed by the two brothers and Collins. I'm so busy looking at them I don't notice John at my side.

'I like a woman with spirit,' he says. 'And a nice ass.' He puts his hand on my backside and squeezes.

And that's it.

My blood runs cold and my breath catches in my throat as I surge with adrenaline and magic. John flies away from me, his body goes slamming into the wall as I intended. But what I didn't mean to happen was making the vase of flowers that decorate the table explode, along with the windows by the front door. Fragments of glass fly in all directions. Everyone covers their heads and ducks down as the air fills with fast-moving shards. A sharp pain stings across my neck, but before I can check what's caused it, a hand grabs my shoulder and spins me around.

'She's losing control!' Hendrix bellows, his fists clenched and pulled back. The surging power inside me explodes once more, and he too slams hard into the wall.

'STAY AWAY FROM ME!' I yell, holding my hand up to get him to stop before I really do lose control. 'For god's sake, stay away!'

'You little bitch,' he growls as he gets to his feet, his eyes on me with a hunger for hurt.'You'll pay for that.'

'I didn't mean it. Just stop, Hendrix. You're making it worse!'

Hendrix is back on his feet and running towards me. I use my magic and pin him to the wall lifting him off the ground with nothing more than a slight twitch of my hand. He grabs at his throat, struggling for air.

'STAY AWAY!' I scream. 'WHY WON'T YOU LISTEN! DO YOU WANT TO DIE?'

My feet come out from under me, and I slam sideways onto the floor which releases Hendrix from my hold.

'ENOUGH!' Grayson orders. He holds his arms up between us. 'Stand down, Hendrix. Lilly, get yourself under control. NOW! I don't want to hurt you, but I won't have you killing my men. Now calm-'

I lift my hand and send Grayson flying backwards as I get back on my feet.

'Don't you dare tell me to calm down,' I warn as I create my fire in my palm. 'John grabbed me, and that animal wants to hurt me. I see how he keeps looking at me. He wants to bite me!' I point at Hendrix and John in turn. 'NO ONE TOUCHES ME! NOT ANYMORE.' I mean it, more than anything.

Gabriel's helping his brother get to his feet, but Grayson's eyes don't leave me for a second.

'You need to stop,' Grayson warns. 'Calm down before you hurt someone.'

I stand firm, unsure what the hell to do. Everyone's watching me nervously and looking ready to attack.

Grayson creates lightning on his hand in response to my fire. He's ready to fight me if he must. I know it.

Gabriel steps between us with his arms raised.

'Please...both of you!' he urges as he looks at Grayson. 'She's frightened and angry. She didn't mean to lash out at you.' He turns back to me. 'Did you, Lilly?' He glances at my hand that still has a fireball ready to fly at Grayson if he so much as twitches. 'Stop,' he mouths, nodding at the fire.

'It was him!' Amara yells, running towards us from the kitchen and pointing at John. 'He was all over her in the kitchen and wouldn't let her leave.'

'Liar!' John insists. 'The bitch kicked me in the nuts as I was getting a glass of water! She's mental! She threatened to slit my throat cos I said she was pretty!'

'Mental?! I'm not fucking mental!' I spit back. 'I'll do more than slit your throat if you touch me again!'

'She came onto me! I swear, Grayson...she was all over me-'

'LYING PIECE OF SHIT!' I go for him, but Gabriel takes my arm and stops me.

'Put the fire out,' he says quietly in my ear.

'He's lying!' I insist. 'I didn't come on to him! I didn't threaten to kill him!'

'Think about what you're doing! Grayson will not let this carry on for much longer.'

I look past him. Grayson's jaw is clenched and twitching. His lightning still crawling over his hands.

'Put out your fire, Lilly,' he urges once more in my ear.

What the hell have I done? Facing off to Grayson, am I insane? He's let me into his home, looked after me. Never mind the fact that he's dangerous. I put out my fire and step behind Gabriel slightly.

'I'm sorry,' I say pathetically. 'I'm really sorry.'

He slides his hand into mine, and I grip it tightly just as Grayson charges towards me. Gabriel steps in front of me completely, acting as a human shield before Grayson can reach me.

'I'm not going to hurt her, Gabriel. Jesus,' Grayson scorns, moving his brother out of the way. 'She's bleeding.'

He pulls off his tie and holds it to my neck.

'The glass cut you. Keep the pressure on it.'

As he holds his tie against the cut, he won't look me in the eye. When he finally does, I see such anger in them it makes me cold.

'I'm sorry, please don't be mad. I panicked. I shouldn't have used my magic against you like that.'

'No, you shouldn't have. It was a stupid, petulant reaction.'

'John's lying, I didn't-'

He raises his hand, silencing me. 'I don't want to hear it,' he tells me. Those dark eyes are angry, so I do as I'm told and remain quiet. He puts my hand on the tie. 'Keep the pressure on it, Lilly. And stay with Gabriel. No more magic. You hear me?'

'I hear you.'

He lets go and helps John back to his feet. 'I'm sorry, John. Did she hurt you?' He's taking his side. Of course he would. Especially after I almost burnt his house down yesterday.

'I'll be fine, sir,' John sighs, smoothing down his wrinkled suit. 'I had no idea she was a witch. I apologise.'

'So, tell me. What happened? She threatened you?'

'Yes, sir. I was just getting a glass of water-'

'He's lying!' I argue.

'Lilly,' Grayson warns darkly. 'Quiet. Carry on, John.'

'I just said she was pretty. And she threatened to slit my throat if I so much as looked at her. She left. I was on my way back to your office. And she attacked me.' The corner of his mouth twitches as he lies through his teeth, and his eyes look smugly in my direction.

Grayson slides his hand in his pockets and looks between me and John.

'One of you is lying to me. And you both know my standing on liars. Especially when they are standing in *my* home speaking them to *my* face. Who is lying to me?'

'She is!'

'He is!'

He glares between us, hands still stowed and a disingenuous smile on his face. One that certainly doesn't reach his eyes.

'Gabriel?' Grayson looks at his brother who still stands beside me.

'Yes, Grayson?' Gabriel replies.

'Make sure Lilly stays exactly where she is. You understand me?'

With a nod, Gabriel looks down at me. His eyes blacken.

'No, please, don't-'

'Stay by my side, Lilly Hooper,' he orders. As Grayson turns his back to us, he leans into my ear. 'Trust me,' he whispers. 'Please. Just trust me.' He waits and I give a slight nod even though I hate that he's taken control of me. I slide my hand into his and grip it tightly, giving him my trust. And he grips me back just as tight knowing that he has it.

'I know you are the liar,' Grayson tells John. 'She has a phobia of touch. Didn't know that, did you? So, why the hell would she be all over a grubby little man like you?' he demands. I let out a relieved breath. He believes me after all.

'I did nothing-'

'Amara and Lilly both said that you grabbed her. I believe those two girls over you any day. Is that how you treat women? You grab them without their consent?'

'I didn't-'

'No means no, John. You know what happens to members of my coven who break that rule. You have left me with no choice.'

John lowers his head and falls to his knees. With his hands together and his head bowed as low as it will go, John starts begging.

'Please. Forgive me, sir. I'm sorry.'

'You think I care if you're sorry? You come into my house, touch what's mine, lie to my face-'

'She didn't tell me she was yours! If I'd known I would never have approached her.'

What? I'm not his!

'Well, now you know.' Grayson grabs John by his throat and pulls him to his feet, squeezing so tight his face starts to go purple.

'Stop it!' I plead. Gabriel's compulsion makes it impossible to move but it doesn't keep me quiet. 'Please, Grayson, don't!'

John's eyes begin to bulge, the veins in his neck rise to the surface and all he can do is claw at Grayson's hands trying desperately to prize his fingers from his throat, but it's all pointless.

'GRAYSON!' I scream. 'STOP! PLEASE! YOU'RE KILLING HIM!'

'No one touches her. Ever.' He sends his lightning through him making John violently judder, his feet an inch from the ground. The poor man wets himself.

'Grayson,' I snarl. 'Stop now or I swear to god I will leave this house and NEVER come back.'

Grayson lets him go with a shove and stands over him, straightening his cuffs as John sobs at his feet.

'Touch her again, or any woman, you will not be this lucky again. Am I clear?'

'Y-yes sir. Thank y-you, sir,' he stammers with a raspy voice.

The two men that came with John scoop him up from the floor. Their heads are bowed and their eyes firmly on the ground.

'Malcolm, I suggest you chose your subordinates more carefully in future. I will not tolerate that kind of behaviour inside my Coven. Am I clear?' Grayson says firmly.

'Yes, sir. I'm sorry,' the dark haired one says, glaring at me with hatred.

'Good. Your plane leaves in two hours. You have your tickets. We will meet again in two weeks when you get back.' He walks over to them and shakes each of their hands. 'I want the Hooper boy found and believe me when I say failure is not an option. Italy is lovely this time of year. Tim. Malcolm. It was good to meet you. Have a lovely rest of the day, won't you.'

Tim, Malcolm and John are shown out by Collins. I hear the door close, and Grayson turns to me.

'You look angry, Miss Hooper,' Grayson smirks. 'Care to tell me why?'

'You nearly killed him,' I say through gritted teeth. 'Are you crazy?'

'He touched you and you reacted with your magic. Tell me...how much of that was intended and how much was a reaction? You think it is acceptable for you to send glass in all directions and slam people into walls? You could have slit your throat! Never mind the fact you almost burnt my house down last night. I did what I did to make sure you feel safe in this house. He won't dare touch you again. No man will.'

'Does that go for you too?' I reply defiantly.

He storms up to me fast, his face right in mine as his eye twitches in utter anger. My feet don't move. They can't. Gabriel's compelled me to stay by his side.

'You can't behave this way, Lilly. You can't talk to me with disrespect. I won't have it.'

'And I won't be claimed by you. I am not yours. I am not your girl. And I am not your witch.'

'You are in *my* house. You are in *my* care.' He's angry. Really angry. But so am I.

'You tortured him. You were going to kill him. I don't want that kind of care.'

Grayson looks at me and pinches the bridge of his nose while closing his eyes.

'I know you have been through a lot. And I am trying really hard not to lose my temper with you. But if you say one more thing to me, I swear, I will not be held responsible for my actions.'

'You have no idea what I've been through...none.'

'Lilly. Just stop talking,' Gabriel warns. But I don't care.

'Yes, Lilly. Stop talking,' Grayson says.

'You know what? Fuck this. I can't go through this again. Another man telling me what to do. How to behave. Gabriel, remove your compulsion. I want to leave.'

'Don't you dare, Gabriel. Tell her to go to her room.'

'You send me to my room, that's kidnapping. Gabriel, let me go.'

'Gabriel...send her to her room!'

'Screw you, Grayson. You can't do this.'

The room's reacting to my anger. The debris all over the floor's jumping around us.

'You think you can talk to me how you please?'

'You think you can claim me as your property? Keep me here against my will?'

'Lilly, please. Calm down.' Gabriel's getting more worried. A series of thuds from Grayson's office tells me my magic is getting beyond my control as his books start flying off the shelves.

'You need to calm down, Lilly,' Grayson warns pointing his finger at me and taking a step forward.

'You need to fuck off,' I reply taking a similar step.

'Lilly, please-' Gabriel calls.

'I'm trying to be patient with you. I know you have had a difficult time. But you will not talk to me this way. And you will not leave.'

'Try and stop me.' My fire erupts on my hand. 'You don't own me. No one owns me.' I raise my arm, ready to attack. 'You dare touch me, and I'll kill you where you stand.'

'LILLY!' Gabriel shouts spinning me round. 'STOP! NOW!'

'GET OFF ME!' I shove him away. He staggers back, but my magic...it's beyond my control and one of the metal pokers from the fireplace behind him shoots across the room and impales him straight through the stomach. Everything around me seems to start moving in slow motion. I hear the shouting of the men around me but pay no attention to them. Gabriel looks down at the metal rod that's gone straight through his body before stumbling back and falling to his knees. He looks up at me with a look of such betrayal and confusion.

No! Oh please no!

I stand speechless, paralysed by shock and horror as he just stares at me.

What the hell have I done?

I don't get a chance to help him, to say a word, to do anything at all before I'm spun around and Grayson's fist slams into my face knocking me out cold.

Chapter 9

Gabriel...

I killed him.

I lost my temper. I lost control. Just as Harry told them I would. The hushed whisperings of the voices around me are angry. Talking about what they should do with me. Someone wants me locked up. He wants me back in chains. Hendrix...he's insisting on it. Telling Grayson I'm a danger to everyone. A risk that they shouldn't be taking. A damaged little girl who doesn't deserve to be here. Who doesn't deserve their protection. No one agrees, but no one disagrees either. I lie here still and silent. My eyes remain closed, and I continue my pretence of sleep. A door opens. The voices disappear as it closes. I'm left alone, too afraid to open my eyes or move. What if I'm back in the dark? Thrown into a pit from which I can't escape once more? What if I'm back in chains? What if I open my eyes and see Gabriel's body? The look I saw on his face as he fell...I'll never forgive myself, so why would they forgive me? I wish they never found me. My uncle was right, I am a monster. Gabriel was nothing but kind. Nothing but sweet and because of me he's dead. Because of my temper and my inability to control my magic Gabriel's gone for good, and if I'm not locked up, I should be. Or even better, they should just kill me. Grayson's more than likely going to. I killed his brother. He's already lost one of his siblings, Bias. And now I've taken the only family he has left.

'I deserve to die for everything I've done,' I sob, still laying with my eyes closed.

'Don't ever say that again. You hear me?'

The stern voice that speaks has me sitting up so fast the room spins. I'm not in chains. I'm not locked up, and what's more, I don't see Gabriel's lifeless body. But his very alive one standing just across the lounge watching me. I propel myself off the sofa and across the room. He winces as I collide with his chest and his hand settles over his stomach as my arms wrap around him.

'Easy,' he laughs softly. I just sob and hold him tightly so thankful and happy that he's alive.

'I thought I killed you!' I cry as he hugs me back.

'It will take more than a poker through the gut to get rid of me,' he whispers in my ear and nestles his face into my neck.

'I'm so sorry. I'm so, so sorry.' I can't stop my sobbing. 'Please forgive me. It was an accident. I swear-'

'I know it was, you daft mare,' he chuckles. 'I'm alright. It's all okay. It didn't hit any organs.'

I've never known relief like it. He's not cross. He's not on death's door. He pulls away and looks down at my tear-streaked face.

'Don't you dare think you deserve to die. Nothing you've done deserves death, understand?' He waits for my response, his eyebrows hitched and a serious frown. 'It was an accident. No one will hold you responsible for it. No one will hurt you-' I pull him back into my arms before he can say another word and continue to cry. He doesn't pull away.

'As long as you're okay, I can face anything Grayson does to me.'

The door opens and Grayson walks in, followed by Collins and Hendrix. Grayson looks at us in each other's arms before gesturing for me to sit. I don't need to be told twice, so I force myself to let go of Gabriel and take a seat on the sofa.

'I'm sorry,' I whisper, too ashamed to look at them. 'I'm so, so sorry. It was an accident. I just got so angry. I'm really sorry.'

'I know you are. I am too.' Grayson takes a seat next to me. 'Listen, Lilly. This isn't working.'

'Are you going to lock me up?' I ask nervously.

Grayson shakes his head. 'No, Lilly. We're not going to lock you up.'

Hendrix shuffles in the background looking thoroughly pissed off.

'Are you going to kill me?' I ask.

Grayson shakes his head once more.

'Are you going to send me away? Because I know I said I wanted to leave but I was just really upset.'

He sighs and looks at the men standing around us. He is! He's going to send me away. They don't want me here. Why would they? I wouldn't.

But I don't want to go.

'Please don't send me away. I have nowhere else to go. I can do better. Please...the Hunters-'

He holds up a hand silencing me.

'No one is sending you away. And no one is killing you or locking you up. But, you are a danger not only to yourself but to those around you.' He sighs once more and slides a little closer towards me. How is he so calm? He almost murdered a man for lying to him. What would he do to someone who nearly killed his own brother?

'Lilly, do you recall us referring to you as a Broken Witch?'

'Yes,' I reply.

'Well, a Break is the result of extreme trauma. It's literally a break. Your personality splits in two. One version is you. You feel everything as you should and are guided by a moral compass. But the other version...they feel no fear, no remorse, no regret.

And they can be very quick to anger, which is pretty much all they're capable of feeling. If they feel anything at all. It's a very rare survival mechanism which kicks in when a witch's emotions get too much. A few hours ago, you lost your temper with me. At your uncle's, you started drowning in all the pain he had caused you. In both cases, the Broken side of you started to appear. All Broken Witches have the same signs. Their hair and eyes lose their colour. The hair turns white and the eyes-'

'Turn lilac,' I finish his words. 'I saw my eyes in the reflection of a broken mirror by my feet at my uncle's house. What does all of this mean?' I ask Grayson.

'It means that if you give in to that side of you, if you let it take control, you will become impossible to reason with and with the power inside you? You would be impossible to stop. Broken Witches don't care about anyone. Not even themselves really. They fixate. Maybe on revenge or destroying their enemies. It's never anything good. You know Toby well. I imagine it comes as no surprise to you to learn that he is a Broken Witch. He gave into his other side a long time ago. He's been Broken far longer than not. He was loyal to us. Even Broken. It came in handy on occasion. His sheer force of will and single-minded focus was very efficient.'

'Until he betrayed us and did a runner,' Gabriel mutters.

'Why did he Break? What happened to him?' Why do I sound like I care? Maybe I do. Maybe learning that there was a reason for why he was the way he was will help me understand what happened between us.

'We're not sure,' Grayson tells me.

'Whatever it was, was violent. Brutal. Sadistic,' Hendrix adds with a cruel smile. 'Right up his street.'

All three men turn slowly and look at him with a *'what's your problem?'* expression.

'What?' Hendrix says with a laugh and a shrug as everyone gives him a glare. 'Don't shoot the messenger. I'm just pointing out the elephant in the room. Little Witch clearly has some darkness in her past.'

'What does he mean?' I ask.

'Like I said,' Grayson says, turning back to me. 'A Break is a result of severe trauma. What he's saying is that something happened to you in your past that made you Break. A single event that you couldn't cope with. You Broke. At some point in your past, you turned. Your hair would have been white. Somehow, you managed to come back. But the risk of you suffering another Break is high because you've already Broken once. When your emotions get too much, there's a risk that the Broken side of you will take over. Which is why I hit you after you hurt Gabriel. I didn't want to risk losing you.'

'W-what do I do?'

Gabriel walks over and sits on my other side.

'Learning to live with whatever it was that happened to you can on occasion help suppress the Broken side. Making it harder for it to leak out and take control,' Gabriel says.

'Tell us what happened,' Grayson says. 'Tell us why you Broke and let us help you learn to cope with it.'

'I don't know what happened,' I tell him. He doesn't believe me. He rolls his eyes and growls under his breath. 'I truly don't, Grayson. I have no idea what may have caused this...Break, or whatever it is that's wrong with me.'

'She's a liar, as well as a liability,' Hendrix retorts. Grayson glares at him. His glare would have me silent but not Hendrix who's getting angrier. He points at me as he tries to contain his frustration as he speaks directly to Grayson, ignoring all of us. 'A Break isn't something you just forget. You can't forget the worst moment of your life. She's clearly lying! She refuses to talk about what happened when she did a runner with Toby. She refuses to admit what happened in that barn. She almost killed Gabriel. She could have killed me! She threatened you, Boss. That can't be tolerated. She needs to be locked up, not given a room with a view and an all-access pass to our home.'

'*My* home,' Grayson says firmly. 'Which *I* allow you to live in, Hendrix. Don't forget that. You weren't exactly house trained when I brought you into my Coven-'

'I never put you or the others at risk. You know what happens if one of you dies-'

'Interrupt me again, Hendrix, and you will be the one I lock up. Do you hear me?' Hendrix lowers his gaze and steps back as Grayson returns his attention to me. He carries on like nothing just happened, but Hendrix stares hatefully over at me.

'Lilly,' Grayson says calmly. 'A Break is an *extreme* trauma. It's not something you forget. Was it Toby? Is that why you don't want to talk about it? Did it happen when you ran away with him? Did something happen to you in that barn?' He leans in closer. 'Does it have something to do with your haphephobia?' He wants to sound like he's driven by concern. But he's so desperate to know what happened.

'I *can't* talk about it, Grayson.'

'I have to insist-'

'I don't know what happened!' I repeat desperately.

'What if you tell me in private. Anything you tell me will be confidential. I promise.'

'I *can't* tell you because I don't know!' I insist. 'I don't remember, okay?' I sigh, knowing that there's nothing to do but tell the truth. 'The truth is...after I left my uncle's house, I have no idea what happened.'

'Explain,' he says with a furrowed brow.

'Toby came to me and asked me to look after something for him. A book. The journal you're looking for. He said he had to go away for a few weeks and that he needed me to keep it safe. I did. I hid it for him in my room. He was gone for over a month,' I sigh as I remember those weeks. And what happened. 'When Toby was away, Harry found out about him. That I was in a relationship and that I'd been sneaking him into the house. He was livid. Things got really, really bad.'

'What did he do?' Gabriel asks.

I shake my head. 'The specifics aren't important.'

'Did he cause the Break?' Grayson asks.

'I don't know. Maybe. He found out about us a few days before Toby came back. Harry beat me something rotten. Toby snuck into my room late at night and saw I was hurt. I told him Harry knew about us. I asked Toby to help me. I wanted to leave Harry's house for good, but I couldn't do it alone. I had no money. No idea how the world worked. No friends or family to help me, just him. I begged him to get me out. Harry was going to kill me eventually. It was the most logical outcome. How much longer was he going to keep me stashed away? Harry was so angry about Toby. So angry.' My train of thought gets diverted to the memories of that week.

'What did Toby say?' Grayson asks. 'When you asked for help?'

'He said no,' I say simply. 'He said I'd made my bed and I had to lie in it. He took the journal, and he left.' An image of his pale face twisted in anger as he hissed awful things to me in the darkness of my room stabs at my heart. I'd never known what heartbreak felt like until that moment. I'd known pain. I'd known fear and suffering, but heartbreak...that was something else entirely. I look into Grayson's eyes. 'He left me there to die.'

'Your uncle said you killed six men at the Miller's farm. That that's why he locked you down in the cellar. What happened there?'

'I don't remember any of that.'

'How?!' he says frustrated.

'After Toby left I cried myself to sleep. When I woke up, my jaw was broken. Three of my ribs as well. I had marks on my wrists that looked like I'd been tied up. I was covered in bruises and...' I wipe the stray tear. 'And there were burns on my skin from Toby's fire.' Gabriel's hands slide into mine and his thumb traces back and forth over my knuckles. It gives me the strength I need to carry on speaking. 'Harry came charging in screaming at me. He dragged me barely conscious into the cellar and tied me up. That's when he told me. Six weeks ago, I'd run off with the boy I'd been seeing. That I'd killed all those people at the barn, that I'd turned into a monster with white hair and purple eyes. He said that I'd become evil and he had no choice but to lock me away. I told him I didn't remember. I thought he was lying. I never really believed him. I thought it was a trick. I was locked down there alone for two years. Toby never came back for me, and I have no memories of what happened between me crying myself to sleep the night he left to me waking up half beaten to death six weeks later.' I look at Gabriel and Grayson both in turn. 'I swear to you. I do not remember.' They both look surprised.

Grayson shuffles as close as possible without touching me. 'The night we found you, you asked your uncle if he killed someone. *Her*.' His dark eyes are desperate for information. 'He said when you knew the answer to that, you went mad. Did he mean that you Broke?'

I nod. 'I guess so.'

'So your uncle believed that you losing this person was the reason for your Break?'

'Maybe.'

'Lilly, who was he talking about? Who died?'

'I know you want answers,' I tell him, looking into his dark eyes pleadingly. 'But I can't talk about that. Not if you want me to stay sane. Okay? Please. I will tell you anything. But I can't talk about that. Not yet.' A single tear slides down my cheek. It's the only other thing I can offer him.

'Okay,' he says gently, tapping my knee. 'That's okay. In your own time. Now, I have something that I think will help you. Something that will keep you, my men and myself safe.' He holds up a leather bracelet and places it in my hand. It's deep red and has delicate Celtic markings engraved on it. I recognise it as the one I saw on Gabriel's wrist on our walk in the Orchard on my first day here. But it's what's sewn straight down the middle in red thread that stops me admiring it any further.

'What's this?' I ask coldly, knowing precisely what it is.

'That, Lilly, is a binding spell. I used the thread from the one you wore at your uncle's to make it.'

I get to my feet.

'You may as well lock me up too,' I snap, letting it slip from my fingers to the floor. 'Put a gag in my mouth. Brand me.'

Grayson picks it up and stands in front of me.

'No one is locking you up. Or gagging you. And no one is branding you. We put poppers on it here, see?' He turns it to show me the fastenings. 'So you can take it off whenever you like. It's not a demand from us, but a request. I want you to think about this carefully. Your control issues almost killed Gabriel. You hurt Hendrix and yourself. And you almost burned to death the other night. And you are clearly not very emotionally stable right now. That's not your fault. But it is a problem. As you continue manifesting your magic, it *will* get worse. One day you will present with Energy.' He wriggles his shimmering hand. 'Emotions can spark a manifestation. You could be arguing with your best friend and end up killing them. My house is usually a lot busier than this, but I daren't have people here with you so unstable.'

I stare at the cuff silently as tears pool in my eyes and stream down my cheeks.

'I'm back where I started.' I wipe the tears, hating their frequent appearance. 'I'm never going to be free. Not really. And I'm sick of crying.'

'This is temporary and mutual.' He holds it out, ready to put it on me but I hesitate.

I look around the room. Everyone has their eyes on the floor, avoiding me.

'Do you all want me to do this?' I ask.

'We all discussed it, and we all agree that this is the best way forward,' Grayson replies.

'But how will I get any better if I can't use my magic?'

'We will practice your magic. Together. It will be controlled and relaxed. It will be safe. I will guide you through Energy when you present with it, and Telekinesis until then. Gabriel will assist you with your Mental magic when that appears, and Collins will train you with Physical when that comes through.' He holds up the cuff once more.

'What about Sight?' I ask.

'That one will be all on you. There is only one other that has had that gift, and he is no longer here to help.'

'Who?' I ask.

'It's not important-'

'Who?' I insist.

They all look at each other. It would be funny if it weren't so frightening. 'Tell me.'

'Toby,' Grayson says finally. 'Toby has Sight as well as power over the Elements.'

This is too much to take in. My head's ready to explode, and in the worst case of bad timing, the glass in the windows start to shake, making everyone shuffle nervously.

'We saved you,' Grayson says. 'We have looked after you. Helped you.' He steps closer. 'Now it's your turn to help us.'

'What if I refuse to wear it?' I ask defiantly.

'I'm hoping that we won't find that out.'

I shake my head and walk to the door and away from them.

'I can't be bound again. I'm sorry, but I can't. First, it's on my wrist then it's in my mouth, then I'm locked away. I can't. I'll leave if that's what you want. But I can't be locked away again.'

'Lilly,' Gabriel calls after me as he follows me out into the lobby. He closes the door behind him so it's just the two of us and he takes my arm stopping me from walking away. I turn and see the cuff in his hand.

'You said you liked it. When we were outside.'

'I do. But not if it makes me helpless. How can I protect myself if I'm wearing that?'

He puts it on himself and holds out his hand.

'Like this.' He simply pulls it off and puts it in his pocket. Unlike the gag I used to wear, there's no triple knot holding it in place. 'See? You want to take it off and use your magic intentionally, that's all you have to do. Wearing this means you don't accidentally kill anyone. That you can sleep without the risk of becoming a barbecue.'

He takes it out from his pocket and holds it flat in his palm.

'I would never let anything bad happen to you. We'll all be with you every step of the way.' He raises the cuff and holds it by my hand. 'It's time you faced what you are. You are the Arcane Witch. You will manifest more magic, and the powers that you do have right now will get stronger. If you don't embrace them, they will control you. And I think it's time you took control back, don't you?'

I look at the cuff. His other hand is resting over where I impaled him. Hurting him was the last thing I wanted to do. It was unintentional.

'Take control. Start your life, right now. You say you're sick of crying? Then stop. In the lobby, you stood up to Grayson. There aren't many people I know that have the balls to do that. Not even I do. Your hair wasn't changing then. That was you telling him that he was wrong and that you won't be owned by anyone. That was you taking a stand. I know you have the spirit to be the best Arcane possible. Now you just need the courage to embrace it. Embrace your pain. Embrace your fears and tell them that you own them. Not the other way around.'

'You think I can?'

'I *know* you can. We've waited five hundred years for you, Lilly Hooper.'

'I must be a big disappointment.'

'You are as far from a disappointment as you could be. What do you say?' he asks, the cuff in his palm.

I give him my hand, and he puts on the cuff. His cuff.

Chapter 10

The leather cuff that Gabriel put on my wrist yesterday hasn't come off. And despite Gabriel's words, it seems to be getting heavier and heavier with every passing moment. I know it's for the best. I know that it's the safest thing for everyone right now, but that doesn't make it any easier.

The raised voices coming from inside Grayson's office stop me in my tracks as I make my way down the stairs alone. The heated tones of the two brothers echo through the slightly ajar door and into the lobby. When I hear my name being shouted, I sneak closer.

'I just don't think it's a good idea!' Gabriel argues.

'Well, I wasn't asking your opinion. I was giving you an order,' Grayson replies. 'I don't like this attitude you have towards Lilly. I won't repeat myself, Gabriel. Back off. I mean it.'

'I'm not doing anything, Grayson! Except help *you* get what *you* want. She needs to feel safe. Not owned or like a prisoner. I'm trying to be a friend.'

'What *I* want? Don't you mean what *we* want? You don't want the Veil down?'

'Of course I want the Veil down,' Gabriel says indignantly. 'Don't be ridiculous. All I'm saying is we need to ease her into this. Telling her about her Broken side? That she's the Arcane, and then giving her that cuff? It's a lot to digest and you know she isn't stable. Trying to find the cause of her Break may very well have the adverse effect.'

'It was your suggestion in the first place. Not mine, and it was the right suggestion to make.'

'I didn't mean for me to go digging around in her head though. I was thinking therapy or hypnosis-'

'Hypnosis?' Grayson laughs derisively at him. 'Come on, Gabriel. She's the most powerful creature alive with a serious trauma in her past and a debilitating fear of being touched. You think hypnosis is going to help her?'

'She won't agree to me using my magic on her,' he says simply. 'She won't even talk about her past, Grayson, I doubt very much that she'll let me see it in full HD.'

'She doesn't really have a choice.'

'I'm not forcing her. She won't talk to me again if I do. I'm amazed she didn't slap me for using it on her yesterday. I'm fine by the way. Thanks for asking,' he adds annoyed.

There's a silence. I shuffle closer to the gap thinking they've moved, but Grayson's voice soon carries through.

'It means a lot to you, doesn't it? That she likes you.'

Gabriel tells him he's ridiculous, but Grayson's being deadly serious.

'I see how you look at her. Don't even think about it,' Grayson tells him sternly.

'I'm not-'

'You're not capable of monogamy, Gabriel. Every week there's another girl between your sheets. She deserves better than that.'

'It's not like that! I like her. As a friend.'

'I need her to feel safe here. I need her focus to be on the spell and her recovery. Not you. She's spent three years being manipulated by a sociopath who somehow, god knows how, but somehow, he convinced her to fall in love with him. That's enough heartbreak for anyone. I won't watch you lose interest in her and move on as you do with every single girl that turns your head. Do you hear me?' There's more silence. 'I said do-'

'I hear you!' Gabriel snaps. 'I don't think of her that way. If I look like I'm flirting it's accidental. If anything, I feel sorry for her. That's all.'

There's another long silence, and I can imagine them glaring at each other. He feels sorry for me? Prick.

'So, what's the plan?' Gabriel asks, breaking the silence and apparently keen to move on.

'Well, she hasn't agreed to help us yet. We need to get her on board. Preferably before anyone else finds out she's here. If word gets out the Arcane is not only alive but here with us, you know *he'll* come for her,' Grayson says. 'Billy will be here this afternoon to organise the men coming back for protection detail. With Lilly wearing that cuff they'll be a lot safer. They are aware that she's completely off limits and not to be approached. I don't want her to be uncomfortable. You know what she's like when men get too close.'

'Yeah well, you made your position on that very clear when you almost killed John for touching her backside,' Gabriel says snarkily. Grayson ignores him.

'She needs to concentrate on getting those powers under control and start her manifestations. Not spend her time hiding upstairs and avoiding everyone. Or crushing on you. We just need to keep her safe and get that damn Journal back before Theo hears we have her.'

Theo? Who the hell is Theo?

'You think he'll come for her? Even with us here?'

'That man would tear the world apart to get his hands on her. He's desperate. Desperate enough to come here, even with us protecting her.'

'You think he'll try to kill her?'

Grayson laughs. 'Oh yes. Theo will try to kill her.'

I swallow past the enormous lump that's developed in my throat. There's a man named Theo who wants me dead? Why?

With a sigh, Grayson says, 'And we're still no closer to finding Toby. It's getting tricky all this.'

'Toby,' Gabriel says his name with venom. 'Don't even get me started on that little freak. This is ridiculous Grayson. I'm getting lost with all these secrets. We should just tell her-'

'Toby!' he says firmly cutting him off. 'Is a complication. One that we will resolve as soon as we find him. She needs to be able to trust us so we will deal with him quickly. We need to keep him as far away from her as possible. At least now we know why he was acting so strangely before he disappeared. He was hiding the fact that he was seeing the Arcane Witch behind our backs. I worry that there are still feelings there. If she sees him, we can't be sure she won't try to protect him. Or worse, run off with him. He knows how to disappear, I'll give him that! And he sure knows how to manipulate.'

The doorbell goes, and before I get caught eavesdropping, I run back up the stairs hoping not to be seen. I only get a few steps before Grayson and Gabriel walk out of the office. I stop and spin round. They both stand in the doorway looking as caught out as me. We all stare at each other for a few seconds before Collins walks straight through the middle of us, glancing at them on one side and me on the other as he makes his way to the door.

'Morning all.'

'Morning, Collins,' I reply as he walks straight through the tension.

He opens the door and greets someone cheerfully. 'Billy. Good to see you.'

'I believe Grayson is expecting me?'

Grayson heads to the door to greet Billy. Their indistinct chatter is of no interest to me. Apparently, it's not to Gabriel either because he starts walking towards me.

'Did you hear any of that?' he asks quietly.

'Any of what?' I reply, trying to sound casual.

'Lilly. This is Billy Songer,' Grayson calls over. I walk past Gabriel, avoiding his stare and head towards Grayson and the man standing next to him. Billy.

Billy's built like a brick shit house, as Mr Simmons would have said if he was here. He has long grey hair with a matching beard and must be in his fifties. But he looks like he could floor even Hendrix with a good punch.

'Pleasure to meet you, Miss Hooper,' Billy's voice sounds like he's smoked twenty a day since he was five. He stretches out a hand.

'I'm sorry, Billy,' Grayson says on my behalf and lowering Billy's hand. 'She doesn't shake hands. I'll explain it all to you shortly. Lilly, why don't you go and make yourself a coffee and come see us in a few minutes.'

They disappear into Grayson's study, closing the door behind them, leaving me, Collins and Gabriel alone in the lobby. I turn and head into the kitchen keen to avoid the third degree over my eavesdropping. Gabriel attempts to follow but is caught by Collins who seems eager to chat.

I make myself a coffee and look out the glass doors across the garden, thinking about what I heard. Whoever this Theo is, he doesn't sound like good news. He wants to kill me? Why? And Toby. What would I say to him if I did ever see him again?

'Morning, Little Witch.'

I turn around and see Hendrix standing a few feet behind me as I nurse my untouched coffee.

'My name's Lilly. In case you forgot. Quit calling me Little Witch.'

He always seems dirty, like he has been rolling in dust and grease for the last ten years and it's stained his skin. The way he stares at me with his mouth twisted in an uncomfortably familiar grin is enough to make me feel violated.

'Do you want something?' I snap. 'Because if you're thinking about trying to hit me again, I would consider what happened to you last time.'

'I was actually going to ask if I could join you for a drink? Build a bridge maybe. Seems a shame to be sitting all alone.' He's trying to make me feel uncomfortable. I know it, but I won't give him the satisfaction.

'I would rather die of thirst than share a drink with you, Hendrix. And I have no interest in building any bridges. Not with you. You want me locked up.'

'I want you gone,' he clarifies, before walking over. But I don't move a muscle. 'You're a risk to everyone here and nothing but a distraction to those two.' He looks at the bandage on my neck from the glass explosion yesterday and takes a deep sniff.

'Your blood smells delicious,' he says longingly, licking his lips. 'I've always wondered what the blood of an Arcane Witch would taste like. Maybe you could let me find out sometime?'

'When hell freezes over, maybe.'

'Grayson will get bored of fucking you soon enough-'

'Excuse me?'

'And once you've brought the Veil down you'll be all alone with no man to protect you. So maybe being nicer to me would serve your future interests.' He runs his grubby finger along my jaw before I slap it away. 'I wouldn't mind the distraction once the spell is done.'

'One, I'm not fucking Grayson. Two, I don't need anyone to protect me, and three,' I step closer and look unblinking into this disgusting, vile creature's face. 'You make me sick. Breathing the same air as you is more than I can stand.'

He grabs my hand and yanks me forwards. I try to free myself from his grip which feels worse than anyone else's so far.

'Get off me Hendrix or-'

'Or what? You'll run to Grayson? Tell him I'm being mean?'

'I don't need Grayson to fight you.'

'You ain't gonna do shit to me with that cuff on. Hear me, Little Witch. If you fuck this up for us, Grayson will be the least of your problems. You step out of line I'll sink my teeth into you so fast-'

'Are you two playing nice?' Gabriel asks as he walks in. His eyes fall on Hendrix's hand on mine, and his eyebrows raise in surprise. 'I suggest you get your hands off her, Hendrix, before I break every single one of those fingers you're touching her with.'

'We're just talking,' he says, letting me go and standing straighter.

'Just get out, Hendrix,' Gabriel orders. Hendrix growls and bares his teeth at me. 'I said get out,' Gabriel repeats.

'Yes...*sir*,' Hendrix walks out looking resentfully at Gabriel as he goes.

'You alright?' Gabriel asks, still watching the door that Hendrix just walked through.

'I'm fine.' I've dealt with more disgusting people than him. 'He really doesn't like me.'

'Do you care?' he asks, sliding his hands into his pockets as he heads towards me.

'Fair point.'

'But a word to the wise, best not piss off the vampire too much. They're not well known for their slow tempers and rational thinking.'

'How does he...you know...feed? Out of curiosity.'

'He has friends that get off on being bitten,' Gabriel says as if it's obvious. 'There's a real fetish about vampires. If you know where to look.'

'So, can he go out in sunlight? Does he hate garlic?'

'What's written in the stories are all fabrications so if people actually met a vampire, they would have no idea how to kill them,' Gabriel laughs.

'So how do you kill a vampire?'

'Planning on offing Hendrix?' He grins as I shrug.

'Are *you* okay?' I ask, gesturing to his stomach.

'Fine. A bit sore, but it'll be healed in a few days. Did you hear Grayson and I talking?' he asks suddenly, holding his gaze and looking me straight in the eye.

'No,' I reply.

'Jesus Lilly, you really are a shit liar,' he laughs. 'Well, I don't want you to worry about anything you might have heard. Okay?'

He slides open the door to the garden.

'Who's Theo?' I ask as he takes a step outside.

'A bad man,' he says simply. 'A man who doesn't want the Veil to come down. That's all.'

'Is that why he would kill me? To stop the Veil coming down?'

'Don't worry about it.' He goes to close the door behind him, but I pull it back.

'Am I safe?'

'You're perfectly safe. He doesn't even know you exist. Fancy joining me as I have a smoke?' He gestures out to the sunny but cold lawn.

Grayson calls my name from the lobby.

'Ahh...the Coven leader calls,' I sigh. I turn and head to the door. But before I get too far from him, I turn back. 'Oh, and Gabriel?'

'Yeah?'

'I don't want your pity. If the only reason you're being nice to me is because you feel sorry for me, you can shove your friendship up your backside.'

He tries to stifle his smile. As do I.

'Good job I don't want anything shoved up my backside then, isn't it?' he laughs and shakes his head as he closes the door.

'Lilly. This is Billy. Billy, Lilly.' Grayson introduces us again as I walk into his office. Billy gets to his feet and gives me a small bow as Grayson walks around his desk to stand by my side.

'Billy is the one who keeps an eye on the Nomads for me and runs security in the house.'

'Nomads?' I ask.

'Nomads are the name of the Descendants that we protect,' Grayson explains.

'And I've selected a handful of the most trustworthy Nomads to be here for your protection,' Billy adds in his husky voice. 'They'll stay out of your way, Miss Hooper, and if you see them just pretend that they're not there.'

I wonder if it's security for protection or prevention. I imagine the Nomads will be here to keep me safe from this Theo. Or the more likely version, to prevent me from hurting anyone else.

'We will start your training in a day or two when you have settled in a bit more. Is that acceptable?' Grayson asks as they both stand there looking at me lost in my own raging thoughts. I nod and look longingly at the door, keen to have some time to sift through all this information I've been given since I've got here. He seems to take the hint and tells me I can go. So, with a nod to Billy and a polite goodbye, I head back to the lobby.

Maybe I'll see if I can find the cliffs. I could see if Gabriel would like to take me. Maybe he'll be more talkative about the whole Theo mystery away from the house. When I step out the back door, I shiver at the low temperature. I don't even know what the date is. Or the month, but it must be winter. The air has that feel to it. It smells cold.

I spot Gabriel and Collins as well as four men I don't recognise, standing by the pool's edge. Although I want to go and see Gabriel and attempt to get some answers, I don't want to meet four more strangers. Instead, I return inside. I'll just go back up to my room.

As I reach the stairs, I hear raised voices. One of which I recognise as Amara's. It pulls me to the front door. Slowly I open it up, peering through a small gap out to the front of the house.

She's standing in the driveway with a tall, well-built man with straggly grey hair, dressed in tatty jeans and a plaid flannel shirt. He looks homeless.

'It's just a couple of hundred!' he says. 'He won't even know it's gone. You can't deny your own father medicine!'

'It's not medicine you want though, is it?!' Amara argues back. 'I'm not stealing money from Collins so you can get drunk. Just go home, Dad. You're embarrassing yourself.'

'Don't you dare speak to me like that!' He grabs her arm and gets in her face. 'You have an obligation to look after me. You being here with him is breaking that obligation. Your place is by *my* side, taking care of *me*!' Her dad slurs and sways. He has that glassy look that all men get when they've had too much to drink.

'My place is here. With them. With him!' she insists. 'Most fathers would be glad their daughters are happy, but not you! You just want me to stay at home, make your dinner and clean up your sick.' She snatches her arm away. 'Well, not anymore. I'm living my life my way, and if you or the other Nomads don't like it, you can all go to hell.'

He screws his face up in anger and hits her with a powerful backhand. The only reason she doesn't fall is that he still has hold of her arm.

'HEY!' I yell, stepping out from behind the door and charging over. 'GET YOUR HANDS OFF HER!' I point at him threateningly when he doesn't let her go. 'DID YOU HEAR ME?'

'Who the fuck are you?' he says, blinking and trying to get a better focus on me.

'Shit,' Amara says under her breath when she sees me. 'Lilly, it's okay,' she says in a panic looking between us. 'I'm okay. Please...' She glances behind me to the door before settling her eyes back on me looking frightened. 'I don't want to make a scene.'

'I said get off her,' I warn. 'I won't tell you again.'

'Who's this?' he laughs. 'A Witch groupie?'

What the hell is a Witch groupie? Pretty sure that's an insult.

'Dad! You can't call her that!' Amara gasps in horror. 'He didn't mean it, Lilly. He's drunk.'

He pushes Amara so hard she falls. 'I'm not drunk.' But an idiot could see he is.

I help Amara to her feet and take hold of her hand.

'You alright?' I ask, helping her brush off the dirt and stones from her jeans. She tries to explain that he's just drunk and didn't mean to insult me.

'I couldn't care less what he calls me, Amara. Trust me, I've been called a lot worse. He hit you! He can't do that!'

My eyes narrow on him. I'm mad. Really fucking mad. He wipes his snotty red nose with the back of his hand.

'Stop being so selfish. Help me! I'll take whatever you have-'

'You better leave.' I point to the dented and banged up Red Corsa that I assume belongs to him. 'Before I show you what happens to a man that hits his own daughter.'

He staggers towards me.

'Who the hell do you think you are?' he says through gritted teeth. 'I'll do what I please to my own daughter.' He grabs Amara's hand and pulls her towards him. Her other hand grips mine in an attempt to stay with me.

That's it. No more. I take off the cuff easily, just like Gabriel showed me, and raise my free hand. Amara's dad flies backwards through the air and slams into his piece of shit red car. I have such a tight hold on Amara, she stays with me and watches with a shocked gasp. I stand in front of her and stare down at him.

'Want to keep pushing me? HUH?' I shout. 'You're not touching her again. So go. Or you'll be sorry.'

He stumbles to his feet breathing hard and heavy.

'You're...you're a witch?'

'You got that right. Now get the fuck out of here.'

Amara tries to pull me back as I start to head towards him. I've faced much scarier men than this. He stumbles back, eyes wide and searching for someone or something to help him.

'I don't have any money, Dad.' Amara's almost crying as she stands between us. She's so afraid. So I stop trying to get past her and step back, hoping to ease her worry.

'Dad, please, you have no idea who you're talking to.'

'Amara, you're coming with me. Let go of her,' he says, reaching out his hand. 'A woman witch? I follow Grayson. Not you. I'll never follow a bloody woman.' He looks at Amara's hand which is still gripping mine. 'She's my daughter. Let go of her. I'll take her if I want.'

'Try,' I reply. 'I could do with a laugh.'

He lunges forward and grabs her hand, making her scream and cower behind me.

'HEY!'

Our yelling seems to have attracted the attention of Gabriel who charges through the front door.

'Oh no, no, no,' Amara's approaching hysteria at his arrival. She turns to her dad. 'Please. Just go before you get yourself killed!'

'What the hell's going on out here?' Gabriel demands, stopping by my side. He sees my cuff in my hand and looks at Amara's dad. 'What's going on, Patrick?'

Patrick smooths down his hair and straightens his shirt before addressing Gabriel.

'My daughter and I were having a perfectly civilised conversation when this whore decided-'

'What did you call her?' Gabriel interrupts. He points at me. 'Did you just call her a whore?'

Amara's hand is trembling in mine.

'Gabriel,' I take his arm as he descends on Amara's dad. 'It's alright. I've got this.' He takes a step back as I turn and face down Patrick. 'I suggest you leave.' I point to Patrick's car. 'Before I do something you'll regret.'

'I JUST NEED A TENNER!'

'I know you're Amara's dad. So, for her sake, I'm gonna ask one more time for you to turn and leave before I show you exactly what I do to men that hit women. But first...' I add as he takes a small step back. 'You're gonna apologise for hitting your daughter.'

'He what?' Gabriel says. 'You hit your own daughter?'

Patrick looks like a deer caught in headlights. His eyes moving from me to Gabriel in utter panic.

'I don't know why you keep looking at him.' I shrug, positioning myself in Patrick's eye line. 'It's Amara you need to be looking at. And I think the words you're looking for are...I'm sorry Amara. I should never have hit you. And I will never hit you again. Because I know that if I do, Lilly will personally shove my head up my ass.' He blinks at me. 'I mean that literally. I will shove your head up your ass. I have the power to do that.'

'I'm...I'm sorry,' he says quietly.

'To her, you idiot. Not me. And the whole thing, please.'

He looks past me to Amara who looks dumbstruck. Gabriel, on the other hand, is stifling his laughs.

'Amara. I'm sorry I hit you. I won't do it again,' he says begrudgingly.

'And the rest,' I encourage.

'I won't...I won't do it again, because I know...'

'Say it...'

'I know that Lilly will personally shove my head up my ass.'

Gabriel snorts, and I find myself grinning at Patrick's beacon face.

'Off you go then.' I nod to his car, and he turns quickly, scuttling away as fast as he can. He jumps in his car and speeds off down the gravel road to the gate. He really shouldn't be driving in that state, but I'm just glad to see the back of him.

Gabriel makes his way over and replaces my cuff on my wrist.

'That, was fucking brilliant,' he says with an enormous grin. 'You're full of surprises.'

'Oh please. Compared to Harry and Toby he's a kitten.'

'I'm so sorry, Lilly,' Amara sobs. She's saying sorry to me? Why the hell is she saying sorry to me? 'He was drunk. He didn't mean what he said to you.'

'Hey, you don't need to apologise to me.'

She looks at Gabriel. 'I'm sorry, sir. Please-'

'Don't call me that,' Gabriel insists. 'I've told you a hundred times. You're a friend, Amara. Not an employee.' He wraps his arm around her as she cries and shakes. 'Shall I fetch Collins?' he asks sweetly. She shakes her head, her face firmly buried in his chest.

'He'll want to kill him. Please don't tell him.'

Amara's eyes are red and streaming with tears as she turns to me. 'He didn't mean what he said to you. Please, don't tell anyone. Grayson won't be happy if he knows he insulted you.'

'I won't.' I rub Amara's back to help comfort her. I saw what he did to John. I'm not that stupid. 'I don't care what he said to me. I care that he hurt you!'

She turns and hugs me.

'Thank you,' she cries. She lets me go and clasps her hand over her mouth. 'I shouldn't have touched you. Oh no! I'm so sorry! Grayson said not to touch you.'

'It's okay,' I laugh. 'You didn't grab my ass. I think you're safe.' Her touch was fine. Not as pain free as Gabriel's, but very bearable. Odd.

'What's going on?' Grayson appears from the front door in the worst case of bad timing. 'Lilly? What are you doing out here? Are you okay?' He charges over, pushing Gabriel out of his way to take my arm. He glances around the driveway nervously. 'You shouldn't be out here.'

'It's my fault,' Amara tells him. 'My dad and I were arguing. She just came out to make sure I was okay.'

'Did he upset you?' Grayson asks. I look to Amara waiting to see what she says, but Grayson tugs my arm. He's talking to me? 'I said, did he upset you?'

'What? No!' I say as if that's ridiculous. 'Amara told him to leave, and I encouraged him to do so. That's all.'

He looks at my cuff. 'Did you use magic?'

I nod. 'Completely in control though. I didn't hurt him.'

'Amara!' Grayson barks aggressively making the poor girl jump and cower away. I watch her fingers grip onto Gabriel's coat tightly. Gabriel rests a reassuring hand on her back. 'My house is not a place for you and your alcoholic father to work through your family issues. If it happens again, I will be forced to intervene. And I'm afraid that your father will not enjoy the outcome of my intervention. Am I clear? I won't have Lilly dragged into your mess. She has been through enough.'

'Yes, sir. I'm so sorry, sir,' she says in barely a whisper, looking at the floor.

Grayson turns to Billy. 'Make sure Patrick doesn't say a word about what he saw here today. Do you hear me? No one can know that there's another witch here.'

'To be fair, sir, he probably won't even remember coming to the house. But I'll take care of it anyhow.' He pulls out a phone and walks away to make a call.

'Can you come back inside?' Grayson asks, pulling on my arm. 'I feel much better with you in the house.' I nod and follow him back inside. Anything to put an end to this weird tension.

We walk through the house to the kitchen where Grayson finally lets go of my arm.

'I need to talk to the Nomads.' He gestures to the four men still out by the pool talking to Collins. 'You okay in here?'

'Fine' I reply. He leaves through the door and is followed by Gabriel, leaving Amara and me alone.

We look at each other with nervous smiles and nervous glances. This is ridiculous. I've spent my life surrounded by people who didn't give a damn if my feelings got hurt. Or if I got hurt. Now everyone is tiptoeing around me terrified to set me off or upset Grayson. I don't want to live like this. I want everyone to be as comfortable around me as Gabriel is. I think that's one of the reasons I like him so much.

I hold out my hand to her.

'Hi, Amara. I'm Lilly. It's nice to meet you.'

She looks at my hand confused.

'What are you doing?'

'Look. You stood up for me yesterday with the whole John thing. I am really sorry you had to see all the mess that followed. I'm wearing a binding spell now, so I won't lose control again. So if you want, I would like to see if maybe, we could be friends.'

'*You* want to be friends...with *me?*'

'Yeah,' I laugh at her surprise. 'What do you say?'

She takes my hand and gives it a shake. Although it feels uncomfortable, it really doesn't bother me.

With a stolen bottle of whiskey tucked under Amara's jacket, we walk past the others and head to the small lake I found on my first day here with the boat tethered teasingly to the shore at the end of the garden. Crossing our legs, we sit and open up the whiskey.

'I never said thank you. For getting me all those clothes. You were so kind, and I was so rude. I was just...' What can I say? I was afraid, jealous, nervous... 'Anyway. Thank you for helping me. It means a lot.' I give her a smile which she returns tenfold.

'You're very welcome. I would have got you some more normal stuff. But Grayson was very specific on what he thought you would like.'

'Well, I accidently set them all on fire so I'm mostly wearing Gabriel's stuff at the moment,' I laugh and gesture to the enormous hoody. 'So, what was all that about with your dad?'

'My dad's such a twat,' she groans. 'I'm so sorry you had to see that. He just turns up sometimes. You shouldn't have got involved. I've put you in a difficult position.' She buries her face in her hands and groans.

I promptly pull them away.

'There's no difficult position. Not for me. A man shouldn't hit a woman, and that's the end of it. A father especially.' I hand her the whiskey and watch her reaction as she takes a sip. Anyone would think she was drinking acid.

'Collins mentioned that you had some trouble with your uncle,' she says, handing me back the whiskey. I like the taste unlike her.

'Him and his mad wife, yeah. Just a bit of trouble.' I take a couple of sips and hand it back.

'Collins also said that they found you locked up.' She sounds a little uncertain if she should admit she knows that.

'Did he tell you anything else?' I ask.

She shakes her head. I don't know if she's lying or not.

'I'll tell you something though,' she says with a big exhale. 'If you think my dad is a kitten compared to your uncle and Toby, they must have been something else.'

'Oh yeah. They were definitely something else. So, you and Collins?' I say happily in an attempt to change the subject. 'Something going on there?'

Her cheeks flush. 'Yeah. We're sort of...dating. He's great don't you think?'

I reach out for the bottle and have another sip. I've not seen a massive amount of greatness. If I'm honest.

'I just wish Dad didn't keep showing up. There's nothing worse than when your drunk dad keeps trying to get you to steal money and booze from the guy you're dating. Bloody alcoholic. He wants me at home looking after him all day so he can do nothing but drink. One day he'll say the wrong thing in front of Grayson, and end up with his throat cut. I'm just glad Gabriel's more understanding.'

'Well, Grayson won't hear anything from me,' I tell her with certainty. 'Can I ask you something?'

'I'm an open book.'

'Do you know about this spell they're trying to reverse?' I ask before taking a sip and offering it back to her.

'Kind of,' she says taking it. 'As much as anyone else I suppose.'

'Would you tell me?'

I'm keen to hear if it's the same as what Grayson's told me.

'A while ago, the Arcane Witch, Rebecca Hooper, put up the Arcane Veil. It's like a wall stopping magic reaching us so we can't tap into it anymore. The spell will destroy the wall, and all the Descendants will get their powers,' she explains it all as if it's a simple enough thing to do and takes another comical sip.

'And then what?'

'Then we can live as what we were intended to be. We have a right to be ourselves. To be free. Living in hiding and with the risk of being scooped up by Hunters every day isn't a good way to live. Grayson, Gabriel, Collins and Hendrix have dedicated their lives to keeping all their Nomads safe. We would all be dead without them. But that will change now you're here. I can't believe I'm having a drink with *the* Arcane Witch!' Giggling, she has another sip and hands the bottle back to me. I don't have the heart to tell her I haven't actually decided if I am going to help yet.

'And you're a normal age? Not a couple of centuries old like them?' she asks.

'I'm twenty-two. A standard twenty-two,' I tell her, not keen to divulge that I actually have no idea how old I am. 'You?'

'Twenty-one. A normal twenty-one.'

'What's it like dating a five hundred year old Witch?' I ask.

'Really good. He's fab. But, you and Grayson...' she eyes me coyly, too nervous to ask what she really wants to ask. So, I save her the trouble.

'Grayson and I are *not* in a relationship,' I say as clearly as possible. 'He's not my type.'

'What is your type?'

'According to them, white-haired sociopaths.'

'You mean your ex, right? Toby?' She nods as I do. 'Yeah, he was a bit weird.'

'You knew him?' I'm suddenly very interested in what she has to say.

She goes very pale very quickly. 'No,' she says defensively. 'I mean, I met him a few times, but I'm just going on what Collins has said.'

'You and he weren't...' I look at her hair. No, her hair's too dark to be the girl Toby would use as a weapon. She scoffs at the mere suggestion that they were a couple anyhow.

'No!' she says adamantly. 'Toby and me? Hell no. I've only ever been with Collins.'

I drink some more and hand it back to her.

'What about Gabriel?' I ask. 'He and Ava seem close.' I'm fishing. I know I am, but she doesn't seem to think anything of it.

'Who knows with Gabriel? He's a lovely guy but definitely not dating material. Can have a nasty temper and not a one-woman man at all.' She takes a sip and looks out to the water. 'How was he with you after you impaled him?'

'He doesn't seem too bothered, if I'm honest. I was more worried about Grayson's reaction. How I behaved and almost killing his brother... not a great start.'

'Gabriel will be completely healed in a day or so. It would take more than that to kill any of them,' she says, brushing it off with a shrug.

Amara is so easy to talk to. We stay out here for hours talking about everything from the weather to clothes, to hobbies. When we get onto the topic of books, we're lost in a world of fiction as we discuss our favourite adventures in detail. She's a big reader like me and enjoyed the *"Grimm Fairy Tales"* too. By the time the sun's gone down, we've finished off the whole bottle of whiskey. We lie on the lawn and watch the stars come out, letting the buzz of the alcohol keep us warm.

'Tell me another one?' she asks again, looking up at the sky. I made the mistake of pointing out Orion and have since been listing the constellations we can see.

'Well that one there,' I point up to the series of stars above us. 'Is Cassiopeia. In Greek mythology, she was a queen that got banished to the sky for all to gawk at.'

'Why? What did she do?'

'She was vain and boasted her beauty was greater than the sea nymphs.'

'Wow. Harsh. Show me another one.'

After a while and countless stories about the origins of the different stars, Collins and Gabriel appear to usher us back inside. As we stumble to the house with our arms linked and the boys following us in, they scold us about excessive drinking.

But we're too drunk to care.

My head hits the pillow and for the first time, I sink comfortably into the bed Gabriel's slumped me into.

'Look at you all drunk,' he laughs. 'You're so cute when you giggle. Did you have fun today?'

'Hmmm,' I reply snuggling down.

'It was good of you to help Amara,' he says, tucking me in. 'I think you've a friend for life there. She could definitely use a friend.'

'I like her,' I mumble. 'She's sweet.'

'Yeah, she is. Do you want a glass of water?' I shake my head and feel the pull of sleep.'Alright then. I'll leave you.' He gently brushes the hair from my drunken face. 'Night, Beautiful.'

'No one's ever called me beautiful before.'

'Well then,' he leans in and whispers in my ear. 'I promise I will never stop telling you just how beautiful you are.'

'You're flirting with me,' I smile.

'Do you mind?'

'Nope.'

'Good. Sleep well, Beautiful.'

As I lie in the giant, musty bed, I sweat.
The room's so hot I can barely breathe
but I keep the blanket pulled up high around my neck.
I don't even blink as I watch the door with nothing but the
moonlight to show me that it's still closed.
When the deadbolt slides across the door at the base of the stairs,
I pull the blanket up higher.
The stairs creak underfoot and then I hear the worst sound of
all.
The deadbolt on my door followed by the creek of its hinges.
'Lills?' he whispers. 'Are you awake?'

'LILLY!'

My eyes spring open as I fight against someone who's trying to pin me down.

I can't breathe for the screaming. The room's dark and someone has me. Their hands are on me, and I can't get them off. I try to reach for my cuff but whoever it is clamping me down onto the bed won't release my hands. I kick and scream.

Pleading for freedom. Panic and terror fill me completely. The light flicks on, and I see it's Grayson holding me down. Gabriel grabs Grayson at the base of his neck and hurls him off me so hard, he crashes with a loud, raging yell into the wall. I fall off the bed to the floor in a heap, panting and shaking, confused as to what's going on.

'WHAT THE HELL ARE YOU DOING?' Gabriel yells at Grayson. Amara and Collins run into view. I reach out for Amara, whimpering her name, desperate for her protection from all these men. She charges past them all dressed in an oversized t-shirt with her legs bare. She falls to her knees and wraps her arms around me. I fall into her and refuse to let go.

'I ASKED YOU A QUESTION!' Gabriel hollers. 'WHY WERE YOU ON TOP OF HER?'

'What are you implying?' Grayson says back a lot calmer than I expected. 'I heard her screaming bloody murder and walked into find her thrashing violently. I was trying to wake her up before she hurt herself.'

'He can't come here!' I cry. 'Tell them, Amara. Tell them they can't bring him back here.'

'Who, Honey?' Amara asks, rubbing my back. 'Toby?'

I fall forwards and cry, clinging to her desperately. 'He can't. Please, don't let him touch me again. Amara, don't let him.' I'm hyperventilating. Shaking. Sobbing.

Terrified.

No matter what she says, it doesn't calm me. Her words of comfort are just words.

'Lilly? Lilly, Look at me,' Gabriel's voice is gentle. He almost sings his words, but it does nothing to ease my suffering. 'Lilly, lift your head and look at me.' Gently he lifts my chin with his finger. He's kneeling beside Amara, his blue eyes full of worry. 'You're safe. I promise. No one will hurt you.'

I look around the room. Collins is watching me from the door. Grayson is standing at the foot of my bed and Gabriel's kneeling in front of me looking calm but concerned.

I'm so confused. My dreams are so real I sometimes forget where I am and who I'm with. The world of the past and the present meld together and sometimes I can't tell them apart.

'Am I safe?' I ask him through my tears.

'You are,' Gabriel tells me with a confident smile. 'You're at The Orchard. You're not at your uncle's house. Harry can't hurt you anymore, and Toby will never get close enough to touch you. I swear it.'

I look at Amara for reassurance. She smiles, nodding in agreement. My body is covered in sweat as I shake uncontrollably.

But it's not Harry or Toby that I was dreaming about. I was dreaming of a far greater monster.

They're all watching me. I must look insane.

'I was having a nightmare.' I can't stand their pity-filled expressions, and the fear from my nightmare is still strong. I need to get that person's face out of my memory. 'Can you go? All of you, I want you to go.'

'You shouldn't be on your own,' Gabriel says, resting his hands on mine to stop them from trembling. I can't help it. I flinch and pull away.

'I'll stay with her. If she wants me to.' Amara looks at me. 'Would you like that?'

I cling to her and nod.

Gabriel takes the hand I cowered away from and uses it to squeeze Amara's shoulder affectionately. 'Keep an eye on her for me.'

'Of course,' she says, still rubbing my back.

'Good night, girls. Don't do anything I wouldn't do,' Gabriel says with a wink as he gets to his feet.

'That doesn't leave much,' Amara says with an eye roll. He walks to the door and holds it open, staring at Grayson who turns and leaves, barging into his shoulder as he goes.

They leave, Collins lingers slightly in the doorway until Amara assures him she's okay.

Now alone, she helps me sit and seeing her genuinely concerned and caring face I burst into tears.

'What on earth were you dreaming about? You're absolutely terrified!'

She pulls me in close and lets me cry. We stay on the floor as she cradles me, rocking me back and forth as I sob.

I don't get any sleep. But Amara does, bless her. She's curled up in my bed snoring away as I sit on the window ledge watching the sunrise. I tried to sleep, but it was useless.

'Morning,' she says with a yawn and a stretch.

'Morning.' I get to my feet and stand in front of her feeling thoroughly embarrassed. 'I'm so sorry about last night.'

'Don't be daft,' she says tossing off the duvet. 'It was nice to sleep in a bed without a snoring man for a change.' I can't help but laugh. I bet Collins has never told her that it's her that snores like a wildebeest. Not him. 'You feeling better?'

'Yeah.' I play with the hem of Gabriel's long-sleeved top that I slept in. 'I have bad dreams. I suppose waking up the house screaming is better than setting the room on fire.'

'I used to have bad dreams too.'

'You did?'

'Yeah. It's okay, I get it. You don't need to explain what caused them unless you want to.' I shake my head. 'Come on,' she says happily, jumping out of bed and taking my hand in hers. 'I'm dying for a coffee.'

Walking into the kitchen, we're greeted by a tired Collins and weary-looking Gabriel. They look at us as we pull up a stool and take a seat with them.

'How the hell do you two look so good?' Gabriel asks. 'You drank a bottle of whiskey and had a disturbed night's sleep. How does that work? I feel like shit!'

'Why do you feel like shit?' I ask.

'Because I was up worrying about you all night.'

'Well, I'm touched by your concern. But honestly. I'm fine. It was just a bad dream.'

'You managed to get some sleep, then?' Collins asks me as he wraps his arm around Amara.

'I did,' I lie. 'Thanks to your girlfriend.'

Collins chokes and wipes the coffee from his chin looking nervously at Amara.

'What?' Gabriel hands me his coffee. It's half gone, but I take it. 'What did I say?'

'You said the G word,' Gabriel laughs, looking at Collins. His elbow gives me a small nudge. 'I don't think they've had that talk yet.'

'What talk?'

'The label talk,' he laughs harder.

'Are you two not...?' They both look awkward and put thoroughly on the spot. Amara glares and shakes her head mouthing, *'Drop it.'* So instead I take a sip of coffee and offer it back to Gabriel who takes it with a wink, enjoying the awkwardness.

'What's a Witch groupie?' I ask.

It's Gabriel's turn to choke on his coffee as Collins leans forwards looking smug.

'Yeah, Gabriel. What's a Witch Groupie?'

'It's nothing,' Gabriel says, still coughing and spluttering.

'Oh *please*,' Amara chimes in. 'That expression only exists because of you.'

He laughs nervously, wiping the table with his sleeve.

'Gabriel has a bit of a reputation with the ladies,' Collins tells me. 'God knows why. I think he's a bit of a prick if you ask me.' Collins has a happy-go-lucky smile on his face, and I know he means absolutely no offence. Gabriel takes none and just shrugs.

'I like women, and for some reason they like me. Being a Witch has nothing to do with it. If they want a piece of this,' he gestures to his body. 'Who am I to say no?' With a more serious look to the other two he asks, 'Can we drop it?'

'You're a bit of a slag then?' I tease, nudging his shoulder. But I totally get it. He's gorgeous and knows all the right things to say.

'Not of late. No. Can we drop it?' He looks at the mug in his hand, and I know everyone is feeling the sudden awkwardness.

'What's the date?' I ask to change the subject.

'The thirteenth,' Collins says glancing at Amara. Why are they so coy? They clearly love each other.

'Of what?' I ask.

They all stare at me like I've just dribbled on my shirt.

'December,' Amara tells me. 'How can you not know what month it is, Honey?' she asks with as much sensitivity as possible.

'There wasn't a calendar in my cellar,' I reply, silencing them all and shattering the easy-going mood completely. For fuck's sake! 'So, it's Christmas in a couple of weeks?' I add cheerfully, retaking Gabriel's coffee. I see Amara watch me and her brow furrow, but I ignore it. 'Are we getting a turkey?'

'We don't do Christmas,' Grayson says distinctly unimpressed as he walks in. He flashes Gabriel an annoyed look as he pours himself a coffee and joins us all at the table. I thought I made the atmosphere frosty... Grayson's just turned it to ice.

'How did you sleep?' Grayson asks, looking at me over the rim of his mug.

'Fine. Thank you' I reply coolly, hoping not to make last night a big deal.

'Good. I thought that we could spend some time talking about those missing six weeks of yours later today. Gabriel's had an idea.' He's not happy.

'Yeah?' I look at Gabriel, knowing full well that whatever this idea is, won't go down well. He isn't happy about Grayson bringing this subject up. 'Tell me.'

'Basically, I can try and use my magic to help you explore your own mind. The memories are in your head somewhere. We just need to try and find them.'

'You can do that? Would...would you see what I see? Would you see all my memories?'

'I would see whatever memories you see. It would be like looking through a photo album, but instead of pictures, it would be memories. We would go into your memories together. I have to be invited these days. There was a time I could just look and see whatever I wanted, but now I have to be welcome.'

'Why?'

'I'm five hundred years old,' he says simply. 'Magic ages even if we don't.'

'What do you say?' Grayson asks. 'Fancy giving it a go?'

There are memories in my head I would rather die than share with anyone else. If Gabriel saw half the things that go on in my head, well. I barely like myself because of my past. And he'd have to tell Grayson, and Grayson would tell Collins, and then they would all know the darkest corners of my mind. I feel my face falling. Dread, swelling in my chest.

'I don't think I could deal with someone in my head like that,' I admit. 'Some things in my past are...'

'Secret?' Grayson says with his eyebrows raised. 'I think we can deal-'

'Private,' I correct him. 'Personal.'

'I told you she wouldn't be up for it,' Gabriel mutters. And I heard Grayson tell him I wouldn't have a choice. I sense a row. Amara and Collins do too, as their eyes flick back and forth between the two brothers anxiously.

When Grayson slams down his coffee mug and opens his mouth ready to start the argument I know we won't win, I say quickly, 'Can I think about it?' His mouth closes. 'Give me a day or two to think it over? Please?'

He nods and smiles that smile. The one I know isn't genuine. But I'll take a temporary win.

'You know what?' Gabriel chirps, carrying on the trend of subject changing. 'We *should* do Christmas this year. It's the first one Lilly will have with us. We should mark the occasion.'

I roll with it. 'It would actually be my first Christmas ever.'

The room goes silent and all eyes land on me.

Why? Why did I have to share that? The looks they give me vary from disbelief to outright pity and I remind myself once more not to talk about my troubled past. If that slight bit of information gets this reaction there's no way digging around in my head is a good idea.

'Well, now we have to make it special. What do you say, Grayson?' Gabriel continues.

'Alright,' Grayson replies. 'But I'm not cooking anything.'

'You never cook anything anyway,' Gabriel adds, giving me a wink.

'I'll do it,' I offer. An idea which they both laugh at. 'What?'

'You burn toast,' Gabriel says, shaking his head as if my suggestion is the most ridiculous thing he's ever heard.

'That was one time,' I murmur as they continue to laugh at me. 'Well Gabriel, maybe you could help me? Show me how it's done?' That shuts him up.

'That's a great idea,' Collins chuckles seeing the look on Gabriel's face.

'That's settled,' I say happily. 'Me, you and the turkey.'

'Fine,' Gabriel sighs.

'Amara, you'll come, won't you?' I add. She glances at Grayson who gives the nod.

'Yay!' she says happily. 'I'll help cook if you like.'

'Oh no!' I insist, nudging Gabriel. 'We've got it, haven't we, chef?'

'I suppose,' he says with a twitch of a reluctant smile.

'We should get a tree too!' I add, getting more and more excited at the idea of celebrating Christmas for the first time. 'I've never decorated a Christmas tree before. Harry hated Christmas. Except for the food. That, he loved.' Shit! What's wrong with me? I sound so depressing.

'Sure!' Gabriel says, bypassing my pathetic admission. 'I'll get one later today for you to decorate. There's a tree lot a few miles down the road. They let you chop the tree down.'

'Oh, that sounds fun! Can I come with you?'

'No!' Grayson says firmly, getting to his feet and not giving Gabriel the slightest chance to answer for himself.

'Excuse me?' I say stunned. 'No?'

'I don't think it wise, Lilly. It's not safe.' He washes out his cup and doesn't even look at me as he speaks.

'Is that an order?' I ask. 'Are you ordering me to stay home?'

He turns and gives a deep sigh. 'I'm afraid so. Yes. It really is not safe for you out there.' He turns and heads to the door like the matter is no longer up for discussion.

'I didn't realise I needed permission to go out?' I call after him. 'Forgive me Grayson, but I was under the impression I was a guest, not a prisoner.'

He slows and stops. Everyone stills and watches us in silence. He turns.

'You are not a prisoner, Lilly. You are, however... a risk.'

'I'm bound!' Annoyed, I wave my wrist in his direction.

'It's not safe,' he says simply. 'The answer is no.'

'But-'

'I SAID NO!' he roars, making everyone flinch and sending Gabriel to his feet to stand beside me. 'You keep making me repeat myself. You keep talking back when I have given you my decision. My answer is no.'

'Then *my* answer is no,' I snap back before I think.

'No?' he asks, the anger piercing his calm voice. Collins takes Amara with him outside into the garden. Gabriel, however, remains firmly by my side. 'Who do you think you are talking to?'

'I could ask you the same question. You want Gabriel to rummage around in my head. Look through memories you know are deeply personal, all so I can help you find a man I have no interest in finding. That's what you are asking of me. All I am asking for is to go out for one hour to pick a Christmas tree and bring it back with my friends. I've never experienced a happy Christmas, Grayson. And I'm sorry, but I won't go back to being forced to stay inside another house for the rest of my life. I'm wearing the cuff like you want. I am not a risk to anyone. Not with the binding spell and you saying that to me makes you no better than Harry'

'I'm not your uncle,' he says sharply. 'I would never lay a hand on you or let you go hungry. Never!'

'He said I couldn't leave the house because I was a danger to others. He made me wear a binding spell because I was a danger to him. Please, Grayson.... tell me how you're treating me any differently right now?' I wait as he stands there. I know I'm drawing a massively unfair comparison. But I'm not asking for the world. Just an hour.

'She's right,' Gabriel adds. 'She isn't a prisoner. If she wants to go out, we can't stop her. At least this way I'll be with her. I'm sure Amara and Collins would come too?'

'I'll wear a hat,' I offer. 'Hide my hair. In case someone recognises me as a Hooper. If that's what you're worried about.'

I know he's worried about that threat too. Even if he won't say. 'You could always come with us?'

'I have better things to do,' he says rather petulantly.

'I won't use my magic, and I'll be good. I promise. Please, Grayson. An hour, that's all.'

'If I say yes. Will you say yes to Gabriel looking into your memories?' He holds that steely resolve, and before I know it, I'm nodding.

'Fine then.' He turns to Gabriel. 'She stays by your side at all times. You hear me? She doesn't leave your sight. If a single hair on her head comes to harm, you will regret it. You are responsible for her safety. If she comes back as anything less than what she is now, you will pay for it. Am I being clear enough for you, Gabriel?'

'Crystal clear, brother,' Gabriel says chirpily. Like there's no tension between them at all as he carries on drinking his coffee.

Grayson leaves. I turn to Gabriel with a triumphant grin. He wears one too.

'You are seriously fearless.' He admires. 'We'll wait for the sun to go down and head out.'

'You want to wait for it to get dark?' I ask.

'Oh yeah. Trust me. You'll want to see this place in the dark for sure.'

Chapter 11

Collins holds the door open for me as I climb out of the car. I see Gabriel do the same for Amara, but she's already excitedly scooting across the seat behind me with a massive grin on her face.

'Wow!' she gasps, her eyes sparkling with excitement as she looks all around us. 'Isn't this amazing?' I see the look of childlike amazement in her eyes that must also be in mine.

We're standing in the middle of an enormous field filled with evergreen trees still growing out of the ground. Some are sprayed to look snowy. Some are decorated with lights, tinsel or stars which twinkle. But most are just a brilliant green. It's a whole world away from my uncle's cellar. Now I know why Gabriel wanted to bring me in the dark.

As the others stand beside me looking at all the decorations and soaking up the atmosphere, I feel like the luckiest person alive! How have I gone from a cellar and chains ...to this?

'Gabriel?' A man wearing a big bobble hat and a red name badge labelling him as Frank calls over. Gabriel heads over to meet him and shakes his hand. They talk for a few minutes after which Gabriel gives him a handful of notes before coming back to us.

'We have the place to ourselves. Most expensive Christmas tree ever, but better safe than sorry.' He wraps his leather jacket further around his body and shakes away the bitter coldness in the air. I tuck my hair further under the black woolly capped hat I borrowed from Amara and double-check the cuff is still firmly in place.

'You're fine,' Gabriel says quietly into my ear. 'Your hair's covered. No one knows you even exist. And the cuff is on. You're fine!'

'Yeah, well I'm not taking any risks. I'm even thinking about colouring my hair. Black maybe, or brunette?'

'Don't you dare,' he says with that half-smile. 'I love your red hair.' He busies himself with the black scarf around my neck, making sure it's wrapped tightly. 'I like seeing you in my clothes. Never had a girl in my stuff before.'

'I'm honoured,' I laugh.

The man in the bobble hat disappears inside a small hut and leaves us to it.

Cheery festive music floats through the air. It's lovely. Peaceful. Happy.

I can't stop smiling.

'It's all so beautiful,' I whisper.

'You think?' Gabriel asks.

'It's perfect. Thank you so much for bringing me here.'

'You are very welcome.'

Collins wraps Amara in his arms and kisses her neck. I knew I saw kindness in his eyes back at Harry's. It's for her. He loves her. And she loves him. It's unbelievably clear in how he looks at her. Like she's the best thing he's seen in his entire life.

'I've never understood the whole tree thing,' Amara says, running her fingers through the needles of the tree nearest to her. 'I mean, who decided to chop down a tree, drag it inside and shove a fairy on the top in the first place? It's like

Easter. Chocolate eggs and rabbits? What the hell's that about? Christianity is weird.'

I stroke the needles too.

'I thought evergreen trees would feel different. Like sharper or something. But they're soft.' I turn to Amara. 'I can tell you if you like? About where the tree tradition comes from?' When she nods, I explain. 'It started as a pagan ritual. Not Christian. Because the evergreen trees stay green through winter, people would cut off boughs and put them in their homes or by their door as a way to entice the sun God back. Then, around the sixteenth century, German Christians took this ritual and amended it to entire trees. Then they started decorating them with what they had to hand. Mainly edible things like gingerbread and apples, which turned into glass baubles and other decorations like candles, coloured paper, foil... stuff like that. Originally, they put a baby Jesus on the top, until it changed over time to an angel. Then a fairy or a star. The tree came to Britain in the 1830's when King Albert married Queen Victoria. He was German you see, so they put a tree up in Windsor Castle in 1841 which started it all off for the British. But the very, very first account of an evergreen cutting being used inside the home was to keep away witches.' I turn to Gabriel. 'Bet a lot of fathers draped it around their daughters' bedrooms whenever you rolled through the village,' I laugh, but he doesn't find my joke funny. 'Maybe I should get one for when Grayson gets annoyed at me. Fashion it into a necklace or something. What?' I ask nervously as he continues staring. 'It was only a joke.'

But they're all staring at me like that.

'What?'

'How the hell do you know all that?' Gabriel asks. 'I didn't even know that, and I'm five hundred years older than you!'

'Yeah,' Amara adds. 'And last night you could name all the constellations as well as tell me the stories behind them. How are you so clever?'

'Mr Simmons taught me. I'm not an idiot you know,' I say indignantly, letting go of the tree and shuffling my feet.

'No. We didn't mean that' Gabriel says, trying to sound casual. 'I just... I didn't really think you were... smart.'

'Wow!' I cross my arms and glare at him with a mix of anger and surprise at how he sees me. 'Way to call me an idiot.'

'That came out wrong. I'm not calling you an idiot,' he insists, embarrassed at the hole he seems to be digging. 'I just thought-'

'Thought what? You know I can read and write. You know I can speak fluent French, and you saw me recognise straight away that the picture you have hanging in the hall is an original Van Gogh that's been missing for years. What about those facts would lead you to believe I wasn't smart?'

'Well, to be fair, you were in a cellar when we found you. And the way you just touched the tree? You've never even seen a real evergreen tree, have you?' He looks to the others for support, but they stare at him similar to me. Like he's an insensitive twat. 'This is all coming out really, really wrong.'

'I can tell you every element in the periodic table, but I've never stepped foot in a chemistry lab. I can name all fifty states in America, but being here is the furthest from home I've ever been. I can name every piece of artwork that Van Gogh, Monet...even Dali, painted in their lifetime, but I've never stepped foot in an art gallery.'

'I get it. I'm sorry-'

'I can even tell you that seventy percent of our planet is covered in water. That for every litre of seawater, there are thirty-five grams of salt. But I've never been to the ocean. I know a lot about the world. But I learnt it from books. Not experience.'

'I'm really sorry,' he says with a sullen face and pity-filled eyes. 'I don't think you're an idiot.'

'Well, I think you are, Gabriel.' I look at them all. 'I'm not looking for sympathy. My life is what is it. Or was, because things are different for me now and I don't want you tiptoeing around me. I won't report anything you say or do to Grayson. I won't flip out or attack you. I'm not going to Break. And I don't want you to be anyone but yourselves around me. If we get on, we get on. If we don't, we don't. But I would like the chance to show you there's more to me than just the girl from the cellar. Okay?'

'Of course, Honey' Amara says, taking my hand in hers.

'Sure thing,' Collins agrees. I turn to Gabriel.

'Hey,' he says with a shrug. 'I only learnt that there was a light in the oven last week. I'm not smart. And I think we've established my brain isn't connected to my mouth. I'm a prat and an idiot.'

'And a slag,' I add.

His mouth curls up into a smile as I ease into a grin myself.

Amara throws her arm around my shoulders and beams at me. 'Shall we go check out some trees?'

'Yes,' I reply happily. 'That would be awesome.'

As we walk off together, I look back to see Collins and Gabriel stand side by side watching us go.

'I really like her,' Collins says with an approving nod. 'She's going to give you and Grayson a run for your money.'

'Yeah,' Gabriel agrees. 'She's really something else.'

There are small trees. Big trees. Real trees. Fake trees. It's a maze of Christmas, and I love it all. Amara pulls off a string of red tinsel and wraps it around my neck before picking up a pink one and wrapping it around hers.

'Who needs a tree?' she laughs. 'We'll just decorate ourselves. Oh, look!' She charges off leaving me to run after her.

'Don't go too far, girls!' Gabriel calls as he stands with Collins smoking.

'We won't,' I call back.

She weaves between the trees and stops finally at a tree decorated in nothing but pink. Pink baubles. Pink lights. Pink snowflakes. It's hideous, but her eyes are lit up.

'You like pink, huh?'

'It's my favourite colour. There's not much pink back home with Dad.'

She links her arm in mine and rests her head on my shoulder as she admires it. I can't help but ask.

'Amara? What was that with you and Collins this morning?' She lifts her head to look at me 'Are you two not a couple then?'

'We are. I think,' as if considering it herself. 'We sleep together. Spend time together and I really, really like him.'

'Is he doing any of those things with anyone else?' I ask.

'No!' she replies, outraged at the mere suggestion. 'I'd cut his bits off if he were!'

'So, you are a couple then?'

'Yeah, I suppose, but we've not said it officially. What about you and Grayson?'

'I told you. We're not a couple.'

She grins slyly. 'He wants you though. He's made sure everyone knows you're off-limits, and he's super protective over you.'

Images of John screaming has my stomach in knots. I really don't need or want that kind of protectiveness. Not again.

We carry on wandering through the trees, arm in arm, admiring all the different decorations.

'So, are you really going to let Gabriel into your memories?' I'm very much enjoying how she is with me. It's straightforward and honest. Effortless.

'I said I would, so...' We stop at a tree covered in black decorations. It's not half as depressing as I would have expected, especially when it's mixed with the odd silver star. 'Gabriel doesn't treat me like I'm about to explode or Break. I like that.

When he sees some of the things that go on in my head, that will definitely change.'

'Is that why you wear long sleeves?' she asks. Again, there's no hindrance to her question. 'So people won't see your scars and feel sorry for you?'

'How do you know about those?'

'Collins. Plus, you're always pulling down your sleeves even though you're covered. It's not hard to put two and two together.'

'Do you and Collins talk about me a lot?' I ask with a laugh. I'm not offended in the slightest. She's impossible to be insulted by.

'Well, you're new and pretty big news, so we do a bit,' she shrugs. 'Why do they want to dig about in that head of yours anyway?'

'Truth is there's a six-week gap in my memory. We're pretty sure that this Break happened at that time and that Toby was involved. He has the journal. They think that figuring out what happened will not only help us find him but help me get this Break under control, so I don't go all...err...' How can I explain it to her?

'White-haired, lilac-eyed, nut job?' Yep, she definitely knew Toby. 'But if it will help with all those things isn't it worth doing?'

We turn and face each other, our tinsel still wrapped around our necks and our noses are getting redder in the cold. I admit to her what I'm most concerned about.

'I don't want Gabriel to see my past. He won't treat me the same. I know it sounds pathetic, but...' I look at my feet. She rubs my arm telling me I can say anything and it won't go any further. 'Well, I like how he looks at me,' I admit. 'I know what everyone says. That he looks at all the girls like that, but no one that nice has ever looked at me like he does. Just Toby and unfortunately Grayson. If he sees my past, there's no way he'll treat me the same.'

'I get it. I was the same when I met Collins. You don't want to be seen as this delicate little flower that can be easily squished.

You don't want to be treated differently or be defined by your past. You don't want to be the girl from the cellar the same as I don't want to be the drunk's daughter.' She nods knowingly. It's a relief that she gets it. That she understands. 'I can't speak for Gabriel, but I don't see you as the girl from the cellar. I see you as the girl that kicked my dad's ass and then got me drunk for the first time ever. As the girl who stood up to Grayson, which I've never seen anyone do, by the way. And the girl that has been super nice to me. Not many people are nice to me. People at home think I'm weak. And annoying,' she adds sadly. Why the hell would anyone not be nice to her? She's so likeable!

'Well, I see you as...' I have a whole speech planned. That she's the girl that defended me against John. Stayed with me all night when I had my nightmare. How she's generous and kind. But something distracts me. I look around not understanding what it is that's drawn my attention.

'What is it, Honey?' she asks, looking around the same as me and taking a step closer.

'I sense magic.' I realise that's the odd feeling. Magic.

'But you have your cuff on. How can you sense magic?'

'I don't know but I can. I'm telling you. I can sense magic.'

'Well, that's just Gabriel and Collins, right?' She doesn't sound sure and steps even closer.

'No. It's not them. It feels...different.'

'How?'

I look at her. Her eyes are wide and anxious.

'When I sense Gabriel, Collins and Grayson, it's a presence. Like a warmth. Protective.'

'And how does this feel?' she asks nervously.

'Like it wants to hurt us. It feels really angry.' I take her hand in mine, scanning all around us for any sign of danger. 'It's not them, Amara. It's someone else.'

'But, there's only one other person with magic,' she says, squeezing my hand. I know. And that's what's got me so afraid.

'Toby,' I whisper his name as I look around us.

I try to sense where he is. The humming in the air as his magic gets closer is overpowering, making it impossible to tell. I'm drowning in it, and it feels violent. Is that what his magic feels like? If I felt like this every time I saw him, I doubt very much that I would have let him get half as close to me as he did. Every hair on my body's standing on end. Every nerve heightened.

'We need to get back to the boys,' she whispers in my ear. Giving my hand a slight tug, we quietly walk away from the black and silver tree and towards where we last saw them. As we walk, we get quicker. Almost running, we pass the enormous pink tree and both look back to make sure no one's following us. No one is. But looking back means we don't see what's ahead and we both slam into someone. We stumble back and look up at a man wearing a big smile.

'Easy, girls,' he laughs. 'Where's the fire?'

'Oh, we're so sorry,' Amara pants, clutching her chest and laughing nervously.

'No problem,' he says happily and glancing around. 'I thought the lot was closed? Should you be in here?'

Amara's giggling nervously as she explains we were just leaving. He's smiling kindly as she babbles on. But I'm watching him. His eyes drift from her to me. Those dark brown eyes look familiar. His dirty blonde hair is short but spikey on the top. A modern cut for a man that must be in his late forties. He's wearing a long black coat that reaches down to his knees with the collar turned up. Beneath the coat, he's wearing a light grey V-neck t-shirt. He looks so familiar it's driving me mad. I glance behind me. There's no one there. No sign of Toby, but I can still sense magic. Stronger than ever. As Amara keeps talking, he doesn't stop looking at me. I take a step back.

'Amara,' I say firmly as I take her with me. 'Amara, we need to go now.'

She stops her incessant gabbling and looks between the man and me. His smile, although still there, is anything but genuine.

'What is it?' she asks.

'We need to go. Now!' I repeat. Every step we take back, he takes one forwards. I'm afraid of him. But I'm not really sure why. The more he speaks, the more familiar he feels.

'You two here alone?' he asks. Amara's hand tightens on mine as she realises that we're in danger. He keeps coming. Slowly following us as we back up, reclaiming every bit of space we create with his familiar, cocky grin.

'I know you,' I say almost too afraid to form words as I try to remember his face. But I still can't place it. 'How do I know you?'

'It's good to see you again, Lilly.' He turns his head to the left and runs his finger down a long scar that goes from his cheekbone and disappears into his hairline. It takes a second, but I get there. I remember him.

'I haven't seen you since you were a child,' he says. 'Look at you. You're a woman!'

'Who is he?' Amara asks nervously.

He's a man I thought lived only in my nightmares. He hasn't aged a day! I remember him kicking down the door to the small cabin my mum and I lived in before we ran away to Harry's. He tried to kill us both, but my magic manifested and I managed to fend him off long enough to get away with Mum. It was me that gave him that scar.

'Lilly? Who is he?' I can hear the terror in her voice. And she should be terrified.

He takes a few significant steps forwards as I jump back, taking her with me.

'Run,' I tell her. 'FUCKING RUN!'

We turn and sprint in the opposite direction as he chases after us. But we don't get far. He grabs Amara by her long hair and yanks her back. Her hand slips out of mine and he slams his fist into her face hard, knocking her to the floor where she lays motionless.

I rush to her, but that only puts me in his reach. He grabs the back of my neck. I go to scream.

'Make a sound, and I'll kill your friend,' he says plainly, lifting his hand which shimmers with the same Energy magic Grayson has. But his is a deep green. His threat keeps me quiet. My feet stumble as he drags me away from her and away from the entrance. Away from the sound of Gabriel's voice casually calling out my name. I'm in shock. Completely petrified into obedience. Like I used to be all those years ago before Toby came into my life.

Come on, Red. Fight him off!

Toby's ever-present voice in my head commands. He's my strength and logic when I have none myself.

Fight him off! NOW!

With my brain suddenly able to function, and now that we're away from Amara so she can't be hurt, I rip off the cuff and send him through the air so quick I would have laughed at the surprise on his face if I wasn't so fucking scared. I take my chance and run as fast as I can back towards Amara.

Turning around a stupidly large tree, I collide with her and we both fall in a heap on the floor. Before we can get back to our feet, he's there. Lifting me by my arm and holding me in a vice-like grip as I try desperately to get free.

'Amara! RUN!' I yell. She does.

'You're coming with me,' he says with an annoyed laugh, as if there's no other option and me merely believing there is, is nothing but laughable. As I try to get his hand off me, he wraps his other hand around my throat. 'The question is, are you coming with me conscious? Or a bloody, broken mess?'

There's a thud. With an angry yell, he lets me go and grabs at his head. Amara's hit him with what looks like a wooden post and he falls to his knees onto the floor. We reach for each other, and hand in hand run past him towards the others.

'You came back for me?'

'Of course I did! Who the fuck is that?!' she demands, looking behind us as we flee. He's coming. I can feel it. 'Is he a Witch?'

'Yes, just keep running!'

Relief isn't a strong enough word to describe how I feel when I see Gabriel and Collins. They're exactly where we left them.

'COLLINS!' Amara screams as we sprint towards them. 'HELP!'

They turn and start running towards us.

'What's happened?' Gabriel asks as we plough into them.

'There's a man back there trying to get Lilly. He has magic!' she tells him.

'Toby?' Gabriel asks.

I shake my head. 'No. It's not Toby. It's someone else.' We all look at the lines of trees, but there's no one there. I can feel him. He's somewhere. Collins takes Amara in his arms and holds her tightly as Gabriel takes my hand and pulls me close.

'What does he look like, Beautiful?' Gabriel asks, scanning the trees around us.

'Light hair. He has a scar on his face.'

'The scar...is it here?' He runs his finger along the side of his face marking exactly where the line is on the man's cheek. I nod.

'It can't be,' Collins says. 'Theo?'

'Theo?' I say the name with dread. 'As in the man who wants to kill me?'

'We need to go,' Gabriel orders, wrapping his arm around my waist. 'Now!'

We turn and start running but my feet come out from under me and I fall, making me lose my grip on Gabriel. I feel it before it happens. The sensation of being grabbed by my ankle, but there's no one there. Nothing's touching me at all! Gabriel lunges for my hand, but I'm pulled screaming back across the dirt, through the trees and away from them on my belly. My fingernails dig into the soil to stop myself, but it does nothing. I try desperately to get a hold of something, but whatever has me is too strong. I'm pulled through the trees and out of sight from my friends as they all yell my name.

Theo's hand grabs my hair and pulls me to my feet.

'A bloody broken mess it is then.'

He slams his face into mine. My nose screams in agony as he lets me go. I fall into a confused daze onto the floor, the taste of blood invading my mouth. I hold my hand over my nose and blood streams through my fingers.

'GABRIEL!' I scream as I try to back away from him. 'GABRIEL, HELP ME!'

Falling to his knees and straddling me, Theo clamps his hand over my mouth.

He ducks down to hide from the others who are running through the trees calling my name and looking for me, but we're hidden. I kick out against him. My fingernails are drawing blood from his hand, but that doesn't do anything to get him off.

'I really don't want to hurt you, Lilly. But I will!'

Like hell! The man wants to kill me! I clamp my teeth down on his hand. He swears furiously before lifting my head and slamming it into the cold, hard ground.

'Stop fighting me,' he threatens, his face in mine. I roll over and try to get away, but he turns me easily and again, slams my head into the floor. Any control I had left over my limbs leaves me. My arms fall limp, and I start slipping into unconsciousness. The world fades in and out of focus as my eyes struggle to stay open. 'Go to sleep, Lilly.'

As I blink up at him, he raises my head again, ready to slam it once more into the ground.

But I see him. Theo doesn't.

Gabriel.

He grabs the back of Theo's neck so tight I hear the bones crunch.

'Get the fuck off her, Theo,' Gabriel orders, his jaw locked in fury. He pulls him off me, and I'm left to lie on the floor in a barely conscious state, looking up at them both.

Amara slides her hands under my arms and starts pulling me away. Collins stands between them and us with his fists clenched and although outnumbered four to one, Theo just laughs. He doesn't even try to fight Gabriel off.

'Oh please,' Theo mocks. 'Your efforts are beyond amusing. You don't think you can actually stop me, do you? You can't control me, Gabriel. I'm far too strong.'

Theo raises his hand in Collins's direction and sends him flying. With his other, he reaches behind him and grabs Gabriel's wrist. Gabriel yells against the pain as he unleashes his lightning, but Theo doesn't stop. All the while, Theo laughs. Gabriel can't maintain his grip and lets go, clasping his red and charred hand looking both furious and in a hell of a lot of pain.

'Just step aside, *boy*. You're not going to stop me from taking her.'

'I fucking am!' Gabriel replies, balling his injured hand into a fist and thrusting it into Theo's nose. His head lunges back and he falls on his arse, grabbing his bloody nose. Gabriel wastes no time and grabs Theo by the scruff of his collar, pulling back his fist again, but Theo sends his lightning at him. He doesn't stop until Gabriel's on his knees, doubled over in agony.

'Oh no you're not.' Theo sends it at him again. Gabriel's howls are filled with agony. I have to help him. I use my magic to send Theo sideways into one of the nearby trees. Gabriel's still on his knees as Collins runs over and gets him to his feet.

'We can't beat him, Gabriel. We have to go!'

Amara lifts me to my feet as I sway and stagger. She has a bruise forming on her face from where Theo hit her and she looks terrified, but that doesn't seem to be slowing her down.

'Come on, Honey. Up you get,' she says. The boys come running towards us, Collins keeping up an injured Gabriel. But behind them, Theo's coming. As soon as the boys are with us, I create a wall of my fire between Theo and us. The raging black and white flames reach head height and every time he tries to go around it I spread it out, keeping him contained.

Theo's hand still glimmers with green light as he looks at us all in turn. Gabriel pushes himself off Collins and takes my face in his hands.

'Are you okay?' he asks me breathlessly. I nod, never taking my eyes off Theo who's stalking back and forth behind the wall of my fire.

Gabriel turns and looks at him, wrapping his arm around my waist and taking my weight from Amara.

'Shall I kill him?' I ask. I sound drunk. My words are slurring from the knocks to my head.

'No,' Gabriel replies. 'We can't. We have to go.' He starts backing away, taking me with him.

Theo stops his pacing and glares at us through the fire with a nasty sneer on his face.

'She's had a Break, hasn't she?' he calls over. 'Her fire just screams damaged. The black and white flames of the unstable witch are the biggest giveaway there is.' His heinous laugh echoes through the night air. 'That's just too good. After all these years of waiting, Grayson ends up with a Broken Arcane Witch. Bet that's pissed him off no end. He doesn't like his women unpredictable, does he?'

'Shut your mouth, Theo,' Gabriel warns.

'So, what happened to you, Hooper? Huh? To suffer a Break, you have to be extremely weak or have suffered something...unimaginable.'

'Come on,' Gabriel says, backing away. 'Don't listen-'

'Do you know what happens to a Witch that gets Broken?' he shouts after us. 'They turn into evil, wicked things. They kill without cause, concern or care in the world. I heard about what you did to your aunt and uncle!' we turn, keen to get the hell away from him. 'I know what happened to your mummy!'

My feet stop.

'I know what happened to your daddy too. He's alive you know. I could take you to him. Just lower the fire.' I turn despite Gabriel trying to pull me on, I shrug off his efforts and look back at Theo.

'My dad's alive?' I call over. The cocky grin and self-assured way Theo holds himself is infuriating in itself. Never mind his words.

'Lower the fire, and I'll tell you where he is. They can't help you, Lilly. Grayson and his band of murderers. But I can. I can help you.'

'I don't need help.'

'You get close to people, and they die. They always die. No one in your life has survived you. Come with me, and I can help you. Make sure you never hurt anyone again. Me and your dad-'

'Don't listen to him!' Gabriel says, still trying to pull me away.

'You have no idea who those people you're clinging to are.' Theo points at Gabriel. 'The stories I could tell you would make you sick.'

'One more word, Theo, I'll rip your fucking head off,' Gabriel spits angrily. 'Don't test me.'

Theo laughs as he looks between us.

'Don't tell me you care about her, Gabriel?' he mocks. 'Like, actually care? Not just need her for your spell or to keep you warm at night?' His bellowing laugh makes me jump. 'Oh, that's just too good. That's *hysterical*.' He looks at me one more time. 'I just want to talk to you. Lower the fire and let me pass.'

I shake my head and grip onto Gabriel's sleeve. I trust Gabriel a hell of a lot more than I do him.

'Fine. I tried it the easy way.' He raises his hand. An invisible force hits me like a wave, knocking me back. My head slams on the floor again. My focus goes. The fire loses its form and starts spreading outwards, giving him a clear path. He has his eyes on me the whole time as he gets closer, with nothing but determination on his face. The others are sent flying out of his path like rag dolls, with a slight wave of his hand. I will my magic to come, but I'm just so out of it from the bangs to my head, nothing happens. He lifts me to my feet and using me as a human shield, turns to face the others. As Gabriel starts to run towards us, Theo presses a blade against my throat.

Everyone stills.

'Let her go,' Gabriel threatens, looking between the knife and Theo.

'No. I don't think I will.'

'Well, you're not leaving with her,' Collins says firmly standing side by side with Gabriel, pushing Amara behind him. My legs can't hold me up. I have to hold onto Theo's arm to stop impaling myself on his knife.

'I can't let you do that spell, Gabriel,' he says simply, digging the knife in. 'If I have to kill her, I will.'

'Don't!' Gabriel says desperately, holding his hands up and stepping back. 'Don't kill her, Theo. Please.'

'I think he likes you,' he whispers in my ear.

'Fuck you,' I snarl back.

'You kill her, Grayson and I will lead a fucking army to your door,' Gabriel warns.

'You will, will you?' Theo laughs. 'How scary.' I feel his heavy breathing on my neck but also the increase in his heart rate. He's more afraid than he's letting on. 'I tell you what. Hand over the journal, and I'll let her go.'

'We don't have the journal,' Gabriel tells him.

'Liar.'

'I'm not lying. I swear. It was stolen.'

'By whom?' Theo asks. Gabriel looks between the man threatening my life and me, but doesn't say a word.

'Take me,' Gabriel offers. 'Grayson will find the journal, and when he does, we can trade. Me for the book. What do you say?'

'Or I could just take her,' Theo says, taking a step back and pulling me with him.

'No! No, don't. Take me. Hold me ransom. Grayson cares about me more than her, you know that.'

Their voices begin to muffle as I stop paying attention. I'm too busy looking at the man that no one else can see, standing right in front of me, almost nose to nose.

'Come on, Red,' Toby whispers with a grin. My own personal ghost. *'Are you seriously going to just stay there and play the little victim? I taught you better than that. All my lessons about pain. Were they for nothing? I hurt you much worse than he is right now.'* He leans in and kisses my cheek. *'Do it for me, Red. Fight. Show me what you're made of.'*

Everything inside me calms as his eyes look into mine. His grin's so familiar, and in this moment, it feels like he's really here with me. But he fades, as he always has in the last two years. My imaginary friend. My subconscious. My Toby. But now, I can finally focus.

Every tree that surrounds us, a good dozen, explodes in black and white flames that reach up high into the sky. The sudden flash of heat and brightness makes everyone but me cover their faces. My magic pulses from deep inside my chest and blasts out a surge of Telekinetic power straight from my body. It's a violent wave that sends everyone hurtling through the air and crashing to the floor. I turn to Theo who's scrambling to his feet. He's looking at the fire swirling around us with terror-filled shock. My eyes are watering from the heat and smoke. I lay out my palms flat. Some of the fire surrounding us gathers in a huge ball of swirling heat in them. I hold it there, sculpting it and assembling all the power I can, creating a huge orb of complete firepower. I feel the resistance as it tries to be free, but it does exactly as I bid and goes straight at him in a streak of black and white fury and heat.

I scream fiercely as it goes. Theo has no choice but to turn and run. It's huge. I send wave after wave of fire at him. When I stop, I'm surrounded by flames. I turn and see Gabriel staggering to his feet. He looks at the chaos around us and then at me.

'STOP!' he yells, shielding his face from the intense heat. 'YOU CAN STOP NOW!' The world spins. Everything starts to move in slow motion. Even his voice begins to fade. My legs buckle, and I fall to the floor unconscious.

Chapter 12

I open my eyes to find I'm in my bed back at The Orchard and surrounded by people. I'm relieved to see Amara, Collins and Gabriel here in one piece. They're dirty and covered in soot and ash. But except for a nasty-looking black eye on Amara, they look relatively unharmed. They linger by the door with a cumulative look of dread. Collins is gripping onto Amara with both hands, and none of their eyes leave Grayson for a second. The Coven Leader is standing at the base of my bed with his arms folded across his chest and a deep furrow on his angry brow. As they watch him, he watches a lady in a white coat check me over. She tells me she's a doctor. Her hands are gentle and careful, but I still flinch when her hand touches my skin.

'I told you!' Grayson growls at her. 'She doesn't like being touched. How many times...'

So, she has the idea to put latex gloves on, and it's bearable. After running her fingers gently over the ridge of my nose and examining the back of my head. She pulls out a small light which she shines into my eyes.

'How does your head feel?'

'Sore,' I reply, blinking painfully against the bright light. She lowers the torch with a slight frown.

'And your vision? Blurry? Do you see double? Anything out of the ordinary?'

'I feel a bit sick. The room's spinning a little. And my head's throbbing.'

She pulls off the gloves and turns to Grayson.

'I suspect a small break on the ridge of her nose which should heal in about three weeks. The bruising will fade by then too.' She directs her next question to Amara. 'You say her head hit the ground hard?'

Amara nods keeping her eyes down.

'How many times?' she asks. 'There are several lumps and cuts on the back of her head so I would expect more than one blow.'

'Three,' I answer for myself. 'I think.'

'Are you worried about a concussion?' Grayson asks.

'She *has* a slight concussion. So keep a close eye on her. If she struggles to stay awake, has any numbness, problems with vision, or bleeding from her ears then let me know as soon as possible.'

'You'll stay here for a few days,' he orders, not giving the woman a say in the matter. 'I want you close in case you're needed.' She gives them a small bow before leaving.

Everyone stays precisely where they are but they watch Grayson nervously.

He's not happy. Not at all. Even I can see that. But they all look at him as if he's a bomb that could blow at any second.

'I'm okay, Grayson. Honestly. I've had worse,' I tell him, waving my hand dismissively and showing him a carefree smile. But the steely glare I get back soon wipes any cheeriness from my face.

'How did he know? Hmm? Not only that we had her, but where you would be? We didn't even know you were going to get that idiotic tree until a couple of hours before you left.' He looks to them as if expecting an answer. But none comes.

'He knew her name,' Gabriel tells him. 'Knew her mum was dead. Her aunt and uncle too. He even said he knew her dad, but that could have been a complete lie. He's not the most trustworthy person. But one thing's clear. Someone in this house must have told him. There's no other explanation. We have a traitor in the house. Someone is leaking information.'

Grayson throws an accusatory look at me. 'Do you know Theo?'

'When I was little, he came into the house where my mum, dad and I lived. There was a fight, but we got away. Mum grabbed me and we ran. Scared the hell out of her. Enough to send her to Harry's.'

'And your dad?' Grayson demands. 'What happened to him?'

'I don't know. He wasn't there when Theo came. After we left, I never saw him again. Mum just said he must be dead.'

'Does any of this matter? Theo knows she's here.' Gabriel's freaking out. 'She's not safe. What do we do?'

'We? Now I'm involved in the decisions that are made in order to keep her safe? Maybe if you had listened to me in the first place, none of this would have happened. You let him get close enough to almost kill her. Whose fault is it this? HUH?' We all jump as he yells. 'Either *you* left her side and this is *your* fault. Or *she* left yours, and it is *her* fault. Because I distinctly recall telling you both to stay together.'

'It wasn't his fault-'

'I turned my back for a moment, Grayson. I got distracted. It was my mistake entirely. Lilly did nothing wrong. Neither did Collins or Amara,' Gabriel says in no uncertain terms.

Grayson charges over and punches him hard in the face.

'HEY!' I bellow, throwing the covers off me so I can get to my feet. 'Don't you dare hit him!'

Grayson grabs his throat and sends his lightning through his body. Amara screams and backs away horrified as I run forward and grab Grayson's other hand, but he yanks it away.

'STOP!' I bellow.

'I warned you,' he snarls in his brother's face. 'Didn't I? If she came back as anything less than she was, *you* would pay the price. You weren't able to protect her because you're pathetic. Useless.'

I take the cuff off and separate them with a wave of my hand. I then put myself between them, protecting Gabriel with my body as the room swirls around me.

'He's not useless. I wouldn't be here if it weren't for him!'

Grayson gets quickly to his feet.

'Move,' he warns. But I shake my head. 'MOVE!'

'No, Grayson. Calm down!'

He starts forwards and I back up, straight into Gabriel who's just barely to his feet.

'GET THE HELL OUT OF MY WAY!' Grayson grabs my arm and hurls me back on the bed, but I miss and my head connects with the bedpost instead. I land in an uncoordinated heap on the floor clasping my forehead. I don't get a chance to gather myself before he's on me.

'SEE WHAT YOU MADE ME DO!' Grayson bellows, lifting me to my feet by my wrist so aggressively, my feet leave the ground momentarily. 'STOP INTERFERING IN THINGS THAT DON'T CONCERN YOU! I'M THE LEADER! ME!'

'GET OFF ME!' I scream in a terrified panic before slapping him hard across his fury-filled face. As he turns back to look at me, I know I'm in big trouble.

'You dare raise a hand to me.'

'I just want you to get off me,' I whimper. 'You're scaring me.'

'YOU DARE!' He twists my wrist and I scream in agony as I'm forced to my knees.

'You're going to break my wrist! Grayson, please...stop!'

'Maybe I should. You're as feral as a goddamn mutt! You need a strong hand to teach you some discipline and respect!'

'Grayson. Get your hands off her, and step away,' Gabriel orders in an extremely formidable and authoritative tone. His eyes are pure black.

He's using his magic.

Grayson's face goes from angry to murderous as he releases his grip on me and steps back.

'Lilly, go to Collins,' Gabriel orders. I run to the door to stand beside Collins and Amara just as instructed. I should be pissed that he's using his powers on me, but I'm just relieved to be out of the way. Amara takes my good hand. She's shaking. I am too. Collins stands in front of us both and gently guides us out of the way but shares our look of horror.

Gabriel's blackened eyes remain on his brother.

'I may not be able to hold a compulsion with you or Theo for long,' Gabriel tells Grayson. 'But a few seconds is all I need. Don't you dare grab her like that. Ever. You hear me?'

'How dare you,' Grayson says slowly. 'How dare you control me. I would turn and run if I were you...*little brother*.'

'I'm not leaving. I'm not running from you. I told you. This is all my fault. I let Theo get close to her. I took her out of the house. Me. I'll take your punishment, Grayson. Not her. I deserve it.'

What? That's all a lie. And he most certainly does not deserve to be punished.

Gabriel's eyes return to blue and Grayson's body becomes his own again.

With a low growl, he storms up to Gabriel and slams a fist into his face so hard Gabriel falls to the floor spitting blood. I rush forward, but Collins holds me back.

'You can't help him,' he whispers. 'You'll just make it worse.'

'Get off me!' I demand.

Gabriel calls my name. 'Don't intervene,' he orders with black eyes. 'You stay exactly where you are and keep quiet. All of you.'

I have no choice but to stand with the others and watch Grayson's *"punishment"*.

I flinch at every thud and every moan as Grayson beats his brother mercilessly. And what's worse is Gabriel does nothing to defend himself. Not a single thing. The urge to throw up as I watch this violence has me clutching my stomach. I hate that I'm so useless. I hate that I can't help him.

I hate that this is all my fault.

When Grayson's done, he stands and looks to us all in turn. There's sweat on his brow and murderous anger in his eyes. He stretches out his fingers, easing out the pain that must be on his knuckles. And Gabriel's blood drips from his hands onto my bedroom floor.

'Does anyone have anything to say?' Grayson snarls.

I can't take my eyes off the bloody mess of Gabriel's face as he lies at the base of my bed, clutching his ribs and coughing. Gabriel rests his finger over his lips. I fight every instinct I have to keep quiet. But I know that if I did argue back, it would be Gabriel that suffers. So, I keep my stupid mouth shut.

'No? No one wants to add anything?' He looks straight at me. 'You think I'm out of line, Miss Hooper?'

Tears are falling down my face. Angry, hateful tears. Right now, I hate him. If I had the strength, the resources or the willingness to walk away from a beaten Gabriel, I would be out of the door, and I would never come back.

'Well, I'm not.' He points down at Gabriel. 'He was supposed to look after you. He let Theo get close enough to almost kill you. It's his fault that you're hurt right now. Not mine. All of this could have been avoided if you had just done as I asked in the first place.' He steps over his brother, pushes Collins out the way and stands so close, I feel his breath on my face. 'You almost died. Your friends almost died. All so you could buy a Christmas tree? Was it worth it?' He stares at me, unblinking and infuriated. 'That's not a rhetorical question, Lilly. I want you to answer me. WAS IT WORTH IT?' He roars, making me flinch and cower back.

'No,' I answer, trying so hard not to let him hear the wobble in my voice. None of this was worth it.

'You need to start trusting me and my judgments. You have no idea what kind of world you live in. How could you? You've spent your life hidden from it. Gabriel knows the consequences of letting me down. And now, so do you. The punishment delivered is fair so I won't hear another word about it. From now on, if you wish to stay in this house and continue having the protection of my Coven, you will stay on the grounds and do as I say. You will let me keep you safe and alive because the fate of our entire species rests on your shoulders! Stop being so selfish and stubborn.'

He waits for my response. How can I respond to this? Part of me wants to apologise, part of me wants to slam my fist into his face. Whose fault is it that Gabriel's hurt right now? Mine. I insisted I go with them to buy the tree. I couldn't fight Theo off as Gabriel offered to trade himself to keep me safe. Theo was right. Everyone that gets close to me gets hurt. Everyone dies. And as Gabriel blinks blood out of his eyes and struggles up to his knees, I have a moment of clarity.

The threats beyond these walls are far greater than I ever thought. Theo's lethal. Then there's Grayson. He thinks I'm his. He was ready to kill John for touching me. Gabriel and I are close. I believe this beating and show of force is as much about getting Gabriel to back off me, as much as it is about keeping his position of leader crystal clear. He could turn me out at any moment. I don't want to leave. This place could be my home. I have friends here. Safety. Acceptance.

I need to start making an effort. I need to fall into line. I need to keep Gabriel safe.

I'll put distance between us. Make Gabriel believe that there's nothing worth protecting in me so he won't end up in this position again trying to defend me.

We can't be friends. Not if it means this every time he tries to protect me.

'Do you wish to stay?' Grayson asks.

'Yes.'

'Then you will do as you are told. Understand?'

I nod. 'I understand, Grayson. I'm sorry,' I say with forced politeness.

'Get back to bed and rest. I'll be up to check on you in a while. And you,' He looks at Collins while pointing at Gabriel. 'Get him to his room.'

He leaves.

Collins gets Gabriel up and helps him out into the landing. When they pass me, Gabriel reaches out his hand to me asking if I'm alright. A ridiculous question to come from a man who's been beaten as he has. I dodge his hand.

'What have I done?' he asks indignantly with blood in his teeth.

'Just stay away from me,' I tell him. I sound angry, but really, I'm frightened. Terrified of getting them hurt. Again. He frowns.

'I just took a beating for you. And what...you're pissed at me?'

'I didn't ask for you to take a beating for me, Gabriel,' I bite back. My hands are trembling, and everything hurts but I stand straight. I stand firm. 'You forced me to stand aside and do nothing.'

'You don't need to ask me to protect you, Lilly!' His irritation seeps into every one of his words. 'I care about you. I protect the people I care about!'

'Yeah?' Well, I never asked you to protect me. I never asked you to care about me.' I see the hurt in his eyes as I spew my venomous lies. 'And to be quite frank with you, you presume too much to think that I would ever want you to care about me. So do me a favour. Stay the hell away from me. I don't want you inserting yourself into my life. Assuming that I need a big man to keep me safe. So, go find someone that does. Because if

you're looking for someone to rescue, it sure as hell ain't me. Go.'
I gesture to the door. My whole body has the shakes. Fuelled
with adrenaline, fear and anger. They all stand there staring
at me with their mouths open. All except Gabriel who looks
thoroughly pissed off. 'You can glare at me all you want,' I tell
him. 'You won't find a swooning mess in here. Your stunt just
shows weakness. I have no time for weakness. Get out. GET
OUT!' I need them to leave. They have to go right now because,
for all my words, which are all complete bullshit, I'm about to
burst into tears.

They back up. Gabriel, brushing off Collins who's helping to
keep him on his feet.

'Fine,' Gabriel spits 'You don't want me or my help?'

'No. I don't.'

'Then I'll go. You can deal with Grayson on your own. You
ungrateful cow.'

As soon as they're beyond the door, I slam it closed with a
wave of my hand, return my cuff to my wrist, curl up on my bed
and scream into my pillow.

*We're outside a door standing side by side and hand in hand.
Toby's is cold to the touch. Like always. Mine, a clammy,
shaking mess.
I tighten my slick grip on him and he, in turn, gives me a
reassuring squeeze.
I stare at the plain, basic white door with a small silver
doorknob. Ordinary, really. Normal. He watches me looking at
it. I feel his stare like a burn on the side of my face.
The house is silent. Everyone's asleep...except us.
This is our time. Ours.
Mine.*

I'm in his shirt and my knickers, and he's wearing just his light grey, faded jeans.

His body is perfect. A chiselled six-pack. Smooth, pale skin. But there are scars on his body. Mainly his back. Not as many as mine but it bonds us together. I suppose.

He lifts my hand and kisses my knuckles.

'Are you ready?' he asks, his eyes shining mischievously in the dim light.

'I...I don't think I can do this,' I whisper, looking at the door. Terror and doubt are filling every inch of me.

'You can,' he whispers, taking my chin and guiding my face to him. 'You have to. Prove to me that you can do this. That you're strong enough.'

'What if I fail?'

'Then...you're not who I thought you were,' he says grimly. 'Go through that door. Do what needs to be done. Or I'll leave, and never come back,' he says simply, looking away from me to the door ahead of us.

My hand tightens on him even more, causing his knuckles to grind together.

He can't go. He can't. I won't let him.

I open the door and go in.

The room's dark.

The only sound I hear is the deep, steady breathing of Harry's maid laying asleep in the bed beneath the window.

I walk silently across the room and stop by her head.

I look at her as she sleeps, so peaceful and tranquil.

'Do it,' Toby whispers in my ear, the same as a lover would whisper sweet nothings. 'She deserves it. She deserves to die. Do it for me, Red. Kill her for me. Kill her for yourself.'

Her eyes flick open, and she goes to scream.

'KILL HER!'

Her shrieks follow me into the waking world. They echo in my ears louder than any screams I've ever created. I bury my face in my hands and push the whole thing away. I force it from my mind and shake it off.

The morning's arrived, and with it, a ray of beautiful sunshine streams through the crack in my curtains. It doesn't suit my mood, which is bleak at best.

When I catch a glimpse of myself in the mirror, I gasp. There's a big gash right across my nose and a bruise reaching from my cheek up to my eye.

Painkillers! I need painkillers.

As I head into the kitchen, I'm greeted by a skinny arse sticking out of the fridge. Surely that's not Amara. I clear my throat. The mysterious girl stands and spins around.

It's Ava.

Seeing her standing in red lace knickers and one of his T-shirts makes my insides feel like they've hit the floor. Even though I know it has no right to. Especially now I've decided that I can't carry on being his friend, let alone anything else.

'Lilly...right?' she says, holding a bottle of champagne in one hand and a large bar of chocolate in the other. When I don't respond, she rolls her eyes and shrugs, closing the fridge door. 'I hear you had a rough night?' She smirks while looking at my nose. 'Gabriel and I are celebrating,' she tells me, holding up the open bottle of champagne. 'Aren't you going to ask what we're celebrating?' Her smugness is making me twitch.

I walk up to her and take the champagne from her hand.

'That you got rid of your chlamydia, finally?'

She laughs and points at my face. 'Sexy. Give me my champagne back?' she asks, holding out her hand. 'Gabriel's waiting for me. I don't want to keep him waiting too long.'

'No,' I turn and stride through the back door.

Fuck her and her celebration. Fuck them both.

I wish I'd put a jumper on over my long-sleeved black top, but I wasn't planning on coming out here, so why would I?

As I walk away from the half-naked bitch who's going back upstairs to be with Gabriel, I tell myself not to cry. The pain in my body from the attack yesterday and imagining Gabriel with her really hurts. I shake my head and will those nasty feelings away. It doesn't matter. I've made up my mind anyway. She's welcome to him. It's the best thing all round.

I walk across the lawn barefooted in the dew-covered grass, seeing my breath in the air and enjoying the taste of the Laurent Perrier champagne for breakfast. When I spot the pool house, I make my way towards it. Thankfully, the door's unlocked.

The hum of the filter and the slight slap of the water on the sides of the pool are the only things I can hear. There's no one here.

Two of the walls are made of nothing but tinted glass. I can see out, but no one can see in. Perfect. The other walls are all dark red brick. The floors too. The pool's an impressive size. Bigger than the outside one. There are several round porthole lights lining the bottom alternating between red, blue, yellow and purple. It's peaceful but most importantly...empty.

Rolling up my jeans, I lower myself onto the edge and dip my feet into the warm water.

Ah, that's heavenly.

I close my eyes and soak in the tranquillity. As I sip this delicious champagne, I wish I could stay in here forever. With my eyes closed, I see images of Gabriel and Ava rolling around upstairs in his bed. Opening them makes it less vivid, but that sharp pang of jealousy is making me want to scream.

There's a light tap at the door, but it's enough to make me jump. Amara pokes her head around and smiles awkwardly at me.

'Morning, Honey. Can I come in?'

I tap the space next to me, happy that she's here. Hopefully, she'll help me take my mind off Gabriel and the mess from last night.

'I just walked past a half-naked Ava bitching to Gabriel about how rude you are. Apparently, you said she had chlamydia?' she laughs. 'Couldn't you have slapped her or set her on fire? I really hate that girl. She's such a bitch.' Sitting herself down next to me she stares at my face with her nose scrunched up. 'No offence, Honey. But you look awful!'

I run my finger along the edge of her black eye. 'You don't look too good yourself.'

'Oh, this?' She shrugs with a sweet little smile. 'I'll cover it with make-up and no one will be the wiser. It doesn't hurt that much. I could cover yours up too if you like?'

'Nah. It doesn't bother me.'

She dips her feet in the water with me as I rest my head on her shoulder with a sigh.

'I've made such a mess of things, Amara. I should never have gone out yesterday. Have you seen Grayson this morning?'

'Briefly. He's still in a foul mood. He was so angry that you got hurt yesterday. It would have been sweet if it wasn't so scary.' She lets out a massive yawn.

'Didn't get much sleep either? I was tossing and turning all night.'

'Not really. I waited up for Collins. He was with Grayson and Gabriel all night talking to the Nomads who know about you, trying to figure out how Theo knew where to find you. He's much scarier in real life. I've heard stories about him, but nothing I've heard does him justice.'

She tells me he's been around as long as the others, but unlike them, he doesn't want the veil down. Odd, because he's a witch. When I ask her why, she says she doesn't know.

'Collins changes the subject when I ask. I know it's not my place,' she says slowly. 'But can I say something?'

'Of course you can.'

'Please be careful with Grayson. He's a very clever and powerful man. He gets what he wants one way or another. Collins and I have seen how he is with you. He wants you, and I'm not sure what would happen if the feeling wasn't mutual.'

'It's not mutual. It never will be. The arse called me a feral mutt and nearly snapped my wrist last night.' I sip my champagne and offer it to her.

'It's eight in the morning,' she scolds. But she holds out her hand anyway. 'I've never had champagne. And yeah, not a great Grayson moment if I'm honest. He's always been... temperamental. But I have to admit, how he was with John and Gabriel was a little extra crazy than I'm used to.'

'Have you heard from your dad?' I ask, handing over the bottle and changing the subject as I do.

'Nope.' She rolls her eyes, sounding like she couldn't care less. 'Grayson said I can stay here for a while with you. So that's cool! He's only doing it to win points, but hey.'

'That's great news.' It really is! I clear my throat and ask, 'Is Gabriel okay?'

'He thinks you're mad at him and he blames himself for you getting hurt. He's also furious at you,' she adds, looking at me sideways. She bites her bottom lip.

'Go on. Spit it out. I know you want to.'

'Well...' she takes a deep breath, 'You were a bit...'

'I was a massive bitch,' I tell her. 'I was horrible, ungrateful and vile.' I look at her as the quizzical crease on her brow deepens. 'Grayson attacked him, Amara. He beat him badly. Because of me.'

'That's...well, that's not, entirely, true,' she says, not believing her own words.

'Yes. It's entirely true. It was all my fault.'

'That's not fair-'

'I could have got you killed.' I run my finger gently along the bottom of her bruised eye once more, hating that she has it and that it's my fault. 'I got you hurt and for what? A tree?'

'Theo got me hurt. With his fist. Which he hurled into my face. Not you. And not Gabriel. Grayson's reaction was completely out of line. And if I'm being honest, so was yours. Gabriel was just trying to look after you, and you threw it back in his face. He cares about you. He was just trying to help.'

'Yeah, he was trying to help me at the tree lot and got hurt by Theo. He tried to help me with Grayson, and Collins had to carry him out of my bedroom. I won't give Grayson a reason to go postal on Gabriel again. I won't. If it means losing him as a friend then so be it.'

'Hang on...' She scoffs and shakes her head as she realises. 'You're pushing Gabriel away to protect him. Last night wasn't about punishment for letting Theo get too close at all. It was Grayson acting out of jealousy. Putting Gabriel in his place. And that scared the hell out of you because...you have feelings for him, don't you? For Gabriel!'

I shrug and avoid her stare. Swigging from the bottle instead of answering her question. But my reaction may as well be me screaming at the top of my lungs that yes...yes, I bloody well do!

'He has feelings for you too,' she says with certainty.

'Not as much as he cares about Ava, clearly,' I mutter, taking a sip of champagne to wash out that bitter taste of jealousy. I groan as she continues to look at me expectantly, her eyebrows raised. We sit in silence and drink the champagne.

'Gabriel's compulsion doesn't really work on Grayson or Theo. I wonder why?'

'No idea. And to be honest, I don't really care. I'm more worried about you. It can't have been nice seeing Ava this morning. Not if you have feelings for Gabriel.'

'Honestly? It sucked. I know he has this reputation with girls, and he said himself he flirts with everyone. But it still feels really shit.' I take a sip of the champagne. 'It doesn't matter how I feel. It would cause nothing but trouble with Grayson, and it's pretty obvious Gabriel doesn't do feelings. He does sex.'

'Good sex I bet,' she says before laughing.

'Yeah,' I laugh too. 'I bet.'

I squeeze her hand and feel like I have a real friend for the first time in my life. I mean, she saved my life last night instead of running to protect herself. Can't get any more real than that!

One bottle of champagne later, we start walking back to the house. As we cross the lawn, we meet Gabriel and Collins heading towards us. The cuts and bruises on Gabriel's face look similar to mine, but days older. They really do heal fast! I wish I could say the same for my guilt over him getting hurt, or my anger that he had Ava here last night.

'There you are,' Collins calls over. 'We've been looking for you everywhere. You alright?'

'We're fine,' Amara says happily.

Gabriel's eyes linger on my impressive black eye as we stop in front of each other. Amara and Collins embrace as we stand a little awkwardly to the side. With a few small shuffling steps, Gabriel's standing close.

'Are you okay?' he asks, running his finger gently along my bruises. 'About last night. I wanted to apologise for what I said to you-'

I move away and out of reach from his touch, hating that I know where those hands have been, and carry on towards the house.

'What's up with you?' he asks, jogging after me.

'Nothing,' I insist, trying not to look into his eyes as I quickly make my way across the lawn. 'I just want to go inside.'

'I know Grayson frightened you last night, but I'm fine! Perfectly fine. See?'

'Yeah, that's great. Excuse me.'

'You fancy a walk?' he asks. 'I could take you around the orchard again. We could talk-'

'No. Thanks.'

He blocks my path and holds me in place by my shoulders. Still, I avoid looking into his eyes, but he waits. So, I look up.

'Are you really still angry at me? I thought last night was just you lashing out. Have I missed something and genuinely pissed you off?' he asks. 'Because if I have, can you just tell me? Trying to guess what a woman actually means when they say *"They're fine"* is arduous work.'

'Can you move?' I barge past him when he doesn't budge and carry on, but he doesn't give up and follows me.

'Did you sleep well?' he asks keeping up with my pace.

'Yep.'

'You spoken to Grayson this morning?'

'Nope.'

'What are you doing today?'

I stop, and so does he.

'What is this? Twenty bloody questions? What do you want, Gabriel?'

His eyes narrow a little, and suddenly he looks very serious.

'I heard you had a run-in with Ava this morning,' he says, folding his arms. I just stand there waiting for him to make his point. 'Well? Did she say something to you?'

'Go ask her.' I walk past him, but he blocks my path again. I groan as I stop.

'I'm asking you.'

'No,' I tell him. 'She didn't say anything. Can you move now?'

He grabs my arm to stop me and leans down into my face. 'You know, I don't have to put up with how you speak to me. No one else would dare treat me with such disrespect, so maybe you could make a bit of an effort-'

'And what? Bow? *sir?*' I yank my arm free. 'I already have Grayson demanding I lick his boots. I don't have the energy to feed two male egos. Tiptoeing around you is the least of my priorities. You want someone to curtsy and tell you what you want to hear? I suggest you go find Ava. Because I'm done being a doormat for arrogant men who use sex as a weapon against me.'

'Oh!' he scoffs. 'So this is about Ava. I knew it.'

'No,' I scoff back.

'You're pissed off that I had her over.' He watches me with his eyebrows raised and looking beyond smug. 'Deny it.'

'I don't care who you have over.'

'You might want to say that with a bit less venom. I might believe you then.'

'I really don't care. Honestly. Like I said last night, I don't want you.' He flinches at my words and the guilt I feel cuts me to my core. 'If you would rather be with her-'

'Than with who?' he asks, stepping forwards as I inwardly slap myself for saying that. 'Than you? Is that what you want to say?'

'No...that's not what I meant-'

'Because it was you that kicked me out of your room after I took that beating. You can't tell me to stay away from you, then get mad when you see me with someone else.'

'I don't care who you're with. Now move,' I warn. Again, he doesn't let me pass.

'Then why are you being such a hostile cow?' With a laugh, he shakes his head. 'I knew you'd act like this when you saw her.'

'Like what?' I'm almost growling at him.

'Like a jealous child. I knew it. You're so predictable.'

'Did you plan this? You wanted me to see her so what...I'd get upset?' I laugh now because he blinks back at me embarrassed. 'If you did then you're pathetic. Manipulative. Clearly, you and Toby spent too much time together.' I barge into his shoulder and walk away. 'Thanks for making this so much easier,' I call back to him.

'MAKE WHAT EASIER?' he shouts after me. 'LILLY! MAKE WHAT EASIER?'

My heart's hammering and I'm shaking with anger as I slam the patio door shut behind me. But if I was hoping for some peace, I was wrong.

'There you are,' Grayson calls, striding in with a large coffee in his hands. 'I wanted to run something past you.'

I don't mean to groan as loudly as I do. My reaction has his eyebrows up.

'Sorry. Long night,' I sigh. 'What can I do for you?'

'Have you ever heard of something called a Bloodstone?' he asks, his tone not quite as friendly, but pleasant enough. I couldn't care less.

'No.'

'Well,' He takes a seat on a stool and gestures for me to join him. I do. 'It's a stone made from the blood of two or more witches. If you and I made one together, it would mean that I could find you no matter where you are. If Theo *had* taken you last night, he wouldn't have got far with you. I would have been able to find you very quickly and bring you home safely.'

That actually sounds like an excellent idea. But he's not done explaining the full purpose of a Bloodstone.

'The second thing it does is give the flow of your magic to me.'

'Excuse me?' This, I don't like the sound of. At all.

'It's not as bad as you think, the stone belongs to you. You have to willingly give it to me for it to work. If you take it back, the link is gone straight away. It is magic based on trust. It has to be mutual. When I'm holding it, I can give you access to your magic or cut you off when you start to get overwhelmed. It only works with the binding spell. You don't want it...you take the cuff off, and you are back in control. What do you think?'

'I may as well just stick to the cuff.'

'But with the stone...I could find you.'

'But you would determine when and if I use my magic.'

'Only when you're wearing the cuff. It doesn't work without you having the binding spell on you.' This is turning into a row.

'Sorry.' I shake my head. 'But no. I need to keep my magic mine.'

He looks disappointed, but not angry. 'Okay. No problem. It was just an idea.' Wow, he took that well. 'There was something else,' he adds.

'What?'

'I wondered if maybe you would like to have dinner with me tonight.'

I don't know what's worse. The way my stomach suddenly drops or the look on his face when he spots how much I don't want that.

'You're upset about last night,' he says as if that's obvious. 'Look. I was angry. I shouldn't have grabbed you like that, and I am sorry,' he says with some serious charm. 'So, what do you say?'

'I say no,' I tell him in no uncertain terms. His eye twitches but that's tough.

'Just like that?' he laughs. 'No?'

'I understand that you're the Coven Leader and have the authority to dish out punishment as you see fit. I accept that, because I want to stay here. But I'm afraid your temper and cruelty has completely destroyed any romantic feelings I might have had for you.'

'I just explained that last night was a mistake.'

'You battered your own brother, and were a second away from breaking my wrist.'

'I would never have broken your wrist.'

'I've done the whole dark, dangerous and angry boyfriend routine. And I'm not interested in doing it again, Grayson. I'm sorry if that upsets you, but I can't do all that again. I don't want to, so no. I will not be joining you for dinner. And if that alters your offer for me to stay here with you, then please let me know. And I will pack.'

Hendrix walks in holding a mobile phone. 'Boss. Billy's on the phone. He has a lead on...err, everything okay?' he asks with a quick look at me. Grayson looks livid. What's new?

'So that's how you feel?' he snarls. 'I lose my temper once, and you strike me off completely?'

'Yes. That's how I feel. And I'm afraid that making me date you is not an order I will follow. So, if that's all, Mr Kendryk, I'm under orders to get as much rest as possible. If you'll excuse me, sir.' I give Grayson a small bow, the same as all his other subordinates. And leave them standing in silence before heading into the lounge, feeling very empowered.

'Hey, Honey,' Amara greets me tiredly, slumping on the sofa beside me. 'So, Gabriel's pissed off with you.'

'Grayson's not too happy with me either. Maybe I should go poke Hendrix in the eye and go for the trifecta.'

She laughs and starts flipping through the channels. Finally, she settles on a film. After a while, I lay my head on the armrest and pull my knees up to my chest. I got no sleep last night. I'm exhausted. Thankfully, with her close, it's not long before I drift off to sleep.

I'm standing in the hall.
Beyond the door, I can hear screaming. Blood-curdling, angry, terrified screams and I know, I know that one of those screaming voices belong to me. The other, to the maid. The third voice belongs to Toby. But he isn't screaming. He never screams. He's laughing.
All of us, out of sight, beyond the door even as we stand here. How can that be?
He's urging me to go in. To do what needs to be done.
'I'll leave,' he says. 'I'll go and never come back. Get in there and do it.'
'I can't. Please. I don't want to,' I cry. I plead.
As we watch each other, him with a sly grin and me, with tears gliding down each cheek, the hall begins to fade into another place.
The concrete walls become wooden planks. The low ceiling becomes high wooden rafters. The grey carpet floor becomes grey stones, covered in blood.

'Lilly...Lilly, wake up!' Amara whispers as she shakes me roughly. I open my eyes which are beyond heavy, thankful that she's pulled me out of the disturbing nightmare. That damn place is burnt into my mind. The thick blood. The need to escape.

The failure to flee. It was the Millers' barn I think. Perhaps my memories aren't missing after all. Perhaps they are just in hiding. Like Gabriel said. If I remember, will I go mad again? Will my hair turn white? My brain's protecting me, but the events may be too strong to be denied their rightful place in my mind.

'Lilly!' Amara gives me another shake, snapping me back to the present. It's dark outside. I've slept all day. I grab her wrists to stop the vigorous shakedown she's giving me and sit up.

'What's the matter?' I moan, rubbing my eyes and trying to wake myself up.

'Something's happening in the lobby,' she tells me.

The angry yells of Gabriel get me to my feet, and together we sneak to the door.

'What's going on?' she whispers nervously in my ear, trying to look out.

'How the hell am I supposed to know?' I whisper back with an eye roll and putting my finger to my mouth. 'Shh. We need to listen.'

'Get him in my office,' Grayson orders as he walks through the front door and into the lobby. Billy, Collins and Hendrix are close behind, along with a handful of Nomads.

Gabriel walks inside dragging a man through the lobby towards Grayson's office. The stranger's hands are tied behind his back, and a gag is shoved in his mouth. But that doesn't stop him making it difficult for Gabriel to keep a hold of him as he kicks and thrashes, trying to get himself free.

'He hasn't said anything?' Grayson asks, watching Gabriel and the restrained stranger disappear into his office.

'Not a word,' Billy replies.

'Who's that?' I whisper in Amara's ear. He looks familiar.

'That's Malcolm,' she whispers back. 'The bloke that came here with that creep John.' We share a look of confusion, before returning our eyes back to them.

'He's supposed to be in Italy. Where did you find him?'
Grayson asks.

'Believe it or not, he was at the Miller's barn,' Billy replies.

'The Miller's barn? As in the massacre involving Lilly?'

Billy nods. 'Yes, sir. The farm and the barn are completely
derelict. The Miller's haven't even been on the land in over ten
years. We found Malcolm inside, ranting down the phone to
someone like a madman. He kept saying he couldn't find it. That
it wasn't there. As soon as he saw us, he smashed his phone and
went silent.'

'Any idea who he was talking to or what he was looking for?'
Billy shakes his head.

'Any sign of Tim or John?' Grayson adds.

'Tim, yeah,' Billy sighs. 'He's dead. Throat slit and his body
hidden in the barn. Been there a few days by the looks of it.
Tim's always been loyal to the cause. My guess is Malcolm killed
him, probably because he threatened to tell us he refused to go
to Italy to look for the Hooper boy. They never left the country.
No sign of John I'm afraid. But, sir...there's something more
worrying.' Billy hands him a folder full of papers. Grayson flicks
through them, his face getting more and more concerned. 'They
go back years. She can't be more than fifteen in this one,' Billy
adds, pointing at something inside the folder.

'They're all of her?'

'All of Miss Hooper, yes.'

What's all of me? What's in that folder? Amara takes my arm
as if reading my mind and holds me in place.

Grayson starts to turn in our direction, so we duck out of sight.

'The girls are asleep. I would rather Lilly not know about any
of this. Especially after yesterday. Come into my office, all of
you.' As they all move, I peek out.

Billy and Grayson are walking into his office followed by
Hendrix and Collins. Hendrix is about to close the door, and

my opportunity to learn what's going on will be gone. Amara tightens her grip on me as I shuffle.

'Don't,' she whispers. 'Grayson doesn't want you to know. It's not worth making him angry again.'

'Stay here. Keep out of sight. I'll be back.'

I charge out from my hiding place and run across the lobby before Hendrix can close the door and jam my foot in it.

'Err, boss?' Hendrix says nodding at me in the doorway. 'We have company.'

'Get her out of here,' Grayson says with the briefest glance in my direction. Like none of this concerns me.

'I don't think so. Grayson, let me in.'

The Nomad that grabs my hand gets a firm slap around the face.

'Touch me again, and you'll regret it,' I warn. 'I have a right to be in there.'

'You want to stay?' Grayson asks. I nod. 'Fine.'

Gabriel's beautiful features are twisted in hatred and malice as he stands behind Malcolm who's on his knees.

'She can't stay in here, Grayson. Get her out!' Gabriel demands, but Grayson simply smiles and shrugs.

'She's not a prisoner remember? If she wants to be here, she has every right.'

'Lilly, you need to leave,' Gabriel insists. 'This isn't going to be pleasant.'

'I need to know what's going on.'

'Fucking ridiculous,' he mutters, looking at me with nothing but hostility. 'Stubborn idiot.'

His words are harsh and the look on his face extremely hurtful. He leans into Malcolm's ear and tightens the grip he has on the back of his neck.

'You better start talking, Malcolm,' he warns.

Malcolm keeps his eyes down and although he's shaking, has blood flowing freely from his nose and a black eye, he holds his resolve. Gabriel yanks his head back by his hair and looks down at him. Gabriel's eyes slowly begin to turn black.

'Your brain is on fire. Your skin is melting. Feel it.'

These words uttered by Gabriel have Malcolm yelling in agony. The more he screams, the more Gabriel smiles. His eyes flick up to me as if to say- you should have gone when you had the chance.

'Start talking, Malcolm, and I'll stop. What are you doing with all those pictures of Lilly? Why were you at that barn? Who were you talking to on the phone?' Gabriel asks the questions slowly. He's in no rush to end his suffering. I can't stand it. The agonised shrieks coming from Malcolm are unbearable. I go to stop it, but Collins takes my arm and holds me back.

'Please don't get involved again, Lilly. Malcolm's gone rogue. We think he had something to do with Theo knowing where to find you,' Collins explains quickly and quietly.

'You think he's the leak?' I ask.

'It certainly looks that way.'

There's a knock on the door. Gabriel's eyes return to their familiar blue. As they do, Malcolm's screaming stops and I find myself relieved. Even though he may very well be the reason I was attacked yesterday. Gabriel looks at me briefly before ignoring me entirely and looking to the door. He's still mad at me. But right now, there are more important things happening.

'Come in,' Grayson calls. The door opens and a Nomad walks in holding more piles of papers. Grayson looks nervously at me as they pass.

'Don't even think-' Grayson's warning doesn't stop me. I snatch one of the papers and in the Nomads efforts to pull them away, he drops them all over the floor.

They're not papers. They're photos. I'm left looking at dozens of pictures...of me! Me at my uncle's house sitting outside in the garden beneath the tree, studying in the library and even sleeping in my old bed.

'Where did you get these?' I ask with hardly any voice. Shock has taken it from me.

'The barn, Miss.'

'Are they all of her?' Gabriel asks.

The Nomad glances nervously between us. 'Yes, sir.'

I lean down and pick up one by my foot. There are slashes all over it.

I take a step closer to Malcolm, but Collins retakes my arm. I glare down at Malcolm who still has his eyes on the floor.

'Why would you do this to my picture?' I demand.

He says nothing.

'Tell me why you have all these?'

I look at the others at a loss for words. What the hell is happening?

'Did you find the men we asked for?' Gabriel asks Billy.

'I did. They're outside,' Billy replies before heading to the door. He leans out into the lobby and starts talking to someone I can't see. 'You three. Inside. Now.'

Three men walk in, heads down and sickly white. They stand by the map-covered wall and stare, terrified, at their feet. I don't know what has me more uncomfortable. The tension, the photos or the fear on these men's faces.

'So...' Grayson says in an eerie calm as he strolls toward Malcolm. 'You left this house to look for Harry Hooper's son in Italy, but never boarded the plane. Instead, you killed Tim and have been skulking around that old barn with hundreds of pictures of Lilly. These photos go back years. Start explaining yourself.'

Malcolm says nothing.

'Have you been speaking to Theo?' Again, Malcolm doesn't say a word. 'Did you tell him she was at the tree lot?' Not a word. 'Why didn't you go to Italy?'

Silence.

Slowly, Grayson turns his attention to the three men.

'Let's start with you then. You are here because I'm told you are close friends of Malcolm's, so I'm going to ask a question. Anyone is free to answer and understand me when I say I won't ask twice.'

He seems so calm he may as well be talking about the weather. As he makes his way towards the men, he picks up his miniature sword letter opener and spins it playfully in his hand, making sure they all see it.

He stops in front of the man in the middle. A well-built man in his thirties. He's almost twice the size of Grayson, but he trembles in fear.

'Joe...right?' Grayson asks. The large man nods. 'Hello, Joe. Let me tell you how this is going to go. I'm going to ask Malcolm a question. If he doesn't give me an answer, *you* will pay the price.' Grayson places his hand on Joe's shoulder and lowers him to his knees. Joe's breathing gets shallower as his shaking intensifies.

I don't like this.

'Grayson, please don't hurt anyone-' I plead, but he holds up a finger silencing me. It's not enough. 'Please. Don't do this. Don't torture them.'

'Lilly,' he says, anger piercing his calm tone. 'You will either stand there quietly, or I will have you taken upstairs to your room where you will stay until I find out exactly who it is trying to hurt you. What will it be? Stay and hear the answers for yourself? Or go and carry on living in the dark.'

I look up at Collins for some kind of support. He takes my hand in his.

'It will be okay,' he whispers quietly. 'Stay by my side. It's alright.'

I grip him tightly.

'I'll stay,' I tell Grayson.

'Good. Now, Malcolm. Did you take these pictures of Lilly?'

I look at Malcolm, whose stubborn refusal to look at anyone tells me he has no intention of speaking.

Grayson points at Joe's forehead with his finger and pushes his head back, slowly exposing his neck. What is he doing?

'Malcolm. I suggest you start talking,' Grayson says. 'Or poor Joe here will pay the price. Tell me, who took the photographs of Lilly? Whoever it was knew that she was alive years ago. Tell me.'

Malcolm says nothing but stares at the floor breathing hard and looking pained.

'Malcolm...please,' Joe says quietly, looking between Grayson and his friend. But Malcolm holds his tongue.

Grayson's hand grips the sword, and in an unbelievably quick and powerful motion, slices open the man's throat. His blood sprays over the man to his right.

I scream and slam my free hand over my mouth as Collins takes an even firmer hold of me. Horror and fear overwhelm me completely. Grayson's not torturing them. He's outright killing them!

Joe clamps his hands over the deep gash, but the blood spews out of him at an astounding speed. He falls in a heap on the floor and twitches as he turns paler and paler until finally, he stops moving altogether.

Grayson doesn't even blink as he steps over him to the man on the right. A man in his thirties with short black hair. He has mist-like blood on his face and is trembling.

'Is he going to kill them all?' I whisper.

'Try and keep calm,' Collins replies quietly. I couldn't react any other way than I am right now! I'm completely in shock.

'Who were you talking to on the phone, Malcolm?' Grayson asks in precisely the same way as he lowers the second man to his knees. His hand grips the blade hilt tighter ready to strike.

'Come on, Malcolm. Carl's your friend. You've known each other since you were kids,' Billy urges, but Malcolm says nothing.

'Mal…' Carl whimpers. 'Just tell him what he wants to know! Be loyal, Mal. We're on his side! sir, please, I'm on your side. Always.'

We all wait, but Malcolm remains silent. Carl's eyes scrunch up as Grayson deals out another fatal swipe. He falls to the floor choking and gurgling on his own blood. My hands have started shaking as Grayson sets his sights on the last man. He's no older than twenty, if that. His bottom lip's trembling as he stares straight ahead. Grayson lets him stay on his feet.

'This boy here is your nephew, isn't he?' Grayson asks slowly, resting the tip of the blade on the young man's neck. 'Surely you won't let him die?' Grayson digs the knife in, creating a red bead that slides down the blade and onto his hand.

'Malcolm, for god's sake!' I plead. 'Just tell him what he wants to know!' I don't even know these people and I can't take it.

'My question to you is this. What were you looking for in the barn?' Grayson asks.

'JUST ANSWER HIM!' I scream, eyeing the knife. He remains quiet but is very agitated. When Grayson raises his hand, Malcolm attempts to move. To get free of Gabriel's grip and help his nephew. But with a horribly smug grin, Gabriel orders him to stay.

'I CAN'T TELL YOU! I CAN'T!' Malcolm bellows.

'Shame,' Grayson says, bored. He starts to bring the knife down.

'NO!' he pleads. 'STOP!'

Grayson stops just as the tip of the blade meets the boy's neck. I'm holding my breath. The boy too as he sits with his eyes scrunched closed, waiting for death.

'What were you looking for in the barn?' Grayson asks.

Malcolm is torn. He wants to save his nephew. But he seems incapable of revealing the answers Grayson and the rest of us are so desperate for.

'Who were you talking to on the phone?'

Tears begin to tumble down Malcolm's cheeks. But still, he remains quiet.

'Did you tell Theo about Lilly?'

'Let my nephew go. And I'll tell you what I can,' he replies.

'Tell me what you know right now, or your nephew dies.' Is Grayson's counteroffer.

They watch each other in silence. Neither willing to concede.

'You have three seconds,' Grayson says simply. 'Three..'

'If I tell you, I'm a dead man.'

'Two...'

'Just let him go!'

'One.' Grayson slices the young mans throat with speed and ruthlessness. The harrowing wail that Malcolm produces is traumatic in itself. But his cries of pain and misery soon turn to yells of hatred and rage as he sets his eyes on the man that just murdered his friends and family. There's such anger in his eyes. If looks alone could kill, we would all be dead.

'You wait. You will pay for this. He'll make you pay,' Malcolm growls.

'Who?' Grayson enquires, cleaning the blood from his blade with the hem of his shirt. 'Theo? That's who you're working for?'

Malcolm turns to me. 'The photos of you belong to him,' he says cruelly. 'He knew you were in that house with your uncle long before you even met him. He watched you for years. Waiting for you to become a woman. You were a child when he first watched you sleep. He said that he loved you even then.

That waiting for you to grow up was agony. He's coming for you, *Red*. And he'll kill everyone here to get you back.'

'What did you call me?' I whisper, suddenly filled with a completely different form of fear.

'You heard me. *Red*.'

'Is h-he mad at me?'

'Oh yeah. But you know him. Pay your dues, he'll forgive you. He'll make you watch as he tears them all apart. He'll make you suffer for a while. But then he'll love you again.' He keeps staring at me. Like it was me that killed his people. Like this is all my fault. 'He wants you. He's coming to get you.'

'Who?' Gabriel growls.

'They won't be able to protect you,' he laughs. 'Not from him and not from yourself. You're incapable of refusing him.'

'I'm not.' I can barely speak, because if he's telling the truth... if Toby knows where I am and he has his sights set on me, I'm beyond screwed. I'm worse than dead. I'm doomed.

'Who's he talking about?' Gabriel asks.

'Toby,' I reply. 'He's talking about Toby. He used to call me that. *Red*.' I briefly gesture to my hair.

'They're coming for you,' he sings.

'Who else is working with him other than you?' Grayson demands as he stands by my side.

'Oh, plenty of people. More than you could ever imagine. He's the rightful leader of this Coven,' Malcolm says, looking Grayson dead in the eye. 'Not you. He has plans. Big plans. And if you get in his way, he'll kill you all. He *will* take his place as leader, and you'll be left in the gutter where you belong, Grayson.'

'How dare you-'

'How dare I?' he scoffs. 'How dare you. How dare you take what's his. How dare you touch *his* woman. How dare you cast him out. You have no idea what Toby is capable of. You have no idea what she is capable of when they are together.' He looks at me with a weird admiration. 'I do. I've seen it. When they are together...they're magnificent.'

Gabriel's eyes go black once more. 'FEEL PAIN!'

Malcolm screams. He screams and cries and thrashes. Grayson takes the bloody knife and starts driving it through Malcolm's palm. His cries are of utter agony.

'WHO ELSE IS WORKING FOR TOBY?' Grayson bellows as Malcolm screams. 'WHAT WERE YOU LOOKING FOR IN THE BARN?'

Gabriel's torture is worse than anything I could have ever imagined. There's blood coming from Malcolm's nose, and soon, his bloodshot eyes are almost completely red as the blood vessels pop.

'STOP IT!' I scream. But they don't. I can't take it. It's too much. There's too much blood. Too much pain. Too much screaming. I do the only thing I can think of and take off my cuff. I toss Grayson and Gabriel aside with a wave of my hands and stare down at Malcolm with terrified tears and a heavy weight on my chest that feels like it wants to kill me.

Malcolm blinks up at me with bloodshot eyes and red streaming from his nose and mouth. The brothers jump to their feet, and the Nomads raise their weapons. I hold up my hands.

'Stop! Just stop!' I plead. 'No more violence. There's a better way.'

'No. There is not!' Grayson snarls. 'Now move aside.'

'You take another step, Grayson,' Malcolm warns. 'I won't say another word.'

I turn back to Malcolm as the others begrudgingly stay put.

'Why would you join him?' I ask. 'He's the devil incarnate.'

Malcolm gets to his feet. Everyone around us tenses and readies themselves to attack and protect me if necessary. But he's in no condition to hurt anyone. And he knows it. I take a step closer. And so does he.

'Where's Toby?' I ask. 'Tell us where he is, and I promise you that no more harm will come to you.'

'Come closer, and I'll tell you,' he says, taking another step forward. There's no fear in his voice. None at all. With another step, he's standing in front of me. Closer than I'd like.

'Lilly...' Gabriel warns.

'Tell me,' I order, holding up my hand in a bid to keep Gabriel quiet.

There's a loud bang. I scream as the window behind Malcolm shatters, just before his head explodes. Blood, skull and brains splatter over Grayson and I, just as he flings himself on top of me as a human shield. We crash onto the floor next to Malcolm and what's left of his head. I stare at his body in silent shock as Grayson lifts his head and looks around. There are no more bangs, and no one else has been hit. But someone's shot Malcolm through the window.

Straight through his head.

Grayson's soon on his feet and barking orders at the Nomads to get outside and find who shot him. Everyone runs around in a mad dash, following his orders, as I just stay on the floor looking at the gaping hole in Malcolm's head. I have his blood in my mouth and in my eyes. I feel its warmth trickling over my skin. I can't move. I can't breathe. How have I ended up in the middle of all this violence and death? I never thought anything could make me feel more afraid than what I lived with at Harry's.

'It's okay,' Gabriel says gently, lowering himself down onto his knees beside me and helping me sit up. 'Look at me. Not him.' He brushes the hair out of my eyes and wipes my face clean with the cuff of his sleeve. 'You're alright, Beautiful. Let's get this blood off. Hey...' he takes my face in his hand and makes sure all I can see is him. 'You're alright.'

'Gabriel,' I whisper as I shake uncontrollably. 'W-what...' I look over my shoulder at the three men with blood still pouring from the gashes in their throats. 'Oh my god. Oh my god.'

'You're alright. Look at me, not them.' He keeps wiping my face clean, but there's too much blood.

The room's in chaos except for us on the floor. He pays no attention to any of it, just me. Even as Grayson kneels next to us.

'Is she okay?' he asks Gabriel as he checks me over and helps with the pointless task of trying to clean me. 'We can't let her be alone. We have to keep her safe. It's the only thing that matters! Toby obviously has people working for him, and he's coming for her. She's gone really pale. I think she's going to-'

I start gagging. A waste paper bin is thrust in front of me as I throw up the little food I have in my stomach. Grayson rubs my back as Gabriel holds my hair out of the way.

'I told you she shouldn't have been in here for this,' he hisses. 'This is too much for her to cope with!'

'Were you expecting someone to splatter us with Malcolm's brains?' Grayson argues back. 'Because if I'd have known, I wouldn't have let her in here, would I?!' He guides my face to his so I can see his dark, concerned eyes. 'It's alright, sweetheart. I won't let Toby get to you.'

I stare at the bodies of four men through pools of tears, either from shock, horror or the vomiting. Toby's got moles in the house. They're working with him to overthrow Grayson. He's coming for me. Who just shot Malcolm? Why?

Grayson looks to Gabriel.

'There haven't been any other shots. And the hit was direct to Malcolm's head. They were aiming for him. Not us. Why?'

'To stop him talking I imagine. We had Malcolm, and if they know us, they'd know we wouldn't have stopped until he talked.'

'Toby wouldn't want us to know who he has planted in the house.'

Torture. Murder. Conspiracy. Threats. It's too much. Way too much. But more frightening than any of that is the idea of Toby setting his vindictive sights on me. I've seen what he does to the people on his wrong side. Better dead than on the wrong side of Toby Smith. Believe me.

He knows I'm here. He's coming, and he will cut down anyone who gets in the way of his target.

Me.

'I need to go,' I say weakly, pushing their hands off me and getting to my feet.

'Of course,' Grayson replies. 'I'll take you upstairs to get cleaned up-'

'I'm leaving. I need...I have to...'

I walk away, stumbling and holding onto furniture as I go to keep myself on my feet.

'Lilly, Lilly wait!' He calls after me as I turn to the front door instead of the stairs. 'Gabriel, stay here.'

The lobby's full of Nomads running here, there and everywhere. They bump into me as I make my way through them straight to the front door.

No shoes and no socks doesn't hinder my determination. I'm outside the front door and sprinting down the driveway to the main gate. When I hear hurried footsteps following me, I spin round and shove Grayson away from me. He looks at the spot where I just pushed him and takes a deep breath to calm himself.

I turn, carrying on with my retreat before he can say anything. He runs ahead of me and stands his ground, holding his hands up to stop me.

'You can't go. I need you to stay. I need you safe.'

'Move. Grayson, I need you to move right now. I'm not fucking about.'

'Neither am I. Come inside and calm down. I'll make you a cup of tea.' He takes my arm and attempts to bring me back.

I snatch it away. 'Tea? Fucking tea? Do you have any idea of what just happened? This violence is worse than anything I saw at Harry's. You promised me safety.'

'I'm trying-'

'There are four dead men on the floor of your office. Three you killed and one shot by an unknown person who could very well have been my former lover. Never mind the psychotic witch who tried to kill me yesterday. A witch you didn't even have the goddamn courtesy to tell me about! Hendrix seems hellbent on hurting me. John was tortured in front of me. And you're so unpredictable, I never know if you're gonna kiss me or hit me!' I shake my head and laugh with a desperate hysteria. 'I can't. I can't! I just can't.' I stumble on the jagged stones as I storm past him, but I don't care. I need to get away, but he runs after me.

'The world is far more dangerous than I am. I assure you. Lilly, you can't go!'

Putting my hand over my cuff, I raise my brow. 'Try and fucking stop me, Grayson. I never agreed to help you. I never said yes when you asked me to help you break down the veil. I am not your prisoner, and I am not your *fucking* girlfriend so move. Let me leave.'

'I'm just trying to keep you safe! For all we know, he said those things to make you run. So Toby can get his hands on you.'

'He has people in your house!'

'I'll find them.'

I try once more to get past, but he stops me.

'Please, Lilly. Please. I just want to keep you safe.'

'YOU CAN'T!' I'm borderline frantic. 'Not from him! And not from you!' I point out past the gate and into the darkness as if he's out there. 'If Toby's coming, I can't be here. I can't be anywhere near him, please …' I can't hold back the desperate tears that are becoming stronger than my anger. 'Please move aside.' I walk past him and get as far as the gate. I give it a shake, but it's locked. I look back at him. 'Open it, Grayson. Let me out.'

'No,' he says, shaking his head.

I close my eyes for a second and take a deep breath to try and calm myself.

'Open it,' I repeat when I open my eyes.

He walks towards me, making me back up. 'I said no.'

I shove him away. He barely moves, but his eyes flash dark.

'OPEN IT!'

'NO!'

Another shove and he grabs my arms pushing me back against the gate.

'I'm getting really sick of your refusal to do as you are bloody told!'

I come apart completely and just burst into tears. I don't struggle against his grip. I don't argue. I just sob.

'I'm so scared,' I confess. 'I can't live like this. I can't. I'd rather be dead.'

He leans in suddenly and lands me with a possessive kiss. An unwanted kiss. I shove him away with all my strength making him stumble.

'What the fuck is wrong with you!' I scream, wiping my mouth and throwing my arms in the air. 'Why would you think that's okay?!'

'Why do you keep pushing me away?!'

'BECAUSE I DON'T WANT YOU!'

I turn back to the gate and rest my head against the bars feeling lost, powerless, afraid and confused. And all I can think about is how I wish it were Gabriel here with me. Not him. I hear his footsteps as he makes his way slowly towards me and he settles his hand on my shoulder. I flinch and shrug it off, gripping the bars and sobbing desperately.

'What the hell am I going to do?' I cry. 'I can't face him, Grayson.' I slide down to my knees, still gripping the bars tight and continue my wailing. 'I'm not strong enough.'

'It will be okay,' he says gently, kneeling down with me. 'You won't have to fight him. We will.'

'You don't understand. What he does...what he turns me into... what if I'm not strong enough to resist him? What if he turns me back into who I was?'

'I won't let him get anywhere near you for that to happen. Please, come inside. It's not safe out here.'

I just sob, shrugging off every attempt he makes to touch me, and cling to the gate, afraid that if I let go, I'll be lost forever.

'Listen. Theo and Toby *are* out there. Not to mention Hunters. You can't leave here without ending up in one of their clutches. You need protection. Let me protect you. I promise, no more violence. No more killing. And I will not kiss you again. I swear. Let us all protect you. There is absolutely nowhere safer for you than here.'

'It's not safe for you if I stay. Any of you. Toby will use the people I'm close to. Amara, Collins...Gabriel. I can't bear to put them at risk. I can't.'

'You let me worry about that. Come on,' he prises my hands from the bars and holds them in his as he looks into my eyes. 'You don't have to face him on your own. If he comes here, he'll find an army between you and him. Trust me. You're safer here than anywhere else. You have to know that. I swear to you, I will never let anyone hurt you. Not while you have my protection.' He stands and helps me up. 'Let's get you inside and cleaned up. Okay?'

There are Nomads everywhere. As we make our way past Grayson's office, Gabriel closes the door so I can't see the carnage inside. Too late for that. It's burned into my brain forever.

'Is she alright?' he asks gently.

'She will be,' Grayson replies. 'Send some tea up, will you? Actually...make it something stronger.'

I avoid looking at him. My eyes are still streaming with tears. Amara and Collins are in the lounge. She seems almost catatonic as he holds her close.

All the curtains in the house have been closed, keeping us out of the unknown gunman's sights while the grounds are searched.

We walk in silence up the stairs. Once we're in my room, Grayson tells me that things will look better in the morning. I don't see how. Those men will still be dead. Toby and Theo will still be out there. Hunters too.

A Nomad brings up a bottle of whiskey with two glasses, then quickly leaves. As Grayson puts a drink in my hand, he assures me that I'm safe and that no harm will come to any of us.

Tell that to the men on his office floor.

'Do you want me to stay?' he offers.

I shake my head, but he stays put. I simply turn and go into the bathroom, closing the door behind me. I hear him leave after a few moments muttering a swear word, and get myself into the shower.

I spend hours rewashing my hair. Every time I do, more blood and brain matter seems to come out.

In bed, I cry until I'm too exhausted to cry anymore. No matter where I go or who protects me, he'll get me. Toby's everywhere. He always was. I can't stay here.

Chapter 13

Trying to sleep's impossible. I'm more awake than I think I've ever been, and feeling uneasy as well as sick to my stomach.

It's dark. I can't see much, but that doesn't stop me sitting on the window ledge with a blanket around my knees, staring out the window. It's raining again. Pouring.

I watch as four bodies are bundled into the back of a truck and driven away. I see Nomads patrolling up and down, up and down. Part of me just expects to see Toby walk up the driveway.

Too much has happened. I'm drowning in all my emotions. Grayson's a cold-blooded killer. There are no other words for it.

I've known him a matter of days, and he's killed so many people. He attacked his own brother right in front of me, and everything he's done has been in my defence. For my protection. Or so he says. Is it always like this? Or is it me? Have I brought this chaos into their home?

This house is swarming with people I don't know. Any one of them could be on Toby's side. He's so manipulative it wouldn't surprise me if they all were.

There's a light knock on the door, but the way I react it may as well have been a bomb. I jump up and stare at the door with my heart hammering and every nerve in my body screaming at me to either run or attack.

'Lilly? Are you awake?' Gabriel calls quietly. I don't answer, but I'm thoroughly relieved it's him and not...well, anyone else. I take two steps toward the door before I stop.

No. I can't run to him. I have to keep him at a distance now more than ever, and besides, we're not exactly on talking terms. His behaviour towards me and mine towards him is at an all-time low. I keep quiet in the hope that he'll think I'm asleep and just go.

After a few moments of standing in the dark, I assume he's given up and gone. With a sinking heart, I return to my window ledge, feeling more alone than ever. Even now, Toby's driving everyone away from me. As I slump down on the ledge, the door opens, and the light from the hall streams in. Gabriel sees me and comes inside, closing the door quietly and making sure no one sees him from the outside.

I watch him as he walks over. He stops at the base of the bed and looks inside my mother's backpack which I stuffed full of clothes a few hours ago. He pulls out a jumper and looks at me with raised eyebrows.

'Are you leaving?' he asks.

'I'm thinking about it,' I say simply. It was a rash reaction when I got out of the shower. I packed it and then got back into the shower still feeling disgusting. Part of me still wants to pick it up and go, but the rest of me is too terrified to do so.

He drops the jumper and takes a seat opposite me on the window ledge. He says nothing, just sits there watching me, listening to the rain hammering the house outside. I return my gaze out of the window, hoping to get control of my anger, jealousy, fear and overwhelming want to be held by him.

'Are you okay?' he asks finally.

I pull my knees up close to my chest and look outside, still avoiding his stare.

'That was a stupid question. It's five in the morning, and you're wide awake. Have you got any sleep?'

'No,' I reply. 'I feel like there's still blood on me. I've had a dozen showers already and every time I close my eyes I see those men dying over and over. As well as Toby's face. It's enough to make me never sleep again.'

'I'm sorry. I knew you being in there was a bad idea.' He pulls up his knees and wraps his arms around them, still not taking his eyes off me. He's reading me in the darkness, trying to gauge me. 'And, I'm sorry that we fought.' He reaches out and strokes my arm gently with his finger. I pull away. So he retracts it.

'I think you should go,' I say quietly, hearing the strain in my voice. 'You shouldn't be in here. Grayson won't like it. Neither will Ava.'

'I don't care what Grayson would like. And Ava means absolutely nothing to me.' He slides down from the ledge and kneels beside me instead. 'I care about *you*! Always. Please-'

'Funny way of showing it.'

'Yes,' he says, looking up at me with the moonlight reflected in his eyes and his hands holding mine.

'Yes? What are you on about?'

'Yes, I wanted you to see Ava. I wanted you to know that she spent the night because I wanted...no, I *needed* to know how you would react.'

I knew it, and I can't hear anymore. I get to my feet and barge past him as he gets to his.

'You're pathetic,' I mutter as I go, swiping up my bag and heading to the door. 'Screw this. I'm out of here.'

He takes my elbow and stops me, but I refuse to look at him.

'I can't do this, Gabriel. Not now.' I pull my arm away, but he takes both my shoulders and refuses to let me go.

'We're not done. You *will* let me explain myself-'

I lunge at him, slamming my fist into his chest.

'Hit me. I deserve it. I know I do! I know what I did was cruel.'

'Why would you want to hurt me like that?' I hiss furiously. 'After everything you know I've been through. I trusted you!'

'Because I had no idea if me being with someone else *would* hurt you! I have no idea if you want me the way...'

'The way?'

'That I want you. Okay? I don't want just to be friends with you. The way you are with me, how we are together... It feels like more than friendship. But you keep pushing me away. So, I had Ava over, hoping you'd realise that you feel something for me. That maybe, you would want to be more than friends. Nothing even happened between us. I got too drunk and-'

'Wow,' I yank my arm free of his impossibly tight grip. I should be thrilled at his confession, but I'm not. He's showing me the man he really is. Manipulative and childish .'How very *Toby* of you. Sleeping with another woman to make me jealous. Nice, Gabriel.'

'I said I didn't! And it's not the same-'

'Oh no? It sure feels similar. The fact that you did or didn't actually sleep with her doesn't matter. Your intentions do. You have feelings for me? Why couldn't you just bloody tell me, talk to me about it? Not sleep, or pretend to sleep with another woman.' The hurt inside is pulling me apart.

'That's what I'm doing now. I spoke to Collins, and he said that I should just be honest and tell you how I feel. That playing games is a bad idea. The man that did that, that's not who I want to be.'

'You're a manipulative, womanising, pretty boy that uses sex and a smile to get what you want. You use your charms to get women into bed and turn them out before the sheets are even warm because you can. I hardly know you, and I can tell that that's the type of man you are. I have no interest in being another one of your conquests and to be honest, Gabriel, I barely want a friendship with you after this. All I see when I look at you is the kind of man who enjoys manipulating women. I look at you, and all I see is Toby-'

'Toby?' His voice is low and furious. His face stern and dangerous. I've definitely triggered him. I'd be scared if I weren't so angry myself. He yanks my backpack from my hands and tosses it to the floor. 'You think I'm the same as Toby?'

'Yes. Give me back my bag.'

'You loved him. Maybe you still do. A full blown, self-confessed sociopath. I'd rather be a womanising pretty boy who's afraid of getting too close to someone than what you are.' He looks me up and down. 'The willing plaything of a man who used you, manipulated you and physically hurt you. Toby doesn't love you. He never did. He obsesses over you because of what you are. An Arcane. The same as Grayson. Without your magic, you're nothing-'

Slap.

I strike him hard. Slowly, he turns his head back, and I can't help it. I just burst into tears.

'Why are you doing this to me?' I sob. 'What the hell have I done to deserve this?'

He holds my face in his hands and looks desperately into my eyes.

'Without your magic, you're nothing to *them*. But to me? Your something pretty damn special. You're all I think about.'

'I want you to get out of my room.' I lower his hands. He has to go.

'You're funny.'

'Please,'

'You're kind.'

'Gabriel, stop. You need to go. I can't deal with this right now.'

'Don't send me away. Please.'

I step back and clear a path for him to the door as he stands there.

'I'm not leaving you. Not until we sort this out.'

'I told you what Toby used to do. And you did the exact same thing. You know full well how I feel about you-'

'That's the fucking problem, Lilly!' he says with complete exasperation. 'I don't know how you feel! I don't have a goddamn clue! All I know is how I feel, and it's driving me insane! Watching you and Grayson get closer...it's killing me!'

'Well, seeing you with Ava killed me!' I want to scream at the idiot, but that will bring others into this room. And it's complicated enough just us two. 'Watching you get beaten by Grayson...it broke my heart. Almost losing you to Theo...it scared me to death. But Toby's coming for me. And if he thinks for even a second that I have any feelings for you, he'll kill you where you stand. That's how I feel. Okay? I care about you, but being with me will destroy you, Gabriel... It will kill you.'

I storm past him and stand with my arms folded looking out the window, trying hard to get myself in control. The silence is deafening. Has he left? I turn, but he's still there. Watching me in the shadows. I can't see his face. I have no idea what expression he's wearing. He takes a step closer, and he becomes bathed in moonlight. Seeing my tears, he comes to my side and takes my hands in his as the rain pelts the windows.

'I don't need protecting, and it will take more than Toby or Grayson to keep me away from you, Lilly Hooper.' There's a sadness in his eyes, and a vulnerability in his words. 'I don't care who stands in the way, I don't want to stay away from you.'

'What *do* you want?' I ask, desperately.

He runs his nose softly along my cheek and holds his mouth close to mine.

'I want to kiss you. I want to hold you. And I know what I did was stupid, but I just had to know if there was even the slightest chance you felt for me what I feel for you.' His lips gently kiss my cheek. He looks back at me through his dark hair and moves his mouth to mine. 'Kiss me. Please...' But before they reach me, my bedroom door flies open.

I panic, terrified it's Grayson. Or even Toby! And push poor Gabriel away from me so hard, he swears, stumbles and falls flat on his backside.

'Lilly?' Amara calls. 'Are you awake, Honey? I can't sleep after everything that...*oh!*' She spots us both in the beam of borrowed light. 'Gabriel...I, err...'

I could slump on the floor with relief that it's her and not Grayson. Gabriel jumps back to his feet and straightens himself after my shove. We both stand there looking guilty as sin, smoothing ourselves down, as Amara looks between us.

'I'm sorry,' her eyes looking between us. 'I thought you would be alone...I'll go.'

'You don't have-'

'Good night!' she chirps, smirking from ear to ear and disappearing so fast I couldn't stop her even if I wanted to.

Gabriel's looking at the now closed door, and then back to me with his eyebrows raised.

'I'm gonna say...ow.' He rubs his elbow and gives a small short laugh. 'That's not where I was expecting that to go.'

'What the hell am I doing!' I hiss, dragging my hands through my hair. 'I can't do this. It's too much too soon. I'm barely out of the cellar, this is just...' All I can do is shrug and shake my head as I slump on the bed and bury my face in my hands. 'You know what...I've barely slept for the last two years. I close my eyes. And all I see is horror. I'm just so tired of being afraid.' I look up at him as he stands above me. 'Gabriel, I'm so tired.'

'I won't push you to do anything you're not ready to do,' he whispers, resting his hand on my shoulder. 'I can't even pretend to understand what you've been through. But let me tell you this. And you can tell me to fuck off if you want. And I will.'

He looks down at me as I look up.

'Whatever you need, I'll do my best to make sure I give it to you. You want space? You got it. You want me to leave you alone? Fine. But only if that's what *you* want, and not because that's what Grayson or Toby wants. And maybe, when you're ready,' he eases into his cheeky half-smile. 'You can snog me instead of shoving me onto my ass.'

He's completely broken all the tension I was feeling as I give a little laugh. His soft chuckle warms my heart.

'There, I made you smile. My work here is done.' He leans down and plants a kiss on the very top of my head. 'I'll come and see you in the morning. I'll make lunch, and take you down to the lake for a couple of hours. The fresh air will do you good.'

My hand wraps around his wrist as he turns. He doesn't move, just waits and watches me.

'If I asked you to stay in here with me, just to keep me company, would you?'

'Are you saying that because you think that's what I want? Or do you really want me to stay?'

'The only time I've felt remotely safe or comfortable in the last decade and a half, has been with you. I don't know if one of Toby's men will sneak in here while I sleep and slit my throat. I don't want to be alone. I want to be with you. I want to fall asleep...in your arms.' I feel myself blush. But he looks so touched.

'I'd be honoured.'

Together, we lay side by side. My head fits perfectly on his chest, and his arm feels sturdy as he holds me close. We hold each other and just...be. The sound of the rain outside, the slow steady breaths he takes and his fingers gently running through my hair are so relaxing.

'You didn't have sex with Ava?' I ask.

'No. I didn't. I swear to you.'

'Good.' I close my eyes as he pulls out his phone and starts tapping the screen.

'*The wife of a rich man fell sick:*' he says. *'And when she felt that her end drew nigh, she called her only daughter to her bedside-*'

'What are you doing?'

Gabriel's staring at his phone and reciting the first line of Cinderella which I know off by heart.

'I heard that you're a fan of the Brothers Grimm. That you lost your book in the fire at your uncle's house.'

'Yeah. It was a first edition illustrated copy. It was...my mum's.'

His arms tighten. 'Close your eyes. I'll read it to you as you sleep.'

'You don't need to-'

'No, but I want to.' He gently runs his finger along my cheek and smiles kindly at me.

'Why are you being so nice?'

'Because I want to be nice to you. Because I need to. And because you have had a really, really rough couple of days.' He returns his attention back to his phone and continues reading.

'I'm still pissed about your stunt with Ava,' I tell him, stifling a smile.

'Quite right too.' He continues, but with a slight grin. I look up at him amazed at how in one minute I think I hate him and in the next...

I close my eyes and listen to his voice as it takes me away into a peaceful sleep.

I jolt awake as the sound of thunder shakes the house. Only with the moonlight can I see that Gabriel's still here. He's lying on top of the covers still facing me, but he's fast asleep.

I lean in to see if he's actually asleep. He doesn't react even as I get closer, and closer. His face is so placid. He looks at peace here. And so beautiful.

I lean in, and with the gentlest touch, I rest my lips on his. I can't help myself. He stirs and I sit up quickly watching him, but he stays asleep.

What the hell am I thinking? Am I determined to get him killed?

'Lilly...' he mumbles in his sleep. He reaches out his hand and slides it into mine. 'Please...'

'Please what?' I whisper back. He shuffles closer.

'Please don't...'

'What, Gabriel?' I ask, brushing the hair from his face. Still, he remains fast asleep. 'Don't what?'

'Don't hate me. Don't leave me.' He stills and continues sleeping.

My heart swells. Leaning down, I kiss his temple. 'I don't hate you,' I whisper in his ear.

I get to my feet and look down at the sleeping man on my bed. The only man whose touch doesn't hurt. Why? How can a man I hardly know have such an effect on me? It's madness but what's even madder is this pit I have in my stomach. This feeling of dread that something awful is going to happen. Not to me, that ship has sailed. But to them. To him. It's more than I can bear. The mysterious gunman. Theo's attack. How long until it's more than a black eye for Amara or a stray bullet goes through Gabriel?

If I want to keep them all safe, I *have* to leave.

Quietly I pull on a pair of jeans, Gabriel's hoody and my mum's boots. I take a pen and piece of paper from the dressing table and write a note.

I'm sorry. I can't stay. It's for the best.
Lilly.

I'm not entirely clear on how I'm going to do this, but before I know it, I've grabbed my bag and I'm out the bedroom door sneaking my way towards the stairs.

The Nomad positioned outside my room has fallen asleep on a chair. His head is tilted back and his mouth's wide open. He's easy to get past, but more Nomads are patrolling the whole house, and they're wide awake. It takes patience and my many years of honed sneaking skills to get downstairs.

The front of the house is crawling with guards. There's no way I'll make it out the front door, so instead, I leave through the back door, and I make it unseen.

Outside, the rain's coming down hard. It's so cold I see my breath in the air. I'm still not clear on my plan. All I can think is this...I care about the people in this house. Some more than others, and I know me being here is putting them all at risk despite what they say. They would never tell me to leave. I'm important to their spell, but what good will I be to them if I end up getting them all killed before the spell can even be done? Perhaps when everything calms down, I'll come back.

Theo wants me. He almost killed Amara and Gabriel at the tree lot to get to me.

Grayson's killed four men since I've been here. Collateral damage in his quest to *'keep me safe'.*

But Toby's coming. It doesn't matter where I am or who I'm with. If he wants me, he's going to get me. And he'll kill anyone who gets in the way of what he wants. Three years we were together. I know what he's capable of. I've seen it, lived it. And what's more, I know what I'm capable of when I'm with him. Because yes, he frightens me and yes, he's a violent and cruel man. But I loved him and followed his lead for years. I don't honestly know what I'll do when I see him again. To say he had a hold on me would be the biggest of understatements. One thing's for sure. I have no intention of being near anyone I care about when he does find me, which I know is inevitable.

The air feels different at night. Colder, uncertain and dangerous. The world's hiding away in the darkness, and I know that somewhere, Toby's playing in it. He always loved games, especially in the dark. He said he was free in the dark, where no one could see him. But I did because I liked to play there too.

With a final glance back at the stunningly grand house that I've been welcomed into and told to treat as home, I pull up my hood and sprint away across the grounds, fighting against tears. I'm going to miss Gabriel and Amara.

But I'm doing this for them. I have to keep Toby away from them all.

I'm soaked through in seconds. The sound of the storm drowns out any noise I may be making, as I run further and further away. I have to dodge several patrols as I make my way across the grounds, and when I come across a huddle of Nomads bitching about the cold and unknowingly blocking my path into the woods, I duck in through the metal gates and into the orchard.

The deep groan of the old rusted metal screams out into the night. I glance back to make sure no one's following.

I'm alone.

If I follow the path through the orchard, it should take me straight to the cliffs. I can follow the coastal path into a town and figure out my next step.

The mud's thick beneath my feet. The rain's falling so hard and so fast it's almost painful on my skin. If it were a degree colder it would be snow, I'm sure of it.

Questions race through my mind. Where will I go? How will I survive? How can I keep myself hidden? Being on my own will be scary, but being with others will get them killed. I'll keep moving. Keep my cuff on so I don't lose control and just stay hidden.

I'll be okay. And so will they with me gone.

I run. Through the trees, over their roots and not once do I look back. I follow the path for a good fifteen minutes until the apple trees disappear and become wild woodland. I stop running and walk through the untamed forest until I come to a wall that towers over me. It must be at least twenty feet high with barbed wire running along the top. Growing through that are thick brambles, reaching over the rim. I hazard a guess that on the other side of the wall is a thick tangled mess of hostile shrubbery.

'Shit.'

I follow the wall. It goes on and on. I walk for another ten minutes until I realise that this wall more than likely encircles the whole damn estate. With a loud, frustrated groan, I slide down the wall and sit with my bag clutched close to my chest.

How the hell am I going to get over that and through whatever lies beyond it?

The sound of a snapping twig has me sitting bolt upright and scanning the darkness to see what, or who, just made that noise.

'Hello?' I call out tentatively, hoping beyond all hope that no one calls back and I'm just imagining it. 'Is...is someone there?'

Nothing. Just rainfall.

Snap!

'Shit.' I jump to my feet in a panic that fills up my chest to such a degree, I can barely breathe.

'Grayson? Is that you?' I start looking frantically around me. Every shape suddenly looks like a person. Every shadow's a possible hiding place.

I drop my bag by my feet and strain my ears and eyes for any sign I'm not alone. My back's flush against the wall but ahead of me is acres of woodland, and I have no idea where I am in relation to the house.

What the hell do I do now?

'It's just your imagination,' I tell myself, hoping to calm my heart which is pounding in my chest. I hear another snap of a twig to my right, which makes me jump a mile.

'Who's there!' I call out. 'I'm warning you...' I put my hand over my cuff. I'm so full of panic, taking it off would be a bad idea. I know that I'll struggle to control my magic if I try and use it now, but I will if I have to.

'Come out!' My voice is quivering and my body's trembling. I don't want to blink in case I miss something. Another snap and I give a small yelp. It's close, but I can't tell where it's coming from. I turn and look all around me but see nothing. No voice calls back. No one reveals themselves, but I know someone's there. I can feel them watching me.

Wait. I can't. I can't feel them, not really. Not like I can with the others. I can't sense magic so whoever is lurking out there...they're not a witch.

'I suggest you fuck off!' I call out into the darkness. 'You have no idea- ARGH!'

I'm body-slammed into the ground from behind and land face down in the mud, as someone climbs on top of me. I struggle to keep my face out of the dirt so I don't drown in the sludge. Their hand wraps around my hair as they sit on top of me. I go for my cuff, but whoever they are, they see and know what I'm planning. They pin my arm behind my back.

'GET OFF ME!' I scream as I thrash beneath them. I can't get free, and the more I try, the higher they pull my arm. It's almost out of its socket. The stranger laughs and yanks my arm higher making me cry out in pain.

'WHO THE HELL ARE YOU? WHAT DO YOU WANT?'

They twist my arm, and I hear a pop. The scream that comes from me is high and blood-curdling as my shoulder comes out of its socket.

'JESUS!' I can't help but sob and yell. It's agony. 'WHAT DO YOU WANT?'

They lean down and put their mouth close to my ear. Their laboured breathing stinks of tobacco. He whispers the words in my ear.

'I want you to kill Grayson Kendryk.'

'I'm not going to kill Grayson,' I repeat for the hundredth time as he pulls me back through the woods towards the house. 'I'm not going to kill anyone.'

He has my good arm in his hand, and he's pulling me on as my dislocated one hangs painfully by my side. We reach the orchard. He hasn't said a word since telling me that he wants me to murder Grayson. I've tried hard to see his face or to get him to talk, but I've failed on both counts as he holds his silence and remains hidden by his hood. Who the hell is he?

We're getting closer to the house, and soon I see the rusty metal gates leading back to the garden. The sun's starting to rise. The slightest hue of orange is peeking out over the horizon, and the rain has almost stopped. When we reach the gates, he pushes me up against the wall, slamming my back hard against the brick and jolting my arm, making me yell.

'Whatever you're planning...I won't do it,' I insist, breathing hard and fast.

He pulls out a gun and rests it on my forehead. I stare back at him defiantly, even as he cocks it.

'Guns don't scare me,' I tell him. 'You'll have to do better than that.'

'You *will* kill him,' he insists. His voice sounds familiar. But I can't see his face under his large hood. 'You have no choice.'

'Or what? You'll kill me? If I so much as even attempt to harm Grayson or any of his men, he'll more than likely kill me anyway, so shoot me. I don't want to kill him and you sure as hell won't make me.' I wish my body would stop shaking. 'Who are you? I know you.'

'LILLY! LILLY, ARE YOU OUT HERE?' Grayson's booming voice travels clear across the air. We're out of sight, hidden just beyond the wall bordering the orchard, and he calls out again. 'LILLY?'

'Is she out here?' I hear Gabriel ask in the distance. *Oh no, not him too!* I can't let him get hurt. I can't!

'Does it look like it?' Grayson snaps back. 'Stupid bloody girl's run off into a world that's full of people that want her dead. She'll be lucky to make it to midday if we don't find her. If she thinks these last few days have been rough, she really has no idea what it will be like if she gets caught by Theo or Hunters. Never mind Toby.'

Shit, how right he is, I think to myself as I stare down the barrel of a gun with my arm ripped from its socket. And that's before I've even made it beyond the boundaries of the house.

'Call him over,' the stranger orders. 'Tell him you're here and you need his help.' I shake my head.

'Fine,' he grunts. 'I'll make him come.' He clamps his hand down hard on my shoulder. I can't help but scream.

'LILLY?' Grayson calls out when he hears me. 'WHERE ARE YOU? WHAT'S HAPPENING?'

He starts issuing orders, telling people to fan out and search the grounds for me. He's heading this way. The stranger gestures towards Grayson.

'Call out, Hooper.'

'No. I won't,' I insist. 'You'll have to shoot me.'

'Oh, you will kill him.' He pulls out a needle from his pocket and holds it in front of my face. 'I was planning on sneaking you into the house before I set you off. But out here will be just fine.'

'Set me off?'

'Hmm. I've heard about your power. It won't matter where we are. One shot of this and you'll be Grayson's very own angel of death. I have to admit...using you as a bomb is genius, even if I do say so myself.'

'A bomb?' I look at the needle. 'What's that?' I ask nervously as Grayson and Gabriel's voice gets closer.

'This...' he says, revealing the needle. 'Is adrenaline.'

'What?' I look at the clear liquid and the point of the needle. 'Why-'

'Your inability to control your magic under stress mixed with a good dose of adrenaline will turn you into-'

'A bomb!' I gasp. 'You want me to lose control and kill him with my magic?'

He laughs. 'Oh yes, Red. Absolutely.' He slams my head into the wall, stunning me, before stabbing the needle into my neck and plunging the syringe down, forcing the liquid into my body. 'Toby sends his love.'

As I slide down onto the floor, holding my head, he pulls off my cuff and disappears into the trees.

It all happened so quick.

My body's already starting to react to the adrenaline.

My heart begins to race. My hands start to tremble and blood's pumping through my body so fast I swear I can hear it. My breathing quickens. I can feel my skin turn hot despite the cold temperature, and I hear Grayson and Gabriel just beyond the wall.

I look up just as they walk through the gate.

'DON'T COME ANY CLOSER!'

'What the hell are you doing out here?' Gabriel demands furiously, watching me as I stumble to my feet. I need to get away. They need to get away! Gabriel starts to make his way towards me.

'STOP!' I yell, holding my hand up to stop his approach. My black and white fire springs to life on my palms.

'What are you playing at?' Grayson demands. Hell, he looks furious. 'Put that fire out. Now!'

'I can't!' I try to extinguish it. The more I try it just gets worse. I'm starting to panic, which only makes the adrenaline more powerful. 'Grayson, I can't.' I look from my fire as I see it spreading up my arms. It's a swelling mass of power inside me charged with fear, anger and pure adrenaline. 'I can't stop it...run!'

He furrows his brow and opens his mouth to argue, but the power inside is building.

'RUN!' I scream, but with the words comes a pulse and I send them both flying through the air away from me. I turn and sprint as fast as I can away from them and into the orchard. My fire's up to my shoulders and spreading down my chest, burning my clothes in a way it's never done before. I have absolutely no control over what it's doing.

'Oh god. Oh god.' I look over my shoulder. Grayson's getting back to his feet, but Gabriel's already on his. He knows. He can see what's about to happen and as Grayson goes to follow me, Gabriel stops him and starts pulling him away.

'We have to get away from her!' he tells Grayson. 'She's gonna explode.'

'We can't just let her go, Gabriel!' he insists, trying to free himself from his brother's grip.

'GO!' I scream at them. 'GET AWAY FROM ME! GET AWAY!' I keep running, desperate to try and keep control, to get as far away from them as possible. They're shouting at others beyond the wall, telling them to run for their lives. Both are waving their arms in the air, ordering people to find cover.

When I turn to look ahead to see where I'm running, Collins appears from beyond the tree line several feet ahead of me. I skid to a stop and so does he when he sees my fire spreading.

'Lilly...what-'

'RUN, COLLINS. PLEASE! RUN!'

He turns on his heel and sprints away.

It's no good. I can't hold it back. There's a massive surge of power from deep within my chest that completely takes my breath away, and with a horrified scream, I explode in flames.

Chapter 14

I t takes a few moments of coughing and heavy gasping before I'm able to open my eyes. I'm lying on my back in the Orchard. The rain's stopped, and it looks like it's snowing, but each of the flakes that settle on my skin leave a trail of grey. It's not snow. It's ash, and I'm covered in a blanket of it.

The adrenaline's run its course, forced from my body in an eruption of magic and fire which has consumed everything around me, leaving charcoal husks in place of trees and a layer of ash on the ground.

With a groan, I roll over and try to push myself up. The slightest bit of weight on my arm has me face down on the ground again. I forgot, my shoulder's out of its socket. I look down and to my horror see that the trees aren't the only thing I've destroyed. The fire was so fierce and covered me so completely, it's left me completely naked and filthy. My mother's boots. They're gone. I've destroyed them. I truly have nothing left of hers.

I can hear yelling in the distance, but it's barely audible over the ringing in my ears and my own self-loathing for letting myself get used in this way. The voices sound miles away, but there's one voice I can hear that's getting louder and clearer with every passing second until he's kneeling beside me. He's trying to help me up. Offering me comfort, asking if I'm okay.

'Collins?' I blink him into focus and see he has ash over his clothes, but also a patch of black, crisp skin on his cheek. He's been burnt. He didn't get away from me quick enough. I reach out to him. 'I'm so sorry-'

'I'm fine,' he tells me kindly.

'I burnt you! I'm so sorry. I never meant-'

He takes my hand and holds it tight. 'Honestly, it will heal. I just caught the tail end of it, that's all. Here, let me help you up.'

Slowly he helps me to sit. As I go to try and cover myself up, to hide my body and the scars that come with it, he's already pulling off his black coat and guiding my arms through the sleeves.

'It's okay. You're okay.' When he gets to my dislocated arm, I cry out, telling him to stop. He looks at it.

'I need to put it back in place. It will feel better when I do. Then I can get you covered properly. I'll need to touch you. Is that okay?'

I nod and brace myself as he places his palm on my chest and tightens his grip on my wrist.

'On three. One. Two-' He pulls hard and I scream.

'YOU SAID ON THREE!' I cry.

'Yeah, I did. But it's done now. Come on, let's get you sorted.' He slowly slides my arm through the sleeve of his coat and starts zipping it up. I hold onto him, trying hard to get myself under control. The world keeps shifting in and out of focus. My head's throbbing, my arm's screaming, and every muscle in my body is beyond tired. I shake my head trying to clear it and remember that the last thing I saw was Collins appearing from inside the Orchard. I'm amazed he managed to escape the flames at all.

'What were you doing out here?' I ask. 'You didn't come from the house.'

'Gabriel woke up and found your note,' he explains as he finishes zipping up his coat. 'We all rushed out looking for you. I got sent to the Orchard. I found your bag by the western wall and was coming back to tell Grayson that you must have gone over somehow.' He gestures to the strap of my bag he has over his shoulder. 'But before I could find him, I saw you sprinting towards me. Then...*boom*! What the hell happened?' He brushes the hair from my face and looks so worried. 'Why on earth would you leave like that? Grayson's furious. Hell, I'm not too bloody happy either. And poor Gabriel. Grayson gave him another beating.'

'What? Why?'

'Because he spent the night in your bed after being ordered not to. And you left under his watch.' He takes my face in his hands. 'You have to start thinking what your actions mean, not just for yourself, Lilly, but others around you. Running off like this? Telling Gabriel that you have feelings for him and then leaving him? You're better than this!'

'I'm sorry. I was wrong. I know that now.'

'Well, it's a bit late for that! Don't you think?' Grayson yells from somewhere behind me.

'Oh shit. Just keep quiet. Lilly. Please,' Collins whispers as he quickly gets to his feet.

Grayson's charging over to us, his furrowed eyes squarely on me.

'She's okay,' Collins nervously calls over. Grayson's stride doesn't waver. Collins places himself between us and tries to talk down Grayson who's clearly furious. 'She's been hurt. Grayson, please try and be-' He's slammed sideways onto the floor with a slight twitch of Grayson's hand before another word can be said.

'I can explain,' I say quickly, trying to get to my feet before he gets any closer, but I'm too weak. Too slow. He reaches me, bends down and yanks me to my feet. He doesn't look at me as he starts pulling me back to the house by my elbow. I pull down Collins' coat which thankfully reaches just above my knee.

'Is that hers?' he asks Collins, pointing at my bag he has tossed over his shoulder.

'Yes, but-'

'Give it to me.'

Grayson snatches it off his arm before Collins gets the chance to hand it over and carries on pulling me towards the rusty metal gate. I struggle to keep up, and with no shoes on, I stumble and wince as I walk over who knows what.

'Grayson...please let me go.' I try to prise his hand off, but he just tightens it and drags me on. 'Let me explain.'

As we emerge through the gate and walk onto the lawn where the damage from my fire doesn't seem to have reached, countless Nomads point large guns straight at me. I see Gabriel, sporting a fresh black eye, pacing up and down in front of them. What the hell was I thinking running off like that? I should have known he would get in trouble. When he sees me, he stops pacing and his brief look of relief goes as quickly as it came. It's replaced instead with annoyed exasperation. I definitely made the wrong call last night.

'She okay?' he asks Grayson as we get closer.

Grayson carries on walking past without answering.

'Where are you taking her?'

'I already told you,' Grayson says plainly as he continues dragging me behind him.

Where is he taking me? I look back at Gabriel who's staring at the floor with his fists clenched looking angry. Even he won't look at me.

'Gabriel, I'm sorry,' I call back as we pass. He looks up and watches us go. 'Please, please believe me. I never meant-' Grayson tugs me forwards.

'Quiet!'

'Grayson, wait!' Gabriel calls after us. With a look over my shoulder, I see he's running after us. 'Maybe you should take a second and calm down.'

'I am calm,' Grayson replies as his hand tightens. 'I am perfectly calm.'

He's not. He's angrier than I think I've ever seen him. I prefer the yelling to this.

'Grayson, please,' I pull against his grip, but he won't let me go. Collins is running after us now as we all make our way swiftly to the back door. 'Please let me explain. I didn't mean-'

'Where's your cuff?' he asks, looking at my wrist.

'I...I'm not sure. Listen-'

The patio door slides open from the inside and a Nomad steps aside to let us past. The kitchen's full of Nomads. They all look down at the floor as we pass.

In the hall, Amara lingers at the bottom of the stairs. She takes a step towards us but Grayson holds up his finger and she stays put. I expect to be taken into his office, but he carries on. To the front door. He kicks it open and continues to drag me on.

My feet hurt as I'm forced to walk over the gravel. I look back. Gabriel and Collins are following us, talking with each other quietly and looking worried. Beside us are two Nomads. One each side. Their guns loaded and ready to fire.

'Where are you taking me?' I ask, glancing at one of the many cars parked up.

'Exactly where you want to go,' he replies with a shrug. He sounds at ease, but his body language is anything but. I look up at him. His mouth's in a tight line and his jaw's rigid.

He walks past the cars.

'I don't understand.'

'No?' Finally, he looks down at me as he pulls me on by my elbow. His eyes drift to my bare legs. I pull down Collins' coat hoping I'm completely covered. His eyes flick back to mine. 'You want to leave, right?

'I did, but-'

'Then today is your lucky day,' he tells me, looking forwards and gesturing to the main gate. 'You're out.'

'What happened with the fire, it wasn't my fault!' I look between him and the gate. 'I didn't want to leave. I had to. For your safety. For everyone's safety.'

'And how did that work out?'

'I was jumped by a man. He wanted me to kill you, but I said no. Please, stop pulling me.' I dig my feet into the stones, but it does nothing to stop him. The closer I get to the gate, the more afraid I become that he's serious! 'He injected me with adrenaline. He knew I would lose control.' He doesn't stop. 'I was just trying to do the right thing!'

We reach the gate. Two men standing either side give a small bow in Grayson's direction.

'Open it,' Grayson orders. Pointing at the entrance.

'Please. Please, Grayson.'

The gate starts to open slowly. The whirring sound has my heart hammering and my magic begins to stir.

Not now, please not now.

Gabriel and Collins join us.

'Grayson. You can't be serious!' Gabriel says. 'She won't last a day out there on her own.'

As soon as the gate is wide enough, Grayson shoves me through it so hard I fall on my face.

'I am perfectly serious,' he replies. I get to my feet as he tosses my bag at me. I catch it and look at him. 'Close the gate.'

My chest tightens when the gate begins to close. I walk back towards them but stop when the Nomads point their weapons at me.

The gate closes with a clank, and Grayson stands close to the bars, looking at me with such disdain.

'I know you're angry,' I say in a forced calm, because, in truth, I'm freaking out. 'And I am truly sorry for leaving the way I did. It was a mistake. One I regretted before I even reached the wall. I shouldn't have gone. I regret it and I won't do it again. I'm sorry.'

I wait for him to say something. But he just glares at me. His lip twitching ever so slightly. Then, he turns and starts to walk away leaving me out here alone.

'YOU CAN'T DO THIS TO ME!'

He turns on his heel and storms up to the gate before punching it out of sheer anger. I jump back.

'I didn't do this to you!' He points at me. 'You did. I'll tell you what I *have* done. I saved your life. I took you from your uncle's house where you lived as a prisoner and brought you here to my home where I have tended to your wounds, fed you, clothed you and protected you from the threats that lie beyond this house, as well as the fears and demons you have inside your own head. I've offered you not only friendship but a family here. And all I have asked from you in return is to stay. To let us keep you safe and work with us to free our people from a life in the shadows. To save us all from certain death.'

'I panicked. There's so much violence here. John...the men yesterday...'

'You may not like how I have behaved, you may think my actions rash and cruel, but I have men, women and children I need to protect. To save. And to do that, I must sometimes be rash and cruel. I need you alive. Malcolm wanted you dead. Or worse, back with Toby. You die...we die. John grabbed you inappropriately. Do you think I should have let that go? You think a man should touch a woman without her consent?'

'No, but-'

'I don't tolerate abusers in my home. In my Coven. And I need you sane. Not Broken. So if I have to punish a piece of scum to stop him grabbing anyone else again, or to prove to you that you are safe from that kind of behaviour here, I will. A hundred times over.' He points at me through the bars. I have to flinch back so he doesn't poke me. 'Now let me tell you what *you* have done!

You have destroyed one of my bedrooms. Thrown Hendrix into a wall. Impaled Gabriel. Burnt Collins. Almost got your friends killed by a man who wants you dead all because you wanted to buy a Christmas tree, against my wishes I might add. And then, as we were spending every second of every day protecting you from Toby, you ran away as we all slept. You were ready to abandon us all to a life of hiding and persecution. Would you like to tell the Nomad mothers that their children may end up in the hands of Hunters all so you don't have to face your ex-boyfriend, you complete and utter coward?'

'I'm sorry-'

'Oh yeah, and you just burnt down my goddamn orchard that has been thriving for centuries! So, go. See how well you do on your own, bearing in mind of course, that you didn't even make it past the wall before some fool managed to nab you and use you to try and kill me. Because that's all anyone outside this coven wants for you. To use you as a weapon or to kill you.' He points down the country lane. 'Town's five miles that way.' He pulls out a couple of notes from his trouser pocket and tosses them by my feet. 'I suggest you get on a bus and keep moving, because if Hunters don't find you, Theo will. That's if Toby and his spies aren't already lurking out there watching you right now, just waiting for an opportunity to get you on your own like last night.' He turns and starts walking back to the house, but not before turning back to me. 'Oh, and do us a favour. If it is the Hunters that get you first, and when they start torturing you for information on any other witches or Descendants, keep our names out of it. You might want to just kill yourself if they do get their hands on you. Believe me when I tell you that you don't know pain till you've been in one of their interrogations. Good luck, Miss Hooper. You're going to need it.' He turns and starts to walk back to the house. Gabriel watches him go.

'You can't just leave her out there, Grayson!' he demands. But Grayson carries on walking away. 'Open the gate!' Gabriel looks at one of the Nomads. 'Let her back in.'

Grayson stops and turns.

'Anyone that opens that gate for her will find themselves joining her. If you so much as step foot beyond that gate, Gabriel, you will not be welcomed back. That goes for everyone. Do I make myself clear?'

'You need her! The spell-'

'To hell with the spell. I won't keep putting our people in danger for someone who doesn't give a damn about them, and she clearly doesn't.'

'That's not true-'

'She has no intention of helping us, Gabriel,' he says, raising his hand to silence me. 'She has no intention of doing the spell. Of saving us all from the death sentence we have for just being born. I have no time or resources to give to people who are selfish and cowardly. So like I said. If you want to go, brother, go. But don't bother coming back.' He waits, looking at Gabriel, Collins and all the Nomads in turn. When no one says a word and Gabriel remains still, Grayson nods and continues walking back towards the house leaving Gabriel looking between us.

Gabriel walks towards me. 'Open the gate. I'm going with her.'

Grayson's too far away to hear him, but Collins does. He grabs his arm and stops him.

'You go, you won't be allowed back. I know you care about her, but you're needed here.' Collins glances at me but avoids eye contact.

Gabriel pulls his arm free. 'She goes. I go. I won't abandon her. She'll be killed if I do. Open the fucking gate.' He walks up to the bars and rests his hand over mine with a perfectly lovely smile. 'I won't leave you. Never.'

'I won't let you destroy your relationship with your brother because of me. You leave with me, and we'll both be dead before the week is out.' My fingers entwine with his. Every time I've left these grounds or been without protection, I've almost died or got others killed. Enough.

'I'LL DO YOUR SPELL!' I shout past Gabriel.

Grayson slows to a stop in the distance, turns and folds his arms.

'Excuse me?'

'Let me back in, and I'll help you bring down the veil. I swear to you.' Gabriel lets go of my hand and steps to one side as Grayson strolls back.

'You'll do the spell?'

'I'll do your spell, Grayson. I'm on your side. I swear it. Please, let me back in. Give me another chance.'

'Will you try and run again?' he asks.

'No.'

'Will you do as I ask? Follow my orders?'

Reluctantly I reply, 'Yes.'

'You will wear another cuff with the binding spell?'

I nod.

'I'll let you back in.' I flood with relief. 'But, there's something else I want from you. Something that if you deny me, I will send you away.' The gate starts to open, and he steps aside.

'What do you want from me?' I ask nervously.

'I want you to prove your loyalty.'

I'm escorted back to the house and sat down in Grayson's office. It's been thoroughly cleaned and no one would know what had happened in here at all. Grayson's opposite me on the other side of his desk and I still have no idea what he wants me to do in order to prove my loyalty. Gabriel pulls up a chair beside me as Collins stands behind him. Both look uneasy, to say the least.

'There is more to the binding spell than just stopping a Witch using their powers completely.' Grayson opens his desk drawer and pulls out a black wooden box. He removes what looks like a bundle of dirty cloth. I notice a large first aid box sitting on the desk beside Collins. What's he going to ask me to do?

'This is a Bloodstone,' Grayson says, showing me a small, clear crystal he's unravelled from the cloth.

'A Bloodstone?'

'Yes. It's a stone used to pass control of when and where you can use your magic to another. If you make a Bloodstone with me for example, I decide when you use your magic but more importantly, when you don't. So, if I see you start to lose control again as you did a few hours ago, I simply will the magic inside you to stop by using the stone, and it will. I can also will it to return to you. Another advantage of making a Bloodstone with me is that I can use it to find you. Like a built-in tracking system. So, if someone gets their hands on you or you get lost, I can find you.'

'What if someone steals it from you and uses it to control me?'

'That's the beauty of a Bloodstone. For it to work, you must willingly give it to me, and it can only be used by the person you make it with. So, if I have the stone, and someone takes it from me, it will be utterly useless.' He slides it across the desk to me.

'What if I take it from you?'

'Then you can use it yourself.'

I pick it up to get a closer look. So, this is the Bloodstone he's been keen on making with me. Except for the way it's crystal clear, it could be any old stone. It's rough, unpolished and jagged. It's quite small. Much smaller than I expected considering the fuss.

'This is what you want me to do to prove my loyalty?' I ask him. 'You want me to make a Bloodstone with you?' Grayson gives a slight nod and sits back in his chair, watching me closely. 'How does it work?' I ask.

'The stone comes from a place called Tintagel. Tintagel was once a sanctuary for our kind. A castle built into the cliffs with its own village where witches lived in peace together. It was our home once upon a time. There is a phenomenon that occurs on very rare occasions. If an item or a place has been exposed to enough magic, it can contaminate it. Tintagel was the home of hundreds of witches for hundreds of years. All had magic, all had access to the Arcane Realm, and over time the land itself became a site of power. Certain stones beneath the ground became connected to the Arcane Realm. They became tools for witches to enhance or store their magic. There are countless ways to use these amazing little stones. But right now, this seems the best use of it.' He nods to the stone. 'This one was removed from deep inside the cliffs many, many years ago. It's the last one known to be in existence. The others were all used up in the war, destroyed by Hunters or simply lost. Tintagel is just made up of foundations and steps now. Humans destroyed it when they turned against us. Pulled it down and threw it into the sea.'

'What about the witches inside?' I ask.

'They slaughtered them all. Every last man, woman and child.'

Hearing that, after creating such a lovely image in my head of families living together in peace, children playing games with their magic out on display... I think my heart breaks a little.

'Places like Tintagel castle, sealed off to humanity, were safe havens. Humans didn't even know we existed. When we left these fortresses, we didn't use magic unless it was necessary. We never killed or hurt humans. We just shared their world from a distance. It worked. But then a few humans learned of our power, and they wanted it for their own benefit. They wanted Witches to fight their wars for them. We told them no. We didn't get involved in human affairs, and they didn't get involved in ours. That was the way of it. So, instead, they decided we were the enemy. They allied with their enemies, claiming that we were the real threat. They attacked our safe havens. They murdered us in droves. Destroyed our homes. Killed anyone who helped us and started the war between us.'

'But you survived.' I feel the tears in my eyes.

'We made difficult decisions to survive. And without the spell that preserves our age and helps us heal, we would all have died. We would never have been able to protect the Nomads. We never wanted to fight humans. We never wanted to kill anyone. They started this. We just wanted to live our lives freely. Without chains and without condition. I think you can understand that.'

'I get that completely.' I hold the stone in my hand and look at him. 'So you want me to bring down the Veil. Return magic back to all the Descendants. People like Amara, and then what?'

'When we have the power to defend ourselves, we'll approach the human leaders publicly, and make a guarantee that we mean them absolutely no harm. That we want this persecution to end and that we will stay out of their way if they stay out of ours. We own a few islands across Europe. They're secluded. We will relocate offshore. We don't want to fight anyone. We just want what's rightfully ours. Freedom. If they refuse us that right, and only if we must, we'll fight for it.'

Freedom. It's all I've ever wanted, and it's something I've never had.

'Why did the Veil get put up in the first place? Why would the witches willingly surrender their magic if they were in the middle of a war?'

'We didn't,' Gabriel sighs, folding his arms across his chest. 'The decision to put up the veil was made by our elders at the time. A small group of powerful Coven leaders. We didn't get a say in it. You know about Hunters, right?' As I nod, he continues. 'Well, before the war started for us, it was well underway for them. They were kidnapping witches in secret. Only a few, and from different countries so we didn't put it all together. But they were actually torturing them for information on our weaknesses. They took mothers and their children first. Can you imagine? "Tell me what I want to know, or watch your baby drown. Tell me what I want to know, or watch your children burn." They got their secrets. They got their information. They discovered the binding method and also, a way to detect magic.'

'Hunters are marked,' Grayson continues. 'Somewhere on their body is something similar to a tattoo. It's a long story on how each mark is created, but the gist is, the tattoo burns hot on the Hunter's skin when close to magic.'

'So when the Veil went up and cut off the Descendants magic, they couldn't detect who was a witch, and who was human,' Gabriel concludes. 'Rebecca Hooper promised that when the time was right, when we had rebuilt our numbers and hidden ourselves amongst the humans successfully, perhaps even created a truce, that the Veil would be removed and we could return to our way of life again. But she died soon after the spell was done, leaving the way to manipulate the Veil written in her journal. We have tried to create peace. But the humans kill anyone who approaches them to try and create a treaty. And Hunters are still active today, with their tattoos. They can't detect the Descendants. But they would detect us if they got close enough. Truth be told, if the Veil hadn't been put up, we would all have died centuries ago. But this was never meant to be permanent.'

'But Hunters will still try and kill us all!' I know that and I've never even seen one. The fear in my uncle's eyes at the mere idea I was discovered, and what it would mean for them, was undeniable. Not much scared Harry. But they did.

'Once we are back to our full strength, they won't be a threat. We definitely outnumber them now. And when we're at our full strength, we will show them that we mean them no harm. That we could start and win a war. But we won't. We'll make sure they know we just want to be left alone. The problem is keeping us and what we are doing, quiet, because if they find out about us now, we will be no match for them. We will all be killed. Us and the Descendants. Anyone who has had contact with us will die.'

Hearing this, I'm ready to practice. I'm prepared to accept what I am. It'll be hard. I'm sure. But I want to be better. I want to start living. There's nowhere else I can be myself or have the chance to learn who exactly I am other than here.

'Okay. How do we do this?' I ask handing back the stone to Grayson, ready to do what needs to be done.

'Only one type of witch can make a Bloodstone. A witch with Sensativa. So you'll have to do this spell for me.'

'I have no idea how to do it.'

'I'll walk you through it. It will be made with my blood and your blood. Our link. I need you to give your blood to me voluntarily.' He pulls out a knife and places a large bowl by my feet.

My eyes widen in shock. 'That's a big bowl!'

'You have to cut, and willingly give your blood to me otherwise it won't work. If you want control back, just take off the cuff, and the link will be severed. The stone only works with the binding spell words. No one else can use it, only the one whose blood made it, and you have to be the one to give or take the stone. No one else can control who uses it but you.'

'And only you will be able to control it? My magic?'

'Yes. Whoever adds their blood will be linked to you.' Whoever? I look at Gabriel who throws me a less than convincing smile as he sits on the edge of his chair.

I get an idea.

Grayson cuts across his palm and squeezes out about half an inch of blood into the bowl then hands me the knife.

'Your turn.'

I take it and hand it to Gabriel who stares at it in stunned silence.

'You...you want me to add to the link?' he says finally.

I nod.

'I don't think that's wise,' Grayson says, 'I'm more than capable of taking responsibility.'

'I know that,' I reply, trying to ignore Grayson's annoyed stare in my peripherals and the sharp edge to his tone. 'But it's the only way I'll agree to this.'

This is bigger than pride. It's about safety. Mine, as well as theirs. Having both of them watching my back feels better than just the one.

'I'm honoured,' Gabriel says clearly taken aback by my request. He slices his hand and adds his blood, ignoring Grayson's displeasure. Finally, I go to add mine.

'How much do you need?' I ask as I hold the blade against my palm.

Grayson stands and kneels in front of me, then guides it instead to my wrist. 'We need a lot.'

'You want me to slit my wrist?' I say, horrified. 'I'll die!'

Collins opens the first aid box and starts pulling out bandages. I look at them all in turn.

Is this a trick?

Gabriel rests his hand on my knee. 'You can do this. We'll make sure you're alright. I promise.'

I close my eyes and hold my breath before sliding the sharp edge across my skin. The coldness of the metal disappears and is replaced instead with warm, thick blood. My heart gets quicker and quicker with every minute as the red liquid trickles freely into the bowl. When are they going to stop it?

I open my eyes. Grayson's watching it intently, but Gabriel's watching me.

'I feel woozy,' I tell them. My head's getting fuzzy and I feel sick. I have to rest my head on Gabriel's shoulder.

'Take a deep breath,' he whispers. 'Almost there.'

'Okay, that's enough.' Grayson pulls away the bowl and puts it on my lap. Collins clamps a cloth down on my wrist and kneels beside me to start stitching me up. Gabriel holds my hand, but

I'm busy watching what Grayson does next. He dips a thick piece of wool into the blood and lays it on his desk.

'I will use this to make you another binding spell,' he says before dropping the crystal into the blood. He hands me a sheet of paper. 'Read this. But say two instead of one here.' He points to a section. 'And while you say the words, let your magic flow into the blood. Like you do when you create fire. But with your Sensativa instead.'

I do as instructed. 'Blood of one, given to another. Power of one shared with two. Et eas tradidit nobis.'

Slowly, the blood begins to disappear. It drains away until, in the bottom of the now empty bowl, sits the crystal. It's no longer transparent but a mix of black and deep red. The colours swirl like there's a rough storm inside it.

'There. All done,' Grayson says, clasping the Bloodstone. 'Even though I will hold the Bloodstone, it belongs to you. If you want to transfer the link to Gabriel, you have to take it from me and willingly hand it to him. We will be the only ones that can control when you access your magic.'

'But only when I wear the binding spell, right?'

'Right.'

That's it. I'm linked to the two brothers. They'll know where I am at all times. They'll control my magic while I wear the cuff and hopefully, I've proven my loyalty.

Grayson, still gripping the stone like it's some treasured possession, looks to his brother.

'Take her up to bed. She looks ready to pass out.'

'Sure thing.'

'And then come back downstairs.' Gabriel nods, Grayson continues to glare at him. 'I mean it. You come straight back downstairs.'

'I've got it,' Gabriel insists, frustrated.

As soon as he's out of sight, I cling onto Gabriel's hand making his fingers turn white as I will the room to stop spinning.

'Why ask me to make the Bloodstone?' he asks quietly. I glance at Collins who's still focusing on my wrist.

'Because I trust you. Why would you want to leave with me knowing that you wouldn't be welcomed back?'

He has a slight grin on his face which warms my heart.

'Because he's an idiot.' Collins finishes taping a thick layer of bandage around my wrist with a sweet smile.

They both help me to my feet.

'I'm sorry again,' I gesture to his burnt skin.

'I told you. It's fine.' He pats my formerly dislocated arm gently. 'How does it feel?'

'It aches,' I tell him, circling the stiff joint.

'What happened to your arm?' Gabriel asks, his eyes narrowed as he looks at my shoulder.

'Nothing,' I tell him, but Collins cuts me off.

'Whoever grabbed her, dislocated her shoulder. I popped it back when I found her. You need to keep it moving, or it will seize up.'

'You are really going through the wringer, aren't you?' Gabriel gently runs his hand over my injured shoulder before looking at my bare legs. 'Did they also take your clothes?'

'That was the fire. Jackass,' I reply.

'Hmmm. Lucky fire.'

'Make sure she keeps moving that arm,' Collins laughs. 'Now if you'll excuse me, I need to get some TLC from a gorgeous brunette and reassure her that everything's fine before she has an aneurysm from worry.'

'Thanks, Collins.'

'My pleasure.' He leaves the room with a smile.

'How are you feeling?' Gabriel asks, trying to put on a serious face. 'Really.'

'Like shit,' I say with a light laugh, trying to make the whole situation less dramatic. 'I really want to go to bed.'

Gabriel scoops me up in his arms. 'I've gotcha, Beautiful. Let's get you upstairs.'

'I can walk you know,' I protest sleepily.

'Yeah, but this is much more fun.'

He takes the stairs slowly, holding me close and looking at me occasionally as my eyes begin to droop. With each blink, we get higher up the stairs and closer to my room, until I feel the softness of my sheets being draped over me.

I snuggle my face into the pillow and close my eyes, too exhausted to stay awake. I stink of smoke and I'm still covered in ash, but I really couldn't care less. His lips on my cheek are the last thing I feel before I fall asleep.

It's six a.m. the next day when I wake up. On my wrist is a watch. An exquisite and probably costly piece, with a white leather strap and a mother of pearl clock face, encased with a diamond-studded rose gold frame. I can't feel my magic, and sure enough when I take the watch off, under the strap and hidden from view, is the blood-soaked thread carefully stitched into the leather with those familiar words.

Nexasanguinum.

I return the watch to my wrist with a sigh. This is most definitely Grayson's taste.

I shower off the stench of smoke, and go for a wander around the house in the quiet, trying desperately to rid myself of the memory of what transpired in Grayson's office. I bump into the odd Nomad here and there who give me polite nods as they stand guard. In the lounge, I find Gabriel hunched over the piano, fast asleep. An empty bottle of whiskey lies on its side next to him. He shuffles slightly, mumbling something incoherently in his sleep. I reach out and stroke the hair from his face and slide a small cushion under his head before heading back to the kitchen leaving him to sleep it off. I still can't believe he was about to come with me. I can't believe I was allowed back in the house after all the crap I've pulled and the trouble I've caused. I guess Grayson really is desperate to bring the Veil down.

Heading outside and across the lawn to the pool house, I'm followed by a chorus of, 'Morning, Miss Hooper,' as I pass various Nomads, all watching me like a hawk. They're everywhere. And they're twitchy. But the pool house is empty.

Perfect.

I walk around the water's edge and notice a music system in the far corner. It takes me ten minutes to figure it out, but soon enough music echoes around the room. I turn it up as loud as it will go and close my eyes. It's quick, fast-paced and catchy. I like it!

I start to sway before spinning and moving around the water, watching my feet and just thinking of nothing but the music. I lift my hands above my head, close my eyes and dance. I feel so much better after sleeping nearly all day and night. The hum of magic in the air gets stronger. I think about stopping, but I don't want to. The door opens and I hold out my hand. Gabriel takes it, wrapping his other arm around my waist he starts dancing with me.

'Get much sleep, Beautiful?'

'I think I was unconscious. Does that count?'

He shrugs. 'Dunno. Maybe.' He looks down at my wrist, eyeing the watch that sits where his cuff used to. 'Do you like your new binding spell?' I hear the slight tinge of annoyance in his otherwise innocent words.

'It's alright. Not very me.' The diamonds sparkle as they meet the light. 'I am so sorry I lost the one you gave me. Your mother gave it to you and I lost it.'

'This one's sparkly though.'

'I don't like sparkly. I much preferred the one you gave me.'

'Don't tell Grayson that.' He gestures to the watch but has a smug little grin. 'Twenty-four grand that cost him. I think he's hoping it'll impress you. Make you like him more or something.'

'Oh well, in that case,' I stop dancing. 'I better go and ask him to be my boyfriend. After all, it's a very pretty watch. Maybe if he throws in a pair of earrings, I'll even marry him,' I tease, letting Gabriel go. But he keeps hold of my hand, spinning me back into his arms as I laugh.

'Ha ha. Very funny,' he says, rolling his eyes.

'Did he say anything about you staying with me?'

'Only with his fists.'

The guilt churns away at me as I examine the black eye he's wearing.

'Don't. Don't you dare apologise.' He reads my mind. 'I wanted to stay. You wanted me to stay. Nothing even happened, and I told him that. He's just jealous because he fancies you.'

The idea of a man like Grayson fancying anyone seems unlikely. He seems more the possess and control kind of man. And I've had my fill of that, thank you.

'How'd you lot have all this money anyway?' I ask, changing the subject and curious to know how they can afford all the luxuries they have.

'We own a ton of companies all over the world.' He shrugs.

'Companies like what?'

'Well, we have our fingers in oil, technology, real estate, retail, and we have a few vineyards in France that make and sell very expensive wine. We've been around half a century. We're very good at making money. And Grayson has a brilliant mind for business. Plus, I can be very persuasive when needs be. Makes business negotiations very easy and very beneficial. Now, if you don't mind, I'm going to dance with you.'

He pulls me closer to his body so all of him is touching all of me and speeds up, leading me around the water's edge. We twirl. We spin. We laugh wildly as he manoeuvres me in ways I didn't even realise I could move, before dipping me low and pulling me back so my face is an inch from his. We're both out of breath, but I couldn't be happier.

He just smiles and looks down at me. His bright blue eyes staring at me through his dark hair.

'Thank you for the dance,' he says.

'Anytime.'

'By the way. Grayson's looking for you. He wants us both in his office.'

'You can't be serious!' Gabriel says with disbelief. 'She's not exactly had an easy couple of days. She needs rest. Not-'

'I agreed for her to visit the tree lot with you, and in return, she agreed to let you look into her memories. I agreed she could stay here with our protection, and she agreed to do the spell,' Grayson argues, sitting with his elbows on his desk. 'We need that journal. Toby has it, and she may well know where he went or where he hid it. But unless we look into her lost memories, we may never know.' He looks between us with an expectant expression, just waiting for either of us to argue. But neither of us do because he's right. I did promise.

'How do we do this?' I ask, dread filling every inch of me. I can barely look at Gabriel. And if he sees anything too bad while he's fishing around my head, he'll never look at me again. And what will we see? What happened in those six weeks?

We sit, cross-legged, facing each other on the floor as Grayson perches on a chair to the side. He watches us keenly, his focus a hundred percent on us. Gabriel reaches out his hands and settles them each side of my head.

'Close your eyes.'

I do.

'Focus on my voice. Try and empty your mind of anything else but my words. And relax.' There's a clock ticking somewhere in the office, but that's the only thing other than Gabriel's voice, that I can hear. Grayson's being as quiet as a mouse. I take a deep breath, relax my muscles, and try my best to close off.

'I want you to think about an event in your life that you want to share with me. A happy memory. Something that makes you smile. Can you do that?'

'Anything?'

'Anything. But preferably a memory that doesn't involve me.'

Hmm. I can do that. I close my eyes and think of my mum. Of her reading to me as I fall asleep.

'Got it?'

'Got it.'

I feel a sudden pressure in my head, like my brain's too big for my skull, but it doesn't hurt. It's uncomfortable and feels wrong. But there's no pain.

'That's it,' Gabriel soft voice fills my ears. 'Don't fight me. It will hurt if you do.'

I take another deep breath and amazingly, my memory plays out in front of me like a movie. And I see things, hear things, that I'd completely forgotten she did. She takes a strand of my hair and twirls it between her fingers. I forget she used to do that.

'Your mum looks just like you,' Gabriel tells me. She did. Except for her hair. Mine's the same red it is now, but hers is a light brown. I always think of her looking so young and sweet. But in my memory I see her looking tired, weary and a little sadder than I recall.

'Okay...' Gabriel breathes. 'Now, I want you to think of Amara, and something that she did that made you laugh.' That's not hard. We're taken to the tree lot, and she wraps tinsel around us both. But that makes me think of Theo and suddenly I'm on the floor as he pins me down watching as he slams my head into the ground again and again. The terror I felt then, hits me just as hard now. And brings up more memories of him. Of him smashing down the door to my mum and dad's cabin and striking my mum as he sets murderous eyes on me. The memories start to snowball, I gasp and pull away from Gabriel's hands which cuts off the link. That was far too real. And judging by the look on his face, it was a little too real for him too.

'You alright?' Grayson asks, looking between us.

'Fine,' I insist, trying to calm my heart rate.

'She got a little distracted,' Gabriel tells him, stretching out his hands. 'Ready to try again?'

Nodding, and more than reluctant, I let him try again.

'Close your eyes. Relax.' I feel his presence straight away. 'Okay, Lilly, I want you to think of a happy memory. With Toby.'

The slightest mention of his name conjures up anything but happy memories.

'I can't. Please-'

'Show me,' he insists. 'There has to have been something he did that made you smile.'

It takes a second, but I pull out a memory. Of him sitting on my bed at my uncle's house, with me on the floor between his legs. He's brushing my hair and working it into intricate plaits, as I hold one of the many history books that Mr Simmons charged me with reading. It's about the potato famine in Ireland. As he plays with my hair, he goes through in detail everything he knows about it. It was one of the most ordinary moments I experienced with him. He brought a box of chocolates with him, and every so often, he pops one into my mouth.

'When was the last time you saw Toby?' Gabriel asks suddenly. My brain reacts and instantly goes to my last memory of Toby. It's the quickest of flashes before I snatch my head away.

'Hey!' I bark angrily. 'That was a cheap shot.' He saw a glimpse. Toby screaming abuse at me, hurling my stuff around my bedroom as I stood there crying. He goes to the window, I fall to my knees and beg for him to take me with him. But he doesn't.

'I'm sorry,' Gabriel tells me. 'It's a nasty trick, I know, but catching you off guard brings honest memories to the surface, rather than selected ones that you want me to see.'

'What did you see?' Grayson asks.

'Not now,' Gabriel says firmly, not taking his eyes off me. He reaches out his hands once more. I lean into them, glaring at him furiously. This is horrible. I feel like I have no control whatsoever over what he's going to see. But I'm pretty damn sure that's the point.

'Close your eyes. Empty your mind. Now, tell me. Do you remember anything about the missing six weeks?'

'No.'

'Harry,' he says. Instantly, a memory of Harry raising his cane pops into my mind. As soon as he sees it, he says 'Christa.' A memory of her hacking off my hair.

'Gabriel, stop it.' I try to pull away, but he just tightens his grip.

'Simmons.'

A memory of Simmons sitting at his desk as I read a book on the floor.

'Amara.'

Her being punched by Theo.

'Grayson.'

Him grabbing me by the gate as he kisses me.

'Hendrix.'

Him leaning in to bite me down in the cellar.

'Toby.'

Him abandoning me.

'The Miller's barn.'

Oh no...

I'm on the floor, crawling like a beast, slipping and sliding across blood.

I pull away so hard, his fingernails scratch my skin. I'm on my feet panting as he remains on the floor.

'That was a hell of a memory,' he tells me.

'It's a nightmare,' I insist. 'Just a nightmare.'

'That's a memory, Lilly. You crawling in all that blood, that happened. If you remember that, and if you don't fight me, I can see the rest. I can get-'

'I don't... I'd rather...I don't think...'

'Grayson,' Gabriel looks at his brother. 'Give us a minute, will you?'

He sits, looking from him to me suspiciously. But he does. He leaves and closes the door behind him.

'Let me see.' Gabriel offers me his hand again. 'And hear me when I tell you that whatever we see, we'll face it together. I'm right here. And nothing will ever change how I feel about you.' He stands close. 'Trust me.'

I'm screaming. But not in fear. It's in complete, undiluted hatred.

My hair turns, from the roots to its tips. My eyes lose their colour and there I am. Broken.

I watch in horror as a version of me seals the double doors to the barn and butchers six men with my magic.

I set them on fire. I tear them apart. I impale them. Cut them.

Their screams and pleas for mercy do no good. I just destroy them. It's carnage.

And when the last man falls silent, and when there's no more blood to seep from their bodies, only then do I stop. I look at the butchery...and I laugh.

Behind me, someone stirs. They pull themselves up, rubbing their head and blinking the world back into focus.

It's Toby. He looks at the death surrounding him, and then at me.

'What have you done?' he whispers. 'You killed them...you...'

My fire erupts on my hands. My clothes and my body are dripping with thick, wet blood. And Toby looks terrified.

'Your turn,' I sneer.

'My turn?' he gasps, horrified, looking at his surroundings. 'Lilly, we were trying to help you! To save you!'

'Too late.'

He hurls a wave of fire at me, which I deflect using my own flames. The last thing I see is him disappearing out the door. When I try to follow, the river of blood has me slipping and sliding as I try to get to the door.

This time, it's Gabriel that lets me go.

The look on his face, it's beyond shock. It's fear.

My trembling hands cover my mouth as I stare at him horror-struck.

'Please tell me that wasn't a memory.'

'I'm afraid it was...' he says quietly.

'No. No-no-no-no.' I just shake my head and start backing away.

'Lilly, calm down-'

'I killed them!'

'It's alright-'

'I killed them all! How could I? Why would I? I'm evil.' I can't get my head straight. The images of those bodies, the feel of their blood on my skin, the way I laughed! He reaches out for me, but I jump back, frightened that I might hurt him. Ashamed, I don't deserve his kindness. I can't take it. No wonder Grayson keeps going to such lengths to keep me from losing control. I have to get out of this room. I throw open the door and sprint upstairs.

'What the hell happened?' Grayson demands as Gabriel calls my name. 'Gabriel, what did you see?'

'Well, she doesn't know where Toby is. The last time she saw him was at the barn.'

'The Millers' barn?'

'Yeah,' he sighs. 'It's there that she Broke. Her uncle was telling the truth. She did kill those men.'

Chapter 15

I can't seem to do anything but sit and stare at the wall. It's been a good couple of hours since I ran off to my room and no one has made any attempts to come and see me. I'm grateful. I need to try and get my head around this. I knew something awful had happened in those six weeks. I'd also had two years of Harry telling me I was a murderer. But seeing it like that, so real and violent...I was a monster.

There's a small tap at the door.

'Yeah?' I say less than enthusiastically.

I expect Grayson, maybe even Gabriel. But it's actually Collins who pokes his head around. He throws me a little smile.

'Can I come in?'

'Are you sure you want to?'

'Course. Is that your new binding spell?' he asks as he sits on my bed beside me.

'Yeah.'

'Nice. Very pretty.' He turns and faces me with an anxious sigh. 'Lilly, I wanted to apologise to you.'

'Why?'

'The way we met. How I was with you. The way I pulled you into your uncle's lounge. I keep having nightmares about it. The way you kept screaming. How afraid you were.' He buries his face in his hand and shakes his head. 'I am so sorry. I had no idea what had happened to you. I had no idea-'

'Hey,' I lower his hand and shake my head. I even keep hold of his hand as I face him. 'You didn't know me. And you were just doing your job. I don't hold that against you.'

'I hurt your aunt. I want you to know, I didn't *want* to do those things.'

'Grayson was ordering you. I know that. I know how it works here and plus, the bitch really deserved it. She was a horrible woman.'

'All the same, I need to apologise. And if my actions have affected your thoughts of me, I would really like to make it right.'

'Has what Gabriel told you affected how you see me?' I ask nervously.

'How did you know he told me?'

'Just a guess.'

There's nothing but kindness in his tone. 'I can't pretend to understand what you've been through. And no one knows exactly what happened to you in that barn, but whatever it was, it's in the past.'

'I killed them, Collins.' I try not to cry. 'I butchered six men.'

'And I am certain that there was a reason why. You're not a monster, Lilly. You're not a bad person. I know that you helped Amara with her dad. I know that you would also sacrifice your happiness to keep my stupid best friend safe. That's you. The Broken version of you, that's not you.' I shake my head, not believing him one bit. It was me. I did it. 'You suffered a serious trauma. We're talking something so bad that you literally couldn't cope with it. The Break is not your fault and what happened after isn't either so please, please don't do this to yourself. I'm begging you. The past is the past. You can't change it. And for the record, not a single one of us thinks any less of you or feels anything but admiration and respect for you. You've survived hell, and you're still an angel.'

'You really think that?'

'I know it.'

I wrap my arms around him and give him the biggest hug, which he returns tenfold. I knew I saw a kindness in his eyes the night we met.

'Thank you, Collins. I needed to hear that. And of course I don't hold how we met against you. If you hadn't have forced me into that room, I'd probably be dead.'

'And I really needed to hear that. Thank you, Lilly. How's your shoulder today?'

I circle it. 'Stiff. But bearable.'

He lets go and grins at me. 'You might want to come downstairs. Gabriel, Amara and I wanted to do something to cheer you up.'

'Amara knows about the memory too?' I fill with dread.

'She does. And she thinks exactly the same as the rest of us. Come on.'

He leads me to the front door. Outside, Amara and Gabriel both get out of his car with enormous grins on their faces.

'Hey, Honey,' Amara chirps as she runs at me. 'I'm so glad you're okay.' She fusses over me, stroking my hair and looking at my face, checking that there's no lasting damage from my adrenaline episode. She then gives me a hard whack on my arm.

'Ow!' I rub my previously dislocated arm. 'What was that for?'

'That's for trying to leave.'

Behind her, Gabriel's completely obscured by a giant tree wrapped in netting.

'Ho, ho, ho,' he cheers in a deep voice as he heads towards us. All I can see are his feet beneath the enormous tree. I laugh heartily as he walks closer and stops in front of me. He peers around the side of it wearing a silly red hat with a thick white trim, and his eyes shine with excitement. The whole show has me in stitches.

'One Christmas tree as promised. Merry Christmas, Beautiful.'

'Oh!' Amara squeals. 'I'll get the decorations.' And off she goes, grabbing Collins and loading him up with boxes from the boot. If she chose them, they're going to be bright! It takes me a few seconds to realise that Gabriel's still watching me with that stunning smile of his.

'About what you saw-'

'Forget about it. We knew that it wasn't going to be pretty. Anyway, what do you think?' he asks, shaking the tree and determined not to dwell. I'm more than happy to oblige.

I step closer and peer around the side of the tree to see him better. The smell of the evergreen needles surrounds me and creates a feeling of nostalgia I didn't even know I had.

'I think that you are amazing, Gabriel Kendryk.'

He beams.

We're joined once more by a heavily loaded Collins and Amara.

'Come on! Let's get this tree up!' she orders, leading the way back inside. Gabriel throws the tree over his shoulder, and I watch them all make their way inside. What did I do to deserve these fantastic, understanding and forgiving people?

'We got a turkey,' Amara says happily, opening all the boxes and bags.

'And the rest,' Gabriel adds. 'We were in that shop for hours, fussing over decorations.' He gestures to all the boxes and bags littering the lounge. I open one and pull out a selection of coloured glass baubles. They're not pink. In fact, I don't see anything pink at all. They're all very classic and elegant colours. Reds, greens, white and gold.

'Well, what kind of five-hundred-year-old Witch doesn't own any Christmas decorations?' Amara mutters. 'Not so much as a piece of tinsel in this whole house. Here, I got this for you.' She tosses me a stuffed Santa with a hat matching Gabriel's. I press his belly, and he wishes me a merry Christmas and starts singing.

'What's all this?' Grayson laughs as he walks in, looking around at the chaos. 'Dear Lord, my living room's going to look like Santa's grotto, isn't it?'

'Yep,' Gabriel says, cutting the netting from the tree, letting the long branches spring free. 'There you go, girls. Have at it. My part's done. I'm going to make myself a drink and sit down.'

'Oh!' Amara says, raising her hand. 'Yes please.'

Gabriel looks at me. 'I'll get you a stiff one. You could probably do with it.' He winks at me before he leaves, letting Grayson make his way towards me. He takes the Santa from my hands.

'How are you feeling?' he asks.

'Like a monster,' I reply. My insides feel like they're squirming every time I think of that memory.

'Well, you're not. I know that whatever you did to them, they deserved. And until we know exactly what happened to you, and why Toby took you to that barn in the first place, there really is no point torturing yourself. So please, just stop fretting and enjoy your Christmas celebrations.' He hands back the teddy.

'When is Christmas? I've lost track.'

'Tomorrow is Christmas Eve.'

I look at Amara who's wrapping bright pink tinsel around Collins' neck, hysterical with laughter as they kiss and cuddle. Guess she couldn't resist the pink after all.

'I feel terrible about burning down your orchard,' I add with a good bit of shame. 'If there's anything I can do to make it right...'

'You can bring down the Veil. Other than that... I forgive you, so you can forgive yourself. It's done, and we're all moving forward. Okay?' He waits for me to give my nod. 'This will be the first of many Christmases together, and we're going to make them all as special as possible for you,' he adds, pecking my cheek. He's being so nice.

Gabriel appears and shoves a beer in my face. I take it and ignore the glare he's giving us.

'Do you like the watch?' Grayson asks, holding my hand and pulling back my sleeve to expose the sparkling accessory.

'It's stunning,' I tell him. 'But it's too much.'

Considering it's essentially a form of restraint, it's way too extravagant.

'No. It's perfect. It suits you.' His thumb traces along the rose gold edge. 'You will get used to having nice things. I'll make sure of that. Speaking of which, I have to pop out. I need to pick up your Christmas gift.'

'But I haven't got you anything!' I say, horrified. 'I didn't think we were doing gifts. And this watch is already so much!' Everything they've done for me and I didn't get anyone anything. 'Please don't get me-'

'Have fun decorating your tree, Lilly,' he calls as he leaves.

The room fills with Christmas music as the others start bellowing, *'I wish it could be Christmas every day'*. They get to their feet and start jumping around, screaming the lyrics in each other's faces and tangling each other in tinsel. Gabriel picks up a red piece and wraps it around me like a scarf.

'Let's get this tree looking as pretty as you.'

Armed with a box of silver stars, I stand at the base of the tree
and start hanging them from the lush green branches, careful
to space them equally apart as instructed by Amara. She's busy
hanging a garland with built-in electronic candles across the
fireplace as Gabriel and Collins are pretending to help, but really
just drinking. A song comes on, and I actually know it. My hand
stills mid-air as an image of my mother springs into my mind.
We're sitting at the base of my uncle's old willow tree at the far
end of his garden, wrapped in blankets. The grass is white and
hard with the morning frost, and our breath looks like smoke in
the air. My mum has me in her arms and she's singing.

O holy night.

The beautiful voice of the woman singing it now is nowhere
near as moving as my mum's. I close my eyes and see her so
clearly. Her long brown wavy hair. Her hazel eyes. Her pale skin
and delicate freckles. Apparently, my hair was once her colour.
But when my magic manifested, my hair turned red. That's what
she said anyway. That my hair meant I was special. I always
thought she meant as a person. But she must have meant as a
witch.

I hear her voice as if she's singing in my ear. *O holy night the
stars are brightly shining, it is the night of our dear Saviour's
birth. Long lay the world in sin and error pining, till He
appeared, and the soul felt its worth.*

I start to sway on my feet gently, from side to side, still
clutching the star as I play it through in its entirety in my head
until the song finishes. I open my tear-filled eyes. Only then do I
realise the room's fallen silent. When I turn, they're all watching
me.

'That was beautiful,' Amara whispers. 'I had no idea you could
sing like that.'

'I was singing?' I ask, embarrassed. They all look so moved by
my emotional display. 'My mum used to sing that song to me
when I was little.' I look at the small silver star in my hand. I

hang it up on the branch and admire the beauty of the tree even though it's only half finished. 'If she saw me now, if she knew what I'd done...she would be so ashamed of me.'

Gabriel guides me towards him, his arms settle around my waist in a most welcome hug.

'No, she wouldn't,' he says. 'And for the record, *we're* extremely proud of you.' We look up at the tree together. 'What do you think of your very first Christmas tree?'

I look up at him. 'I love it.'

The sun's gone down and the stars outside are not the only things twinkling. The lounge has been transformed with elegant lights, delicate decorations and festive charm. Amara and I are happily sprawled out on the sofa by the warm fire as Collins and Gabriel arm wrestle. Telling him he doesn't want to embarrass him anymore after beating Gabriel for the fourth time, Collins sits next to me and begins chatting away.

'Rock climbing, abseiling, bungee jumping...I love it all,' he tells me.

'I can't imagine anything worse than jumping off a cliff with nothing but a piece of elastic to save me,' I tell him, amazed that anyone would willingly do this...and enjoy it! 'But I suppose it's not as scary if you can heal.'

'Don't get any ideas, woman,' Gabriel says as he pushes himself off the sofa. 'After you set fire to our orchard, I think we can call it a day on your adventure sports.' He walks past, taking the empty bottle out of my hand. 'I'll get us all another beer.'

I glare at him as he goes. That was uncalled for. What's his problem?

'Something you should know about Gabriel,' Collins says, watching the empty door before turning back to me. 'When things frighten him, make him nervous or upset, he tends to come across as cruel or angry. The angrier he is, the more vulnerable he's feeling. And when it comes to Grayson, the opposite tends to be true. He has a smile that you just can't trust. Just remember that. I have a feeling you'll need to.' He pats me on my knee before getting to his feet. 'Food! We need food!' He follows Gabriel outside, so I settle my head on Amara's shoulder. I know that smile Grayson wears. I see it far too often.

'You're all Gabriel spoke about today. Lilly this and Lilly that. I think-' She stops talking when they both walk back in. Collins with a load of crisps and Gabriel with a bottle of whiskey and four glasses.

'Let's get this party started!'

The music gets louder, the laughing gets more intoxicated, and it's not long before we're all on our feet dancing around the tree. When Amara trips and lands on her arse, we all watch her lying in a heap giggling, before Collins scoops her up, laughing to himself.

'And I think we'll call it a night,' he says cheerfully while she tells him drunkenly that he's *"so pretty"*. 'Come on, you. Bed.'

It's just Gabriel and I left as her giggles fade up the stairs.

He makes his way over, taking the glass from my hand and putting it down on the table.

'Dance with me.'

His arm wraps around my waist, his hand slides into mine as he pulls me close. I lean against his chest and listen to his heart thumping as he settles his chin on the top of my head. I hold him tightly and feel so safe in his embrace. Slowly, he leads me around the base of our Christmas tree. I can't silence the raging argument I'm beginning to have with myself. I love how it feels in his arms. I want to stay in them forever. But the risks are still there. Toby. Grayson. Theo. And now...me. That monster that I know lives in me. As the song ends, I slow and pull away.

'I should probably go to bed,' I tell him, avoiding looking him in the eye. He leans down. His lips go for mine, but I move. So instead he plants a gentle, lingering kiss on my cheek.

'Sweet dreams, Beautiful. Thank you for the dance.' He waits for me to lift my head. When I do, he smiles. 'At your pace,' he says. 'Everything at your pace. Goodnight.'

With a small bow, he turns and leaves the room.

I can't seem to face the idea of going to sleep. I don't know who'll visit me in my dreams. With a shudder, I leave the Christmassy room and walk around the house in the dark, nodding to the odd Nomad still on duty.

I go into the games room and practice shooting pool. When I'm bored of that, I lean over the bar and take a bottle of whiskey before going into the Victorian conservatory to feed the fish. After, I head to the library.

The sheer size of this room and the number of books it holds still amazes me. I walk along, swigging my whiskey and stroking the bindings. The smell of these books is more intoxicating than any of the flowers in Grayson's giant greenhouse.

'Can't sleep?' Amara asks, closing the door and making me jump. She walks over to me in one of Collins T-shirts, her hair's a ruffled mess, but she smiles. I shake my head and offer her the whiskey. 'No...dear lord.' She actually gags. 'I've had enough. I've no idea how you manage it.'

The clock gives a small chime telling us it's three in the morning. 'Merry Christmas Eve, Amara.'

'Merry Christmas Eve, Lilly,' she says happily holding her arms open. We have a lovely hug. 'Is it okay?' she asks. 'When I hug you?'

'It's fine.'

We sit squashed up together on one of the sofas as I continue sipping the whiskey.

'Did Toby rape you?' she asks when I'm mid-sip making me cough and almost choke.

'Jesus. You don't hold back do you?' I could laugh at her bluntness. 'Where the hell did that come from?'

'I think I'm still pissed... did he? Is that why you don't like being touched? Is that what he did to you in the barn?'

'No. Toby didn't rape me. He did a lot of things, but that wasn't one of them. Can we talk about something else?'

'Sure.' She rests her head on my shoulder. 'Like what?'

'Tell me what it's like being a Nomad.'

'Hmmm, well, Nomads live off the radar. We don't own houses or pay taxes because we don't want to be traceable, and we don't want to live a human life. So we live in camps. Big tents or cabins set up on land owned by Gabriel and Grayson. We have running water and electricity, so it's not horrendous. But it's not the nicest. Towards the end of the war, after the Veil was put up, there were so few of us left. Grayson and Gabriel gathered all the survivors together and promised to protect them. Hunters knew the family names of the survivors even if they couldn't use their stupid tattoos. They also have their blood, and they use it to see if their prisoners today are related to the known families from half a century ago. If we get discovered, we'd all be carted off to the Hunters' cells and put to death. So, we live in secret camps. Each camp has a leader.'

'Billy?' I assume. She nods.

'Well, the leaders take orders from the brothers and pass them onto us. You have the men who are the muscle. They protect the camps and work for the brothers. And then there are the women. We fall under one of three categories. A fighter, a wife or a breeder. We get to choose what we become.'

'A breeder?' I can't hide the disgust in my voice, and her expression mirrors it back completely. 'Why would anyone choose to be a breeder?'

'Witches are born with access to one or two realms of power usually. It was very rare to have more. Except you, born with the lot. The Hoopers always had multiple realms of power and all Arcanes have been Hoopers, so your bloodline is gold dust. Some realms of power are more desirable than others. Elemental and Mental are good ones to have. Sight too. If for example, I was keen for my child to have a specific realm of power, I would find a man whose bloodline has it. So, if Collins and I had a kid, they would have Physical or Telekinetic magic because that's what Collins and my ancestors had. The Jaynes tended to be Telekinetic so either way, it's a good match. Breeders just want to produce as many kids as possible with as many realms of power as possible. So they may end up with seven kids with different dads and an extremely powerful brood when the Veil comes down.'

'That's vile.'

'You're telling me!' she huffs. 'Then you get wives. The women that marry young and look after the men and the camp. Men at the camp don't do cooking or cleaning. They work for Grayson or sit about drinking, so they would probably starve to death if left to their own devices. And then there are the fighters. They work for the brothers and protect the camp. My mum was a wife. She wanted me to be a wife too, so when I came of age - thirteen, by the way - Mum and Dad wanted me to start looking for a potential husband.' She shakes her head as she recalls a memory that makes her scoff in disgust.

'Dad took me to this social thing at a beach a few miles away. They lit a big fire, played loud music and got hammered. I remember sitting at this campfire freezing my ass off as these teenagers all got drunk and started trying to flirt with me.' She shudders and rolls her eyes. 'After a couple of hours of telling them all to piss off, I went looking for Dad, but couldn't find him. So I just went home.'

She goes quiet and her eyes sort of glaze over. A look of horror washes over her face, and her voice changes into an unrecognisable, hollow version of itself. 'I turned up and saw my dad with my two uncles, standing outside a flaming mess where our tent used to be. They were just standing there watching as everyone else tried to put it out.' She looks me in the eye as tears start to fall down her pale cheeks. 'My mum and little sister were inside. They didn't make it out.'

'Oh, Amara,' I take her hand in mine and squeeze. 'I am so sorry. I had no idea!'

'I saw him smile, Lilly. Dad was smiling as they burned.'

'Why would he be smiling?'

'I found out a few years later that she'd been with another man. My sister wasn't his. I confronted him, but he denied he did anything. After the fire, he was unbearable. He would get drunk and hit me. Accuse me of being someone else's child and called me useless because I was fifteen, not married, not knocked up and not training with the men. I didn't fit in. I hated all of them, but with no money and being the last female in my family, I couldn't leave. Not without a fight. One I wouldn't win, so instead, Dad tried to offer me to men for money.'

'Jesus, Amara!' I gasp. She's such a happy and upbeat woman. How can she be this sane and rational after all that?!

'I knocked out the first guy he tried to sell me to with a bat. That's how I met Collins. Because I struck a man and violence wasn't tolerated between camp residents, they called for Billy to pass punishment. Collins just so happened to be with him, and when I explained why I did what I did, I was forgiven. Collins made it clear that prostitution and forcing sex on anyone wasn't tolerated and the consequence would be death if it happened again, so that was that.'

'What did he do to your dad and the guy who tried it on with you?'

'He punched Dad so hard he didn't get up for two days. And then he broke every single one of the guy's fingers,' she laughs. 'Collins and I started dating soon after. There's no pressure to be anything but myself with him. I don't need to pop out a dozen kids or do his laundry. I'm not told to protect the camp or run errands for the brothers. I can just be me, and the best thing is... he's happy just being with me. Just as I am.' She sighs a content little sigh like it's a weight off her chest, before looking at me. 'So that's my story.'

'I can't believe you went through all that. You're a hell of a woman! No wonder Collins adores you.' She beams when I say that, but it soon fades as she looks me in the eye.

'I don't have any friends. I never have. Not until you. I don't fit in with the people back home. They all think I'm stuck up.' She takes a deep breath and lets out a relieved sigh. 'Talking about it feels good. Therapeutic. You should try it. Maybe talking about your past will help with your nightmares.' She takes my hand and gives me an encouraging smile.

'Okay,' I say with a deep readying breath. I can't make myself worse I guess. 'But this goes no further. Everyone looks at me like a victim enough. Promise?'

'Promise.'

'Well, I lived with my mum and dad in this little cabin somewhere. I don't remember much about it except it was surrounded by trees. There was a small lake at the back of the house. I would paddle in it with my mum, while my dad would catch fish.' I smile fondly at the memory of my young life. And wonder how different everything would have been if we could have kept hold of that.

'I always remember the smell of rain and rotting leaves, but not in a bad way. It's a lovely smell. Natural. At night, we'd sit by a fire, and they would tell me stories. Mum had this book that she absolutely loved. *"Grimms' Fairy Tales."*. She would read them aloud to my dad and me. One day, while my dad was out, Theo came to the cabin. He forced his way in and tried to get to me, but Mum wouldn't let him. He got so angry as I cowered in the corner. He struck my mum, knocking her to the floor. And I just lost it. I manifested my first realm of power and sent a carving knife at his head without touching it. It sliced across his cheek, and when he was down, Mum grabbed me and we ran. I never saw my dad again.'

'Where did he go? Did he run? Did he-'

'I thought Theo may have killed him, but I don't know for sure. Theo said he was still alive but...I don't know. Mum took me to Harry's house and spent over an hour begging him to let us in. He did finally. He put us up in the attic together and barely spoke to us. We were there maybe three months before she died. Harry said it was my fault. He said I lost control of my magic and killed her, but I don't remember that at all. What I do remember is it was New Year's Day. We watched fireworks out of the attic window before we went to sleep. When I woke up, she was dead on the bathroom floor with her head caved in. I was five.' I look at Amara expecting to see judgment or disgust, but I don't. I see horror and pain. Sympathy even. 'I don't think I killed her. If I did, it was an accident. I loved my mum.'

'Of course you did!' she insists as if the idea I didn't is absurd.

'She was great. Really fun and extremely loving. But Harry always said she was unhinged and a lunatic. I never believed him. Considering how he treated me...he was the lunatic. After that, Harry let me stay in the house. I was a risk. If anyone found out that I was a witch and related to him, we would all have been taken by the Hunters. So instead, he kept me in the attic. Suppose he didn't have the guts to just kill me. When he put the binding spell around my wrist, I was allowed downstairs, but always supervised. He hired Mr Simmons. An ex-army man. His job was to keep me in line and keep me out of the way. Simple enough really. I knew never to take the spell off. The pain Harry would inflict on me was never worth it.'

'Mr Simmons gave me a routine which we followed every single day. Up at seven, breakfast at eight. At nine I was taken into the library for lessons which ended at four. Ten past four was dinner, eaten in my room. Last night's leftovers, if there was any. If not it was bread and water. The attic door would be locked at four fifteen and not unlocked again until eight the next morning. If I needed the toilet...tough. The attic had no insulation, and the window was nailed shut. In the summer, I would be dehydrated and exhausted from the heat. In the winter, I would get sick from the damp and cold. One year I got pneumonia. Mr Simmons snuck me in some antibiotics. He was docked three weeks' salary when my uncle found them, and I got ten lashes and a weekend in the garden shed with a bucket and one of the dog's old blankets. Harry believed he could beat the disobedience out of me. Not that I was ever disobedient. Not really. Sometimes I got so hungry I would have to steal food from the kitchen. If he caught me, I got lashed. If I got under his feet...lashed. If he got drunk and angry... lashed. He used his belt most of the time. Sometimes his fists and on the rare occasion his walking cane.'

'Didn't your aunt try and help you?'

I laugh at that. 'No. Once, when I was eight, my aunt got this god-awful haircut. I laughed. So she cut mine off out of spite. One year she put on all this weight, and Harry told her she was turning into a fat pig. She asked me if I thought she was fat. I said yes, so she made me eat a block of butter. Totally worth it.'

'Bloody hell,' she says under her breath.

'So that was every day. The same thing over and over. I think if things had just carried on like that I would have been okay. Yeah, I got beaten. I hurt. I was lonely but otherwise...yeah, I think I was okay.' Now my eyes glaze over and the horrified look that was on Amara's face a few moments ago is now on mine.

'And then, along came Ryan.' I haven't said his name in years. It feels like there's barbed wire in my throat as I do.

'Who's Ryan?'

'A boy my uncle hired to do some work around the house. He found out I was a witch and blackmailed me.' The floodgates seemed to have opened, and it actually feels good to say these things out loud. To someone I trust.

'What did he want?' she asks.

I take a breath, ready to tell all about the young boy, Ryan. 'He... well he...' But the breath seems to get stuck in my lungs. The words, trapped in my throat. She remains quiet, waiting with slightly furrowed eyes. 'Toby saved me from Ryan,' I tell her, not able to say any more on the matter. And she doesn't push it. 'He was so gentle and kind with me. He was the most stunning thing I'd ever seen. He said he would come back every day to see me and he did. Every day. When Mr Simmons would go to his room for lunch, I would go to see him down the end of the garden.'

'How did Toby save you?' she asks.

'He made Ryan disappear.' I shrug. 'Toby told me he had feelings for me soon after. He was sweet, kind, gorgeous.' I can't help but grin. He was like a piece of perfectly sculpted marble. My smile fades, because for all the beauty he has outside, inside he's as ugly as a person can be. 'But Toby manipulated me. Controlled me. Made me do things... that I would never have done. Things that I can never take back. Things I regret every day.'

'What sort of things?' she asks, sounding apprehensive. Her sweet expression, the "*You can tell me anything*" look, wouldn't be there if she knew.

'He has this way of making you think that he's right. That his madness and twisted logic makes sense. I was so lonely and empty. No one wanted me. Everyone hated me, but not Toby. The way he looked at me was unlike anything I'd ever experienced. He talked to me, wanted to know me, wanted to look after me, and after so much hurt, I clung to his attention like an idiot. I *had* to make him happy. I *had* to do what he wanted, or he might leave and I'd be alone again. It's what my life revolved around. Keeping Toby happy. Fucking pathetic,' I scoff at my own pitiful desperation. Hating myself and the words I'm saying. 'The first few months, he was gentle and sweet. He would sneak into my room with treats. Chocolates, cakes, whiskey. We would lie on my bed, side by side, and talk for hours. He never tried anything with me. But things changed when he saw me after one of my uncle's beatings. He said I was weak, but that he could make me strong. If I trusted him, he would teach me to be strong and unafraid.'

'How?' she asks, apparently unsure if she wants to even know the answer to that question.

'Harry would hit me, so Toby would hit me harder. He said if I could handle his beatings, I could handle Harry's. He started to teach me how to fight. We would sneak out to the end of the garden and practice punching, kicking, and soon he took off the binding spell and started practising magic with me. He was obsessed with getting another realm of magic to manifest and when he got my fire to come through, he was so thrilled. Our first kiss was during one of those lessons. In the dark under the moonlight beneath a giant willow tree. Very romantic. As the days and weeks went by, he wanted more and more. More kissing. More touching. But I hated the idea of him seeing my body. He started to get nasty. He wanted our relationship to be physical and the more I put him off, the less he would come and see me. I was just so bloody lonely. So empty. I would have done anything to keep him in my life. So finally, I agreed to let him see me with no clothes on. I agreed to let him touch me. And...it was nice. I didn't ever think that being with a man could be nice.' I give a shrug. And then I pull up my sleeves and let her see me. She traces her fingers along my marks and whispers a swear word. I lean forward and show her my back. Her sharp intake of breath is followed by her hand laying flat on my back.

'Oh, Lilly. You poor girl.'

I sit back and carry on. 'I thought that once he saw my scars, he'd think I was repulsive. That he wouldn't want me. But that's not what happened. He loved my scars. I mean...really *loved* them. They turned him on. He stayed with me, and I was just happy he didn't think I was ugly. How pathetic is that?'

'That's not pathetic, Honey. That's abuse! That's complete manipulation.' Her hand entwines with mine. 'Your scars do not make you repulsive. Not at all. What happened after that?'

'I gave him everything he wanted without any form of argument or reluctance. I just handed over my will. It didn't matter if I didn't want to do what he wanted. I had to do it. It was like a compulsion. The need not to be alone overtook everything. First, he wanted to see my body. Then he wanted to touch it. Then he wanted to add to the scars like he was marking me as his.' My hand rests on my inner thigh subconsciously. She sees the slight act, and I promptly move my hand away. But I can feel his *"mark"*. His handprint burnt into my flesh. Bastard. I didn't even put up a fight.

'Once, he snuck me out of the house in the early hours. He gave me this tiny little silver dress with no back and a pair of heels I could barely walk in and took me to a nightclub. On the dance floor, some guy touched me. It was harmless, but Toby didn't like it. He *really* didn't like it. He beat the guy half to death then pulled out a knife and cut his throat from ear to ear. I watched him lying in a pool of his own blood with this look of terror in his eyes, and I did nothing. I didn't try and stop Toby. I didn't try to save the guy. I just accepted it all. Toby took my hand and we ran out before the police arrived. Even though he pulled me out of there quick, he wasn't afraid. I remember how funny he found it. As we ran away, he couldn't stop laughing. He told me that he would kill anyone who ever tried to touch me and that he would never let anyone hurt me again. No one had looked out for me like that, and instead of being horrified, I just felt lucky that I had someone who loved me that much.' I take a second, hating the feeling of loss that suddenly washes over me. I'll never be loved like that again. Not now. Not if he's coming after me. I miss it. A bit. 'What's a bit of pain compared to that, Amara? What's a broken finger or a black eye to the feeling of utter love and devotion? Of protection and passion? Why did I love him when he enjoyed hurting me so much? Why did I put up with the humiliation, the manipulation and the fear he would inflict on me?' I hear the words, and for the first time I know the answer. 'Because without him I was nothing. I was empty. I felt no joy, no excitement, no hope for the future. I felt nothing! I would take fear and pain with a little bit of love over nothing any day. When I finally felt confident enough with our relationship, I asked him to help me leave my uncle's house. Help me set myself up so I could live without being found by Hunters or Harry. He said no...and left me.'

'Why? Why wouldn't he help you?'

I shrug because I still have no idea.

'I remember him leaving and then...nothing. I woke up six weeks later in the cellar where I stayed for two years. Till Grayson, Collins and Hendrix found me. Harry said I killed six men in those six weeks, in a barn. He said my hair turned white and I was an unrecognisable monster. I thought that this recurring nightmare I had was just that. A nightmare. But it's a memory. I killed those men.'

'Something awful happened to you in those six weeks, Lilly. So awful that you Broke. And when you think of everything that you've been through you have to wonder...What the hell could have happened to you that was worse than all that?' She's completely understanding and calm. How? Why are they all being so nice?

'Part of me wishes that I could find Toby and get some answers. Especially since he was the last person I know who had the journal they're all so keen on finding. And another part of me wants to run and hide.'

She exhales deeply, puffing out her cheeks as everything I've said sinks in.

'You need to stay as far away from Toby as possible,' she says. 'If Grayson wants to find him and that book, then he can find them himself.'

'Do you think they're only interested in me because I'm a Hooper?'

'What do you mean?'

'You said it yourself. Hooper blood is gold dust. If the Nomads are as obsessed about bloodlines as you say, wouldn't Gabriel, Toby and Grayson want the best?' I wait as she thinks it over. 'Do they have kids?'

'Not that I'm aware of.'

'That's a little odd, isn't it? Why do you think that is?'

'Well, Collins says he doesn't want kids until the Veil's down. If we had a kid together now, for example, he'd be stuck at the age he is and be forced to watch his child and his partner grow old, get sick and die. He says he couldn't bear that. When the Veil's down and we're safe, reconnected to the Arcane realm, he says he wants to undo the spell. You're a Sensitive. You can undo the spell he did with the others that keeps him young. Maybe Grayson and Gabriel feel the same, which is why they don't have any kids. Or maybe they do have kids. I have no idea. But I doubt that Gabriel is thinking about that. Grayson...maybe. But not Gabriel. I have never, ever seen him care about a girl the way he cares about you. And I can see it as clear as day that you have some serious feelings for him.' She sits and looks at me with a solemn face. 'You spent the first twenty-two years of your life miserable, Lilly. I think you have earned a shot at being in a happy relationship. Don't you?'

Chapter 16

'**M**orning.'

I sit up too fast, surprised to hear Gabriel's voice. He laughs as I pull my duvet up around my neck and groan. 'Here. I made you a coffee. Thought you might need it after the bottle of whiskey you and Amara polished off last night.'

'Thank you.' I take it gratefully and drink it down. He gestures to the end of the bed where there are several bags heaped up in piles, as well as boxes. 'What's all that?'

'Well, I couldn't sleep, so I did some online shopping last night. You don't have many clothes, especially since you accidentally set fire to them all the other night with your nightmare. So I brought you some. An amazing thing, online shopping. You click a few buttons and someone delivers what you want to your door a few hours later.' He looks thrilled as he gets to his feet and tosses me one of the many, many bags. 'Jeans. Long sleeves. Boots. And just a few dresses. If there's anything you don't like, or that doesn't fit, let me know and I'll change them for you. But...' he looks to his feet but has the cheekiest grin ever. 'Can you still wear that?' he asks, nodding to the top I'm wearing. 'I love that you sleep in my clothes.' I lower the duvet and he's right, I'm sleeping in one of the tops he lent me my first day here.

'You didn't have to do this.' I'm so taken aback by his kindness.

'No. But I wanted to.' He gives a small bow and doesn't hide how happy he is as I smile. 'Merry Christmas Eve, Beautiful.'

Tomorrow is Christmas Day. I can't leave the house. Not without putting everyone at risk, so I spend the day crafting gifts. And I craft hard. Growing up, I spent a lot of time on my own, trying to find ways to entertain myself. Turns out, I'm rather good at making trinkets from not much at all. So that's what I do. By the end of the day, there are four little presents wrapped beneath the tree from me to my friends. Yep, that's right.

Friends!

One for Amara. One for Collins. One for Grayson and one for Gabriel. Then I spend the evening doing something utterly amazing. I sit in the lounge with them all having fun. Playing board games. Watching films. Drinking mulled wine and eating a ton of chocolate. Everyone is super relaxed. Even Grayson. There's no magic talk. No Nomads bursting in with a drama. No blood. It's just...normal.

We end the night watching A Christmas Carol. And as everyone starts to fall asleep on the various armchairs and sofas, Gabriel, who's sitting beside me and sharing a blanket that covers both our legs, slides his hand into mine. No one else can see. Not that anyone is even awake. Not even Grayson who has had his fair share of whiskey. His fingers entwine with mine and mine with his. He has such a lovely smile as he looks at me. And I feel perfectly happy too. We continue watching the film, hand in hand. And I fall asleep with my head on his shoulder.

'MERRY CHRISTMAS!'

I'm greeted with a more than enthusiastic chorus as I walk into the kitchen the next morning. Everyone holds up a glass of champagne and beams at me as I'm adorned with a Santa hat and a glass of champagne for myself.

'Merry Christmas,' I laugh, holding up the flute before we all take a sip.

'Right!' Amara says, 'You two have a dinner to cook. I know you said that you would do it, but I just want to go through a few things before you start. No one wants to be ordering a pizza on Christmas Day.'

Gabriel stands next to me as we listen to Amara's instructions about turkey and vegetable timings. I'm too busy picking at peanuts, pretzels and orange chocolate slices to pay much attention.

'Hey!' Gabriel calls over, throwing a tea towel at me. 'Head out of the clouds and fingers out of the chocolate. We have a dinner to cook and Amara's instructions are confusing the hell out of me.'

She goes through it all with me instead. It all seems simple enough. When she leaves, we get to work.

'I like your dress,' he says, nodding to the knee-length red dress with long lace sleeves.

'Why thank you. I was given it as a gift.' I grin.

'Well, whoever bought it for you has excellent taste.'

The day is perfect in every way. We eat, drink and play cards together. Except for Hendrix, who lurks in the corner watching the festivities from afar. And the Nomads, who continue their silent patrolling. We all go outside to watch Collins give Amara a bright pink beetle, and in their moment of absolute bliss, Collins takes her face in his hands, looks straight into her eyes and says,

'I love you.'

With tears of joy, she says, 'I love you too. Completely.'

'Now,' I say nervously as I hand out my gifts. 'I had one day, no money and could only use what I could find. So forgive me for their.... well...crapness. I hope you like them.' I shrug.

'With everything that's happened, I would have thought gifts would have been the last thing on your mind,' Collins smiles, taking the small envelope I hand him. He opens it and looks at me with a *"She's crazy"* kind of look.

In his hand is a small picture.

'It's St Bernard of Menthon,' I explain, gesturing to the hand-drawn picture.

'And who's he?'

'He's the patron saint of travellers. Specifically, climbers. If you carry this with you when you go rock climbing or abseiling, he'll protect you.' I shrug, knowing it's rubbish. But it's all I could think of.

Amara takes the drawing and looks at it.

'You drew this?' she asks, her eyes scrutinising my work as I nod. 'Bloody hell,' she hands it to Gabriel who nods approvingly.

'That's impressive, Lilly! You have a real talent.'

As he hands it to Grayson to look at, I give Amara her gift.

'Holy hell!' she gasps, unrolling the large sheet I hand her. It's a hand-drawn map of the constellations I can remember and where to see them in the world.

'You enjoyed stargazing with me so I thought you might like it.' I wait nervously, but she absolutely beams at me.

'It's such a thoughtful gift!' she says. 'This must have taken you ages!'

'Do you like it?'

'I love it!'

I hand Grayson his gift.

'It's a bookmark.' He suddenly notices and smiles. 'With one of the flowers from my greenhouse pressed into it. It's lovely, Lilly. Thank you.'

But it's the gift I've made for Gabriel that I'm most nervous about. He opens the wrapping paper and holds it up with silent awe.

'Ohh...Lilly,' he gasps. 'It's beautiful.'

It took me hours to get right. It's a necklace made of dark string with a handmade pendant. I found the smoothest black pebble I could and used a small chisel to carve an image of angel wings onto it.

Gabriel...like the angel.

I used to do it at Harry's. I made quite a collection. But this one is my favourite by far. And the detail I managed to create is truly something special. Because he's special.

'You made this?'

'I did. Do you like it?'

He slides it over his head and beams at me. 'I love it!'

Amara has bought me a new pair of Dr Marten boots that lace up my calves, telling me, 'I know they won't replace the ones you lost the other night, but I think your mum would definitely have approved of these.'

I pull her into a hug and tell her I love them.

Collins has bought me a lovely leather jacket which I'm positive Amara chose, and then Gabriel hands me his gift. Well, gifts. The first is a small box wrapped in bright blue wrapping paper. I can't help but notice that it's the exact same shade as his eyes. I almost don't want to rip it. But the excitement has me tearing at it.

'What's an iPod?' I ask, reading the words on the white box. Gabriel takes it from my hands and opens it up. After a moment of fiddling, I have an earbud in my right ear and music playing just for me.

'I've loaded it up with hundreds of songs for you,' he says, handing me back the small square device. 'As well as audiobooks so you can listen to them while you go to sleep.' His fingers linger on mine ever so slightly. Then he hands me his second gift. It's larger than the iPod and this time wrapped in red wrapping paper. Almost my exact hair colour. I open it up and stare at the gift in amazement.

'Oh...Gabriel. This is...it's...it's amazing.'

In my hand is a book. But not just any book. The most important book in the world. Well, to me anyway. The crimson of the cloth-bound hardback is a little faded, and the edge of the spine is a bit thin, but the gold lettering and illustrations across the front are pristine. I open it up, and except for the doodles I added as a child, the book could be my very own.

The Brothers Grimms' Fairy Tales, illustrated by Arthur Rackham.

It's the same as the one I lost at my uncle's home. Inside are all the stories my mother would read to me before bed. My fingers gently feel the pages as I lift them to my nose. It smells like an old book. A well-used, musty smell. To some, it would be repugnant. But to me, it's my mother's arms around me as we revisit the story of Cinderella for the hundredth time. My absolute favourite. Tears prick at my eyes and a lump forms in my throat as my longing for those embraces and sweet kisses goodnight weigh heavy on my chest. But in a good way.

'I'm sorry,' Gabriel says worriedly. 'Is it wrong? Was it a bad idea? I just thought...when you told me about how your mother used to read it to you...I thought you might...shit. I fucked up. I'm sorry.' He goes quiet, but when I look at him, and he sees the happy tears glide down my face. He relaxes and breathes a small sigh of relief.

'I love it, Gabriel,' I whisper. 'Thank you.' I close the book with the utmost care and clasp it close to my chest. 'I love it. I really, really love it. It's amazing. So thoughtful and meaningful. Truly.'

'Is it the same edition?' he asks.

'It is. It's as close to the real thing I'll ever get.' I reach out and take his hand, giving his fingers a gentle squeeze. 'Thank you.'

'Merry Christmas,' Grayson says, almost thrusting a black box tied up with a silver bow in my face. I'm reluctant to put down my book, but I need both hands to open his gift. I unwrap the delicately wrapped bow and open the box.

Inside is an elegant white gold necklace with a pear-shaped, brilliant green emerald.

'It matches your eyes perfectly.' Taking it from my hand, he moves behind me and lifts my hair so he can put it around my neck.

'It's lovely,' I tell him as I look at the clearly costly gift. 'Thank you, Grayson. It really is very pretty.'

The gift part of the day is done, and we all resume chatting, drinking and eating. I, however, remain quiet, sitting in the armchair by the fire with the book open on my lap, reading Cinderella. Everyone around me is engrossed in their activities. Amara and Collins are in each other's arms, kissing and giggling quietly to themselves. Hendrix is sitting with Grayson and Gabriel, and for once, all three men look at ease and relaxed. They're even laughing and joking. Occasionally, Collins will join in with whatever anecdote they're telling. I love watching them all. I love hearing their laughter. I love that my belly is full. That I'm warm and safe. Wanted. And as I look at them all with a smile firmly on my face, I notice that someone is watching me. He has an affectionate smile and warm eyes. He raises his hand and rests it over the necklace I gave him earlier today.

By midnight, we all call it a night. I've had the best Christmas Day of my life. Scratch that. The best day of my life full stop.

We bid goodnight to Amara and Collins on the first floor and Gabriel, Grayson and I continue up to our rooms. On the top of the landing Grayson takes my elbow, keeping me with him as Gabriel continues towards his room.

'I do hope you enjoyed today,' he says.

'I did,' I tell him. 'I absolutely did.'

'I'm so glad.' He glances at Gabriel who seems to be taking a phenomenally long time getting to his door. 'I wondered if maybe you would like to join me for a drink?' He looks at his bedroom door. 'I have a comfortable sofa and the finest whiskey. If you fancy it?'

'Oh, that's really nice of you to offer,' I say with as much casualness as I can muster. 'But I really am tired. I'm just going to head to bed.' Only then does Gabriel open his bedroom door and go inside.

Grayson kisses my hand like a gentleman and wishes me goodnight before I turn and go to my room.

It's really been a fantastic day. I'm completely blown away that a day could even be like that! I pull off my clothes and pull on Gabriel's top before crawling into bed. Sinking into my pillow, I yawn and stretch out but freeze when I hear a light thump from inside my bathroom.

There's someone in there!

The door opens, I sit up quickly and go to scream. But instead, I'm left laughing and shaking my head.

'What the hell are you doing in there? Did you really just climb in through my bedroom window?' I whisper.

Gabriel chuckles and gives a small shrug as he walks over and perches on the edge of my bed.

'There are Nomads outside your door. I don't fancy another black eye from my jealous brother so I thought I would go old school and sneak in.'

He taps the jewel-encrusted diamond that dangles on a white gold chain around my neck.

'Do you like the gift Grayson brought you?' he asks.

'It's stunning,' I reply. 'But it feels a little like I'm in his debt with it on. Like I should be grateful for receiving such a clearly expensive gift and in return, let him feel a little more ownership over me. Does that make sense? I don't ever want him to say "Well, I brought you a ridiculously expensive gift the least you could do is let me...whatever". I hated it when Toby used to do that.'

He reaches behind my neck, unhooks the necklace and holds it in his closed fist.

'Better?'

'Much,' I sigh happily. 'What are you doing in here?'

'I didn't get to say good night.'

'You snuck in here to wish me goodnight?' I say rather disbelievingly.

'And to see you in your pj's. I love seeing you in my clothes and those little shorts,' he teases, raising his eyebrows suggestively. 'Plus, I'm worried about you. It's not been an easy couple of days for you.'

I lie down and hold out the book he gave me.

'Read it to me?'

He takes it and settles next to me on the bed. I snuggle into him and lie silently as he reads. His hand rests on my waist, then in my hand which he holds affectionately.

'Can I stay in here with you?' he whispers when the story has ended.

'I would love it if you stayed with me.'

He lays beside me and holds me close. 'Goodnight, Beautiful,' he whispers. 'Merry Christmas.'

'Merry Christmas, Gabriel.'

My eyes fling open. A feeling of dread washes over my entire body from my head to my toes. I feel sick with it. Gabriel's still by my side fast asleep with his arm draped loosely over me. The clock tells me it's three a.m. I've been sleeping a matter of hours but now I'm suddenly wide awake. It wasn't the mumblings of two Nomads on guard out in the hall that woke me. It wasn't even my nightmares. It was something else. Something that has my senses on high alert.

I sit and look around the room. Nothing here is cause for concern. But still I know, deep down, something's wrong. I can sense something. Someone.

And they don't belong here.

I sense Gabriel. I can even sense Grayson a little as he sleeps across the hall and Collins below. But there's someone else. The more I concentrate on my Sensativa, the more I know that there's someone outside this house who shouldn't be here. I stand and pull on Gabriel's black hoody that's draped by the foot of my bed and head to the window. It's snowing hard. There's a thick layer of white on the ground.

I peer through the curtains and see a man standing below on the gravel driveway, cast in shadow, as the full moon dimly lights the front of the house. He stands there, hands in his pockets looking straight up at me, with a hood pulled over his face. As I watch him, he pulls the hood down, and my heart begins to hammer hard.

'*Toby.*'

He's standing there, bold as brass looking straight up at me with his sly smirk firmly in place. The white snow falls on his equally white hair, and he raises his hand giving me a little wave. I close the curtain and step out of sight, focusing on steadying my breathing.

He's out there.

I pinch myself hard. I must be dreaming.

I pinch again.

No, I'm not asleep. He's really out there.

He's done sneaking about and finally, he's come for me. I look outside again, peeking through the curtain hoping I'm just imagining it. Nope. He's still there. He gestures for me to come down and puts his finger to his lips.

I'm frozen.

He places his hands together as if pleading with me before settling his hands over his heart and pointing at me. He would do that every time he left. He would stand beneath my window, look up at me and rest his hands over his heart to wordlessly remind me that he loved me. I would always do it back.

There he is. The man who saved my life. The man who gave me a reason to live. The man who ruined me.

I can't help it. Part of me wants to go to him. That lonely lost little part of me that belonged to him. That still, belongs to him.

A gentle hand rests on my back as Gabriel stands beside me. My hand grips his t-shirt as if I'm anchoring myself to him. To stop my old self resurfacing and taking over.

'What is it, Beautiful?' he asks, looking at my white knuckles. 'What's the matter?'

I stand back, pressing myself into him. His arm wraps around my waist. I can't take my eyes off Toby who's still looking up at me.

Gabriel opens the curtain further to see what it is that I'm looking at. His arm tightens around me and I feel him go rigid.

'*Bastard*,' Gabriel hisses. 'Don't worry. He won't get to you.'

Toby, seeing that I'm not alone, loses his self-assured grin and glares at Gabriel loathsomely.

'That's right, you little shit,' Gabriel mutters. 'I'm here too.'

Toby points up to us both and slides his finger across his throat.

'He's come to get me. Gabriel...what do we do?'

'He won't get anywhere near you. Stay here. You're well protected.' He turns, but I grab him.

'You can't go down there! Are you insane?' I pull him away from the door. 'He'll kill you!'

'I'm going down there, Lilly. We've been looking for him for years. We need the journal, and we need to stop him from hurting you anymore!' He goes to leave, but I yank him back. My hands are bunching his t-shirt in my fists.

'I'm going!' he insists.

'You can't!' I almost plead. 'Gabriel, he will kill you!'

'HE'S HERE!' Gabriel yells towards the door. 'TOBY IS HERE. OUTSIDE THE FRONT OF THE HOUSE!' He looks down at me sternly. 'Stay put. This won't take long.'

He turns on his heel and runs out of the room before I can stop him. The two Nomads watch him leave the room with extreme confusion, before turning their attention to Grayson, who has joined Gabriel out in the hall.

I look down at Toby as he shakes his head. His loathing written all over his face.

The Nomads inside the house have sprung into action. Grayson's barking orders from out in the hall, telling someone to stay up here with me. My bedroom lights are turned on by a Nomad who has a large gun at the ready and stands beside another equally well-armed Nomad. Looking back outside, I see Toby's turned and started running. But not away from the house.

'HE'S COMING INSIDE!' I yell. Toby's hands are covered in his fire as he shoots it skilfully at those around him. I have to shield my eyes it's so bright against the night sky.

Amara barges into my room, ignoring the armed men and sprints to my side. Her hair's a mess, and she's wearing one of Collins' oversized T-shirts. I take her hand, desperate for comfort as we watch the fight unfold below.

'Collins has gone down there,' she tells me. I can hear the absolute panic in her voice. 'Oh no, Lilly. He's really here. Toby's really here.' I tighten the hold I have on her hand as she looks at me. Those big eyes of hers are brimming with tears. 'He won't kill them, will he?'

I can't meet her gaze because yes, if Toby wants to kill them, he most certainly will. But how can I say that to her? Instead, I look back out of the window. I can't see him anymore, but we hear one hell of a crash below and feel the house shake.

'He's inside,' I realise.

We abandon the window and turn to the door. I head towards the hall, desperate to see what's going on below us, but the Nomads stop me.

'RED!' Toby's voice booms clear across the yelling and the chaos of the fight below. The sound of his voice and the anger that comes with it, has my insides plummeting like cement in water. 'RED, YOU COME HERE NOW!'

Amara's hand tightens in mine. 'Don't even think about it,' she warns.

'I WON'T STOP COMING FOR YOU!' he calls. 'I'LL NEVER FUCKING STOP!'

'YOU WILL IF YOU'RE A DEAD MAN,' Collins bellows back over the sound of smashing glass and splintering furniture.

The look of fear on Amara's face is heart-breaking. She's shaking, as the man she's only just declared her love for, risks his life to try and stop Toby. A psychopath who's here only because of me. This isn't right! Gabriel and Collins are down there as I hide away up here like a coward. Any harm that comes to anyone tonight is squarely on my head.

'Move,' I tell the Nomads.

They stand straighter and hold their guns clearly in view, reminding me that they're armed.

'Sorry, Miss Hooper. More than my life's worth to let you past.'

I look past them standing on my tip-toes. There are more Nomads in the hall, all pointing their weapons at the top of the stairs, standing in lines just waiting for the fight to come up to us. It sounds like absolute chaos below. I hear Gabriel yelling. Telling Toby to stand down, but the violence continues.

'Why don't they just shoot him?!' Amara sobs.

'They won't shoot him. They need him alive to find the journal,' I tell her.

'How are they going to stop him then?' she cries even harder, tears streaming down her face. 'Gabriel's orders clearly aren't working.'

I can't stand the panic in her voice. We hear a pain-filled yell echo through the halls.

'Collins,' she sobs 'That was Collins. Lilly! We have to do something.'

She's right. I won't be the reason anyone dies. I run back inside my room, take my new boots from the bottom of my wardrobe and put them on.

'Miss Hooper,' one of the Nomads warns as I finish lacing them up. 'I won't allow you to leave this room.'

Boots tied up to my calves, I get to my feet, completely ignoring him. I take off my watch and shove it into Amara's hand, letting my magic return to me in a mighty wave.

'Keep this safe for me,' I tell her. 'I'm going down there.'

'You can't go down there!' she says, horrified, trying to hand me back the watch. 'He's here for you!'

'I can't let people die because of me, Amara. Not anymore. And besides, I have my magic. I'll be fine,' I lie, determination coursing through my veins.

'Lilly...you're in your pyjamas,' she says, pointing at my blue and white striped shorts and Gabriel's top.

'I don't care. It will be okay. I promise.' I kiss her cheek and hug her. 'If he gets up here, hide. You hide and don't come out for anyone or anything until it's safe. Promise me.

'I promise.'

I turn to face the Nomad.

'Move.'

'No, Miss Hooper. You are to stay put. Grayson's orders.'

'Move,' I take a step forwards. 'Before I move you.'

'Miss Hooper. You will not leave this room,' the Nomad repeats.

'Oh no?'

With a wave of my hand, I send the two Nomads flying into the wall so hard, they fall to the floor in a dazed heap. I step over them and walk out into the hall. I won't hide up here and listen to the people I care about get hurt or die. No way. I walk forwards to at least eight men, all armed and dangerous, standing guard at the top of the stairs.

When they see me coming, they turn their weapons on me.

'YOU CAN NOT GO DOWN THERE!' one of them shouts. 'STOP!'

'No,' I reply as I continue walking straight at them. I channel my magic, sending them all into the air and smashing them hard into the wall with a blast of Telekinetic power that explodes from inside me. Some are unconscious. Some are staggering back to their feet, but I have a clear path. I walk through them, stepping over the slumped bodies as I go. Amara calls after me but stays exactly where I told her to.

I make my way down the stairs to the first floor which is empty and then down into the lobby. The table in the middle is a charred mess, and there are unconscious and injured men all over the place. Most have burns on their skin and some look like they've been slashed by a knife. I don't see Gabriel, Collins or Grayson.

'Where are they?' I ask one man who's tending to a friend. He doesn't say anything. 'Gabriel and the others...where are they? Where's Toby?' I demand. I create my own fire on my hands as a warning. 'Tell me where the fuck they are.'

He points towards the kitchen. 'They drove Toby out the back door. He's run off towards the cliffs. They've gone after him. There are men with him. Three of *our* men, they turned on us.'

I take off at a run, straight through the throng of the injured and the random patches of fire and into the kitchen, not caring who he's with.

The garden's in darkness. There's a thick layer of snow on the ground and my breath hangs heavily in the air, but that doesn't stop me. Ahead is a line of men, evenly spaced out, creating a protective barrier around the house. They're all pointing their weapons into the night.

On the patio are three dead men. Toby's men I assume, judging by the lack of care anyone is taking with them. Grayson's and Gabriel's voices carry clear over the night air, and the odd flash of torches tell me they're searching for Toby down by the orchard.

Why are they looking there?

I look to my right. To the woods. I can sense him in this direction. It's getting fainter, but I'm positive.

They're looking in the wrong place.

I turn and sprint towards Toby, leaving them all behind. I know it's stupid. I know it's dangerous for me to go after him alone, but I would rather put myself in the line of fire than Gabriel or Collins. Even Grayson. I have my magic. I can handle Toby. I knew the man for years. I can talk him into reason. And if I can't? Whatever happens, it will be away from them. Away from the people I care about.

We need the journal. But more than that, I need this never-ending threat to be over. He said it himself. He won't stop. I know he won't. He never did. When he gets something in his head, it becomes an obsession, and I can't live in fear like this for the rest of my life. Who knows when I might get another chance to end this.

At least if I'm chasing him, he's not sneaking up on me.

I soon disappear into the darkness. I wasn't seen and as I run I can feel I'm getting closer to him. The snow's falling so hard it covers my tracks almost straight away. The humming in the air gets stronger as I go. The sound of my feet in the snow and the heavy breaths I need to take to keep myself going, are soon all I can hear, as the voices of the others fade into the distance. I keep going. Running till I can't anymore. So I walk. He's still moving. So I carry on following. As I always did.

After what must be another hour, the snow has slowed. I can see the slightest trace of Toby's footprints as I emerge from the woods and come face to face with the enormous wall. I was right. It surrounds the whole estate.

Where the hell has he gone? His footprints go up to the wall and then stop by a bush. As I get closer, I notice there's a small hole in the wall hidden behind it. I climb through and come out onto a thin country road with no streetlights. If it wasn't for the full moon, I think it would be pitch black.

His presence is still here. He's walking ahead of me in the distance, but I can't see him, just his trail in the snow. I carry on, desperate not to lose him and terrified to catch up with him. The adrenaline's eased and the bitter night air on this Boxing Day morning is starting to take effect, as I begin to shiver. I'm relieved I put on Gabriel's hoody before I left. His scent has been my only comfort. But a hoody, pyjama shorts and Doc Marten boots aren't effective against this level of cold.

Ahead in the distance to my left, I spot the silhouette of a man walking alone across a field.

Toby.

He's heading towards a parked car on a dirt road just ahead of him. He's planned his escape well. But I can't let him get away. This has to end.

'TOBY!'

My voice echoes in the vast emptiness around us. He stops. Slowly, he turns.

I continue walking towards him and he heads my way too. I keep telling myself to be brave. To be strong. To be careful. When he's about ten feet in front of me I stop. So does he.

We face each other for the first time in two long years.

He's just as entrancing as I remember. Folding his arms across his chest, he looks at me with that mischievous grin of his.

'There you are,' he says. 'I knew you'd come. Eventually.' He reaches out and beckons me forwards with his finger. 'Come here.' I stand frozen. 'Come on now, Red. Don't make me ask twice. You know I never liked repeating myself.'

My feet start to move. I'm shaking as I make my way towards him. I'm nervous. Terrified, but compelled to go to him. My old self is resurfacing, and I obey. Just as I always did. As I get closer, he remains as he ever was. Cool, calm and entirely in control of everything around him. Myself included. It was one of the most alluring aspects of him. No matter what was happening, no matter the chaos or the risk. He enjoyed the situation, whatever it was, and made sure everything went the way he wanted it to go. He was in charge. Always. I was sure the world only turned because he wanted it to. Physics be damned.

His skin is just as pale as I remember. His lips still a deep red and his eyes an unnatural violet. But the most unusual thing about Toby has always been his hair. It lacks any colour except the whitest of white. It's a little curly and falls just above his eyes. He's twenty three. A little older than me. I can't look away. And neither can he. He comes to me, his hand brushing my arm as he positions himself with his body flush against my back.

'Long time,' he says in my ear, moving my hair out of the way so his lips can get to my neck. They're cold. Like his hands which he slides under my top to caress my stomach. I should push him away. Make it clear that I have no interest in his hands, his lips or his words. But I don't. I'm thrown back two years when I was completely and utterly obsessed with him. When I was so happy to have someone look at me the way he did. Like everything between then and now just isn't important.

I'm finding it hard to steady my breathing and organise my thoughts. His touch is too distracting. It always was. He's beyond reason. Beyond sense. He was everything to me. *Everything.*

'I've missed you, Red,' he whispers longingly in my ear. 'Have you missed me?'

'No.' My mouth is dry and every nerve on fire. My voice is barely a whisper as I stand in his arms not knowing what the hell to do. Now he's here, I don't believe he wants to hurt me. But I always thought that. Until he did.

'Are you trying to hurt my feelings?' he asks sweetly, his lips pressing into my neck. 'Why would you want to upset me like that? Of all the people in your life, I'm the only one...the *only* one, that ever gave a damn about you. When your aunt starved you, I fed you. When your uncle beat you, I tended your wounds. When Ryan put his hands on you, I killed him.'

'Don't say his name.'

'When you tied a rope around your neck and tried to take your own life, I saved you. Or have you forgotten all that?' His hand slides up my back. His fingers are tracing the scars he knows so well. 'I know you inside and out. I know every dirty little secret. Every dark desire. Every single one of these marks on your delicious body. Your battle map. Remember that, Red? What I used to say about your scars?'

'Yes,' I reply in the same weak whisper. 'I remember.'

'Tell me. Tell me what I used to say.'

'You...you would say that you loved my scars.' I look at him over my shoulder. His lilac eyes bore into mine. 'You would spend hours running your fingers along every single one of them. Making me tell you who had given that specific one to me and why. Even the ones you put there.' His fingers continue to trace the marks as his grin grows. 'You called them my battle map.'

'Only the strongest could survive what you've been through. I was proud of you. Proud to be loved by you. I still am.' His chin settles on my shoulder. His hands hold me firmly around my waist as we just look at each other. 'You do still love me, don't you?'

I did. My god I did. He was like a drug. The strongest heroin. Completely addictive. An incredible high and just like any good addiction, he completely took over my life. Made me do things I would never dream of, but most of all... he was destructive. I'd spent my life alone and suffering. I'd spent my life hated and feeling nothing but fear and loneliness. Then he came along and everything inside me ignited. I *finally* came alive. He had me in every way. Heart, mind, body and soul. Of all the women in the world he could have chosen...he chose me. Despite my scars. Despite my situation. Despite my fear of touch. He decided to want me.

That was until he left. That night, everything fell spectacularly apart.

'Tell me. Tell me you still love me.' He watches me as I stare back at him in silence. His smile starts to disappear, and his nails dig into my hips. 'Don't make me repeat myself. Tell me-'

'I don't,' I tell him. My voice slightly more my own but still timid and wary. His eyes frown and his smile goes altogether.

He spins me quickly and holds me in place, his hands gripping my hips painfully tight and his nails digging in deeper.

'That's a lie.'

'It's not.'

'I know you. The real you. Gabriel doesn't.'

'Gabriel has nothing to do with this.'

'He was in your bedroom,' he snarls. 'You think he would want you if he knew the truth about you? About what you've done?'

'What you made me do,' I correct him.

'Is that what you tell yourself to help you sleep at night?'

'I don't sleep, Toby. I can't. I'm haunted by the things you made me do.' I try to prise his hands off me, but he jabs his fingertips into my skin hard, making me wince.

'You can act like the victim with them. But don't you dare pull that shit with me. I know the real you. I've seen the darkness that's in your soul. It was there long before I came along.' He leans in. 'And I love it. I love you. What can we be in the dark, Red?'

'I'm not playing that game with you.'

His nails dig deeper but I don't make a sound.

'What can we be in the dark, Red?' Small, powerful fires springs to life on the tips of his fingers, burning my skin.

'Toby, stop!' I gasp, grabbing his wrists to try and push away.

'What. Can. We. Be?'

'Whatever we want! Get off me!' I plead, trying to get away. His fire goes, and his grin returns.

'What can we do in the dark?' he asks.

'Anything,' I reply. His motto.

'Red,' he says with a desperate longing. 'My Red. Always and forever. You shouldn't be locked up behind high walls and guarded by pathetic wannabe witches. Told where you can go. What you can do.' He releases his vice-like grip, peeling his nails from under my skin so he can run his finger slowly and sensually down my cheek. He's so close I can see every shade of lilac in his mesmerising eyes. 'Come with me. Be free with me. Let's show the world, and Grayson's Coven, exactly what we can do.' He takes hold of my chin. 'Name a place. I'll take you there. I won't make you bring down the Veil. I won't hide you away. There are no rules with me. There never were. You'll be happier than you've ever been. I guarantee it.'

I'm a second away from agreeing. Leaving all this behind. The Veil, Theo, Grayson and his unwanted affections, his rules. Perhaps Toby *is* the answer. But I remember my fear at the idea of Toby coming for me. I remember his violence and manipulation when we were together, and I inwardly slap myself because here we are again. I'm exactly where he wants me to be, and the only one that's going to suffer is me.

What the hell am I doing?!

I reach up and hold his hand. Then, I guide it away and step back.

'I say no, Toby. I'm not going with you. The Orchard is my home now.'

He looks at me like he has no idea what he's looking at. Like I'm a bewilderment. I am, because I've never, ever said no to him. Not until today. And it's more terrifying than anything I've ever done in my life.

No one says no to him. No one.

The familiar dangerous flash I remember so well, lights up his eyes. The corner of his mouth twitches as well as his hand. A subconscious act as his instincts tell him to attack, but his reason tells him to hold back. I know his reason will lose out soon enough. But I don't need to keep him happy. I have no interest in trying to make him stay. To prove that I'm enough for him. Because I'm enough for *me*.

That's all that matters.

And when I'm with him, under his influence, I'm not me. I'm Red. I'm his.

No more.

'I'm not coming with you, Toby, because I don't love you.'

'Are you sleeping with him?' he says through gritted teeth. 'Is that it? You let him fuck you?' He takes a menacing step closer as I stumble back. 'Answer me, Red. Are you fucking him? ARE YOU SLEEPING WITH MY BROTHER?'

'Y-your what?' I reply in a stunned gasp. 'Your brother?'

He scoffs at me. 'See? You have no idea who they are. None. And they don't know you. You think Gabriel would look twice at you if he knew the *real* you?' He steps closer, his fists clenched. 'If he knew about Ryan?'

'Don't. Don't you dare-'

'He wouldn't. Trust me. I've known the man my whole life. He likes his girls strong. If he knew what you let Ryan do to you for all those years, he would see you as pathetic. Damaged. Second hand.'

'He knows I loved you. If that hasn't put him off, nothing will.'

'Shut your mouth,' he snarls.

'No. I won't. Not anymore.' I stand straighter. Stronger. 'I need the journal. Rebecca Hooper's journal. Where is it?'

'After everything I did for you. After everything I sacrificed... you turn your back on me like this?'

'Where's the journal?'

I see him start to lose control over his reason as his jaw tightens and his eyes twitch. And I'm so angry that he may be related to them and no one told me!

'GIVE ME THE GODDAMN JOURNAL!' I scream.

That's his last straw. All reason leaves him, and his instincts take over as he charges me. I don't get a second to react before he body slams me into the ground and wraps his fingers around my throat.

'I GAVE YOU EVERYTHING I HAD YOU UNGRATEFUL...' he lifts my head and slams it into the ground. 'LITTLE...' again, another whack. 'BITCH!' *Thud.* He leans down into my face and tightens his grip so I can't breathe at all. 'You betrayed me. No one betrays me. Never. Tell me you're sorry. Tell me you love me and I'll forgive you. TELL ME!'

'Toby...' I gasp, whacking his hand that's wrapped around my throat. 'You're killing me.'

'I'll see you dead before I see you with another man.'

I claw at his hands and try to kick him away, but he's always been too strong. He laughs as I struggle for breath and pointlessly try to loosen his grip. His hands may as well be made of stone.

I grab the hand he's choking me with and set it alight with my magic. I'm released as he lets go and stumbles back.

'Please,' he scoffs as he creates more fire in his palm. His flames are just like mine, black and white. 'I taught you how to manifest fire. I taught you how to control the movement of objects around you. I gave you the will and the strength to channel your magic, and you think you can use it against me?'

'Was it you?' I gasp, massaging my throat. 'Did you do it?'

'Do what?' he laughs angrily.

'Did you kill her? Was it you?' I sit up. 'Tell me what happened. I killed people in the barn and then you ran. And when I woke up back at Harry's, she was gone.' Tears sting my eyes and fall fast and plenty down my cheeks. 'What happened when we left Harry's house that night?'

'Is that all you remember?'

'Tell me what happened.'

'My little spies told me you had no memory of those six weeks. Part of me didn't believe it, but you don't. Not a clue.' He shakes his head. 'You're not ready. Trust me.'

'TELL ME WHAT HAPPENED TO HER!'

'NO!' He seals his lips together and takes a moment to try and calm himself. 'I'm not talking about that. I'm not.'

'Just tell me-'

'I SAID I'M NOT GOING TO TALK ABOUT IT!' He's deadly serious and I know that there's no way in hell he'll talk without some violent persuasion. My fire springs to life on my hands. He glances at them briefly before choosing to ignore them completely. 'I'm going to give you one more chance. Tell me that you still love me and I will take you back. I'll give you the life you always wanted. You want to live abroad? Rome or Jamaica perhaps? I can take you there. We can live by the beach.' He looks at me with a forced smile, but I can see the anger raging beneath his surface. 'Come away with me.'

I shake my head. 'I'm not leaving the Coven. I'm bringing down the Veil. I'm staying with Gabriel and to be honest, I would rather be back at Harry's than be with you. Just give me the journal and run. Because they're coming for you. I may not want you dead, Toby. But if they kill you, I won't shed a tear.'

He lunges at me with a furious yell and again, I'm on the floor. And again, his fingers are wrapped around my throat. He squeezes.

'You're mine. Mine. MINE! You will NOT leave me. Not for anyone. Not again. ESPECIALLY, NOT FOR HIM!'

I grab his hands with my inferno. But he just yells against the pain and tightens his grip. I try to buck him off. I kick out my legs. But it does nothing.

Behind him, someone's running straight at us. Toby doesn't see. He's too busy trying to kill me to notice, but I see him.

It's Gabriel.

He runs full pelt towards us, bends down and swipes up a fallen log. When he reaches us, he strikes Toby over the head knocking him off me and pulling me to my feet. I gasp for air, breathing it in fast as I cling to Gabriel.

He wraps his arms around me.

'Are you okay?' he asks in a breathless panic. I nod and cough. 'Jesus, girl. I thought you were as good as dead.'

I've never been so relieved to see him. He kisses the top of my head and pulls me close to his body, as we both turn to face Toby.

Toby stumbles to his feet, reaches up and touches his head. There's blood on his fingers. When he sees Gabriel, he looks livid.

'Get your hands off my girl, Gabriel.'

'She ain't yours. Not anymore. You can't beat both of us, and you know it.'

'Come here,' Toby orders me through gritted teeth. I cling to Gabriel and shake my head.

'She doesn't want you anywhere near her,' Gabriel says equally as vicious. 'After everything you've done to her.'

'I've done nothing! Whatever they told you, whatever lies they've put into your head, don't you believe it, Red.'

'We haven't said a thing about you. Your actions towards her have proved what a sick, depraved little freak you are.'

Toby laughs and points to himself. 'You think *I'm* the sick, depraved one?' He shakes his head. 'Oh, you have no idea what that girl is capable of. I could tell you stories that would turn even your stomach, Gabriel. Shall I?' he asks me.

'Go to hell.'

He looks instead to Gabriel.

'And what about you? Does she know about you? What you've done? Why didn't you tell her who I am? Hmm? That you and me are brothers!' Gabriel glances at me briefly before returning his full attention to Toby. 'You think she would be clinging to you right now if she knew the truth? If she knew about Rose? Hmm? You're the biggest liar I know, Gabriel. And she's so full of shame and secrets I'm amazed there's room for anything else.'

Who the hell is Rose? I want to ask, but now is most definitely not the time.

'Shut your mouth,' Gabriel says firmly. 'Another word and I'll-'

'You'll what? Kill me?' Toby laughs. 'You've been looking for that journal I took for years. You'll never find it. Not unless I want you to. I didn't bring it with me if you were wondering. I'm not that stupid.'

'One day with me, you'll talk,' Gabriel snarls. 'They always talk.'

'What more could you do to me? Hmm? Torture me? You've done that. Maybe you could banish me from the only family I've ever known? Oh wait, you did that too. Perhaps you could betray me and toss me to the Hunters to save your own skin?' He slams his hand against his head. 'How could I forget, you already did! I know. Maybe you could steal the only woman I've ever truly cared about.' He looks at me. 'Did he tell you I Broke because of him?' I look between them as Toby becomes more and more unravelled. 'The Hunters took him. They had Gabriel in their cells for six months. Torturing him. *I* was the one that snuck into their cells. *I* was the one that got him out.' Toby turns to Gabriel. 'I carried you for miles. And then they caught up with us.' He points at Gabriel with more hatred than I ever thought possible. 'And you jumped on that horse and fled like the coward you are. You left me there on my own.'

'It wasn't like that, and you know it!' Gabriel argues. 'I told you to get on that damn horse with me. I told you that we needed to run. You refused. You were hell-bent on fighting them, even though I told you I could barely keep my eyes open.'

'You left me.'

'*You* left *me*!' Gabriel yells back. 'You put me on that horse, turned around and tried to win an impossible fight. As soon as you threw that fire, the horse spooked and bolted. I came back, but you were gone. They had you. We went back to where they kept me, but you weren't there.'

'Six years,' he says hatefully. 'They had me for SIX YEARS, GABRIEL. I BROKE IN THOSE CELLS!'

'We looked for you–'

'You and Grayson want Rebecca Hooper's journal?' Toby interrupts. 'There's only one thing that will make me hand it over. One thing that will make me turn around and leave you to your plans in peace. Hell, I'll even tell you where Theo's camp is if you like? I found it you see. I could tell you right now, and you could eradicate them. Wipe them off the face of the earth. Him and his traitors.'

'Is that so?' Gabriel says disbelievingly.

Toby nods and smiles smugly.

'What do you want?' I ask. He's offering everything we want. The book. Theo. For him to leave us in peace.

He turns and looks at me. 'You, of course. I want you back.'

'Not gonna happen.' Gabriel stands in front of me as a barrier.

'You give her to me. I'll make sure she does the spell and brings down the Veil for you. I swear it. But, then I get to keep her, and you leave us alone.'

'I don't want you to keep me.'

'I don't really care what you want, Red. So...Brother? What do you say? You get it all. If I get her.'

I watch Gabriel nervously.

He won't, will he?

'You're not touching her again,' Gabriel vows.

Toby creates fire on his hands. 'You've turned the only woman I've ever loved against me with your lies and started fucking her in the house I used to call home. You've turned me into an outcast. I've lost everything because of you, Gabriel. I'm going to make you pay.'

'You lost everything because you're sick. You're a sick, twisted little boy. A psychopath. And you're not touching my girl ever again.'

As he says that, my heart swells. Despite the situation.

'Your girl...' Toby repeats the words with malice. *'Your girl?'*

'Yes,' Gabriel says firmly, taking my hand in his. *'My* girl.'

Toby charges forwards with an enraged cry, as Gabriel shoves me out of the way. I land on the floor and Toby sends him down with a punch.

'I don't need my fire to kick your ass.'

Gabriel's up again, holding the same heavy log he used to knock Toby off me. He slams it across Toby's face, and he goes down. Gabriel brings it down on Toby again and again, shouting and yelling. Toby kicks him straight in the knee, making Gabriel's leg buckle, giving him time to hurl himself on top of him. There's blood streaming from his nose and a large gash across his eyebrow, but that doesn't slow him down. I watch him wrap his hands around Gabriel's throat and start banging his head on the ground over and over again, just as he did with me.

'STOP!' I use my magic to hurl Toby away from us and run so I'm standing between them. Toby scrambles to his feet as Gabriel rolls onto his front, shaking his head and trying to regain his focus.

Toby and I stand to face each other. I create my fire on my hands.

'You won't hurt him. I won't let you.' My fire doubles in size. The logs and rocks on the snow-covered ground begin to tremble as my fists clench. 'Last chance. Tell me where the journal is.'

He's looking anxiously at my fire, then at me.

I pull my hand back, ready to send my flame towards him. But before I can, he sends out a blast wave of fire and heat straight at Gabriel and I, which hurls us both several feet back through the air. Toby watches me as I try to get to my feet. I have him in my sights, but the pain-filled moan I hear from Gabriel, who's slumped on the floor, distracts me. He's bleeding. A thick trail of red is flowing freely from beyond his hairline.

'Gabriel...' I run to him as he lies on his back, blinking blood out of his eyes. 'Stay still. Don't move.'

'I'm alright. Lilly, I'm fine!' he insists as I fuss. He lowers my hands and looks at my face, scanning it for injury. 'Are *you* okay?' he asks in a panic. 'Are *you* hurt?' I shake my head, and we wrap our arms around each other.

I almost forget Toby's still there. He watches our intimacy and looks...heartbroken. Genuinely devastated.

I look at him filled with hatred. 'I'm going to make you pay,' I threaten, letting go of Gabriel and getting to my feet. Gabriel's right by my side, his hand in mine as we face Toby together.

Toby glides his hand through the air. A wall of fire springs to life between us. I stand and watch him through the flames. He watches me right back.

'I'll spread it to you if you so much as move,' he warns, gesturing to the fire.

Gabriel attempts to move, but I keep him by my side.

'You're still there you know,' Toby tells me. 'Still in my heart. Still in my head.'

'We can't let him go!' Gabriel whispers.

But we have no choice. I won't risk his life.

'I'll be back for you, my love. This isn't over. And you...' He looks Gabriel square in the eye. 'You're going to pay. You're going to pay big.' Toby turns and walks away. I watch him go.

I *let* him go.

He gets into his car and speeds away. The brake lights disappear out of view, and Toby's gone.

Gabriel looks to the corner where Toby just disappeared and then to me.

'You just let him go? How could you just-'

'Don't,' I say firmly, watching the darkness of Toby's escape route. 'Just...don't.' I look up at him as he frowns. 'He's your brother?!'

Chapter 17

'Do you have your binding spell?'

'No,' I reply. 'I gave it to Amara before I left. Did you hear me?'

'I heard you. Do we have to do this now?' he groans.

'We kinda do. *Is* he your brother?' I fold my arms across my chest and wait as he struggles to meet my stare. 'Gabriel!'

'His name is Tobias. Tobias Kendryk, okay? But we called him Bias. And yes, he's our little brother,' he sighs.

'Why the hell would you not tell me that! Grayson told me your brother was dead! What-'

'Bias is dead to us. Okay? That man isn't our brother. Our brother died in the Hunters' cells centuries ago. Whoever that is...they're not my baby brother.'

'You should have told me!'

'We couldn't. When you met Grayson at your uncle's house, you said that if he was one of our men, you couldn't trust us. How would you have reacted if you knew he was our brother?' He drags his fingers through his hair and looks up at the sky. Snow falls on his lashes and sit there, too cold to melt. 'I told Grayson to tell you. But he said no. That you needed to trust us first.' He lowers his gaze and I see a terrible sadness in his eyes.

'I'm sorry we lied to you. But that man isn't my Bias. *That's* Toby. And he's not my brother anymore.'

He waits for me to say or do something. I feel so let down by him. So stupid that everyone back at the house knows who he really is while I remained clueless.

'I'm sorry, Lilly. Please. I didn't have a choice.'

'What now?' I sigh, looking around the darkness.

'We have no money. No phone and we're stuck in the middle of nowhere, miles away from the house,' he says.

'Helpful. Don't you know where we are?' I ask, wiping the snow from my legs before it melts and makes me even colder than I already am.

'I think so. Let's get somewhere warm before you freeze to death. Why the hell are you in shorts?'

'I was in a rush. It was a spur of the moment decision to run after him.'

We start to walk. Where to? I have no idea. I take his hand in mine.

'You still want to hold my hand?' he asks, glancing at our entwined fingers.

'Yes,' I grumble. 'You prat.'

'Hey, I'm not the only prat here. Running off? Facing him alone? Letting him go? All very prattish things.'

'Prats together then,' I laugh as he wraps his arm around my waist and holds me close.

'Looks that way. Come on, I know a place not far from here where we can get in the warm. It's far closer than the house.'

Finally, we get somewhere close to civilisation. We come onto a real road. One with actual lighting. He pulls me on quickly and soon we arrive at a place called *The Starlight Hotel*.

'Thank God,' I say under my breath as we head towards it. 'I can't feel my legs.'

When we get inside, Gabriel greets the elderly man behind the counter by name.

'Earl,' he says with a slight nod. 'Can I get a key to my room, please?'

'Of course,' Earl replies, sliding over a chub key. 'Rough night?' He glances at the various cuts and bruises on Gabriel's face, and my odd wardrobe.

'Car trouble,' Gabriel replies, taking the key. 'Thanks, Earl.'

He takes my hand and leads me down the tartan-carpeted hallway to a room at the end of the hall.

'I have a permanent room here. We can get warm and take a minute to get our shit together.'

Inside, he locks the door, flicks on the light and sits me on the large double bed. He takes the duvet and wraps it around me before pouring us both a large glass of Scotch. He hands me mine and kneels in front of me and starts massaging my legs, encouraging the blood to return.

There's a leather sofa against the wall, facing a television. A desk with a few books and a couple of bottles of Scotch, and an open wardrobe full of his clothes.

I look at them curiously.

'What exactly is the purpose of this hotel room? Please tell me this isn't your love nest,' I say, imagining in an instant all the girls he must have had in here.

'No,' he says, still rubbing my legs. 'It's my Grayson-free nest. I don't know if you've noticed, but life in that house can be a little...intense. Sometimes I need a break. You're the first girl I've brought here, if you must know.'

Hanging over the wardrobe door, I spot an item of clothing that completely contradicts his claim. It's a roll neck cable knit long-sleeved jumper that would reach down to the wearer's thighs. And it's my favourite colour. A lovely deep red.

'So, that's yours?' I joke, nodding to the very feminine jumper. His face falls completely.

'That belonged to a friend,' he says gruffly.

'A friend?'

'Yeah. A friend. That's all.'

'Where is she?'

He turns and says merely, 'Gone.' Then he takes a deep breath and moves on. 'Drink the Scotch. It will help calm your nerves.'

I didn't realise I was shaking so violently. And not just from the cold.

I turn to Gabriel. 'I genuinely thought that if I could get him alone, I could reason with him. I should have stopped him. We need that journal, and I just let him go. I've let everyone down.' I close my eyes and slump.

'You can't reason with a madman, Lilly,' Gabriel replies. 'He tormented you for years and called it love. You did well to face him. Don't get me wrong, it was stupid. Bloody stupid. But brave.' He strokes my cheek. 'We'll figure it out. We'll get the journal and get him out of your life for good. Without handing you over. Somehow. A shower will warm you up. You're even more pale than normal, and shivering like hell. You're mad, running out in shorts in December.' He puts on a little smile. It's a sad little smile. It's not his familiar grin. 'You look hot in those boots though,' he adds, getting to his feet. I look back at him feeling utterly ashamed of myself for yet again doing an idiotic thing and getting him hurt.

I stand and take his hand in mine. 'I'm sorry, Gabriel.' With my other hand, I gently feel his cuts and bruises. 'Please forgive me for getting you hurt again.'

'It's nothing. I'll heal,' he says, moving away from my touch. He doesn't even look at me. 'A shower. That's what you need.'

He heads into the bathroom and turns on the shower. The sound of the water is the only thing that breaks the silence. I wait, but he doesn't come out. After a while, steam starts making its way through the open door into the bedroom, but he's not in the shower itself. I can tell by the steady stream of water. What is he doing in there?

Leaving the duvet behind, I follow him in. He's standing with his head bowed, gripping the sink. My presence goes unnoticed. I observe his unusually sombre behaviour.

'I heard you giving Toby orders when he got into the house.' I say quietly. He looks at my reflection through the bathroom mirror, instead of turning to face me. 'Why didn't it work?'

'Grayson and Toby learnt how to fight my compulsion, after years of practice. It's all about strength of will and mental stamina. I told Toby to stop, and two seconds later he was moving again. Clearly, he's got a hell of a lot better at it since I saw him last.' He starts needlessly washing his hands which he does for a ridiculously long time.

'Who's Rose?' I ask. Gabriel's hands stop mid-soaping for a few seconds and then he carries on like I hadn't said a word. 'Is it her jumper you've kept hold off? Is she the girl who's gone?' He doesn't answer.

He turns off the tap and starts drying his hands, still avoiding the questions or making eye contact with me.

'Gabriel, please talk to me.'

'I should call Grayson. Let him know we're okay. There's a phone...' He turns and goes to walk past me. I stand in the doorway stopping him. 'Can you move please?' he says with a sigh.

'Can you answer my questions?'

'No,' he says, glaring at me. He steps forwards, but I stand firm. Short of him lifting me off the floor, there's not much he can do.

'Please don't shut me out. Talk to me.'

'Rose was someone I let down. A long time ago. Centuries ago,' he snaps. 'She trusted me, and I failed her. And no, that jumper didn't belong to her. It belonged to a friend, who I lost.'

'Lost?' I ask. 'What does that even mean?' I'm getting tired of the deflections.

'It means that she was in my life. And now she isn't.'

'Did you love her?'

'Just drop it, Lilly!' he says frustrated. 'Have I asked about your scars? No. Have I demanded an explanation for what I saw in your memories about the barn? No. When Toby, of all people, called you depraved, did I demand an explanation? I haven't demanded to know anything. Not a single thing.'

'I'm not demanding. I'm asking-'

'There are things in your past that you're ashamed of and can't face. Things that you regret. I would never, ever corner you like this and insist you tell me. You're completely out of order.'

His words are harsh but his eyes. There's a fear in them I've never seen there before. He's terrified and lashing out. Just like Collins warned me he would.

'Gabriel, that's not what I'm doing. I just-'

'Is it too hard for you to believe that I have a past that I regret?' he says over me. 'That there are things I've done that I would change if I could? Things I can't bear to talk about?'

He steps back and shakes his head. 'No. Because all you think about is yourself.'

'That's not fair!'

'I look at you as the person you are now and the person you're turning into every day. I have no interest in the person you were. Not with Toby, or Harry, or anyone else. I wish that you felt the same about me. But clearly, you don't. I can't change my past. So, if that's what you're going to use to judge the person I am now, then this will never work. Because, to be honest, you would hate the man I was. You would loathe him.' He charges past me back into the main room.

I turn and follow him.

'Gabriel... just calm-'

He spins around fast, struggling to contain his growing anger.

'You were a bloody idiot going after him tonight. You were an idiot running away the other night, and you are an idiot for thinking that he wouldn't hurt you.'

'I know-'

'Do you? Do you really? Because it looks to me like you can't wait to get yourself killed. Well...' he charges up to me and points a shaking finger in my face. 'If death is what you're after, it's not going to happen. Do you hear me? I won't fucking lose you, Lilly Hooper. I won't-'

I grab hold of his hair and pull his face into mine. My lips land on his, hard. He pulls back, his eyes looking at me with uncertainty at my sudden act. But I keep a tight grip on his hair, knotting my fingers through it tightly and stepping closer so my body is flush with his.

'Kiss me,' I tell him. 'For God's sake. Fucking kiss me!'

He lunges, wrapping one arm firmly around my waist as his other slides behind my ear. He pulls me in. His tongue caresses mine in a desperate kiss that consumes me completely. He starts pushing me back. My legs hit the bed as my hands grab at the hem of his t-shirt. I pull it off quick, keen not to let our lips be apart any longer than necessary. The necklace I gave him rests on his chest. He does the same, pulling off my top and throwing it to the floor so his hands can stroke and caress as much of me as possible. His belt joins our clothing. As do my shorts. I fall back on the bed and take him with me, pulling down his jeans and wrapping my legs firmly around his waist, keeping his as close as possible. He moans my name as he traces kisses down my neck. Then lower, across my chest, my stomach, and then between my thighs.

Falling to his knees, he runs his hand along my boots, from my knees to my ankles, which he lifts and rests on his shoulders as he continues kissing me. I can't stop the heavenly moans. My fingers entwine in his hair as I writhe in pleasure. On and on it goes until I can contain it no longer. As I let out a pleasure-filled moan, the lights flicker. The television turns on as does the radio, and the books on his desk tremble. The room comes alive as I climax. He crawls back on the bed and gets on top of me, kissing me wildly as he rests his body on top of mine and positions himself between my legs.

'Tell me you want me,' he breathes through his kisses. 'Tell me.'

'I want you,' I moan. 'Since the moment I saw you. I want you now, Gabriel.' He looks down at me, filled with want and passion. I ask, 'Do you have protection? I don't want to get pregnant.'

'You won't,' he says, his hair falling over his brilliant blue eyes. 'You never will with me. I can't have kids. I've never been able to.' He waits, watching my reaction. 'Is that a problem? For the future?' My worries that he only wants me to further his bloodline vanish.

'The future? You think of us like that?' I say, absolutely taken aback that he would.

'Of course I do,' he tells me as if it's the most obvious thing in the world. 'Don't you?'

I pull him back down to my lips which are smiling, loving his words, his touch, his kiss and his soul. When I feel his body in its entirety, when we finally become one, I know without a shadow of a doubt.

I've fallen in love with him.

The smell of him surrounds me like a blanket of comfort. The scent of his hair and his cologne. The feel of his skin on mine. I can't help but smile as I watch him sleep soundly next to me, nose to nose. He breathes slow and deep. His hair's even more of a mess than usual and even sleeping, his face is beautiful. I play with the pendant resting on his chest. He's still wearing it, and that makes me so happy. We're completely entangled in each other as we were when we finally stopped exploring each other's bodies and fell asleep long after the sun came up.

I lean in, my face less than an inch from his and all I want to do is kiss him. He's the most perfect thing I've ever seen.

'What are you doing?' he asks, making me jump a little. His eyes remain closed, but a smile appears on his lips.

'Watching you sleep,' I admit.

'That's a creepy thing to do.' He flicks his eyes open. They smile with the rest of him. 'You look beautiful in the morning. Have I ever told you that?'

'No, you haven't. May I say that you too, look mighty fine.' I take a deep breath and just can't believe that a man this beautiful, inside and out, would ever look twice at a mess like me. What must he have thought? He saw all of my scars. He saw everything.

'Hey...what's the matter?' he asks softly, stroking my face.

'Did they bother you?'

'What?'

'My scars? Did they...distract you? Put you off?'

He smiles and shuffles closer. 'Did it feel like I was put off at any point?' He runs his hands down my back, letting his fingers gently glide over my marks. 'I got a bit distracted when you made the light bulb explode.' His face buries into my neck and he starts kissing my skin. 'And you in those boots...hmmm, that was definitely a distraction.' He sits suddenly and whips the duvet off the bed, tossing it across the room altogether. Then he looks down at me. 'You are perfect. Absofuckinglutely perfect.' He leans over me with his hands pressing into the pillow as he nudges himself between my legs. 'Does it feel like I'm put off now?' he asks.

'Nope. Definitely not,' I giggle, running my hands up his chest.

'Kiss me,' he says, working his own magic with every bit of movement he makes. I grab his hair and pull him down so I can kiss him hard.

'I really should call Grayson,' he grumbles, lying behind me with his face snuggled into my neck. I have no idea what time it is but the sun's going down. We've been in our cocoon all day, and it's been bliss. He gets up with a groan and starts pulling on his underwear.

'Does Grayson know about your home away from home?' I ask, sitting up.

He shakes his head. 'He will when I give him the address to pick us up.'

'What if we get a taxi back to the house?' I saw a load of cash stuffed in one of his drawers when he paid the pizza delivery guy. 'He doesn't need to know about this place. That way you get to keep it as your sanctuary.'

He throws me a wink. 'I like the way you think.' He reaches over and grabs my hand, pulling me to my feet. 'Get that sexy little ass of yours in the shower.'

When the cab pulls up outside the main gate to The Orchard, we get out and share a look. A nervous, apprehensive look. I didn't want to leave our bubble, and neither did he, but we've been missing for an entire day. It's going to be hard enough explaining why I ran off, never mind where we've been for the last fifteen hours or so.

'Ready?' he asks.

'No,' I moan.

He scans my face which is scrunched up in thought. 'What are you thinking, Beautiful?'

'I think that we shouldn't tell him, or anyone, about last night. I think we keep it simple. We separately followed Toby but met just before he ran off. He got away and we found somewhere to sleep. Then you hailed down a ride. I don't want to upset

Grayson. It's pretty obvious he has feelings for me and I don't want to upset him. Or make him cross. Last time he was angry, he beat the shit out of you.'

'True. But at the same time, I don't want to stop seeing you.' He looks at the access panel which opens the gate and thinks. It feels like forever as he decides what he wants to do. 'We can keep things between us for now? See how things go in private?' He looks at me and waits. 'Secret sex is always better,' he adds with a wink.

As I chew my lip, he takes my hand and takes on a serious expression.

'You're not just another notch on my bedpost. I know what people say about me. But it's different with you. You do believe me, don't you?'

I nod and give his hand a squeeze. I'm suddenly terrified. Now I've had him, I can't bear the thought of losing him. I love him! But there's so much mess around us. It seems impossible.

'Lilly, I want this. I want you. Please don't get cold feet on me now. We can make this work, but it just needs to be kept on the down low for a little while. When the time's right, we won't need to sneak around. I'll talk to Grayson in a day or two and figure this out. Okay?'

Again, I nod. He taps the code in, and the gate slowly starts to open.

Walking down the long gravel path, the house finally comes into view. Ahead of us, dotted around in groups and all chatting to each other, must be three dozen Nomads. They all turn to face us as we walk up the path together. A few go inside and shortly afterwards Grayson comes out. Seeing I'm okay, he visibly sighs with relief before yelling.

'WHERE THE HELL HAVE YOU BEEN?!'

He charges towards us and pulls me into a hug before shaking me.

'What the hell were you thinking going off like that? And you!' He lets go of me and turns on Gabriel. 'You couldn't use a phone and let me know you two were okay?' But he pulls him into a hug too. 'Where's Toby? Did you find him?'

'We did, but he got away,' Gabriel says as his brother lets him go. 'I'll fill you in inside. It's been a hell of a night, and I'm sure Lilly could do with a good night's sleep.'

'Are you alright?' Grayson asks me.

'I'm fine. Tired but otherwise okay.' He looks at me for a moment as his brain ticks over. I know he's dying to ask a million questions but he won't with all these people around us, listening to every word. Placing his hand on my back, he gives me a gentle nudge towards the house.

'Get inside. I'll feel much better with you inside.'

Yeah, because I was safe inside last night.

The mess in the lobby's been cleared. The charred table's been removed, and the blood's been mopped up. You would never have known that Toby was here. Or Tobias.

Billy nods when I see him standing inside Grayson's office. He comes out to greet us.

'Miss Hooper. Nice to see you in one piece.'

'Thank you, Billy.'

'Lilly,' Grayson says. 'How about you go get some rest. It's late, and you must be exhausted. I'll have some food sent up to you if you like?' he says kindly. This is weird. I was expecting yelling and threats. Demands to know where we'd been and what we'd been doing but instead, he's reasonable.

'I'm fine, thank you.'

'Here.' He pulls out my watch from his trouser pocket and hands it to me. 'Please keep it on. I don't think my nerves can take losing you again.'

Collins appears from the kitchen followed by Gabriel. Collins looks relieved to see me and heads straight over. I meet him halfway and we hug each other.

'Thank goodness you're okay. You scared the hell out of me running off like that.'

'I'm so sorry you got caught up in all that last night. Are you okay? Did you get hurt?'

'Don't be daft. I'm fine, just glad you two are okay.' We let each other go.

'Where's Amara?'

He keeps looking over my shoulder at Grayson.

'She's upstairs asleep,' he says, forcing a smile. 'She's been awake since you left, but she crashed about an hour ago. She'll be relieved to see you.'

'I'll leave her to sleep. Can you ask her to come find me when she's awake?'

'Of course.'

He pats my arm before Grayson calls over. 'Gabriel. A word in my office before you head up to bed.' He goes into his office leaving the door wide open ready for him.

Gabriel looks down at me. My worry must be apparent.

'Everything will be fine,' he insists. 'I'll tell him what went down so he's all filled in and that will be that. Stop fretting. Go get a shower and some rest.'

With a little wink, Gabriel leaves and follows Grayson into his study.

'C'mon,' Collins says. 'I'll walk up with you.' Collins takes my arm and starts leading me upstairs. I don't miss the glares from the odd Nomad as I go past.

'What's up with them?' I ask Collins quietly.

'Grayson wasn't too happy about you getting past them. He had words. Loud, angry words. Plus, you did kind of slam them into the wall before you left.'

'Oh yeah.' I forgot about that.

Once inside my room, Collins closes the door, turns and takes my shoulders. His face is more severe than I've ever seen it.

'Lilly, no matter what happens, no matter what Grayson says to you or how kind he is, you can't tell him that you and Gabriel slept together.'

'What?!' He's caught me completely off guard. 'I don't know what-'

'Gabriel told me just now. After I told him that Grayson went absolutely fucking mental when he realised you two were gone. It wasn't your safety he was worried about. It was the fact you two were alone together. I've never, in all my time with him, seen him so unstable. He killed the two Nomads that were posted at your door and terrified Amara half to death. He kept accusing her of letting you leave. He was adamant that she knew where you two were and demanded she admits to knowing that you two were in a secret relationship which of course she denied. He even frightened me.'

'I'm so sorry. Is she okay?' I gasp, horrified.

'She's fine. Shook up, but okay.'

'He really killed those two men?' I feel awful. How could I be so selfish?

'He did. He's told us all not to tell you that though. He doesn't want you to see him as the type of man who kills out of anger.' He rolls his eyes.

'Bit late for that. I just wanted this to be over. I thought I could get the journal for him.'

'This is about more than the journal. This is Grayson and his pride. He wants you, and if he knows that Gabriel had you, I dread to think what will happen. He doesn't take rejection well. He said that if anything happens between you and Gabriel, he'll banish him.'

'Banish?'

'Send him away. He won't be allowed back to the coven, and if he did come back, he could be killed.'

'He could do that?'

'It's what he did to Toby! And they were really close.'

'You mean Bias, his brother.' I add with raised eyebrows. He blinks at me in surprise. 'Yeah. He told me. Not cool, Collins. And when Amara wakes up, you can tell her that I'm not happy she kept it from me either.'

'I'm sorry. It's just, how you reacted at your uncle's house...'

'Yeah. I know. But still.'

'Grayson's been kind to you. I don't want that to change, and I won't have Amara caught in the crossfire or watch as Gabriel loses his family, his home and his coven. Gabriel agrees. He was horrified to learn about his brother's reaction. He knew it would be bad, but banishment? No matter what, Grayson can't know about you two. Please, I can't lose him. I can't lose any of you.' He waits for me to say something.

'Of course. I won't say a word. I promise.'

'Good,' he says with a relieved sigh. 'And you're alright about the whole Bias thing?'

'I would have killed you all if I'd known,' I laugh nervously. 'The way I was. You did the right thing.'

'I hope so.' He turns to leave. With his hand on the door handle, he stops and looks back at me over his shoulder. He looks even more concerned.

'What is it, Collins?'

'I don't want to speak out of turn. Gabriel's a good friend of mine. He's a good guy when he wants to be. He's good to you. Amara loves you, and I love her, so I'm going to give you some advice.'

'Okay.' Where's this going?

'Gabriel doesn't have the best track record with women. He chases them down, and when he gets what he wants, he tends to lose interest.'

Oh. That's where this is going.

'I love the guy,' he says. 'But he can be a real dick to the women he dates. And if Grayson threatens him, he may not choose you. I just want you to be prepared for that. I know you've been through hell with your family, and with Toby. I don't want to see you get hurt. Just... don't put all your hopes on Gabriel. I would hate for him to let you down.' He gives a small bow and keeps his eyes on the floor. 'Night, Lilly.'

'Night, Collins.'

He leaves and closes the door behind him. I stand at the end of my bed with my fingers knotted together and a weight on my chest that's almost crippling.

After a night tossing and turning in bed, I get up with the sunrise and have a shower. Amara didn't come to see me. I've been left alone all night. No one has come to check on me, and by no one, I really mean Gabriel. I know it's not like he can come and see me easily, but still. I've missed him.

I trace my fingers along my skin, just as he did as he held me in his arms last night. I tingle and smile at the mere memory of it all.

I'm in love.

I'm completely besotted. But he may not be, and I must prepare myself for that. He may not be willing to risk everything for me.

And he shouldn't.

When the sun rises, I head downstairs for a cup of coffee. But hearing someone playing the piano in the lounge, I stop. The melody's beautiful and floats through the lobby, luring me in.

My heart swells as I stand there silently watching Gabriel play. The man is full of surprises.

'You know...it's rude to stare,' he says as his fingers slow to a stop.

'How long have you played?' I ask.

'A while,' he replies, his back still to me.

'You play beautifully,' I tell him, heading over to perch on the stool beside him.

'Thanks.' He glances at me and smiles. A smile which I return tenfold, especially when I see he's unharmed. Grayson didn't go postal again. Thank goodness.

I rest my fingers on the keys before he takes his away. I start to play. I haven't played for years, but it's a skill I haven't lost. My fingers move without effort as I play Beethoven's Moonlight Sonata and I feel his eyes on me.

'This was my favourite piece to learn,' I tell him as I continue to play. 'I found it beautifully sad.' I smile, looking up at him. My fingers still move, and I don't miss a note. But the smile I get back is less than enthusiastic.

'I had no idea you could play the piano,' He looks back at my fingers.

'Mr Simmons taught me. Him and his metal ruler.' I turn my attention back to the keys. 'He also taught me this one.' I stop and start another melody.

'Is that Danse Macabre?' he asks. 'You're very talented.' He sits in silence as he watches me till I'm done. 'That was lovely, Lilly. Thank you for playing for me.'

'My pleasure.' I rest my hands on my lap and look over hoping to catch his eye, but he keeps his eyes firmly on the keys. I don't know if it's me and my paranoia about what Collins said last night, but he seems a little off. 'How did it go with Grayson last night?'

'Fine,' he says simply. 'I told him everything we agreed to tell him. He was pissed that we both went off on our own, but he's glad we're okay.'

'He didn't hurt you, did he?'

'No.'

'And he doesn't know...' I gesture between us.

'No.' He gets to his feet. 'No, he doesn't. He made it clear that he wouldn't be happy if anything did happen, but no. He has no idea. I'm really sorry, Lilly, but I have to head out. I have a busy day, and I'm already running behind.' He leans down and gives me a kiss on the top of my head. As he goes to leave I take his hand. He stops and looks down at me.

'Are you okay?' I ask. 'You seem-'

'I'm fine,' he says with a shrug. 'I just have a shit ton to do today.' He pulls his hand free which I try to keep hold of. 'I'll see you later though, yeah?' He turns and leaves the room. I watch the empty doorway. That weight in my chest is getting heavier. It lifts a little when Amara pokes her head around the door.

'Amara,' I say with utter joy.

She, however, bursts into tears and comes at me with her arms wide. I meet her in a hug and do my best to calm her down.

'I was so worried about you,' she sobs into my neck. 'Grayson was so cross, and no one could find you.' She gives my arm a sudden whack. 'WHAT THE HELL WERE YOU THINKING GOING AFTER TOBY ALONE LIKE THAT! ANYTHING COULD HAVE HAPPENED!'

'I'm sorry,' I tell her, rubbing my arm. 'I never meant to get you in trouble.'

'HE COULD HAVE KILLED YOU, LILLY! DO YOU HAVE NO GODDAMN SELF-PRESERVATION?'

'Stop screaming at me. I said I was sorry.' Tears are streaming down her face and I have no idea if she's angry, frightened or sad. I guess all three. And I don't have the heart to tell her off for lying about who Toby really is.

'SORRY? SORRY? YOU'RE A BLOODY IDIOT! YOU COULD HAVE DIED!'

'My feelings exactly.' We both turn to see Grayson in the doorway. He folds his arms and looks at Amara. 'Morning, Amara. I understand you're upset but can you refrain from screaming and hitting the Arcane?'

Amara wipes her tears quickly and composes herself.

Lowering her head a little, she says, 'I'm sorry, sir.'

He looks at me.

'Good morning, Miss Hooper. Did you sleep okay?'

'I did. Thank you.' Amara's gone pale and seems to be shrinking. She's afraid. I subtly move so I'm between them. 'You?' I ask him.

'Perfectly well now I know you're safe.' He starts towards me. Amara starts backing away. 'Listen. Gabriel told me what happened.'

Oh no. He stands in front of me, reading my face.

'Would you mind giving me your version of events?' he asks, baiting me into revealing some unknown secrets, I'm sure. He's testing me. But I know what Gabriel told him. We practised it all the way home.

'I heard the fight. I wanted to help. I thought I could talk Toby down. Maybe get the journal. Your Nomads wouldn't let me past, so I took off my binding spell and forced my way through. I didn't give anyone a choice. Amara tried to stop me, but I didn't listen.' His smile goes for the briefest second as he looks at her over my shoulder, but it returns as soon as he's looking back at me. I hate that smile. It's far from genuine. I carry on. 'You were all looking for him in the orchard, but I knew he was in the woods. I didn't want to lose him or put anyone else in danger, so I followed him alone. I caught up with him. We fought. He attacked me, but Gabriel found us and got him off. They fought, but Toby pinned us down with his fire. I tried to stop him, but I wasn't strong enough. He ran. He didn't have the journal with him.'

'Hmm. Exactly what Gabriel said. What happened after?'

'It was cold, and we were lost. We had no money or phone, so Gabriel broke into an empty old farmhouse. We fell asleep waiting for morning. We were so tired we slept most the day before waving someone down and heading back to the house. That's it.' His eyes furrow a little and we all stand in silence. Finally, he breaks eye contact. I held my poker face well I think.

'Toby should never have got that close to you in the first place,' he says. 'He lived here with us a long time before he left, so he knows this place like the back of his hand.'

'There's a small hole in that big wall. It's behind a bush. You wouldn't know it was there without looking for it. I'm pretty sure that's how he got in here.'

'Is that so? Hmm. I'll have the whole wall searched and the hole filled. He had friends helping him last night. Three of the Nomads we had in the house were his. You know better than most how manipulative he can be, but I promise I'm doing everything I can to make this house safe. When the Veil is down, there are a hundred spells I could do to protect us all, but until then I'm constrained. I hope you can forgive me.'

I can't help but look over at Amara in shock at his calm reaction to all this. The look on her face tells me she is too. He gives a small laugh at our response.

'Don't look so surprised. You did the best you could. We all did. Him getting away can't be helped. I'm just glad my brother found you and kept you safe. Anyway, I was hoping we could do some practising together today. If you feel up to it?'

'Of course.' He stands aside with a gesture for me to follow. After a final hug with Amara and a promise to catch up later, I follow him to his office.

Grayson sits on the floor of his office with his legs crossed and takes off his tie.

'What are you doing?' I laugh as he beams up at me.

'Sit with me,' he says, tapping the floor opposite. Following his lead, I sit and cross my legs. This is weird.

I notice his eyes drift to my neck and his brow furrows. He glides his finger across his own throat.

'You're not wearing the necklace I bought you for Christmas. Do you not like it?'

My hand flies to the place where I know the necklace should really be resting, out of politeness if nothing else. I'm sure it cost a small fortune.

'No, it's on my dresser. I just forgot to put it on today. That's all. But I do love it. It's gorgeous.'

He accepts my explanation and swiftly moves on to the topic at hand.

'You seem to be able to control your Telekinesis well. I have a fair few Nomads that can testify to that,' he says with a chuckle. Not at all acknowledging that he killed two of them for my getting past them. I won't reveal that I know. It will get Collins in trouble. 'Would you mind demonstrating it for me?' he asks, dropping his tie between us. I feel the warm surge of my magic when he gives me access through the Bloodstone. I make the tie rise above our heads and perform little circles and swirls before laying it gently back down.

'That was remarkably controlled. Well done. Can you do it with your eyes closed?'

'I can try.' I close my eyes and feel out for the tie. When I hear a smash, I open my eyes and see a lamp on the floor by the wall at the other end of the room.

'Apparently not,' he says, looking at the pieces on the floor.

'Shit. Sorry.'

'No problem.' He turns back to me. 'Can I ask you to try and refrain from swearing?'

'Oh, I didn't think it bothered you.'

'It doesn't really. But you're so...' He smiles, 'Sweet. It doesn't suit you.'

'Erm, okay. I'll try.'

'Let's see your fire.' He carries on. 'Hold out your hand.' I lay my palm flat and my fire springs to life, covering my skin.

'Can you make it a normal colour? The fact that it's black lets others know that you have suffered a Break. Nothing to be ashamed of, but let's just see.'

'How do I do it?'

'You need to calm yourself. Inside as well as out. Think of a time or a place when you were happy. That should help.'

I look into the fire and try. But it remains the unnatural black and white.

'Never mind,' he says kindly. 'Can you use it to light the fire in my fireplace?' He scoots over so I have a clear view of the tall grey fireplace and I reach out my hand. The fire shoots across the room and lands in the grate like water thrown from a bucket. Extinguishing the fire in my palm, I smile proudly. He nods his approval.

'So that's Elemental and Telekinesis down. Well done. We have four other realms to manifest together. Sensativa isn't something for you to build on, so it's not something we need to practice. Sight, Energy, Physical and Mental is what we have to focus on. There are a few methods we could try, but usually, it's raw emotion that kicks it in. Remind me again, you presented Telekinesis first, right? Tell me about it.'

'I was little,' I start. He leans back on his hands and listens intently. 'Maybe four. I was playing in my room when Theo came into the house where my mum, dad and I lived. He was yelling at my mum, trying to get past her to my room, but she wouldn't let him. He shoved her, and she fell. I remember this sudden feeling of fear in my stomach that made it hard to breathe, and when he saw me, a knife from the counter flew across the room straight at him. It cut his face, and while he was trying to get himself together, Mum grabbed me and we ran.'

I remember it clearly. Too clearly. His face, his voice then my terror as I experienced my surge of magic for the first time.

'So, fear. And your fire came a couple of years ago?'

'Yes,' I say uneasily. Oh no, please don't ask me about that.

'Tell me about it.'

I inwardly groan and feel my face redden as I look down at my hands. 'It's a bit... personal.'

'Anything you say is between us. I would never tell anyone else, and I won't judge you for it.' He rests his hand on my knee. 'I promise.' He pulls it away and sits waiting.

'When Toby knew I was a witch, he became obsessed with teaching me stuff. He would try and get me to make fire, but I told him I couldn't. He tried different ways to... encourage it.'

'What methods did he try?'

'Fear, at first. I told him about what happened with Theo, and he thought it would work again, but I always knew he wouldn't let anything too bad happen to me, so it didn't work. Then he tried anger, but that didn't work either. Getting angry was hard. I thought very little of myself back then. Then he tried...positive encouragement.'

'Positive?'

'Sex,' I say it quickly.

'So, when your fire manifested, you two were...'

'I was having...' I clear my throat and fail to say the word.

'You were having an orgasm?' he says sounding nothing more than polite. I nod and continue staring at my hands. This is so embarrassing. 'Okay. So, fear and pleasure have been your motivators so far. Well, there are other things we can try.' He reaches into his trouser pocket and pulls out a folded piece of paper. He opens it up and hands it to me.

'What's this?' I ask.

'It's a list of motivators. Now, there are a few, and if there are any you don't want to try then that's fine, but I thought we could start at the top and work our way down. Fear and pleasure are on there, but the same motivator doesn't usually trigger multiple manifestations.'

I look through the list.

Meditation. Hypnosis. Joy. Surprise. Pleasure. Sadness. Fear. Anger. Hatred.

And the last one.

Pain.

'Pain?' I look at him suddenly feeling very nervous. 'You want to hurt me?'

'No. Of course not. These are just the main triggers. I'm going to start with this one first.' He leans over and points to Meditation. 'We don't have the journal yet, so we have time to experiment. I'll see if I can get your Energy to manifest using meditation. Collins will help you to manifest Physical and Gabriel will work with Mental. Happy to start today with me?'

'Okay.' I refold the paper and hand it back.

He describes what his lightning feels like to use. How it feels crawling on his skin and how he uses what he calls mental willpower to control it. He lets it streak briefly over my hand. It hurts, but not massively.

'That's because I wasn't trying to hurt you,' he tells me.

'Can I ask how you manifested your magic?' I ask.

'Well, I was five. My mother and father were witches so I knew I would be one too.'

'Is that how it works? If your parents are witches, their children will be?'

He nods. 'Two magical parents make a magical child. If a human and a witch have a baby, they will be a human child.' He leans forward, resting his elbows on his knees. 'Magic usually manifests with heightened emotions. It can be something as simple as being startled to something big, like fearing for your life. Most witches present young. A child's emotions are always felt strongly. They feel sadness, joy and anger stronger than adults. Well, Gabriel was maybe a week old and he just would not stop crying. We got hit by a storm. The rain fell and fell. Back then, there were no roads, just dirt tracks, and the only way to leave our village was over this narrow little bridge that went over a wide stream. One night, Gabriel got a fever. There was a medicine woman a mile or so away. On the other side of the bridge. My father was away, so our mother bundled us up on a horse, and we made our way to her. The bridge was washed out. Gabriel was getting worse by the minute. Mother had Energy magic. She reached out and used her lightning to strike down a tree hoping to use it as a bridge, but it missed and fell into the water. I was so afraid. The weather was apocalyptic, and my new little brother was going to die. The tree moved. I wanted it to move, and it did. We got across and to the medicine woman. She treated Gabriel, and he was fine after a couple of days.'

'You manifested your magic to save his life?'

'Of course. I'd do anything for my little brother. Consciously or subconsciously. I love Gabriel more than anything. Even if he does give in to whims and flights of fancy all too often without thinking it through.'

'He does?'

'Just ask the dozen or so young lady soldiers that used to be stationed in this house.' He tries to make the comment sound flippant. But I know it's well placed. 'Gabriel's fleeting attention and then his almost instant dismissal of far too many young Nomad ladies has led to many banishments unfortunately.'

'Banishments?' I repeat the word quietly, almost too afraid to say it too loudly.

'Yes. You see, he knows exactly what to say and what to do with the fairer sex. It's almost magic in itself to witness. They fall in love with him. Almost in an obsessive nature. Then he drops them. On more than one occasion, the spurned lady has turned violent towards him. Stalked him. Become very inappropriate or even attacked his new conquest. These actions have led to several dismissals on their part. Mainly because I can't very well sack my own brother. I need him. Not just because he's one of a handful of people with magic but also because he is the only real family I have left. So, you see, that's why I have forbidden him to chase after you.' He flashes me a sympathetic smile because I'm sure the look on my face is nothing short of crestfallen. 'I don't mean to presume that you and he are anything more than friends. I've been assured that you aren't. But I can't banish you if it all goes horribly wrong. It's impossible. You are far too dangerous to face such a cruel and dangerous world on your own. And there are far too many enemies beyond these walls who would gladly see you dead. Toby's visit, the attacker the night you tried to run away, Theo's assault at the tree lot...these are just three men of hundreds that would tear the world apart to get their hands on the last Arcane Witch alive. So, if things did get nasty between you two, which they would, believe me, I would have no alternative. I couldn't send you away. I would have to send Gabriel away, and that would simply break my heart.'

I have to quickly regroup my rampant thoughts so I don't look like a dumbfounded fool. With a small, insincere shrug and disingenuous nod, I pretend that I understand his reasons. Maybe it's not acting. Could I really just be another in a long line of women that Gabriel has chased down and dumped? Everyone seems to think so. Amara has been very truthful about his past. Collins too. Even Theo has made similar remarks. What if it's not his past? What if it's his pattern? To make girls crazy about him so when he moves on, they're driven insane by jealousy. I admit the thought of losing him now is a painful concept. A very painful concept. Unbearable in fact.

'So yes, I know it seems crazy to insist that nothing more than friendship transpires between you two. And it may smack of jealousy.'

Too right, I think to myself.

'But there is a very serious reason behind it. You have been through enough, and all I want is for you to be happy here. I want this to be a safe place. Not only for you physically, but mentally and spiritually too. The idea of watching you look on as Gabriel continues using women, after manipulating your already very fragile heart, causes me pain. That is why I have forbidden it. Can you understand that?' He looks at me expectantly. What the hell can I say to that?

Nothing. I can't say a single thing because I've already done everything he was afraid of. I've slept with Gabriel. I've fallen in love with him. And now, perhaps it wasn't my imagination. Maybe it's the beginning of the brush off he seems to favour after successfully getting what he wants. Shit. I'm so confused. And as my brain continues to sift through the mess of self-doubt and worry, Grayson's watching me keenly. I snap out of my train of inner thought and smile, nodding understandably while my insides squirm with uncertainty.

All of a sudden, he slaps his palms on his knees, making me jump violently.

'Come on, let's get to work.' He makes me sit in an odd pose with my hands cupped together, palms up. He's very particular about how I should be breathing and what almost every part of my body should be doing.

'Visualise the power. See the lightning. Feel it on your skin.'

This goes on for a couple of hours. By the end of our session, I've come to the conclusion that Grayson's method, although much more relaxed than Toby's, just won't work. I remember my manifestations. One driven by the kind of terror only a little girl who's scared for her mum can muster. The other sparked by the pleasure only a woman can feel, when the person she loves tells her they love her for the first time, while making her body feel absolute passion and pleasure. Grayson wants to use meditation and sheer force of will.

It will be a massive waste of time.

He walks me to his office door and opens it like a gentleman.

'We made good progress today,' he says. As I unintentionally roll my eyes, he insists with a smile, 'We did. Honestly. It may not feel like it, but we're moving in the right direction.

'If you say so,' I sigh.

'I do. Go and get some rest, Lilly. You've had a hard few days.' He continues to hold his easy smile as he gestures for me to head upstairs. As I turn to leave, he takes my arm gently in his hand. I look back at him and once more he's looking at my neck. He takes his finger and runs it ever so slightly along my clavicle.

'Wear the necklace I gave you, will you? It will really look stunning on you.'

I nod and step back away from his touch which as ever makes my skin turn to fire.

'I will,' I tell him. 'Thank you for your lesson today.' I turn and leave him standing in his doorway. He remains there, watching me until I'm out of sight and heading up the second flight of stairs.

The sun's gone down. I watched it set from the sill of my bedroom window with a single headphone in my ear. Gabriel's iPod gift with an endless stream of music is in my hand.

There's a slight tap on the door.

'Come in,' I call.

It's Amara. And I'm thrilled to see her. I give her the mother of all hugs, and thankfully, she hugs me back. She seems to have gotten all the yelling out of her system.

I tell her everything that happened. Everything. Both with Toby and with Gabriel.

'You should have told me who he was,' I tell her.

'I was under orders not to. And then you told me what he's done to you, and I couldn't. I asked Gabriel to tell you. But he said no. I am really sorry.' She looks so worried as she watches me. 'Please don't hate me.'

'I don't,' I sigh. 'It's done now. In the grand scheme of things, it doesn't really matter.'

'Talking of Toby, he said that he would give you the journal if what...they hand you over to him? Get back together with him? What does he want exactly?' she asks.

'He just said he wanted me back. That he'd get me to bring down the Veil, but he gets to keep me afterwards. Just being that close to him made me feel dirty. I was so glad Gabriel was there.'

'So, are you and Gabriel a couple now?' she asks. She's been very keen to know all the details of mine and Gabriel's time together.

'Not sure,' I tell her. 'We're keeping it very quiet whatever it is, so not a word. Collins knows but other than that-'

'I get it. I'll take it to my grave.'

'I am so sorry that I got you in trouble with Grayson.'

She lets out a long breath. 'I'm not going to lie, he scared the hell out of me. I thought he was going to use his lightning on me.'

We're summoned downstairs for food by a Nomad before we can talk anymore.

In the kitchen, Gabriel and Collins are sitting side by side picking at a pizza. I take the seat next to Gabriel thrilled to see him.

'How was your day?' I ask.

'Fine. Yours?' he says, barely looking up from his pepperoni.

'Alright. I missed you.' I go to take his hand, but Hendrix walks in, so I retreat.

'Glad to see you're in one piece, Little Witch. Going after the little freak alone? Very brave. Did I say brave?' He pours himself a vodka. 'I meant stupid.'

'I don't remember asking your opinion,' I reply, taking a slice of pizza. Hendrix laughs and just stands there.

Gabriel's phone buzzes in his pocket. He glances at the screen and then at me, before getting to his feet and leaving to answer.

'Wonder who that could be,' Hendrix says with a derisive snort, before carrying on drinking his vodka.

What does he mean by that?

Gabriel doesn't come back. I hear the front door open and close. That's the most interaction I have with him all day. Even Amara seems bemused at his behaviour. I call it a night and head to bed, hoping tomorrow will put him in a better mood. Maybe Grayson was tougher on him than Gabriel's letting on. Or worse, he's giving me the brush off. God damn it, I hate feeling like this.

I decide that I'll talk to him about it tonight when everyone's gone to bed. I'll sneak into his room and make sure he's okay. I bid goodnight to Amara and Collins and head up to my room. I wait upstairs, watching the door and straining to sense Gabriel. But by three am there's still no sign. He doesn't come home all night, and the only sounds I hear are the Nomads on duty as they walk up and down the hall.

'PLEASE!' she screams 'PLEASE STOP!'
But I don't. I think maybe I never will.
She keeps screaming. Calling for help. For me to stop.
Her blood is dripping onto my feet. Seeping beneath the thin black straps of my stilettos.
My fingers are knotted in her long blonde hair as I once more lift her head and slam her not so pretty little face onto the cracked and broken mirror on the wall.
She's already lost two teeth. They're by my feet.
She tries to untangle my hands. To push herself off from the broken glass that I keep forcing her features into.
But I'm fuelled with anger. With jealousy.
'I'm sorry,' she cries. 'I didn't know. He didn't tell me.'

I know that. Of course I know.

But that doesn't stop me.

I just keep thrusting her fucked up face into the remains of the mirror, again and again.

I'll be damned if she leaves with us tonight.

I'll be damned if I'm forced to share him with another woman.

He's mine.

MINE!

With a final, forceful slam from me, she closes her eyes and falls limp.

I drop her like the sack of shit she is and watch her lying unconscious,

bleeding and disfigured at my feet.

I wash my hands, dry them with paper towels, step over her and leave the bathroom.

When I reach the exit to the club, I nod politely to the bouncer who smiles and gives me a wink.

The only interest I have is in the man watching me walk towards him, with his hands tucked in his pockets and a sly smile on his face.

'Where's our friend?' he asks, looking behind me for the stray tart he picked up inside.

'She changed her mind,' I tell him, wrapping my finger in the waist of his black jeans and pulling him closer.

His hands settle comfortably on my hips. 'Looks like your stuck with just me.'

He leans in and kisses me hard.

'I'm never stuck with you. Come on, Red, we have another three hours until we need to get you back home before anyone realises you're gone.'

'Where to now?'

Please not to find another blonde to join our party.

'To a hotel.'

'Just us?'

'Just us.' He wraps his strong arm around my waist and leads me out. 'By the way,' he says with a soft laugh. 'You forgot to clean her blood off your feet.'

'Morning, Honey.' I wake to Amara lying beside me in my bed. She's under my covers and holding two cups of coffee. One she hands to me.

'How do you manage to sneak in here all the time?' I laugh.

'Not hard. You sleep like you're dead. You know, *when* you sleep.'

I sit up and rub the sleep from my weary eyes and hopefully the image of that poor young woman I horribly disfigured after she got caught up in the middle of one of Toby's games. And slap bang in the centre of my angry, violent, possessive rage.

According to the clock, it's eight am. I got five hours of uneasy sleep.

'Thanks.' I drink it down. Strong and hot. Perfect.

'So... have you spoken to Gabriel yet?' she asks.

'No. I haven't seen him since he left the kitchen yesterday. You?' She shakes her head. 'He was a bit off with me yesterday.'

'He's probably just trying to make sure Grayson doesn't suspect anything. Give it a day or two. I'm sure he'll go back to normal. Talking about Grayson, how's he been with you?'

'Super nice actually. I think he's just relieved Toby didn't kill me or that I didn't run off. Yesterday was actually nice. Apart from being ignored by Gabriel,' I sigh and rest my head on her shoulder. 'I really hope he hasn't changed his mind about me. Just my luck. The first man I fall in love with is a psycho and the second man I fall for changes his mind.'

She sits up so fast she spills coffee all over the bed. 'You love him!'

'Keep your voice down!'

'Sorry,' she whispers. 'You're in love with him?'

I'm not ashamed. 'Yeah. Pretty sure I am. Actually, I'm completely positive I am.' Her face lights up as she pulls me into a hug.

'That's amazing! I'm sure he feels the same. I'm sure of it!'

'I'm going to tell him. Just be honest and tell him. Fuck it, right? Grayson doesn't need to know. We can keep it secret. Until the time is right. Right?'

'Right!'

We drink our coffee snuggled up in bed and then lay under the covers whispering for a while about the men we love. It's very girly, but lovely. She then heads down to Collins' bedroom to get dressed.

Dressed and ready to face the day, I head out into the hall. Closing my bedroom door behind me, I make my way to the stairs. Amara's on her way back up, singing happily to herself. She is so happy about my revelation, she's started making plans for double dates and joint holidays. When she reaches the top of the stairs, I hear Gabriel's bedroom door open. My spirits lift, and I fill with excitement. I've missed him. I take a deep breath and try to contain my grin. This is it. No more fucking about. I'm going to tell him. I'm going to walk straight up to him and tell him in no uncertain terms that I've fallen in love with him. That I'm willing to do whatever needs to be done to be with him.

From where I'm standing, I can't see him. But one look to Amara and I can tell she can. Whatever she sees takes her happy smile, and instead, she turns even more pale than usual. When she spots me, she looks ready to faint. She runs to me, takes my arm and starts pulling me back to my room.

'Go inside,' she says desperately. 'Go back to your room, Honey.'

'What are you doing?' I ask, pulling my arm free as she tries to drag me back into my room.

She takes my hand and pleads desperately, 'Honey, please. Just go back to your room.' She's in full panic mode, pulling and tugging at my arm. She looks down at my wrist. 'Where's your watch?'

'I took it off when I showered. I just forgot to…what's wrong with you?!' I pull my arm free with a big yank. I don't like being manhandled and she's starting to piss me off. She keeps glancing over my shoulder.

'Amara, what the hell is wrong with you?'

I hear a soft little giggle from behind me. From the direction of Gabriel's room. Amara closes her eyes in defeat.

'Oh, Lilly,' she whispers. 'I'm so sorry.'

I turn. There at the top of the stairs is Gabriel. But he's not alone. He's with Ava.

And they're together.

She's in his arms. He's shirtless and kissing her neck as she playfully laughs. Her hands are all over him. And heartbreakingly, his are all over her. She stands on her tip-toes, and they kiss. He holds her close. It's passionate. It's intense.

It's devastating.

I feel like I've been gutted with a carving knife and my insides are spilling out onto the floor. He sees me. The bastard gives me a polite nod and then goes back into his room like he's not just betrayed me. Like he hasn't just taken every word he's ever said to me and turned them into nothing more than meaningless lies used to do precisely what everyone warned me about.

He bedded me. And he's left me.

Ava lingers at the top of the stairs smirking at me as a tear slides down my cheek. Amara takes my hand which stops me from launching myself at her.

'Morning, Lilly. Amara,' she says smugly, tucking her coat under her arm. 'Lovely day...don't you think?' she laughs as she leaves. I hear her all the way down the stairs. Laughing.

Tears continue to stream down my cheeks as Amara tries to talk me into going back to my room. I'm rooted to the spot.

I thought we were together. I thought I meant something to him. But Collins was right. He got what he wanted, and he's moved on. Back to her. I turn and look at Amara who seems devastated for me.

'Please. Please tell me I imagined that, Amara. Tell me you didn't just see that.'

'Honey...come back inside. He's not worth a single tear.'

The old me would have turned on my heel, returned quietly to my room and silently cried out of sight. I would have thought that I probably deserved it. That I got the wrong end of the stick.

But not this time.

I look back to his door, and the strangest thing happens.

I get angry.

I get really, fucking angry.

Chapter 18

'Come inside,' Amara pleads quietly. 'Take a second to calm down. I'm sure there's an explanation-'

'An explanation?' I almost hiss the words at her. 'Are you that naive or are you just pretending to be?' I snatch my hand out of hers, wipe my tears and start heading towards Gabriel's room. She runs after me and stands in my way.

'You can't go in there and start yelling. Grayson will hear you. He can't know about you two, Lilly, please.'

'Move,' I tell her. 'Move, or I'll move you.'

'I'm not a Nomad you can boss around.' She stands firm, blocking my path. 'I'm your best friend. You don't have your binding spell on. You might lose control. And if Grayson hears you and figures out what happened between you, Gabriel will be banished. He may be a dick but you don't want that for him, do you?'

I barge past her and head to Gabriel's door.

'You have no idea what I want for him.'

I barge in without knocking and slam the door closed behind me.

He's sitting on the edge of his large four poster bed with the sheets wrinkled and the duvet on the floor. This scene hurts like hell.

His elbows are resting on his knees with his hands clasped together. He looks up at me and says nothing. Not a word. I don't look away from him. I can't.

'You slept with her?'

He just keeps looking at me.

'Of course you have.' The evidence is everywhere. 'Why? Why would you do that?'

He gets to his feet still half naked and looking tired.

'It was just sex. Calm down.'

I'm ready to attack. To scratch and claw at his pretty face. But when I see her bra lying at the foot of his bed, pain pierces my anger. I think I'm going to be sick. Every breath I take gets more constricted and every time I blink, more tears fall.

'Are you crying?' he asks, scowling at me like he's making sure he's seeing tears. 'Oh, shit, Lilly. If I knew you were going to get so clingy, I would never have slept with you.'

'Fuck you.' My voice is strained. Struggling to break through the sobs that are clawing up my throat.

'We never said we were exclusive. We had a good time, didn't we? I thought that's what you wanted?' He picks up his t-shirt from the floor and covers himself before walking away to another room. I follow him into his bathroom. He washes his hands and splashes water over his face as I watch him in the mirror. He doesn't even turn to look at me.

'This doesn't make sense. Everything you said to me? You thought of us having a future...what was all that? A trick? Lies?'

He holds the ridge of his nose before running his hand through his hair with a groan.

'Look, I like you. I do. We spent a fantastic night together, but that doesn't make us a couple. We're not an item, and I don't do exclusive. I never have. You knew that. It's not a secret, my lifestyle. I like sex. I liked it very much with you but if I'm honest...' he pauses.

'Spit it out. Be honest with me, Gabriel. For once at least,' I snap, wiping my tears.

'Well, you have a lot of baggage. The nightmares, the trust issues, the scars.'

'You said you didn't care about the scars.' I can't hide how much that comment hurts.

'I don't really, but it's what comes with them. All your drama, and then there's Toby. You're clearly not over him. I'm really sorry I've upset you. That wasn't my intention. But hey, if you want to hook up again? Maybe when the Veil's down, then I'm up for that.' His words and disinterest are killing me. 'But if it's monogamy, love and a relationship you're after...that's just not my thing.' He gestures to the door. 'I think you should go before you make even more of a scene.'

I'm trying to read him, to see any hint of a lie, but I don't think I can.

'Did Grayson threaten you?' I ask in one last-ditch attempt to make sense of what's happening. 'Is that what this is? Did he find out about us and threaten you with something? Because if he did just tell me. I can pretend to hate you if that's what this is about-'

'No,' he laughs, making his way back towards me and resting his hand on the door handle. 'If Grayson knew you and I had slept together, I would be getting the beating of a lifetime and banished from my family home. Which is just another reason why a relationship with you is a terrible idea.'

He's so calm. He looks like he could be talking about the weather, not crushing what's left of my heart.

'Put it behind you, focus on the spell. That's why you're here, right? To do the spell.' He gestures to his bedroom door. 'You really should go.'

'How could you do this to me? I thought you wanted to be with me.'

'Even if I did want a relationship with you, which I don't, I wouldn't pursue it. My life would be too complicated and to be honest, well, you're just not worth it. I'm sorry.'

I do it before I think. My fist slams into his face and knocks him clear on to the floor.

'Jesus!' he snaps, wiping the blood from his nose. 'Calm the fuck down!'

I just start hitting him. Punching and slapping him as he cowers on the floor, covering his face with his hands.

'YOU PIECE OF SHIT! YOU UTTER BASTARD!' I scream. With every word, I hit him harder. I cry and yell as he tries hard to protect his body from my attack. 'Do you have any idea what it took for me to open up to you? To get the courage to trust someone again? I let you into my heart and my bed, and you fuck another woman less than twenty-four hours later! You're a sick, perverted excuse of a man.' I finally stop hitting and stand up straight panting, trying to catch my breath. 'Everyone warned me. They all told me you would do this. Everyone knows what kind of man you are. You're a goddamn whore. A manipulative, vile whore. You're worse than Toby.' I look down at him as he lowers his arms to look up at me. He's furious.

'Compare me to Toby again. I dare you.'

'No problem,' I snarl. 'You're both egotistical whores who seem to enjoy making women suffer.'

'Lilly. I'm warning you.' He slowly pushes himself to his feet. His eyes not straying from mine one bit.

'You're nothing but a sad little boy with no self-worth which is why you feel the need to manipulate and fuck as many women as you can. To validate yourself because without your looks, your charm and your lies...you're nothing. Just like Toby. Two peas in a twisted pod. You know what? You're worse than him because he never lied about who he was. I never thought of him as a good man, but you...you had me thinking you were a misunderstood saint.'

'I'm nothing like him. Shut your mouth.'

'Oh yes you are,' I laugh spitefully before sneering the next words in his face. 'You two deserve each other as brothers.'

I scream as he lunges at me and slams me against the wall pinning my wrists up by my head.

'Keep talking. See what happens.' His tone chills me to the core. He gives me a shove, pressing me harder into the wall and tightening the grip he has on my wrists.

'Let me go.' I've never, not once, been so afraid of him.

'You think you can talk to me like this? You think you have the right to barge in here-'

'Get off me Gabriel,' I try to hide the fear in my voice and make myself sound threatening.

'You've told me what you think of me. Now it's my turn. You're nothing more than one of life's permanent victims. You're so desperate to be loved. So desperate to be wanted, that you'll take the attention of any man who looks your way. Even sick little psychopaths like Toby. The only person to blame for everything that's happened to you is you, Lilly. Your uncle, your boyfriend, everyone in your life has taken what they wanted from you and left you in the gutter because you let them. Because you're weak. Why would I ever choose a girl like you to spend my life with? Why would I want a Broken, scarred, unstable little witch like you?'

'Get off me, Gabriel.' There's no anger in my voice. It's barely a whisper. What he's just said to me, I never for a second would have thought he felt this way. My whole body has started to shake, and still, he holds me. 'Please. Please get off me. You're hurting me.'

'I'm barely touching you!'

'It hurts, please...'

'I said I'm barely touching you!'

'STOP TOUCHING ME! PLEASE, GABRIEL! IT'S BURNING MY SKIN! YOU'RE HANDS FEEL LIKE FIRE!'

His grip loosens, and his venomous expression starts to fade. Replaced instead with a look of horror.

'It hurts. Please, please you're hurting me.' I look at his hands that are now gently holding my wrists, but they may as well be covered in razor blades.

There it is. The pain. The hurt that I knew would come. His touch has become the same as everyone else's. The trust has gone.

'Get off me,' I sob. 'Please, stop touching me.'

He doesn't know what to do. He lets me go and stares at his own hands as if they're foreign objects. I flinch violently at every one of his movements. He has me cowering away from him. I've never felt so betrayed. So hurt. So afraid. Not even with Toby.

'I'm sorry. I'm-' He touches me, and I freak out completely.

'GET AWAY FROM ME!' I scream. With the words come a huge surge of power. My stomach feels like it's been punched with a fist as I double over. Gabriel lets me go and staggers back with wide eyes. He looks down at his feet and hands in bemusement.

'You took control of my body,' he breathes. 'You've manifested your Mental magic.'

I hold my belly, trying to regain control of the magic inside me.

I look up at him through my hair, my vision blurred through the heavy brim of tears and my entire body's shaking. That's all he can think about? That's all that matters right now? My magic? At this moment in time, I couldn't give a shit about any of that. I've just lost the man I love. I've been shattered into a hundred pieces after I only just started putting myself back together. All those things he's just said, the pain I felt as he touched me…I've lost him for good. This hurts more than anything Toby ever did to me. More than what anyone's ever done to me.

'You think I deserved it?' I say painfully. 'You think I deserved to be beaten? To be starved? You think I deserved to be raped, Gabriel?'

'R-raped?' he whispers. 'You were-'

'I didn't. I didn't deserve that, and I didn't deserve this.' I open the door. 'I'll never forgive you for what you've said. For what you've done to me. Never.' I leave the room, slamming the door behind me as I go.

'She fell asleep about an hour ago.' Amara's voice wakes me. I'm where I was when I fell asleep. Lying on my bed with my head on Amara's lap. Her fingers are still stroking my hair.'She caught Ava and Gabriel together.'

'Yeah. He told me.'

'She was on her way to tell him she was in love with him,' she says. 'How could he do this to her? He has feelings for her. I know it!'

'You know what he's like, Amara' Collin replies. 'Gabriel's not exactly reliable when it comes to women. But I have to admit, this is cruel. Even for him. Especially after everything he told me. I thought this time was going to be different. I thought he really liked her.'

I don't want to hear any more. I get up and walk into the bathroom.

'Lilly,' Amara calls after me. 'Honey, please talk to-'

I slam the door cutting her off. 'You can go now,' I call out as silent tears fall down my cheeks.

'I don't think you should be alone.'

'I really want you to leave. Both of you, please just leave.' I sound so emotionless. I feel numb and distant. Like I'm feeling too much, and my body can't cope, so it's just cutting it all off.

'I love you, Honey. Remember that,' Amara says, before leaving. I hear the door close and look at my reflection in the mirror. My red eyes are puffy from crying, and the dark circles are worse than ever. But most of all I just hate how pathetic I look. That I've let someone do this to me. I thought there was a ray of light at the end of this shitty tunnel called life. I thought that finally, I'd reached a point where I didn't have to worry about getting hurt all over again. What else do I have to go through until I can be happy?

Or is it me? Am I just unlovable?

And now I've manifested a new realm of power. Grayson will be thrilled, but I also know that I'm going to have to practice and hone this power with Gabriel. In Grayson's office, he said that Gabriel would help me manifest my Mental magic. How right he was. Screaming at Gabriel to get off me could easily have been another sentence. Get lost, drop dead, go fuck yourself. This is a dangerous power. I look at my wrists. The last place he touched me and I can still feel the white-hot sting from his betrayal on every inch he touched. It hurts. It will always hurt.

'Lilly?' Grayson calls gently through the bathroom door. 'Can you open up please?'

I wipe my eyes and clear my throat. 'Just a sec, Grayson.'

'I have to insist. Please open the door.'

I can't do anything to rid myself of these red eyes, and I can't say anything to convince him to leave, so I open the door. Grayson's sitting on my bed and taps the empty space beside him. I sit.

'So, I just had a chat with Gabriel. He said you two had a fight a couple of hours ago. That you got quite upset and that you hit him. Is that true?' He doesn't say any of this with anger or annoyance. He's completely calm and even comes across as reassuring.

'Yeah,' I reply. I'm just like one of the girls he described to me in his office not even twenty-four hours ago. God, he was so right.

'Are you alright?' he asks.

'Fine.'

'He also said that he had to restrain you and that when you told him to get off, your eyes turned black. He seems to think you manifested your Mental magic. Is that right?'

I nod, keeping my eyes down hoping he doesn't see how distraught I am. Gabriel may have broken my heart and let me down, but Grayson can never know why. He won't send me away. That's been made clear. Gabriel could lose his home, his family or get another beating from Grayson. Even after everything, I don't want that for him.

'You must have been really angry at him.'

'I'm sorry I lashed out. It won't happen again.'

He rests his hand on my back gently as he shakes his head. 'I'm not angry at you. I'm not even going to ask what the argument was about, but I'm sure I can guess. You thought you were special and then you saw him with Ava this morning and realised you weren't.'

'Something like that. Let me just say...you were right. I should have listened.'

'Well, I won't pry. I just wanted to make sure that you are okay. Mental magic can be scary and confusing.' He gives me a comforting smile which falters ever so slightly when he sees how upset I am. 'I am so sorry you got caught up with Gabriel like this. I tried to keep you apart. I could see you falling for him from the start, and I dreaded this happening. He's my brother. I love him dearly. But I've seen this too many times. Girl after girl falling for those blue eyes and charming smiles, only to be trampled on. He can't be loyal to one woman. Never has been able to. I'm just glad you saw him for what he is before it went beyond flirting.'

'You're not angry at me?'

'No. of course not. You see him for what he is now, and that's what matters. I just hope you're not angry at me.'

'Why would I be angry at you?'

'Because I've behaved like a jealous, possessive idiot when I had no right to. I only acted that way because I'm very keen on you and I know you deserve better than him. I think you are the most beautiful, strong and brave woman I've ever met.'

'You do?'

'I do. When we kissed, I admit I could see us having a future together, and when I saw your feelings grow towards my brother instead, jealousy got the better of me. I'm sorry. Would you like me to ask Gabriel to leave? I don't want you to be uncomfortable.'

'No,' I reply sadly. 'This was his home long before it was mine. It's fine. It was just a misunderstanding. That's all. Believe me, I'm crystal clear about him now.'

He gets to his feet. 'Don't stay up here all day. This is your home as well as his. Don't let Gabriel take that from you.'

'Grayson?' I call after him. He stops and turns. 'Is there any possibility that I could stay somewhere else? Maybe with the Nomads or at a hotel? Just until we get the Veil down.'

'I'll be honest with you. That can't happen. I want to tell you that I can keep you safe here with me, but I think we can both agree that's not a hundred per cent true. This house is patrolled by dozens of men. There are three witches and a vampire here, and even with all that, Toby has managed to get to you. What chance do you think you would have out there alone? Theo, Toby, Hunters...I can't risk losing you. Not this close to bringing the Veil down. Never mind the fact that I am still, very keen on you.' He smiles coyly before walking back to me. 'I'll make you a deal. Stay here. I'll talk to Gabriel and make sure he doesn't have any more of his girlfriends over. We can ask if Amara wants to move in, keep you company. And together we'll get the journal and break down the Veil. When that's done, I'll buy you a house. Anywhere you like. I'll make sure you have enough money to live out your days in comfort, and with the Veil down I'll be able to keep you hidden. How does that sound?'

'That's a very generous offer, Grayson. I couldn't accept so much.'

'I insist. All I want is for you to be safe. To be happy. Please, let me keep you safe. Let me try and make you happy.'

I nod and accept his offer. It all feels like a million years away anyhow.

'We'll start practising your new power and get to work on looking into your memories. Okay?'

'Does it have to be with him?' I ask.

'I'm afraid so. Gabriel's the only one that can teach it to you. We'll wait a few days for you both to calm down before we start. Deal?'

'Okay,' I agree. 'How come I could control him? He can't control you or Toby so why did he do what I told him to do?'

'He's not had to practice fighting compulsion, has he? Not like Toby and I.'

'How do you expect to get the book from Toby?' I ask.

'We'll get it. It may take time, but we'll get it.' He pats my arm and bids me farewell before heading out the door.

I slump down on my bed and stare at the ceiling. If my heart weren't in pieces, I would be excited by his offer. But the idea of staying here as they try to figure out a way to prise that book from Toby's hands is more than I can bear. Weeks, months, maybe years of watching girl after girl falls for Gabriel as I linger in the background...the one night stand that never left.

I'm a fool. There's me falling in love with Gabriel while all he wants is a warm body to distract him for a while.

I'm an absolute idiot.

My stomach growls loudly as the hunger pains continue to build. I've spent all day hiding away upstairs. I can't face Gabriel. I can't face anyone. I keep bursting into tears and then exploding with rage. My emotions are wreaking havoc on me. An ever-changing storm of pain, anger, sadness and grief. Stolen sleep, a missing appetite and a heavy dragging in my chest, where I'm sure my heart used to be, has left me only capable of lying on my bed staring up at the ceiling. My brain is no friend to me. My thoughts don't offer me comfort or solace. Instead, they replay Gabriel's words over and over.

I'm one of life's permanent victims. So desperate to be loved and wanted that I'll take the attention of any man who looks my way. The only person to blame for everything that's happened to me is me.

Because I'm weak.

When the words aren't proving torturous enough, my brain shows him with Ava in full HD, intercut with *our* time together. Memories that are now just a perverted joke. I'm stuck in this house. Pinned in at all sides with no hope of escape until the Veil is down and my enemies defeated. But my enemies are numerous and not all have a face. Toby, Theo and even Hunters I can see. But my immature awareness of who to trust, my faith in mankind and fear of trusting another person, they are foes I have no idea how to face. Let alone defeat.

My thoughts are deafening. This room is far too quiet. I force myself to my feet and order myself out of this room. I walk the hallways. I explore the library and revisit the blackened room that I destroyed in my first few days here.

Amara and Collins fall silent in an instant as I walk into the kitchen and they put on these big, pity-filled smiles. I open cupboard after cupboard until I find what it is I'm looking for.

I pour myself a large glass of whiskey, down it in one and pour another before sitting at the table with them.

'How's it going?' I ask less than enthusiastically.

'Fine,' Amara replies. 'Are *you* alright?'

'Fine.' I drink the whiskey and pour another.

'You should have something to eat,' Collins says. 'That's a lot of whiskey on an...' I drink it down. '...empty stomach.'

They share a worried look.

'Don't start.'

Amara shrugs. 'Wasn't going to. I'll have a drink with you.' She holds her hand out for the bottle, but the sudden appearance of Gabriel has me clinging to it. We all stare at him. Amara looks filled with hatred as she glares daggers at him. He stops dead when he sees me. Then his eyes drift down to the bottle in my hand.

'Have you eaten today?' he asks. I pick up the bottle and pour another drink for myself. As I drink it, he scoffs. 'Very mature.'

I pour another before he storms over to me, snatches the bottle from my hand and tosses it in the sink.

'We might not be friends anymore, but I won't let you drink yourself into a coma,' he warns quietly in my ear. I look up at him as he towers over me. 'What I said to you, that wasn't okay. I was angry and I didn't mean it. I'm sorry.'

I lean up, so my face is close to his. 'Bite me, Gabriel. Shove your apology and your concern up your arse.'

'Has she eaten anything today?' he asks the others while not looking away from me. They don't answer. He turns his angry glare on them. 'I asked you a question. Has the Arcane Witch eaten today or not?'

'No,' Collins replies, glancing apologetically to me.

Gabriel returns his stare to me.

'Eat.'

I can't help but laugh as I get to my feet. I walk to the cupboard and instead of pulling out the box of cereal, I take the bottle of wine from the top shelf. It's been opened, but there's at least half the bottle left. I pull out the stopper and start chugging it. He watches and twitches with anger until he can't take anymore. His eyes go black.

'Put the bottle down, Lilly.'

I have no choice but to obey. I slam it down on the worktop and open my mouth ready to start hurling abuse at him, but I fall silent in a second when behind him, through the door walks Ava.

'Sorry to disturb, but we really should be going, baby.' Her enormous grin and smug eyes land on me.

His eyes return to blue, and they look anywhere but me.

I can feel it. The desperate sobbing is coming. I have to get out of here. I won't let them see me cry. I leave, barging into his shoulder and walk out the back door as fast as I can.

'Lovely to see you again, Lilly,' Ava calls happily after me.

I hear a commotion and turn to see Amara slamming her fist straight into Ava's face, before being dragged off by Collins. She shrugs him off and turns to Gabriel.

'You're a fool. A bloody fool.' She points at Ava. 'You two deserve each other and believe me, Gabriel,' she squares up to him even though he stands a clear foot over her, but hell, she looks fierce. 'You go near my best friend again, you so much as look at her, I'll cut your dick off myself. I don't give a damn who you are.'

I can't help but gasp as she only goes and slaps him.

'AMARA!' Collins yells, grabbing her arm. She turns and slaps him too. 'What the hell did *I* do?'

'You defended him. You have shit taste in friends, Collins.' She storms past them all and comes outside to me. She wraps her arm around my waist and leads me out into the garden and far away from them all.

'You just hit two witches and punched Ava in the face!' I say in awe.

'No one messes with my best friend,' she says.

I wrap my arm around her and hug her as we walk.

'I bloody love you, Amara.'

'I love you too, Honey.'

The television's on, but I'm not watching it. My eyes aren't even focused on it. I'm huddled up in the corner of the sofa in the lounge, trying hard to get my brain to stop thinking. Amara hands me a sandwich, but I can't stomach it.

'You haven't eaten all day. Please try.'

I shake my head and carry on starring at the screen.

It's late. Grayson comes in and wishes us a good night as he goes to bed. Collins follows shortly after. He tries to kiss his girl, but she brushes him off. She's still pissed off with him.

The house gets quieter as it gets later. In the early hours of the morning, I sit in the dark with the television on mute as she sleeps soundly next to me. Soon, the sun begins to rise. I haven't moved all night. The sandwich she made me remains untouched. The lettuce browning and curling as the bread dries out. The grandfather clock chimes. It's eight am.

Gabriel didn't come home.

All I can see is him and Ava together. I imagine him with her right now. Kissing her how he kissed me. Whispering all the beautiful things he said to me in her ear. Making her fall for him. It's enough to make me want to scream.

Add the fact that Toby's breathing down my neck and that I have another realm of power to learn to control, it's all a bit much. Perhaps I should talk to Grayson about Toby's demand. Me for the book. Maybe I should just give Toby what he wants. He can have me. Do what he wants with me. I'll bring down the Veil and just go back to how we were.

Collins walks in holding two plates in his hands. He puts one on the floor by Amara and kneels in front of me with the second.

'I made you some breakfast,' he says. I look at the full English and my already knotted up stomach clenches even tighter. I shake my head. He puts it beside Amara's and looks back to me. 'You love him, don't you?' he asks sadly.

'Yes,' I reply. My throat constricting and my eyes beginning to brim with tears. 'So much. I wish I didn't.'

He holds out his hand. I take it. This small act of kindness unravels me completely. I can't hold them back.

I cry. I fall apart. He holds me. He tells me to let it out. To cry. That it's okay.

I cling to him and just sob.

Two days have passed since I broke down in Collins' arms. Two days of avoiding people, not sleeping, of only managing a liquid lunch. And two days of not seeing any sign of Gabriel. Grayson tells me he's probably at the Nomad camp with Ava since he told them she's no longer welcome here.

I can't keep wallowing. I can't keep playing it all over and over in my head. We're done. That's it.

Get over it, Lilly.

I had to borrow Amara's jumper this morning. Weirdly, a load of my stuff has disappeared from my wardrobe. Not sure where it's gone. I don't really care to be honest. Her clothes fit just fine. So it doesn't matter.

'Miss Hooper?' A young man in his mid-twenties calls, jogging after me as I stroll across the snow covered lawn. 'Miss Hooper. Can I have a word?'

I recognise him as one of the Nomads that was in the hallway when Toby came to the house.

'What do you want?' I ask as I carry on leisurely walking across the lawn. He catches up to me and takes hold of my arm. 'What the hell are you doing?' I demand, snatching my arm away and giving him a shove. 'Don't you dare fucking touch me!'

'I need to talk to you about Gabriel,' he says, ignoring my words. 'It's urgent. Here. It's for you.' He holds out a mobile phone. *'I'm so sorry,'* he mouths.

I take the phone and hold it to my ear thinking maybe it's Gabriel.

'What?'

'Hello, Lilly. How are you?'

Fear courses through me like icy water, but yet I start to sweat. Just the sound of his voice, the way he says my name, the fact that I'm standing in what's supposed to be the safest place on earth for me and he's still able to talk to me, is terrifying.

'Theo...' I whisper. The Nomad who handed me the phone continues to watch me. He looks around us, making sure we're alone. There are plenty of Nomads in sight but none in earshot.

I don't know what to say. I stutter over the hundred questions in my head so the only words that come out are. 'What do you want?'

'I'm going to need you to do something for me,' Theo says. 'I need you to come and see me.'

'Why would I do that?' My voice trembles despite how hard I try to settle it.

'Because, if you don't, Gabriel will die.'

Chapter 19

Everything around me slows. I look around me, just to make sure that Gabriel isn't in fact here. But he's been gone for almost two days. No one's spoken to him. I knew something wasn't right.

'You're lying. You don't have Gabriel,' I insist.

'Oh no? Say hello, Gabriel.'

I hear someone getting a beating. Their groans and grunts as they get hit come down the phone.

But that could be anyone.

'He's a stubborn bastard. One moment,' Theo says, before the phone goes quiet. Then I hear a blood-curdling yell, and I know it's him. Theo has Gabriel!

'What do you want?'

'I told you. I want you to come and see me.'

'Grayson will never let me.'

He laughs a cruel mocking laugh. 'No. He won't. I'm impressed that you have him so devoted to looking after you considering he's only just met you. He's got you very well protected there. I don't like it. So, I want you to change it.'

'Change it?' What the hell does he mean?

'Yes. I know you've promised to help him break down the Veil. Now I want you to tell him you've changed your mind. That you will never help him and that you think he and all his men deserve to die. You tell him that if he tries to stop you from leaving, you'll kill him.'

'He'll kill *me*, Theo. You can't be serious.'

'He won't kill you. He may not be very nice to you in the future, but he won't kill you. With Grayson as your enemy, you'll need me to look after you. Or your life simply won't be worth living. And don't even think about trying to tell someone what's happening. You see the man standing in front of you?' I look at the Nomad. 'His name is Adam. He's a very loyal Nomad but also a devoted husband. Adam's wife is currently a guest of mine, and he'll do anything to keep her safe. Adam knows where I am, and he's going to bring you to me. He's under strict orders. Here are the rules. You're not to talk to anyone about what's happening. You're to do everything Adam asks. You're going to make one hell of a scene when you leave and when you have left the house, you're going to come quietly. Adam will keep me updated at particular times. If he's late calling or picking up the phone, or if you break these rules... Gabriel and Adam's lovely wife will die. Do you understand?'

'Yes,' I whisper. 'But how do I get out of here? There are Nomads everywhere.'

'You're a witch, Lilly. Use your magic. Adam will take it from here. Be a good girl. See you soon.'

'LILLY! DON'T YOU DARE-'

The call ends and Gabriel's voice is cut off. I give Adam the phone. What the hell do I do now? Gabriel and I may not be in a good place, but I can't just abandon him. Or Adam's wife.

'What now?' I ask.

'I have a car parked out the front of the house. A little way down the lane. We need to get to that. I'm so sorry, Miss Hooper, but I have to do this. I can't let Clara die.' I look into Adam's eyes. They're completely filled with fear. 'I can't let her stay with Theo. Just like you can't let Gabriel stay there. Theo's evil. Please, please forgive me.'

'It's okay,' I tell him. 'I understand. We'll get them back, just give me a second.' I need to calm my thoughts. I need to rein in my panic. I take stock of our situation. 'There are dozens of armed Nomads between us and that car,' I say quietly. 'Never mind Grayson, Collins and Hendrix. I'll never get us past them all.'

'Miss Hooper...we *need* to get to that car.' He sounds as fearful as I feel.

I drag my hands through my hair in desperation.

Fuck fuck fuck.

'This is impossible.' I have to push those ideas out of my head. It *can't* be impossible. It *has* to be done.

Adam holds out his hand.

'I need to take your binding spell.' I give him the watch which he slides into his coat pocket. My magic rushes through me like an old friend. No longer feeling like an uncontainable force, but a part of me. I feel stronger, safer. Perhaps it's because I know I *must* be strong. That I *must* be in control. Gabriel's life depends on it.

'Do I have to make a scene? Can't we just try and sneak out?' I ask hopefully.

'No,' he says simply. 'If Grayson isn't your enemy by the time we leave, then Gabriel and Clara will die. Theo made that crystal clear. We're being watched. I don't know by whom, or even how. But he'll know. I'm sorry, we don't have a choice.'

'I know. All that matters now is getting to Gabriel and your wife and making sure they stay alive. When we get back, we'll explain why we left to Grayson. He'll understand.' I can see by the look on his face he doesn't believe that for a moment.

'Maybe you, but not me,' he says quietly. 'We need to move.'

I take a deep readying breath and accept that this is going to happen.

'You better stay close. We'll go through the house. It will attract attention which is what Theo wants. When we're through the front door, we'll head to the front gate. The wall's too high to climb so the gate is the only option. Stay by my side. Keep up...and don't die,' I tell Adam who nods.

We turn shoulder to shoulder and face the house.

I'm filled with purpose. It overpowers everything else. We're getting the people we love back from Theo, and if I get the slightest chance, Theo's a dead man.

We walk across the lawn and towards the house. No one outside stops us as we go. In the kitchen, two Nomads stand by the kettle drinking coffee. They nod politely at us but say nothing as we continue to walk. In the lobby, it's the same. Plenty of people, but no one says a word.

Grayson's office door is open. Inside he's talking to Billy and Hendrix. I hear his voice, sounding very serious and full of authority and they nod in agreement to whatever it is he says. Adam takes hold of my elbow and gestures to the men in the office.

'You have to go in there. Theo made it very clear you have to turn him against you.'

'Easier said than done, Adam' I whisper. 'I've seen him kill and torture people for insulting him!'

'He won't kill you. He needs you alive. Just go in, tell him what Theo wants you to tell him, and then we get the hell out of here.'

Terrified, I stand in Grayson's doorway and clear my throat. He looks at me with a sweet smile, happy to see me.

'Everything okay?' he asks, still sitting behind his desk. Hendrix and Billy are sitting opposite watching me. I'm so busy panicking I forget to speak. 'Lilly?' he says, with a slight laugh. 'Can I help you with something?'

I know what I have to do, but when I do it, all hell's going to break loose. There's just no other choice.

'I'm leaving.'

His smile falters.

'You want to go out for a walk? Get some air? I'll come with you.' He starts to get to his feet.

'No,' I say quickly, holding my hand out to stop him. 'I'm not going for a walk. I'm leaving the house. I'm...I'm... leaving you and your Coven.' His smile goes completely, and he continues to get to his feet slowly. Hendrix and Billy look between us watching the conversation.

'Can I ask why?' Grayson asks coldly.

Adam clears his throat quietly behind me as I stand here silent. I know what I'm supposed to say, but the reality of saying those words to a man like him isn't easy.

'Lilly!' Adam whispers quietly. 'Say it!'

'I've changed my mind,' I say quickly, almost tumbling over my words. 'I won't help you bring down the Veil. After everything you've done, all the people you've killed... I think you...' *Oh, bloody hell*. With a deep breath, I just say it. What else can I do? 'I think you and your men all deserve to die. Why would I ever help you?' I step back in anticipation of his reaction. I expect yelling, lightning, violence but he just continues glaring at me. 'I'm not your prisoner. I'm leaving this house, and you're not stopping me, Grayson. If you do, I'll kill you myself.' Grayson's eyes flick down at my wrist before they turn on me with savagery.

'Where's your binding spell?'

'Gone.'

I've done what I was told. I've said the words, and now all that's left is to go. I turn quickly and head to the front door. I push it open.

'MISS HOOPER!' Grayson bellows as I stand just inside the threshold of the house. 'I strongly suggest you turn around, apologise and get up to your room before I do something *you* will sorely regret.'

I stay standing and look out ahead of me to the driveway. A quick scan shows me at least twenty Nomads between us and the gate.

'Lilly. Turn around,' Grayson says firmly. I turn. So does Adam. He's so close I can feel his body trembling and hear his terrified breathing. Grayson looks at him. 'What are you doing so close to her? Step away.' Adam stands firm at my side. 'I SAID STEP AWAY!'

I wrap my hand around his wrist and pull him so he's standing behind me. 'He can't. I've used my Mental magic on him. He has to do as I've said. I need him to drive me away from here.' Hopefully, that will help Adam after all this is done. 'I'm leaving, taking him with me and you're not stopping us.'

I step back and turn to leave when the door slams shut in my face. I look at Grayson over my shoulder. His hands are covered in lightning, crawling across his skin, like snakes weaving between his fingers.

'I won't let you leave.'

'I'm not asking your permission.'

'Is this because of Gabriel? Is this because he's upset you?'

'No,' I reply. 'This is because of you, and what you've done.' I create my fire, letting it flicker away on my hands as a clear warning.

'You're not going anywhere.'

Here we go.

He starts towards me. I send two streaks of fierce fire towards him which land at his feet and spread outwards, creating a tall barrier of black and white flames that reach the ceiling, cutting him, Billy, Hendrix and the Nomads off from us. It's completely in control. I shatter the glass around us into hundreds of shards and send them all soaring through the air, making everyone dive to the floor. When they're down, I blast the front door off its hinges with a wave of my hand and grab hold of Adam, who's swearing and looking at the chaos in shock.

'Run!'

Together, we sprint outside and towards the gravel driveway. Four Nomads on my left turn and point their weapons at us. Two aim for my legs while the other two aim for Adam's head. Before they can open fire, I slam them with my Telekinetic magic, sending them violently sideways. Their sprays of bullets fly into the sky as their bodies hit the ground hard.

We never stop running. I turn and create another wall of my fire in front of the door, sealing the Nomads and Grayson inside. I swipe my hand widely through the air feeling a slight resistance, like my arms moving through water, as I send a wave of energy at the group of Nomads on my right who are rushing towards us, launching them backwards.

I see trucks and cars parked all along the driveway. They would be able to follow us!

So I set them all on fire and hurl them across the lawn like blazing tumbleweeds. I don't want to kill anyone. I just need them to get out of my way and make sure they can't follow. When one of the cars suddenly explodes, the Nomads close by get thrown through the air in a blast wave of fire and heat.

Men and women are screaming and shouting. There are explosions and fire surrounding us, all of my own making. Holy shit! I'm amazed at what I'm able to do with my mind so focused. I never thought I would be this...powerful! We keep running. I look back and see Grayson along with Hendrix and a handful of men making their way out of a broken window from the lounge, bypassing my wall of fire by the door and heading straight towards us. Grayson doesn't look at the fire, the hurling vehicles or his men lying on the ground. His eyes are firmly on me. And they're murderous. His fists are clenched as he walks towards us with purpose. He raises his arms.

'Adam...GET DOWN!'

Grayson's lightning streaks towards us and I have to push us both onto the floor as it flies above our heads. We stumble to our feet and sprint towards the gate.

'KEEP RUNNING!' I scream, pulling him with me.

I uproot trees, lighting their branches as they fly overhead, and toss them behind me.

Anything to slow our pursuers down.

When the gates come into view, I raise my hand. They come away from their hinges as if hit by an invisible bulldozer and spiral through the air. They land across the road, forty feet away, in a twisted and tangled mess.

How am I capable of any of this? My magic is so much more than I thought it was.

We run through the gap I've made and onto the road.

I take a second to look back, hoping to see where everyone is.

It's chaos! I've left behind a war zone of destruction, and in the middle of it all is Grayson still charging towards us. He holds out his hand and an invisible force slams into me. I fly backwards through the air, letting Adam's arm slip from my grasp and I land on my back in the middle of the road. Pushing myself up with a groan as my body throbs from the impact, I make another wall of fire across the hole where the gate once was as Adam helps me get to my feet.

'THE CAR'S DOWN THERE!' He has to yell so I can hear him over the noise.

He gestures down the lane.

We turn and run. I throw tree after tree into the middle of the road, creating blockades so they can't follow us in the cars I didn't manage to burn. They won't get through that mess.

Or so I think.

The wall protecting the house starts to shake and groan. A single brick shoots out past our heads. Then another and another. Grayson's breaking through from the other side.

There's a loud animalistic growl.

'Shit! LOOK OUT!'

Hendrix hurdles over the twenty-foot wall and lands skilfully on the grass verge before sprinting towards us. I can't help but scream when I see his bared teeth and jet-black eyes coming straight for us. He runs at remarkable speed, like an animal chasing its prey. All the while, the bricks continue dislodging themselves from the wall, making a passage for Grayson and his men to get through.

Hendrix is moving too fast. We'll never outrun him. I shove Adam forwards.

'Get in the car, open the passenger door and start the engine!' I order. 'I'll hold him off.'

Adam nods and sprints ahead as I stop and turn to face the Vampire. He looks thrilled to finally have the chance to cause me some pain. With a silent prayer to a god I don't believe in, I try and use my new power.

If fear is an incentive...well, I have plenty of that. Before he gets close enough to grab me, I shout.

'STOP!'

He does. Every muscle in his body goes rigid, and he can't move.

It worked!

'Protect us, Hendrix,' I order. 'Fight anyone that tries to stop us. But don't kill anyone.'

'You fucking bitch. Grayson will tear you apart for this.'

I have nothing to say to him because he's probably right. He gives the angriest yell I think I've ever heard as he turns. His fists are clenched as he stands between us and Grayson's oncoming attack.

I run to the black Vauxhall with the open passenger door and throw myself inside. Adam slams his foot down and speeds off down the country lane. As we turn the corner, the last thing I see is Grayson emerging from the hole in the wall and Hendrix charging at him.

'We did it!' I pant.

'Not yet we haven't.' He looks over his shoulder. Turning to see what he's looking at, I see a car speeding after us.

Shit!

'How?'

I climb into the back seat as Adam pelts it down the country lanes.

'What do we do?' he asks with a quaking voice.

'Keep driving!' I tell him. 'Don't stop.'

I count five cars behind us and catching up fast.

'You better do something, Miss Hooper. If we get caught-'

'I know, Adam! Believe me, I know!' He'll be killed, his wife will be killed, and Gabriel will be killed, leaving me at the mercy of Grayson alone. What can I do? I don't want to throw the cars. That could kill the people inside. I need to stop them from following, but how?

We're on a simple country road. On my left is the boundary of the house with hedges and a wall that reaches high above us. To our right are vast open fields. There's nothing to throw at them. Nothing to block the road with. The road! If I could destroy the road, make it impossible to pass...

As we race away with Grayson and the others gaining on us every second, I turn my attention to the tarmac.

I close my eyes and reach out with my magic, feeling it building up from my chest and spreading through me like a wildfire. I build it up and build it up, making it stronger till I can't keep it inside anymore. I fling open my eyes and expel it from my body directing it to the ground, willing destruction. The tarmac splinters and cracks, like the earth beneath it is shifting. As we drive, the splintering road chases us but never touches our tyres. The cars behind continue to follow, driving over the broken and uneven ground. I clench my fists determined to do this. Determined to stop them. When I open my palms, the road behind me collapses with a loud, horrific crash, making a ditch ten feet deep and stretching way out across the surrounding fields at phenomenal speed. The first three cars don't stop in time and crash below. The others screech to a halt as I continue to make my enormous trench. Before we fly around another corner, I see Grayson get out of one of the cars.

He has no choice but to abandon it and watch us drive away.

'Did you see that?' I say breathlessly. I look at the chasm I've made. 'How did I do that?'

'You're the Arcane Witch, Miss Hooper. That's nothing. The last one levelled a whole town. So the story goes.'

He's breathing hard and fast as we drive. We're both shaking. Both full of adrenaline and fear, but we did it. No one follows.

A whole town? Jesus!

'Give the Miss Hooper thing a rest, will you?' I tell him as I continue to look out the back window, watching the road. 'I think we're past formalities. My name's Lilly.'

We join a motorway, and when I'm sure we're not being followed, I climb into the front seat next to Adam. He pulls off the motorway after a few miles and drives into a large service station where he parks up, gets out and opens my door.

'Follow me.'

We abandon the Vauxhall for a silver Ford. He holds open the front passenger door for me. I get in and so does he before we drive calmly away. As we travel, he keeps glancing at the small clock on the dash. When it reaches eleven twenty-five, he pulls out his phone and dials.

'We're in the Ford,' he says. 'No. We're not being followed. Yes, she followed the rules. She caused some serious havoc and most definitely turned Grayson against her.'

'I want to talk to Gabriel,' I demand, knowing that he's talking to Theo. Adam looks at me before handing over the phone.

'How's it going, Lilly?' Theo asks.

'I want to talk to Gabriel.'

'No-can-do, sweetheart,' he says smugly. 'Well done. Part of me thought you wouldn't make it.'

'Prove to me that Gabriel's alive,' I insist.

'He's alive, and he'll continue to be as long as you do what you're told.'

'What about Adams wife?'

'She's fine. See you soon.' He hangs up. Adam holds out his hand for the phone. I shove it in his hand.

'What does Theo want me for?' I ask. 'Does he want to kill me?'

Adam shrugs and carries on driving.

'Where are we going?'

Nothing. I sit back in the seat and do the only thing I can. Wait.

After more than two hours, he pulls into a small carpark with two other cars and no people. He turns off the ignition and sits. When the clock turns to two thirteen, he calls again.

'We're at the reservation.' He nods and hangs up before getting out of the car and walking around to my side. He opens the door. I get out and follow him to a black jeep.

We get in and drive for another hour or so in silence.

My fingers are knotted together with nerves. I'm praying Gabriel's okay and that I didn't badly hurt anyone back at the house. I hope Grayson understands and forgives me for what I had to do. I hope I get the chance to fix this. I don't regret the choices I've made. The way things ended with Gabriel and

I would never stop me trying to save him. No matter how hard you try, you can't just remove love.

The sky's getting darker as the sun begins to set. We've driven through town after town, and now we're slowly making our way down a rough bit of road lined with high hedges and no street lights. It merges into a dirt track, and we're thrown around inside the car as we go over the frozen ground. Adam stops and turns off the engine.

He leaves the headlights on and waits.

His phone rings.

'Yes?' He listens and nods as I sit beside him. I'm miles away from the house, alone and about to be handed over to Theo.

'Yes. Okay.' Adam hangs up and swivels in his seat to look at me. 'Please hold out your hand.' I do as I'm asked and he replaces the binding spell. My magic leaves me in an instant, and a realisation hits me. Grayson has the Bloodstone. He may be hours behind us, but he'll be able to find me now.

'Turn away from me and put your hands behind your back,' Adam orders.

'Why?'

'Because if you don't, I'll have to call Theo and tell him you're not following the rules. Please, Lilly, just do as you're being told so we can save the people we came here to save.'

I turn and put both hands behind my back. He ties them together tightly with rope and returns to his seat, looking ahead of us into the darkness.

He says nothing, does nothing. We just sit there. Until the phone goes again. This time he gets out of the car to answer it, telling me to stay put. He slams the door and walks to the front of the vehicle and into the headlights. As he faces ahead and talks to Theo, I suddenly see six men emerge from the darkness and walk straight towards us.

I'm so outnumbered and now have no magic.

What the hell am I going to do?

Adam hands the phone to a man with long grey hair combed back into a ponytail. He's wearing a red plaid shirt with a thick, black woollen jacket. The man places the phone to his ear. He's nodding, talking to Theo and gesturing at the men around him. The tallest of the six makes his way to my door and opens it.

'Get out!' he barks, grabbing my arm and yanking me out so fast I stumble and trip. He pulls me back to my feet before leading me towards the man with the ponytail, not giving me a second to compose myself. I'm stopped in front of him. The ponytailed man looks me up and down.

His green eyes bore into mine.

'Miss Hooper,' he says. 'Nice to meet you.'

The ponytailed man then proceeds to pull out a gun, points it at Adam and shoots him right between the eyes, without a flicker of any hesitation or regret at all.

I scream as Adam's body slumps to the floor by my feet.

'He did everything you asked him to do!' I yell.

The shooter turns his attention, and the gun, to me.

'Theo's waiting for us. If you try anything, I will shoot you and he'll kill Gabriel. Do you understand me?' He cocks the gun and raises his eyebrows. 'Well?'

I nod quickly, eyeing the barrel of the gun that's still smoking.

'Good.'

Chapter 20

The man's grip on my upper arm gets tighter the further we walk into this thick heavy forest. There are no pathways or distinguishable landmarks, but the ponytailed man seems to know exactly where we're going. I stumble over jagged rocks, fallen logs and deep snow, struggling to keep up.

Three men have guns pointing at me, their fingers resting on the triggers. More men join us in stages as we walk, appearing from the shadows and positioning themselves around me. All of them are armed with weapons.

What do they think I'm going to do with my hands tied behind my back and the binding spell on my wrist?

Finally, after maybe half an hour of stumbling and being manhandled by the brute that has hold of my arm, I start to see more than the dark silhouettes of trees and hear more than our footsteps and breathing. Ahead of us is the border of a camp filled with tents. There are small fires, lanterns and torches. People are talking amongst themselves in hushed, nervous tones about *the witches*. There must be a hundred men and women here at least. The men walking around me close in and another takes my second arm. The trees begin to clear, and soon the people in the camp see us. They fall silent as they watch me being led in and step back like I could explode at any second. The way they look at me, like I'm the most disgusting, vile thing they've ever seen, not only pisses me off but makes me laugh a little. They can think what they want. They don't know me. And if they've hurt Gabriel, they really won't want to know me either.

The ponytailed man glances back at me. Seeing that I'm still here and satisfied that I'm well contained, he carries on walking ahead.

So, this is Theo's camp and his band of followers. Surrounding us are dozens of tents all different shapes and sizes. Large campfires are being used to cook what smells like chicken soup, and lines hang from tree to tree, suspending clothes in the air just like the maids at my uncle's house used to do when drying sheets. It's obvious they all live here.

'We're always on the move,' the ponytailed man tells me. 'We never stay in one place for long. We have your friends back at The Orchard to thank for that.'

'Yeah well, I'm sure that if you didn't attack us or you know, kidnap us, they wouldn't be so hell-bent on trying to find and stop you,' I snipe back.

He gives a small laugh.

'Something funny?'

'No.' he looks back at me. 'You just remind me of someone I used to know. She had your defiant spirit too.'

The air begins to hum. It gets stronger and stronger the further into the camp we go. There's magic here. Gabriel, but also Theo. I feel them both. When the ponytailed man goes into the largest of the tents, it's not Gabriel who walks back out with him.

It's Theo.

He smiles at me with a nasty sneer, looking cocky and smug as I stand here surrounded by his men, utterly defenceless.

I'm every bit the rat in a trap.

Slowly and purposefully, he walks towards me. I want to stand tall and be unafraid, but he scares me so much I can't help but retreat. The hands on me tighten as I slowly back up. There's nowhere to go.

I'm completely surrounded.

Stopping close in front of me, Theo gives a small laugh before sighing in contentment. 'Lovely to see you again, Lilly.'

'I wish I could say the same.' My mouth is drier than a desert, and I feel myself trembling. But I try my best to be brave. Or at least look it.

'I have to admit, it's a weight off my mind seeing you in restraints, safely under my control.'

'It looks more like smugness than relief, Theo.'

'Perhaps. It has been difficult getting to you. Well done for getting away from The Orchard and Grayson. Adam told Jensen that you caused a lot of havoc. I'm thrilled.'

'Jensen?'

Theo steps aside so I can get a good look at the man standing behind him.

The ponytailed man who led me here.

His green eyes look tired. His grey hair is thick and smooth. He has an attractive, mature face but looks entirely battered by life.

'Lilly Hooper, meet Jensen Hartley. My right-hand man.'

I look him up and down with as much disgust as I can muster.

'Pleasure.' I look at Theo. 'He murdered an innocent man tonight. Adam did everything he was ordered to do, and he killed him anyway.'

'Adam wasn't innocent. He was a Nomad,' Jensen says.

'You don't get to talk to me,' I spit. 'You've played your part. The relevant people are talking now.'

Theo laughs.

'Where's Adam's wife?' I demand.

'Dead,' Theo tells me, not caring one bit what he's done.

'Where's Gabriel?'

'He's here. But first, you and I are going to have a chat-'

'I'm not listening to a word you have to say until I see Gabriel with my own eyes.' The man holding me starts to walk forwards, but I dig my heels into the dirt so he can't take me with him. 'I said I'm not going anywhere till you show me Gabriel!'

Theo gives a small scoff at my stubbornness. He slides his hands in his pocket with his chest puffed out slightly and that nasty, condescending grin on his face.

'If I show him to you, will you behave?'

'Yes,' I say begrudgingly.

He nods and gestures to the tent he emerged from a few moments ago.

'Take her in to see him. Hope you're not squeamish about blood.'

I'm led to a khaki green tent that looks more like a house. It has a slanted roof and probably covers eighty square feet. It must be military. It certainly looks it. The other tents, although none could be called small, look tiny in comparison.

Jensen holds open the flap of material that acts as a door, and I'm led inside by the two men still holding onto me.

Inside are crates of food, pots and pans, shelving units stacked with books and a large table in the centre with a few chairs around it. It looks like some kind of office or storage space. Above our heads are three lanterns hanging from the ceiling. There's more than enough room to stand up in here. You could probably fit forty single beds inside and make it a dorm of some kind. There are two large wooden poles buried deep into the ground, reaching high into the canvass roof acting as support for the shelter. And right in the centre, on his knees, with his head bowed and hands tied behind his back around one of the poles, is Gabriel. His hair hangs over his face and there's blood splatter on the floor around him.

'What have you done to him?' I say in quiet horror.

I take a few hurried steps closer, but the men holding me won't let go. I pull against their grip, but it just makes them tighten it.

'Gabriel?' I call out nervously, terrified that this is all a cruel joke and he's dead. He stirs but doesn't look up. I fill with relief. He's alive. 'GABRIEL!' I bellow. His head shoots up, and he sees me. Horrified surprise etches across his battered face. He's badly bruised with a large cut above his left eye. A mix of fresh and dried blood covers his face, and there's a steady drip of red falling from his nose. 'Jesus, Gabriel.'

He shakes his head. 'No. Lilly...what are you doing here?' He looks at the men surrounding me. 'Let her go. GET YOUR HANDS OFF HER!'

'There. You've seen him. Out.' Theo opens the door and gestures to the men holding me to take me back outside. I struggle against their grip, desperate to get to Gabriel, but they won't let me go.

'GET OFF ME!' I scream. 'GET THE HELL OFF ME!' I thrash against them.

'Take her to my tent,' Theo orders. Despite all his injuries and how much pain he must be in, Gabriel tries desperately to get free of his restraints and yells for them to get off me.

'YOU LAY ONE FINGER ON HER, THEO, I'LL RIP YOU APART!' he bellows as I'm dragged out of the tent. 'DO YOU HEAR ME?!'

I dig my feet into the ground, so they lift me off the floor and carry me to another tent a few feet away.

Once inside, I'm lowered back to the floor. I don't give up trying to get back to him. I pull and kick. I yell and threaten. Theo stands in front of me and with a mighty blow, backhands me right across the face. White spots blight my sight and the metallic taste of blood seeps into my mouth.

'You said you would behave, so stop fighting us,' he says. 'Things will go better for you both if you do.' He leans in closer, his eyes staring straight into mine. 'Unless you want me to go back and resume my one-on-one time with your boyfriend?' He waits patiently as I rein in my emotions.

I'm seated on a chair and held there by my shoulders as Theo walks around, picks up a stool from beside a small fold-out table, and sits opposite me.

I shrug off the hands that hold me in place.

'Get your grubby mitts off me. I'll stay put.'

When they let me go, I turn to Theo, hating him more than I've ever hated anyone. He's killed innocent people. Hurt Gabriel. Turned Grayson against me and there he sits looking happier than ever. He tells the men to leave, except Jensen who remains by the door. I sit on the stool, hands still tied behind my back and the binding spell still firmly in place. I wait to see what he wants from me.

Surely, he doesn't want to kill me.

Or I would be dead already.

'Talk then. Say what it is you want to say and let us go.'

'You're treating me like the enemy,' Theo says, crossing his legs and picking off a piece of lint from his knee. 'I'm not the bad guy here Lilly. The bad guys are the ones you've been playing house with for the last few weeks.'

I can't help but laugh which makes him frown.

'Care to share the joke?'

'Well, for a start, the men I've been playing *house* with... haven't kidnapped me or tied me up. They haven't taken someone I care about hostage and threatened to kill them unless I did what they wanted. They haven't attacked me, and they never attacked my mum when I was little, starting a chain reaction that destroyed my entire life.' I sit back and glare at him. 'You brought me here to talk, so talk. But I have very little interest in anything you have to say to me.'

He laughs and looks at Jensen.

'I like her. She's got balls.' He leans forward, resting his elbows on his knees. 'Listen, Lilly. The only reason I'm giving you a chance to listen to what I have to say and not just taking what I want from you is that I promised someone that I'd at least try to get through to you. To get you to see reason. Show me some courtesy and-'

'Who?' I ask. 'Who did you promise?'

Another smug laugh as he shakes his head.

'No one you know. We're getting side tracked. Let me just start. What do you know about the Veil?'

'Nothing. Never heard of it.' The venom in my voice is palatable.

Theo sighs. 'Do you know *what* you are?'

'I'm told I'm a pain in the ass.'

His sigh turns into a grunt.

'That I can believe. Do you know why Grayson and Gabriel are so keen to have you in the house with them? You ever wondered why they've tried to keep you hidden?'

'Probably because there's a lunatic on the loose that wants to beat them half to death and try to kidnap me in a...what did you say when you grabbed me at the tree lot? A bloody broken mess?'

'Okay. Theo...this is getting us nowhere,' Jensen says calmly from behind me. 'Can we just tell her about the vision?'

'Fine,' Theo grunts, getting to his feet to stand over me. 'You want to see what the people you call friends want for us all? You want to see where helping them will lead?'

He reaches out, his hands going for my head. I flinch, but he's quick. He places his hands over each of my temples, the same way Gabriel did when he looked into my memories. The sensation of electricity shooting through my mind, stuns me as my brain is bombarded with images. Images of death, destruction and a world on fire. People are screaming, and children are dying. In the roads are blackened and charred bones.

It's the end of the world.

Theo lets go, and we're back in his tent.

'What was that?' I whisper, utterly horrified. He doesn't answer but gives me a moment to let what I just saw sink in. 'WHAT WAS THAT, THEO? WHAT KIND OF MAGIC WAS THAT?!' I'm yelling as I approach hysteria. I could be sick at what he's just shown me.

'That got your attention then. That is the future.'

'The future? You can't see the future.'

Can he?

'No. I can't, but I know someone who did, and he showed me that vision. Once shared, a vision can be passed on. Now, you can show someone too. If you like. We have to stop that vision from ever coming true. That's where you come in.'

'Me?' I still can't get over the horror he just showed me. I'm no stranger to death, but that was something else.

'Yes. You. Grayson, Gabriel and Collins want to bring down the Veil. If it comes down, *that* will be the result.'

'How on earth could that be the result of bringing back magic? How can I trust that was even a real vision?' Nothing about him screams trustworthy, but I also hear the desperate denial in my voice. 'The people I know would never let that happen.'

Sighing impatiently Theo explains. 'I'm sure you're aware of the war that took place five centuries ago?'

'I'm familiar. Humans attacked us.' My words come out slow and uncertain. 'They wanted to wipe out the Witches.'

'That's right. Humanity wanted to use us for our magic. They couldn't persuade us to help them willingly, so instead, all across the world, the human leaders gathered. Kings, queens, emperors... they all decided that we were the enemy. That we were the ones who posed a risk to them, instead of each other for a change. Their hatred unified them for the first time in history. Do you know why?'

'The same reason people always turn on each other, I imagine. Fear and jealousy.' I give the tent a quick look to see if there's any other way out of here. But there's just the one, and that's guarded. I'm keen to keep him talking, at least while he's in here, he's not out there hurting Gabriel.

'Spot on,' he says with the same enthusiasm Mr Simmons would have when I answered his questions correctly. 'Humans created Hunters. Human children, raised to fight us. They were then unleashed onto the world, all at once, in one giant synchronised attack across the whole world. An average witch settlement consisted of between fifty to three hundred witches at that time, and of course, the odd ones were living amongst humans. Some married outside a coven and had families with non-magic folk, or hid the fact that they were magical completely, so we can never know for sure how many witches there were. But, in England, there were four of these magical safe havens. I lived in Tintagel with my family when the attack happened. We were the Elders. The most powerful family, therefore, we were the ones in charge. My wife and three children.' His eyes glaze over as he disappears into himself for a second. Soon, his eyes return to me, and he carries on, ignoring whatever memory he was just lost in. 'Four thousand soldiers turned up at Tintagel in the dead of night. Soldiers, who for twenty years had been trained to kill us. I woke up to the sounds of screams and the smell of fire. Four thousand soldiers against three hundred and twenty witches, who had never killed a single person in their whole lives. Never seen war. Most of them had never even left Tintagel. It was chaos. Seventy of my people were younger than eighteen. Thirty-three of them hadn't even reached the age of manifestation, and twenty-eight of them were elderly. That left less than two hundred able bodied men and woman to protect the children and the elderly, while trying to fight them off. Needless to say, it was a bloodbath. For them and for us.'

This is difficult to hear. He shakes off the memory and takes a deep breath.

'The survivors fled. From my home, there were a total of fifteen survivors. My children and I included. My wife didn't make it. We found other survivors from other settlements, and together we hid. We spent years looking for any other witches and helped them all hide too. But it wasn't enough. Hunters were killing everyone. Witches, outcasts, people that got in their way. Three years after the initial attack, we were in the middle of what the world called...the scourge. Every human was on the hunt for witches in exchange for money. Even those who had once been friends. I watched them publicly torture and execute anyone convicted of aiding us. They showed no mercy. Not to women, not to children. No one.' With a deep breath, he carries on. 'I was leading a new Coven with the help of a man named Arthur. Arthur Collin. His son, you've met. When Rebecca Hooper, your ancestor, came along, she performed an immortality spell on a selected few, in the hope that we would survive long enough to save the people whose lives had become dependent on us. Sadly, Arthur wouldn't do the spell. He said he was too old to live forever, so his son volunteered instead. While we protected them, Rebecca started to create the Veil.' He pauses for a second and looks at me expectantly. I just wait for him to continue.

'She sealed off witches from their magic. We would all become effectively human and no longer be traceable. Hunters can track us down. They're marked-'

'With a tattoo, I know. It burns hot when they're close to magic.'

'We sacrificed our way of life and our magic to save our lives. They couldn't tell who was a witch and who wasn't. The immortality spell we did before the Veil went up keeps us alive and makes us almost impossible to kill. It also kept our connection to the Arcane Realm open. Everyone else lost their magic after the Veil was created. We didn't. We began to integrate the recently human witches back into the human world. Arthur and I spent years travelling all over the country helping them start over. Right up until he died. It was a long time until I realised the truth about Grayson and Gabriel.'

'What truth?' I'm almost too afraid to ask.

'Turns out they weren't too keen on living the human life. They wanted revenge against the Hunters. And it soon became evident that their need for retribution and power was far more important to them than survival.'

'What did they do?'

'They started breeding the Descendants,' he says.

'Breeding?'

'Yes. Breeding. They wanted to ensure that as many children as possible were being created. You see, Descendants having children with other Descendants is the most absolute way to ensure the birth of a witch, so that's what they did. They found the men and women that Arthur and I had hidden, and told them that if they didn't procreate, they would lose our protection. But if they did, if they swore loyalty to them, that they would be rewarded with wealth, power and ultimately...their magic. Of course, we're talking about people who had watched their families die and their people tortured. A lot of them were angry enough to agree. Soon enough, they'd rebuilt the coven. We'd lived in peace for decades without magic, so when I found out the truth, I demanded to know why they were doing this.' His eyes narrow on me with a nasty look. I'm not going to like what he has to say, but I bite anyway.

'Why were they doing it?' I ask.

'Grayson and Gabriel were breeding them to create an army. They're doing exactly what the humans did with Hunters. They're training them to fight. I tried to stop them so they shunned me, took control over the majority of the Descendants and vowed that they would bring down the Veil. Those who stood with me, who wanted to live the human life and stop Grayson and his plan, became what *they* call Traitors. Those who followed Grayson, who want their magic back to destroy their enemies, became Nomads.'

Jensen stands beside me, looking down as I sit here with a clear look of shock on my face. Amara said it. The women are either fighters, wives or breeders. She told me that the Descendants were obsessed with bloodlines.

'But there aren't enough Nomads to create the kind of destruction you showed me,' I tell him.

'Have you ever been to one of the Nomad camps?' Jensen asks. 'You have no idea how far Grayson's network reaches, Lilly. The camp your friend Amara comes from, is just one of thirty-eight in England alone. He has groups all over the world. Thousands of them! When the Veil falls, every single one of his Nomads will get their magic in one fell swoop. A hundred thousand, ten hundred thousand...who knows how many brand-new witches will suddenly be in the world. We're talking five hundred years of focused breeding. And all of them will turn the rage and the anger Grayson has brainwashed them with, towards the humans.'

'Humans they want to destroy,' Theo says in a morbid conclusion. 'The vision that I showed you is the result.'

There are so many questions rushing through my head. So many, none of them come out of my open mouth.

Theo looks frustrated at my speechlessness and snaps, 'Your ancestor Rebecca died putting up the Veil and now it's all going to be undone because of you. The Nomads aren't just helpless people who are missing a piece of themselves. Grayson has no intention of leading them off to a cosy island to live out their days in peace. They are a cult brought up from childhood to hate humanity. They train every day for a war that hasn't happened yet, based on hate and enticed with promises of greatness for their loyalty and service. They're led by two of the most evil and malicious men I've ever known. And they're intent on starting a war, destroying humanity in its entirety and creating a new world of magic with Grayson as it's leader. That's why they've taken you in and protected you. Because you are the only one who can take down the Veil. I know you aren't a fool. I know you know that you are the Arcane Witch and that Grayson has asked you to help him bring down the Veil. I also know that you've agreed, but you can't. I can't let you.'

'They wouldn't.' I shake my head violently repeating the word no.

'Five hundred years ago humans fought with a blade. But now they have guns, bombs and nuclear weapons. Magic and today's modern warfare?' Now he shakes his head. 'It will destroy everything. You're the Arcane Witch. Lilly. *You* cannot let this happen!'

Theo's watching me intently. Jensen's looking at me the same way. Waiting for my reaction. But there's something here that doesn't make sense.

'If I'm needed to break down the Veil, why not just kill me? Why try to reason with me?' I lean forwards. 'You need me for something. What?'

'There's a way that we can stop it for good,' Theo says. 'A way that we can ensure that humanity and Descendants can both survive.'

'Killing me would do that, wouldn't it? You need an Arcane Witch to bring down the Veil. Don't get me wrong, I don't want to die. But why wouldn't you just kill me? You had the chance at the tree lot.'

'Perhaps killing you would stop it all. Or maybe killing you will bring down the Veil. Your family's blood created it. If you died...truth is none of us have any idea what killing you would lead to. And Arcane Witches always find a way to survive. Look at you! Popping into existence five hundred years after the Veil's creation. So yes, I could kill you and prolong this never-ending war between Grayson and I. Let him have another five hundred years to build on his already unbeatable army until another Arcane Witch pops up. Or you could help me end this now.'

I have no idea how on earth I could ever help him. I'm still struggling to believe anything he's saying.

'What would I need to do?' I ask. 'For argument's sake?'

'It's drastic,' he warns. 'But there's a way to taint the magic in the Arcane realm so if the veil's destroyed and magic returns, Grayson's army will perish instead of becoming Witches again.'

'It would kill them?' I ask, stunned. 'I don't understand. It would just kill his army?'

'It would kill any and all Descendants.'

'But, that would kill you, your men. You said that you can save the Descendants and the humans.'

'I can protect those who deserve to be protected. I promised my men that their loyalty will ensure that protection. The men and woman outside, who Grayson calls Traitors will be safe. They will survive. Swear your loyalty to me, promise to help me stop them, and I will give you the same guarantee.'

'Wait. What you're saying is all the Descendants will die unless you specifically save them?' Images of Amara and Collins laughing in each other's arms break my heart. Gabriel along with thousands of people I haven't even met. Is he serious? 'Why the hell would Rebecca create a spell that can kill all the descendants anyway?'

'Because she knew that this was a possibility. She knew that Witches may start a new war. And if they did, they had to be stopped. So, will you help us?' he asks.

I burst out laughing. I don't find anything about this situation funny in the slightest, but the fact he is actually asking me to help him murder thousands of people, to help him after everything he's done to me and is still doing, is just unbelievable!

'No!' I laugh. 'Absolutely not! You're fucking insane. I won't be responsible for killing god knows how many people.'

'I'm the only one left speaking any sense. Even your father agrees with me!'

'My father?' My laughter stops as quickly as it started.

'Yes. He's one of my men. Who do you think wanted me to try and reason with you? Join me, I'll reunite you!'

I don't believe him. Not one bit. 'No thanks,' I tell him plainly.

'I'm not lying. He's here-'

'He could be the king of England, and I honestly wouldn't care. I don't know him. And he doesn't know me.'

'Grayson cannot be allowed to succeed. That vision-'

'That vision could be the outcome of anything,' I insist. 'I've read up on the theory of Sight back at The Orchard. That could be the result of your poison spell or just humans being humans and killing each other. Hell, I don't even know if that vision is true at all! For all I know, you're doing this because Grayson took your place as leader of the Coven. Is that what this is all about? Payback?'

He gets to his feet so fast, his chair slides out behind him.

He's trembling with anger.

'You think this is about petty payback?' he says with a fierce indignity.

'Well, all I'm saying is while you all live out here in the woods, shitting in a hole in the ground, Grayson has two swimming pools and running water. I wouldn't blame you for being a bit...jealous. I don't believe you. Or that vision. They told me their plan. When we're strong enough to protect ourselves against Hunters, we'll get our freedom. Peacefully. If not, then we'll take it. That's our right. It's everybody's right to be free.'

'You have no idea what they are capable of. How could you? You're just a child. Let me tell you what will happen if that Veil comes down. That dreadful vampire Hendrix? He'll be able to turn as many humans as he wants. All the Descendants in the world will suddenly have immense power. Most of them are Nomads and they'll follow Grayson in his war against the humans. There won't be any winners. We'll all just kill each other.'

'I know a girl from one of those camps. She would have told me if they were an army. I think...if that vision is true, that it's more than likely the humans that cause it. Not us. Not me. I spent my life at the mercy of a very nasty group of humans. They're more than capable of destroying the world all by themselves!'

'What do you mean?' Jensen asks. 'Living at the mercy of nasty humans? You were with your uncle...weren't you?'

'My uncle was evil. You know what? If my father is here like you said, you should get him in here. I would love to show my gratitude.'

'Gratitude?'

'Oh yeah. Leaving me alone with my uncle? He has some serious explaining to do. Harry starved, beat and tormented me for almost two decades. My entire body is a map of his cruelty. The only people who have shown me any kindness or compassion are the people you want me to kill.'

'You have people you want to protect? That Amara girl, right? I'll protect her too,' Theo offers.

'Tempting,' I sneer. 'But I still won't be responsible for genocide. I'll talk to Gabriel and decide for myself if you're telling the truth. If I think for a second that he's lying, then I'll refuse to do his spell. But there's no way in hell I will ever do yours. *That*, I can guarantee.'

Theo lowers himself down to my eye level. His dark brown eyes swirl with anger.

'You think you're in love with him, don't you? That maybe he loves you too?'

'Ha. No. I really don't think that. He's a prick.'

'Well, let me tell you something about your precious Gabriel.'

'I know everything I need to know about Gabriel. Believe me. The good and bad.'

Theo has something nasty up his sleeve, and in my current situation, there's fuck all I can do but listen.

'Something you don't know about Rebecca Hooper was that a few months before she completed the Veil, she gave birth to a daughter. When the spell was done, and she had passed on, her husband and daughter disappeared. He wanted nothing more to do with any of us. But he left something behind. Rebecca's journal. Inside, she wrote down all her own spells. Hundreds of them, all of her own creation. The journal contains every spell that could be used with the Veil, plus who knows what else. Rebecca was unlike anything I'd ever seen. She could do magic that no one else could, and she wrote all of it down. Clear instructions for becoming the most powerful creature on earth. Problem was...no one could read the bloody thing.' He starts to pace slowly up and down in front of me. 'I had it for years and couldn't translate it. No one could. Not until I met a man by the name of Quinn. He was an Irish fella. A Descendant and extremely clever. I showed him the Journal, and he said it was written in a language that only the Arcane Witch can decipher. A language that no one even realised existed. Arcanian.' He stops pacing and points to me. 'So only *you* can read it.'

'Oh.'

'When Grayson heard about the journal and what it contained, he was thrilled. Not only did it hold the answer to bringing down the Veil, but it had spells within it that he had only ever dreamt of! Of course, spells can only be performed by a Sensitive. But he still wanted it. When he also learnt that it couldn't be read by anyone other than an Arcane Witch, he went looking for the next best thing. Rebecca's daughter. Rose Hooper.'

My stomach hits the floor. All the blood drains from my face. Rose! The name Toby hurled at Gabriel. The name that filled him with so much shame and regret, he couldn't talk to me about it. She was my ancestor.

'But...you said no one had magic. Did she have magic? Could Rose read it?'

'She couldn't. She wasn't an Arcane. Her father was human, so she was born human. But that didn't stop Grayson. They found her when she was twenty and they tortured her for years. Tore her apart from the inside out. When I found Rose, she was empty. Her eyes glazed over like a zombie. And I knew Gabriel was in her head. He had hollowed her out. Tormented her and twisted her thoughts so she would bend to his will completely. She couldn't read the book, but she knew what her father had told her. That only a Hooper Arcane Witch with magic could ever manipulate the Veil.'

Jensen kneels beside me and looks at me comfortingly. Theo's playing the bad cop. Jensen's trying to be the good one.

'Do you know how you were born with magic, Lilly?' Jensen asks gently. I shake my head. 'It's really very simple,' he says. 'When a Hooper falls for a person of magic descent, a Descendant, and if they have a baby, that baby will be born an Arcane. Put simply, your mum...a Hooper, fell in love with a Descendant and he, in turn, loved her. Together they had you. She was the first Hooper to have a child with a Descendant since the Veil went up. Before that, Hoopers only ever married humans which is why there hasn't been another witch born. Hoopers were against Grayson and his plans. They did everything they could to make sure that an Arcane Witch was never created. Rebecca made it so that love on both sides would create an Arcane, so *that* child would be loved and protected and hopefully, guided into making the right decision for our kind.'

'Well, that didn't happen. At all. My dad abandoned me. My mum died. And my uncle kept me locked in his house my whole damn life so he could use me as his personal punching bag.'

Theo pulls his stool closer so he can sit directly opposite me.

Wearing the smuggest grin yet, Theo says, 'Rose told Gabriel what they had to do. They were left with a problem. They needed an Arcane Witch with magic so they could read the Journal, and then use that witch to break down the Veil. The problem was, the only way to make an Arcane Witch with magic was to get a Hooper to fall in love with a Descendant. So, Gabriel got in Rose's head. Twisted her thoughts and memories. He aimed to get her to fall in love with Grayson. She was locked in a dungeon, her hands chained together and tethered to a wall, three months pregnant with Grayson's second child when I found her. She was adamant that she loved him. It's all that she would say. I managed to fight through Gabriel's compulsion and when I did, all that was left was a young woman who had been held against her will and forced to produce children in the hope that one would be an Arcane. You can make people do pretty much anything. But falling in love is something no one can control. But that didn't stop Gabriel from trying. He made her compliant. Messed her head up, hoping to trick her into loving his brother and then stood by as Grayson forced her to have his children.'

My stomach turns before I gag.

'Yeah...made me sick too,' Theo says. 'But love...you can't fake it. You can't force it. His plan was never going to work. Grayson's children would be the same as any other Descendant. Magic free. So, I did what anyone would do. I put Rose out of her misery.'

'You killed her? When she was pregnant?' My stomach turns again. 'What about her first child?'

'Grayson tried to get his son's magic to manifest. But it didn't. It never would. Rose didn't love Grayson. The boy died in the effort.'

Oh my god. Oh my god.

I can't breathe. I can't take this. He has to be lying. He *has* to be!

Theo continues, 'What none of us knew, was that Rose had a daughter with her human husband, before Grayson and Gabriel got their hands on her. We never saw another Hooper again. Well, not until your uncle and his parents moved into that house on the Moors. Turns out, they had spent the last few hundred years hiding from us. Making sure that if any Hooper had a child, it would be with a human only. Until your mother. Tell me, Lilly, has Grayson shown a romantic interest in you?' he laughs 'Of course he has. The idea that his children could be Arcanes would be too hard to pass up. What was his reaction when you started falling for his infertile brother instead?' He continues to laugh as tears prick my eyes. This isn't funny. All of this is hell.

'Will you help us?' Jensen asks as Theo continues to laugh.

'No,' I say firmly as the tears spill over and slide down my cheeks. 'I will not help you.'

That shuts Theo up.

'I just told you that Grayson abused-'

'I know what you just told me!' More tears slide down my face. He's told me that Gabriel's a cruel, manipulative, evil man and my heart which is already in pieces, shatters even more. And Grayson is even more evil than I ever thought possible. 'I'm not going to help you murder thousands of people. I won't read your journal, Theo. I won't tell you what it says. I won't kill anyone and that's the end of it!' I tell him hatefully.

He looks at Jensen, and they share a disappointed look. Theo returns his attention to me.

'Fine. Have it your way. We'll keep this simple. I'll ask you some questions which you will answer. Question one. Where's the journal?' he asks tiredly.

He doesn't know Toby has the Journal.

'I don't know.' One thing's certain. If that journal contains as much information as he says, there's no way in hell I want it near him.

'Gabriel said it was stolen. Who stole it?'

'Like I said. I don't know.'

'How many of the seven realms of power do you have?'

I shrug, not looking away as his eyes read mine.

'Your uncle had a son. Where is he?'

'You hoping that he'll help you?' I shrug. 'Sorry, no idea.'

'Look, Lilly. I'm doing the best I can with what I have. Inside that Journal could be a million ways to return magic to the world. For all I know you might not even be needed. We're all going on the word of a young woman who was tortured and had her brain addled with. So, having you and finding that book is the only guarantee I have to stop this. I can't let you die. I can't let you go, and I need answers to these questions so I can save the world. Tell me, where is the Journal?'

I lean forward so I'm sitting on the very edge of my chair. He leans in too, hoping that I'm about to share a delicious secret.

'That's it. Tell me what you know,' he says with a forced smile. 'You can tell me.'

'Screw you, Theo.' Not quite what he was hoping for. 'Seriously. Go fuck yourself. You won't kill my friends. I won't let you.'

Jensen and Theo stand over me.

'Take her into the main tent. I'm going to get my answers one way or another.'

I'm taken back to the sizeable military-style tent, shoved to my knees and Jensen ties my hands to the second post opposite Gabriel. Gabriel's watching me intently, but I can't even look in his direction. I'm too afraid to look into those blue eyes that have always been of such comfort to me. Now if I look into them, I think I'll be sick or want to tear them out. He's not the man I thought he was. He's not a man at all. He's a monster. Him and his brother.

Theo kneels in front of me. 'I'm going to get the answers I want. One way or another.'

'Bring it on.'

I watch him as he stands. He opens his mouth to say something, but his name is called from outside. With a final sneer, he leaves. Jensen's still fiddling with the ropes around my wrist, making them unbearably tight.

'Lilly...' Gabriel says slowly. 'Are you alright?'

'Don't talk to me.' Repulsion is evident not only in my words but my face.

'Have they hurt you?' he asks.

'I said don't talk to me, Gabriel.' I keep my eyes down hoping not to see him at all. Hoping to get my head together and organise my thoughts, but all I can see is the darkness of the cellar I was in the last time I was tied up. Then I can't stop thinking about Rose and what they did to her. What Gabriel and Grayson put her through. I know what it is to be abused. To be touched by a man that you can't stand. How could he do that to someone? I really don't know him at all.

Jensen finishes tying me up and kneels in front of me with an expression similar to that of an annoyed parent.

'Is there a reason why you're looking at me like that, Jensen?' I ask hatefully.

'You should consider being more co-operative,' he says. 'Things will go much better for both of you if you are.'

'And I suggest you get your patronising face out of mine. Things will go much better for you when I get rid of this binding spell if you do.'

He gets to his feet with a sigh and looks at Gabriel.

'Talk some sense into her, will you? I know you don't want to see her get hurt.'

'You touch her I swear-'

I start to laugh. I can't help it. They both fall silent.

'You think he cares about me? You think he cares about anyone other than himself and his stupid brother?' I glare at them both. 'All Gabriel cares about is what's between his legs and making Grayson happy. Coming here to help him was the biggest mistake of my life. And that's saying something.'

'Oh dear,' Jensen says sarcastically. 'Take it things aren't too good between you two then?'

'You could say that.'

Jensen walks over to Gabriel and kneels down. I watch despite myself. Jensen doesn't hurt him, but simply pulls out the necklace from around Gabriel's neck that was tucked under his shirt. He lets it hang there. It's the necklace I got him for Christmas. He's still wearing it. Why? Gabriel's looking at the floor as I look between him and the necklace.

'I think there are significant feelings between the two of you. I know you made this for him. Gabriel? Please try and get her to see sense. Or things will get very unpleasant very quickly. I can give you a couple of minutes, but Theo will be back.' He turns and leaves us alone.

The tent rustles in the wind, and the distant mumbling of the people outside are the only things that distract me from the unbearable silence between us.

'Why are you still wearing that?' I ask. He shakes his head. What the hell does that mean? 'Why are you wearing that, Gabriel? Look at me.'

He lifts his head. His eyes look so angry which takes me by surprise.

'Why the hell did you come here?' he hisses. 'What the bloody hell were you thinking? You're the Arcane. Do you have any idea how stupid you coming here is? Do you know how important you are?'

'Don't you dare. Don't you dare tell me how important I am.' I bite my lip, seal my mouth shut and rein in my temper. Arguing now is pointless. Absolutely pointless. 'I can't believe I trusted you. Can't you get us out of here? Use your compulsion and get someone to untie us or are you completely useless?'

'I'm bound. Same as you. There's a cloth tied around my wrist so yeah...I'm pretty fucking useless.' He glares at me. 'What did Theo tell you?'

I look at him and can't hide the disgust on my face.

'What did he tell you?' he asks again.

'Don't talk to me, Gabriel. Don't fucking look at me.'

'They're going to come in here any second and start asking questions, Lilly. Now isn't the time to bicker.'

'Bicker?!'

'They want the journal.' He ignores my indignant reply. 'And whatever they want it for won't be good.'

'There's a spell in the journal that will kill every single Descendant on the planet,' I bite back. 'So yeah, Gabriel...not good. He wants to use me to kill you all while saving his Traitors.' Again, the tent falls silent. I'm almost vibrating with anger.

'Are you sure?' he asks quietly.

'Of course I'm fucking sure. If he finds that Journal, we're all screwed. He'll kill us all, so when he comes in and starts asking questions, just keep your mouth shut. Okay?'

'He's going to use torture.'

'I'm sure you'll survive.'

'For fuck's sake!' he barks. 'Will you take this seriously?' He tries to get free of his ropes. I know better than to try. My ropes are so tight I can barely wriggle my fingers. When he fails to get free, he looks at me. 'If he starts on you, I'm telling him.'

'No, you bloody won't! If I do the spell, it will kill every single Descendant and Witch, except the select few he chooses to save. If you make me responsible for genocide, I will never forgive you. Mainly because we'll more than likely be dead!'

He stares at me defiantly, and I look back at him in equal measure.

'You need to stop glaring at me.'

'I won't sit here and–'

'I have this stupid watch on. It won't be long till help gets here so whatever Theo does to us, we'll just have to deal with it because he can't know who has the journal. Your twisted psycho of a brother will come soon and get us out of here, then you can go back to screwing whoever you want. And I can tell you both to shove your spell, and your Coven, up your ass. You're a couple of absolute nut jobs and the further away I am from you, the better. I'm so done with you and Grayson.'

'I won't let you get hurt–'

'End of discussion.'

'No, it's really not–'

'I SAID END OF!'

Theo's voice is just outside. Gabriel's angry eyes glance to the door before settling back on me.

'I will not sit here and watch him carve you up.'

'Well, that's exactly what I'm going to do for you,' I spit back equally as hatefully. 'Let me be clear, Gabriel. I don't want your help or your protection. I don't even want to share the same air as you. You're the worst person I possibly could have got involved with so take your own advice. One night together doesn't make us a couple. It doesn't mean anything so drop the act. You just keep your mouth shut and for once, do the right thing. Grayson will be here soon. Can you do that? Hmm? Put the rest of the magical world ahead of your own needs for just a little while?'

We carry on glaring at each other, but just before the door to the tent opens he gives the slightest, most reluctant nod.

'Good.'

We both turn to look at Jensen who's followed closely by Theo. Theo claps his hands together enthusiastically and grins.

'Right then. Let's get started, shall we?'

Gabriel's eyes never look away from me even though I know Theo's making his way slowly towards us. The plastic groundsheet rustles with his every step. The wind outside starts to pick up and batters the sides of the tent, but inside Gabriel and I are sharing an odd calm before the storm. I know that whatever's coming next will hurt. And so does he. But it will be temporary. Grayson, although a monster, will be here soon.

Theo fetches a stool from the edge of the tent, places it between us and sits facing me.

'Are you ready to start co-operating?' he asks.

'I've already told you. I don't know where the journal is,' I reply.

'I thought after having some time to think it over with the man responsible for the torture of Rose Hooper sitting opposite you, you would change your mind. Guess I was wrong.'

Gabriel's eyes widen as he looks at me. Yeah, I know all about Rose and what he did.

'Guess so.' I shrug. I'm covering my fear and hiding the fact that I think Gabriel and his brother are nothing less than ruthless savages, better than I thought I would.

'Hmm.' Theo looks at Gabriel over his shoulder. 'She's a feisty little thing, isn't she?'

'You have no idea,' Gabriel replies. 'Listen to me, Theo. I know you want the journal, but we don't know where it is. Lilly doesn't know-'

'You expect me to believe that?'

'I've told you a hundred times. It was stolen. I don't know who by or where it is now. If I did, we would have it!'

Theo gets to his feet and puts the stool to one side.

'Well, we'll soon find out who knows what.' He walks towards Gabriel. 'I think it's safe to say there are definitely feelings between you two. Any idiot can see that.' Theo looks back at me over his shoulder. 'But she didn't know all the facts before, did she? She didn't know about Rose. I know because I watched her gag when I told her. So, tell me, Lilly-?'

'You're a real piece of work,' Gabriel spits. 'Telling her *your* version of everything. Turning her against me. You didn't tell her your role in all of that though, did you?'

His version? How could there possibly be a different version of what happened?

'Just tell me where the journal is and save yourselves the pain.'

'We've told you-'

'I know the lies you've told me, Gabriel,' Theo interrupts. 'And I was speaking to her. I will ask one more time. Lilly Hooper, where is the journal?'

He looks at me over his shoulder once more and waits. When I remain silent, Theo turns suddenly and punches Gabriel hard in the face. Blood splatters on the tarp floor and I can't help but gasp.

'Where's the journal?'

'Like the lady said,' Gabriel replies before spitting blood at Theo's feet. 'We don't know.' He returns his eyes to mine.

Theo lands Gabriel with another punch to the face.

'Sure about that?' Theo asks, anger seeping through his calm exterior.

'Positive,' I tell him. 'Hey, maybe Ava knows. You should bring her in here instead of me.' I look at Gabriel. 'I bet she'd tell them anything they wanted to know to keep your face pretty.'

There's blood between his teeth and a fresh flow falling from his nose. Another punch. I jump but keep my poker face. This is hard to watch. Harder than I thought.

'Tell me where the journal is, Lilly. Or things will get much worse.'

'She doesn't know anything,' Gabriel answers for me. There's a look of comfort in his eyes. He's telling me it's okay with nothing but a look.

'I think I need Lilly to tell me that.'

Theo grabs Gabriel's hair and lifts his head, making him look at me with blood pouring from his nose and mouth. I tell myself to stay firm. Be strong. Gabriel's laughing, spitting blood on the floor and making Theo angrier.

'You came all this way to save him, Lilly. And now you're going to let him suffer like this? All you have to do is tell me where the journal is.' He slams Gabriel's head hard into the wooden post. I wince at the thud. He does it again and again. 'Where-' *thud*, 'Is-' *thud*, 'The-' *thud*, 'Journal?' *Thud*.

He lets him go. Gabriel shakes his head clear and blinks a few times before I seem to come back into focus.

I'm completely in Theo's sights as he grimaces at me and says. 'All you have to do is tell me where the journal is and I'll stop.'

'I don't know anything.'

Theo walks to me, crouches down with his elbows on his knees and looks me in the eye. 'If you tell me what I want to know now, I'll make sure that your friends will be kept safe when the spell is done. How's that?'

'Oh, well, in that case...I'll tell you. It's up Jensen's arse. You should go look for it.'

Theo looks at Gabriel and me before glancing at Jensen briefly over my shoulder.

'I think perhaps we need to change tactic. Jensen my friend, would you like to stay or leave for this bit?'

The next bit? Why would he want Jensen to leave? What's he planning?

'I think maybe Gabriel's the weaker link here. Do you agree?'

I look behind me to see Jensen standing by the door with his arms folded and a deep furrow on his brow.

'I agree,' he replies. 'Do what you need to do.' He stands firm.

I think it's my turn.

Theo gets to his feet and stands by my side facing Gabriel. Slowly he starts stroking my head. The sensation of his hand on me is unbearable.

'Tell me, Gabriel. Where is the journal?' Theo continues running his fingers through my hair as Gabriel watches. The blood drains from my face. In fact, I think it's drained from my entire body. I repeat to myself *don't pass out. Stay strong. Hold your ground.* 'Telling me what I want to know will save you...and her, a lot of suffering.'

Gabriel twitches at his words. The slow and gentle stroking continues. He's showing Gabriel exactly how easy it is for him to touch me. And how there's nothing anyone can do about it.

'You don't like me touching her, do you?' Theo says smugly. No, he doesn't. Gabriel's eyes flash dark as they leave mine and look at him. 'I'm not hurting her. But I could be.'

Gabriel's breathing gets heavier. Each breath is deeper than the last, but he says nothing.

'Where is the-'

'We don't know, you psychotic shit,' I hiss. Theo wraps his fingers in my hair and pulls. I give the slightest yelp as he pulls a fist full of my hair higher, lifting my backside off the floor.

'I'm not talking to you anymore, Lilly,' Theo says with a nasty grin. His eyes are firmly on Gabriel. 'I'm asking him. Tell me, or I hurt her.'

Every muscle in Gabriel's jaw is rigid. He's shaking with anger.

'Doesn't care about you, huh?' Theo laughs.

I do my best to hide my pain as Gabriel watches every single one of Theo's actions and my reactions. Those blue eyes don't look anywhere else.

'We told you. We don't know.'

Every word that comes out of Gabriel's mouth is filled with utter contempt. It sends a shiver down my spine. Thankfully, Theo lets me go. He kneels next to me and makes sure he's facing Gabriel. Softly, he runs his finger down my cheek. I flinch away, making him laugh. His hand goes lower. When he slides it under my T-shirt, I freeze.

What the hell is he doing?

He looks at me with smugness and then to Gabriel.

'Tell me,' he says.

'I don't know,' Gabriel replies.

Pressing his palm into my stomach, Theo creates his green lightning. It shoots into my skin from his fingertips in an agonisingly hot surge. I can't help but scream. The high-pitched shriek is uncontrollable. Much like my body's reaction. There's too much pain, my body doesn't know what to do so it thrashes about violently until he lets me go. My muscles are still screaming from the shock and where his hand was feels red raw.

'Gabriel? Feel chatty yet?'

'Touch her like that again-'

Gabriel doesn't get to finish his threat. Theo's hand is on my stomach once more as he sends his lightning across my skin. He continues on and on despite my desperate screaming. He stops for a few seconds, long enough to ask his question. When the same answer is given, his lightning returns. This pattern goes on for so long I'm hoarse when he suddenly loses his cocky composure and yells in my face.

'JUST FUCKING TELL ME!'

My quickened breath turns into mockery. Laughing at Theo and his attempts to get us to talk. Yes, I'm in pain. Yes, I'm afraid. But compared to what I've been through in my life...this is easy.

'You think this is funny?' Theo grabs the back of my neck and ensures all I can see is his face. 'This isn't a game! Can't you see I'm the one in the right here?! I'm trying to save the world!'

I look up at him while wearing that nasty grin I remember Toby used to wear so well. Even now, after everything, I look at him and his lessons for a way to cope with pain.

'I had a home,' I tell him. 'A family that loved me and I lost it all because of you. You made my mother seek shelter with a man who tortured me my whole life. You want me to murder the only people who have ever shown me any kindness on the say so of your shady vision. You've kidnapped Gabriel and I and are currently torturing us. So tell me again how you're the one in the right! Because you destroyed my world. Destroyed it!'

'I don't find pleasure in this,' he says. 'But I won't stop until I get the information I need, so do yourself a favour and just give it up. You will eventually. Everyone does.'

'You think so? Well, why don't you let *me* tell *you* a story? I had this boyfriend. He would make me practice my magic for hours and hours till my head was pounding and my nose was bleeding. He thought pain and anger fuelled my strength and believe me when I tell you he wanted me strong. So that's what he did. For hours. For days. For years. He'd push me to every conceivable limit. Snap my bones. Burn my skin. Break my spirit. Meanwhile, my uncle and his wife would beat me and starve me for kicks, so trust me when I tell you, *Theo*. Your pathetic attempts to hurt me are nothing, *nothing*, compared to what I've been through in my life. I've been submerged in pain for as long as I can remember. It's as common to me as sleeping. So, do your worst. You can't do anything to me that hasn't already been done, and Gabriel? You can do what you want to him. I couldn't care less. Keep asking us a question that we simply don't know the answer to. Keep drawing blood because that's all you'll get from us. Blood. We don't know where the journal is.'

Theo isn't impressed with what I've said. Especially when he looks into my eyes and knows I mean what I say. Slowly he gets to his feet, not once looking away from me until he turns and stalks to the edge of the tent towards one of the tables. After a few minutes of rummaging, he finds what he's looking for and turns back to us.

'I see the problem. You're not afraid of pain because you know it won't last. You also know I won't kill you, so let's try something else.' Theo holds out a pair of small iron bolt cutters and points them straight at me. 'Gabriel can heal. That's true. But you can't. Not until your Physical magic comes in and I know that hasn't happened by how pathetic your attempts have been to get free. You want to know what I think?' He walks back to my side and kneels. The cold steel of the cutters rests on the base of my little finger on my right hand. I struggle to swallow the nervous whimper that wants to come out. 'I think that you're tough. That you'll put up with most of what I could do to you out of spite alone. But Gabriel won't be able to stand by as I chop off little pieces of you. I think that he'll talk.'

'You're wrong,' I insist. My words aren't directed to Theo. I'm making sure Gabriel knows I still mean what I said. No matter what, Theo can't know who has the journal. 'We can't tell you what we don't know.'

'Physical magic lets you heal,' Theo growls in my ear. 'Get shot, get stabbed, break a bone, and in a day or two no one would ever know. But losing a finger, a hand, an arm... the bleeding will stop. But that part of you will never grow back. Physical magic or no Physical magic.' He clamps the cutters down a little, drawing blood and making me fight a yell against the slow torturous cut. I keep my eyes on Gabriel. His eyes are wide and afraid as he starts to struggle against his restraints. He watches Theo. And Theo watches him.

'Tell me, Gabriel. If you care about young Miss Hooper's wellbeing, you will tell me what I want to know.'

That's eerie. Those are the exact words Grayson told my uncle before having Collins chop off Christa's fingers.

'Tell me, Gabriel!' Theo says. 'TELL ME!'

Gabriel seals his lips together, his body rigid and his eyes start to brim with tears. Are they sad or frightened tears? Maybe it's both. I know that the tears that are trying to spill out of my eyes are.

'No?' Theo leans into my ear. 'Tell me and I'll stop.' He clamps down the cutters a little further, but I refuse to let the yell out. My lips remain shut even if my tears have spilt out. I struggle to swallow against the urge to throw up.

With a deep breath, I sit straighter and defiantly tell Theo. 'Go screw yourself.'

Theo growls, and as he does, he clamps the bolt cutters closed.

Snip.

The sound of the metal blades meeting and the small thump as something lands on the floor is swiftly followed by a blood-curdling scream.

My scream.

Gabriel's yelling, threatening him with every form of violence possible and pulling against his restraints.

I can't stop the screams. They just keep coming. I have to mentally slap myself to get them to stop. It takes a few moments to get myself back under any form of control. The hot, sharp pain settles and turns into a deep, agonising throbbing. My head slumps forwards as I focus on getting my breathing back under control. When I lift my head and return my attention to Gabriel, he looks in shock. He's whiter than white and shaking.

Theo stands. He walks purposefully towards him and drops a small pink and bloody digit by his feet. My little finger.

'How about now?' Theo asks smugly. 'You going to tell me who has the journal or shall I continue?'

Gabriel looks at my severed finger and slowly lifts his gaze to the man standing in front of him.

'You're a dead man.'

'No. I'm very much alive, and I'm going to chop her up, and put her in front of you piece by piece.' He returns to me, grabbing the back of my neck roughly and unleashing another series of lightning shocks. This time it travels down my spine. My legs kick out as I struggle to control myself against the pain he's inflicting. He's yelling at Gabriel, demanding answers to his questions. Gabriel's furiously yelling back, telling him to stop. Telling him over and over that he doesn't know and all I can do is scream against a pain that's spreading through my whole body.

I don't know how much more I can take.

'PLEASE! DAMN IT, THEO, STOP!' Gabriel yells desperately. Theo lets me go with a shove. I blink through the tears to get Gabriel into focus. I'm crying despite myself.

'TELL ME!' Theo yells.

I hang my head and can't help the weak laughter that comes from me.

'What could possibly be funny?' Theo demands.

What's funny is this whole situation. I lift my head and look at Gabriel who's agonising over watching me suffer.

'This is what Grayson did to my aunt and uncle when he met me,' I tell him with a laugh. 'I was in your position. Talk about Karma.'

'Stay with me, Beautiful,' Gabriel soothes, thinking I've gone mad from the pain. But I haven't.

'Oh, bite me, Gabriel,' I snap back. I look up at Theo, and although I have tears streaming down my face and I'm in so much pain I could pass out...I smile. 'Is that all you got?'

He takes a deep angry breath and gives me a powerful backhand. The hard sting stuns me. I taste blood in my mouth. He's split my lip. I lick it clean and turn back to Gabriel. He mouths the word *"please"* to me. I give the slightest shake of my head. He returns his attention to Theo.

'Theo...she's been through so much already. You have no idea. Please-'

'Shut your fucking mouth, Gabriel. Hearing your voice is worse than this nut job hacking off my finger,' I tell him angrily.

Theo laughs.

'The only words I want to hear from either of you are... *"Theo, the journal is..."* So, until that sentence comes out of one of your mouths and is completed, we'll carry on.' He lowers himself once more to his knees beside me, picks up the bloody bolt cutters and rests it on my ring finger next to the stub where my little finger once was.

I wince as the blade sinks into my skin.

'Theo. Maybe this isn't the way,' Jensen says from somewhere behind me.

'Violence is all these people will respond to. I tried it your way, Jensen. I tried to reason with her, but she can't be reasoned with. This is the only way to save the world.' The tent falls silent and the pitter patter of rain starts. I take some very difficult breaths, preparing myself for what's coming. I'm determined not to scream anymore.

'Please. Please, Theo. Stop,' Gabriel says desperately.

'Tell me what I want to know. And I will.' He closes the cutters a fraction, and I can't help it. I give a small whimper and look up at the ceiling desperate to keep my composure.

'Theo just stop!'

'TELL ME!'

He closes it more and I scream out.

Gabriel looks at Theo pleadingly. 'Dad, please. Don't do this. Stop.'

Only now do I break my intense lock with the ceiling to look between the two with wide eyes.

'Did you just call him dad?' Neither of them looks at me. Neither of them answers me and Theo keeps the cutters exactly where they are.

'You think calling me *"Dad"* will evoke some kind of sympathy? That it will make me feel sorry for you?' There's nothing but hatred in Theo's voice. 'You and your brothers should have been drowned at birth. The only thing that will make this stop is you telling me who stole the journal. She has nine fingers left ...*son*.' Theo clamps down the cutters even further. 'Want to make it eight?'

I feel the blood seeping across my hand as I whimper against the pain.

'Tell me who has the journal, and I'll stop. I swear. Look at her, Gabriel. Help her.'

Gabriel looks painfully at me. He's losing his willpower. I look at Theo whose face is close to mine.

'Fuck. You.'

I scream as he slams the blade closed and severs a second finger. Theo throws the cutters to the floor and grabs my mutilated hand. His green lightning erupts over it. I can't hear what he's yelling over at Gabriel because my screaming is deafening. Ignoring my pleas for him to stop, he makes the pain worse. I think I'm going to die. He goes on and on until my voice is barely there anymore. I don't know how long it goes on for until finally, my body stops thrashing.

The last thing I see before I black out is Gabriel trying desperately to get free and help me.

The sheets cover us completely as we lay on our sides facing each other.
The bed smells of him. His scent. Vanilla and sandalwood.
'Aren't you tired?' I ask.
Gabriel shakes his head. 'Why would I want to sleep when I can lie here and watch you?'
'Let's stay here,' I sigh, brushing the hair from his face. 'Let's not go back to The Orchard.'
'What, live here in this room?' he asks with a soft laugh.
'Yeah,' I reply. 'We can stay under these sheets and forget the outside world completely.'

He pulls me closer and lies on his back so I can rest my head on his bare chest. I listen to his heartbeat. The slow and steady thump, thump, thump is comforting.

It's been such a long night. An emotional and physically draining night.

Running through the woods after Toby. Gabriel and I finally giving into how we truly feel. I still can't believe I'm here with him. His arms wrapped around my body and his legs entwined with mine. It's all I've wanted since I first laid eyes on him.

Lilly and her Gabriel.

Finally.

'Lilly? Are you still awake?' he asks.

His fingers are running through my hair. I'm on the verge of sleep.

'Lilly?' He leans into my ear and whispers. 'I've fallen in love with you.'

I jump at the loud clap of thunder. Slowly, my consciousness returns. My brain awakens and starts registering everything. Where I am. Who I'm with. What I'm feeling. And what's happened.

I twitch my hand. Holy hell, it's painful. Very painful. I shift my legs. They're filled with pins and needles. As I move, the blood rushes through them and starts waking them up. Everything sounds like it's a million miles away. The rain. The tent. Gabriel's voice. I groan and slowly lift my head to blink him into focus. We're still in the tent. Still tied to the posts. There's a storm going on. Thunder shakes the ground and lightning flashes from outside. I see Gabriel's mouth moving. His concern filled face. But I can't get a grip on what he's saying. It takes a few moments to wake up properly, and finally, I hear him clearly.

'Look at me,' he says. 'Are you with me?'

'Yeah,' I groan. 'I'm here.'

I'm sweating. My hair is plastered to my face, and the pain in my hand's unreal. I look at Gabriel as I slump against the post with my hands still tied behind my back. In front of him are two of my fingers, lying in a small puddle of blood on the floor, left there to mock him.

'He cut my fingers off,' I say in utter disbelief. As I look at the two digits, it really hits me. 'He cut off my fucking fingers!' I look at Gabriel. 'Your dad cut off two of my goddamn fingers!' I look around the tent, ready to hurl every insult and threat I have at Theo. Which to be fair won't do much. But swearing and shouting will definitely make me feel better.

'I know it's a stupid question, but how are you feeling?' Gabriel asks me.

'Like I've had two of my fingers cut off! How do you bloody think?! What a stupid fucking question, you utter prat.'

As soon as I see the look of misery on his face, my anger eases. I sigh heavily and slump back against the post.

'I'm thirsty,' I tell him in a much calmer manner. 'And I have one hell of a headache. That lightning is bloody agony!'

'You're telling me,' he mutters in agreement. 'And...your hand?' he asks.

I wiggle the remaining digits. 'Sore. Really sore. Now I get why my aunt was screaming so much. What happened? Where are they?'

'You passed out. Theo was about to cut off another finger when Jensen threw him off you. He said he was going to come back when you woke up. Finish what he'd started. Unless...'

'Unless what?' I see the look on his face. Regret.

'I'm sorry. I couldn't let you go through anymore.'

He looks so ashamed of himself. I'm ashamed for him.

'You told him, didn't you? Who has the journal?' He nods and looks at the two fingers on the floor in front of him. My anger's back. 'You bloody idiot! All we had to do was wait it out. You knew help was coming!' I can't even look at him. I'm so angry.

'So, what now?' I demand. 'There's no reason for him to keep you alive is there! He's going to kill you. Keep me here. Find that book and make me commit mass murder. Your dad!' I scoff. 'Nice bloody family you have. Two raging psychos for brothers and a lunatic for a dad. And then there's you. I don't even have the words to describe you.'

'I panicked. You have no idea what it's like to watch someone you care about suffer!' He sounds angry now.

'Someone you care about? Don't make me laugh.'

'I do care about you.'

'I must have missed that while you were lying to me about who Toby was, screwing Ava and telling me I'm one of life's permanent victims. That I deserve everything that's happened to me. What about this, huh? Do I deserve to be missing two fucking fingers?!'

He goes quiet as I brim with anger. Anger at him, at Theo, at this whole situation and how helpless and useless I am.

'I don't deserve this. You deserve it. You and Grayson. You deserve death for what you've done.'

'Theo won't kill me. He can't,' he says after a few moments.

Again, I scoff. 'I don't think he feels very paternal towards you. And you're not immortal. You can die, Gabriel!'

'Yes, but he won't kill me. The spell that we did, the one that keeps us all young... it's linked us.' He can't stop looking at the fingers.

'Will you stop looking at those and focus on the current situation, please? What do you mean it's linked you?'

He tears his eyes away from the fingers and looks at me instead.

'Basically, if one of us dies, we all die. Theo won't kill us because he doesn't want to die. Grayson, me, Collins, Theo and Toby are all linked to the same spell,' he sighs and leans his head back as I take in what he's saying. 'No one else in the world knows that. It's one of our most guarded secrets.'

'Oh well, I'm honoured,' I sneer as I pull at the rope around my wrists, but all that does is anger the wound on my fingers. I can feel something wrapped around my palm. I move, looking over my shoulder as much as possible and see a blood-soaked bandage covering the stumps. I suppose they wouldn't want me to lose too much blood. They need me alive after all. I really can't believe I've lost two fingers.

'How long was I out?'

'I'm not sure. An hour, maybe a little more.'

'The cuff went on about an hour and a half before that,' I tell him. He nods understanding what I'm saying. Grayson will be here soon. I long to feel my magic. To get free of these restraints. To get somewhere safe. To leave them all behind. Grayson wouldn't give me access. Why would he? He has no idea what's happening. As far as he's aware, I've just done a runner.

'I'm sorry,' he says again.

'It's done. We just need to get out of here and find the journal before Theo does.'

'Not that. Us. I'm sorry about what happened. What I said-'

'I really couldn't care less what you think of me because, to be honest, my opinion of you is in the toilet. Everything that comes out of your mouth is a lie,' I tell him. 'Theo told me about Rose. About what you did to her. No wonder you wouldn't tell me. I would never have slept with you if I knew. I would never have stayed in that house if I knew what you had done.'

His eyes fill with shame. He swallows painfully and starts chewing on his lower lip.

'What exactly did he say?' he asks.

'That you and Grayson tortured her. That you got in her head trying to make her fall in love with Grayson and that he got her pregnant twice as a result.' He doesn't say a word. 'I was chained to a wall for two years, Gabriel. Alone. In the dark. What you did to her...' I shake my head, fighting the bile in my throat as

I think of it. 'That and the fact that you're trying to start a war with humanity-'

'A war?' He looks at me like I'm insane. 'We're not trying to start a war!'

'No?' My voice drips with sarcasm.

'No!' he repeats flatly. 'We train the Nomads. Sure. We teach them how to defend themselves because no one else will. When the Veil comes down, Hunters *will* come looking for a fight. And yeah, we'll fight back. But we won't go looking for trouble. I don't want to live through another war. I don't want to kill humans. I don't want to kill anyone! But I will if they come after me. Or the people I care about.'

'And Grayson? What does he want?'

'He wants power. He wants to the be the strongest. Being the leader of a new generation of Witches is all he's wanted since the Veil was put up. We have the islands ready, Lilly. We have our future homes waiting for us. If he starts planning a war before magic returns, I'll stop him. We *all* will, I assure you. No one wants a fight. Not me, not Collins, not the Nomads... no one.'

I'm not sure if I believe him, but I see nothing but honesty and genuine truth on his face.

'I swear to you. All we want is to be free. If humans leave us alone, we will leave them alone.'

'Do you trust Grayson?'

'With the Veil? With succeeding in returning magic? Yes. I trust him. We *must* be free. The alternative is death. Grayson will get us there, that I'm sure of. The veil *must* come down. Do you know what will happen to us all if we don't? This will seem like a holiday compared to what Hunters will do to us.'

'Did you do those things to Rose?' I ask quickly before I change my mind.

I was hoping for denial. But instead, he lowers his head and gives a small nod. Everything inside me feels like it's slowly turning to ash and crumbling. These people are not what I thought. Grayson and Gabriel are wicked men. Is there anyone good on this planet?

'I hate you more than anyone else on this planet.'

'Yeah well, I hate me too,' he mumbles.

There are voices outside the tent. They're getting closer. It's two men, and it sounds like they're arguing. Gabriel looks past me to the door. I look over my shoulder towards the sound of their voices. I can't see anyone but I know that whoever it is, they're not happy and they're coming this way.

'What now,' I groan.

'Sorry, gents,' says a third voice from outside. 'No one's allowed in. Orders direct from Theodore and Jensen.'

'I only need a few minutes,' says one of the men that were arguing. 'No one needs to know.'

'Sorry, Jay. Answer's no.'

'I just want to look him in the eye. Do you know who that is in there? What he's done?'

'I'm well aware, but this is bigger than your own personal vendetta. Take your brother, turn around, and leave. No good will come of seeing him.'

There's a scuffle before someone gets punched hard. I hear them hit the floor.

'Gabriel?' I whisper, my body twisted so I can see the door. 'What's happening?'

'I don't know, but whatever it is, keep quiet,' he says sternly. 'Don't say a word. Let me deal with it.'

The flap that acts like the door is pulled open. A man with short ginger hair walks in followed swiftly by another man. He too has ginger hair, but his is a little longer. These must be the brothers who just knocked out our guard. The one with short hair looks straight at Gabriel like he wants to kill him.

'Well, this can't be good,' Gabriel says when I turn to look at him.

'Jay, please,' the one with longer hair says, pulling on his brother's arm. 'We shouldn't be in here. Jensen will have our heads-'

'I'm not going anywhere,' Jay replies. He doesn't blink as he stares daggers at Gabriel. 'Do you remember me?'

Gabriel looks him up and down then shrugs. 'Should I?'

Jay charges forwards, his fists balled up and shaking he's so filled with anger and hatred. His brother runs after him, grabs his arm and holds him back.

'Get off me, Tom!' Jay hisses, trying to pull his arm free.

'This won't achieve anything!' Tom says desperately as he's dragged forwards by a determined Jay. They stop between us, facing Gabriel. All I can see are their backs. Jay's panting. His shoulders are rising and falling quickly as he looks down at Gabriel. I peer around them to get a more unobstructed view and see Gabriel looks as confused as me.

'What did you do?' I ask him. 'Sleep with his wife? Let your brother keep his sister in your basement?'

'You're not helping, Lilly.'

'I wasn't trying to.'

With a groan, Gabriel looks up at the two of them. 'Do I know you?'

Jay looks between us with utter disdain. Like we're the filthiest vermin ever to exist. But he settles his attention on Gabriel.

'You really don't remember me?' Jay squats down making them eye level while wearing a cruel sneer. 'Nothing about me looks familiar?'

Gabriel looks. He really looks but shakes his head. 'Sorry mate. No idea.'

'Six months ago,' Jay starts as Tom lingers by my feet watching the door nervously. 'You and a group of your Nomad scum raided one of our camps.'

'Did we?'

'You did,' Jay spits back. 'I was there. So were my two brothers.'
He gestures to Tom. 'We got out. But our oldest brother didn't.
Nick. You killed him.'

He holds eye contact with him but keeps quiet.

'Are you going to deny it?'

'I'm sorry if-'

'There's no *if*, Witch scum. You came into our home and killed
my brother.' Jay's face gets redder as anger takes control. He
pulls out a knife from his jacket pocket and gets to his feet. I
stare at the blade, but Gabriel keeps his eyes on Jay.

'You killed my big brother. You're an abomination that should
have died centuries ago but yet here you are. Contaminating the
world with your poisonous words and you,' he looks down at me.
'You're worse than all of them.'

'Me?' What did I do? I have no idea what you're on about!'

'You have the chance to end all this. To destroy their species
and yet you refuse. You make me sick.'

'They're your species too,' I remind him. 'You're a
Descendant.'

'Stop talking, Witch bitch.' He takes a step towards me with
that knife in clear view. 'I heard Theo cut off two of those fingers
of yours. Maybe I should make it three!'

The mere threat makes me feel faint. I've only just woken up
from my last torture session. I can't face any more. Not yet.

'Actually...' Gabriel says arrogantly with a cocky grin. 'I think
I do remember your brother. Long ginger hair, tied back in a
ponytail...right?' Jay stops walking towards me. 'Yeah. Yeah, I do
remember.' Gabriel starts to laugh as if remembering something
funny. 'Yeah. He was the guy who pissed himself as he opened
fire on his own men.'

'Shut up!' Jay snaps.

'A full-grown man pissing himself,' Gabriel laughs. 'That was
worth the visit to your camp alone.'

Jay turns his back on me and faces Gabriel instead.

'I heard he cried for his mummy.' Gabriel keeps on goading. Insulting him, his brother and the camp in general. Calling them pathetic, weak little children until finally, Jay can't take anymore. He yells and charges forwards, the knife pointing straight at Gabriel ready to go into his neck.

'NO!' I scream. Gabriel's tied up. What the hell can he do against an armed madman?

As soon as Jay's in reach, Gabriel kicks out his leg in a large swiping motion knocking the irrational Jay to the floor. As he lies on his back, dazed and winded from the hard fall, Gabriel lifts his foot and slams his boot down on Jay's face, knocking him out cold leaving the knife to lay in his limp hand. Tom runs forwards to help his brother, but Gabriel puts his heavy boot on Jay's throat and presses down.

'One more step, Tom, and I'll snap his neck.' He's suddenly extremely serious. All the mockery that was just there has gone. This was his plan all along.

Tom freezes and I'm watching everything with bated breath. Gabriel nods to the knife by Jay's hand.

'I want you to pick up that knife, and cut through her ropes.' He presses down a little harder with his foot. 'If you try anything, Tom, I will kill your brother. Do you understand me?'

Tom nods looking petrified and slowly makes his way over to the knife, keen to stay as far away from Gabriel as possible. He scoops it up and walks back to me, not taking his eyes off Gabriel and his brother.

As Tom starts cutting my ropes, Gabriel says, 'For the record. I didn't kill your brother. My men and I did go to your camp. And only because you had taken two of our people hostage. Two young girls, who you tortured for three days, might I add. I set up a perimeter of your men and ordered them to open fire on anyone who attempted to follow us after we left. Your brother was one of those men. I remember him. If your brother died, it was because of your own people trying to get past him. Not us. I also have no idea if he pissed himself.' Tom doesn't say anything as he cuts. And neither do I. Because that seems remarkably fair, if that's what happened. Once free, I toss the rope as far away from me as possible before taking off the binding spell watch. My magic comes back in the most welcome rush.

'Give her the knife,' Gabriel instructs.

Tom does as he's told and I get to my feet, knife in hand. I sway a little, but I'm so full of determination and adrenaline I push past my wooziness. With all the strength I have left, with all the anger and hatred that's currently coursing through me, I pull back my fist and slam it hard into Tom's face. He spins before he falls and lands face down. He doesn't get up.

I turn my attention to Gabriel. The knife still in my hand. Slowly he moves his foot away from Jay's neck as he looks up at me. I don't rush to him. I don't ask if he's okay. I just look down at him.

'Are you going to help me get free?' he asks.

'Did you free Rose?' I ask back.

He shakes his head and lowers his gaze.

'No. you didn't.' I take a step back. 'You don't deserve to be saved. You don't deserve freedom or peace.'

'You're probably right.'

'Goodbye, Gabriel.'

'Bye, Beautiful.'

I turn and start to walk away.

When I reach the tent door, he hasn't said a word. No pleading for me to free him. No attempts to explain anything. Nothing. I can't help but look back.

There he sits. Tied to the post, still bleeding and still silent, but watching me. I know what he's done. To me. To Rose. And there's probably a million other things that would turn my stomach. I know he's far from a good man and yet... I can't walk away. The truth is, I love a man that doesn't exist. I love a lie. But still, I love. I know I have to leave. I have to walk away for my own safety. But I can't. The idea of never seeing the version of him I knew up until the night we came back from his hotel room hurts more than Theo's lightning. More than losing a finger. More than my uncle's cane. My insides are being torn to pieces at the mere idea of never seeing my Gabriel again. Not the man I've come to know in the last few days, but *my* Gabriel. The man who held me so I could fall asleep. The man who read to me. The man who defended me. Who made me laugh. Who looked at me like I was the most beautiful thing he'd ever seen.

But they are one and the same.

All I can do is stand by the door and let those silent tears slide down my cheeks as I struggle to decide what to do.

'It's okay,' he says. 'I understand. Go. Run.' He nods to the door. 'Get as far away from here as you can. Don't stop. Never stop running. From Theo, from Grayson, from Toby. Find somewhere and disappear.' Tears tumble down his cheeks. They land on his lips which smile sweetly and blend with the blood. My feet shuffle back, but still, I don't leave.

I could turn and run. Disappear. My binding spell is in my pocket. All I need to do is destroy it and Grayson would never find me. The Bloodstone would be pointless. I could cut my hair. Colour it. Make myself a new person. I'm a survivor. I could do it. Leave the world of witches behind. Leave The Orchard. Leave them to their violence and battles. I could finally be free. As I turn and reach out to pull open the door I freeze. If I leave, *they* will never be free.

'Lilly, go,' he says firmly despite a quaking voice. 'Go before Grayson gets here. Before Theo knows you're free.' When I don't move, he shouts. 'FUCKING GO!'

'The night we spent together. At the hotel,' I turn and look him in the eye. 'Did you tell me you loved me?'

He just keeps watching me as another tear tumbles down his cheek.

'Did you?'

'Please...just go.'

I turn and walk back to him, kneeling by his side and shake my head.

'No,' I say simply. I wipe my tears away with my sleeve and shake my head. 'Not until I understand.' I rest my hands on his head. 'Let me in. Show me'

'Show you what?' he asks.

'Who you really are. You said Theo told me his version. Turned me against you. You treated me like trash, but you clearly care about me. I don't want to hear more lies. I want to see the truth.' I hold his head firmly, one hand each side of his face, and look into his eyes which are staring straight back at me.

'Just leave,' he says. 'Save yourself.'

'I can't,' I admit, trying hard not to just burst into tears. 'I can't walk away from you. Not yet.'

'Why?!' he asks desperately as his tears spill over my thumb. 'Everything I've said, all the things I've done-'

'They don't make sense! I need to see for myself who you are.'

'I'm a wicked man.' He looks me straight in the eye. 'I'm evil. I manipulate and lie to get what I want. You were no different. I wanted to fuck you. I did. Now I want you to go.'

His words are cruel, but they're lies. I can see it in his eyes. Like when he was goading Jay to try and protect me.

'No,' I insist. 'You keep pushing me away, and I don't understand so please...please. If you have ever cared about me, let me in.'

'I never cared about you.' He pulls his face away from my hands. 'Just go!'

'I can't!'

'WHY?!'

'Because I love you!' I sob. His eyes flick up to mine in shock as I say those words.

'What...what did you just say to me?'

'I told you that I'm in love with you, Gabriel. I do. I love you completely. And I know you told me you love me too. At the hotel. I remember it. You told me, then you broke my heart. You did something unspeakable to Rose, but I see how much pain it causes you. I need to know that a good man *can* care about me. Not just cruel, evil men that hurt me, so please...' I cry desperately, begging for him to help me. Holding his face in my hands and resting my nose against his, I say, 'Please let me see why you've done the things you've done. Please let me see that the man I love *is* a good man.'

'I'm not a good man,' he whispers. 'Looking into my memories will not bring you comfort.'

'I'm not seeking comfort. I'm seeking the truth. Show me, or you will never, ever see me again. And I will never forgive you. Not for what you did with Ava or to Rose. But for turning your back on me when I love you and need you as much as I do right now.' I tighten my hold on his head and channel my magic into his mind. 'Let me in. Show me Rose. Show me us. Show me the truth.'

Chapter 21

I smell damp, mould and rot. I see rats crawling across a grey stone floor, sniffing and scratching as they search for food. I'm in a room I've never been in before. I know I'm not really here, it's nothing more than Gabriel's memory. But it's so real. I reach out and feel the cold, wet stone of the walls. The ceiling's stone too, and it arches high above my head. The room's dark. Lit only by a small fire burning in a fireplace ahead of me. Despite that, it's cold. The sound of metal scraping along the stone floor makes me turn. Behind me is a woman. She's sat cross-legged on the floor. Her hands are cuffed together in thick iron and a heavy chain trails from her wrists to the wall where she's been tethered. Just like mine used to be. Her long beige cotton dress is filthy and torn. Her brunette hair reaches her waist and is plaited together so it falls down her back. She's trembling as she looks at the floor. The sound of a key unlocking a heavy door makes her head fly up. She looks straight at me, and I know straight away who she is.

Rose Hooper.

Her face, her eyes, they're mine. Only her light brown hair is different. She gets to her feet and starts to back away. I turn to see what she's looking at so warily.

'Fuck!' I gasp as I too start to back away.

Gabriel, Grayson and Toby are all standing in an arched doorway beside an open heavy wooden door watching her. They're wearing clothes from centuries ago. White cotton shirts that fit loosely. Dark, heavy waistcoats, and small blades on their hips. In their hands are torches of fire. Of course, there's no electricity. This must be almost five hundred years ago. The most startling thing about all this is seeing Toby. His hair is dark brown. Not white. This is before his Break. He lingers behind the others watching, looking nervous, almost timid. When Grayson speaks, he jumps. This is as far from the Toby I know as can be.

'She's a Hooper, that's for sure,' Grayson says calmly, looking Rose up and down with ease. 'No magic though. Her hairs not the tell-tale red.'

'It's not right,' Toby says quietly, looking nervously at the ground. 'Keeping her in this horrible place.'

My Toby wouldn't give a damn. He would enjoy seeing her this way. Misery makes him happy. When it isn't his.

'We have to keep her hidden, Bias. No one can know she's here. It's not like we can take her home. Gabriel?' He looks at the version of Gabriel standing next to him. 'We need to know what she knows. We need to know what needs to be done to return magic. Do what you need to do.' Grayson turns and leaves. Toby follows with his head down. Gabriel waits by the door until they're gone before looking back into the cell at the frightened girl who looks eerily like me.

I watch as he walks towards her. The closer he gets, the more frightened she becomes and the further she backs up. But there's nowhere for her to go. He puts the torch into a holder on the wall and faces her.

'Hello, Rose,' he says. 'Do you know who I am?'

She nods, clearly petrified as he stands there so calm.

'Do you know what we want?'

'Yes,' she whispers. 'But I don't know anything. I swear.'

His eyes go black. 'Rose, come here.'

She does. Her eyes glaze over as she walks towards him, stopping close. Her face is expressionless. All the fear that was there a moment ago has gone. He strokes the hair from her face and looks her over before settling his eyes on hers.

'Rose, tell me what you know.' He places his hands on each side of her head and closes his eyes. 'Let me in. Show me.'

'Hi.'

I jump. Gabriel, my Gabriel is standing by my side. He looks at the other version of himself currently digging through Roses' head.

'What are you doing to her?' I ask.

'Looking into her memories. Like you are with me right now in the tent. I did this every day for three months until I finally saw what we needed.'

The room keeps fading in and out of focus. Each time it returns he's there, looking into her mind. Each time she seems paler, dirtier, thinner and emptier. This long passage of time and her deterioration passes in front of my eyes in moments. But also, intertwined with these memories, is Gabriel sitting with her, wrapping blankets around her, feeding her, keeping the fire burning as big as possible and even once, he comforts her as she cries. He brings her books, clean clothes, and they sit and talk like friends. But she's still his prisoner.

'Why did it take so long?' I ask.

'Mental magic allows me to control others. Their actions mainly. But it also allows me to dig into people's minds. Alter their way of thinking. But I could never get them to say something they didn't want to. I could get them to repeat me. But not answer me. Their secrets remain just that. Their secrets.' He looks back to Rose. 'I got to know her pretty well. She was sweet. Stubborn, but sweet. Grayson refused to let her out of that room. I tried to make it more comfortable for her. But I was limited in what I was allowed to do.'

Suddenly, we're no longer in the dungeon where Rose was being kept. We're outside in the sunshine. Grayson and Gabriel are standing side by side looking out to a lake. My version of Gabriel lingers back with me.

'What have you learnt so far?' Grayson asks.

'I learnt that we need an Arcane Witch to break down the Veil,' Gabriel tells him. 'And that there's only one way to make an Arcane Witch while the Veil is still up.' Grayson watches him, hungry for information. 'A Hooper has to fall in love with a Descendant and produce a child. Only love on both sides and the heritage of magic will do it.'

'This moment right here,' I look to my side, to *my* Gabriel. 'This is the moment that I regret most of all. I should never have told him that. I didn't think for a second that he would do what he did.' He looks at me with such pain and shame.

'What did he do?'

Gabriel looks back to the younger versions of the two. 'You'll see.'

'So all we need to do is get her pregnant?' Grayson asks with a shrug. 'Easy enough.'

'No, not easy enough. Love, Grayson. There has to be love. That's what I saw.'

'What you saw?' he asks with a mocking laugh. 'That's what she thinks. That's Rebecca and her father telling her that. Who knows if that's the truth or not.'

'Grayson, a child won't be enough!' Gabriel insists. 'It must be conceived with love and there's no way in hell that girl will love anyone but her husband. Her *human* husband. I can see the devotion inside her as clear as I can see the ducks on the lake.'

Grayson shrugs and looks back out to the water.

'Hmm. I'll figure something out. Did you discover anything else?' Again, Grayson looks at Gabriel who shakes his head. 'Fine, then go.'

'I want to have her moved,' Gabriel insists. 'I've prepared a room for her in the house. I won't keep her locked down in that pit any longer. It's not right and you know it.'

'Thirty years ago, we lost everything. And we are still losing everything. If anyone finds out we have a Hooper, we're as good as dead. If Hunters don't come, Theo will. So no. She won't be brought out of that pit because all it will take is for a whisper of her existence to come out, and we'll be swarmed by enemies.'

'I don't care. Grayson, I won't leave her down there.'

'And if you move her, I'll banish you,' he replies sternly. 'So think about it very carefully. Because I don't give second chances. Not anymore.'

Gabriel turns to leave but hesitates. 'Grayson, don't do anything drastic.'

'Drastic?'

'We don't do...that. We don't touch women. Not like that. Never.'

'I know,' Grayson replies as if that's obvious. 'I said I'll think of something. We'll figure it out. Don't worry yourself, little brother.' Gabriel leaves looking back at his brother over his shoulder.

The image fades. These are Gabriel's memories so without him here I can't see what happened next. Instead, the sunshine turns to moonlight. The lake becomes an old cabin. Inside I hear the soft giggle of a little girl. The other version of Gabriel is hiding behind a tree, looking in through the window. I look. Inside is a man. He's reading to a little girl who's sitting on his lap.

'I knew Rose had a daughter with her husband,' my Gabriel tells me as he watches himself observe the little girl. 'Her name was Poppy. She was a sweet little thing. She and her father lived in Wales. Rose tried so hard to keep her hidden from me when I went inside her mind, but I found her.'

'What did you do?' I almost daren't ask, but he looks at me and shakes his head.

'Nothing,' he says. 'I did nothing. I pretended like she didn't exist. I didn't tell Grayson. I didn't tell anyone. I saw a look in his eye when I said that a child was needed. It was a dark look. A cruel, callous and desperate look. The war had changed my brother. He was always cold and distant. But after our mother died the night of the first attack, he changed. He could be wearing a smile on his face when he was far from happy.' He looks back to Poppy. 'When I saw his reaction by the lake, I think I knew what he was planning. But I didn't dare admit it to myself. I love my brother, I never thought for a second...' He loses his train of thought, or maybe the ability to speak because I know what he's going to say. I know that Rose ended up pregnant.

'So, you didn't tell him about her daughter?' I ask hoping to encourage him on.

He shakes his head. 'No,' he says. 'I didn't tell Grayson about Poppy because he would have wanted her too. And I promised Rose I would keep her safe. I couldn't protect her, but I could protect her daughter.'

The image fades, and again we're in the dungeon but this time on the other side of the door. It's been locked. Gabriel's key doesn't work. Grayson appears behind him.

'What are you doing, little brother?' he asks.

Gabriel turns and gestures to the door. 'I came to talk to Rose. See if I could find out any more information, but my key-'

'I thought it best we let her rest. Let her gather herself. Have a break from you digging around in her head for a while.' Grayson stands to one side and gestures for him to leave. 'I will let you know if you are needed.' Gabriel looks back at the door before reluctantly leaving.

'Grayson sent me to Ireland the next morning in search of a man called Quinn. A few months later, when I came back...'

The image fades, and it's the dead of night. Gabriel's sneaking down the corridor towards Rose. He opens the door and stands in the entrance looking horror-struck. I stand behind him and see Rose, lying on her side on an old bed with a prominent bump on her belly. He turns and storms down the corridor. The next thing I see is him yelling at Grayson. He's hurling abuse at him as Grayson simply sits there.

When Gabriel has finished, Grayson merely says, 'I didn't force myself on her, Gabriel. I simply gave her a choice. Give me a child and then she can leave, or stay here forever in that dungeon. She chose to give me a child. The deal is done.'

'What the hell kind of choice is that? You nasty, manipulative bastard. You don't even love each other!' Gabriel argues. 'It won't work!'

'We'll see.'

I look at my version of Gabriel who still stands by my side in horror. What kind of a choice is that? Give me a child or stay here a prisoner forever! That's no choice at all.

'What happened next?' I ask him.

The image fades, and I'm watching Grayson sitting at the end of a small bed. Laying under a grey blanket is the pale body of a little boy. He can't be more than four. He isn't moving. My insides feel like they've fallen flat on the floor as I realise... he's dead. The poor little boy with dark brown hair, is dead.

'Grayson tried and tried to get his magic to spark. I kept telling him it wouldn't. I kept trying to make him stop. Then I was caught by the Hunters and I wasn't there to protect him.' Gabriel looks at the scene before us with deep sorrow. I can hear it in his voice as well as see it in his eyes. 'Without me there to stop him, he just kept pushing. Using more and more aggressive methods. He was so small. His little body just couldn't take it.'

I think back to the list Grayson gave me and the last item on it. Pain. He tortured his own son to death.

Grayson stands and looks at his version of Gabriel who lingers by the corner of the room.

'We'll try again-'

'No,' Gabriel insists. 'This isn't right. You promised to let her go years ago, and she's still down there. You gave her your word! We need to forget this and get Bias back. Grayson, Hunters have our little brother. We need to get him back and let her go!'

'Rose will stay there until I get what I need. What *we* need. We *need* an Arcane Witch.' There's a determination in Grayson's voice so absolute even I know that there would be no talking him out of it. 'And I'm looking for Bias. I'm doing everything I can-'

'Bull shit!'

Grayson hurls his fists at Gabriel and warns him that if he says another word, he'll stop the search for their youngest sibling and Gabriel will be locked up as well as Rose. The world shifts again and once more we're down in the dungeon with a very pale, very thin and very broken looking Rose. Gabriel spoon feeds her soup as she stares at the wall and wraps a blanket further around her body.

'It didn't work,' Gabriel tells her sadly. 'He didn't manifest.'

'I told you it wouldn't,' she says quietly.

'He was a brave little thing-'

'Don't,' she says sadly. 'I don't want to know anything about him. Please...don't.'

'He wants to try again,' Gabriel tells her. 'I've told him-'

'It won't work. I don't love him. I love my husband.' She closes her eyes as tears fall down her cheeks. 'I want to go home. I want to see my daughter.'

He rubs her back. She doesn't push him away but instead leans on his shoulder. After a moment, she looks at him with a spark in her eye that wasn't there a moment ago.

'You can make me!' she says as if she's had a brilliant idea. Gabriel's brow furrows as she nods. 'Yes. Yes! Get in my head. Make me love him and then when the child's born it might have magic. Then you can undo your compulsion and let me go.'

'I can't. It won't work!'

'You have to try!' She takes his hand in hers and looks pleadingly into his eyes. 'Gabriel, please. My little girl needs me. I'll do anything to get back to her. I know you can't get me out of here. I know that, but you can help me do this. Get in my head. Make me believe I love Grayson and then I can go home to my family.'

He tucks her ratty hair behind her ear as he struggles with this decision.

'What if it doesn't work?' he asks.

'If this child has magic then I know it will be loved and cared for by him. If it doesn't, then kill me. Hide Poppy and her father. End this.'

'I won't kill you,' Gabriel tells her.

'Please, please help me!'

I can see his internal struggle and see the evident desperation on her face.

Finally, he nods and says. 'I'll tell Grayson that I'll do this on the condition he releases you when the child is born. No waiting to see if they manifest. Agreed?' She smiles and nods as he gets to his feet and leaves.

As he walks back along the corridor and away from the cell, I turn to my version of Gabriel.

'What happened next?'

He looks at himself with such disgust and shakes his head.

'I did as I promised. I got in her head. Made her believe she loved him, but I knew it wasn't real. It was just words. Conditioning at best. And besides, Grayson didn't love her. It wasn't going to work, but she wouldn't listen to me.' He looks at me, and I hate the pain I see.

'Why didn't you break her out?'

'I couldn't get her out without losing my place in the coven. I would have been banished or ended up in the cell next to her. And every time I said the slightest thing Grayson didn't like, he called off the search for Bias. Back then, they were everything to me. Grayson, Bias, Collins, the Nomads. They were my whole life. And our only drive was to break down the veil. It was all that mattered. It's no excuse, none whatsoever. There's not a day that goes by that I don't wish I could go back and just haul her out of there. I wish I had. So much, Lilly. It's the biggest regret of my life. I honestly thought I had no choice. I tried to make it better for her, but really all I did was...' he looks at himself as he disappears out of sight. 'Nothing. I did nothing for Rose but get her killed.' He looks at me as the image fades and we're standing in a void of blackness. 'When she was five months pregnant with the second child, when I saw her little bump, I knew I would be burying another niece or nephew in a few years. So, I did the only thing I could think of. I sent word to Theo.'

I watch them meet. Gabriel tells him that Rose is in the cells. They make a deal. That Theo will get her out safely. That Gabriel will make sure the door is unlocked, that the guards will be gone and that he will leave the key to her cuffs by the entrance to the cells. He gives Theo all the money he will ever need to get her and her family safely away from all of them, and Theo agrees to it all. They even embrace and say that they will meet again after it is done and try to build a truce. But they both agree, no matter what, that Gabriel's involvement is never to be discovered. Gabriel is the key to keeping his brother under any form of control.

I watch another memory of Gabriel undoing the compulsion and telling Rose the plan. That a man named Theo will come and set her free. He tells her to be ready to run and that soon, she will be home with her family once more.

'Grayson will kill you!' she says. 'You'll end up down here instead of me.'

'Whatever happens to me is well deserved. I'll do everything in my power to keep you and your family safe.'

'Come with me!' she whispers. But Gabriel shakes his head.

'I need to stay with Grayson. I need to make sure that he doesn't do anything like this ever again.'

The image fades into another, and I wish to god it hadn't. My version of Gabriel grabs my wrist as we stand side by side, but it's not to pull me away. It's for support. He's afraid.

The younger version of Gabriel is on his knees sobbing and in his arm's, is the lifeless body of Rose. Her throat has been cut from ear to ear. Her hand lays lifeless over her belly. Over her little bump.

'Theo killed her. He didn't even try to get her out,' my Gabriel says in barely a whisper. 'He just slit her throat and left. That wasn't the plan. That wasn't what we agreed.'

I see the grief and guilt plainly. Not on just the younger version of him, but my version too.

'He had every chance to get her out, and he didn't. He wanted Grayson to see that his efforts were pointless and that he would stop him no matter what. He killed her to prove a point. Nothing more. And I let him in. I led him to her. I should have just got her out myself, damn the consequences.'

I can't help but slide my hand into his as he starts to cry.

'What happened to her daughter?' I ask. 'What happened to Poppy?'

The world fades, and we're back at the cabin where I saw the young girl, but this time we're inside the cabin. Gabriel is watching a man pack. Roses husband. He's throwing clothes into a case as if his life depends on it. Gabriel hands him a satchel. When he opens it, it's full of money.

'I've secured passage for you both to Spain,' Gabriel tells him. 'When you dock, you look for this man,' he hands him a piece of paper. 'He will give you details for your new home. It's all paid for and it's in your new names. Here,' He hands him an envelope. 'New identities. You can sell the house and move on from there if you like. You never have to tell me where you're going if that's what you decide, but please know that your family will always have my protection no matter what. I'm sorry, William. I tried to get her out. I tried-'

William punches Gabriel hard in the face, and he falls to the floor.

'Bullshit,' he barks angrily. 'You left her there because you're a damn coward. My wife was a good person. She was a saint, and you let your brother defile her and your father kill her. POPPY? COME HERE, CHILD!'

Rose's little girl runs out from another room. He takes her hand, and together they leave the cabin, leaving Gabriel on the floor with a bloody nose.

'I've hidden every Hooper child from Grayson since then,' my version of Gabriel tells me. 'I hid them all, from everyone. Roses daughter was named Poppy. She had a daughter, Dahlia. Dahlia had a daughter, Jessamine and so on and so on. Five centuries of girls and the odd boy, all born with one human parent and all named after flowers in honour of Rose. I helped them hide to protect them from Theo. And from Grayson. I've never forgiven myself for my part in what happened to Rose. I lost track of the Hooper's seventy years ago when your great-grandparents left the house I bought them in Russia suddenly. Forty years ago, a couple bought a house in Dartmoor. Your grandparents. They had a son. Harry Hooper. When Grayson got wind of them, we all went to see Harry after his parents died. Grayson made Harry an offer. Come with us, find a woman, marry, settle down. But he was already in love. With Christa. He knew that we needed a child born of love. He said that if we left him alone, let him live his life his way, that he would have a child and give it to us. We could bring it up any way we wished. Grayson agreed. He thought if it was a girl, he could win her over from a young age. If it was a boy, there were plenty of Nomad woman who would love to have a Hooper baby.'

'So, you left Harry alone? Let him live his life? Why didn't you come and get his son?'

'He had his son in secret and sent him away as soon as he was born to live with close friends. It wasn't until Harry's son left for France a few years ago that we learned he even existed. We tried to find him but couldn't. That's when Grayson went to your house. It was one last-ditch attempt to change Harry's mind. We needed more Hooper children. Grayson was determined to find a Hooper girl and make her fall in love with him so his child would be an Arcane. He offered Harry women, more money, more prosperity, but he said no. Then Hendrix found you, and suddenly Grayson had what he needed. A ready-made Arcane Witch. We guessed that your mum was another secret child. Like Harry's son. The Hoopers made sure their children knew about us. They told them what happened to Rose and they feared us. Rightly so. Your mum must have been raised away from the house, or we would have known about her. About you.' He looks to the ground, his body slumped in sadness. 'I refused to go to the house that night because Grayson would have used me to force compliance on your uncle, and I just couldn't. I couldn't do that to someone again. In truth...I have no idea if I could go that deep into anyone's mind now. It's been so long since I've tried. And so that brings us to the second biggest regret of my life.' He looks at me as I stand here in silence, waiting to hear what else he could be guilty of. 'I regret that it wasn't me that found you. I regret not being there for you that night. I regret not keeping a close eye on the Hoopers because if I'd have seen for a second what they were doing to you, I would have got you out of there so fast. I would have kept you safe. From all of them. Your uncle. Toby. Grayson.' A tear falls down his cheek as he searches my eyes for any sign of what I'm thinking. 'Say something,' he pleads.

I'm in tears too. Not only seeing the truth for myself but seeing how much it's clearly affected him. Regret is a hard thing to live with. The mistakes we make and can't change are the hardest things to bear. I can live with what was done to me, just. But the things I've done to others...they're what haunt me. They're what keep me up at night because no matter what you do, you can't change the past. But, you can try and make it right. And I believe he's done precisely that.

I face him and make sure he's looking at me when I say, 'You could have done more to help her, but you did everything you could to make it right.' His eyes close as yet more tears fall. I stroke his face as he leans his forehead against mine. As he does, the world around us changes.

'What are you looking at now?' he asks.

'Us.'

I feel my hands in the real world nervously hold his head tighter. His anxious breath lands on my skin and I feel it here, in his mind. Everything fades from us. The cabin disappears, and instead, we're standing on the top landing back at The Orchard. It's night time, and Gabriel is pacing back and forth. He stops when the sound of a door opening reaches his ears. He looks nervously over the top of the stairs. I follow suit, my version of Gabriel lingering behind me.

'That's me,' I say quietly. 'Weird.'

I'm watching myself walk quietly and nervously along the landing looking at all the artwork on the walls. It's the night I arrived. Gabriel watches me, and with a readying breath, he silently goes down the stairs after me. I see our first interaction from a bird's eye view. How I stand there silently as he tries to talk to me. How I tuck myself in looking timid and wary.

'You were waiting for me?' I ask turning to Gabriel standing behind me.

'You were in Grayson's arms when I first saw you,' he says. 'He carried you upstairs. You were filthy. Tiny. Frail. He laid you on your bed and I helped him sort you out. We washed you. Tended to your wounds. Dressed you in clean clothes. I saw your scars. It broke my heart.'

'You said Grayson washed me.'

'I know. I didn't want you to be uncomfortable around me. I saw how you hid your scars. I worried that if you knew I'd seen them, you'd avoid me. And I really didn't want you to avoid me.'

All this time worrying about what he might think if he saw them, and he already had. And he didn't care. He paid no attention to them when we slept together either.

'What happened after?'

'Grayson went to fetch more bandages as I sorted out the welts in your wrists from the chains you were kept in. You opened your eyes and looked at me. You just blinked a few times. Then you looked at my hands that were touching you, and you smiled. You wrapped your fingers in mine and said... "Wow. It doesn't hurt." Your eyes closed and before you fell asleep, you asked me my name. I told you. You called me your angel.'

'I did?'

He nods. 'You did. You said it again when we met in the hallway. Gabriel, like the angel. From that moment, I was spellbound. I had to get to know you.'

The landing fades, and I'm back in his bedroom. He's looking out the window. Below, on the grass, is me again. I'm talking to Grayson, lifting my hands up and down. Soon enough, Grayson goes back inside, and I start walking towards the end of the garden. Gabriel turns and almost sprints out the door.

'You followed me out to the orchard?' I watch as he sprints across the grass after me.

The room shifts and we're back in Gabriel's bedroom. He stumbles to the bathroom holding his ribs. When he flicks the light on and looks at his reflection in the mirror I gasp. He's been severely beaten.

'The night Theo attacked us at the tree lot,' I say out loud. 'This is after Grayson attacked you.'

'Yeah,' he says. 'Can we not look-' I hold up my hand as Grayson appears in the doorway. The two brothers share an awkward and frankly angry stare through the mirror before Gabriel turns and faces him.

'This ends, now!' Grayson warns. 'You're getting too close to her.'

'She's not yours, Grayson. You can't-'

'I will say this once and hear me, little brother. You are not to get physical with her. You are not to kiss her. You are not to touch her! She's too fragile for you to be screwing around with her. I won't have her ask to leave because you have made this an uncomfortable place for her to be.'

'And that's the reason you don't want me to get close to her?' I hear the disbelief in Gabriel's voice.

'I'm the one who saved her. I'm the one who can look after her. I'm the one she kissed. Not you. Me and her...we're supposed to be together. So back off. You don't deserve her. You're nothing but a little boy who uses women and discards them like trash. She knows that. Why else would she have slammed the door in your face tonight? She knows you're not enough for her. She knows how pathetic and useless you really are. She told me herself, so here.' Grayson hands him his phone. 'Call Ava. She's who you are supposed to be with, Gabriel.'

'Lilly told you that?'

'Yes. She did. She's not interested in you. She's just too polite to say it to your face.' He turns and leaves without giving Gabriel a chance to speak. He looks at himself in the mirror.

'I never said that to him,' I tell him. He still isn't looking at me. 'Why would you think I would say that to him?'

The scene shifts.

Outside in the garden, Gabriel's smoking furiously as he sits on one of the chairs by the outside pool. His knee is jiggling up and down, and Collins is sitting watching him. He still has the bruises on his face. It's the morning after the attack. The morning I saw Ava in the kitchen and had a row with Gabriel.

'What the hell is going on with you, man?' Collins asks. 'I've never seen you so angry before. Yelling at Lilly like that, what were you thinking? She hasn't done anything wrong.'

'She just hurled abuse at me!'

'And since when do you care what a girl says to you?' Collins laughs.

Gabriel runs his fingers through his hair in desperation, and a kind smugness becomes clear on Collins' face.

'So, you've finally realised you like her then?' he laughs softly.

'Like her?' Gabriel replies.

'You know exactly what I mean, man. Don't play the idiot. You like, *like* her. I'd even hazard a guess at saying maybe, this time, this girl...you may even love her?'

Gabriel goes to protest. But the words don't come as he shakes his head and laughs nervously. But the two boys share a look. Collins' face remains as happy, as Gabriel's slowly descends into defeat. With a groan, he leans back in the chair.

'I can't stop thinking about her, Collins. I've never felt this way about a girl. Normally it's...'

'Wham, bam, thank you, mam?'

Gabriel nods. 'But Lilly... She's beautiful. Fiery. Powerful and yet so fragile. I just want to look after her, you know? Wrap her up and hide her away.'

'If she heard you say that, she would probably kick your ass.'

'Oh, I know,' Gabriel chuckles softly. 'But that's why I think so much of her. Look at everything that girl's been through. All the loss and the pain. She's been betrayed and abused by literally everyone in her life. Except for her mother who let's face it, fuck knows what happened to her. And yet she smiles and laughs. She wants to go out into the world. She wants to be independent and even after all the misery, she still sticks her neck out for others. To help others.' He looks so proud as he speaks. Collins nods in agreement.

'She stood up for Amara with her dad. That took some guts. And not to mention your brother. When she stood up to him in the kitchen about going to the tree lot!' he puffs out his cheeks in an exasperated breath. 'She definitely has some balls on her. She's more than a match for you, mate.'

'Yeah well...Grayson. He's threatening me to stay away from her because he's got his own plans. Not only is she the Arcane but she's fucking gorgeous. He's not happy that we get on. He's livid.'

'He's jealous. But she clearly feels something for you. Not him. That's tough, but that's the way it is.'

'You say that. But she told me she doesn't want to be anything more than friends.' Gabriel takes another puff of his cigarette. 'After last night and our fight just now, I don't think she even wants that anymore. Grayson's forbidden us being anything more than acquaintances, and yet she's all I can think about.'

'Is that why you asked Ava to stay last night?' Collins asks. 'Because Lilly says she doesn't want you that way? Because she hurt your feelings last night? Or should I say your ego.'

'Ava wants me. Lilly doesn't,' he grunts. 'I just thought...arggh. I don't know what I was thinking.'

'You were thinking that sleeping with that wasp of a girl would make Lilly jealous, realise how much she wants you and fall into your arms.' Gabriel confirms Collins' words with nothing but a look.

'I didn't even sleep with her, truth be told. I downed a bottle of whiskey before she got here and passed out. I woke up with her sleeping next to me in her underwear.'

MJ LAWRIE

Collins laughs. 'You have no idea how women work, do you. I have to say, a bit of a dick move, mate. Even if you did pass out. Lilly still thinks you slept with her.'

'I've never wanted to actually...try, with a girl. You know? I've never been knocked back before either. Nomad girls are easy.'

'Not all,' Collins mutters as an affectionate glint shimmers in his eyes as he thinks about Amara.

'Amara's unique. You're lucky, man. I'd kill to have that. A girl that looked at me like she looks at you. I wish Lilly looked at me like that. But she doesn't. She slammed the door in my face last night after I took Grayson's beating, and now she's being a right little bitch! Why shouldn't I be with Ava, huh? I know where I stand with her. She wants me. I know that. Lilly? Fuck knows what she wants.'

'You're an idiot,' Collins laughs. 'She's being a bitch because you slept with Ava. Or she thinks you did. She's hurt,' Collins says simply. 'And she told you to do one last night because she was forced to watch you get a beating from Grayson for simply trying to protect her. You think maybe she's pushing you away because she doesn't want you to get hurt? Or maybe the fact that she's frightened of getting close to another man since the last man she had a relationship with was your twisted little brother? Who, by the way, we need to tell her the truth about. Amara is giving me some serious grief about us making her lie.'

'You think she's trying to protect me? You think she likes me?'

'I know that seeing you with Ava drove her crazy and that watching you get hurt almost killed her. I had to hold her back, or she would have jumped in the middle of you two. And believe me, I've seen how she looks at you. She cares for you. A lot. But playing games isn't going to win her over.'

'What... what will win her over?' he asks timidly, staring at his fingers.

'Gabriel Kendryk, are you asking me for advice on girls?' Collins teases.

'I'm not asking for girl advice,' he clarifies, looking Collins in the eye humbly. 'I'm asking for Relationship advice. How do I get her to be...'

'Be?' Collins encourages, eager to hear what word he is planning to use to explain what he wants.

'My, my err...' Gabriel coughs and clears his throat. Collins tries to hide his amusement. 'How do I get her to agree to be my girlfriend?' he finally says. Funny, it's clear he's never used that word in this context before. 'Stop bloody laughing.'

My heart swells as he talks so intimately about me with his best friend. I look at my Gabriel who still lingers behind me and can't help but smile.

'Listen. Grayson clearly wants her. And we all know he won't let you be with a girl he wants. But, as long as he doesn't know, until you figure out a way to make it sit well with him, I say go for it. Quietly. Be honest with her. Tell her how you feel. Explain why you did what you did with Ava, or failed to do, and stop playing games. And tell her about Bias before someone else does. If you feel strongly towards her, just bloody tell her, mate! Stop pussyfooting around it.' He gets to his feet. 'But you better be serious about it. She deserves better than just being a notch on your bedpost, and I'll never hear the end of it from Amara if you screw her over. Never mind the grief you're both gonna get from Grayson. You're risking a hell of a lot by pursuing her. She better be worth it.'

'She is worth it. She's definitely worth it.'

'Then go for it.'

He turns and walks away leaving Gabriel alone.

'You tried,' I say quietly before I turn to look at him. 'You came to see me after Malcolm died and tried to explain, but I wouldn't listen. Then we argued.'

He nods. 'You were too angry to hear anything I had to say. Which made me upset and instead of admitting what I wanted to admit, I hurled abuse at you. Like I always do. I don't like feeling vulnerable, and when I do, I lash out. Anger's easier I guess.'

'Show me the rest. Show me how it went from this... to the end.'

I see myself standing in the lobby by the foot of the stairs. It's when we came back from spending the night together at Gabriel's hotel room. I watch Gabriel tell me that he's going to talk to Grayson. That he's going to tell him what happened with Toby and that I shouldn't worry. He turns and goes into Grayson's office as I'm taken upstairs by Collins.

Inside his office, Grayson sits behind his desk and gestures for Gabriel to take the seat opposite, which he does. I stay close, keen to see what happened here.

Gabriel explains his version of events as we agreed. That he followed Toby alone. Found that I had done the same and by the time he caught up with us, Toby and I were fighting. He tells him that Toby fled and we were lost. He also tells him that I know who he really is. As he explains, Grayson has this look on his face. Like he doesn't believe a word of it. Gabriel stops talking and watches his brother with unease.

'And that's it,' Gabriel concludes. 'We found somewhere to keep warm and get some sleep then came home.'

My Gabriel is by my side watching the conversation. I glance at him as he stares at the floor not keen to watch what he's already lived, but I'm desperate to see.

Grayson taps his fingers rhythmically on the desk and never looks away from Gabriel. The smile he has on his face most certainly doesn't reach those dark eyes as he looks across the large desk filled with papers and books. Slowly, he leans back into his chair and rests his hands together on his lap.

'Gabriel. I need to know if something is going on between you two,' he says.

Gabriel shakes his head. 'No. Nothing but friendship. I told you, we followed-'

Grayson holds up his hand silencing him.

'Brother, please, don't lie to me. I see how she looks at you. I see how you look at her. I can't deny that it hurts me to see you two connecting the way you do, especially when you are aware of how I feel towards her,' he pauses. 'But, I can't stand between you two if you both want to be together.' Grayson's eyes narrow slightly on his brother, but that smile is still there. 'Is that what you want?' he asks. 'Do you want to be with her?'

Gabriel leans back in his chair. It creaks as he does and he bites his lower lip ever so slightly. I can see how he is trying to gauge what his brother is thinking. After a moment Gabriel shrugs.

'I like her. I do. She's unlike anyone I've ever met. I know that you have feelings for her-'

Again, Grayson holds up his hand silencing him. Gabriel falls quiet immediately.

'Yes, I have feelings for the girl,' Grayson says. 'That is true. But you are my brother. I love you and if being with her would make you happy, then who am I to stand in the way. Especially if she feels the same about you.'

'Really?' Gabriel says astounded.

'Of course,' Grayson insists. 'But if it's just sex, just physical then I will insist that you stop. She's far too fragile to be used and dropped like so many of your other...conquests. But if it's real, if you think that what you feel for her is genuine...' he pauses and takes in Gabriel's reaction. 'Is it?' Grayson asks. 'Do you genuinely feel for her? Is it more to you than just sex?'

Gabriel looks at his hands which are knotted together, and I feel a pit in my stomach.

'Gabriel, I need to look out for her interests. If you want nothing more from her than sex, then you need to walk away and leave her be.'

'I think I'm in love with her, Grayson.'

I hadn't realised that I'd been holding my breath and when he says that, I almost gasp.

'Actually, I'm positive. I've fallen in love with her. And I think that maybe, she loves me too.' I can't move. I can't breathe. Gabriel just admitted he loves me to Grayson.

'What makes you say that?' Grayson asks. There's a sharper edge to his voice, and those eyes are getting darker, but Gabriel doesn't realise. He doesn't see.

'Last night,' Gabriel says with a happy smile. 'It was unlike anything I'd ever felt before. It was real.' Their eyes meet. 'I love her, Grayson. I want to be with her. No one else. Just her.'

I turn and look at my version of Gabriel who avoids looking at me entirely. He runs his hand through his hair and turns his back on the memory. Turns his back on me.

'I don't understand,' I say quietly.

Grayson starts to laugh a cruel laugh filled with mockery. I turn.

'You?' Grayson says through his laughter. '*You* love her?' He continues to laugh as Gabriel sits and says nothing. His smile's gone and is instead replaced with a look of hurt and anger.

'It's not funny,' Gabriel tells him.

'Oh yes, it is. She's the Arcane!' Grayson scoffs. 'She is the most powerful witch alive. Her bloodline is sacred. You think that you are worthy of even looking at her? You think she would ever love a man like you?'

'I've done more than look at her,' Gabriel bites back. Grayson stops laughing as he realises.

'You have slept with her then.'

'It's none of your business.'

Grayson slams his hand down hard on his desk making Gabriel and I jump. I can't stop watching. I can't tear my eyes away. Grayson points at his brother.

'I told you, I made it clear what would happen to anyone who touches her. You disobeyed me.'

'You going to kill me, brother?' Gabriel demands. 'For being in love?'

'No. You know I can't do that. But I can banish you.'

'I love her, Grayson. Banishing me won't change that.'

'No, it might not. But banishing you will separate you. It will leave her here alone... with me.'

'What do you mean by that?' Gabriel gets to his feet as Grayson stays sat in his chair. 'Tell me what you mean by that!'

'I mean that she is the last Hooper alive. Save for Harry's son who is still missing. We can't let her bloodline die out and you, *little brother*, are incapable of producing children. Sending you away will give her time to see that she doesn't need you. Not when she has me here to keep her safe. To keep her warm.' His mouth twitches into a nasty smile.

Gabriel's fists clench. 'You won't do what you did to Rose again. Not to her. Not to anyone.'

'You'll be on the other side of the world, *little brother*. What are you going to do to stop me?' When Gabriel lunges forwards Grayson sends him flying backwards through the air with a simple wave of his hand. As he scrambles back to his feet, Grayson gets to his and calmly walks around the other side of his desk.

'Calm down,' he says, gesturing for Gabriel to stop. 'I would never hurt Lilly. This may come as a surprise to you, but I do actually care about her. I might even be in love with her too.'

Gabriel stands looking ready to tear Grayson's head off. His fists are balled up and every muscle in his body is rigid, while Grayson seems entirely at ease.

'I'll tell you what. I have an offer for you.'

'I'm listening,' Gabriel snarls.

'Break it off with Lilly.'

Gabriel shakes his head. 'Not going to happen.'

'You *will* break it off with her. You *will* back off completely. I don't even want you to be her friend. If you do that, and in six months, if she still shows no interest in me, then I will let you two be together.'

'She won't want you.'

'Well then,' Grayson shrugs. 'You have nothing to worry about. You back off, let her decide if she wants you, or me. For the sake of our future, we need to see if there is any chance of creating more Hoopers. Her bloodline can't be allowed to die out, and with me, she could have the most powerful children possible.'

'You think you can get her to fall in love with you, don't you? That she'll give you Arcane children?'

Grayson smiles. 'She would already be in my bed if she hadn't met you. The kiss we shared the night I saved her was real. I felt it, and so did she. But then she met you. All sparkling blue eyes and charm. I have thousands of lives to protect. I have obligations. Responsibilities. While I was keeping us all alive and safe, you won her over. You made me the bad guy. Telling her she can't go out. That she needs the binding spell. You agreed with me that I was right, but you never backed me up. That's going to change. Starting with you telling her that last night was a mistake-'

'No. No way.'

Grayson groans and folds his arms. 'You have two choices. Choice number one, tell her it was a mistake, break it off and back off. You will stand aside and give us a chance to work. If after six months she still wants you, then fine. I'll back down and you two can be responsible for the end of the Hooper bloodline. But at least you'll be happy.'

'Or?'

'Choice number two. I banish you. Have you sent to the other side of the world forever. You will never be welcome back in any Coven. You set foot back in England, and I will have you locked up for the rest of your days in a pit where no one will ever find you. And I will ensure that Lilly will be mine. I will ensure that she produces children for me. One way or another.' His words and tone are nothing less than evil. 'She *will* do my spell. She *will* bring back magic. Lilly *will* love me. If given a chance,' he adds with a shrug. 'And just so you know, if you even think about telling her about this conversation, I'll know. That girl can't lie to save her life. And I will make sure she never sees you again. And if she fights me, turns against me, or tries to leave, I'll lock her up and never let her out. You hear me?'

'That's why?' I say through sad tears. 'That's why you left me?' He says nothing. 'But, you didn't say anything to me. You didn't tell me it was a mistake.'

'I couldn't. I'm a good liar, but I'm not that good. How could I say that to you after everything you've been through? I just...I was so scared of you getting hurt. After Rose...' He shakes his head and keeps his eyes on the floor. He can't even look at me.

The memory merges, but we're still in the office. Grayson's sitting at his desk again as Gabriel stands opposite, looking agitated and pale.

'She's upset,' Grayson tells him. 'I can see that, but it's not enough. Did you tell her that it was a mistake?'

'Yes,' Gabriel lies. 'And I've stayed away as you wanted.'

'Hmm. Well, there's something else I want you to do.' There's a knock at the door. I turn and see it open. In walks Ava. She closes the door behind her and stands beside Gabriel who watches her with confusion.

'By something...I mean someone. I want you to sleep with her,' Grayson says, pointing at a smug Ava.

I feel my heart breaking, but not because of what I know came next, but because of how horrified Gabriel looks.

'I'm not sleeping with anyone, Grayson. That's never going to happen. That wasn't part of the deal.'

'I'm changing the deal. You will spend the night with Ava and make sure Lilly knows about it.'

'She hates her. Please, if I do this, Lilly will never forgive me.'

Grayson's smile tells me that he knows that. Ava runs her hand down Gabriel's arm and flutters her eye lashes at him.

'It's nothing we haven't done a dozen times,' she says softly. 'We're good together, you and me.' He shrugs off her hand, but still, she tries. 'Baby, please, we make sense.'

'What? Because neither of us can have kids? You were an easy lay. Nothing more. Lilly is everything to me.' He turns to Grayson. 'You said that if after six months she still wants to be with me, you would give us your blessing. If I do this, she'll never forgive me. She'll hate me.' Grayson merely shrugs. He doesn't care. 'I don't want to be with anyone else. I don't want to have sex with Ava!'

'You will. And you will say whatever you must to break Lilly's little heart. And I mean break it, Gabriel,' he says, pointing his finger at him. 'Or you can pack, and she will never leave this house again,' Grayson replies.

The room fades, and we're in Gabriel's bedroom. My version of Gabriel is leaning against the door, still refusing to watch as the memory version of him paces up and down, while Ava sits on his bed.

'This doesn't have to be a big thing,' she says, taking off her jacket and kicking off her shoes. 'We're fantastic together. You know it.' She stands and pulls off her top and stands there in her bra, with a self-assured smirk and lust-filled eyes.

He stops pacing as she strolls over to him.

'What are you doing?' Gabriel asks, looking at her half-nakedness.

'What we do best.' She un-hooks her bra and lets it fall to the floor.

'I'm not actually going to fuck you, Ava. Lilly just needs to think that I did.' He bends down and picks up her red bra before thrusting it back into her hands. 'Get dressed.'

He continues pacing. Ava doesn't look happy. She drops the bra again and her eyes flick over in his direction.

'If you don't,' she says slowly and with a good amount of arrogance. 'I'll tell Grayson that you refused.'

He stops and faces her with a face of thunder. Slowly and seductively she walks back to him.

'If you don't, he'll send you away.' She starts unbuttoning his shirt. 'If you don't, Lilly will be left here all alone, and you will never see her again.' She finishes unbuttoning his shirt and slides it down his body to the floor. She sees the necklace I gave him hanging around his neck and taps it lightly with her finger. 'Aww. Cute.'

The look of hatred on his face is clear.

'I can't have children. Neither can you. We're both outcasts just for that.' She starts kissing his neck. Her hands caress his chest, tracing the definitions of his abdominal muscles. 'No one else wants us. We may as well be together.'

'Get off me, Ava.'

'What does she have that I don't?' she purrs, still working his neck and her hands going to the buckle of his belt. 'Apart from scars, nightmares and crippling fear of being touched. Can't be fun screwing a girl covered in all those marks-'

He grabs her by the throat suddenly, but she only smiles. She even places her own hand over his and encourages a tighter grip.

'She's a freak,' I whisper as I watch this horrible and ugly interaction. If I thought I hated her before, I beyond loathe her now.

'Say another word about her, and I will kill you,' Gabriel threatens hatefully. 'Lilly is a million times the girl you are. Than you will ever be.'

'I want you,' she gasps beneath his grip. 'And I won't stop till I get you, so make love to me now or say goodbye to your home, your family, your coven and Lilly for good.' She snatches his necklace and tosses it to the floor. 'Your move, Gabriel.'

He throws her onto the bed and unbuckles his belt. He's furious, and whatever is about to take place between them will be far from loving, gentle or meaningful. I turn and look at my version of Gabriel at a complete loss for words. He was forced to sleep with her. They gave him no choice. He did it to protect me. To keep me safe from Grayson. When I turn back the memory has faded, and the deed is done. Ava looks thrilled, but Gabriel seems broken.

She has her ear pressed against the door, and with a huge smile, she whispers, 'She's coming! Remember, you have to be cruel. You have to break her fragile little heart.'

He gets to his feet and the rest I saw. I watch the kissing and cuddling on the landing. I see my face and the second my heart does in fact break. A light goes out in my eyes. Gabriel sees it too, before he turns and goes back to his room. Inside, he walks to his bed where he sits and buries his face in his hand.

He sobs.

When he hears my footsteps outside, he wipes his tears and composes himself. I watch our fight. I watch as I cry and say awful things to the man who was forced to be physical with someone against his will. I watch as I call him an egotistical whore who enjoys making women suffer, when in truth he was trying to protect me. I watch as he loses his temper and grabs me when I compare him to a man who spent years abusing me. I watch as his words eradicate the trust I had in him and see myself flinch and recoil from his touch. I see him realise it too, just before I manifest Mental magic. When I slam the door behind me, he slumps to the floor on his knees staring at his hands in horror.

'I've lost her,' he says, scrunching up his hands. 'I've really lost her.'

He looks heartbroken at the door I just left through. The door where I now stand and where my Gabriel stands, refusing to see any of it. As he has for almost all of these memories. As one version of him cowers in an emotional mess on his bathroom floor and the other shows me nothing but his back, I reach out and take his arm so I can guide him to look at me. As he turns, his eyes don't leave the floor of the bathroom. And the room shifts once more. He's in his room shoving money into a bag and making phone calls. I follow him as he sneaks into my room and throws some of my stuff in the same bag.

'What are you doing?' I ask.

'Getting ready to leave,' he says quietly. 'I was going to take you away. Just...grab you and go. Explain it all on the road. But, Theo grabbed me before I could. I'm so sorry. I am just...so sorry. What I said to you. What I did.'

'They forced you,' I say in a quiet, pain-filled whisper. 'Grayson and Ava made you do this.'

'I had to keep you safe. I can't...I *won't* let you go the same way as Rose. I can't let that happen again. Not to you. Not to anyone.'

'You tried to save Rose. Her death was not your fault.'

'All of it was my fault,' he says in a sad conclusion. 'I wanted to make sure you didn't suffer like her. I wanted to keep you safe. I wanted to tell you how I felt about you, but I couldn't even do that properly. Every time I tried and felt the slightest bit of rejection from you, I hurled abuse at you. I said vile words that I knew would hurt you.'

'And I pushed you away. I was afraid of you getting hurt. I never wanted to push you away. I had to. Grayson...he's too dangerous.'

He has tears brimming in his eyes, and as hard as he tries, he can't stop himself from breaking down.

'Oh Lilly. Everything I've done. All the ways I've let you and your family down.'

The room starts to fade into darkness. His devastated tears begin to echo as it all drifts further and further away.

When I open my eyes, I'm on the floor of the tent. My hands are still each side of his head, and we're still alone.

Words fail me.

All I can do is look at him as tear after tear falls down my cheeks. They fall down his too, and I wipe them away with my thumb.

'Look at me,' I whisper.

He shakes his head and sniffs as he quietly cries.

I lower my hand and let it slide down his arm. A trail of goose bumps follow my fingertips. Leaning forward, I reach behind him to the ropes binding his hands behind his back. When I feel them, I burn them, setting him free. He tries to guide me away from him.

'Don't touch me, Lilly. Please don't.' He gently takes my wrists and pushes me away. 'I know it hurts. I don't want you to feel that. Not because of me.'

I move so I have one leg each side of him and hold his face in my hands. My bleeding, bandaged hand missing two fingers throb as I touch him, but I don't let it stop me. I make him look up at me. The tears in his eyes make them look so much bigger. So much sadder, but he watches my skin on his with a look of marvel.

'Well, would you look at that...' I stroke his cheek. When his hand rests over mine, I wrap my fingers around them. 'No pain. None.' I smile, despite my tears. His face buries into my neck. His arms wrap around my waist. I'm holding him so tight, and his grip on me is equally as solid. We sit in silence embracing each other.

'I want to ask you something,' comes a gentle whisper in my ear.

'Anything.' He's just shown me the darkest corners of his mind. He can ask me anything.

'In my room, when we fought, you said that you'd been beaten, starved, abused.' He lifts his head, and two pain-filled blue eyes look deep into my soul. 'You said that you'd been raped.'

'I don't want to talk about that.'

'Please, tell me. Was it Toby?'

'No,' I reply. 'It wasn't Toby. It was someone else.' He waits. He tries to hide the pain of knowing that such a vile act was done to me, but he wants to know. And he has a right to know. 'Harry hired a boy to work on the house one summer. Ryan. He let him live with us, so he did the work cheap. He was eighteen. I was fourteen. He figured out I was a witch soon after he moved in and he blackmailed me. He said that if I didn't do what he wanted, he'd turn me over to the Hunters,' I say it in a single breath, not giving myself a chance to back out of admitting it to him.

He swallows a lump as his eyes glisten with tears. 'Fourteen?' I nod.

'How long?'

'He lived with us on and off for two years.' My insides squirm and I feel dirty in my own skin just talking about it.

'You don't need to tell me anymore if you don't want to.'

'I went to a maid and asked her for help. She was the least cruel of the lot. But she refused. She said...'

Gabriel's eyes narrow. 'She said what?'

'She said I should be grateful.' He goes rigid and a violent hatred springs to life in his eyes. 'She said that considering I was a filthy witch, I should be grateful any man would ever want me.' His breathing increases. His fingertips dig a little harder into my body like he's keeping me close, frightened to let me go. 'I couldn't take anymore,' I admit. 'Harry and Christa. Ryan. The misery each day offered. The blackness at the end of the tunnel. It was too much. So, I took a bed sheet to the end of the garden, tied one end to a tree, the other around my neck, and I jumped.'

'Fucking hell. Christ! My poor girl.'

We lean in, resting our foreheads together as tears slide down my cheeks. It's painful. But feels like a weight's been lifted off my chest.

'That's how I met Toby. He found me hanging. He cut me down and got me breathing again. He saved my life. When he found out about Ryan, he disappeared for two days. I thought he was disgusted. That I would never see him again. But he came back. He told me he'd killed him. I never saw Ryan again.'

'At least he did one thing right by you.'

'Maybe. But now, I owed him. He saved my life, and he said that it was his now. Every word he said to me was exactly what I wanted to hear, and soon, he had me wrapped around his finger. But I guess everything changed...no, I changed, the night we first slept together.' I watch Gabriel, trying to read his reactions.

Should I stop talking? He probably doesn't want to know.

'Tell me,' he encourages. 'You can tell me anything.'

'Toby took me downstairs, to the room of the maid I asked for help. And he made me kill her. I dream about that night all the time. I killed her, Gabriel. I murdered a woman. I didn't want to. I really didn't. But once I started, and when she stopped moving, I felt good. Like I'd got my payback. After that, I did everything Toby asked me to do. Everything. Whether I wanted to or not and I can't help but think...'

'Think what, Beautiful?'

'That if I hadn't have gone into her room that night, if I hadn't let Toby talk me into it, if I hadn't handed myself over to his will, then maybe I wouldn't have done all the other horrible things I did with him. I beat people. I disfigured a girl who I was jealous of. I tortured people because he wanted me to. I watched him kill people and did nothing to stop him. I killed those men in the barn-'

'You are not to blame!' he insists, taking my face in his hands. 'You have been through so much. More than I could ever have imagined. You were alone in this world and horrifically treated by everyone around you. All you knew was violence and pain. Toby capitalised on that. He manipulated you instead of helping you. I don't blame you for your past. Never. And no one worth a damn would.'

My shame has me pulling away. My disbelief of his words has me shaking my head. But he grabs my face once more and looks sternly into my eyes.

'You are not to blame. Do you hear me? None of that was your fault.'

'Yes, it was. Gabriel, I'm not a good person.'

'You are the best person. Look at me.' He lifts my head, trying to catch my lowered gaze. When he has it, he tells me in no uncertain terms, 'I love you, Lilly Hooper. More now than I ever thought possible. And I promise you that I will never let any man touch you that way ever again. I will never lie to you. I will never manipulate you. And I will never, ever leave you. When you see those memories in your dreams, I will wake you up, and you will be in my arms. I will keep you safe from the ghosts of your past, and I will build such an amazing life with you that they'll fade away. They'll be replaced by beautiful, happy memories.'

He lifts his head and looks at me. Our faces are so close our noses are almost touching.

'I'll protect you from your past. And I will not let anyone, Grayson included, keep us apart. I love you, Lilly. So fucking much. I can't lose you.'

I smile a relieved smile. 'I love you too, Gabriel. More than anything. Anyone. Ever. You will never lose me.'

I lean in and find his lips. We kiss. It's a desperate and loving embrace. All our fears, pains and forgiveness go into it. And I do, of course I forgive him just as he forgives me.

The whole world falls away. It's just us. As it should be. And now I know. I know what kind of man he is. I'm certain. Yes, he's made mistakes. But he has done all he can for me. He's not given up trying to protect me so like hell will I give up on him. He seeks redemption. He doesn't need to seek it from me.

It's all meaningless. This tent and the tortures we've endured. The men outside who brought us here. The never-ending deep pain in my hand. Grayson. Theo. Toby. Our pasts.

They don't matter one bit. Not right now. We've finally found each other, and although our path has been far from easy, I fear our struggles have only just begun. But that can wait.

His heart hammers as he pulls my body flush with his. He's holding me like if he loosens his grip for even a second, I'll disappear. When we break our tender kiss, his arms still keep me close. Finally, he looks at me. His hand still cupping my cheek and those blue eyes filled with such emotion.

He takes off his leather jacket and carefully puts it on me, guiding through my mutilated hand.

Gently, he kisses it.

'I'll make them pay for doing this to you,' he says with a murderous glint in his eye and a deep hatred in his voice.

'Give me your binding spell,' I tell him, opening my palm. He takes off the cloth around his wrist and places it in my hand. I put my watch in there too. All twenty-four thousand pounds worth. He watches as I create my fire and burn them to nothing.

'We can't be bound anymore. Without the binding spell, I'm no longer linked to Grayson through the Bloodstone,' I tell him, looking up to watch my fire reflect in his eyes. 'I don't care what he threatens us with. He won't come between us again.'

'No one will, my love.'

'Say that again,' I say with a grin.

'My love. My girl. My Lilly.'

With our magic and with each other, Theo and Jensen's men don't frighten me. It's them who should be afraid because I'm pissed. If anyone gets in the way of our well deserved happy ending...they're going to wish they'd never been born.

'Let's get the hell out of here,' he says.

Gabriel takes my hand, and together we turn, walk out of the tent and into the rain.

Chapter 22

We walk slowly. Purposefully. We're not hiding. We're not slipping away into the darkness.

Not this time.

Hand in hand, we step over the unconscious guard at our door and almost straight away we're spotted by two men. They start backing away from us before turning on their heel and running in the opposite direction yelling for Theo and Jensen.

'Witch!' they yell. 'The witches are free!'

Gabriel's hand tightens on mine as we look at each other.

'Ready?' he asks.

'Absofuckinglutely,' I tell him, squeezing his hand with mine.

The camp has filled with panic. People are running in all directions. Some outright flee as others turn and run straight at us. They position themselves. Placing their bodies strategically so we can't pass. So we can't escape. We stop and face a wall of men all pointing their guns straight at us.

'HOLD YOUR FIRE!' Theo bellows from somewhere behind them. The men make way, parting like a biblical ocean as he walks through, followed closely by Jensen.

Theo laughs when he sees us. He looks nothing more than amused at our sudden appearance. 'Where do you two think you're going?'

The magic within me is buzzing with desperation to get out, and his arrogance makes it even more desperate. He grimaces at us and gestures for the men behind him to come closer. Their raised guns point straight at us, but it's Gabriel who laughs now.

'Move aside, Theo. You know as well as I do that you won't shoot us. You won't kill us.'

I let go of Gabriel's hand so mine can erupt in fierce black and white fire. Theo eyes it nervously, showing me a flicker of doubt. He's not as confident as he was.

I run through what he can do in my head, or rather, what I saw when he attacked me at the tree lot. Telekinesis and Energy. I have to prepare for those. His hands. That's where the magic comes from with those realms of power. So as Gabriel watches the men, I don't take my eyes off Theo's hands. His left-hand twitches and before I give him the chance to send that agonising lightning our way, I raise my fire covered hand lifting him off the ground and hurling him back into the crowd of people behind him. It feels incredible to be using my magic. And using it against him feels fantastic as I show him a glimpse of what I'm capable of.

'You owe me two fingers, you arse hole,' I say viciously as his men lift him back to his feet.

'I'll take more than your fingers you little bitch.' He's angry, humiliated at being knocked down, and it fuels his attack. He raises his hand and shoots his green lightning at my chest knocking me onto my back before I can react. Winded I roll over and see him charging towards us. Jensen and his men follow suit, yelling and shouting.

Gabriel's eyes are black as he orders men close by to point their weapons at the oncoming wave of men. Five Traitors turn and raise their guns to their own people. But to my horror, the men running at us just raise their own weapons in retaliation. Gabriel has Jay's knife in his hand as he helps me get to my feet. My fire's gone out. I'm not as strong as I would like to be.

'You alright?' he asks quickly, stroking and scanning my face for injury. With a nod, we turn back to the fight about to break out in front of us. The five men under Gabriel's control are standing with their weapons raised. They all tremble and yell at their comrades, their family... to please, stop!

But they don't.

'Gabriel...what do we do?' I ask, clinging to his hand and watching a wave about to crash into a wall.

'What I must to keep you safe.' He looks at the men he has under his control. I know what he's about to do. And I don't stop him. 'FIRE!' he yells. 'SHOOT TO KILL!'

Gabriel takes my arm and runs to the side away from them, dragging me alongside. The air fills with the sound of gunshots. Countless bullets being fired from dozens of guns echo all around us. Stray bullets splinter trees and pelt the ground around us, but by some miracle, we're not hit by a single one. I look back over my shoulder. Men start to fall from the wave of Theo's men charging at Gabriel's puppets. They continue to race towards us, merely jumping over their fallen friends. Theo's men return fire and two of Gabriel's puppets go down. There are too many of them. I stop and turn. With a wave of my hand, I knock the front line of Theo's men to the side. But there are so many more behind. I do it again and again. Knocking them over like bowling pins, but for everyone I slow down, another two pick up the pace. I feel the toll of my exhausted body. More men fall as I continue to batter them with my invisible force and Gabriel's puppets knock down a good few with bullets, but the wave of men just keeps rebuilding.

'They're coming, Gabriel!' I call out as his puppets fall. Theo's men trample their bodies as they continue to descend on us.

Their skulls cave under the heavy footing of the countless men charging over them.

'Your fire!' Gabriel calls over the sounds of yelling, screams and rapid gunfire. He still has a tight grip on my arm, and he's pulling me quickly away from them as they chase us down. 'Build a wall. block them!'

I stop, skidding to a halt so I can face them. I reach out both my hands and a stream of fire explodes from them. I direct it to the ground which ignites straight away creating a wall of fire. But it's weak. Barely waist height and maybe fifty feet long. That won't do anything to stop them. I stagger on my feet as the world spins. Gabriel wraps his arm around my waist and pins me to his body, taking all my weight.

'You alright?' he asks, looking between me and the army on the other side of the fire still charging at us.

'I...I'm too tired. I'm not strong enough.'

The air fills with the sound of more bullets. When one flies between our heads and splinters the tree behind us Gabriel pulls me down. I fall gladly. I need a second to breathe and get my strength. He cups my chin and lifts my face. I see fear in his eyes.

'We have to run. You're not strong enough to fight.'

'I don't think I can run. My body's exhausted.'

He turns, fretfully looking beyond my pathetic attempt at a fire barrier.

'Fine,' he says gruffly, getting to his feet and hauling me up with him. He scoops me up in his arms. 'Then I'll carry you.'

But before he takes even a slight step, we see the most unusual thing. Theo's men stop dead just before they reach my flames. They turn a complete one-eighty and sprint away.

'Is that it?' I ask disbelievingly, watching them flee. 'This small wall of fire and they give up?'

Gabriel secures me and watches in uncertainty himself.

The air twinges around me. The familiar hum that tells me when magic is close. The men aren't running away from us. They're running towards someone else.

'Grayson...' I tell Gabriel. 'He's here. Collins too. I can feel them.'

I'm not sure what I should feel. Relief? Or fear at his arrival.

'Are you sure?' he asks. I nod and he looks exactly as I feel. Conflicted. Unsure.

'What do we do?' I ask. 'Everything he's done. To you, to me, to Rose...do we stay? Do we leave?' I make him look at me. I need to see his eyes when I ask. 'The Veil, what do we do?'

'The Veil needs to come down,' he says quietly as if to himself. His eyes shift a little to the side and he chews his bottom lip. He's thinking. I can see his thoughts racing a mile a minute behind his eyes which is exactly why I needed to see them. To know what he's thinking. They return to me and look certain.

'The Veil needs to come down. You won't be safe until it does. None of us will. Theo won't stop. Grayson will never let us be as long as it stands and we will never defeat the Hunters without our full strength.'

'But Theo's vision...the war...'

'We will not let that happen. No one wants to fight. Not once we get what we need. What we all deserve. Theo's lying. He has to be.' He looks me dead in the eye. 'If the Veil stays up it will be a lifetime of running. Fighting. Hiding. For all of us.'

'Agreed. But what about Grayson?'

'Let's just get out of here alive first and then we'll deal with Grayson together.' He slides his hands into mine. 'As a couple. As one. Unbreakable. He won't split us up. We'll do the spell and go. Once he has what he wants, he'll have no interest in us.'

'What if he follows through on his threat. What if he sends you away?'

'Then I'll take you with me, and he can kiss his Veil spell goodbye.'

Part of me wishes that we could just do that. Just up and leave. But I know it wouldn't be that simple. We'd never stop running. We'd be hunted on all sides. Two of the most wanted people in the world. I'm not a hundred per cent convinced that staying is the best idea, but I agree about the Veil. It must be destroyed if any of us are going to have a chance at a normal life. I trust him and his plan.

'Are we agreed?' he asks. 'We have to be in this together. All the way.'

'I'm in. Together. All the way.'

There's a terrible explosion followed by the screams of men and women. He pulls me down to the ground to keep us both out of the line of fire.

'I have to go. You stay here-' He gets to his feet, letting go of my hands but I pull him back down with me, gripping his t-shirt tightly in my fists. I don't want to let him go.

'Stay with me,' I plead.

'I have to fight,' he insists, prying my hands away.

'You go, we may never find each other again. Grayson could send you away. Theo could get one of us. We *have* to stay together. We *have* to! Gabriel, please...' I couldn't sound more desperate. I *am* desperate. 'I've only just got you. I can't lose you.'

'You're never going to lose me,' he says with a comforting smile. He tucks a stray strand of hair behind my ear and rests his palm on my cheek. 'The devil himself couldn't separate me from you. Not now you've said that you love me. I won't let you leave, even if you asked me to let you go,' he grins. 'I love you. I'd die for you. I'd die without you and believe me, I'll destroy anyone who tries to separate us.'

'You mean that?' I ask, amazed that he clearly loves me enough to sacrifice everything.

'Absofuckinglutely.'

Despite being in the middle of a battle and surrounded on all sides by multiple threats, I can't help but smile and pull him in for a kiss which he returns tenfold.

Renewed yelling and increased gunfire fill the air, drawing our attention back to what's happening. In amongst the crowd of men, bodies go flying in all directions and blue lightning streaks around them, knocking Theo's men down to their knees.

Grayson's coming. I can feel him getting closer and although I'm relieved for the help, I've never been more anxious.

'You stay here,' Gabriel says with a kiss on my cheek. 'Stay safe. I'll be back for you.' He lets me go and turns back to join the fight.

'No!' I pull him back and hold his face with my bloody hand. 'I'm coming with you. I'm fighting,' I insist.

'Your body is too weak. You've been through too much. You go into that fight, you won't come out.' He rests his hand on my cheek. 'I need you safe.'

'I'm safer with you. Gabriel, please!'

'You're exhausted. You can't-'

'Then make me strong,' I tell him. 'Compel me. Give me the strength I need. I won't resist you.' He shakes his head, a deep frown on his brow. 'Gabriel Kendryk, you do as I'm asking and you do it now! I won't stay here and hide. I won't do nothing. I want to fight. I need to be by your side.'

He looks conflicted, but finally, he gives a small nod. He gives me what I ask for. As he always has. He trusts me.

His eyes go black.

'Lilly. Fill your body with adrenaline. Release it as quick as it's created. You send it through your body, to your muscles. Pain and tiredness will not stop you. Your muscles may want to give up. You may want to fall down. You may want to stop, to give up, to sleep, but you won't. Your magic is strong. You're filled with strength. You won't stop fighting the enemy until you're safe.'

'How will I know when I'm safe?' I ask. I feel strange. Like I'm in a daydream. All I know is that I must obey his words. It's all that I know. His words are law. Gods law. I must obey.

'When I tell you that you are,' he says, pulling me in for a loving, possessive kiss. As he does, I feel the adrenaline he's ordered to fill me, course through my body. My heart races. My breath quickens. I feel like I could tear the trees up from their roots with my bare hands. The wall of fire triples in height and burns hotter. When we break our embrace, his eyes are back to their usual, stunning blue.

We turn and run back to the fight. I make a break in the fire and we sprint through it. Theo sees us and starts coming at us. I send my fire streaking through the air straight at him making him barrel roll out of the way. I do it again, throwing it at him over and over so he can't get to his feet. Gabriel runs at him and slams his fist into his face. As he draws his fist back for another attack, Theo raises his hand, propelling Gabriel backwards into a tree. He's barely hit the ground when he's set upon by three Traitors. Theo gets to his feet and starts charging towards him. He can't fight them all. I run and plant my feet firmly between them as Gabriel gets back to his feet and fights his attackers. My hands are flaming. My body filled with forced adrenaline and all I can think about is causing Theo as much pain as I can, while keeping the man I love safe.

He smirks at me with intense hatred.

'You're in my way, girl.'

'You're not getting anywhere near him,' I state, like some fierce warrior.

'I thought you had more morality than this. After everything he's done, and you still fawn at his feet.'

'Stop talking, Theo. You don't know your son. You have no idea who he is. And you pretending to be the hero? It's boring me.' I raise my hand, fire ready to fly as he raises his electrified hand.

'Let's do this, little girl. You and me. Let's see who comes out on top.'

Before either of us can do anything, someone else gets to him first. Theo goes stock still and starts juddering violently as blue lightning, not his green lightning, streaks all over him. It shoots over the entirety of his body making him shudder and fall to his knees. His eyes roll into the back of his head, and he slumps onto his side unconscious.

Behind him, is Grayson. He looks at his father who lies at his feet and scoffs.

'I come out on top,' Grayson says to the unresponsive heap. 'Always.'

He lowers his hand slowly, the lightning fading and he turns his glare to me. He looks angrier than I've ever seen him before. Around us, the Nomads and the Traitors are fighting. Guns and fists. Knives and axes. Anything and everything is being used as a weapon, and yet Grayson pays no mind. His eyes are on me. And now I know what he is capable of, what he wants with me, I feel nothing but distrust, sickening dislike and an overwhelming need to protect Gabriel from him.

Gabriel floors the final of his assailants and runs to me. He's so worried about my safety, he hasn't noticed his brother. As he strokes my face, runs his hands down my arms and asks me over and over if I'm okay, I can't stop watching his brother, who surveys every one of his touches. Gabriel finally notices my distraction and turns to look. He sees Grayson and his palpable anger. All three of us are stuck in this triangle of tension. Grayson turns suddenly and hurls his fist into a nearby Traitor's face. He turns his back on us and continues to fight. His lightning is shot skilfully through the multitude of battling bodies, and he hurls men and women through the air, like leaves in a breeze. Gabriel and I share a look of unease.

Some of Theo's men turn away from Grayson and the Nomads and instead turn on us. I spin Gabriel so he can see the danger coming straight at us.

'Stay here, Beautiful.'

Gabriel pulls out the knife and turns to fight them off. Running straight at them, leaving me behind. Theo's on the floor not moving, but soon he's joined by Jensen who shakes him awake. Theo's disorientated, but not for long. He and Jensen are both on their feet and looking straight at me in an instant.

'Shit.'

I go to run towards the Nomads. To Gabriel. To anyone on my side. But with the first step I take, Theo raises his hand. I'm slammed by what feels like a sledgehammer that hurls me through the air backwards. I land ten feet away on my back, winded and sore. The pain doesn't matter. I can't let it. I force myself to my feet, not giving into the hurt. I see them both walking straight at me with a clear focus. They're going to take me down. Nothing is going to get between them and their target.

Me.

I raise my hand to use my fire, but Theo's too fast and I'm too weary. Despite Gabriel's compulsion, without which, I'm sure I would be a floppy heap on the floor. I'm hurled another ten feet back, slamming hard into the ground and rolling another few feet from the force of his attack. They're still coming towards me. They haven't broken or slowed their descent one bit. I get to my knees, but again I'm hurled backwards. Another full-frontal slam of energy which has me spinning a full three-sixty and landing face down in the dirt. They're separating me from them. Getting me as far away as possible from anyone who would help me.

I'm winded. Exhausted. Terrified. I cough and gasp as I roll over. I look up at the tree canopy overhead as Theo and Jensen tower over me.

'Well, hello there,' Theo muses cruelly. 'Here. Let me help you up.' He wraps his hand around my throat and lifts me clear off the ground. My feet hover inches above the mud and slush as I kick out. I can't breathe! He tightens his grip. My brain feels like it's going to explode from the pressure. I claw at his hands as I fail to get any sort of breath.

'THEODORE!'

He turns with me still in his grasp. Grayson hurls a streak of blue lightning straight at him. It hits him square in the chest and makes him lose his grip on my throat. I fall to the floor and scramble away as fast as I can, still gasping for air.

'Get your hands off my Witch,' Grayson warns.

Jensen helps Theo get to his feet.

Theo turns to Grayson and opens his arms wide and laughs loudly.

'If you want her, son... you're going to have to get through me!'

'Not a problem, *father*.'

Streaks of lightning start flying in all directions as Theo and Grayson hurl it at each other. A mix of the brightest blues and the starkest greens, light up the darkness. Behind them, Gabriel's eyes are black, and men are screaming in pain letting him punch, kick and snap necks.

'GET ME THE HOOPER WITCH, JENSEN!' Theo's voice calls over. He's locked in a vicious battle with Grayson who won't let him past. Every attempt he makes to get to me, Grayson thwarts. And it's driving Theo mad.

Jensen has started walking towards me. Behind him, a dozen armed men have turned in my direction. Traitors. And they're coming straight for me. I push myself to my feet still struggling to get a good breath and ready myself. Gabriel appears from the mass of people and throws himself between us.

'You want her, you'll have to get through me,' he warns Jensen.

Through the crowd, Collins joins him. 'And me,' he says, standing side by side with his best friend.

'Very well,' Jensen says darkly. 'I have no problem making you bleed, Gabriel. You have no idea how much I want to hurt you.' Jensen raises his hand high in the air. When he lowers it, the men behind him charge. And so does he.

But Collins and Gabriel...they're unbelievable! Every hit, stab, kick, duck or weave is perfect. They're deadly weapons on their own, without need of guns or magic. But with Collin's added strength, his punches are killers. One Traitor falls and his head is at a one eighty-degree angle. They stop some from getting to me. But not all. A few men get past and start running straight at me. Soon I can't see anyone I know. Just the enemy and they're all coming for me with Jensen front and centre.

My brain kicks in. I get ready to fight. But Jensen stops. He almost skids, he stops so fast. Suddenly, he looks afraid, but it's not me he's looking at. It's something, or someone, behind me.

'You...' Jensen whispers.

'Me,' the voice behind me says. A voice that has me spinning so fast I feel dizzy. I stop dead when I see who it is. His malicious grin and confident stance have me stock still in shock.

'Hey, Red,' he says coolly. 'Need a hand?'

Toby looks past me to Jensen and his men. His sly grin twists into a menacing grimace as he pushes me behind him and releases a powerful surge of black and white flames, twice as intense as anything I could ever produce.

Jensen's reflexes are remarkable as he dives out of the way. Fire explodes from Toby, wave after wave after wave, pulsing from him in a ferocious attack, knocking down the men coming at us and burning them alive. I hear their screams of horror and agony as it slams into them over and over. Toby laughs a low, cruel laugh as he watches them burn, before slowly turning to me. My eyes flick between the charred, still alive, still screaming men behind him. And at the man himself.

Slowly, confidently and with a carefree swagger, he walks towards me. I'm so shocked at his sudden appearance that I just stumble backwards in silence. My back hits a tree, and still, he descends on me until I'm all but pinned. He reaches out and runs his finger along my cheek and to my mouth.

'My Red. My girl.' He smiles dreamily, distantly, like his mind is somewhere else. He looks at the lip he traces his finger along, then down at the rest of my body. That wanton glint sparking in his eye as his face is illuminated by the flames still devouring Theo's men. Suddenly, his eyes flick up to mine, and he gives a small laugh.

This is bad. Very bad. I know the motives of everyone here. I know who wants to help me. Who wants to hurt me. But Toby...knowing what he wants is impossible. An environment like this? A war zone, a battle of magic and weapons...he'll be loving every second. He's in his element. Where most men would wince at the sight of a man slowly burning to death, he would watch in wonderment.

'W-what are you doing here?' I breathe, watching every single one of his movements.

'I came for you. Of course.' He taps my lower lip playfully and smiles. 'You want that journal, right? Rebecca's journal?'

He's in no rush. He's not concerned one bit by his surroundings. His entire focus is on me as I continue to try and back up. But my back is flush against a great oak. I turn, ready to run but he slams his hand by my head, placing his palm on the bark. I can't get past, and I know better than to try. He steps closer as I shrink back. I watch the reflection of his fire in his lilac eyes that survey me with deep interest. His face is in mine. An easy smile on his lips. Everything that's happened tonight and only now do I cower. Only now am I truly afraid. The fight may as well be a million miles away. I swear, I can't even hear it anymore. All I can hear is his breathing which is slow and steady. All I can see are the playful intentions swimming behind his eyes. As always, when he is with me, the rest of the world disappears. It's only us.

Whereas before, it was sensual. Intoxicating. Obsessive.

Now, I'm paralysed with fear.

'Come with me,' he purrs in my ear, leaning in and running the tip of his nose along my jaw. 'Come with me right now, Red, and I'll give it to you.' His pale eyes stare straight into mine. 'Come with me and I'll give you the journal. If you don't, I'll hand it over to Theo in exchange for my safety during his spell and everyone you know will die.' He slides his hand in my hair. 'Tick tock, Red.'

I look over at the battle. They're still fighting, and the fire has caused untold casualties. I can't see anyone I know. No Gabriel. No Collins. No one. Just bodies on the floor and strangers fighting each other.

'Well?' Toby asks. 'What's it gonna be?'

Toby has my hand firmly in his as he pulls me after him. We run through trees, over fallen logs and wade through a stream. Only when the sound of everyone else is far in the distance does he slow and finally stop. My legs buckle and I fall, struggling to catch my breath. I've been tortured and not slept. I've had a physical and emotional marathon. That sprint has just taken every last ounce of energy I had left. If I wasn't under Gabriel's compulsion, I might very well be unconscious.

Gabriel. The mere thought of him back there has my heart in knots. Is he okay? Does he know I'm gone? If he's worried about me, he won't focus on what's happening around him.

I need to push those thoughts out of my head. I'm with the most dangerous man in the world right now. I need every ounce of my focus on him. I need to get the journal and get away from him, back to Gabriel. I'm a fool if I think for even a second that Toby will willingly hand it over and let me leave.

Toby kneels beside me as the rain continues to fall.

'You okay?' he asks, his voice seemingly concerned but I know better. He doesn't do concern. It's a lie. A manipulation. Just like everything that comes out of his mouth.

'I need a second,' I pant, falling forwards so my hands are in the mud. Every breath I take in burns my starving lungs. No inhale is big enough as I gasp and wheeze. When he places a gentle hand on my back and starts slowly rubbing it, I go rigid before hastily shoving him off. He falls back and lands on his arse still watching me.

'A thanks for saving my life may be nice,' he says petulantly.

'Don't touch me,' I warn. 'Don't you dare touch me, Toby. Ever.' I'm making that clear now.

I sit up, wipe the hair from my face and look at him. His white hair is soaking from the rain. He's out of breath, just like me. Seeing those Lilac eyes this close makes me uneasy. All I want is to turn and run. But he has the journal, and I need to make sure that I keep it as far away from Theo as possible. And him away from Gabriel.

'Where's the journal?' I demand, my erratic breathing beginning to calm.

'Manners.'

'Fuck my manners. Where is it, Toby? Or should I call you Bias?'

His eye twitches like it always did just before he would lose his temper. A small tick that I picked up on quickly when we were together. I would back down, apologise for whatever action or word had caused the twitch and hope that he would let it pass without punishment. But that was then.

'My name is Toby. Bias is long dead.'

'Where is it?' I repeat.

'Give me a kiss, and I'll tell you,' he replies with a smart grin.

I don't have time for this. The man I love is fighting a war. Collins too. They're all I have, and I won't sit here playing games with my psychotic ex as they risk their lives.

'It doesn't have to be on the mouth,' he says, raising his eyebrows suggestively. 'No one kisses me like you do.'

I lose it completely and lunge at him, pinning him to the ground with a leg either side of his waist. I start searching all his pockets. Toby just laughs and lets me look, his hands up in a condescending surrender.

'If you want to tear my clothes off, all you have to do is ask, Red. I'm more than up for a bit of rough and tumble with my best girl.'

I slap his face hard making him laugh more.

'WHERE'S THAT DAMN JOURNAL YOU VILE PIECE OF SHIT?' I yell in his face. I keep searching. Looking in his inside jacket pockets, the waistband of his trousers, but it's not here. I slam my fists into his chest. 'LIAR!' I thump them into him again and again. 'GIVE ME THE JOURNAL, TOBY! TELL ME WHERE IT IS!' I've lost control of my anger and I just keep hitting. My bloody hand is screaming at me to stop, but Gabriel's compulsion makes me not give a damn. My anger and hurt are much stronger than a simple bit of pain.

He rolls over quickly. I scream as he throws me to the floor and pins me beneath him.

'Calm down, will you?'

'Get the hell off me,' I warn with complete venom.

He looks down at me, the rain dripping off him and onto me. As I lie beneath him, that sly grin on his face gets wider. His fingers tighten around my wrists which he has pinned up by my head.

'Like old times,' he says seductively, pressing his hips between my legs.

'You have three seconds to get off me, Toby, or-'

'Or what?' he asks, leaning down to my face so his nose rests against mine.

He slides his hands from my wrists into my palms and entwines his fingers with mine. I wince as he touches the fingerless hand, but he doesn't pay any attention. He knows it hurts. He presses his fingers over the still bleeding wound and waits for me to react.

But I don't. I won't plead with him to release me.

Pleading never worked. Never.

'I just saved you, and all you have for me are threats?'

I don't fight. I just lay beneath him knowing that I'm more likely to get answers if I'm the little compliant thing he knew.

I relax the anger I feel on my face, slow my breathing, look him deep in the eye with as much fake passiveness as I can muster and say sweetly, 'Thank you for saving me, Toby.'

'You are very welcome,' he says. 'Now, about that kiss...'

I reach up and push my lips against his quickly for a kiss that lasts less than a second. There. That's all he's getting. Even that small bit of contact feels beyond familiar and the old me, the girl he made in his image, rears her head.

Wouldn't it be easier just to give him what he wants? You know there's no point fighting him. You never could say no.

But I tell her to fuck off. I push her back down deep inside where I hope she stays. I'm *not* that girl anymore.

'Humph. Well, that was a bit shit,' he grumbles, but thankfully he sits and pulls me with him, not pushing for another.

He straddles me with my legs between his. One of his arms snake around my waist as the other sweeps the hair I have plastered on my face, out of my eyes.

'Damn, I've missed you. You're even more beautiful than I remember,' he purrs, tracing his thumb across my lower lip.

His calling me beautiful feels wrong. Ridiculous. That's not his word. It's Gabriel's. But I hold his eye contact and remain placid. He pulls me closer, using the arm he has wrapped around my waist and I have to fight the urge to slam my forehead into his nose.

'What have you got yourself into, huh? I leave you alone and you end up in the snake pit. It's alright. I'm here now.'

He speaks as if he's my hero. My saviour. Rescuing me from a situation I was silly enough to get myself into and only he is smart enough to get me out of.

'I want a real kiss,' he says, looking at my mouth.

But it's never just a kiss with him. He won't let it go. If he wants to kiss me, he will. And if he refuses to tell me what I want to know until he gets it, then he won't say a word about the location of the journal. So instead of prolonging the inevitable, I lean in and his lips touch mine. His lips move slowly. Gently. I stare at him with my eyes open and kiss him back. Barely. Hoping to keep him calm and at ease enough to tell me what I need to know. Praying all the while that I don't throw up. I tell myself not to hit him. Not to push him off. To just let him do this in the vague hope it gets me what I need. His hand slides under my top and his skin meets mine. I can't help it. I flinch. The familiar pain that comes with unwanted touch explodes. He stops in an instant and opens his eyes.

'Did you just flinch?' he asks, menace clear in his voice. 'I've touched every part of you. I've made you feel absolute pleasure and now...you *dare* flinch?' He stares straight into my eyes. 'You're playing me. You don't want to kiss me at all.'

He's not buying the act. I don't blame him. I never was a good liar, and he could always read me so well.

'I need that journal, Toby,' I tell him, hoping perhaps reason will work. That perhaps, if he does love me still, he will help me because that's what *I* need. 'Please. My life depends on it. I need that journal.'

He grins his nasty grin and slides his hand up, cupping me beneath my top. His eyes close as he loses himself in the feel of me despite knowing full well the reaction I'm having. I feel sick to my stomach. Violated.

'Come with me and your life won't depend on it,' he says with a deep longing.

As if it's that simple. That tone would have me bending to his will every time a few years ago. The idea that he needed me. The idea that a man this sexy, this powerful and this intense would need me was everything to me. He didn't care about anyone. No one mattered. No one registered on his radar. He honestly didn't give a damn who was hurting or why. Except me. For a girl who had been unloved and unwanted since the age of five, that was powerful. Hell, on some level, it still is.

But now, I'm able to hear it for the lie it is. The manipulation. I was weak. An easy target. A powerful weapon he wanted to mould. Recreate in his own image. I know that now. I just have to keep telling myself that.

'Come back to me, Red. And I swear no one will ever get close enough to hurt you again.'

But they will. *He* will. And being away from Gabriel would kill me. My heart wouldn't survive.

I lower his arm and push it out from under my clothes, all the while never looking away from his face.

'I'm not going anywhere with you,' I tell him firmly. 'I would rather die.'

'Tone...Red.'

'You don't frighten me anymore, *Tobias.*'

His grin turns to a sneer. It's as familiar to me as all his other expressions. His arm stiffens as I try to push it away. I have to settle for keeping it an inch from my body.

'My name is Toby,' he says. 'And I still frighten you.'

'You said that you would give me the journal if I came with you. I'm here. Now give me the journal.' I shove him in the chest. 'And get the fuck off me.'

'What's wrong with you?' His tone is chilling. 'How dare you speak to me with such disrespect.'

'I never dared to speak to you how I really wanted to speak to you. I never had the conviction or self-worth to tell you how I truly felt about all those things you did to me. But now I do because the person who loved you, the person who needed you, craved you...she isn't here anymore. Inside this body is someone new. And she doesn't need anyone but herself.'

Damn it, Lilly, stop shaking!

'Oh yeah? And what about Gabriel?' he says through his teeth. His jaw's clenched and his eyes more dangerous than I've ever seen.

'I don't need Gabriel,' I tell him. 'I *want* Gabriel. And that alone makes him mean more to me than you ever did.'

Suddenly, he reaches out and wraps his fingers in my hair, yanking my head back hard.

'You even hint that you're leaving me for another man, I will kill you. Do you understand me?'

I don't fight. I don't panic. His grip isn't tight, nothing more than a warning. One sign of weakness and I'm done for. That's what he likes. What he loves. The fear he evokes in others. Watching them beg and plead for him to show mercy is an aphrodisiac. So, he never shows them mercy. He would never ease up. I stare back into his angry face, defiant and unbothered.

'You've known him a matter of weeks. Me and you...we have years of-'

'I'm not interested in hearing what you have to say. Me and you? Whatever we were, we're done. Anything I had that resembled love for you, is dead. And it's never coming back. So kill me, or get. The fuck. Off me.'

'How dare you,' he growls keeping his hand exactly where it is. 'How dare you talk to me like this. After everything I've done for you, you ungrateful-'

'Everything you did for me? You ruined my life!' How is he so delusional about what we were? About how he treated me?

'I saved your life,' he argues. 'You were hanging from a tree when we met. If it weren't for me, you'd be dead.'

'And because of that, you think you own my life? You think it's yours to do with as you like? Just because you saved my life, does not make it yours.'

'You had no life before you met me so don't pretend otherwise. You longed to be wanted. For someone to care, and I did. I still do!'

'You cared?' I laugh in his face. 'You manipulated me. Abused me-'

'Abused you?' he says shocked.

'Yes! What you did to me was abuse. I just didn't know any better. But I do now. I thought you loved me.'

'I did. I do!'

'No. You didn't. I know what love is now, and what you and I had...it most certainly wasn't love.'

'You know what love is now?' he repeats my words darkly. 'Are you telling me you love him?'

'His name's Gabriel.' I see the hatred he has for the man whose name I just said, but that just spurs me on. 'And yes. I love him. Very much. He's a hundred times the man you are.'

'Is that right...' he says menacingly with narrowed eyes. He's started to shake with anger. 'I tell you that he's the reason I Broke. Theo tells you that he brainwashed your ancestor into sleeping with Grayson. He fucks another woman when he's with you and you still fall for his lies? Are you that desperate to be loved?'

'How do you know that?' I ask quickly.

'Know what?' His grip on me eases in his momentary lapse of concentration. He's slipped up, and he knows it. I manage to push him off with a large shove and scramble to my feet in a hurry. He, on the other hand, slowly gets to his feet. His fists are clenched, and I can see he's struggling to hold his temper.

'How did you know that Theo told me about Rose? That Gabriel slept with another woman?' I hear the anger in my voice.

I step forwards, and he surprisingly steps back. I guess he's not used to me fighting back.

'Are you working with Theo? Have you sunk so low as to side with a man who wants to kill every single Descendant on the planet except those he deems fit to save?' I look around half expecting Theo to appear. But he doesn't. No one does. It's just us. 'Answer me, Toby. How do you know all that?'

'I'm not working with Theo. Yet. But unless you start behaving, I will. I'll give Theo the journal, and you. I swear it.'

We glare at each other. Both emanating hatred and anger. He sighs and ruffles his hair before turning and showing me his back. I watch his shoulders rise and fall as he takes a deep breath. When he looks back to me, he seems more relaxed. In control.

'Red, this is getting nasty. I don't want to fight with you. That's not what I came here for.' He walks back to me, removing any space between us and takes my hand. Looking deep into my eyes he says, 'I came here to take you somewhere safe. No one matters to me like you. No one is as important to me as you.'

'Only because I'm the Arcane,' I retort.

'No. Not because you are the Arcane. Because you're you. I know I've said and done some things. Bad things, but you know what I'm like when I lose my temper. I can't help it. You shouldn't push my buttons. You know better than that. Look at me. Can't you see how much I love you? How much I need you? I'll die without you.'

That charm used to get me every time. He usually pulled it out after he did something particularly cruel.

'How do you know those things?' I ask again, ignoring his blatant attempt to win me over.

That fake smile goes as quick as it came. As I knew it would. I wish I had this clarity back when we were together.

'If you're not working with Theo, you must have been listening to us when Gabriel and I were in the tent to know those things.'

I push his hand away as it all starts to make sense. 'You were, weren't you? You were hiding outside the tent! Did you stand there and listen as Theo cut off two of my fingers?' I brandish my wounded hand in his face. He looks at the stubby mess and scoffs, making me angrier. 'Did you laugh as I screamed? Huh?' I shove him again when he laughs. 'You hid out of sight like a coward as we suffered, when you could have helped us! Didn't you?'

'Yes,' he replies heartlessly. It angers me that it upsets me.

'Why?'

'Because you needed to see that no matter what Gabriel says to you, he can't protect you. Not like I can!'

'Protect me,' I scoff, shaking my head. 'You never have and you never will.'

'That's a load of shit!'

'Is it? I saw the photos of me as a child that you took. You knew I was in that house for years. Malcolm told me.' He goes to argue. 'I don't want to hear it. I know that you knew I was there. And that you just left me there until I was old enough for you not to become a paedophile before you started your sick idea of courtship. The only reason you looked at me twice was because you knew I was a Hooper witch. The Arcane.'

'That's not true-'

'When I asked for your help the night you left me. Where did you go? Because if you loved me, if you wanted to protect me, you would have taken me away from that hell hole my uncle had me in. Instead, you abandoned me and I lost everything. I lost you. *Her*. Six weeks of my life. And then, I lost two years rotting in my uncle's cellar. Alone. So where was your protection then? Where was your love?'

'I thought you were dead!' he insists. 'As soon as I knew you were alive and at The Orchard, I came for you. I came on Christmas night and saw you with him!'

'You came for me? You wanted to bloody kill me!'

'Only when I saw you with him! I'm the only one that truly loves you. Me. You belong to me, Red. No one else. Gabriel doesn't love you! Gabriel will never care about you the way I do.' His words tumble out of his mouth at a rapid, desperate and angry pace. I'm not interested in hearing about how he loves me. I don't give a damn how he feels or what he thinks. I need answers, and it's obvious he's deflecting.

'Harry found out about us,' I continue, not letting him change the subject. 'He was furious with me. You came back. I had a bloody nose and a bruised eye. Harry had broken my wrist. I told you everything. I told you he knew about us. You saw my bruises. I told you...' my words start to get stuck in my throat because this is where the pain, the real pain in my life lies. 'I told you what he wanted to do to me. I begged you for help. Pleaded with you to get me out of there before he could carry out his threats. But instead of helping the woman you claimed to love, you went mad. You trashed my room and left saying you were done with me. That it was my fault. That whatever Harry did, I would deserve.'

'I...I made a mistake,' he says. For the first time ever, I see a hint of sadness in his eyes. I hear remorse in his voice, but it's too late for that now. I live with that every day. And so should he. 'What else do you remember?' His eyes keep flickering between me and his feet.

I shrug angrily, tears joining the rain that streams down my face.

'I woke up six weeks later locked in the cellar with these.' I lift my top, showing him the two ugly scars on my stomach. He looks at them for only the briefest of seconds before diverting his eyes back to mine once more. I see that sadness take root and grow.

'What happened in those missing six weeks, Toby? What happened to us? Why did you leave and not come back? Why did I kill those men? Why do I have these scars?'

'If I tell you. If you know what happened, you can never un-know it, Lilly.'

I can count on one hand how many times he's used my real name.

The first was when he discovered the truth about Ryan.

The second was when he first saw the full extent to which Harry would beat me. As I lay on my bed, face down and my bloody back exposed to the air, he washed the cuts clean and comforted me through the pain.

The third was the night he left me.

And the fourth is just now, when he's getting ready to tell me why.

He lifts his face and I shudder as his whole body slumps making him look vulnerable. It's an entirely foreign set of emotions to see on him, and it terrifies me.

What story could he have to tell that would make a man like this look so broken? What could make him this lost?

'Are you sure you want to know?' he asks.

I nod, unable to speak.

'I did come back for you,' he admits.

'You did?'

'Of course I did,' he says sincerely, locking his gaze with mine. 'When you told me...what you told me. I panicked. It wasn't my finest moment I know that, but there was a reason why I left-'

'You're a coward, that's why you left.' There's no reason good enough to hear why he abandoned me when I needed him most. None.

'Maybe,' he says before nodding 'Yes. I was a coward but after a night fighting with myself and facing some hard truths, I came back to your uncle's house. I came back for you. Ready to face my responsibilities. I was going to do the right thing by you.'

'And then what happened? When you came back for me?' I ask nervously.

'I took you away. Just as you asked. We left together in the dead of night with what little you owned. Your mother's necklace and your Brothers Grimm book,' he hesitates. 'But...'

'But what?'

'Well, something wasn't right. I thought you'd be happier than you were. But you just sank into yourself. Locked yourself away. I took you to a little cottage and for the first three days, you refused to come out of the bathroom. I had to sleep on the floor with you because you wouldn't leave. You were terrified. Absolutely terrified. Worse than I'd ever seen you. I planned to take you abroad, but I needed cash. More than I had on me. I left to fetch it and asked my friends to watch you. Men who wanted me as their leader. Not Grayson. Men I trusted. I went back to The Orchard and stole the money I needed. I left you safe and sound, fast asleep. But when I came back, you'd gone.'

'Gone? Gone where?'

'Home,' he says. 'You'd left to go back to Harry's.'

I can't help but scoff at his words. At his version of events. At his lies.

'You're telling me that instead of staying with you, a man I loved. Instead of going to a whole new country with you to start over, I went back to a man who had abused me my whole life? Who wanted to deal with me like he would his dog? I would never have gone back. Never.'

'You did. You bloody did go back!' he insists, annoyed that I would dare call him a liar. 'You left me a note. A goddamn note, Red. That's how you broke it off with me.'

'I would never have gone back there, Toby. Not after I knew what Harry was planning.' I'm positive he's lying. But the solemnness of his expression, the lack of argument...he can't be telling the truth. Can he? 'What did this note say exactly? What possible reason would I give to go back willingly?'

'The note you left me said that you were afraid of a lot of things in life. But terrified of two. Just two. The first was losing control of your magic. Of losing yourself and hurting innocent people. You said that being out in the world, which was full of too much uncertainty, was too much of a risk. That the person you were when you were with me, was too much of a risk. And then you wrote that the second thing that terrified you, was-'

'Hunters,' I finish his words because I know what terrifies me most. The mere idea of ending up in the hands of the sadistic humans who called themselves Hunters was the main reason I stayed at my uncle's. The other was that I knew I couldn't control myself. Just ask my dead mother.

'You thought that we would be caught and taken to the Hunters' cells. We all know what that means for people like us. For Witches. It's a fate worse than death. You knew that, and you couldn't face it. It's why you locked yourself up in the bathroom. You were convinced they would find us. You didn't want to be free!'

'But I still wouldn't have gone back. Why would I go back there when I knew what Harry was going to do? Why would I go back?'

'You wanted to go back because deep down you thought he was right. Because you didn't want *her* to suffer as you had suffered. Because every night you prayed never to wake up. You prayed to die in your sleep, peacefully, rather than spend another day living in fear. And every morning, you wished that you had never been born. And you couldn't stand the thought of her ever feeling the way you felt. You said that you couldn't do that to her and that you wouldn't let her end up in the hands of Hunters.'

'I saw what happened in the barn. I saw myself kill those men!'
'You remember the barn?'
'Bits. What happened.'
'Oh God. I hoped you hadn't remembered that.'
'Why? What did you do?'
He shakes his head. 'It's what you did, Red. You won't be able to live with it.'

'Tell me.'

He sighs, and spills. 'When you left, my men called me. We chased after you and caught you. I had to knock you out. You wouldn't listen to reason! But you kept waking up and using your magic against us. We got caught in a bad storm. We took shelter in that bloody barn. You woke up.' He looks at me warily.

'Tell me.'

'You slaughtered them. You knocked me out. You killed my men as they tried to look after you. And you went back to Harry. Willingly. And you let him do the procedure. Willingly. Those scars are cuts he made so you could never...Lilly...you can never have...Christ. I'm so sorry to tell you all this.'

'No...' I whisper as grief and shame overwhelm me as I finally hear the truth. 'Please tell me you're lying.'

'I'm not. You went back-'

'No.' I shake my head and start to back away, like I can in some way escape the truth. Make him the liar. Keep him the coward. For every step I take back, he takes one forwards. As I shake my head, he nods. 'No' I repeat, pleading with him for it not to be true.

'Yes. I wanted to take you away. I wanted to give you a life. Both of you, a life.'

'You're lying.'

'I'm not.'

'YOU ARE!' I scream. My magic seeps out unchecked making the stones around us dance across the ground and the thick trunks of the trees groan as they bend and shake. He pays no mind, keeping his full attention on me.

'I'm not lying to you, Lilly,' he says in a complete calm. 'You want to know who was responsible for her death? Who had killed her?' I stop backing up when I hit a tree. He stops descending on me when there's no more than an inch between us. He reaches out and tucks a stray piece of hair behind my ear before settling his hand on my cheek.

'It was you, my love.'

'LIAR!' I sob.

'You killed her. It Broke you, but you did do it. You killed her, Lilly. You killed our unborn daughter!'

Chapter 23

Those words have me clutching at my chest and struggling to breathe as I sob desperately. I shake my head over and over. He's lying. It wasn't me. It wasn't.

He catches me in his arms as I fall and eases me gently to the ground. I collapse into his arms, bury my face in his chest and cry harder than I've ever cried before. Because now I know.

It was me.

The heat had broken, and we were experiencing a summer storm like no other. The sun hadn't reached beyond the clouds in three days. The rain hadn't eased one bit, and I hadn't seen Toby for the last week when Harry hurled open the door to the library where I was practising the piano with Mr Simmons. Harry stood in the doorway, filling it with his enormous frame. His beady little eyes didn't leave me as he slowly stalked closer. I remember how afraid I felt because he was angry. Very angry. But not his usual yelling, screaming, angry. This was an eerie, controlled fury that seeped into the air so much you could taste it. I stood and slowly backed up until I bumped into Mr

Simmons, who, ever the loyalist to Harry, held me in place so I couldn't escape.

Harry towered over me. His nostrils flaring and his lip twitching.

I asked what I'd done to make him this way, I'd actually been behaving of late. Much more than usual, because I'd felt so poorly. Heat stroke, I'd thought. Exhaustion from the immense heat I was enduring in my stifling attic room.

He asked me, rather boldly, an unusually personal question.

When did I last have a bleed?

When I asked him what he meant, he growled in my face, 'Period. When was your last period?'

I remember laughing because of the whole situation. How my uncle, who only spoke to me when he was screaming, was asking me about my monthlies. But when he continued to glare and continued to wait for me to actually answer, I thought back. My stomach hit the floor and only then did I notice the box of tampons he had clasped in his hand. The unopened, unused box. I hadn't needed this month's supply because, to my horror, I realised, I hadn't had my period this month. Oh hell, or last month. My eyes widened in horror and I felt faint. Harry grabbed my arm and hauled me speechlessly to the ground floor bathroom, where on the toilet lid, waiting for me, was a box.

A pregnancy test.

He watched as I peed on the stick and with bated breath, I waited. The first line appeared and then, so did the second.

I was pregnant with Toby's child.

Harry didn't say a word as he steered his view from the stick in his hands, to me. And then, he punched me. He'd never punched me before. I'd received many backhands, and I was familiar with his belt and walking cane. But he always thought a punch was too much to deliver to a woman. Not this time. I went down hard. He'd busted my lip and damned near dislocated my jaw. Instinctively, as I pulled myself up, I wrapped my arms across my belly, protecting the baby I'd only just learnt was there. And despite the shock and fear I was feeling, I knew, beyond a doubt that I had to protect her. *Her.* I never thought of my child as a boy even though I only had her inside me for such a short time.

He demanded to know who the father was. He refused to let me leave until I told him. It took three more punches to the face before I started to talk. I had to protect my child. It was all that mattered, so I sang. I answered every question he threw at me.

He asked me if the father was a witch.

I said yes.

He asked if I loved him.

I said yes.

He asked if he loved me.

I said yes.

That angered him even more. It makes sense to me now. The baby would be born with magic. He hated magic.

Harry wrenched me to my feet and threw me as hard as he could out into the hall. I left one arm covering my belly and used my other to break my fall. I heard the snap of my wrist and screamed at the pain it caused.

Harry didn't care. Mr Simmons neither as he stood watching his employer hurl his pregnant niece around the house.

When Harry shoved me into my bedroom, he tossed the pregnancy test at my feet. He called me stupid. Selfish. He called me a whore. He said I had no idea what I'd done. How my actions had put everyone in danger and that there was no way he was going to let all his hard work at keeping me away from the world go to waste. Not only that, but to bring another witch into it. He told me he was sending for Mr Jennings. That he would take care of it.

Mr Jennings was a half-rate vet who tended to Harry's dogs and horses on the cheap. For a vast increase in wages, he would rid me of my...problem. That's what Harry said. That's what he thought of my baby. Nothing more than a problem he wanted a butcher to rid me of. That night, Toby came. I told him. I showed him the test and pleaded with him to help us get away before my uncle's vet could terminate our baby. Undoubtedly, the father of my little girl would feel the same. Surely Toby would level this house to the floor at the mere suggestion of such a thing being done to the woman he loved. And to his child.

But that isn't what happened. Not at all.

Toby flew into a rage. He trashed my room. Snapped the pregnancy test in two. Pushed me away from him when I reached out for his hand. This was my mess, he said. He had given me the pill, if I'd forgotten to take it, it was my fault. He said he didn't want a baby. Not with me. Never with me.

And then he left.

The pain I felt when I watched him climb out the window was indescribable. But it wasn't my abandonment that broke my heart. It wasn't his anger to me that had me suddenly loathing him. It was what his refusal to help meant for her. For our child. He had turned his back on her. Effectively sentenced her to death. I remember watching the rain come in through the still open window. The darkness only giving way to lightning as the storm continued for its third night. And I remember thinking...no. I won't let this happen. I won't let anyone touch my child.

I pulled on a jumper. Pulled up the hood and went to the window. As I looked out into the night, I couldn't see the man who had just fled from us. I couldn't see anything, not until another streak of lightning shot across the sky. I saw his small frame making its way quickly across the vast fields away from us. Away from me. I watched until he disappeared.

And now, so would I.

But instead of fleeing through the open window before me, I hesitated. Fear gripped me. The same fear that had me trapped in this place for all these years. The fear of what lies beyond these walls.

Hunters.

And so, I lingered. One leg over the ledge, one still planted on my bedroom floor. I don't know how long I stood there. And I have no idea what I did next. Because the next memory I have is waking up in my uncle's hidden cell beneath the house, with chains around my wrists and too many cuts and bruises to count. But the most significant pain of all was when I lifted my top and saw the mass of heavy bruising across my stomach and the two wounds which looked like cauterised cuts. I knew, without needing to hear it from a gloating Harry, that I was empty. That my baby was gone. I didn't know how. I didn't know why. And as Harry closed the heavy door to the prison I was destined to remain in for another two years, I let out a scream that contained all my grief. A cry so filled with heartbreak that I wanted to die then and there.

Over the years, Harry had told me the story of how I had fled in the night. Of how he looked for me and finally found me. He told me I'd gone crazy. Murdered people. Butchered them. That if it weren't for him, I would be with Hunters right now. Not here. He told me he didn't know what had happened to my baby. That it was gone before he found me. But now I know. I came back. I let him take her.

Harry lied.

Toby lifts my face and wipes my tears. 'I'm so sorry. I told you that you wouldn't want to know.'

'Why didn't you come back for me?' I cry 'Why didn't you stop me?'

'I did come back for you. I followed you. But I was too late. Harry and Simmons told me that there was a complication. That you had a bleed and died.' His eyes glimmer with a deep sadness.

Like the idea of my dying hurts him too deeply to ever put into words. 'I was banished from my coven. Gabriel and Grayson knew I'd taken the journal. They knew I'd taken all the money I could get my hands on. They were looking for me, and with you gone there was no point in sticking around. I left. I was heartbroken. I'd lost the woman I loved and my child. I was drowning in grief and guilt.' His hands settle each side of my face as he stares into my eyes. 'I should have taken you as soon as you told me about the baby. I'm sorry that I didn't.'

He's apologising to me? Why? It's all my fault. This is all on me. I deserve those two years of isolated hell. I deserve a lot more than that for my pathetic cowardice.

'When I heard that you were alive and at The Orchard, I came back to take you away so we could be together again. But instead of you being happy to see me, you were with him. You'd moved on to the man who ruined my life.' He takes my hand and lightly kisses my knuckles. 'Come with me,' he says. 'Let me look after you. Let's try this again. Let's be us again.'

The rain is falling so hard, I can't tell the difference between my tears and the rain. I'm so confused. So lost. I feel like there's no gravity and I'm spinning erratically into orbit with no means of ever returning to earth. I can't cope with all this. It's too much. Too confusing. I don't know what to do, how to feel or how I will ever get over the revelation that I'm the one responsible for losing my child.

I bury my face in my hands and let out a loud pain-filled scream before slumping forwards and sobbing uncontrollably. This ache I have in my heart for the baby I lost, explodes, just like it did the day I awoke in the cellar.

'Lilly?' he says softly, pulling my hands away from my face and looking at me. 'I lost her too. We need each other to get through this. To mourn. Together.'

I sink into his chest. A place that has always been so familiar, and cry. He holds me close, his face in my neck. I cling to him, just like I used to, and he tethers me to the ground.

'It's my fault, Toby. You should hate me. Everything I've done...you should hate me.'

He lifts my face and looks into my eyes.

'I could never, ever hate you. I love you,' he says in an absolute. 'I always have and I always will. Three years of devotion I gave you. I know I didn't do it right. I made mistakes. I was cruel and violent. But I swear to you, I will never raise a hand to you or force you to do anything you don't want to do again. Living for two years thinking you were dead, it killed me in more ways than I thought a man could die. But now you're here.' He rests his hand on my rapidly beating heart. 'You're right here and I know I never want to let you go again.' He slides his hand behind my ear. 'I forgive you for what you did. I forgive you for being with Gabriel. I forgive you for choosing them over me. And I forgive you for what you did to our baby. Come back to me. There's nothing about you that I don't know. There are no secrets you need to keep from me because I lived them all with you. I accept you and everything you are. No one else will. Don't you see that?'

He leans in and rests his forehead against mine.

'You don't need to pretend with me. I know who you truly are and I love you.' He kisses my lips. Just a quick peck as he watches and waits for me to accept him. He leans in again, kissing my lips for a fraction of a second longer and this time, my lips kiss him back. The third time he leans in, I don't hold back. The damaged girl desperate for a connection and the dangerous man desperate for her. It's like it was. His kiss is a hungry, passionate embrace that I've missed. And for a moment, it's just as it was before everything fell to shit.

But then, something clicks inside. An image. Me in the barn, covered in blood as my hair turns white. I Broke in the barn. Not at Harrys.

I pull away.

'What's the matter?' he asks, caressing my face and searching it, hoping to see what I'm thinking.

'You're lying to me,' I whisper as I struggle to understand.

'What?' he asks, with a nervous laugh.

'You're lying. I-I Broke in the barn. Gabriel and I saw it. When he looked into my memories. We saw it together-'

'Gabriel,' he snarls. 'Fucking Gabriel. It's always him, isn't it?' he says, anger piercing his voice. 'Good boy Gabriel with his pretty fucking eyes and sad little smiles.' His fingers tighten in my hair as he fills with anger at the mere mention of his brother's name. 'You're mine. Not his. Mine!'

'Let me go.' I try to push his hands away once more, but he wraps his fingers in my hair and holds on. 'Toby... stop it.' He leans in, his mouth going to mine once more. 'Get off!' I tell him, but he still comes in. His lips land on mine and all I can do is dodge his kiss which is getting more and more aggressive. 'I SAID GET OFF ME!'

His face hardens, and all the kindness that he put there has gone. He tugs sharply on my hair, yanking my head back and starts screaming in my face like a madman.

'NO!' he yells 'I'M IN YOUR HEART WHETHER YOU LIKE IT OR NOT!' Another yank of my hair. 'YOU DON'T GET TO STOP LOVING ME. NOT UNTIL I LET YOU.' Another yank and he starts climbing on top of me, pushing me into the ground. 'I'M DEEP UNDER THAT SKIN OF YOURS AND IF YOU THINK I'M GOING TO STAND ASIDE AND LET SOMEONE ELSE CLAIM YOU AFTER ALL THE YEARS I GAVE YOU,' he leans into my face and snarls. 'Then you can think again, Red.' He breathes fast and fiercely as he hovers over me, effectively pinning me beneath him. 'Now you will kiss me, you will tell me that you love me and you will leave with me. You owe me that much at least.'

He's insane. He's genuinely insane if he thinks that this is how love works.

'I want you to listen to these words, Toby, and know I mean them with every fibre of my being,' I speak calmly and with absolute conviction. 'I don't want you anymore. And I don't love you anymore. And I know that you are lying to me.'

'I don't care,' he says back, just as definite. 'I love you, and that's all that matters.'

'I'm not leaving here with you. I'm staying. With Gabriel. And you will tell me the fucking truth!'

His hands go to my throat and tighten. He cuts off my air entirely and shakes me before leaning in my face as I try desperately to get the smallest bit of air into my lungs.

'I told you, didn't I? That I'll see you dead before I see you with someone else.' He waits for me to speak, but I can't. I can't breathe! 'DIDN'T I?!' he yells, throttling me hard. I claw at his hands, but it does nothing to release his grip. I grab at his face with my nails. I scratch right across his eye and down his cheek. I draw blood, but he doesn't stop.

'YOU'RE MINE!' he screams, wringing my neck even harder. 'MINE OR DEAD! HOW MANY TIMES DO I HAVE TO TELL YOU!'

I have to get him off. I have to! He's going to kill me. For real this time. My magic pulses inside me as I channel it and use it against him. But no fire comes. There's no hurling of his body through the air. My magic doesn't come from my chest. Not this time. It comes from my head. A heavy, painful throbbing at the base of my skull is accompanied by the sensation of a red-hot poker through the centre of my brain, and somehow, I don't know how but somehow, I'm inside his head. It feels different than it did with Gabriel because this time, I'm not welcome. I feel the resistance like a wall slowly closing in on me, pushing me further and further away from the memory I seem to have found myself in. But I'm stronger. Stronger than I even knew. I need to know the truth. Nothing will stop me. I push that invisible wall away and walk into his memory with ease.

I wish I hadn't.

I'm standing in a place I know well even though I've never been here before. Not that I remember anyway. Piles of hay and broken farming machinery line the wooden walls. It's raining. Drops of water fall through the cracks in the roof. The beams are slightly off their centre. The same as every time I dream about this place.

The Miller's barn.

I look down at my feet, expecting to see the familiar coating of thick red blood. But it's not blood I see. It's me. I'm looking at myself lying on the floor of the barn with my wrists bound above my head by chains attached to the floor. Someone's holding my feet down as I try to kick them away. It's a girl.

The girl.

Toby's other woman. The hood of her jumper is up, and her face is covered, but I know it's her. Her hair falls out the front as it did when he had sex with her in front of me. Around us are six men. Their arms are folded as they encircle us. Watching with an eerie silence.

Standing over me...is Toby.

'You can't have a baby Lilly,' he says. 'I can't let you.'

I see tears falling down his cheeks. He looks like he's in so much pain, so conflicted and afraid. Very unlike the Toby I know. I can tell this isn't a ploy. This isn't him pretending. This is genuine. I can feel it. I look down at the terrified version of me lying helpless at his feet.

'She's yours!' I cry. 'She's your baby. Please, Toby. I'm sorry I left. I won't do it again. I swear. I'll come with you if that's what you want. We can be happy! Don't listen to that woman. Listen to me!'

'We can't have this baby,' he repeats, shaking his head and sniffing as he continues to cry. He takes a step back.

'If you don't want her, fine!' I sob. 'You'll never see us again. Please, please don't hurt my baby. I'm begging you. I'll do anything just, please. Let me go. Please...' I look up at Toby who's lifting up his foot. It hovers directly over my exposed belly. The version of me on the floor looks up at him and pleads one last time, 'She's all I have. Don't take her away. Toby...please.'

'I'm sorry,' he says. 'I am so sorry. But you can't have this baby. You can never have a baby.' His eyes start to change as his heartbreak seems to take over. They're getting darker. Turning a deep hazel, like they were in Gabriel's memory before he Broke. He's returning back to his former self before he suffered a Break.

The girl notices too and panics.

'FOCUS! DO IT!' she screams. 'YOU HAVE TO!'

He blinks, and in a second, he returns back to the cold, hard version of him I know all too well. His eyes remain lilac. He raises his foot higher still.

'HELP ME!' I scream at the men. 'HELP ME!'

But they don't. Not a single one of them.

I watch it with as much horror now, as I did then. The version of me on the floor screams. She pleads for him to stop and although I know that this is nothing more than Toby's memory, I too scream and charge forwards as he thrust his boot towards my stomach.

I don't see the impact.

But I know it happened.

The memory disappears before I can see the brutal attack and I'm back in the forest with his hands around my throat and the rain battering our bodies.

I look up at him. His eyes are wide in shock. His face even paler than usual and in the momentary lapse of concentration, he's forgotten to keep his grip on my throat.

'It *was* you,' I whisper.

He lets me go and scrambles away, desperate to distance himself from me. I sit and look at him in utter disbelief.

'That...that wasn't what it looked like,' he says in a panic. 'How did you do that?'

I get to my feet and look at him. He jumps up to his and takes a step back. My breathing's slow and deep. Every muscle in my whole body is rigid and filled with adrenaline.

'That wasn't-'

'It was you. Not Harry. Not me. You.' I take small steps towards him, and he almost falls over he stumbles away from me so fast. 'Those men I killed, they helped you murder our baby. You had your tart pin me down so you could kick our baby to death, you evil, manipulative...I'm going to kill you.'

I hear the yelling from the fight getting louder. They're getting closer to wherever we are, but right now I couldn't care less. If the Traitors think they're going to get between us, if the Nomads believe they are going to capture Toby, they can think again. He's mine.

He's a dead man.

Toby looks back over his shoulder towards the noise of the battle, but we're still alone. For now.

I hold out my hand.

'Give me the journal,' I say in the coldest tone I think I've ever had. I'm filled with anger and hatred. Every inch of me is consumed by it. My magic's screaming, demanding freedom. Demanding blood. I hold it back, stopping it from spilling out of me. I have it under control because I'm in control. I see with a clarity that I've never had before.

Toby Smith has something I need. When I get it, he will die.

'You're new to your mind magic,' he says, taking another step back. 'What you saw wasn't real.'

But I know it was. It was another snippet of the missing six weeks. A fragment that tells me everything I need to know. I didn't want that baby gone. I wanted her. He took her in the most brutal way possible. And his other woman helped. She held me down and helped him. Those men too. Suddenly, I feel no remorse over what I did. None. If they were here now, I'd tear them apart all over again.

I take a step towards him. There's no fear in me. There's no doubt. For every cumbersome step back he makes, I take a solid, confident step forwards. I have nothing else to lose.

'Give me the journal,' I repeat.

'No,' he replies. Although I can hear the nervousness in his voice as I descend on him slowly, his face still looks as composed as always. Like I'm the one being crazy, and his job is to calm me down.

'Oh, Toby...I wasn't asking. I was telling. You *will* give me the journal.'

The trees around us erupt in flames from the roots to their tips. The rocks and boulders around us rise off the floor. My fire snakes around my wrists, slithering up my arms like serpents. Now his eyes narrow on me. Now he's getting angry.

'That fire... that's mine. I gave it to you.' He creates his fire too. 'You're nothing without me, Red. Just a shell. A victim. A pathetic girl swinging from a rope. You think Gabriel actually wants you? With your scars and fear of being touched? Does he know about Ryan? Huh? You think he would want you after hearing about that?' I stay quiet as he spews his venom at me, desperate to upset me. To make me cry or lose focus, but I won't. Nothing he says matters to me. Not anymore. 'I did what I did for a reason.'

'What possible reason could you have?'

'Because I saw you die!' he says. 'I had a vision soon after we met, of you, pregnant. And dying. I couldn't let you die. I love you too much!'

'That's your excuse? You did it to save my life? What about the cuts you made? What about the scars on my belly?'

'I had to make sure that you could never get pregnant again. And now you can't. I'm sorry it went down like that, but I had no choice. You wouldn't agree to an abortion!'

The fires grow in height. The roots of the trees begin to groan. He glances around him nervously.

'When I'm the Coven leader, I want you by my side. That's the plan. You and I, but if you don't fall into line right now, I swear...no matter how much I love you I will put you down myself.'

He stops and waits for my reaction, but I just continue to stand there with my arms alight and my breathing slow and steady. I have nothing else to say to him. I have no more emotions to feel, other than the need to tear him apart.

'I did it to save you!'

'I'm going to kill you,' I tell him. 'Slowly. Painfully.'

He looks at the forest that blazes around us. At the fierce black and white flames that smother the trees, and then he looks back to me.

'So that's it? You choose them over me? You choose Gabriel over me?' he asks.

'No, Toby' I reply. 'I choose me.'

With a roar, my flames become a deep red all at once. The heat intensifies tenfold as the flames climb higher, above the tops of the trees into the air, making a ceiling of fire above our heads.

Without another word, I hold my hands close to my chest before opening my palms and shooting the most powerful stream of red fire straight at him. He reacts quickly. Doing the same with his black and white fire.

The flames clash between us.

'LILLY, STOP!' he yells as he struggles to stop my red fire crawling closer. It consumes his flames bit by bit as I continue to direct it straight at him. His feet slide back in the mud as the force of it starts to overwhelm him, and I know he can't hold me off much longer. Especially when this isn't half as draining on me as it seems to be for him.

'LILLY...' he stares at our fire. 'PLEASE!'

'Please?' I say curiously. 'Please what?'

'STOP!' His feet slide back further as my red flame claims yet more of his white. He looks behind him to a tree a few feet away, covered in my magical fire. My new red flame. *My* flame, not his. I step forwards. More of the white is consumed by my red, and his feet slide back again. He's no more than a foot away from the flaming tree, and there's less than a foot of his white now.

'YOU CAN'T KILL ME.'

'Yes. I can. I really, really can,' I say simply.

My red fire is at his fingertips. The tree an inch from his back. He looks between the two, and for the first time ever I see real fear on his face. I see my fire reflected in his eyes. That, and the realisation that he's about to die.

'IF YOU KILL ME, THEY DIE TOO!' he yells.

The sound of the battle is getting louder as they all head towards us. Nomads and Traitors alike. But I don't care. The devil and his hellish army could be coming this way and I wouldn't flinch. I wouldn't stop.

'YOU KILL ME,' he yells. 'GABRIEL WILL DIE! COLLINS, GRAYSON... THINK ABOUT IT. YOU CAN'T KILL ME WITHOUT LOSING EVERYONE YOU CARE ABOUT!'

He looks between me and the fire both at his back and his front. But still, I hold my ground.

He takes a few deep breathes and in a much calmer voice says, 'They're fighting. Can you hear them? The yelling? The gunfire?

They need your help. Gabriel *needs* your help. What if Gabriel gets hurt? What if he gets shot?'

I look over to the sounds of the fighting. I'm filled with the need for destruction, *his* destruction, and I'm so close. There's barely any white fire left. My red fire's so close and I know I could cover him in it and watch him burn.

But he's right.

Killing him will kill Gabriel, and I'll be damned if he takes anyone else I love from me.

I lower my hand. My fire fades. The trees extinguish in a second. He slumps back against it with a sigh of relief.

But I'm not done.

I walk to him, grab his head, and with a yell of utter hatred, I dive back into his mind.

I know what I want. I know what I need. Finding the journal is all that matters now. It drives every instinct. Takes over every thought and as I hold his head, the answer comes in the quickest of flashes.

When I hear Collins in the distance yelling my name, I let him go. I hear Collins yell again. But this time it's an anguished cry filled with pain.

I've neglected the battle for too long. I've abandoned not only the man I love, but my best friend's partner. *My* friend.

I look at Toby who's staring at me with wide, panicked eyes. I can't kill him. But I can't just let him go. Leave him to disappear into the shadows again. I can't let him get away with this. He knows I know where the journal is now. If he gets to it before I do, I may never get my hands on it.

'I told Gabriel about Ryan. I told him about the maid. He knows. And he still loves me. Fuck you, Tobias Kendryk.' I slam my hand on his face and create my fire. He screams as I burn my handprint into his flesh. Just like he did to me all those years ago on my thigh. As he yells, I reach out my hand and summon a large grey rock and slam it hard into his face, knocking out several teeth and breaking his jaw. He falls to the floor and looks up at me. I pull out his leg before lifting my foot and stomping down with all my might on his knee. I hear a stomach-turning snap as he shrieks, grabbing his leg and choking on his own blood. I raise the rock again and bring it down hard on his skull with an almighty yell. He falls to his side. He's out. Completely unconscious.

I look at the bloody broken mess of the man I loved. The devil.

'Don't go anywhere,' I tell his unconscious body before I turn and begin the long run back to the camp.

He'll be out for a while, and if he does wake up before the Nomads can get to him, he won't get far. Not on that leg.

I have to get back to Gabriel. Part of my heart has been broken for good. I need to see him. I feel like I'm slipping away. I can't give in to my Break. I can't. If I could just see his face, I know I'll be okay.

The heartbreak will just have to wait.

Chapter 24

As I return to the camp, I see bodies on the ground. Nomads and Traitors alike. My eyes take in as much of the carnage as possible. Looking at as many faces as I can to make sure that none of the bloody, tangled mess of people is anyone that I care about. But none are faces that I recognise.

But there are still people fighting. Dozens. More. Theo and Grayson are in the centre of it all. Their lightning never stops. It covers both their hands as they send it to the other. They yell, throw punches and try desperately to knock the other one down with their magic. Grayson even starts using Theo's men as weapons. Hurling them at him like cannon balls. Yanking them suddenly from their own fights to be used as blunt weapons. They yell as they fly towards their target, but Theo merely swipes his hand and sends his men into the battle raging around him, uncaring of their fates. Theo's men try to protect him. As does Grayson's men for him. But each man knows precisely where each threat is coming from and the attackers don't stand a chance. They barely distract the witches, father and son, mortal enemies.

Grayson and Theo are both so lethal, so skilled, so fast, that neither of them gets close to winning.

I flood with relief when I see Gabriel. Alive and looking savage as he fends off attacker after attacker. Each time he strikes a man, he speaks. I can't hear the words, but the man who falls isn't the same man who rises. They turn on their own and fight beside Gabriel. Some take their own weapons, and use them on themselves, sliding blades across their own throats or putting pistols in their mouths. Most are more afraid of attacking him than Grayson. There's blood splattered all over his clothes but other than that, except for the injuries Theo inflicted, he seems unharmed. He keeps scanning the crowds. Looking frantically between each punch.

'ANY SIGN?' he bellows at Collins who's in the distance, snapping necks, punching men so hard they don't get up, and firing a gun into as many as possible. I see him looking sporadically around him, searching. 'CAN YOU SEE HER?' Gabriel yells. 'CAN YOU SEE ANY MORE FIRE?'

'NO!' Collins calls back before slamming his fist into another man's already bloody face and once more scanning the space around him. 'I CAN'T SEE HER ANYWHERE!' Collins has a large red patch on his shoulder. If I were to hazard a guess, I would say he's been shot.

Gabriel's face looks panicked for a brief moment as he once more looks rapidly around him.

Hendrix lets go of a man who he has hold of from behind and drops him lifeless to the floor at his feet. There's a thick pool of blood in his mouth from where he just tore the man's throat out. He too starts frantically looking around him. His black eyes land on me.

'THERE!' Hendrix shouts, pointing straight at me. 'SHE'S OVER THERE!'

Gabriel's head spins round so fast he stumbles. Our eyes meet across the battlefield, and he looks beyond relieved when he sees me. He smiles, but his smile soon fades and shifts to concern when he sees my tear-streaked face, red puffy eyes and clothes which are covered in mud. I don't smile back. I can't bring myself to feel happiness. Just relief. But as I linger at the edge of this battlefield, as I look around at the violence, at all the fighting and death, my eyes fall on the man responsible.

Theo.

He sees me.

He points and shouts over the din, 'GET THE HOOPER WITCH!'

Theo's men all turn to me. Their eyes hungry for the capture their master so desperately wants.

Grayson looks at me. He tells me to run. Gabriel starts making his way to me, but Theo's men block him at every opportunity. They almost bundle him, dragging him down into the mud like dead weights so he can't reach me.

Inside me is a whirlwind of emotions. None are good. Heartbreak. Grief. Anger. But the hatred I have inside me is unrivalled. It drowns out everything else. I look at Theo with tunnel vision. The battle may as well be a million miles away. The noise fades away. All I can hear is the blood rushing through my body and my deep, steady breathing. I hear myself give a low, guttural growl and for the first time in a long, long time, there isn't an ounce of fear. There's no dread. There's no panic. I'm completely focused. Completely in control as my hatred shifts from Toby, to the men who now threaten my friends and the man I love. I've lost so much already...no, I've had so much taken from me. And I refuse to see a single one of these men, my family, suffer any more injury at the hands of the people who have terrorised and mutilated me.

I am in no mood for mercy. No mood for forgiveness.

They're going to pay.

Theo's going to pay.

Grayson throws one hell of a punch towards Theo while he's distracted with me, but Theo catches his fist in his hand and slowly turns to face his eldest son.

Gabriel's under a heap of Traitors. Collins is there, pulling them off while defending himself from attack, and Hendrix is making his way towards me.

'Stay behind me, Little Witch,' he says gruffly when he reaches me. He turns to face the men charging towards us. 'I'll protect you.'

I rest my hand on his arm and guide the vampire aside.

'I don't need protection.'

I hold out both my hands palm side up and raise my arms. As I do, the air fills with yells as all the Traitors, all the ones I can see, leave the ground and shoot upwards into the night sky as if gravity has all but abandoned them. I leave Theo and Jensen where they stand so they can see exactly what I'm capable of.

As they fly through the trees, bits of branches and debris fall to the floor as they slam into the canopy above us and far beyond. Everyone who remains on the ground, my family and the Nomads, Theo and Jensen, stops still to watch as countless Traitors soar up into the night's sky.

They go higher and higher until they're out of sight and no one can hear their screams. It's suddenly eerily quiet.

'Holy fucking Christ,' Hendrix mumbles, craning his neck to see where at least thirty men have disappeared to.

The Nomads gather and look to the heavens too. But no one can see a thing. I've sent them far, far away.

For now.

All my attention is squarely on Theo. I don't look anywhere else. And he, in turn, looks only at me.

I have a confident, holding all the cards kind of look. He has an angry, loss of the upper hand expression. Which I love. Immensely.

The corner of my mouth hitches in a smile, not too dissimilar to Toby's come to think of it, and I give a small scoff of laughter at the look on his face.

He tears his eyes away from me and looks upwards, as does Jensen who's made his way to his master's side. And then together, they stare at me in stunned silence.

All their allies, their comrades, their friends...are gone, leaving them hugely outnumbered.

And I take a tremendous amount of joy in telling them so.

'Four witches, one vampire and at least two dozen Nomads...against you, and Jensen.' I take a sharp breath in through my teeth and shake my head cockily. 'I don't like your chances.'

I see Grayson in the distance quietly laughing to himself, looking between me and the sky with pride.

'Did you know... that if a man falls from high enough, they can make a hole in the ground twelve inches deep?'

'You're unhinged,' Theo calls back.

'Probably.'

'Where are my men?' Jensen shouts, storming forwards and pointing into the sky. He only takes a couple of steps before Theo takes hold of his shoulder to keep him away from me.

I look up and laugh, 'They'll be back. Soon.'

'Why are you fighting for them? Why would you take their side?' Jensen shouts back. 'I don't understand!'

'They didn't torture and mutilate me,' I reply simply. I ball up my fists, cutting off the magic that's keeping his men high above us. The sounds of their yelling start to come back into range as they plummet down.

'Save them!' Jensen orders.

They all fall through the trees screaming. Their arms and legs flailing.

'LILLY!' Jensen bellows looking up. 'PLEASE, SAVE THEM!'

I open my palms and stop them before they hit the ground, leaving them a meter or so in the air. The men reach out, desperate to touch the floor but I keep them there. Hovering in the air close to safety but also a million miles away from it.

'Put them down,' Jensen says, taking a cautious step forward. 'You don't want to do this. Listen to me,'

'Jensen, you can't reason with madness.'

'WE TRIED IT YOUR WAY! STAY OUT OF IT, THEODORE!'

He looks back to me, trying to keep calm. He wants to reason with me.

'We're sorry we hurt you. You have to see, we did it for the greater good.'

'The greater good?' I laugh. 'No. You did it because you could. You know what I can do?' I grin.

I send them all back into the air again as I laugh hysterically. '*Weeeee*.'

'What do you want?!' Jensen asks in desperation, watching as his men once more disappear high above our heads. 'Tell me what you want.'

'My fingers back.'

Theo's lightning crackles. I shake my head and tut three times, not hiding how fun this is.

'If you so much as sneeze, Theo, you'll be scraping bits of your men's bodies out of the dirt.'

'For god's sake,' Jensen hisses at Theo over his shoulder. 'Just stand down. Please, let me talk to her.' He turns back to me. 'How does this end?' he asks. 'What do you want?'

'I told you. I want my fingers back.' There's nothing he has that I want. I know I'll never have my fingers back. Like I'll never have my little girl back. All this pain inside is fuelling a cruelty and malice that I can't get under control. I don't want it under control because when I stop feeling it, I know what comes next. Pain. Suffering. Misery. Grief.

I close my palms once more, making sure he sees. The sound of his men crashing through the trees make them all look up. Grayson and the others, Jensen and Theo, all turn their attention to the sky. They all look at the canopy and wait.

'You don't have to do this!' Jensen tells me, holding up his hand to me in surrender, all the while looking up at the sky. 'They don't deserve to die!'

'I would rather kill Theo if I'm honest,' I say with a slight shrug. 'But since that would lead to my family and the man I love dying too, I'll settle for *your* men, and enjoying as you watch helplessly.'

'*They're* not your family. *Your* family would never want you to do this. Your mum would never want you to be a killer.'

'Far too late for that, I'm afraid.'

Theo's eyes narrow on me. I take a step forward, and so does he. His hatred of me and the power I hold over him right now is written all over his face. And I'm enjoying it very much.

'Lilly,' Theo warns. 'You will let the men go. You don't want to kill them. This isn't you.'

'You don't know me. Hell...I don't know me.'

'Lilly?' Gabriel calls over. I glance at him quickly as I keep my attention on Theo. He looks worried. 'We have the upper hand now. You can let them down.'

'Like hell!' Grayson snaps. 'Drop them to the floor. Kill them!'

'This isn't her, Grayson,' Gabriel argues as he points at me. 'She's going to Break. Look at her!'

They all stare at me. I must look a sight. I wonder if the misery I've felt tonight is visible. Is it in my eyes? Is it written on my face? I feel like it's covered me completely, but I won't let it inside. I can't. Not yet.

Maybe I am going to Break. Perhaps all this is too much and what I'm feeling now is me giving in. I look down at the ends of my hair, but they're still red. Not a hint of white. Yet.

'Lilly. Calm down,' Gabriel pleads.

I return my attention to Theo and seeing his hate-filled face refuels my anger.

'It all started with you, Theo,' I tell him. 'And it will end with you, on your knees.' I gesture to the floor. 'Beg.'

He scoffs at me and shakes his head.

'You want me to save your men? Get on your knees and beg me.'

'I will never beg you for anything,' he snarls. 'You won't kill them. You don't have it in you.'

'Just shut up, Theo!' Gabriel barks angrily. 'Stop goading her. I won't lose her because of you.' He looks back at me, hand outstretched. 'Come here, Beautiful. Calm down and let's go home. Me and you.'

When I don't move, his eyes start to go black.

There's a loud groan as a giant oak tree falls on its side, landing with a thud between Gabriel and I. He jumps back as I stare at him.

'You stay exactly where you are. And don't even think about using your magic on me,' I warn. 'Or the next tree won't miss.'

'Lilly, please...'

I look back to Theo and Jensen, ignoring the look of betrayal on Gabriel's face. He can't stop this. I won't let him.

'Where were we? Oh yes. Theo, you were about to beg for the lives of your men.'

Jensen looks between me, Theo and the sky. He knows, like I know, that Theo will never beg. Usually, I know that I could never kill all these people. That I could never willingly watch as others suffered. But that was before. Before I learnt that the man I loved beat me until I lost our unborn child after making me believe her death was my fault. Before I discovered the truth about what happened to Rose at Grayson and Theo's hands. Before I was cut. Before all this. Now, I'm not sure what I'm capable of.

I will not be controlled. I will not be manipulated. I will not be hurt anymore. My pain, my suffering, my loss... I choose not to feel it any more.

'Coming after me, my mum and the man I love, was the biggest mistake you will ever make.'

I lower my hands, letting them fall limply to my side and with this action, the magic I was using to keep them in the air, goes.

'Lilly...' Jensen steps forwards, his eyes upwards. 'Lilly? What are you doing? Raise your hands. Lilly...'

We hear them coming back. The slow screams of the plummeting men get louder and louder. Everyone's eyes are up. Everyone's except mine and Theo's. We watch each other with such contempt it contaminates the air.

'Lilly, please, don't let them fall,' Jensen pleads.

'Funny, I think I heard Gabriel beg Theo to stop cutting off bits of my body. But you didn't stop him. Did you?'

'I did! I stopped him when you passed out!'

'Very big of you.' I take a deep breath, letting it out in a long, slow breath. 'Let the fun begin.'

The first man hits the ground with a hollow thud, like a watermelon smashing into concrete.

'Humpty Dumpty sat on the wall,' I sing.

Thump.

'Humpty Dumpty had a great fall,'

Thump.

Theo's eyes widen in shock as he looks away from me and to the corpses lying in front of him. He really didn't think I would do it.

'All the king's horses,'

Thump.

'And all the king's men,'

Thump.

I step forwards and they both back away.

'Couldn't put Theo's army back together again.'

'STOP THIS!' Jensen bellows. 'STOP THIS NOW!'

The bodies fall like the beginning of rain on a tin roof.

Thump...thump...thump. Thump. THUMP!

I never look away from Theo, and he never looks away from me. I have a smile, but he looks murderous. The bodies fall one after the other. Each with a horror-filled cry that gets louder until it stops suddenly with a thump.

'You evil little bitch!' Theo spits.

'That's me alright. Let me show you how evil I can really be.'

The camp erupts in violent red flames as I slowly walk towards Theo. All I can hear are the flames roaring around us and the screams of the men as they plummet to earth. When I reach Theo, he does nothing. Just stands there looking ready to explode.

'Maybe this is what causes your vision,' I say in a sweet, calm voice. 'Maybe it's just me finally getting sick and tired of being the victim. Maybe it's me, fighting back.'

'Your hair's turning,' he says in a very forced calm. 'You need to calm down.'

'And you,' I reach out and grab his hand with mine. 'Need to scream for me.'

With my other hand, I grab two of his fingers. The same ones that are missing from my hand. And I snap them. Pressing them back so hard the crack of his bones echo around us. As he yells, my fire explodes over my hand and spreads onto his. He shrieks and tries to free himself, but I hold onto him with every last bit of strength I have left. Gabriel's compulsion is still working. Pushing my body beyond its limit, not giving in to the pain or the exhaustion.

With his free hand, Theo grabs my arm and releases his lightning into it but the pain my fire is causing has him on his knees in agony.

'There you are,' I say calmly. 'On your knees after all.'

The more he fights, the more intense my fire grows until all I can smell is his burning flesh, and all I can hear are his agonising yells as I turn his hand into a charred black mess.

'I doubt very much that this will heal,' I laugh, letting him go. He falls on his side, in too much pain to move. I kick him hard in the face. He lands on his back. I proceed to slam my foot into his face again and again until he's a bloody, broken mess that doesn't move. Behind him, I see Jensen running towards us. I spin round and come face to face with him. He stops. His eyes look between my face and my hand. He doesn't dare come any closer, but I would love to see him try.

Around us, the men continue to fall. My fire's everywhere. I can't see any of the Nomads. I can't see anyone but Jensen standing terrified in front of me and Theo unconscious at my feet. I step over him and walk towards Jensen. He tries to back away, but there's nowhere for him to go.

'This isn't you,' he says.

'You don't know me,' I remind him.

'I did. I knew you well, Lilly. Many years ago. I knew your mum. She wouldn't want this for you. Stop. Calm down. Please.'

'Who are you?' I ask. 'Is it you? Are you my f-'

I'm suddenly hit by a wave of energy and fly sideways through the air, slamming into the ground and skidding a good few feet before I stop and start to get back to my feet. When I look back, Jensen's pulling Theo up. He's awake, but barely. Enough to use his magic against me. They turn like cowards and start running into the woods. But they're both in my sights. They're all I can see. All I can think about. I want to tear them apart. I want to peel the skin from their bones. I want them to suffer.

As I go after them, I'm cut off as Gabriel runs between us and holds up his hands.

'Whoa! Stop, Beautiful.'

'Move,' I warn. When he stays put, I scream. 'MOVE!'

'No!' he says firmly. 'I need you to calm down. Now, Lilly!' He's looking at my hair.

'Move aside,' I order, but he shakes his head. 'Move aside, or I will move you myself.'

'I'm not letting you go. Your Break is taking over! Your hair's turning white. I've only just got you back. I'm not losing you now.' He takes a step towards me. 'Look at me. Let me see those beautiful green eyes of yours. Not these empty violet ones. Please...come back to me.'

'They can't get away!' I tell him. I've started to shake. 'THEY HAVE TO PAY!'

'NOT IF IT MEANS LOSING YOU!'

I stop looking past him and instead look at him. His smile, his worried eyes, his bloody face. He takes another step closer, then another. Each bit of space removed between us takes away the anger and the hatred until he's close enough to touch.

His hand reaches out and strokes my cheek.

'I love you,' he says. 'Look at me.' His gentle hand rests on my waist. 'I love you.'

Grayson's in the distance calling our names, but neither of us reacts. Our eyes remain locked. Gabriel's smile stays firmly in place.

'I have to kill-'

'I love you.' He rests his hand over my heart, leans down to me as his eyes begin to blacken and rests his mouth close to mine. 'You're safe now, Lilly. Stop. It's over.'

My body suddenly feels unbearably heavy. The forced adrenaline leaves me beyond exhausted. His compulsion is gone. I couldn't chase after Theo even if I wanted to. Both my arms wrap around his neck as my legs become too weak to hold myself up. He holds me close, keeping me on my feet and breathes a sigh of relief as he runs his fingers through my hair. It stops turning ashen and returns slowly to red. I feel myself once more. And my god, the pain. It's almost too much to bear. I cling to him desperately.

'Don't let go,' I whisper.

'Never.'

I pull him in. Our lips meet, and we hold onto each other desperately. My hand runs through his hair. I'm flush against his body as we stand amongst the flames.

His eyes flick open as our kiss slows. He's smiling, but then he looks over my shoulder and frowns. His eyes widen in horror.

'NO!' he yells before hurling me to the floor.

A loud bang echoes through the woods as I fall, and I watch as something hits him in the chest. He stays on his feet but staggers.

What the hell just happened?

His fingers rest on his shirt, and when he pulls them away, there's blood. A pool of it spills out of him and down his shirt faster and faster. I would scream if I could.

He's been shot!

He looks down at me and falls to his knees. I catch him in my arms and hold him close. The patch of red on his shirt gets bigger. I clamp my hand over the wound and scream for help. I scream so loudly I think the whole woods can hear me, maybe the entire world! Gabriel's hand rests over mine as I try to stop the bleeding.

'Look at me,' he says weakly. I pull him even closer as I sob. This can't happen. I can't lose him, not now. Not ever! 'I love you, Lilly. So much. I have since I first saw you.' His eyes start to close. With each blink, they stay closed for longer.

'I love you too!' I cry, pulling him closer and closer to my body. 'Don't you dare leave me.' He reaches up and strokes my face.

'You be strong. You stay you.'

'Don't say goodbye. Don't you dare. You promised. Nothing can separate us. Nothing!'

His hand falls limp by his side.

His eyes close.

Grayson skids to a stop on his knees beside us and pushes his hand down firmly over mine, trying to stop the bleeding. We share a look of utter panic.

'FIND THE SHOOTER! NOW!' Grayson orders the Nomads who all turn and run in the direction of the bullet. 'He'll be okay. He'll be okay.' But I hear the fear in his voice. I've never heard fear in his voice, but it's there now.

Collins kneels beside me and all I see is more fear. I can't take it. Looking at two of the strongest, bravest people I know and seeing them so terrified as they watch the increasingly pale Gabriel. Instead, I look down at the man who lies bleeding in my arms.

'Stay with me, Beautiful,' I tell him, leaning down and kissing his forehead. I kiss his cheeks, his lips, all of his face. His chest is still rising and falling. He's still breathing, but he's losing so much blood!

'Get her out of here!' Grayson orders, watching my actions with hatred. 'Before that shooter comes back! Get her away, Collins!' Grayson reaches over and actually pushes me off. I land on my backside, but in an instant, I have Gabriel back in reach.

'I'M NOT LEAVING HIM!' I scream in his face, shoving *him* away. 'Get your hands off him.'

Nomads have started surrounding us. I don't care. I'll tear them apart if they try to touch me.

'Collins!' Grayson barks. 'You get her away from my brother now.'

'Collins... if you touch me, you'll regret it,' I warn, not taking my eyes of Grayson. Collins stays put. A wise decision.

'I know what you did. I know everything. Rose. Ava. All of it.'

'Gabriel lied-'

'I saw it. I looked into his memories and saw it all. And I'm warning you now, Grayson Kendryk, you try to separate us, you try to hurt us or you so much as think about threatening any of us, Collins and Amara included, I'll do to your men what I just did to Theo's. I'm not bound and I'm not fucking about.'

'Don't you dare threaten me.'

'I'm not threatening. I'm promising.' I look at Collins as I hold Gabriel close. 'He forced Gabriel to sleep with Ava by threatening to do to me what he did to Rose. Did you know that?'

'Err, Rose? Who's Rose?' Collins asks, looking between us blankly. 'Rose as in Rebecca's daughter? What did you do to

Rebecca's daughter?' His blankness is replaced instead with suspicion and caution as he watches Grayson. He has no idea about any of it!

'Enough, Lilly. My brother's been shot. He needs medical care.' He gestures for three of his men to join us. 'Get him into a car and back to the house now. Call the doctor and make sure she's there when you arrive.' They nod and watch me as they take cautious steps forwards.

'I'm going with him.'

'Like hell.'

'I wasn't asking your permission, Grayson.'

'Stop acting like a child. The man you claim to love is bleeding to death. Unless we get him to a doctor, he could die. We will all die! So you will let him go, let the men take him and stop acting like a selfish fool!'

He's right. Gabriel's injured. He has to be treated.

I look at Collins. 'Will you stay with him? Promise me you won't leave his side. No matter what.'

'But...what about you?' he asks quietly, glancing at Grayson.

'I can look after myself. Gabriel needs you now. Just, keep him safe.'

Collins nods and vows that he will. So, reluctantly and with a final kiss, I let Gabriel go and watch as they carry him away. Collins firmly by his side. But before he leaves, he looks at Grayson.

'I'm letting you know this right now, Grayson. If you hurt her, or Gabriel, you'll be sorry. You hear me?'

'Go,' he growls at him angrily. They leave and he turns his attention to me. 'Jesus! Lilly, you're missing two fingers!'

'I want to go with Gabriel.'

'No. You're staying with me.'

'I want-'

'Someone just tried to shoot you! He pushed you out of the way just in time and took the bullet himself! You are staying with me! What the hell were you thinking coming here?'

Now I know what Gabriel was looking at so strangely over my shoulder.

'Theo took Gabriel and was hurting him. He threatened to kill him. I had no choice. I had to come.'

'There's always a choice! The problem is you don't think clearly when it comes to him! I can't risk losing either of you. Not now we're this close to bringing down the Veil. Damn it...You could have died!' He grabs my chin and looks at the cut still stinging from Theo's backhand. He's shaking with anger. Very unlike him. He lets me go and points a finger straight at me, his voice low and full of warning. 'You will listen to me and obey me. You and Gabriel will not be together. Not until the Veil is down at any rate.'

'You can't do that,' I tell him adamantly.

'You will be kept close to the Nomads and to me. Where I can keep you safe. From yourself as well as the Traitors and Hunters. Do you hear me?'

'No!' I shake my head.

'Gabriel will be taken to a secure location for treatment. When he is recovered, he will be leaving England. That's the end of it. Gabriel is leaving, and there is nothing you can say or do to change my mind. I need you to focus on the spell, and I need him to stay alive. Both will be considerably easier if you're not running around sacrificing your lives for each other. When the Veil's down, you can do whatever you want.' He turns and starts walking away. He doesn't get far. He stops when a wall of red fire springs up in front of him. I make it curl into a circle so he has nowhere to go.

'We're not done here, Grayson,' I say firmly.

Slowly, he turns. If he was angry before...now he's livid.

'This has nothing to do with the Veil. Or his safety. This is about your jealousy. You want me, and it kills you that I don't want you. Sending him away won't change how I feel about him, but it will make me hate you. Even more than I already do.'

He glances at my wrist. 'Where's your binding spell?' he asks.

'Destroyed,' I answer simply. 'Don't pretend that you took me in out of the kindness of your heart. You need me. So let me make my position, and your position, clear. I no longer have a binding spell and I never will again. I'm too strong for you to try and force one on me. I could level this place and hurl your men into the sky like I did with Theo's. I could walk away from the spell and refuse to do it.' He opens his tight-lined mouth to hurl back his own threats. 'But...' I interrupt before he can say a word. 'I want to bring the Veil down. That goal we share. I want all of our kind to be free. But it's like this. I'm in love with him. Not with you. And he loves me. Not Ava.' His mouth twitches when I say these words. 'If you send him away, I'll go too. And you'll have to find another way to break down the Veil because I will refuse. You can hunt us down. You can threaten us. But if you do, I will destroy everything you have built.' I stand and wait. 'Either let us be together and get what you want, or try and keep us apart and lose everything. Your move.'

Grayson takes a second to organise his thoughts. He seems to get them in line as he looks at me through my ring of fire keeping him penned in.

'Gabriel will leave. But, he can come back to us when I have the Journal. When I have it, he can come back. That way, it eliminates the amount of time you two can be used to manipulate each other and get us all killed. Now put this fire out.'

'I know where the Journal is,' I tell him, folding my arms and narrowing my sights on him.

'Excuse me?'

'Toby was here. He still is. I know where the journal is, and where he is.'

'That's a bit of a coincidence,' he mutters.

'It's the truth. I can get you the journal tonight. I can start on the Veil tomorrow. In exchange for your word that Gabriel can stay at the house and you give us your blessing. If you don't agree, I'll never tell you where the Journal or Toby are, and I won't help you do your spell. If you try and screw me over once you have the journal...well, you've seen what I can do.'

He nods. 'You have a deal. Give me the journal and Gabriel will be back at the house tonight. You'll have my blessing, as long as you're careful and don't end up in a mess like this again.'

I could fall to the floor in relief.

'I have no intention of getting in a mess like this again. Believe me.' I walk to Grayson and extinguish the small circle around him. I stretch out my hand, and he shakes it, sealing our arrangement.

'If you betray me, I'll make you sorry,' he says.

'Right back at ya,' I reply just as menacingly.

He tightens his grip on my hand and starts pulling me.

'Where are we going?' I ask.

'You tell me. You'll take me to the journal now. I want you by my side until I have it in my possession.'

'And then you take me to Gabriel?'

'Yes.'

As we walk to his car, I notice there's no sign of any of the bodies that fell into my new red fire. They've been consumed by the sheer intensity of the heat.

I almost lost control completely tonight. My hair started to change, but it didn't change fully. I'm still here. Gabriel tethered me down, brought me back. We're finally going to be together. We'll get the journal. Do the spell, and then my life can really begin in a world where we don't have to hide anymore.

Chapter 25

As we drive, Grayson says very little. He listened intently as I told him about Theo's plan to wipe out the Nomads as well as his theory about Grayson starting a war. And since then he's been very quiet. The rain's started to really come down and the window wipers are going like crazy.

It's just us.

Grayson either sent the rest of his men back home to look after Gabriel, search the woods for the mysterious shooter, or make sure Toby's secure while we fetch the journal.

Toby.

I still can't even start to process the truth about him. About what he did. Every time I think about it, I want to explode in a fiery rage and in my case, that's a very real probability. Either that, or turn this car around and go to the house to rip his head off.

I shake my head, ridding myself of the harrowing images I saw in his mind. Occasionally, I notice my hand covering my belly as if still protecting the life that was once there. I lower my hand and rest it idly on my lap, telling myself over and over not to think about it. Not yet.

What if Toby tells them everything he knows about me? I can barely live with the horrors of my past, let alone knowing that everyone else knows about them too. I can't face Toby hurling the memory of my lost child at me like a weapon. I need to tell Gabriel. It will be better coming from me. When he's better, I'll lay it all out. Like he did for me tonight.

It's the right thing to do.

I've started to shake. I'm covered in blood. Mine and Gabriel's. I can't get the image of him falling to the floor out of my head. The way his blood spread across his shirt so fast. I think that will haunt me forever. My hand's bleeding through the bandage which is now just a red mess and it hurts like hell. I take a deep breath, hoping to stop my increasingly violent shakes.

'Are you cold?' Grayson asks. He's watching me anxiously as he drives.

'I think I'm in shock,' I admit, looking down at my mutilated hand and trying to rid myself of everything I learnt tonight. My head's a mess. I'm a mess.

He turns up the heating and hands me a flask he had in the driver's side door.

'Drink this and try to calm yourself. It's sweet tea. We'll fetch the journal and get you back home as soon as possible. A nice hot bath and some seriously strong painkillers will do you a world of good.' He looks down at my hand. 'I'm so sorry that Theo did this to you. We looked for the fingers but couldn't find them. I thought we could try and reattach them for you, but sadly the tent you were in was destroyed. The fingers too I imagine.'

'It doesn't matter,' I mutter before I sip the tea. Truth is I'm not ready to face everything right now. My hand, Toby, Grayson. 'I like the sound of a bath and some painkillers though. A stiff drink would be most welcome too.'

He gives a small laugh. 'I bet. Drink the tea for now. It will help with the shock,' he says before returning his full attention to the road. I look out the window sipping it and see a streak of lightning in the distance. There's one hell of a storm going on outside. I wonder if it's raining at the house. I wonder if Gabriel's awake. I hope he's okay. I know he's alive or Grayson would be dead too, if what I was told about the spell linking them all is true. I'm just so desperate to get back to him and see how he is.

'I'm sorry,' he says.

'Sorry?'

'For threatening to send Gabriel away as I did. I just...' he continues looking out at the road.

'What?'

'I was scared. I've never been scared before but knowing you were in danger and seeing you so hurt...I was terrified. Then you two kissed and jealousy got the better of me. The truth is, your safety and your happiness *must* come first. I know that. Not only because of how important you are, but because of how much I care about you. In the heat of the moment, I forgot that. But please believe me when I say that I am sorry and from now I'll be nothing but supportive of your relationship. And, I'm sorry about Ava. And for what happened with Rose. It was a difficult decision-'

'I really don't want to talk about any of that. I won't pretend to understand what you did, and I certainly can't forgive it. Not Rose and not what you forced Gabriel to do with Ava.' I look him right in the eye. 'I don't trust you. You put on this front. That you're a good man, just misunderstood. But you're not. You're selfish, manipulative and frankly despicable. This is a business arrangement, that's all. If I didn't need your help with the Veil and stopping Theo getting his hands on the journal, Gabriel and I would be gone. So let's not pretend to be friends. Don't try and be sweet. I know what you did to Rose. I saw it all through Gabriel's eyes. Thanks to my new power. So just drive.'

'I may do things that others see as cruel or unpleasant, but I only do what I must to keep us all safe and to keep us all alive. I have to make the hard decisions.'

His attempts at sounding reasonable are pathetic.

'If a man said to me, have sex with me, or I'll hurt the man you love...what would you call that?' I ask him. He keeps glancing between me and the weather-beaten road. 'Because I would call that rape. Forcing sex...is rape. You raped Rose.'

'I never-'

'You aided in Ava raping Gabriel.'

'That's ridiculous!'

'What, a woman can't rape a man?' I scoff. 'I know what you are. And even if I hadn't met Gabriel, I would never have fallen for a man like you. And if you attempt to start a war...I'll stop you.' My voice is as cold as ice. My stare as resolved as could be. 'I'll destroy everything you've built. I'll tear it all down. You hear me?'

He says nothing before turning back to the road.

'I have no intention of starting a war. What I told you about our plans for our people once the Veil is down, is the truth. I swear it,' he tells me. 'I would never lie about that. You can ask any of the Nomads. No one wants to go through that hell again. The war killed my mother. I won't lose anyone else.' And I believe him. There's no hint of a lie in his voice and it's also what Gabriel said too. 'And I didn't rape Rose.'

'I'm not talking about it with you anymore.

'I didn't-'

'I said stop talking.'

An hour of silence and we turn off the country lane to drive down a long and very bumpy private road. The car comes to a stop. He turns off the engine and looks at me.

'You sure it's here?' he asks.

'If this is the right place, then yes. It's here.'

'How can you be sure?'

'I saw it. In Toby's head. I know that he's hidden it here.'

Grayson can choose to believe me or not. I'm not going to argue or explain how I can be this sure. I know. I felt it like an absolute truth. There's no doubt in my mind that according to Toby, the journal is hidden here.

The Miller's barn.

Straight ahead of us, illuminated by the full beams of Grayson's headlights, is an enormous piece of neglected farmland with an old rust bucket tractor and the shell of a car straight ahead of us. Beside those is an old, weather-beaten barn with double doors and red peeling paint. Half of it's covered in overgrowth, but there's a clear path leading from the road where he's parked the car, to the doors of the barn.

'Does it look familiar?'

'Not particularly.'

'Come on. Let's get this over with.' He opens the glove box, pulls out a torch and goes out into the rain, closing the door behind him.

I get out and follow.

We walk quickly, almost running towards the barn. The rain's relentless!

By the time we reach the doors we're both soaked. They groan and creak as they open, making the whole barn shake. Once in, Grayson slides the door closed and we brush-off the rain to minimal effect. Together we turn.

He glides the light from the torch over the inside of this rundown, old building.

The air feels colder in here, unnatural almost. I look around the room I've seen a hundred times in my dreams. It's a big old structure with wooden planks for walls that don't quite fit together and a high roof with more than a few leaks. It's all being held up by makeshift beams.

There are a couple of rusted through pieces of farming machinery with vicious spikes and rotor blades. In the far corner are a few old tires piled high next to some empty black barrels and a pile of dry, rotted straw. The place stinks of damp, dust, oil and stagnant water. The smell gets stuck in the back of my throat.

The grey concrete floor is filthy with dirt and grime. It's stained by something too, creating dark brown and black patches all around us. It takes a moment to register what it actually is.

'That's not paint, is it?' I whisper, looking at the floor.

'No. The floor's stained with blood,' Grayson tells me, looking at the large stain under our feet.

'The men I killed...'

I see a metal hoop bolted to the floor in the very centre of the room with a chain attached to it. This is where I was when Toby attacked me, while the mysterious girl held down my ankles.

'Some of this is your blood,' he tells me, showing me the dark patches on the steel and snapping me back to reality. 'Hendrix could smell it when he came here a few days ago.'

I back up knowing why my blood would be here and wanting to be as far away from it all as possible. I can't face this right now. I just can't, so I turn away and scour the rest of the building.

'Malcolm was shot. Like Gabriel was shot tonight,' I ponder aloud. 'Do you think that was a coincidence? Maybe it was the same person? Maybe that bullet Malcolm took was meant for me, just like tonight's bullet was.'

'The bullet that hit Malcolm was meant for Malcolm. It was very precise. They would have had you in their sights as well, so no, that one wasn't meant for you. But tonight's bullet was.' Grayson continues looking around the barn. 'When Billy found Malcolm here, he said that he was on the phone. That he kept saying that it wasn't here. That he couldn't find it. I bet he was looking for the journal. Hopefully, he was looking in the wrong place, or we're back to square one.'

My eyes become fixated on the metal hoop hammered into the ground once more. I can hear my pleas for mercy ringing in my ears and see the look of betrayal and fear in my eyes. After a moment Grayson clears his throat, and I crash back to reality. He's watching me with anxious eyes.

'Everything okay?' he asks. 'You look like you've seen a ghost.'

'I'm fine. I just want to get out of here. The place gives me the creeps.' I turn away from the blood-stained floor, keen not to think about any of what I saw in Toby's mind. 'Well, let's see if he was looking in the wrong place.'

I make my way over to an old tractor tucked away in the corner with two large rear rubber tyres that are almost as tall as me. The engine makes up the majority of the machine, and I'm sure it's more rust than metal. Between the two tyres is a metal seat. I climb on top and start to slide off the metal case that covers the engine, careful not to use my injured hand. Grayson keeps the light on me so I can see what I'm doing.

'Do you need a hand?' he asks.

'No,' I groan as I struggle with the weight of it.

Screw this. I use my magic and send the seat hurtling through the air. It falls to the floor with a loud bang. I look down but can't see much.

'Here.' He reaches up and hands me the flashlight.

I use it to look inside the machine.

There are metal pipes and various gears. But no journal. I slide my hand down and feel. Maybe it's underneath. I panic when there's nothing there but the engine. I reach further down but still feel nothing but metal.

'I saw it! In his head, I know the journal's here. I saw him hide it in this exact spot.' My sudden vigorous rummaging makes Grayson nervous.

'If it's not in there, if this was a trick...' his voice is tainted with anger. My fingers feel the spine of the book, and I slump with relief. Leaning down even further so my entire arm is lost beneath the engine, I grab hold and pull it out.

'Got it,' I sigh thankfully.

The thick book with thin pages, similar to that of a bible, looks just as I remember it. Except the hard, red leather cover is a little dirtier than it was with some oil stains and dust. The faint silver seven-pointed star is still embossed on the cover. Seeing it is a weight lifted off my shoulders.

We have the journal. Toby's secured. I've finally managed to learn to control my magic. Gabriel's at home safe and sound, and I'll be with him soon. Everything is finally falling into place.

'How did you not find this? You've been here a few times. Didn't you search it from top to bottom?'

'Sorry. We didn't think to dismantle the tractor. Can you give it to me please?' Grayson's looking up at the book hungrily. He stretches his hand out expectantly.

'I'm going to keep hold of it. I'm sure you understand,' I tell him, holding it close to my chest. 'You can't read it anyway.' I jump down and walk past his angry stare. But what's he going to do? Nothing. That's what.

'Shall we go?' I ask, striding towards the door and placing the flashlight in his expectant hand instead of the journal.

As I walk, I notice that he's not beside me. Or behind me. I look over my shoulder and see him still standing where I left him with a far from genuine smile.

'You alright?' My eyes scan the room for any indication of why he's just standing there looking at me. 'Grayson? What's...'

In an instant, the room spins wildly around me, and I stumble a little. My arms fan out in a vague effort to return my sense of equilibrium. I stop myself from falling as the room settles a little and I try to shake off the immense dizziness.

'Are you okay?' he asks, his tone cold and disinterested.

I look over at him as he blurs in and out of focus. He puts the flashlight on the floor before slowly, purposefully walking towards me. Each one of his footsteps echoes loudly around me and with each dull thud, I flinch.

I back up. Something is wrong. Very, very wrong. My feet are clumsy. My skin suddenly clammy. My heart is going a mile a minute and I can't organise my thoughts. There are two of him. Three. I have no idea. I can't see properly.

'Stay...stay the fuck...what have...'

I create my fire on my hands and as he gets closer, I send it to him. But he dodges my clumsy efforts easily and laughs as I stumble and stammer. He continues descending on me, and I, in turn, continue drunkenly backing away until my back hits one of the makeshift posts holding up the roof. The whole barn groans as I make the slightest contact with the shoddy support beam. I can't focus on more than one thing. Watching him, keeping myself on my feet, staying awake. In a second he's in front of me, looking down at me with a cold stare.

'It's working a bit quicker than I expected,' he boasts.

'What have you done to me?' I slur. I reach out to push him away but the room takes another wild spin, and it's too much. I can't tell up from down. My legs buckle. I fall. My flames disappear as Grayson catches me in his arms. He holds me close to his chest, one arm around my waist and the other in my hair holding the back of my lolling head.

I try to push him off. I try to scream. But I can't. He pulls my hair so I have to look up at him.

'It's okay,' he says with complete and utter calm. 'You'll be okay.' He lowers himself to his knees and takes me with him. I'm pulled into his lap where he starts gently rocking me back and forwards. 'I slipped a little something in your tea. It will wear off soon,' he shushes me as if comforting me. Tears sting my eyes as I lie helpless in his arms. He's drugged me. He's tricked me. And I'm all on my own. No one even knows where we are.

I'm slipping. Falling into oblivion. My body's already gone there, and now all I can do is wait for my mind to follow. I try to get him away from me. I call for my magic, but it doesn't come. It's faded too. My muscles. My voice. My magic. It's gone. They've left me all alone with him.

With every blink, my eyes stay closed longer. My arms fall limp at my side. All I can do is lie in his arms. He brushes the hair from my face, leans down and lands a delicate kiss on my lips.

'You should have listened when I warned you not to threaten me. Because, my dear girl, I always come out on top.'

His soft laugh fades away as I lose all ability to stay awake.

I can smell smoke. I feel a warmth on my face, but the rest of me is shivering. Slowly I blink open my eyes, terrified of what I'll see when I open them. Nothing good, I'm sure.

I'm lying on the floor of the barn. There's a fire in a neat circle in front of me, lighting the room. The sound of rain pelting the barn roof is almost deafening.

But I can still hear the crackling of the twigs as they burn.

My hands are tied together above my head. There's a leather belt wrapped around my wrists and they're tethered to the same metal hook that I saw in Toby's mind. A wash of horror covers me inside and out as not only the memory of what happened here last time hits me, but also why Grayson would want me tied down this way.

I pull at the restraints, but it's no good. I'm stuck.

Everything's spinning. My vision's blighted by black spots that fade in and out of sight. As I try desperately to focus, I see Grayson standing at the opposite side of the fire. He's looking into the flames, lost in thought, before his eyes redirect straight to me. He has a severe face, full of concentration.

'You're awake already?' he says poking at the fire with a long stick. 'You have the constitution of an ox, clearly. I gave you enough to knock you out for hours.'

'What are you doing?' I ask nervously. He doesn't answer. He keeps his focus on the stick in the fire. I try once more to get free, despite feeling like I have a bottle of whiskey and half a box of sleeping pills in my bloodstream.

'You drugged me?' I ask in a panic. He says nothing. 'Untie me!' I demand as firmly as I can without vomiting.

Again, he says nothing but keeps his focus on the fire. He won't talk, but I don't need to be told that I'm in serious trouble. I keep trying to get free. Pulling and pulling against the restraints.

I look at my hands bound together above my head and what I see has me convinced I'm hallucinating. I blink until I get my vision a little clearer.

That's not possible. It can't be.

On my right wrist, I see a cuff. A brown leather cuff with Celtic engravings carved into the flesh, and in a deep red, almost black thread, the word Nexasanguinum is sewn through the very centre.

It's my old cuff. The one given to me by Gabriel to act as my binding spell after I set fire to my room when I first arrived.

The one that was stolen by the man who shot me with adrenaline and pushed me towards the house, hoping I would explode and take out Grayson.

How? How is it here?

He sees me looking at the cuff with extreme confusion and then at him, all the while everything is still swirling and fading in and out of focus.

I roll over and get clumsily to my knees as the fog slowly starts to clear. If I can't slip out of the belt then maybe I can get the binding spell off.

I start going at it with my teeth. It's held together by poppers. I can get it off. I undo the poppers, but the bastard must have sewn the damn thing shut while I was sleeping. I bite at it like a rabid animal, determined to get free and hurl my magic at him.

He sees me struggling.

'Stop that!' he barks, pointing at me as I continue. 'I said stop it, Lilly. Or I'll come over there and pull your teeth out!'

'Fuck you!' I garble, mouth full of leather.

Why can't I get this bloody thing off?!

He heads towards me when I keep trying. I don't take my eyes off him as he charges over, but there's nothing in heaven or hell that will stop me from trying to get free. I'm still frantically pulling at the thing with my teeth as he reaches me. He grabs my hair and yanks my head back hard, so I let go.

'GET OFF ME!' I scream. 'GET THE FUCK OFF ME!'

'No,' he says simply. 'And what have I told you about that mouth, hmm? A delicate little thing like you shouldn't have a filthy mouth.' He slams me down onto the floor on my back before he slides my body away from the hoop my hands are attached to so my arms are stretched out as long as they can go above my head.

I'm reliving the memory I saw in Toby's head. Tied down and stretched out. Helpless. But the only life in danger right now is mine.

He sits on me with a leg either side of my waist. The sleeves of his white shirt are rolled up to his elbows, and there's blood from the battle splattered all over him, drying and flaking. All I can do is kick my legs out as violently as I can and scream as loud as my voice will allow but I'm not strong enough to get him off and there's no one around for miles to hear me.

'Shhh,' He looks down at me with a self-assured grin. 'Calm down, Miss Hooper. Trust me, you're not going anywhere.'

Like hell! When I let loose one hell of a blood-curdling screech he jumps, his features contort in hateful anger at my complete disobedience. He slams a hand over my mouth and pinches my nose shut.

'I said, calm down.'

I'm kicking and thrashing. Thrusting my hips up to buck him off me, but all he does is raise his eyebrows and wait.

'Stop struggling, and I'll let you breathe.' He's not messing about. He's cutting off all my oxygen. 'I mean it. Thirty seconds roughly until you're unconscious. So lie still willingly, or I'll just keep squeezing.'

I stop kicking and force my legs to go limp. I fight my instincts and hope he keeps his word and lets me go. As soon as I'm still, he releases his grip, allowing me to gasp in the air greedily.

'Good girl,' he says softly, stroking the hair from my face.

'The cuff,' I pant. 'How have you got my old cuff?'

'You're clever. Think about it,' he says with a small, condescending laugh.

It was stolen. Taken by a man who broke into the grounds. As I look up into his eyes, which are thoroughly amused, he watches me racking my brain trying to understand.

'The man who attacked me. You got it from him.'

'Obviously,' he drawls.

'You caught him? You...I don't understand.' I look around the barn and pray for something, anything that will help me get out of here. Nothing. I'm on my own. Completely. 'Tell me, Grayson. Explain!'

'I saw your bag.'

'Bag? What bag?'

'After Malcolm's head exploded, you said you wanted to leave. That night, while you were in the shower, I saw the bag you packed. I knew you wanted to leave, but you see...I couldn't let that happen. I needed you to stay right by my side. But...' he presses his finger to his lips as if thinking before pointing briefly to his head. 'I needed you to *want* to stay. You're a stubborn little thing. You wanted to be all stoic and self-righteous, putting the safety of others before yourself. You were right, your presence in that house puts us all in danger. So I had to make sure that you wanted, *needed* to stay.' He taps the side of my head. 'I needed you to think that the only way to keep everyone safe was for you to stay.'

'What did you do?' I ask, even though I'm damn sure I don't want to know the answer.

'You didn't think that it was ridiculously easy? Your escape? Sneaking past my men unseen? Making it to the outer edge of my estate unchallenged?' He leans down and laughs. 'You went exactly where I wanted you to go. Exactly where John was waiting for you.' He sits again, his thighs pressing hard against my hips. His cruel eyes never leave sight of my face, which is probably looking horrified as the reality starts to set in.

'John? The guy who grabbed me in the kitchen?'

'The guy I ordered to grab you. You see, not much happens in that house unless I want it to. I needed you to see how much of a risk you are to others without my protection. And what better way, than to make you into a weapon that could destroy the man I knew you were falling for. And not to mention Amara, of course. John did everything perfectly. He made you lose control so I could get the cuff on you. Then he showed you exactly what would happen if you did leave me. I needed you to understand how dangerous you really are. And then you begged me to let you stay. Only then would I get what I needed. Something to make sure you could never, ever run from me again.' He reaches to the collar of his shirt and pulls out the deep red Bloodstone that he has hanging from a chain.

'The Bloodstone?' I look at it dangling there. 'You think I'll willingly keep a binding spell on? You're delusional. You can't keep me chained up. Gabriel won't let you. Neither will Collins. You'll lose your entire Coven and I'll refuse-'

'Yeah, yeah. You'll refuse to do the spell. I know. I know. But I have no intention of keeping you tied up. I do, however, plan on keeping you on a very tight leash.'

'Oh yeah?' I snarl, getting more and more murderous thoughts with every one of his words. 'And how do you plan on doing that when I can kill you where you stand.'

'With your magic, you can kill me where I stand. Without it...' he laughs a low, cruel laugh. He has something planned. Something terrible.

He pulls out a knife from his pocket. I eye it nervously as he holds it in front of me.

'Are you going to kill me?' I laugh, knowing full well he won't. He needs me.

'I could never kill you. That's not what this is for,' he says, looking at the knife lovingly. 'This is for your new binding spell.'

'My what?'

'I watched you almost destroy my house and toss my men around like they were nothing but ants in your way. You took control of Hendrix. He almost killed me before I knocked him out, and then there was your rage-filled mass execution of the Traitor army. Well, it's safe to say I can't have you running around with all that power. Power that you have barely scratched the surface of. You may use it against me. I mean, that new fire of yours!' he whistles through his teeth. 'That's something special. You're already more powerful than me, and you still have three more realms of power to manifest. You could leave me and my coven a smouldering wreck if you wish.'

'I *want* to bring down the Veil!' I shout. 'I *want* the Nomads to be free! I do. That's the truth. But if you don't untie me right now, I will fucking destroy everything.'

But he shakes his head, ignoring my threats completely.

'Maybe that's what you want *now*. To bring the Veil down. To be part of the new world. But what if you decide you want to rule the Coven? What if you change your mind? The truth is I need to keep you close. I need to keep you where I can see you or at least where I can find you. The cuff worked temporarily, but I need something more...permanent.'

'Permanent?' I look at the knife in his hand. 'Grayson... what are you going to do?'

'What I should have done the night I met you.'

He takes the knife and uses it to slice the sleeve of my shirt off before holding out his hand and sliding the blade across his palm. I wince as he cuts deep. Blood pools thick and fast in his cupped hand until it spills out between his fingers and drips onto my exposed forearm.

'What the hell are you doing?!' I gasp. It's repulsive. Wrong.

'Don't move,' he orders as he rests his bloody palm down by my wrist. Slowly he smears a thick streak of his blood along my forearm. It's enough to make me gag.

He drops the knife and looks at the fire. He reaches out his hand and the long stick he was poking into the flames a few moments ago soars through the air, landing in his outstretched hand.

It's not a stick at all, but a metal rod. The end of the rod is glowing red hot and stretches out in a series of long curves. The heat of the metal compared to the chill in the air has it steaming and groaning as the metal expands.

He brings it closer for a visual inspection. I see it's not just curving. It's letters.

It's a word.

Nexasanguinum.

It's the binding spell.

'What the hell are you doing!' I demand, not taking my eyes off the glowing metal. He continues looking at the rod and nods approvingly.

'Yes, this will do nicely.' He looks down at me. 'I had this made when I met you,' he says. 'Just in case you misbehaved. I never wanted to brand you, Lilly, but you really have left me with no choice.'

'Brand!' I start to struggle again. 'Don't you dare. DON'T YOU FUCKING DARE!!!'

I'm pulling at the restraints around my wrist as if my life depends on it. It does. If he brands me, I'll be helpless forever. I'll lose my magic.

I'm screaming. Pulling so hard I think my wrists will break, but I don't care. I kick out my legs. I try and buck him off, but all of my efforts are less than pointless. He merely watches and waits.

'Are you done?' he asks as my efforts start to slow. I'm not getting free. Not with force. Reasoning is all I have left.

'Don't,' I plead. 'Don't do this, Grayson. If you brand me, I won't have my magic. I can't do your spell without my magic.'

'Don't worry about that. I've used my blood.' He gestures to the thick streak of red on my arm. 'The brand and my blood will link us, just as the blood in the Bloodstone has. Hence why I was so very keen to make this with you. You see, the Bloodstone gives me control of when and if you have access to your magic. It works with the binding spell. A binding spell like this,' he uses the red-hot metal to gesture to the cuff on my wrist. 'Or a binding spell seared into your flesh with this.' He hovers the rod an inch from my eyes. The heat makes them water. 'Unless...'

'Unless what?'

Again, his eyes drift down to my chest and a slimy smirk appears. With his free hand, he runs his thumb across my lower lip.

'Would you reconsider furthering your bloodline with me?'

'I can't.'

'Then this is the only way.'

'Grayson, stop! Listen to me! I can't have kids. I can't!'

'You can't?' he asks, unsure if he can believe me.

'The scars on my belly, Toby made them. So I couldn't have children. I can't further the bloodline even if I wanted to. And I love your brother.'

He leans down, his thumb still resting on my lip. When his nose rests against mine, he gives a small laugh.

'You expect me to believe that?'

'If you force yourself on me, I'll tear you limb from fucking limb.'

'Are you threatening me?'

'You better believe it.'

He laughs a little harder and looks longingly at my lips. 'And I believe you. Truth is, the doctor told me that you may not be able to conceive when she saw your scars. The positioning of them would make it unlikely. So you're useless to me in that respect. And you have made it clear that you don't care for me that way. And Collins, as well as Gabriel will leave if I refuse to let you be together.' He sighs and gives a shrug. 'But, you are still my Arcane. I need you. And I cannot allow you to leave me or my coven.'

'Well,' I have to force myself to speak. 'That's not your choice, is it!'

'It's not yours either.'

'Everything you said, that you'll give us your blessing, that you'll back off, it was all lies.'

'No. It wasn't. I give you my blessing. You and Gabriel love each other. So be together. I not only allow it but encourage it.'

'Then let me go, put down the branding iron and take me back to Gabriel. I'll forget this ever happened.' That's a lie. He's not getting away with this. Not at all. 'Let me go, Grayson.'

He sits up and looks around him at the darkness of this horrible place. It's tainted here. I can feel the evil in the walls. The things this place has seen and may yet still have to witness. But he doesn't get off. He doesn't lower the iron. He's thinking.

'This will work. You and Gabriel will stand by my side. You will have each other, and I will have your magic to use as I wish,' he tells himself. 'If I don't brand you, you'll leave. I'll lose everything. This is the only way.' He sits back and holds the brand over my arm. I can feel the heat already and it's unbearable. 'I won't let you leave me. You or my brother. You'll stay, bring down the Veil, help me destroy the Hunters as well as

Theo, and we will find your cousin. He can further the Hooper bloodline instead of you.'

He can't do this! As Grayson starts manoeuvring the glowing metal above my blood streaked arm, I begin to scream again, but this time its threats.

'YOU DO THIS, I WILL FUCKING KILL YOU!'

'WATCH YOUR GODDAMN MOUTH, LILLY!' he bellows. 'I WON'T ASK AGAIN!'

'You're a dead man. Brand or no brand.'

'Is that so?' he laughs. 'Let me put your position in a way you will understand. You will have no magic unless I deem fit to give it to you. You can't run because I will find you-'

'I will never read your journal,' I warn. 'You do this to me and I swear I'll never read your damn journal! Fuck your spell.'

'I warned you about your foul mouth. Swear one more time, I'll cut your damn tongue out.'

I lay beneath him terrified. Beyond terrified. But I pull my courage together, what there is of it and repeat my warning.

'Grayson,' I say firmly, even as I shake all over. 'If you brand me, I will not do your spell. I mean it.'

'Oh yes, you will,' he says in a forced calm, taking his aggressive pointing finger and using it to gently tuck my hair behind my ear. 'Because if you don't, if you hinder this spell, if you try and run or fight me in any way, if you so much as vex me, Lilly Hooper, I will make sure Amara knows nothing but misery, pain and suffering till the day she dies.' His eyes get darker and darker as he issues his threats. My heart almost stops at the idea of her being hurt. But he's not done. 'You will behave and do exactly as I ask of you because if you don't, I will lock up Gabriel and have bits of him handed to you every time you disobey me. As well as Collins.' He looks me right in the eye. 'You will stop with the vulgar language and the disrespect, or you will be the reason your friends suffer and die. Now,' he leans in closer. 'You look me in the eyes and tell me if you think I'm bluffing.'

I know he's not. I know with every fibre of my being that he'll do exactly as he threatens. Gabriel knew too, which is why he went to such lengths to push me away.

'AM I BLUFFING?' he bellows in my face making me sink back further into the floor, ignoring my words completely. 'You could have had the nice Grayson. I tried to give him to you. I was sweet. I was caring. But that wasn't enough for you. So this is who you get.'

'This is the real you. Everything else was just a lie.'

He shrugs and turns his attention back to the brand.

I turn primal.

'GABRIEL WILL KILL YOU IF YOU DO THIS TO ME! HE WILL FUCKING KILL YOU!'

'Then you better persuade him not to.' He stands, wraps both his hands around the hilt and positions the glowing hot metal an inch from my arm. He looks at me. 'I'm sorry.'

'No, you're not,' I say with an angry, lost sob.

'No,' he shrugs. 'I'm really not. You should have just fallen in love with me like you were supposed to.'

He thrusts the rod down and slams the hot metal into my skin.

My screams are beyond desperate and filled with such agony. The cracking of my burning flesh is nowhere near as bad as the smell. It's like burnt meat on a grill. He presses it harder into my skin making my shrieks even more desperate. Losing my fingers is nothing compared to this pain. My whole body feels it. Every nerve is screaming out with me. My legs judder and I thrash. There's smoke coming from my flesh. It makes my eyes water and burns my nostrils.

As the sizzling eases, he peels the red hot metal from my skin taking chunks of melted flesh with it and casts the branding iron to the floor, out of reach. I lie between his legs as he towers over me, staring at my arm.

He did it! He actually did it!

He branded me.

The binding spell's been seared into my arm forever. My eyes go up where just beyond the mark is the blood-soaked bandage that covers the empty space where two of my fingers should be.

I can't say anything. I can't cry. I can't scream.

I lie here, completely and utterly silent with my mouth open in shock. He reaches up to my wrist and removes the cuff with a swipe of his bloody knife. When it's gone, I still can't feel my magic.

He smiles happily and undoes the belt around my wrists before getting to his feet.

Slowly, I roll over and wince as my arm screams out in protest at every single piece of movement.

I sit myself up, holding my arm gingerly with my hand. The word Nexasanguinum is blistering. It's an angry, redraw and charred black mess that hurts beyond comprehension, but as I look up at Grayson who stands with absolute smugness, I fill with hatred.

I don't care if I have no magic. I don't care he's muscled and skilled at fighting.

With a scream, I charge at him hard, slamming into his chest and knocking him to the floor.

'I'M GOING TO FUCKING KILL YOU!' I shriek, my fists slamming into his face again and again. But with one punch from him, I fall off his body and land on my side. When I go to resume my attack, he grabs my arm, right over the brand mark. A fresh bout of agony shoots through my body and a high pitched, blood-curdling scream explodes from deep within me. He tightens his grip till I can't take any more and fall subdued on my knees, a sobbing and gasping mess.

'I'll let that outburst pass,' he says. 'But I meant what I said. You and Gabriel are free to be together. I will not interfere. Not at all. In return, you will bring down the Veil for me. And if you try to leave, I will find you with the Bloodstone. And Amara, Collins *and* Gabriel will pay the price.' He twists my arm making me sob against the sheer agony. 'If they turn against me, they will pay the price. But if you all do as you're told, you can all live happily ever after. And no more swearing. Do you hear me? I won't have my Arcane sounding like an uncouth peasant.' When I don't answer, he twists it further. 'DO YOU HEAR ME?'

'I HEAR YOU!'

He lets me go with a shove. I pull my arm close to my chest in a bid to protect it. As he starts collecting his things, I watch him.

He picks up his jacket and puts it on. 'Now, let's get home and see how your beloved is, shall we?'

Chapter 26

I jolt awake when Grayson stops the car. I'm sweating and shaking. My whole body is in agony and I'm so tired I can barely move. He turns off the engine and looks at me. He just looks at me as I struggle to keep my eyes open, and without a word, he gets out and heads to my side. Slowly, he opens the door. He has to catch me as he does. I have no energy left. I hate that he carries me inside the house. We pass the Nomads who are clearing the mess I made during my escape and the hateful stares I get don't bother me one bit.

'Morning, Boss,' Hendrix says happily as we walk into the lobby. 'Jesus. You look like shit!' he adds when he sees me.

'She was in the middle of a war zone, Hendrix. What do you expect her to look like?' He heads into his office, taking me with him. He lowers me gently into a chair and kneels in front of me. Hendrix follows.

'I want to know everything that happened when we left. Where's Toby?' Grayson asks him, stroking the hair from my damp face.

'Not here. Boss' Hendrix replies. 'All they found was blood. Nothing else.'

I don't believe it. There's no way. I broke his leg. He can't have got away on his own. It's impossible!

Hendrix looks me over. His eyes settle on my arm which I hold protectively to my chest. But he doesn't say a word. He simply waits for Grayson's orders.

'That's unfortunate,' Grayson says, with an angry glance in my direction. He looks at Hendrix and gets to his feet. 'Where's the doctor?'

'With Gabriel.' The mere mention of his name has my heart hammering.

'Is he okay? Is he awake?' I ask. I go to get to my feet, but Grayson pushes me down with a firm hand on my shoulder.

He's here. Part of me wondered if Grayson would lie about that too and send him away nonetheless.

'He's still out cold, but Doc got the bullet out, and he'll be okay in a few days. Collins is up there with him too. Refuses to leave his side. Amara as well.'

Well, that's a relief. Everyone is okay.

'I need the doctor down here when she is finished with him. Go tell her that.'

He disappears and leaves Grayson and I alone in his office. When he puts a drink in my hand, I put it on the desk untouched. I'll never trust anything he gives me to drink again.

'I want to see Gabriel.'

'You will. I promise. First, you need sorting out. I can't have any of those wounds getting infected.'

The doctor arrives and fixes me up. I'm sewn, bandaged, and dosed up on painkillers.

'All done?' Grayson asks.

'Yes, sir. All done,' the doctor replies. 'She's as fixed up as can be, but getting used to life minus two fingers may take some time. Her hand and arm will need dressing daily, and I'll leave some medication for her. She'll be in a large amount of pain for a week or so. Best not to touch her right arm if possible. And keep an eye on her for signs of shock or PTSD. She has been through one hell of an ordeal tonight.'

'You will stay with us for the next few days. I want all your attention on my brother and his girl,' he tells her. 'You got that?'

She grips her black bag and gives a small bow. 'Of course, sir. I am at your disposal. I'll be in the room I stayed in last time.'

Grayson stands aside as she leaves. I watch her go wishing more than anything that she would stay. But she doesn't. Grayson shuts the door and starts walking towards me.

'Someone found Toby and took him,' I tell him, keen to get all this out the way so I can go upstairs and see Gabriel. 'I broke his leg and gave him a hell of a whack. I messed his face up too. It was probably the shooter. It's too much of a coincidence.'

'Perhaps. We will keep looking. We may not need him for the journal, but we do need to eliminate him as a threat to you. He will come after you for payback. I meant what I said. I'll do whatever it takes to keep you safe.'

'Toby's mine.' The words come out as a growl. 'If anyone's going to kill Toby, it's going to be me. Not you. I owe him a hell of a lot of pain.'

'What happened between you tonight?'

'Nothing I want to tell you.'

With a sigh, he carries on. Not pushing. 'Theo and Jensen both got away too, as well as a fair amount of their followers. So we have that to deal with. The bodies of the men you killed were destroyed in that impressive new fire of yours, so there's no trace of us at all for the Hunters to follow.' He doesn't mention the men they killed. Just mine, as he goes through his report swiftly and without any encouragement for questions. To be honest, right now I don't care.

When he puts his hand on my knee, I slap it away.

'Touch me again, I'll break your fingers,' I warn.

'Look, I know you're angry-'

'Angry? I'm beyond angry, Grayson. You branded me!'

'It's done now, and my warnings still stand. And watch your mouth. I won't be spoken to like that. Not by you. Not by anyone. Do you understand?'

I look straight ahead because if I see his face, I fear I'll want to slam my fist into it. 'I need to get some sleep,' I tell him.

He places the journal on his desk and taps it with his finger. 'We'll start on this tomorrow.' From his trouser pocket, he takes out a small, folded piece of paper and opens it up. From the same pocket, he also produces a pen. On the paper is a list.

Meditation. Hypnosis. Joy. Surprise. Pleasure. Sadness. Fear. Anger. Hatred. Pain.

'So...' he says, gesturing to the list with the tip of the pen, running its nib across each and every word. 'Which one caused your Mental magic to manifest?'

'Fuck you.'

'Tell me.' His eyes flash darkly, the same as they did in the barn and reluctantly, I lean over and point to the list. My finger landing on sadness. He ticks it off. 'And fear was with Theo when you presented your Telekinesis,' he muses, putting a neat tick beside the word *fear*. Then he gives a derisive snort. 'And pleasure manifested your fire when you were with Toby.' Again, he draws a small tick beside the word and looks up at me as he folds it neatly away back into his pocket. 'I can't wait to see what motivates you next time.'

'Can I leave now?'

'Of course. You rest up. Go lay in your lover's arms,' he adds with a slight eye roll and condescending tone. 'And tomorrow, we'll start work on the journal. You should be excited! It's the beginning of a whole new world. None of it would be possible without you.'

'I hate you, Grayson,' I reply without looking at him.

'As long as you and your boyfriend behave, I couldn't care less.'

I get to my feet, swaying and staggering as I do. But he doesn't try to help. He's wiser than that. I leave the room and head upstairs. It's slow work climbing three stories. But when I see Gabriel's door, I sigh in relief. It's slightly ajar. When I open it up, Collins and Amara both jump to their feet. As Amara rushes towards me, I hold out my hand.

'I really, really need you both to go to bed,' I tell them. Collins looks at my heavily bandaged arm and goes to ask me something. 'Please. I am asking you both to leave. I need you both to leave. I will talk to you in the morning. I can't deal with anything else tonight. Not a single thing. Please.'

Amara heads over first. There's a deep concern in her eyes, but she nods and kisses my cheek as she passes.

'I'll be in to see you tomorrow,' she whispers. 'I love you.'

'I love you too,' I tell her. She leaves. And it kills her to do so.

As Collins passes, he leans in and pecks my cheek.

'Are you safe?' he asks.

'For now.'

'Are we?' he asks, nervously looking at Amara.

'For now. Don't leave her side, Collins. Not for a second. You hear me?'

He nods and glances at my arm. 'Not now. Please,' I say quietly. 'I can't...'

'Alright, Lilly. Okay,' he soothes, taking my uninjured hand in his and giving it a squeeze. 'I'll be back first thing. If you need me, you just yell.'

He leaves, closing the door behind him.

Gabriel looks asleep as he lies in his large four-poster bed. But I know he's unconscious. He's bare-chested with a square patch of bandage covering the spot where he was shot. As I head over, I take off my filthy clothes, leaving them in a trail behind me till I'm in nothing but my underwear. When I reach his bed, I slide in next to him, careful not to wake him. If he can even be woken up at this stage of his recovery. I stroke his face softly and watch him sleep before leaning in to kiss his cheek. His head moves suddenly, and instead, it's his lips I kiss, and he kisses back. But he doesn't open his eyes. He just mumbles my name.

'I'm here,' I tell him. 'You're safe. I promise. I'll keep you safe.'

'I love you, Lilly,' he says sleepily, his nose against mine.

'I love you too.' I rest my chin on his shoulder, my head sinks into his pillow and my good hand grips onto his limp one. 'We're going to get through this. Together.'

As I lie beside the man I love who has a hole in his heart, and with the brand throbbing on my arm and two fingers missing from my hand, I make a vow.

I will find Toby and his mysterious woman. I will make them pay for what they did. I'll learn all of Rebecca Hooper's spells and when I get my magic from Grayson, I'll know how to use it to my full advantage. I'll hunt for a way to remove this brand. I'll practice as hard as I can. And somehow, I'll remove the immortality spell from Grayson, Toby and Theo. And when I do...they'll see exactly what I'm capable of.

Because I will not give up. I will not roll over and let them win. I will never stop fighting.

Never.

They're going to pay for everything they've done.

And no one, I mean no one, will be spared.

End of Volume One.

THE
LAST
WITCH

II

M.J.LAWRIE

Continue reading
Vol 2&3 are available now!

Also by
M.J.LAWRIE

The Last Witch Series

A dark, paranormal fantasy romance series.

The Verity Duology

A dystopian, romance, fantasy.

The Stolen Fae series

A dark, MFM, paranormal romance fantasy.

Printed in Great Britain
by Amazon

34448864R00326